BRONX HEART
JERUSALEM SOUL

A Novel

Bronx Heart Jerusalem Soul

A Novel

Rayna Sue Harris

Acknowledgments gratefully made for brief use of lyrics to "You'll Never Walk Alone," by Oscar Hammerstein, music by Richard Rodgers, copyright 1945 &1956 by Williamson Music, Inc., New York, N.Y.; for excerpts from President John F. Kennedy's televised address to the nation, October 22, 1962; and for the American Consul General's Notice to American Citizens in Israel, May 23, 1967.

M

ISBN-13: 9781534834828
ISBN-10: 1534834826
Library of Congress Control Number: 2016910259
CreateSpace Independent Publishing Platform
North Charleston, South Carolina

To my Grandchildren- May the legacies of your forebears bring you wisdom and joy. Treasure them as you go on to create your own!

TABLE OF CONTENTS

Prologue · ix

Part One   Bronx Heart - Jerusalem Soul · · · · · · · · · · · · 1

Part Two   Jerusalem of Gold and Steel · · · · · · · · · · · 323

Part Three The Law of Return · · · · · · · · · · · · · · · · 461

PROLOGUE

Everything was high in Jerusalem- the endless rolls of mountainous slopes were majestic and breezes flowed throughout the city. The air was crystal clear, full of fragrance of pine forests and essence of blooming wildflowers. It was easy to breathe in, and Tyra Miller enjoyed gulping it, feeling her lungs expand and invigorate her. The sun was high and strong, and its comfortable, dry heat radiated within the narrow streets of shuks, decrepit neighborhoods of Mea Shearim and Romemma, and twisted, bullet-marked streets of Mussrare. Mountain waters were pure, and made her freshly shampooed hair fly-away and unmanageable, but she loved the way her soft tresses tickled the nape of her neck. The sky was high- a gleaming, cloudless expanse of deep pure blue as far as the eye could see, sheltering the modern stone and glass structures of the western side: the Knesset, the museum, Hadassah Hospital at Ein Kerem, and the campus of the Hebrew University in Givat Ram, where Tyra studied, and the dorms, where she lived.

Tyra felt she truly belonged in Jerusalem. On one hand she was close to God and able to wrestle with Him on an almost daily basis, shouting out her anger toward Him for all the suffering she had witnessed. On the other hand, she continually struggled to release herself from all the bitterness that had accumulated within her since she was a little girl, for that bitterness, she knew, was eating away at her soul. It made her hard rather than resilient, unnaturally tough rather than admirable, and she missed too much of whom she really wanted to become because of it.

Tyra belonged to Jerusalem like kreplach and knaidlach in chicken soup. She struggled to observe ritual and free herself from it at the same time, and she always was searching for some spiritual peace, a sense of meaning that she felt more intensely in Jerusalem than anywhere else. She still hadn't found the redemption she was seeking. And time was running out.

PART ONE

BRONX HEART
JERUSALEM SOUL

ONE

BON VOYAGE

Tyra Miller, squeezed in the middle of the back seat of the old Chevy Impala between her grandmother, Hana, and sister, Jessie, could hardly breathe. They left plenty of time, so she knew they wouldn't be late despite the stop and go traffic on the West Side Highway. But she was queasy at all the unknown possibilities about to unfold.

Her reverie was broken when the driver behind them honked relentlessly, as if Sid had someplace to go. Tyra loved her father's unwavering patience in these situations. He waved his arms in a wing-like motion in front of the rear-view mirror as if telling the rude driver behind, 'Fly above me.' Kaye laughed at Sid's composure. She, too, was crowded in the front seat between Sid and her father, Lazer who took up most of the row, being as stout as he was.

Without warning, Tyra's eyes welled up. *How she would miss them all, even Jessie, with their constant bickering and antagonism,* she thought. This is what she wanted, fought for. Yet now that the moment was…

"Here she is! What a beauty," Sid said, as he parked the car in the lot at the pier and pointed to the S.S. Ashrei, the modest ocean liner that would take Tyra to Israel.

The family boarded the ship, roamed the sun decks and lounges admiring the charm and luxury and descended to Tyra's cabin waiting for the slew of relatives and friends to show up for her grand bon voyage party.

When the time came for the ship to pull up anchor and head out to sea, Tyra kissed everyone goodbye. Dawn, her best friend from high school, hugged her so tightly and wouldn't let go, that Kaye had to pull her off Tyra to get her turn. Tears flowed easily from everyone.

Sid was the last to speak. As he hugged her, he said, "Don't forget, now…"

"I know, Daddy. I promise. I will come home when the year is up. No foreign entanglements." She laughed. "If it weren't for you convincing Mom, I wouldn't be going, so I promise, promise, I won't get you into trouble with her. I'll come back!"

They hugged tightly and tears welled up again in their eyes. The final horn blew and all the visitors scurried off the ship.

Tyra fought for a spot along the rail of the deck so she could catch the last glimpses of her family below on the pier. The excitement and nerves of the morning's packing and rushing turned to a fearful pit in her stomach. *I'm really doing it, going away,* she thought. Could she really leave for an entire year? Nearly twenty-one years old, she had never seen her grandfather, Lazer, cry before. The European master of a struggling existence, he stood there with tears in his eyes. *Please God, don't let anything happen to Grandma and Grandpa,* she prayed. *Don't take them away from me.* Yet she was taking herself away from all of them: her parents, her sister, her whole universe filled with devotion and loyalty.

She finally attained what she wanted all her life- an opportunity to immerse herself in Jewish studies- Hebrew language and the great literature spanning three millennia, literature from the Talmudic age, the Golden Age, the ghetto, and the moderns- Bialik and Shenhar, subjects ignored and opportunities denied in the New York public school system. Yet sailing away from all that was not only familiar to her, but comfortable despite the suffering and disappointments she witnessed, represented a journey toward freedom. No, not just an ordinary journey, rather a flight to freedom, a fulfillment of the yearning to do things, to feel, to become who she was without being watched, without making account, without feeling guilty for her good fortune. Only at that moment on the deck, as she cried and waved goodbye, she didn't know she was running away, and if she did, she could not realize how foolish it would be to think she could leave her heart behind.

When she first told her parents she wanted to go to Israel, they said she was just looking for an excuse, a pseudo-intellectual pretense to distance herself from the disappointments and encumbrances, the obligations and guilt of their family life. But she didn't believe them. "This is the Sixties. It's time for expanding one's horizons, for change," she countered.

She stood on the deck. Baggage, a multitude of pieces, was stacked and strewn around the various decks. There were hard-sided valises, duffel bags bulging into misshapen and tautly stuffed heaps, and heavy, black trunks with silver colored trim and latches. Tyra had one of each type filled with clothes, books and appliances for the year. An extra valise was crammed with packages of tissues and rolls of toilet paper. "The paper's like cardboard in Israel," her college friend, Zelda, told her. Since she was allowed four pieces of baggage, she filled one with paper goods, and would take a good bit of ribbing during the year because of it. In the end, she would be redeemed, as the contents of that valise would serve as a two-fold blessing.

The wind was blowing and the sun was hot. The New York sky was unusually blue and the harbor water was its usual murky brownish-green. Tyra looked pretty in her blue and gold sleeveless suit, although she wished she had a little jacket as she was chilled by the wind. Her straight brown hair had been swept up and rolled into a cluster of loose curls atop her head. The hairdresser placed a gold bow in the front, softening her high forehead, and she looked elegant, and a bit sad. Tyra zoomed the camera lens on the pier and filmed her family. Sid splurged on a good Super 8 camera for her and since Tyra wasn't particularly adept at handling equipment, he patiently showed her how to load the cartridge, zoom the lens, more than once, in fact, several times, more accurately, many times. But for all her slowness to adapt or her klutziness, he hardly ever yelled and she loved her father for that. He knew that once she finally got it, like the fractions he taught her by dividing up M&M's into different colored piles over and over again when she was a child, she would get it for good and the knowledge would stay with her.

Tyra's parents never really traveled together. Trips to the Catskills in the summers were about as far as they would be able to go, and that was for the sake of the kids, and Grandma Hana and Grandpa Lazar, who always went along. Life was hard for Sid and Kaye, and Tyra promised to take the best movies for them, so they could all share her trip. Only Sid would write occasionally, especially in the beginning, "Don't shake the camera so much," or "Focus longer on the subject- you fly by so fast we get dizzy. Count to seven." And Kaye would add, "Don't take so many pictures of the ruins. Give the camera to a friend and have them film you. We want to see you." You could feel the pleading from the words on the page.

On the deck as the shower of confetti waned, she stared across the wake for the last look of her parents, and Jessie, until they all turned into a blur, both from distance and from the tears that clouded her vision. She filmed the Statue of Liberty and Ellis Island, and a little scared, a little sad, went down to her cabin on the lowest passenger deck. Later that night, she passed by the ship's photo gallery, and found the picture the ship's photographer took of her on the gangplank. Tyra liked the photo—she thought she looked elegant in the new suit, and gentle. It was at that moment she realized, by filming her folks crying and waving farewell on the pier, the first thing they would see on the movie film she would send to them would remind them of the sadness of her departure.

She wound her way down the narrow flights of metal stairs, hoping her three cabin mates would be nice and like her, and that at least one of them would want to be her roommate in the dorm in Jerusalem. Come October when regular university classes would begin, the American students from the program would be assigned Israeli roommates in an effort to affect cultural understanding and learning. In the meantime, they would choose their own roommates from the friendships made during the voyage.

Tyra couldn't understand why she felt insecure. She had plenty of dates in high school and college, more even than she could keep track of. Still she felt like a follower, a non-descript outsider waiting to be included, to know she was wanted by others, never pushing her way into places or things she wanted herself.

When she entered the cabin, three young women were sitting on the floor. The bunk beds were full of half-emptied suitcases, and the floor was cluttered with all the essentials they needed for a two-week journey: make-up and toiletries, clothes, clothes, and more clothes. Mostly summer clothes, but some warmer things. The Atlantic storms could be cold and rough, even in summer. Floral bouquets, those fragrant going away presents from their friends and relatives, filled the small nightstands. She saw right away, she could never manage to keep her things neatly arranged in such a little box, and she was relieved. Just like the room she shared with Jessie at home.

"Hi. We just met each other, and we are trying to decide whether to laugh or cry. A year is a long time. I'm Bella. This is Miriam and that's Olga. What do you say?"

7

"I'm Tyra, and I say, "Let's eat!""

They laughed so hard, tears came down their cheeks. Four kooky girls, happy and sad, excited and anxious at the same time. They hit it off, and Tyra's doubts from a few moments before dissipated as they drank leftover champagne and gobbled chocolates, compliments of the Ashrei.

The cabin was cluttered, but a porthole allowed in a good amount of light, even though the sea came up to the halfway mark. As luxurious as the ship was for Tyra, her cabin was on the lowest passenger deck. Between the endless ocean and the constant rolling of its waves, she felt queasy, and took a Dramamine. "I need some air. Anyone want to come with me?"

"I'll go for a walk," Bella said, and they grabbed their jackets. As an afterthought, Tyra plucked a pink rose from one of the bouquets, and stuck it in her hair.

Bella Wishinsky was taller than Tyra and broad-shouldered. Her dark hair was thick and curly, not quite past the nape of her neck. Her complexion was olive, like Tyra's, and there was an exotic look to her. She came from Cleveland, although her accent indicated she was born somewhere in Europe- Romania, Tyra found out later.

By the time they reached the Winter Garden on the top deck, Bella had conversations with at least ten sailors and deckhands. Not just a "hi," but real conversations.

Tyra was almost envious of Bella's exuberance and confidence. "How can you always laugh and make such small talk to so many strangers at once?" she asked.

"Because my father never did. It's a long story. I'll tell you sometime. But it gets easier the more you do it. Here, try," and she pushed Tyra right into a passing waiter, a good-looking Israeli who was carrying a tray laden with bar drinks.

"Oh my God," Tyra cried out. I'm so sorry. It's so hard to walk- the decks don't stay still for me," and she helped him steady the shaking glasses clanking against each other.

He laughed. "Eets oo-kaay. Is that how you say in American?" Showing off his repertoire he added, "See you la-ter, al-lee-gator. What's your cabin number?"

"Right," Tyra called as he left to serve the drinks.

"I'm going to kill you, Bella," and she knocked into her side, and they walked away arm in arm, laughing.

The girls split up after dinner, each wanting to explore the night and for Tyra it was the newness, the independence she wanted to contemplate.

"I flirted with five guys tonight. How about you?" Bella asked Tyra when they met up in the Winter Garden. Peyton Place was on the television in the lounge, and Tyra stood transfixed at the image of Mike Rossi, how many hundreds of miles away from land?

"Well, how many?" Bella pressed.

"Let's see. I was supposed to meet Robert at ten, but I got lost. He must have left before I got there. I hear these continentals are very independent. But his friend Roger was there instead. He's a waiter in the first class dining room and he sneaked me in for dessert. The cake was scrumpt...."

"Tyra, I don't care about the cake."

"Okay. I was supposed to meet Charlie at eleven on the crew's deck, but Roger wouldn't leave me alone, so I told him I was going to the ladies' room, and left him hanging. He had some line, so he deserved it. Charlie, now Charlie..."

As Tyra continued to describe her rendezvous during the evening, Bella counted them off on her fingers. "Well, that makes six for you," she said when Tyra finished.

"I wasn't counting, Bella. All I know is that I had a blast."

"Well, all I know is that I'll have to work harder tomorrow night," and they both cracked up.

All those years growing up, Tyra knew people considered her pretty and refined, but she thought herself to be scrawny and shy. They thought she was kind but she felt meek and dull, a useless observer wishing she were a productive doer. Now barely a day away from port, from all that was familiar to her, she felt a surge of energy and vitality. With flowers in her hair, she popped out of the ship's corridors, into elevators, sneaked into the crew's staircases trying to meet up with Roger or avoid Charlie or put Robert in his place. She felt like a celebrity, a performer in a hilarious scene of I Love Lucy. And all the while a childlike levity and an awesome freedom, both of which she had never before known were pulsing through her entire body.

Then she met Eitan. It was after the midnight snack. Tyra left a group of friends and went out to one of the decks for some fresh air. She grasped the railing, holding herself steady against the waves that were smacking against the sides of the ship. Once again, she was awed by the massive space above, the darkness interspersed with glittering bursts of stars and streaks of the moon's light. She leaned against the railing, weakened by nature's strength and lit a Tareyton, struggling to keep the match alight in the wind. When she glanced below at the crew's deck, she saw a sailor standing on the deck, one foot up on a ledge, his left hand holding his head, looking out toward the sea. His hair was thick and curly, big and high around his head, the new look. He was stocky, strong and broad-shouldered. He was not as tall as she would have liked, but then, she never saw an Adonis in the Bronx. She couldn't take her eyes off him until he turned around, looked up and saw her. He flicked the remains of his cigarette in the air over the railing into the sea and smiled. He withdrew his foot from the ledge and started walking to the stairs.

"Come down," he said.

"It says, 'Crew only'."

"I show you the work," he said in his thick Israeli accent. "No trouble."

"I bet," Tyra said, stomping her cigarette on the deck. She looked around as if she had just robbed a bank, and when she saw no captain or leaders of the group were around, she ducked underneath the chain that blocked the staircase with the sign that said, "Crew only," and held on to the railing for dear life as she hobbled down the slippery metal steps to introduce herself to Adonis.

His name was Eitan and he recently finished his army service. He got a job working on the bridge of the ship. He wanted to see the world and save some money to help his family before he would settle down in Israel. Tyra spoke in Hebrew and Eitan was impressed with how grammatically correct she spoke. "It will be hard for you to speak like Israeli," he said. She took that as the insult it almost was. But he was so cute.

She held onto his hand as they descended down the "crew only" staircase to the crew's quarters on the lowest deck. If she had thought her cabin, which she shared with three other women was tiny, Eitan's cabin which he shared with five other shipmates, looked like a long and narrow cigar tube, only the cigar within it had more room to breathe than these poor overworked sailors. The bunks were stacked one on top of the other, three high, and despite the porthole, the cabin was dingy, cluttered and smelly from men who were apathetic about their hygiene, as for the most part their women were "knots" away, and socializing with the passengers was forbidden at the risk of one's employment. They dressed up for the days in port. That's why most of the young Israelis worked on the ship- to see the world for free.

She looked out the porthole and saw nothing but dark ocean and its white froth. As if she were watching the tumbling inside a washing machine, she sat mesmerized by the water covering the round glass in rhythmic circular splashes.

They sat on his bed, and she felt every rock and sway of the tireless ocean as he showed her photographs of his family and told her stories about them. She could tell that he missed them. This to her made him seem more real, more honest, for with all the flirting she had done since she boarded ship, she didn't know whom she could trust, and dismissed all of it but for the good time it was.

After a while it was hard to concentrate on Eitan's photos and the stories that accompanied them, and Tyra was surprised she started to feel queasy at these depths. For the past three days during the fierce Atlantic storm that attacked the ship as it steamed toward Gibraltar, Tyra walked the decks, even the highest ones which were slick with ocean foam and salty rain. With camera in hand, sliding and grabbing onto the rails for dear life, she filmed the waves as they washed aboard, and the sailors as they struggled against the sharp winds to tie down the deck chairs. She had been taking Dramamine since the start of the voyage, just to be prepared for such a moment, and had felt fine. While most of the passengers were suffering in the belly of the Ashrei, Tyra was spry, out-and about, even able to eat apples and crackers. She even thought she would be able to hold down some real food, but she didn't want to take the chance.

Tyra felt comfortable with Eitan. He was friendly and didn't make any untoward advances, but the ocean made her woozy. The longer she sat on Eitan's bed, the more she felt like she was inside the drum of that washing machine, tumbling about, no longer able to hold the sea within. He told her he had the day off when the ship would dock in Piraeus, and she was glad he asked her to spend it with him. She liked him on the sea, where he dared to lose his job if he were caught with a passenger, and she was eager to see what he would be like when she would have her feet on the ground.

"Let's go," she insisted and as she wobbled out of his cabin. He held her back at first, so that he could check to see if the corridor was clear.

TWO

FULL PLATES - EMPTY POCKETS

"Daddy, Daddy," Tyra cried out, tugging on her father's hand. "I can't breathe." They were somewhere between the sixth and seventh floors of Manhattan Orthopaedic Hospital, and the ten-year-old's pace had slowed considerably as she dragged one heavy leg after the other on the staircase, her skinny fingers resting on her thighs, as if each step was steeper than the one before.

"Sh…, sh…," Sid said, putting his finger on his lips. "We don't want that old biddy to find us."

It was a delicious game they played, two criminals stealing into a room at Manhattan Orthopaedic Hospital where children were not allowed, beating the system, taking the prize. Jessie would be proud.

"Only two more flights, Kiddo. You can do it. We can get to the *ruf* if we wanted to," he said with the remnants of his Chicago accent. "Tell ya what we'll do. Let's rest a minute."

When they reached the landing of the ninth floor, Sid looked through the glass insert of the door, and motioned to his daughter that the corridor was clear. Now the real challenge began. As they had rehearsed, Sid wrapped his black wool coat around Tyra, hiding her inside. She would put her feet on top of his and become the "pot-belly" that he would clutch as he'd waddle laboriously from the stairwell to Jessie's ward, his slight build and nimble demeanor betrayed by his secret forbidden cargo weighing on his shoes. There they would meet up with the rest of the family.

Partners in crime, they would pull a good one over Nurse Slater. Tyra was trembling with as much thrill as fear, and her heart felt like it would bust out of her chest. She was excited by the danger, yet secure in her conspiracy with her father, who had been furious when the head nurse kicked Tyra out of the ward the time before. "Don't worry, Kiddo," he told her afterward, "I'll take care of you." Tyra loved her father for his courage. After all, if Miss Slater caught them, she could scold him, too, and make him sit in the corner!

It had been two weeks prior when, sheltered in between her parents, Tyra walked into the ward to see Jessie for the first time since the operation. Kaye explained that Jessie would be in a white plaster cast from head to toe, and she wouldn't be able to move on her own accord; but even that simple description couldn't prepare Tyra for what she saw in front of her that day.

The ward was huge- six hospital beds on each of its two long walls. In each bed, lay nearly identical Caspers. The room was filled with a dozen white ghosts, all lined up in two rows, twelve white jumbos in a carton, each unable to move on her own, dependent on the help of a parent or, after visiting hours, a nurse or worse, Slater. So many teenagers, in the prime of their adolescence: months filled with unattended parties and proms, void of boyfriends, filled with lonely nights spent in the company of TV instead of dates. Pretty faces whose deformed bodies were wrapped in cases of hard, massive white plaster.

Some packages big, some smaller, depending on the stage the patient was in during the long spinal fusion process—all to rectify the adolescent curse of scoliosis.

Jessie was wrapped in the bulkiest, heaviest white body cast there was, as she was a new patient. Just a few weeks since her surgery, only her face and the top of her shaven head were visible. It was the most comfortable when the head was newly shaven, for as the hair grew in, the scalp got itchier, and since it was impossible to shampoo, lest water get on the inside of the cast and dampen the cotton stocking underneath, making it clumped and matted and causing even more itching, heads were shaved regularly.

Jessie was at the threshold of the tortuous procedure. She was fifteen years old and had decided to make her life better. She had a good attitude; she was chipper. She would show them. No one would need to feel sorry for her. No. She was brave. She was strong. Most important, in just a little over a year, she would be straight, and she would smile through it all.

Scoliosis was a hard thing for a young child. Usually it was a disorder that affected adolescents, but Jessie was stricken at the age of four. The doctors didn't know what if anything would help Jessie's condition or prevent it from getting worse as she grew. Kaye was willing to try everything, every little suggestion that promised even an inkling of help she jumped on. She took Jessie to a chiropractor, a physical therapist. She enrolled Jessie in swimming lessons, dance class, posture exercises, everything. Once when Jessie was about eleven, a therapist told Kaye that Jessie should stay still in bed for twenty four hours, five days a week.

Kaye was desperate that Jessie should grow up to be normal and have a good life. But no matter how she tried to explain to Jessie that it would be worth it to do this awful thing today in hopes of improving the future, Jessie wouldn't agree. She kept popping out of bed. "I want to go to school, Mom." Kaye scolded her and told her to get back to bed.

"She's impossible," Kaye cried to Sid once when he came home from work. "She won't do anything to help herself.

Sid talked till he was blue in the face to get Jessie to cooperate.

"It's my life and I don't want to spend it in bed," she screamed.

"That's it." Sid dragged her to the bed and tied her wrists and ankles to bedposts. "Do what the doctor says!"

But for hours Jessie screamed, bumping the mattress with her body, flagellating as much as could despite the restraints.

Finally, Sid went into the bedroom. "You win. I can't put on a muzzle on you, too. You're doing more harm than good." He untied the knots. "Jessie," he said as she was sitting up, straightening her clothes, "I'm sor…" He stopped in the middle, then started again. "Listen, you're a tough girl. Don't you worry. You're going to be just fine." He pulled her to him and wrapped his arms around her in a gentle hug.

"I know I am. Don't **you** worry," she said.

He told her he was going to build a trapeze for her, so she could stretch and exercise. He installed metal chains under the archway of the kitchen and attached the ends of the wooden rod to each side. Tyra loved to swing on it more than Jessie. She learned how to thrust herself up so she could sit on the pole, and then she hung from her knees. The view of the ceiling as she hung upside down was a thrill. The more she practiced, she was able to lower herself and hang by her ankles. She even had dreams of the circus and handsome trapeze artists. Jessie hardly ever swung on it. In fact, it seemed she deliberately wanted to use it only when Tyra was on it. "You're always kicking me off, just for spite," Tyra yelled. "You don't

even like it. I hate you." Tyra would feel bad because Jessie was
so crooked. Then she would feel even worse, because despite
everything, she wouldn't apologize.

"Hi, brat. How does it feel to have the bedroom all to yourself?" Jessie said with a big smile.
 "I wish you were home, Jessie."
 "Sure, sure. Bet the room is as neat as a pin, Miss Prim n'
Proper. Anyway, I'll be home in a few weeks. They're sending
me in an ambulance. Want to bet I'll get the driver to put the
siren on for me?"
 She wondered how Jessie could be so bubbly when Tyra
herself was horrified by the cast, the smells, the whole scene.
 Kaye took out a new-fangled wide-mouth thermos filled
with a homemade concoction somewhere between baby food
and stew. The full body cast covered the chin and neck, and
made chewing an impossible chore. But that didn't seem to
bother Jessie, lousy eater that she was. "Oh! Ma. I don't want
to eat," she complained.
 "I stand on my feet and cook and mash, and you don't
appreciate anything," Kaye countered. Still she felt obligated
to provide nutritious homemade meals as if Jessie would
become stronger and recover faster, and she brought ther-
moses and care packages to the hospital everyday.
 Then Kaye glanced at Tyra and shook her head in utter
despair and frustration. "And you, young lady, stop biting your
nails. You don't want to look like a baby, do you?"
 As if the head nurse overhead Kaye admonishing Tyra, the
portly woman entered the ward and walked straight toward
Jessie's area.
 "So what do we have here? Don't tell me you're sixteen,"
Nurse Slater said, "sitting here chomping on your nails,
too." The roar of her voice made everyone turn and stand at

attention when she stomped into the ward. "Out, missy, out. Go sit in the hall. Your parents will get you later."

Kaye tugged on Tyra's hand, and kissed her on the forehead. "Be good, Tyra. We'll come soon."

Tyra walked to the row of chairs near the elevator bank. It was Christmas time and the halls were decorated with bells and Santas, wreaths and bows. There was a big tree at the end of the hall, dressed in sparkly tinsel and blinking lights. It was Hanukah, too, but there wasn't a Menorah or even one dreidel in sight. Christmas carols were playing softly in the hall, and Tyra tried to close her ears. She sat down in a chair along the wall which faced a row of large windows overlooking the East River.

When Miss Slater passed by on her way to the Nurse's Station, she handed Tyra a big, red and white striped candy cane, wrapped in cellophane. She wanted to smile big, and say thank you so as not to offend Miss Slater or get her angry. But she couldn't move her lips. She studied the cane for a long time, crinkling the wrapper in her hands. She decided not to eat it, assuming that, since it was a Christmas candy, it wouldn't be kosher. She sat perfectly still, her legs crossed at her ankles, reflections of the hall lights bouncing off her shiny black patent leather Mary Janes. She didn't want to mess up the neat arrangement of chairs, lest she get yelled at. She sat still until she heard the tooting of a ferry from the river. She thought about walking over to the window. She fidgeted a bit and glanced left and right, and observing the stillness of the corridor, she got up and took a few deliberate steps toward the window, but she started to breathe heavy and before she could get close enough to see the Circle Line ferry full of happy tourists waving, smiling and taking photographs, she ran back in fear to the hard chair. Oh, if only she could have been standing at the side of the deck, the splashing spray brushing against her cheeks, the wind whipping through her dark brown hair! A loud echo of a door slamming somewhere in the hallway startled her. A blonde nurse soon passed her by and smiled. The toot-tooting of the horn was hardly audible by now, and as Tyra realized she let her opportunity pass her by, she started to cry. She didn't think she would be brave enough when the next boat passed by either. She waited in the hall as still as frozen water. The only sound she made was the crinkling one as she toyed with the candy cane. She was bored and wondered what her parents, grandparents and Uncle Sheldy were doing with Jessie in the egg carton ward. What were they talking about? Were they making fun of her? They were probably having a good time. Oh, she was so angry! She wanted her mother, and was scared in the damp hall that smelled of pine and peppermint, and ether and rubbing alcohol. Smells that made her gag. Then she was ashamed of her selfishness, and decided to think about everything, her entire universe, for she knew she couldn't get into trouble for thinking.

Her childhood was half good, half sad. Plates were full, too full, but pockets were empty. There was an abundance of love to go around, but despite that, it had seemed to Tyra, in her youth and naiveté, that other families had normal lives and good times, while the Millers suffered with punishments undeserved, struggling to get by each day.

Tyra always wanted to have a room of her own, a private spot where she could do what she wanted and put her things in places where she thought they belonged. But she had to share the bedroom with Jessie. Her parents slept in the living room where they opened the convertible every night. Jessie took control of everything; after all, she was older. If Tyra liked the room dark, Jessie opened the blinds. If Tyra wanted it cold, Jessie shut the window. She bossed Tyra around as well. "Do this, go here, not that," she would say. Jessie was an expert at giving directions, and seemed to have the knack of knowing just how to make Tyra's life difficult.

In the endless, frustrating cycle of maintaining the room in a civilized manner, the more Tyra hung up her clothes and put her things away, the more Jessie scattered about her belongings. Books, so many books- Cherry Ames, R.N., Nancy Drew and countless novels.

But now that Tyra had the bedroom to herself, it didn't feel so good. She was lonely and even afraid to fall asleep when *Green Man's* shadow was on the ceiling.

She lived in a pre-War building on Tulip Avenue in The Bronx. The architecture was intricate and graceful, with rosettes jutting out from above the second story windows. The bricks were a rich, golden brown except for the dark brown quoins, which graced the corners from the ground to the roof. The structure was built in the shape of a U, with a courtyard in the middle, and knee-high hedges growing out of cement planters lining the entranceway. The lobby was spacious, like the Concord's or Kutscher's in the mountains, with two steps off to the side just for the wall of mailboxes. The staircase alongside the mailboxes was wide, its marble steps sleek and cold.

When Tyra would leave her grandparents' apartment on the fifth floor, she would sashay down the majestic flight to her fourth floor apartment as if a book were perched on her head, starting with her right foot, then bringing the left to the next step, pausing briefly before continuing with the right. She would stand tall, just as her mother would say during all those posture exercises when she and Jessie would parade back and forth in the living room with books balanced on their heads. The doctors said Jessie needed to do those exercises, and Tyra followed along, as usual. "You're the *me-too girl*," Jessie would chide and taunt, "always me-too." On the stairs at night when the halls were quiet and Tyra was alone, she would pretend to be a princess. In her own little fantasy, the hand-me-downs she wore transformed into long, flowing skirts of chiffon, and her imaginary entourage escorted her along her graceful descent. She was always careful not to hold on to the wrought-iron black banister, its side decorated with engraved scrollwork poles, preferring to carry herself perfectly balanced. But if she heard the elevator door open or a footstep echoing in the hall, she would cut short her secret ritual and spring back to reality, skipping noisily the rest of the flight.

Despite the sophistication of the architecture, the innards of the building were not particularly luxurious. The elevator was always getting stuck, and the old appliances in the apartments were constantly on the blink. The ovens never got hot enough and the refrigerators never kept food cold enough. Her grandmother complained to the landlord when he came for the rent every month. "My baking, by the time the top gets brown, the insides is rubber." And he would say, "Soon, Mrs. Siegel. Soon." Soon never seemed to come and Hana's complaints were as reliable as the rent money she handed to him every month.

Tyra lived on the fourth floor near the staircase. The one bedroom apartment was roomy and had high ceilings. The windows faced a vacant lot to the south. When a new apartment building was built, Tyra watched the construction workers build one floor at a time. The new building had only four stories, and the red brick façade was flat and sleek, without columns or pilasters. The building lacked distinction or style, and there were no adornments around the windows. But the appliances inside the apartments were new and efficient. Both buildings were graduated along the incline of the steep 219th Street hill.

When Tyra stuck her head out of the bedroom window and looked west to the right, she could see the Horseshoe, the four foot high gray stone wall entrance to the park. The tall Obelisk Memorial to the veterans of the World Wars stood in the middle, with fresh, vibrant flowers always surrounding it. Stiff soldiers in starched uniforms with braided epaulets and shiny buttons used to march down Bronx Boulevard and pass by the monument, laying wreaths at its base and playing taps on Armistice Day and Memorial Day. The steps from the Horseshoe led to the playground. The wide bicycle path traversed the length of the park from Gun Hill Road to the South and 233rd Street to the North. Beyond the park and parallel to the bicycle path was the narrow, winding Bronx River. On the other side of the river lay the curvy, tree-lined Bronx River Parkway which went up to Scarsdale, and on top of the slope behind the parkway were the railroad tracks of the New Haven line that led south to Manhattan and north to somewhere Tyra never had been.

Tyra's mother, Kaye, was an effective peacemaker, always leading the two girls to find solutions to their sibling rivalries in a way they could both accept, even if a little begrudgingly. Sisters. It was already embedded in her- this thing about sisters. "I always wanted a sister," Kaye would say. That's probably because she only had two brothers, and what she romanticized about having a sister was better than it really was. "Sisters take care of each other. Remember, friends come and go, but Jessie and Tyra are forever."

But sometimes it didn't seem it would ever be that way. Once when Jessie and Tyra walked up the hill to Mr. Cohen's candy store on the Avenue, Tyra asked Jessie for some money to buy a Tootsie Roll. "No, Tyra. You can't have any," Jessie said as she picked out two Archie comics for herself. Tyra was steaming, and she tried not to cry. She looked around. When she saw Mr. Cohen standing with his back to her stacking up some bags of chips, she edged over to the candy counter, nervously lifted a five cent pack of Bazooka and slipped it in her pocket. As the sisters walked back home, Tyra's heart beat faster and faster and the further she went, the more ashamed she felt. When they reached the middle of the long block, at the little church with the big cross on top, next to the house with the friendly cocker spaniel, Sandy, who Jessie always stopped to pet, Tyra did a quick about face, and as she ran back to the store, Jessie screamed as she looked up from Sandy, "Hey, where'ya going?" But Tyra ignored Jessie. She was too scared thinking about how she could put back the pack of gum.

"Forget something?" Mr. Cohen asked when she walked in.

"Just looking," she whispered, and Mr. Cohen turned to the cash register. Tyra quickly put back the small pack of gum, her heart pounding so fast, she thought it would pop out of her chest. She left the store quickly, tears running down her face. That night, she lay in bed, tossing, unable to sleep. She had thought if she returned the gum without being caught, it would be as if she didn't steal it at all. But it didn't feel that way. When Kaye passed by the bedroom, she heard Tyra's thrashing.

"What's wrong, sweetie?" She sat down on the bed next to her daughter and began stroking her hair. It took a while for her to confess.

"Jessie always bosses me around and I hate her." Then she told her mother about the gum.

"You can't blame other people for your wrongdoings," Kaye said. "You have to be responsible for your own actions. But I will talk to Jessie, and tell her to treat you more like a grown-up. Go to sleep, now. You're forgiven, but don't do it again."

Kaye was also a neatnik. She wanted everything to be in its place, but the small apartment was cluttered and messy. Sid would try to sneak in a variety of pets and that drove Kaye crazy. Once he packed the cutest black and white cocker spaniel puppy inside his jacket, and rode on the train all the way from Manhattan to the Bronx without the conductor having a clue. Kaye had a fit when Sid called out "Surprise! I'm home!" that night. But Jessie loved animals and she loved the puppy from the moment Sid pulled him from his jacket and put him in Jessie's arms. Only after several months, Lucky, as he was named, kept peeing all over the apartment, and Jessie and Sid kept sneezing because their allergies were acting up. Poor Lucky, he had to go.

A while after Lucky had been given away, Sid and Jessie went shopping on the sly for a parakeet. When they returned home with the bluest blue parakeet, Kaye screamed, "Always a million *tchotchkes* lying around the house. And now you want another *tchotchke* flying around the house!" But Jessie was so excited, and when she leaned her cheek into the bird's beak, Kaye saw the bird took to Jessie as she did to him, and she melted. She said Jessie could keep the little *tchotchke*, as long as the cage was cleaned regularly. When the pretty bird nuzzled against Jessie's cheek, she told him he was no ordinary *tchotchke*, but a very special one to her, and that was how he became to be known as Tchotchka.

Eating was a big thing and Kaye made delicious food. But the portions she gave were enormous, far too much for young ladies to consume in a month, no less at one sitting. But Jessie and Tyra would sit, until they finished, or pulled off some trick which made it seem like they finished. They would scrape food into their napkins when Kaye wasn't looking and stuff them into the built-in potato bin underneath the window, or Jessie would excuse herself, and flush a napkin stuffed with food down the toilet. The family always struggled to make ends meet, and Tyra could never figure out how such little money could buy so much food. Kaye would always say that it was a sin to waste food. She peeled potatoes carefully, so that only the thinnest layer of skin would be removed, leaving all the meat of the vegetable. It was the same with cucumbers, too.

One morning, Jessie ate her oatmeal, the food she despised the most, and went into the bedroom to get ready for school. Tyra switched her full bowl with Jessie's empty one, as payback for some of the bossing she had endured. She and Jessie were halfway up the hill when Kaye caught up to them, huffing and puffing, and dragged them back to the house. Jessie protested and said Tyra tricked her, but Kaye didn't believe her, and insisted she finish the leftover cereal. Tyra knew she would have to pay dearly for this prank, but the more Tyra observed Jessie gag and struggle with each additional spoonful, the more she regretted the swap. Even so, she didn't have the guts to confess.

The best thing about the nightly suppers was that Tchotchka, their deep-sky blue parakeet, would make the rounds at everyone's plate. Tchotchka was the only one in the family who had his own private room, but he hardly ever stayed in the cage. He flew about the house, free, like a jungle bird, and perched on the high moldings, or hopped onto this or that one's shoulder, nuzzling at an ear, then pecking a cheek. He'd swoop onto the dinner plates and nibble away at mashed potatoes, lamb chops or steak that were cut into miniscule bits just for him. Bright as he was, he had a tremendous vocabulary. Not only did he say his name, but "yummy," "thank you," and "come here, Jess." Tchotchka jabbered all the time, just like Jessie.

Once, while Jessie was bathing him, he slipped out from her grip and tried to fly. But his wings were already wet, and

25

he smashed against the mirror, then banged himself on the sink, and finally fell with a thump onto the white tile floor. He was a mess, bruised from head to tail, his eyes black and swollen, and he was shivering. Kaye called the vet who gave a grim prognosis, being that Tchotchka was in such bad shape. But Kaye lined a tissue box with a soft terry washcloth, and laid him in the small cozy place. She put the heating pad under the box, and gave him sips of water from an eyedropper. Tchotchka couldn't stop shivering. Kaye filled the dropper with whiskey, and gave him a few drops at a time. He seemed to like that the best! They huddled over him, keeping vigil. After a week of whiskey, prayer and intensive care, he nibbled at some seeds, which the family rightly took as a sign that the crisis was over. Tyra used to hear people refer to her mother as Florence Nightingale, and she finally understood why.

Kaye had a shapely Marilyn Monroe type figure, and she curled her long dark hair in intricate, flattering Hollywood style up-dos. Tyra thought her mother was beautiful, but Kaye said she was always self-conscious about her left eye, that, till this day, it didn't blink or close all the way because of the facial polio she had when she was four years old. She didn't remember much of that experience, except that she lay on a cold bed surrounded by doctors and nurses she didn't recognize who prodded and pinched her with instruments and needles for reasons she didn't understand. She felt like she was being swallowed up into the unknown, alone and terrified by the faces hovering over her in a big, cold hospital room with ugly, olive green shades covering a giant window. She hated that shade of green. She eventually recovered from the polio, although it left her with a subtly asymmetrical twist in her face embodied by a slanted left eye and an upturned eyebrow. It also left her with an everlasting distaste for the color green. In the beginning, it turned her stomach whenever she saw it, but as she grew up, she just avoided it as a matter of habit, and this explained why there wasn't a touch of green anywhere in the house, not even a plant.

Sidney was one of five brothers. They grew up, lanky orphans, fending for themselves, looking out for each other, protecting themselves against the Irish hoods in the rough south side of Chicago. Only two of the brothers married. One died in the battle of Normandy. The one who lived in California loved alcohol, and the youngest in Brooklyn loved the racetrack.

During the war, Sid worked in a Brooklyn shipyard. It was then that he came down with tuberculosis of the kidney. If only he could have gotten the new antibiotic drug, he wouldn't have had to have a terrible operation to remove his kidney. But penicillin was scarce, and whatever there was of it went overseas to the soldiers in the war. He spent a year at home recuperating; he couldn't work, and there was no money.

Those were hard times for Kaye. It was then that she had noticed Jessie's shoulders were uneven and the left hip was higher than the right. It was unusual for a four year old child to have scoliosis, but the doctors said it was *idiopathic.* Whenever doctors couldn't explain something, they said, "idiopathic." They were, though, able to explain that because Jessie was so young, her arms and legs would still grow to normal length, but her torso would be stunted, and the more the spine would curve and rotate, the more pronounced the hump would become. They said surgery wouldn't be an option until Jessie reached adolescence, and in the interim, all the physical therapy, exercise, and even a metal brace wouldn't prevent the curvature from worsening. Nothing would improve the existing curve. The more the doctors explained, the more Kaye understood just two things: help was a long, long way off, and the older Jessie got, the more she would suffer.

To boot, Kaye had become pregnant with Tyra just before Sid's surgery. Tyra loved to hear her mother tell her that she was so happy she was already pregnant before she found out about Jessie because she would have been too afraid to have another child, and that she couldn't imagine life without her Tyra.

"Do you know what your name means?" Kaye would ask Tyra. *Tyareh*, in Yiddish, means dear, like expensive, fine. And it's such a perfect name for you. You are so special and dear to me. And don't ever forget that. I can't imagine my life without you." She'd say that all the time and Tyra never tired of hearing it.

Lucky for Kaye that her parents lived in the same building. Hana and Lazer Siegel lived in Apartment 5F. At that time, before Tyra was born, Lazer worked twice as hard and Hana cooked double portions to feed Kaye and her ailing family. "Manna from Hana," Sid quipped appreciatively whenever his mother-in-law came into the apartment with bundles of freshly-cooked food.

Hana Siegel stood at a petite five feet tall. She was stout, with a full, flabby bosom and a thick waist. Her eyes were set wide apart and deep with hazel tint, her subtly curved small nose smack in the middle of her two high boned, fair-complexioned cheeks, all together her features, topped with a silvery crown of fine neck-length hair, composed a portrait of a regal woman who worked too hard in her shapeless cotton housedresses, and had far less than her goodness deserved.

Lazer Siegel's obesity was accentuated by his mere height of five feet, seven inches. From the back, a round bald head encircled by a band of wispy hair leftover from times past topped his broad shoulders and flat *toochuss*. His thighs and calves were exceedingly slim and shapely. By contrast, when looking at him from the front, he appeared to be an oversized beach ball, so wide it was impossible to find a shirt large enough to fit comfortably without having sleeves that reached the ground. Hana and Lazer married when they were both very young, and they had been married for a long, long time. In the wedding portrait which hung on the living room wall, Hana was a slim, pretty brunette, and the now clean-shaven Lazer had thick, wavy hair and a well-defined mustache.

Hana and Lazer were a perfect couple in that they both worked hard and wanted a better life than they had in Europe for their American-born children. She cooked and cleaned, and he labored at his tailoring day and night. He also assumed the extra burden of supervising Hana's housekeeping, passing judgment on whether she got the best merchandise for the lowest price, or if she ground the whitefish and pike for the weekly gefilte fish fine enough to be succulent without being so fine as to fall apart. In other words, he drove her crazy.

He was a stubborn man with a strong temper. Everything had to be done his way because he was always right. He would yell and shake his arms in the air, and the color of his cheeks would turn as reddish-blue as the sweet Malaga wine he would bless on Friday nights. Though he never laid a hand on Hana, he would slap his palms on the closest inanimate surface to make his point.

Lazer worked hard in the garment district's sweatshops when he arrived in America, and within just a few years, he was able to bring over his mother, four brothers and two sisters, one by one.

Many times Tyra would walk with her grandfather up the steep hill and then the ten blocks north to the post office. She would help him carry bundles of clothes, fabrics, and shoes that he would send to his cousin Barak's family in Israel. Once Lazer walked around the apartment, clutching the letter Manya, Barak's wife, sent, as if it were a spool of golden thread, his face beaming. "I don't know you in person, but I love you like a father," Manya wrote in Yiddish.

Lazer didn't have a formal education, but he knew the ways of the world and how to get by. He was a pious but practical man. He never would, God forbid, shortchange or overcharge anyone, and he always made sure his craftsmanship was of the highest caliber. He would come home from his job in the city, and open up the Singer sewing machine which was in the corner of the bedroom. He would pedal the treadle for hours making the most beautiful suits and coats with fur trim for his customers. But every Friday, just before sunset, he would cover the machine and Hana would sweep the scraps off the floor, in honor of the approaching Sabbath.

Lazer walked to the synagogue every Saturday morning. He didn't know how to read the Hebrew words from the prayer book, but he sang them by heart. He would hold the *Siddur* in front of his eyes pretending to read, proud that no one could tell the difference. He sat in the same seat, always, which was close to the altar, and if ever someone else sat in it before Lazer came, he automatically got up when Lazer entered the sanctuary. Asthmatic and with a heart condition, the rabbi gave him permission to ride the elevator on the Sabbath, on account he lived on the fifth floor, and it was hard enough for him to breathe.

As stubborn and strict a man Lazer was, Hana was as soft and sweet. Tyra loved her grandmother with all her heart. She could tell Hana everything. Tyra doted on her, making sure she looked beautiful. She would shampoo Hana's yellowish hair with bluing rinse, and roll fine, thin tresses into curls. While her hair was drying, Tyra would pluck a few course white hairs from Hana's brows so that the arch was crisp and neat. By the time Tyra applied a subtle touch of makeup- eye shadow, powder, rouge and lipstick and polished her nails, she would unroll the curls and brush them into soft waves that framed Hana's face. Tyra would give Hana the once-over to make sure everything she did was perfect. Despite the furrowed lines reflective of a hard life, and a double chin, Tyra compared her grandmother to the ivory face carved in the cameo Hana wore on special occasions.

Tyra spent hours teaching Hana how to tell time, but she never got it. For her, as long as grocery shopping was done before *As the World Turns* began, she knew the day was going well, and she didn't need to prepare dinner until *The Edge of Night* was over. "Tyra, enough with the clock, already. Better paint my nails, yet." She did manage to speak a decent enough English. Of course, when the adults didn't want the kids to hear the latest gossip, they spoke in Yiddish. But, unbeknownst to them, Jessie picked up the language, and eventually understood every clandestine word. When she was in a particularly nice mood, she would let Tyra in on the secret. Otherwise she would torment Tyra. "I know something you don't," she would say, another weapon in the older sister torment stockpile.

It was amazing to Tyra how her grandmother, who ate mainly radish skins and potato peels in Poland, could cook such wonderful food. In America, food was everything. "*Myna kinder vil essen.*" Lazer would say the words, not merely as a promise, for promises could be broken, but with the conviction of a solemn covenant, and Hana would cook until the oath was fulfilled. Hunger was in the past.

Tyra adored her grandmother, but she was embarrassed by the way Hana would call her. Once, they were shopping in different aisles at the Woolworth's five and dime on the avenue. Tyra was fingering the miniature decks of cards with the different designs on the backs when she heard her name, "Tyraleh, Tyraleh," billowing through the store. She ran towards the voice, and when she met up with Hana at the pots and pans counter, she said, "Grandma, please don't call me that. What if the kids from school should hear?"

But Hana said, not understanding Tyra's plea, "Tyraleh, you are my special Tyraleh, my joy. I don't know what else should I call you?"

Tyra spent many afternoons in Hana's apartment while Kaye was busy with Jessie. After school Tyra would sit at the kitchen table doing her homework while Hana was cooking the evening meal. "Here, Tyraleh," this is just the way you like it," Hana would say as she would hand over a warm onion roll straight from the tin cookie sheet, or a slice of pot roast, juicy with pieces of cut carrots on top. Sometimes Hana would wipe her hands clean on her half apron and sit down at the table to rest for a few minutes. She would tell her little granddaughter stories of her life in the old country: Her father, a lawyer, was a divorced man. His first wife was very religious who constantly fought with him because he used to work on Shabbos. They divorced and he married Hana's mother and they had five sisters- Grandma and all the great aunts. They lived in a small, crowded house and had many chores. One of the father's grandsons from the first marriage was named Sid, and that is how it came to be that Hana was the aunt of her son-in-law.

The smells of warm cinnamon-sugary coffee cakes or hot onion rolls filled the house and the hallways as Tyra would deliver samples to Bashke on the sixth floor, or Sadie, next door. Once Tyra was in the elevator bringing some mandelbrot to Hettie on three, and Mrs. D'Amato came in on four. "What's your Grandma making today? It smells out of this world."

When Tyra told Hana what Mrs. D'Amato said, Hana took a few cookies from the baking sheet, wrapped them in wax paper, and tucked the little bundle in Tyra's palm. "Do me one more favor, please. Take this to Mrs. D'Amato."

Tyra protested, but Hana insisted. "I know you don't want, but she was nice; maybe things will get better." Hana always wanted peace.

When Hana came over with her sisters from Europe, they were taken in by an aunt who lived in Harlem. The aunt found work for Hana as a maid, and took Hana's entire salary in exchange for room and board, leaving not even a few pennies for Hana to save a nest egg for a vestige of independence.

Hana marveled at the wonderful kitchens she saw, with stoves and sinks that had running water, and most of all the fully stocked cupboards with canisters overflowing with flour, white sugar as well as brown, and jars of seasonings and marmalade. The ladies taught her how to make their favorite dishes, and Hana learned to cook recipes from the Old Country in the new land.

Hana's aunt matched her up with Lazer. He was of sturdy build, a little stocky, with a dark mustache and a thick head of wavy, black hair. "But there's no magic," Hana cried to her aunt, "and he yells so much if he doesn't get his way." Her aunt could care less. "Magic, shmagic. He's a hard worker, a good man. You'll learn to love him." But Hana was young. Even a girl from the Old Country knew about magic.

Over the years, Hana learned how to stand up for herself, to answer back, and even if she were afraid, she'd never show it.

"Grandma," Tyra said once after she overheard one of their arguments, "you don't love Grandpa?"

"Oy, Tyraleh. You say such crazy things." Hana groaned. "I had three children by him. A man who takes care of your children, and gives them a better life, what's there not to love?"

They had been sitting across from each other at the kitchen table, and Hana clasped Tyra's hands in hers. "Tyraleh, remember what I say. You're a pretty girl, and in a couple years you'll go with lots of fellas. Be smart. Wait for the magic, and make sure he doesn't raise his voice."

In a good week, when Hana would manage the household expenses particularly well, she would put aside the few left-over coins in a handkerchief and hide it in her nightstand. Someday in the future, she would spend her *k'nipple* on something special. The stout, gray-haired matriarch who didn't catch magic, would, at least, one day buy a dream.

"Tyra, you're so quiet lately," Hana asked one afternoon. "What's the matter?"

Tyra was sitting on the radiator, looking out toward the park and counting the trains that were passing by. She loved the view from her grandparents' living room window. She could see everything that she could from her bedroom window downstairs, but in 5F she saw the full expanse, straight on, and didn't have to strain her neck.

"Grandma, I've been trying to tell you something, but it's terrible." She hesitated and finally, almost in tears, blurted out, "Mommy doesn't love me anymore."

"Why you say that, Tyraleh? Mama adores you. She always says how much you help."

"She's never here. I guess she just loves Jessie more."

"Tyra, you're old enough to understand that Jessie is sick and your mother is trying to do right by her," Hana said.

Tyra pondered what her grandmother had said, and turned her gaze toward the park.

The next day, Kaye asked Tyra to join the usual afternoon excursions. "But you must agree to come every afternoon for two weeks. Promise?"

One day they trekked to a neurologist's office. Tyra came into the treatment room with her mother and sister. Jessie lay on a table and a contraption above her was lowered from the ceiling toward her body. Pins and needles, they said. Actually it looked like something from the Spanish

Inquisition, but the tingling it caused was supposed to stimulate her muscles.

Another afternoon, they went to an indoor pool. It was in a hospital in the city, and it took a long time and several trains to get there. Someone was working with Jessie in the pool, stretching her arms and legs, while Tyra and her mother were standing around the damp, humid enclosure.

The worst were the three visits Tyra made to the chiropractor, whose office was on the other side of Gun Hill Road. Each time, Tyra went into the examination room and watched the friendly, heavyset doctor give Jessie adjustments. They didn't seem to be too bad until he made her sit up and he turned her neck all the way until it cracked.

Whenever he could, Kaye's youngest brother, Sheldon, arranged his work schedule so that he picked up Kaye and Jessie at the chiropractor's office. Otherwise they'd have quite a schlep home by bus. He drove them home the times Tyra was there, too, and each time, like clockwork, just as they reached the midpoint of the Reservoir Oval, she would get nauseated. There was a sharp curve in the road that in combination with the dark olive color of her uncle's car made her throw up.

After that third visit, Tyra put her arms around Kaye and asked for permission to stay with her grandmother the next day. Kaye placed her hand on top of Tyra's head the way Lazer did on Friday nights to say the blessing. "I know it's hard. Everything will be alright," she said, and granted Tyra's request even though the two weeks weren't up.

Things were starting to get edgy around the house. Marvin, Kaye's other brother, was getting married and asked Jessie and Tyra to be flower girls. Tyra couldn't wait for the fitting sessions; she paraded around the house in the pink organdy gown Lazer was making for her, like Chandra in *The Enchanted Garden,* her favorite library book. "Take it off before the pins get loose and tear the ruffles," Lazer would yell. Jessie's matching gown was blue, a shade darker than powder, but not as deep and rich as Tchotchka's blue. Jessie always got in trouble for showing up late for her fittings. She'd strut in saying, "I'm here, Grandpa," as if she were on time and Lazer's blood pressure wasn't as high as the ceiling. She would stand there forever while Lazer would make a tug here, and put a pin there; lift the hip an inch, and put a shoulder pad on the other side, spin her around and even out the entire hem. It wasn't just that Lazer approached his sewing as an artist; he had come from the place of pogroms, and knew full well the nature of man and what it was like to be scorned for being different. He was a tailor, and would do his best for his beloved Jessie, to mask her deformity from the world so she would have a chance for a normal life.

Jessie and Kaye had a huge blow-up about the wedding procession. Instead of the sisters walking down the aisle side by side, as was the custom, Kaye thought Jessie should go first, so Tyra, by walking behind, would hide Jessie's back a little. Jessie wouldn't hear of it.

"I am that I am!" she screamed. It was right after they saw Charlton Heston in *The Ten Commandments,* and she pronounced those words in that deep, intimidating voice, just like God's.

"Do what you want!" Kaye shouted back.

Finally, the wedding day arrived. The aisle was long, and Tyra didn't exactly walk alongside Jessie, nor did she follow precisely behind. She just did a wishy-washy stagger, a little off to the side and trailing slightly. The whole thing was a disaster. Jessie sprinkled pink petals onto the white carpet, and Tyra bent down and picked them up. By the time they reached the *chuppah,* Jessie's basket was empty and Tyra's was overflowing. Tyra thought the crowd was laughing because marriage was so much fun but when Jessie called her stupid as she passed by, Tyra knew otherwise. Jessie made her way to the reception hall where she flirted with the band members and waiters, and Tyra went to the lobby where she sat down on a big winged chair and cried until she fell asleep. Petals from the overflowing basket lay bunched up on her lap.

Marriage was a step up for Marvin. He moved to the Mt. Eden section of the Grand Concourse, the premier neighborhood, the Scarsdale of the Bronx! One afternoon the Miller women visited Marv's family—he had two sons by then, and were sitting on folding chairs in front of the building, when Sheldy, the perennial bachelor, stopped by from work just to say hello. He looked all dapper and spiffy, his dark curly pompadour Brylcreem slick and perfect. A little girl, maybe six or seven, fell on the metal spiked fence in front of the hedges and opened her inner arm from the wrist to the elbow. Blood was gushing out of her and she was screaming. Sheldy tore off his suit jacket, scooped the girl in his arms and ran to Lebanon Hospital on Mt. Eden Avenue, three blocks away. After the girl's mother got to the emergency room, he came back, plodding along, his white shirt soaked with blood. That was the bravest thing Tyra ever saw.

Her father did an even more courageous thing. Sid risked his life for a stranger, only Tyra didn't witness it personally. Sid was ashen when he got home one night. He'd left work at the Sixth Avenue Deli, and when he got to the IND station, he saw a man lying on the subway tracks and heard a train approaching the station. Sid jumped onto the tracks, careful to avoid the third rail. "I dragged him into the hollow space under the platform. He was heavy, and unconscious, and I rushed because the train was coming. It was pitch black and noisy and the station was vibrating so much, I thought the platform would crumble on top of us. But you know New York; she's built like a rock. I couldn't see anything, but I swear I felt rats crawling around. Then the banging of footsteps echoed through the tunnel as people went in and out of the train. Finally the train pulled away. By the time the tracks were clear, some policemen were there and they pulled the guy up as I hoisted him, and they pulled me up, too. They took him away on a stretcher and I got on the next train. I sat down and when I thought about what I did, I started to shake."

"What if something would have happened to you?" Kaye said.

"Just goes to show you, girls," and he clasped each daughter's hand, "if you ever need to take a risk, know what you're doing. Always know where that third rail is."

"Was he a drunk, Daddy?" Tyra asked.

"What difference does that make? He was there, honey. He was just there."

Tyra left the kitchen, her face stinging from her stupidity. How could such a hero, she thought, have an idiot for a daughter?

Her parents were a perfect couple. Kaye knew what things needed to get done, and Sid knew exactly how to do them. Just as Lazer wanted to provide nourishment for his children, Sid yearned to give his daughters the college education he missed. He would have been an engineer had he gone to college. He was always tinkering with the tubes of the television set, laying them out on the floor and studying the schematics, having the patience to test each one until he found and replaced the bad one. Kaye fell in love with Sid the first time she laid eyes on him, but she was only fifteen and he was twenty-one. She opened the door and there he was, just in from Chicago, looking for his Aunt Hana Miller Siegel. Sid had that Frank Sinatra aura about him- skinny, wearing a long coat and a charcoal gray felt hat that had that indentation on top and a squeezed in hollow on each side in the front, perfectly aligned with his sunken cheeks below, and slightly tilted on his head in a debonair, flirty sort of way. Only Frank's features were classic and blended into the rest of his face, while Sid's eyebrows and nose were prominent, and Sid couldn't carry even one note of a tune. Kaye had heard that none of the Miller boys were the marrying type and she used that to her advantage, growing up fast, and in the meantime, learning how to entice Sid. By the time she was nineteen, she got what she wanted.

"You can't marry him," Lazer said, swinging his arms in the air. "It's too close. Mama is his aunt. It's not he's not a good boy," Lazer pleaded. "But my sister, Edith, also married a cousin; they had a Mongoloid, and they had to put him away. Such a *shanda*."

"Papa," Kaye argued, "That's an old wives' tale. Even the Bible permits it. Besides, he's only a half-cousin. Mama's father was divorced and Sid is a grandson from the first marriage. It's far removed. Don't worry so much."

Hana already loved Sid like a nephew. He was good-natured and soft-spoken. To love him like a son would be easy.

On the day Lazer realized, that for all his domineering and obstinate ways, he could not withstand the potent combination of his wife's tenacity and his daughter's relentless declarations of love for Sid, on that day, he began to sew the most magnificent wedding gown of soft white satin, embossed with tiny fleur-de-lis, closing in the back with fifty satin buttons and matching satin loops straight down the spine, and pulled in tight at the waist, with puffy shoulders and tight long sleeves which came to a point right up to the base of the middle finger. Not even Frank and Marilyn could have been more glamorous, and for the wedding portrait, Kaye gazed at Sid, giving the right side of her face, her perfect, beautiful side, to the camera.

⸻

I n the afternoons, the courtyard and sidewalk were filled with kids horsing around and all the hubbub of the congested streets. When the bells of the Good Humor or Bungalow Bar trucks were heard from down the block, a cacophony of voices would yell, "Mom," and heads, scattered randomly throughout, would pop out of windows. Women would take coins folded inside paper napkins, secured with string or rubber bands, and toss the little packets for the children to use for the ice cream on its way. Women who lived in apartments facing the alley would visit neighbors with street front views, and borrow the windows from which they would toss coins to their children. But it wasn't always that way, friendly and blissful.

When Tyra was little, she, Jessie, and Miriam, the only other Jewish girl in the building, hung around together, despite the fact that they were years apart in age. They were shunned by the other kids and were used to being called names, but one day when they entered the courtyard, the taunting crossed the line. The Italians started to surround them, chanting in loud and haughty unison, proud of their pre-meditated attack:

> Jessie, Jessie, hunchback bump
> Jewish bitch, a camel hump.

In a flash, Donna Bracco ran up to Jessie and kicked her right on the hump of her back, hard, so that Jessie fell on her face.

The bully, Donna, was all the while buoyed by the cheers and foot-stomping of the other kids, Walter D'Amato, included. Jessie's face was scraped and bloodied, and although Tyra and Miriam ran over to her, she shooed them away and got up on her own. She was hurt and could hardly walk, but stood up as tall as she could, and the three got to the elevator, seared by the hatred, still hearing the slurs behind them.

The sisters reached their apartment and Jessie walked straight into the bathroom. She slammed the door and stayed there for a long time. Kaye sat at the kitchen table, holding her head in her hands, waiting for Sid to come home. She whispered, "I should have listened to Papa. I should have listened to Papa." She used to say that every now and then, but that day, she said it twice. Tyra had the bedroom to herself for a change, which was good. She was a coward, too afraid to help and too inept to stop the brutality; at least she would be able to cry alone.

Later the Millers, all four of them, marched down to the Bracco's apartment on the ground floor. Sid's body was stiff and his face was taut. When Mr. Bracco opened the door, Sid pointed his finger right into his face and said, "If you don't care about the filth that comes out of your daughter's mouth, that's your business. But if Donna ever lays a hand on my Jessie again, God help you all."

Mr. Bracco apologized and told his daughter to do the same. She muttered something, but there was a snicker in her tone.

Sid's chest heaved and his cheeks turned bright red with anger.

"Come on, Hon," Kaye said as she gripped Sid's shoulder and tugged him away from the front door. Sid backed away. As the Millers started to walk across the lobby to the elevator, the Bracco's door slammed shut behind them. The sound of a crisp slap and a loud wail seeped into the hallway.

After that incident, things got better and the Italian kids were friendlier. Camille Menotti was the first to suggest a get-together. That very next Sunday, after church, Camille asked Tyra to come down to her apartment, which was on the third floor. It was the exact layout as her grandparents', but only in reverse, as Camille's apartment was on the other side of the courtyard. Many of Camille's relatives were milling about and the kitchen was hot from steam coming out of big pots on the stove. The smell was rancid: pungent sausage and the sour smell of Parmesan and Romano cheeses mixed with mounds of chopped meat and tomato sauce in a huge pot made Tyra wince. When she saw a glass jar labeled Pig's Knuckles on the top of the cabinet she stopped dead in her tracks and felt faint. Camille pulled her by the shoulders into the bedroom she shared with her brother Gregory. A heavy floral print curtain split the room in two. Camille had the window on her side. Gregory was six years older than Camille and far more studious than the other boys in the building. He wanted to study engineering in college.

"It's good you girls got friendly," he said. "Christ was killed a long time ago, before Tyra was born. It wasn't her fault." Just to prove the point, Gregory took down the heavy black bible from the shelf and flipped through the pages until he found what he was looking for. "Here, look at this," he said as he pointed out a passage to Camille and read it aloud as she followed. "See, it was the Romans who did it, and you should put Walter and the others in their place when they say otherwise." Tyra could barely digest the concept when she was thrown from that lurch into another.

"Yeah, yeah. Come on, Tyra," Camille said. "Let's play Parcheesi until dinner."

Dinner. Tyra was paralyzed by the thought. Such a price for friendship. She could barely concentrate on the game and the moment of dread came at three o'clock, on the dot, when the girls were called into the living room for the Sunday feast. Tyra wanted to leave, but Mrs. Menotti insisted she stay, and Tyra sat in a folding chair next to Camille at the console table that was opened up to fit all the relatives. Actually, the living room looked just the way Tyra's grandmother's looked when her family came for a big holiday or Shabbos dinner, only Tyra liked the smell of her grandmother's house better.

Mrs. Menotti put a huge portion of spaghetti on her plate, dumped a big ladle of meat sauce on top, and dropped a blizzard of cheese on an ever-growing mountain of food. Tyra looked down at it. She wanted to run away, but she didn't know how to without hurting anybody's feelings.

After everyone else bowed their heads and mumbled some words, Mrs. Menotti called out: "Eat, everyone, Enjoy. Tyra, you too, eat." She might as well have been Kaye.

Tyra stared at the food in front of her, and drew her fork to a clump of spaghetti at the edge of the plate. It was still pretty yellow, and there was just a bit of sauce and cheese on it. She twirled it on her fork, squeezed the insides of her nostrils together so she wouldn't smell it, and put it in her mouth. Actually she was surprised that it tasted pretty good.

"Mom," she said later that night. "I did a terrible sin today," and confessed how she ate treif at the Menotti's.

"Tyra, there will be many times when people will want you to do things you know you shouldn't. You'd better learn to stand up for yourself, because no one else will. Just do it in a nice way. Try to sleep and don't worry so much. A mistake doesn't count if you learn from it. There are bigger problems in the world."

A few weeks after that incident, Camille asked Tyra to go to church on Sunday, "just to see what it was like- to genuflect and eat a wafer- it wouldn't really be communion for you,"

Camille said. Tyra passed by the church a million times. It was on top of the steep hill on the way to the avenue. The front of the building was composed of large, abstract-shaped stones with a tall steeple and big cross. In the spring the lawn was a palette of bright colors from the blooms of the gardenia, lilac and chrysanthemum bushes.

"It wouldn't be respectful if I just watched, and I can't kneel. But maybe we could go to the park when you get back." They prayed differently, and although Camille ate fish and Tyra ate chicken on Friday nights, they still rode their bikes the same, and Tyra was happy for that.

The best times were the yearly preparations for Passover. Hana's house during the changeover from *chumatz* to *Paisadicah* was an arduous task. How Hana could cook such massive quantities of food for the Seder meals was a miracle. Stock pots and utensils soaked in the bathtub for three days. The cartons of eggs, half of them brown-shelled, half white, sitting comfortably in the rows of indented cups of cardboard trays stacked one on top of the other were stored on the fire escape. "Don't worry," Hana would say, "it'll be cool enough," and the March or April air always seemed to cooperate.

The housework was backbreaking, but Tyra always found security in knowing that year after year, things would be the same, and being Hana's best helper, she would bask in her grandmother's compliments. Hana would give her the tiny key to the mahogany china cabinet in the foyer where the Passover things were kept. She would open the glass doors carefully and bring out the stacks of fancy dishes to the sink. Jessie washed, because she was the oldest, and washing was more prestigious than drying. Tyra dried dutifully and together they meted out a rhythmic cycle of efficiency. When the silver was polished and the blades of the knives were shiny and free of streaks,

Tyra would begin to set the long console table in the living room, making sure to put her special tan and blue checkered Kiddush cup at her place. The cup was in truth, a creamer, a remnant from an old set of *fleishig*-meat- dishes, and since it never contained anything dairy, Hana kept it aside just for Tyra to use on Passover.

The house was packed for the two Seder nights. On the first night, Lazer's brothers and their families would come. Great Uncle Shockneh was Tyra's favorite. He owned a chicken market on Jennings Street, in the southeast section of the Bronx. He would always put a bag of little yellow chicken eggs in Lazer's weekly order of Shabbos chickens. Shockneh's wife was stern and cold. She never showed an interest in Tyra. Shockneh was the most religious of all the brothers, and the only one who was childless.

On rare occasions when Tyra would accompany Lazer to the market, Shockneh, wearing a big white cap on his head and wrapped in a bloody apron with feathers stuck to smudges of dried blood, would lift her up and spin her around. She loved to be twirled, but held herself stiff, making sure that her body would not touch Shockneh's apron. "*Kim aryn, viber. Haysa* chickens. Come in, women. Hot chickens," he beckoned on the street to bring customers into the back of the market. In the front of Shockneh's stall, Tyra could see rows of dead, naked birds lined up in the showcases, ready for soup pots and from the back, she could hear the clucking and flapping of chickens before their ritual slaughter. She tried to put aside the necessary cruelty of life- after all, she loved Hana's *g'demptke* chicken, stewed with all those fresh, colorful vegetables, but she shuddered at the poor creature's bloody slaughter. She'd run next door, to Abie, the pudgy dairyman who was bald except for one dark strand of hair hanging down from the middle of his head. He'd always roll a paper cone and fill it with fresh, creamy pot cheese for her. There she would tarry, observing the shelves of creams and cheeses until Lazer would call for her when he finished his business with his brother.

The last year's Seder was the best. Aunts, uncles, cousins- everyone sat on metal chairs squeezed around the table, except Lazer, who had the big softly upholstered armchair at the head of the table. As always, Hana was exhausted and barely able to move, no less open her mouth when it would be time to eat. Blessings and songs, prayers and stories, noise and commotion, the Seder night was electric, like a fuse box sizzling with too many crossed wires. Even Tchotchka attended in his little travel cage. Jessie let him out to fly, and he hovered around the moldings until he caught sight of egg-water, matzah and celery, the ceremonial edibles before the meal. He swooped down, hopping from place to place, pecking at a celery stalk or a piece of farfel. But as soon as he stumbled upon the Kiddish cups where little puddles of wine sat in the saucers, drops spilled commemorating the plagues God wrought upon the Egyptians, Tchotchka only wanted to drink, and he sipped from one saucer to the next. When he quenched his thirst and tried to fly, like a feather in a tornado, he swirled around until he flopped on the tablecloth in a drunken stupor.

"*De faigeleh es shickah,*"- the little bird is drunk- Uncle Shir called out, and everybody laughed as poor Tchotchka flapped his wings against the glasses and nearly fell to the floor.

Lazer interrupted his reading of the Hagaddah. His bulbous cheeks were red as he stood up and yelled, "*Machst mir meshugge. Epicursim.*" Appalled at the sacrilege, he sat down again, with one hand on the book and the other making a fist in the air. "We need finishin' the Seder," he said, and ordered Jessie to put the bird back in the cage while she was running after the poor thing, trying to catch him before he would get hurt. In all the commotion, Sid began to sing a

46

majestic rendition of "Go Down, Moses" in his deep, baritone voice. He couldn't carry a tune, but he wanted to make the Seder more interesting for the children. Everyone joined in, everyone but Lazer, who continued mumbling quickly a combination of Hebrew and Yiddish syllables as he flipped pages he could not read. After all, the faster he'd finish, the sooner they would eat. Jessie, in her usual defiant way, refused to put Tchotchka back in the cage. She held him in her lap, and let him sleep away his hangover in the palm of her hand.

Year after year the Seder would end with Jessie and Tyra dancing a hora in the foyer. They would stomp their feet as hard as they could, and when, like clockwork, Mrs. Longo, the downstairs neighbor, would bang her broomstick on the ceiling just to show her annoyance, Tyra and Jessie would dance and stomp their feet with even more fervor, giggling while everyone inside clapped and sang *L'shanah habah b'Yerushalayim.* Next year in Jerusalem.

That was Tyra's universe—a world where children were cherished and neighbors looked out for one another; a world of unlocked doors and fire escapes; of double parked cars and blaring horns; of clotheslines on the rooftop and wet laundry flapping in the breeze; a world of winters sledding down the slopes of Bronx Park and skating on the frozen river; of summers picnicking at Orchard Beach or loafing in cool Catskill bungalows; a world of counting trains rumbling toward the city and parakeets bathing in bowls of lime Jell-O; of name-calling and back-kicking; of playing potsy and hop-scotch on the sidewalk, and ring-a-li-vio and stickball, of chasing after Spauldeens in the gutter and catching them before they vanish into the sewer; a world of doctor's appointments and hospital stays, of hospital beds and bedpans, of stretchers and ghosts.

Blessed art Thou, Lord our God, King of the Universe, who has bestowed upon the Millers abundant love...and heartache.

The gong thundered out of nowhere and scared Tyra half to death. Visiting hours were over and there was a flurry of footsteps in the corridors as the wards were emptying out. Tyra saw her folks way down at the other end, walking slowly, turning around to wave back to Jessie. Poor Jessie. Kaye turned around and waved one extra time. Then she looked ahead and reached her arms out toward Tyra. Tyra got up and ran toward her family. It was time to go home.

THREE

ALIYAH - UPWARD

When they reached the Acropolis, Eitan stood in front of the Parthenon. He struck his pose, his chest leaning over a bent leg, his chin resting on his palm, his elbow supported on his leg. "Move, Eitan," Tyra said. "It's a movie camera." Tyra didn't know how to say movie in Hebrew. She would have to ask someone. But he just stood there in a silent pose, his eyes glued on her, his heart smitten. She could tell. He looked like Adonis himself, in front of the ancient pillars, and her hand started to shake. Only a week away and in love. Not possible, she thought. Yet she knew, even if she loved him, she would not get emotionally involved! After all, he was sailing away a day after they were to land in Haifa.

Tyra knew her mother would catch the picture shaking while she was filming him.

Wednesday, July 13, 1966- 2 A.M.

Hi all,

Five hours from Haifa and can't sleep for the life of me. All the luggage is piled high on the decks. There's hardly any room to walk around. But I'm the only nut on deck. I want to write about Greece and the last day on board because once I get to Israel I'll be so wound up (I'm excited already) that I'll probably forget the past five years! Oh! I see Eitan. I'll finish later....

10 P.M.

In Jerusalem now. This has been the longest day. Standing on the deck as dawn was breaking was awesome. The sea was calm and a hazy land mass appeared way off in the distance at about 5:50 A.M. That was my first glimpse of the Holy Land and I couldn't help but feel so humble- it was like I was in a dream. I was so nervous, too. How could I ever find the relatives among all the crowds at the port? The passengers were congregating on the decks, hanging over the railings as if to get closer to Israel- it was like a scene from the movie Exodus.

The ship docked with thuds and groans against the Haifa pier, and instead of finding God, I saw smokestacks, factories, railroads tracks, and I was so let down. I'm so stupid. Why should I have thought Israel's harbor would have been spiritual when it looked worse than New York's?

I walked up and down the pier and paged the family several times, and finally I saw a dress that looked familiar! I ran over to the woman and sure enough it was Manya and we fell into each other's arms. Barak told me I have a home for as long as I am in Israel, and Hadas said she will meet me at the central bus station in Haifa next Friday and take me to their house in Tel Paran. Irit is in Jerusalem and I will meet her there. I felt badly as they waited since six o'clock at the port to see me. We spoke in Hebrew, and Hadas told me my Hebrew is very grammatically correct! Barak asked for everyone and said that Grandpa is the watchman of the family. They gave me your letter. I was so happy to hear from you.

The ride from the pier to Jerusalem was long but beautiful. We were all so tired that is was hard not to doze off now and then. As we came closer to Jerusalem, we rode through the mountains- the hills are embedded with rock walls and rows and rows of trees. Jerusalem is built on top of a mountain.

After dinner, Bella and I and a few boys from the program walked around town. We came across a memorial park in honor of the soldiers from the neighborhood who died in the War of Independence in 1948. We sat there for a while. The night air is cool and refreshing, but for the first time I felt kind of lonely. I guess it was the rush and excitement of today. Also, the voyage seemed to be a suspension bridge between two worlds, and therefore I was neither here nor there. Now I am here- definite and concrete, and I am a little unsure of myself and how things will turn out this year. I have my plans, but in my head, I keep hearing Grandma say in Yiddish, Man plans and God laughs.

Tomorrow we get up early for a tour of the university. I will continue then.

Tyra

Hi again,

The campus is gigantic. It takes a good half hour to walk from the academic buildings on one end to the dorms on the other. The buildings are constructed to be cool and airy. The land is hilly so first there are large stone pillars upon which the actual buildings are supported. They are strictly modern- rectangular with glass walls for lobbies. Stunning! The lawns are thick with rich grass, large flowers, bushes and trees. There are fountains and statues everywhere. There is a stadium, an amphitheatre which is surrounded by a cliff of red and brown rocks, a sports building in the form of a butterfly, and get this, a shul shaped like a mushroom dome in stark white! I wouldn't have been surprised if the dorms were built like space-ships because frankly, I feel like I'm out of this world!

The campus is set on a hilltop, one mile from Jordan on one side and a mile and a half from the border on another. Because the land is deserted, it's hard to tell where Israel ends and Jordan begins. But don't worry- I won't stray!

The university surroundings are just magnificent. In Lisbon, some scenery reminded me of Route 17. In Greece, one intersection resembled Claremont Parkway and Webster Avenue. But here, the land is unique. The campus is lush and fertile, but the hills around are composed of dry soil with rows and walls of stones and scattered pine trees. The weather is hot and dry but the afternoon breezes are cool and luscious. We took a three hour walking tour of downtown Jerusalem. I stopped into the post office and it cost $1.30 to mail one letter. I guess the mail will be the biggest expense this year. We walked so much until we hit a wall- turns out that is the Jordanian border- right there in the middle of town!

I am going to Barak's for Shabbat and then the program arranged a two week tour of the country. Then Ulpan starts and I will finally get my taste of the Hebrew language. Will write after the weekend.

All my love,
Tyra

Lazer and Baruch Schpiegelman were first cousins. They grew up in the same town in Poland. Lazer was sixteen years older than Baruch, and after he came to America, he tried to send for Baruch, but Baruch wouldn't come. He was a Zionist, and he wanted to go to Palestine. In the thirties, it was Lazer who helped Baruch and Manya flee from Poland. Lazer looked after them, even from America. Tyra remembered walking with her grandfather as they carried bundles of clothing to the post office to send to them, for times were hard and necessities scarce in Israel.

Baruch changed his name to Barak when he got to Palestine. Baruch, the word means Blessed in Hebrew, and has its place in many prayers, but he liked the sound Barak more, that hard "k" at the end, especially since the word meant lightning. He changed his surname too, from Schpiegelman to Sagal, which denotes the act of acquiring or adapting. His name became a part of the new man, more Sabraesque than spiritual, more powerful than religious. He was an easy-going liberal, a chaleh and wine on Friday night kind of Jew.

The acquisition of Barak's new place in the ancient homeland was bought and paid for in courage and deeds, actual and concrete. He fought for independence in 1947 and 1948 with nothing more than a worn-out pair of overalls for a uniform, a rifle and a bit of cunning to help him survive. He was from the old-time school of Zionists. He was an idealist and worked hard for communal benefit. Jews, he felt, should always have a place, safe from the anti-Semitic, oppressive world.

He named his two daughters for the colorful blooming flowers of the homeland. Though they were born in the same neighborhood, nursed and weaned in the same house, the oldest, Irit, was born in Palestine, the youngest, Hadas, in Israel. He was proud of his girls, and gratified that he had been able to bequeath his love of Zion to them as if it were as indisputable as his genes for blue eyes or brown hair.

They were total opposites, one sister shy, obedient, the other stubborn and overbearing. Irit was a lot like Jessie. She talked fast and argued about politics and culture. She was outgoing and vibrant, but unlike Jessie, who had no interest in food, Irit ate with gusto and often. Target practice was her favorite pastime during her basic training in *Zahal*, the Israel Defense Force. Hadas was gentle and idealistic. She was a nervous wreck until she found out she was accepted in an army sponsored teacher-training program. She wanted to spend her required military service teaching young immigrants how to adjust to Israeli life in an Ulpan Absorption Center. She had a lot in common with Tyra.

Manya and Barak treated Tyra like a third daughter. She loved them for watching over her and filling the void of being away from her own family. She loved the way Manya made potions of herbs and mud from the Dead Sea called shomrim to protect her complexion and clear up her acne, which got worse whenever she spent time in the humid atmosphere of the Haifa outskirts where the Sagals lived.

Tyra found Manya to be sentimental. She would complain that, "Irit is so far away, studying in Yerushalayim. I haven't seen her in a month."

"What should my mother say?" Tyra countered softly, trying to comfort her. "She's heartsick, and we can't even speak on the phone." A three-minute overseas call cost more than Tyra's weekly living expenses.

Barak loved Tyra from the moment they met on the pier in Haifa when the Ashrei made port. "You are the first to come from America. Others will follow. You are the bridge." He squeezed her so tightly, she could hardly breathe.

Sunday, July 17, 1966 9 A.M.

My dear parents and sister,

The last time I wrote was Thursday night and I'll continue from there. Bella and I arose at seven, ate breakfast and left for Haifa. It was strange at first since we were unsure of the connections, but the people we asked were wonderful. I asked the local bus driver to tell us when we reached the Central Bus Station in Jerusalem. Knowing Hebrew is a great advantage, and when Israelis see that you are trying to speak their language, they become interested in you and want to converse. Then we took an express to Tel Aviv, and from the Central Station in Tel Aviv, we took another express to Haifa. The trip was comfortable. There was no air-conditioning, of course, but it was breezy and delightful. We saw everything from moun-tains to seashore. The trip took three hours. When we got to Haifa, Bella left for her family. The station was right near the port and I walked down to the pier to see the Ashrei which was due to sail at noon. For some silly reason, I wanted to see what it was like for you watching her, and me, sail from port in New York. She looked so huge and lovely, but I wasn't going to stand around for more than an hour in the heat and humidity for such sentimentality, so I made my way back to the bus station to get to Tel Paran. Hadas had said she would meet me downtown, but I'm on my own now and wanted to find my way by myself. I passed some stores and stopped into a camera shop to get film for the movie camera. One roll costs 26 pounds or thirty cents short of nine dollars. I don't think I'll be buying much film here! I passed a bakery and bought a cake for the family.

I told the bus driver the address, and he told me he would let me know when to get off. After twenty minutes, I got a little nervous, and reminded him. He screamed in Hebrew, "Don't worry." A man sitting behind me heard me tell the driver the name and address I needed and he said he knew the Sagals. Isn't that amazing? We got off the bus together and he took me to the house. He lived a bit farther down, so it was kind of him to get off with me.

Tel Paran was a small Arab town built on a mountain slope before the War of Independence. Houses are not laid out in an organized fashion with blocks and streets. Houses peek in and out of crevices and their addresses have nothing to do with logic. There are only dirt paths, no paved roads or sidewalks. I don't know how I would ever have found their house if not for this nice stranger.

It turns out that he works with Barak. Manya told the man he did a wonderful mitzvah. We were talking over some iced tea Manya served, and he told us that only two weeks ago, his seven year old daughter was run over by a bus and is recovering. It was so fantastic- he must have so much on his mind and yet to go out of his way for me like he did.

It's obvious that Barak made the right decision. He never would have been happy if he immigrated to the States. It would be like Grandpa becoming a butcher like Uncle Shockneh, instead of a tailor, where his true talent is. Barak wanted Manya to change her name too, to something more Sabra-ish, but she outright refused. 'It's all I have left of the world I knew,' she told him. They make a perfect couple- she holding on to the past and he moving forward.

The house is large, the furniture what there is of it is simple and the facilities are primitive. The dining room has a table and six chairs and shelves for books and records. There is a record player and a telephone, which is the one real luxury they have. There are alcoves in the bedrooms for closets, and you might remember the fabric Grandpa sent a while back- orange grapes and beige leaves on a blue background- well they used it to cover all the closets and for curtains throughout the house. In an instant I was surrounded by it and had a fit of homesickness!

There is a small room just for the toilet. In order to flush, you have to turn a knob to fill the tank- it takes a few minutes, and then pull down a chain. I never saw a contraption like that in my whole life! It's a hot, sunny room and there are lines of ants crawling all over. There is a large room for the sink and shower- there's no shower stall. The showerhead is attached to the boiler and there is a drain in the middle of the floor. If the rooms weren't large, the place would be horrible. There's so little stuff in it that at least there's room. It isn't the best, but there's no problem as far as food and clothes go. A lot of East African families live in Tel Paran. There's a huge cultural difference, but the Sagals are very sweet and get along with everyone. They want me to come every Shabbat and tell me their home is mine. In fact, Manya wouldn't let me bring a dish from the table to the sink or do anything to help around the house. But you know me. I insisted on helping out.

Am I writing too much? You must tell me if I take up too much of your time. I think it might be abnormal to write in such detail, but I feel that since I am the first in the family to travel so far, it's my duty to let you live vicariously through my adventures- it's all so wonderful and exciting. Especially armed with my movie camera, I can be the Miller Roving Reporter!

Love,
Tyra

During one of the first tours after she arrived in Jerusalem, the camera and the film in it was almost confiscated. At the Modi'in checkpoint in the Judean hills, the ancient site of the Maccabees, a lieutenant told her to stop filming the outpost, the soldiers manning it and the Jordanian hill across the alley. "Security," he explained. But the tour guide was a stickler, and wanted to take the film from her right there on the spot. The officer interceded and said it would be all right to wait until the cartridge was used up and send it to him afterward for censoring instead of ruining the whole of it right there and then. Of course, the guide had forgotten about it afterwards and Tyra sent it home with a warning. "For family only. Don't let strangers or spies watch it- or we could all go to jail!"

By the time she got to Dimona, she was even more brazen. Despite the warning sign with a picture of a skull and crossbones, and the words *Asur L'tzalem-* Photography Forbidden- she scanned the vast, arid space enclosed by high barbed wire fences. If it weren't a nuclear power plant, why the warning? Always denied, always known. But she made sure the guide was out of sight. The little girl from the Bronx who couldn't wrangle permission from her older sister to buy a candy bar stood up against the entire Israel Defense Force!

Further south, in the scorching wadis near Solomon's mines, near where crazy Azariah stood over a small blue flower, the camera met its match. Azariah looked disheveled, dressed in his customary soiled pair of baggy overalls, the twenty-eight year old American expatriate as he extended his hand to every student crossing over the steep, dry riverbed, warning, "Precious flower. Do not crush Hashem's precious flower." Can you imagine- one lone flower growing in a vast wasteland? And one kook protecting it! All of a sudden, there was a loud explosion and Tyra and the students standing near her ducked for cover. After some moments of silence, they lifted up, expecting perhaps to see Jordanian soldiers across the thistly expanse of underbrush and sand standing on Harei Adom- the Red Mountain Range- so named because the shadows of the setting sun cast a deep red hue over the graceful slopes, or thieving Bedouin nomads ransacking their camp. But there was none of that melodramatic excitement. Tyra saw that her camera battery exploded from the heat or perhaps the sun's glare. The camera's insides were all corroded from the residue. Such trouble.

The train ride was the last straw. Sid wrote her that the three-hour trip from Jerusalem to Haifa wasted a lot of film. "All the trees look alike. One minute of the Mediterranean is enough." But for Tyra, every wave crested on the shore with a different thickness of foam and a tempo all its own, the rhythm of the centuries at once stable and irregular. Every olive tree had its own history. Who knew who may have planted it- Jeremiah or

Michah- and every terrace was cleverly designed and built with back-breaking labor so as not to waste one precious drop of rain. Sid didn't realize that when Tyra hung out the window to capture an approaching tunnel on the other side of the mountain slope, her head was nearly reaching into Jordan, as the tracks hugged the Jordanian border as they descended the steep, stony Judean hills. It was Tyra's favorite way of traveling to her relatives in Haifa, but by April of 1967, service was suspended because it became far too dangerous. Terrorist units operating out of Syria repeatedly sabotaged the route between Jerusalem and Tel Aviv during nighttime mine-laying infiltrations.

July 18, 1966 9 P.M.

Dear Mom, Dad and Jessie,

If you were my children, boy I would be worried! I haven't heard from you since I got here. If you haven't written, I hope it's because you were away on vacation and had too good a time to write.

I'm resting in the room tonight. Thank God they gave us a free night. We hiked in the Judean hills all day and I was so filthy, I couldn't wait to shower. I washed some laundry and all I have left is to set my hair. The sun is so strong here, I am so dark. At least my complexion is better.

We had breakfast at 7:30. I had a hard-boiled egg, four pieces of bread and butter and get this- a glass of milk! Anything's better than Turkish coffee. As soon as classes start and I'm on my own, I'll buy some instant coffee. It's pretty good but costs $2 for eight ounces. The prices are high which is a shame for the Israelis who don't have very much money.

We started the day by hiking four miles on the Burma Road. This was a road constructed by children and old folks in three days during the War of Independence. It was the major supply route between Jerusalem and Tel Aviv because the main highway was too exposed and vulnerable to Arab attacks.

The entrance to the Burma was steep, stony and slippery. We passed an Arab village which of course is deserted now. I was glad I didn't take the camera because I could hardly keep my balance. At least I walked off breakfast, and I could tell from the way I've been eating here, this is going to be a fattening year, so the more I hike, the better. I did get the feeling that it was a terrible war and winning it was a great achievement for the Israelis.

Almost every tree and shrub is planted by man. Israel's hilltops are green. In back of them you can see Jordan's sandy, white mountains. The contrast is stark. The hills are made of stone and I found out that the rock formations that I mentioned previously are not natural, but were constructed as terraces to catch the rains and irrigate the mountains. Otherwise, all the water would roll down to the valleys leaving the hills dry and barren. Some of these stone stepladders are two thousand years old but we couldn't distinguish them.

I almost started to cry at our last stop at the John F. Kennedy Peace Forest Memorial. Fifty one columns of Jerusalem stone- one for each state and the District of Columbia- are built in the form of a tree stump which is a symbol of Kennedy's life cut short. It's set atop a mountain and surrounded by interloping slopes and valleys. Just awesome. They love him here. I remember that awful weekend not long ago when he was killed and we all sat around the TV without moving. It was like the closest thing to sitting shiva (seven days of mourning). Thank God, I could only imagine what that is like!

I must get to my hair now, so I will close. Take care.

Love to all.

Tyra

Tuesday July 19, 1966 11P.M

Hi-

Today we toured many points of interest in Jerusalem and the surrounding areas. We started at Mt. Hertzl which houses the tombs of some of the leaders of the State. It is also where the Jerusalem National Military Cemetery is. The entrance is constructed of steel which looks like charred wood and remains of artillery. Each grave is set a little higher with a ridge of stone bricks surrounding it. At the head of each is a large flat stone which has the national seal and name and date. The State kept the bodies of each battalion together- it felt that since these people knew each other and fought together, they should remain together. There was one memorial dedicated to 33 men between the ages of 19-29 who were on a sabotage mission during World War II and sank in their destroyer. There is a huge stone shaped liked a destroyer with the names of all these men. The slab is set in a pond of water.

There is another memorial dedicated to 140 men who died in a submarine also during World War II. There is slab of stone shaped like a captain's bridge set in the water, and from it you can look ahead and see a huge triangle of land- that's the front of the ship and it's pointed toward Jerusalem.

We stopped at the grave of a thirteen year old boy who was killed during the Israeli War of Independence. I got the feeling that these guys who fought and died knew what they were fighting for and wanted to accomplish their mission. They must have been driven by such a sense of purpose. They wanted Jerusalem and Israel. I was thinking of Viet Nam and I don't think our boys know why they're there. Somehow, "making the world safe for diversity," is too vague and just not enough.

The whole conception of the cemetery was so warm and in such good taste. One could see the compassion for the dead soldiers and their families who come to visit.

We continued on to Yad V'Shem. It means Everlasting Monument as it is written in Psalms. It is a memorial to the Six Million killed in the Nazi Holocaust. The first building was a very dark one of stone brick walls. On the floor were the names of the concentration camps and in the corner, an eternal flame flickered dimly on the mosaic floor. It was so quiet you could hear only footsteps echoing. It was depressing to look at all the pictures you've seen over and over before. I was sad, angry, and bitter. And then when I got outside again into the bright sunlight and as we started riding in the bus, things got back to normal- it doesn't change you- you just go on as before. The memorial is on top of Mt. Zicharon- Mt. of Remembrance- and the view was of overlapping slopes all around.

From there we went to Hadassah Medical Center. The Marc Chagall stained glass windows based on Jacob's blessings to the twelve tribes of Israel from Genesis were displayed there as the huge walls of the chapel. They are absolutely stunning and so symbolic and unique.

The medical school consists of a seven year program, six of learning and one of interning. Students enter right after high school graduation. There is also a three year nursing program.

We continued to the Notre Dame Monastery in Jerusalem. From its roof you could see the wall and Jordanian border on three sides. The border is about four blocks from the building. Part of the roof is used as an Israeli military post. The other side of the building is in Jordanian territory. It was amazing- even pictures weren't allowed because it was so close to the border. In fact, there is a story that a nun was on the roof, looking over the ledge, and her dentures fell out of her mouth onto the ground into Israeli territory. The soldier who retrieved them couldn't just give them back to her. It became a whole diplomatic episode and took about three months for the UN to resolve the issue. The poor nun must have had to eat baby food all that time! Can you imagine the craziness here! If only people could just get along.

Then we passed the Mandelbaum Gate. That's another crazy story. During the war, Jordanians got control of this Dr. Mandelbaum's house. Israeli soldiers pushed them back halfway, and of course, just when Israel makes headway, the UN calls for a ceasefire, and right then and there, smack in the middle of the house, the line is drawn- Israel on one side, Jordan on the other- and the poor Mandelbaum family never saw the inside of their house again.

We had lunch at the university and then went to Har Zion- the place of David's Tomb. It was an ancient structure- very dreary and cave-like. We stood in front of the coffin and the rabbi there blessed all of us. In the very same area we went into the room of the Last Supper and the church in which Mary was supposed to have died. There is a life size statue of her in her deathbed. It's surrounded by marble pillars and carvings.

Finally we got back to the hotel, had fifteen minutes to shower, eat dinner and then went to the National Museum. It's a beautiful place not far from the university and I'd like to go back and spend more time there.

Yesterday I went to see Irit and she wasn't home. Tonight Irit came to the dorm and I wasn't there. I think I'll be going to Barak's for the weekend. I want to get in touch with Rabbi Singer soon.

Traveling around these past few days I saw construction sites all over. There's such a great need for housing and schools. They're so busy working hard to make everything work out, and there's so much to be done. Take care. Love,

Tyra

July 24, 1966

Dear Tyra,

 I can't tell you how much your letters mean to me. I know how busy you must be and really appreciate all the details you write. I spent my entire life in the Bronx. I was born here- went to school here, got married here, worked here, had you and Jessie here. The furthest I ever traveled was to the Catskills. Even Daddy is worldlier than I am, being that he was born in Iowa and grew up in Chicago! I guess my life is pretty ordinary. You write with such gusto and detail- you appreciate every flower- every mountain range in Israel that you climb and I can feel your exhilaration. Between your descriptions and all the movies you send back, I get a real sense of Israel and how beautiful a country it is, almost like I am there. Only I miss you so much. Thanks for taking me around the world with you!

 The week in the mountains was restful, and it was good for Grandma and Grandpa to get away. Grandpa so enjoys the "fresha luft". It seems the cool, breezy mountain air is the only thing that hasn't changed. The bungalows are not the same as they used to be. Time must have flown by when I wasn't looking. All the children are grown up. Your friend Michelle is engaged- her mother told me she got a teaching job in a good neighborhood and her fiancé is a lovely boy from a well-to-do family. He's in medical school. The wedding plans are going well and they are excited and waiting for a December wedding. Some people have all the luck. There were just a few younger children that came back and the place actually was pretty dull. We did get to see a show at the Brown's Hotel. Things are changing, that's for sure.

 Your uncle came to visit on the weekend, but even his sons gave him a hard time and wanted to stay in the city. Sheldy came with the two little ones. It was the baby's first outing since the bris (circumcision). He is adorable.

So who is the Greek god you're in love with already? You're too practical to use up so much film otherwise. Was that in Greece? I'm dying to know about the guy!

Love,
Mom

Tuesday, July 26, 1966 8:45 A.M.

Dear Jessie,

I tried to time this letter to arrive on your birthday so I can wish you a year of happiness and success. Remember that night when we were in bed talking about what we should do- you didn't know whether to accept that new position at Manhattan Orthopaedic Hospital and I didn't know whether to go to Israel. The actual making of the decision is the most difficult. One has to choose a fate for herself not knowing what it will bring. I was afraid it would be hard for me to adjust, not so much to a new environment, but being away from my family for so long. So far, I think I made the right choice, and I hope, Jessie, your decision will be good for you, too. Since you start your new job on your birthday, I wish you lots of success and satisfaction. Next year we will celebrate together.

Now, Mom and Dad can join in. I spent the last weekend in Haifa and I feel bad because I think I gave you the wrong impression about the Sagals' life. I was too hasty to judge the way of life in a country way different from our own. I can understand why. On Wednesday I left one of the most luxurious ships and on Friday I came in contact with an Israeli home for the first time, so I was a little shocked. But now, from what I can see, life is very different here. The pace is slower and more casual. People wear shorts to work! We never wore shorts except in the mountains. Here that's all you see in the streets of the cities.

But modern Israel is so young and trying so diligently to solve her many problems. A big one is that her manufacturing facilities are underdeveloped. Everything made in Israel is for mass consumption and is simple, not only in style but in quality. Even in the best furniture shops, the furniture is without richness and detail, just plain and practical. The clothes also are made without the workmanship that we're used to. Grandpa would plotz! It's amazing that the poor quality demands such high prices. Israelis try to buy everything from furniture to cosmetics from abroad even though they are more expensive.

What I have observed is that the Sagals have a good standard of living. They don't struggle for the necessities and they can afford things many other families cannot. They bought a telephone for the equivalent of $400 three years ago, and last time I was there Barak bought a record for Hadas. But of course there are many things they don't have. So I would say they are in the middle of the Israeli scale.

Today is the second part of placement exams, but many of us are fasting and were excused until Thursday.

It was exciting to be in Jerusalem for Tisha B'Av. I learned of a legend that goes like this and it applies to me and your future grandchildren! There is a special blessing for those people who come to Israel during the three weeks before Tisha B'Av. Those who come at this time will be happy all their lives and even more so their children will live to see the rebuilding of the Temple. Last night being Tisha B'Av, many of us went to different shuls in Jerusalem. I went with some girls to Hachal Schlomo. It is a majestic building, but too crowded, so we went to Beit Hillel, which was also crowded, so we went to Har Zion. In the book of Lamentations, it is written that the people would go up to the mountain and weep on the destructions. Har Zion, being the only ancient place left in Israeli territory, has taken on a great momentum and is an important place for Jews in Israel today. On Erev Tisha B'Av there is a major pilgrimage to the top of the mountain. Walking from shul to shul I felt like an outsider. I felt like a wandering Jew which I suppose is a terrible thing for a Jew to say in Israel.

There are many steps leading up to the mountain. They are made of stone bricks and there are stone walls for banisters. The way was lit with torches and it was very dark except for the flames' reflections. There were little glass boxes with lit candles strung from wires attached to the trees lighting the way. At the top, a crowd of people gathered on a level piece of land. The chief Rabbi of Israel stood on a platform and spoke of the ruins of centuries ago and the ruins in our own time, in Europe. Tall palm trees surrounded the field, and their blowing fronds against the dark sky and the flames from the torches was an awesome and eerie sight. Some cantors sang and we sang Ani Maamin together. Then services were over and everyone scattered about, running to see David's Tomb and the other sites on the mountain. The hubbub was totally incongruous with the mournful spirit of the fast, and except for listening to the rabbi, I wasn't inspired. In fact, I was let down. I'm glad I went, though. The next afternoon, six of us sat on the lawn and read the Book of Aichah. Then it felt like Tisha B'Av.

I hope all is well. Take care. Love to all.

Tyra

July 30, 1966

Dear Mom, Dad and Jessie,

We spent the past two weeks touring and I am exhausted. For such a tiny country it's amazing how much there is to see and learn. Every inch of land is filled with Biblical history and modern stories of bravery and hard work. It seems nothing, even to this day, comes easy to our people, and I feel so privileged to be part of it. I am so happy that I came here to study this year. Yet I feel like all that has been developed and accomplished was just handed to me on a silver platter and I didn't do anything to earn it. In any event, the vacation's over and I will be studying my tail off as classes start next week. I hope to speak fluently and write literary papers by the end of the year.

There are twenty levels of Ulpan and I placed in the seventeenth which is almost the top. I was really happy. I guess graduating with Honors really meant something after all!

My roommate Bella and I get along great and we have a lot of fun together. We've been going into town, seeing the sights on our own, talking to shop owners, and of course eating! Everyone eats in the streets here, while they're walking. We wouldn't be caught dead doing that in the Bronx. The Yemenite falafel stands are the best- deep fried chick pea balls stuffed into fresh doughy pita bread- falafel is to Israel what Coke is to America. I came here like Twiggy and I'll come home like Kate Smith!

It's amazing to see policemen, firemen and garbage men, knowing they're all Jewish. I don't think I've ever seen any Jewish garbage collectors in New York! And here the streets are full of soldiers, girls, too, and they look great in dark khaki skirts, and all of them are so young- they look like babies and they walk around with rifles on their shoulders!

The streets are full of motorcycles. Hardly anyone has a car. The motorcycles even have cute little sidecars attached to them-with enough room for a wife and a baby, as that seems to be the most popular mode of private transportation.

I have the opportunity to study with the most noted archaeologist, Dr. Yigal Yardin. He is the one who discovered the ruins of Masada! I am registering for the Intro to Archaeology course he is teaching. I know it's not literature related, but it's a thrilling opportunity I can't give up. We will be going on field trips and digs. Can you imagine me slaving in the desert!

I am so excited to see Rabbi Singer- they invited me to spend next Shabbos with them. I can't wait.

Take care. Love to all.

Tyra

FOUR

A Prayer and a Wing

Tyra was setting the table for dinner when Kaye sprung a new one on her.

"Grandpa thinks you should go to Hebrew school when classes start up again."

The old European rabbi had died around Thanksgiving and the board of directors finally, after interviewing numerous candidates, agreed on a new one to take his place, Rabbi Norman Singer.

"Ma, you can't do that to me," Tyra said as she put her fingers to her mouth. She pleaded with her mother, "You know how much I hated it. Rabbi Landau used to slap his ruler on my desk when I got my letters mixed up. It's not my fault the *hey* looks like the *chet* and the *zayin* is almost the same as the *gimmel.*"

"This rabbi is different. Grandpa says he's young and modern. He just graduated from Yeshiva College, and he has a pretty wife and a baby girl. At least, give it a chance. Then we'll see. Besides, Jessie will be home from the hospital soon and it'll be good for you to get together with your own friends after school. And stop biting your nails, for God's sakes. How many times have I told you, `Hands make the first impression.'?"

It was a raw February afternoon when Tyra walked up the hill to White Plains Road and then north three blocks to the synagogue. She was cold, and huddled in her coat as she entered the modest, narrow split level house that had been converted to a shul. Up a few stairs was a plain sanctuary, fitted with wooden pews on the right, and a raised women's section on the left. The benches of the women's section were cordoned off with a four-foot high *mechitzah-* divider-which was decorated with open scrollwork on the top. In the back, there was a small classroom. Downstairs, there was a kitchen, two lavatories and a large all-purpose room. She did not know it at the time, but this place was to become a second home, a personal sanctuary, and it was here the direction of Tyra's life would slowly solidify and remain with her forever.

She saw the back of a tall, broad-shouldered man writing on the board as she stood by the doorway of the classroom. Rabbi Singer must have felt her presence as he turned around to acknowledge her. She was stunned. He was young, good-looking, had a thick head of dark, wavy hair, and he sported a mustache, grown, Tyra assumed, to add age to his boyish face. A rabbi who looked more like a movie star–like Clark Gable or Gregory Peck. A rabbi! This wasn't going to be so bad after all, she thought.

"I can tell you're going to be a good student," Rabbi Singer said after they introduced themselves. "You're a few minutes early, and most students, I've been told, never even come on time." Tyra liked him immediately.

One by one the neighborhood boys, half of whom she knew, trickled in. Eleven and twelve years old, they were there to learn their bar mitzvah lessons. The rabbi made it quite clear throughout the hour and a half that he was developing a three year curriculum of serious study that would intensify with the attainment of bar mitzvah rather than culminate with it. The young generation, if he had anything to do with it, would understand the wisdom of the law and participate in its beautiful tradition. The era of merely memorizing foreign words from old prayer books was over. Judaism was alive, and no one could make that more clear than the dynamic Rabbi Singer, the teacher who cared more about the questions his students asked than the answers they gave.

Tyra kept turning toward the door throughout the lesson, and when she got home, she told her mother in no uncertain terms that she wasn't going back.

"Why?" Kaye asked. "He wasn't nice?"

"He's okay. But I'm the only girl."

Kaye found the right things to say, as she always did, and they really did make sense to Tyra. "Maybe as more families hear about the rabbi, some new girls will register. Besides, women always outnumber the men. You, my dear, are in a unique spot. You'd be smart to enjoy it!"

Tchotchka had been missing Jessie so much these last weeks. Even Kaye's piano playing didn't cheer him up. No one could play *A Mother's Prayer* like Kaye. The musical staffs wrapped around her like a lush mink stole, the kind the ladies of Congregation Anshe Shalom wore on the High Holy Days, and stuck to her like a second skin. The yearning notes and wailing chords sifted through the air, slowly, hauntingly, as Kaye's fingertips struck the ivory keys with the burden that was in her heart. Tyra loved most, the way her mother's left hand would cross over the right and play the high notes with agile, lingering trills. Someday Tyra hoped to play piano like that. Whenever Tyra practiced, Jessie would suddenly decide to read. "Stop banging. You sound awful anyway," she would yell.

"I like being mediocre," or "I'm never as good as you," Tyra would answer as she would cry and run into the bedroom.

When Jessie would come home from the hospital, the console would be closed. Kaye sewed long tablecloths together which she would use to cover the intricately carved Chinese Chippendale top. All the medical things Jessie would need near her hospital bed would be stored on it: alcohol, calamine, witch hazel, combs, make-up, a back-scratcher and an emesis basin.

Tyra would try to coax Tchotchka onto her finger, but he would merely nip at her. His seed went mostly uneaten and the bells of his spinning wheel were silent. "She'll be home soon," Tyra kept repeating, knowing he was smart enough to understand. Tchotchka just sat on the gravel paper covering the bottom of the cage, chirping over and over, "Where's Jess? Where's Jess?"

Family was like a puzzle, made up of many parts, each a different size and shape, round or narrow, straight and even curved. But when all the pieces fit together just right, the picture was complete, perfect. Now a piece was missing and things did not feel right. Soon Jessie would be home. The living room would be as it never was before, and no one really knew what to expect or how things would be. The family heart was broken, yet at the same time, filled with hope. Only one thing was certain, together they would manage, learning one day at a time what they would need to do to get by. Soon the family would be complete.

Just as Jessie had predicted, the ambulance came with its siren blaring, and the neighbors were there in force to greet her. As the attendants were wheeling the stretcher from the elevator to the apartment, Tchotchka chirped, "Here's Jess. Here's Jess."

She took over the living room, her hospital bed in the center, in front of the television set, so she would be able to watch. All her personal items were set on top of the piano. The bedpan was put on the floor next to the pedals. Tyra's piano lessons would have to wait.

Tyra was going to sleep on a cot in the foyer, and such a sorry circumstance finally provided Sid and Kaye with a bedroom for themselves.

Tyra went to Hebrew school day after day without saying another word about it, and finally Kaye just had to ask if other girls showed up. Tyra told her there was only one other girl, Elaine, but Rabbi Singer was wonderful and she would continue her studies.

Tyra would walk to shul with Lazer on Shabbos mornings. He would hold her hand and ask her what Rabbi had taught that week, and she would tell him what she had learned. On the way home it was her turn to ask him questions, and he told her stories of the old country, and how hard he worked in the sweatshops after he arrived in America so he could bring over his mother and siblings from Europe. Tyra loved best the way he told of how he met Hana, that when he saw her for the first time, he thought she was the most beautiful girl in the world.

When they arrived, Tyra would sit next to Rebbitzen Vicki in the women's section. The sermons were what she enjoyed the most. She took note of how Vicki concentrated on her husband's words, how she nodded when he spoke forcefully, and she did nod often. It was a romantic love story, one that Tyra dreamed about for herself. She would make a good rebbitzen one day, too.

The rabbi's voice was passionate, and he connected the weekly Torah portion to the issues of the day. Since Sid always talked politics in the house, Tyra felt somewhat knowledge-able about what was going on. Rabbi Singer pounded his fists on the lectern, and you could even see fine sprays of saliva coming from his mouth, because he spoke so quickly and with great fire. But he did not instill fear. He challenged him-self as much as he tried to uplift his congregants. He criti-cized the new breed of American-Jewish authors who seemed to find solace in deprecating their Jewishness, and enhance their popularity by assimilating into the mainstream and dis-tancing themselves from their heritage. He warned the older generation that they had to explain to the children the mean-ing of the *mitzvot*- commandments; that it wasn't enough to force them to observe rules without understanding their sig-nificance. "They deserve to understand. Otherwise, we will lose them." He advised the congregation not to be swayed by those who questioned their American loyalty just because they were Jewish as well. "We love the country we were born in or came to. How many of you or your sons served in World War II?" he asked, and you could see waves of movement as heads nodded throughout the congregation. He said that the Jewish people would be loyal citizens in whatever country they lived, and for effect, he turned to the corner behind him and pointed to the American flag. And then, for more effect, he turned to the opposite corner and pointed to the Israeli flag with the blue Magen Dovid in the middle, and continued, "but no matter what that country would be, our *neshumas*, our essence would be Jewish."

But Rabbi Singer's sermons about Israel were the ones Tyra loved the most. "We are no longer a people in exile. The Diaspora is over," he exclaimed with pride. Tyra would nod in agreement because she learned about the Babylonian exile and studied the words of the prophets Ezra and Nehemiah. The rabbi would describe how dangerous and difficult it was to live in Israel—water was scarce and the land was barren. Israelis didn't have televisions in every living room or a phone in every house. When he spoke of the tailor among them who sewed clothes and sent them to his *mishpacha* in Haifa, Tyra beamed looking over the mechitzah to get a glimpse of Lazer. Rabbi told of the others who were better-off and bought bonds for Israel's defense. Once he said that the Talmud Torah class was going to lead a campaign for the Jewish National Fund, and asked Tyra right then and there to be chairman and organize the students who would canvas every Jewish home in the neighborhood. "Our congregation doesn't need fancy chandeliers," he said, pointing to the simple fluorescent lights overhead, "or plush carpets. But we will send enough money to Israel so a forest could be planted on the hills of Jerusalem. Our brethren know that we support and appreciate their sacrifice. We will not leave them alone to fight those who would destroy us- we will not be silent." Rabbi Singer, like an alarm clock, woke up the congregation and reminded them of their covenant with God and their obligations to humanity. Tyra was inspired to do some good in the world.

In the late Shabbos afternoons, when Tyra knew the Rabbi would have awakened from his traditional nap, she would visit the Singers. They would sip hot tea together and talk about everything. Everything, that is, except what was truly in her heart, for she could not bear to expose her selfishness for having opportunities denied to Jessie. Nor could she admit her guilt for wanting those opportunities. So discussions about Rashi and Rambam, and debates pitting Hillel's compassion against Shammai's exactitude sufficed, bringing Tyra joy and warmth, as the Singer's toddler ran between them vying for attention.

The rabbi called Kaye one day to invite her to come to services. "It's important for children to see their parents participate, to show by example," he said. "I understand that your husband works, but you...."

"Rabbi, I have a better idea," she interrupted, not happy and too tired to care about this new demand placed on her. "Why don't you visit us and see what's doing here?"

He said he would, and he did one day, and he was shocked at what he saw.

"It's not easy for a child to be cooped up, lonely and suffering," Kaye told him.

"Nor for her mother, either," he said. "Jessie's a spunky young woman. We'll see what we can do."

"It's a mitzvah to visit the sick," Rabbi told the teenagers in the youth group at the synagogue, and after a long discussion on friendship and compassion, the Rabbi led the twenty or so teenagers singing and dancing through the neighborhood, right to the Miller's apartment.

"You didn't come to the meeting, so the meeting came to you," Bernie, the president quipped to Jessie. From then on, hoards of kids came to visit, after school, before work, before their dates, on their way to the movies.

The late afternoons, when Tyra returned from Hebrew school were the worst times of the day. Tyra wanted to watch "The Bingo Game," her favorite television program. Jessie wouldn't stand for it. "The Secret Storm is on," she yelled. "I have to find out what happens."

"Can't you miss it one day?" Tyra cried.

"I had surgery. When you have surgery, you can watch what you want." Over the next months that became Jessie's mantra: She had surgery and Tyra deserved nothing.

Everyone in the youth group sent Jessie cards, too. Tons of cards. It was Tyra's job to bring them up from the mailbox.

Then she, Jessie and Kaye would string them together and Sid would hang them like streamers from one side of the room to the other.

Once Tyra threw an entire handful she brought up from the mailbox at Jessie. Tyra came into the lobby from school and Patrick, the mailman, told her he was glad she happened by. "Too many cards to fit in the box," he said as he handed her the stack. She took them from him, but inside she was stewing. She failed a math test that morning. She had been out of school the week before with a fever and sore throat, missed the whole unit on fractions and walked into a surprise quiz. Nobody sent her any get well cards. "Here's your mail," she said when she walked into the living room, and flung the entire handful at Jessie, although most of them landed under the bed. "Pick them up right now," Kaye screamed. "Why can't you girls get along?"

About a week later, Tyra saw one envelope addressed to her as she sifted through the mail in the lobby. She ripped it open and sat down on a step to read.

Dear Tyra,

You know everything that I am writing about because you live here and you know, too, nothing very exciting happens. I know you have been disappointed when you bring up bundles of cards for Jessie and you never get any mail for yourself, but I wanted you to know how much I appreciate the things you do for all of us around the house. Jessie appreciates it too, even though sometimes she says things she doesn't mean. You are grown up enough to know how hard it is for her, and we just have to help each other get through hard times.

Tyra read each of her mother's words as though it were a nugget left behind in the pan, bringing immense joy to the miner who found his gold. By the time she turned to the final page, a reluctance to finish overcame her, and she read it more slowly than the rest.

I've spent so much time writing these six pages of chit-chat. I hope you enjoyed your very own letter, but please don't expect me to do this often. There is laundry waiting for me to fold and food for me to cook. I love you.

Mom

Despite everything, the house was cheerful, noisy, and always smelled of fresh-baked cakes and cookies. Kaye wanted the kids, especially the boys, to have something to eat.

"Listen to this, Rabbi," Tyra said after class one day, and started to chant a *haftorah.* She was glowing because she knew the melody and the words by heart and her rendition was almost flawless.

"Tyra, what is this? You're wonderful."

She saw he was a little wary. "Rabbi, I want to have a bas mitzvah. I studied the portion that falls on the Shabbos of my twelfth birthday, and I want to chant it from the altar."

Learning the *haftorah* was a great achievement, and to know it by heart, an enormous feat. Rabbi Singer was truly impressed and told her so. "You learned it by yourself and you recited it perfectly. But you know girls don't come up to the *bimah.*"

"That's not fair. I study harder than the boys. They don't even try. Why can't I? Aren't I worth the same?"

"Probably more, but it's just not done. Women have a special role in the Jewish home, and are very highly regarded."

"I see how Grandma slaves in the kitchen. By the time she sits down at the Passover Seder, she's too exhausted to eat. She might as well be a slave in Egypt!"

"You are my number one student. And you will be the very first bas mitzvah of Congregation Anshe Shalom. You won't be able to chant, but I can guarantee you will be very proud."

She was no match for him and figured that she got the best deal she could. He promised her a special day. His sermon would be about Tyra and her family, and after services the entire congregation would partake of a sumptuous Kiddush. Because Rabbi trusted Hana's kashrut, he would allow all that she would cook and bake for the occasion- her wonderful kugels and soft, sweet cakes, into the shul. A rabbi's trust, that was the greatest honor of all.

That was the Rabbi's plan, and she trusted him. But she had one other idea all her own, and knew she'd best keep it to herself for the time being. That was a survival technique she had learned over the years starting when she was a child, when Jessie was put in charge of watching her. Tyra would tell Jessie during afternoons in the park or summer days in the Catskills, "I want to climb the tree," or "I want to roller skate." But Jessie wouldn't allow any of it. "Can't do this. Can't do that," she would holler. Tyra, smothered by the curse of obedience, didn't do anything she wanted.

After being denied everything important to her, and tired of merely complaining about how she hated being bossed around, she learned to take her chances and did as she pleased without asking for approval. So plain her imagination, so ordinary her desires, she rarely got into trouble, and even if she did, the consequences were hardly as dire as the sting of disapproval or confrontation which she dreaded in the first place. Time and again, Jessie would call her a sneak, but she could live with that.

The timing would be perfect for the bas mitzvah. Jessie would be out of her body cast; at most, she might need to wear a smaller walking cast. She would be straight and the whole family would celebrate in shul.

One day after school, Tyra and Elaine took the crosstown bus to Jerome Avenue. There was a special shop Tyra wanted to check out for a bas mitzvah dress. She fell in love with the first one she picked off the rack and tried it on. If only it would fit. The bodice was pleated and fit low on the waist. The skirt was flared and when Tyra twirled around in front of the mirror, the crinoline underskirt crinkled and the soft gold fabric shimmered as the reflection from the overhead lights bounced off the mirror. She saw it was perfect. Elaine told Tyra she looked too skinny in it, but for Tyra the dress was perfect and she was happy. The owner agreed to put it in the back room until Kaye could come to take a look. Tyra couldn't wait.

"Let's get a soda," Tyra said, and while the two girls walked over to her great uncle's candy store around the corner, they talked about the bas mitzvah party that Kaye told Tyra she could have on Saturday night after the kiddish. The boys from Hebrew school and Tyra's girlfriends would come to the house for a real party, with dancing to romantic songs sung by Johnny Mathis and The Platters. That was what they were most excited about. "You mean Rabbi is coming to chaperone. That's awful," Elaine said, but Tyra didn't mind. "Is not," she said.

"Hi, Uncle Izzy. We've been shopping for my *bas mitzvah* dress," she called out when they walked into the candy store.

"A *bar mitzvah*– for a girl?"

"*Bas mitzvah*, Uncle Izzy. I'm going to have a *bas mitzvah*."

"What a *meshuggenah* world! Things keep changing," Izzy said, shaking his head.

"Well, sit down, girls. Two chocolate malteds coming up, with lots of ice cream. Don't your mothers feed you? For God's sakes, when you drink tomato juice, you look like a thermometer!"

Tyra loved Uncle Izzy. He was married to Hana's sister, Minna, and not nearly as religious as Tyra's other great uncles, Lazer's brothers. But he was certainly a riot. Everything was a joke to him; he was loud and he made everyone laugh. Every time he and Aunt Minna visited Hana and Lazer, he would squeeze a few dollar bills into Jessie and Tyra's palms. Kaye taught the sisters early on to protest and refuse, but Izzy would never take the money back. And as the sisters got older, the singles became fives.

Tyra and Elaine were chatting at the counter when they heard Izzy yell over to a couple of the neighborhood boys who came in and stood by the rack reading comic books.

"Why don't ya' buy the books first, ya' flat-foot floogies? And tell your mothers I put enough ice cream in your malt-eds, ya' skinny balinks!"

Izzy turned to the girls and chuckled, loud enough for the boys to hear, "Be smart. Find yourself some good boys, not like those cheapskates!" He laughed. "Am I invited to your bas-s mitzvah?" he asked. "It don't matter because I'm comin' anyway."

When Jessie returned from one of her hospital check-ups, and after the ambulance attendants transferred her to her hospital bed and left, she called to Tyra to bring Tchotchka to her.

"In a few minutes. I'm almost finished with my math."

"You never do anything for me," Jessie screamed. "You selfish brat!"

"You've got nerve. `Change the channel, bring me a drink, change the channel again, get me a book, go to the library.' Excuse me for living, Miss Queen of Sheba." Tyra stormed out of the kitchen and slammed the door to the bedroom. She was startled to see Kaye sitting on the bed, crying.

"What's the matter, Mom?"

"The x-rays showed the fusion didn't take. The doctors want Jessie to stay in the cast for another three months. Maybe the extra time will make her spine stronger." Kaye clasped Tyra's hand. "If it doesn't help, Jessie will need to go through the whole operation again. Her spine won't be strong enough to support her. I wish you wouldn't fight."

Tyra ran over to her mother and wrapped her arms around her. "Don't cry." After a short hesitation, she cried out loud, "Oh, no! What about my bas mitzvah? Jessie won't be able to come. Ma, that's not fair." Tyra started to cry. "I don't want a bas mitzvah anymore."

"Tyra, please, not you, too. I'm beyond my limit today. We'll figure something out. Stop crying, please. Go, keep Jessie company or set the table, please."

"Here's Tchotchka, Jessie," Tyra said as the parakeet hopped from her finger onto Jessie's. "I'm sorry about the operation."

"Don't worry. You can have your bas mitzvah. I don't want to go to it anyway," Jessie said, propping the bird onto her chin-band, where he nuzzled against her cheek and wiped away the single tear that managed to escape from Jessie's usual bravado.

"Tchotchka," he chirped. "Here's Jess. Pretty Jess."

It was Sid's idea to build a stretcher for Jessie. Then after the ceremony in shul, Jessie could participate in a grand celebration on the roof. He measured the elevator and the doorway from the stairwell to the roof to make sure the stretcher would fit inside. When he told Kaye it just wouldn't be for the bas mitzvah but that Jessie could be strapped in and taken up to her grandparents' for a change of scenery or to the roof for some fresh air whenever they wanted, he got a big hug!

Tyra sat in the women's section with Kaye, Hana and a host of her aunts and cousins. Sid, Lazer and the uncles were sitting in the front near the altar. The Rabbi spoke of Tyra's accomplishments, and she looked down, humbled by his glowing and exaggerated words. She didn't deserve to be praised when it was Jessie who had the courage. "Look up," Kaye said and kept poking her. "Be polite."

When Rabbi started to tell the congregation of Kaye's devotion and resilience, she too looked down. "Look up, Mom," Tyra nudged, "Look up," and they laughed quietly, clasping their hands together. Tyra knew her time was coming, but she fought the jitters within her. When Mr. Bloom, one of the elders chanted the *haftorah*, Tyra sang along softly from her seat. She moved her lips precisely, enunciating each word clearly. She didn't anticipate that one by one, the women, even the *Rebbitzen*, would hum along, and the mellifluous, collective feminine voice floated toward the altar, for even Rabbi lifted his head up from the *Chumash Tikkun*, looked toward the women's section and smiled at Tyra. Her bas mitzvah was better than she expected! Lazer though, didn't know what to make of hearing his granddaughter's voice during the recitation of the *haftorah*. He was the one who insisted Tyra go to Hebrew school in the first place. He squinted, half in confusion, half in disapproval, perhaps realizing once again, how far from Europe he had come, and how new this world really was.

Rabbi Singer was right. Services were beautiful. But not perfect. There was no such thing as perfect, except for a dress or the weather. Tyra ached because Jessie was back in the apartment, isolated and denied, still in the big cast. It was a terrible blow when the doctors told them the fusion didn't take and she needed to stay in bed even longer. Tyra knew everyone else was thinking about Jessie, worrying that she might need another operation. They tried not to show it, not to spoil the day, but it was there. The ache that festers because a piece of the puzzle isn't where it's supposed to be—the expectations that whither into disappointments—the imperfection of life that rips a family apart as much as it binds them together—and the burn Tyra didn't know how to quell, that kept growing deep within her confused and helpless soul.

The weather was perfect for the rooftop kiddush. The entire congregation walked back to the house for the celebration. Sid and a few neighbors carried Jessie up the narrow flight of stairs from the top floor to the roof. The men were struggling under the weight of the cast and the bulk of the stretcher, but Jessie was laughing and flailing her arms as she greeted the neighbors. She acted like she was Cleopatra being carried on her throne by courtiers, waving to throngs of her adoring subjects. "Hold on, hold on!" Sid hollered. Then she clutched Tchotchka's travel cage, lest he fall.

The neighbors and the congregation celebrated all afternoon. The platters of food Hana and Kaye prepared were laid out on two long aluminum folding tables, and all of it was tasty and wonderful. The wine was sweet and the rabbi said the blessings. Catching her off-guard, Sid put his arm around Kaye's narrow waist and to the beat of his off-key humming, led her in a few tender, awkward steps of the rumba. Kaye laughed radiantly, and for a few hours, the Millers basked in the limelight.

From the roof on that clear day, they could see the Manhattan skyline, and as dusk approached, the lights of the city began to sparkle here and there. The women on the roof intuitively knew the streets along Broadway would be filling up with ladies dressed in gabardine suits with fox collars or mink stoles, and slim skirts falling just below the knees. Their stockings fit snugly, the seams perfectly straight in the middle of their shapely calves; they stepped gracefully in high-heeled alligator shoes with straps buckled around their ankles; ladies whose arms interlocked with the arms of their gentlemen, well-dressed men who escorted them to theatres or restaurants or nightclubs. Ladies of the city who were having the time of their lives, and who could blame them for their good luck or begrudge them their good fortune?

And the women of the roof, in their comfortable cotton housecoats, with their men sitting on cardboard boxes nearby, trumping pinochle or knocking gin rummy, with their children hiding-and-seeking inbetween the elevator shaft and electrical boxes. Women of the roof who were living the life of their times, staying within their place, calling to their children, "Don't get to close to the edge."

Trapped on the rooftop, all of them. Tyra's day to shine clouded with worry over Jessie. Worse still, Jessie had never had a chance to shine. And Tchotchka alongside her, pecking and pulling at the latch of his cage door, would surely wing his way to the trees if he could, and flourish in the freedom of the park before coming home. Tyra one day, too, would fly to the other side of the world.

FIVE

HOLY

Saturday evening, July 30, 1966

Dear Dawn,

The voyage was great. Met an adorable crew member, really sweet. The last night he told me he loved me! I know he wants to go to America and I don't want to be taken in. He docks again in Haifa in August so we shall see!

Spent the first week in Israel touring and was totally exhausted. The nicest and most relaxing thing we did was to go swimming at Tantura Beach in the Mediterranean. The water is so clean and warm and you can see the mountain slopes on both sides of the beach. Oh, was that fantastic!

Classes started Monday and we had placement exams. There are six levels and I'm in five- the next to the highest and although I didn't think I'd care which level I'd be in, I was really very happy because you know me, I always want to be the best. I study for five hours each day. I have three teachers- they're all young girls who just graduated the university educational program.

The university is a beautiful place. The campus is larger than all the city colleges combined. There are gardens with fountains, pools and statues all over. On Monday we move into the dorms. Until then we've been staying at a hotel- not a luxurious American hotel, but an old fashioned Israeli one where you have to beg for a clean towel once a week. I saw my dorm room on Thursday. It's all very exciting and can't wait to get settled, although I'm not looking forward to packing tomorrow and unpacking Monday. On Tuesday our hold luggage arrives and although our room is very lovely I have no idea at all as to where everything will go. My roommate is a very sweet girl named Bella. She's a junior and was one of the three other girls in my cabin on the Ashrei. The kids in the program are all very nice and I have a lot of fun with them. They're all pretty young and even though we're about the same age-they're mostly juniors and there's quite a difference. However I'm having a good time.

I'd like to collect the letters I write this year, so please save them. It should be interesting to read next year what I felt this year. Hope you write real soon and tell me about your summer and everything else too. Regards to all. Be good.

Love,
Tyra

August 1, 1966

Dear Tyra,

Not much going on here, so just a few words to keep you from worrying about us.

It's been a hot summer and all the strikes made everyone's temper even hotter. The only thing good about the newspaper strike is that the house isn't cluttered with all your father's papers all over. Train fare rose a nickel to twenty cents and they called in the National Guard to stop the riots in Chicago. A serial killer murdered eight nurses in Chicago, too, which was just so frightening and awful. Things aren't safe anywhere, it seems. Hanoi threatened to try American prisoners of war as war criminals, so God knows where that will lead. On a lighter note, Mia Farrow is marrying Frank Sinatra, and there is a big fuss about how she will be written off Peyton Place!

You would be interested to know that there is a Jewish group in Rockaway protesting the postage rates to Israel. An airmail letter cost .25 per ½oz. to Israel and the organization claims that the rates to the Arabian countries are cheaper. I hope they win.

Today Jessie is 25 years old and as I am sitting here and thinking, I can't help but feel a little blue that she doesn't have what other girls her age have. Most at 25 are married and have children already but such is life. What is meant to be is, and all those good wishes you wrote her I, too, hope and pray for. I guess all I really want is for my children to be happy and that Daddy and I enjoy some nachas from the both of you.

I felt bad leaving Daddy and Jessie but it would be silly not to take advantage of being in the mountains for a few days of rest. I told them they would have peace and quiet without my nagging. The louses- they agreed! Grandma and Grandpa are enjoying the weather here and look rested and brown from the sun. They went to a show Saturday night at the Majestic Hotel and enjoyed it.

Jessie started her new job today. I will call home later to find out how her day went. Her last day at her old job was pleasant- they took her out to lunch, made her a party and gave her a pretty pin. I hope this new job turns out good for her.

Thank God, Grandma and Grandpa are holding their own, cooking and yelling as always. Daddy is still working too hard. Sorry but I can't think of anything else right now. Love you so much.

Mom

August 3, 1966

Dear Mom, Dad and Jessie,

Well, I can tell you of one more strike – I am no longer your vicarious tour guide. My fingers are so cramped up from all this writing. For such a small country, there is so much to see and I observe so much, my mind is swimming!

*I sat next to a snotty American high school girl on the bus from Tel Aviv last week. She was on a seven week tour and complained about Israel's faults- the same things that are wrong in America- it's okay there, but here, everything is supposed to be **holy** and perfect. I gave her the third degree and although I found her to be annoying, I'm glad I met her because it showed me how involved I am with Israel- that I am not just looking at the landscape. And what the most ridiculous thing was, is that I was appalled myself at something I witnessed last week when I went to a concert at Binyamai HaOoma- the new National Concert Hall in the heart of Jerusalem. The hall is beautiful and modern but simple- no formal drapes on the stage and the lights stayed on during the performance which was Berlioz' Requiem and quite wonderful. Before the music began, a man got on the stage and welcomed the audience for about a half an hour. The people got very impatient and started clapping so that he couldn't continue. I was shocked at this outburst of rudeness. But to the spoiled girl on the bus, I defended everything!*

Love,
Tyra

August 8, 1966

Dear Tyra,

The best news to tell you is that Jessie's job is really working out well for her and I've never seen her happier. I'm sure some of the surgeons who operated on her pulled some strings to get her this job. Some penance for screwing up the results. The part she loves most is working with the juvenile patients. She needs to measure their breathing capacity with big, intimidating equipment, and the kids are afraid when they come into the lab. But Jessie shows them how the machines and tubes work and spends a lot of time with them, and they actually like coming to her after a while. Some of the doctors mentioned that the kids aren't so afraid of them anymore, although there is one lab worker that doesn't agree with Jessie's approach. Hopefully, he won't spoil things for Jessie and Jessie will keep her mouth shut and not make trouble for herself. God forbid things should be good for a while.

On a sad note, Estelle, Mrs. Janolsky's daughter, from the sixth floor committed suicide last week. It was just horrible. We can't believe it. She was in the middle of a divorce, and she lost her job. It was all too much for her, poor thing, and she jumped. Everything was hush-hush. No one from the building was allowed to go to the funeral (the rabbi said funerals are not the same for those who commit suicide). Rumor had it that Mrs. Janolsky was hysterical and threw herself into the grave. Grandma can hear her screaming upstairs all day long. She blames her husband- after all these years, and although he loved his grandchildren and accepted and grew to love Gregory, Mrs. Janolsky blames him for Estelle's troubles. The youngest daughter is only seven, and already has so much sorrow. Who will take care of her? Her grandmother is on her way to a nervous breakdown.

No one knows another's pain. It must be awful for a mother to lose a child, and a child to lose a mother. No one had even the slightest notion. Who'd ever think? What happened got me thinking- of all the things in my life that overwhelmed me- when Daddy had his surgery and almost died while I was pregnant with you, all Grandma's illnesses and pain, Jessie's struggles and heartaches, and the money problems- so many times I wanted to run away, all the times I screamed, and the worst, when I would ring up my arms to God shaking my fists, asking why, but despite all that, I never once, God forbid, thought of ending it- I couldn't even bear to think of not being with all of you. Poor Estelle, and her children.

Anyway, sorry for the bad news, but you wanted to be kept informed. Take care of yourself and please, be safe.

Your letters are such a treat for us. I get home late from work every Friday night- you know my boss- all the books have to reconcile to the penny for the week- but after we finish Shabbos dinner at Grandma's, we sit around the living room and even though we are all so tired, I read your letters, and I have to read extra loud for Grandpa as his hearing is getting worse. He loves every detail you tell about Barak and his family. As much as he would love to go to Israel, he knows your letters are as close to Barak as he will get. I think he still wishes Barak would have come to America instead but that's the way it is. Daddy laughs and calls your letters the Miller's version of the Fireside Chats!

In fact, why don't you number the letters so we can read them in order. The Israeli postal system is erratic and your letters come out of order. I'm saving them in a filing box just in case one day you want to write a book!

We miss you, but know you are doing what you want and hope you are having a good time. Just be careful.

Love,
Mom

Tyra got off the bus, looked around the new surroundings and asked the first person she saw for directions to the address she needed. The middle-aged man took the paper from her hand and pleasantly pointed. "After you get to that street, make a left, and in two blocks, go right, and the building will be right in front of you. Wish the Singers *Shabbat Shalom* for me."

She was stunned that first, he answered her in English, native English, and second, that he knew the Singers. She got to the home and was embraced by Vicki and the children, the youngest grabbing on to her, jumping up and down.

"Children, give Tyra a chance to breathe," Vicki said standing in the doorway. She looked wonderful. Israel so agreed with her.

"Tyra, Tyra," Rabbi Singer bellowed as he came into the salon and gave her a big hug. "So you are finally here. Come, let me show you around," he said, taking the small valise from her as Vicki shooed the children into the kitchen to finish the chores before Shabbos.

"So, I understand you will be studying here this year?"

"Yes. At the university. I majored in Hebrew at Lexington College and will be starting my master's now here."

"I see you found a way to get what you wanted after all," he laughed. "I'm proud of you."

"It wasn't easy convincing Mom to let me major in Hebrew. 'There isn't a great need for Hebrew scholars in the world,' she argued, but I told her I loved the language, that Hebrew is a phenomenal language. Did you know you can take the same three letter root, let's say *write* and put it in the reflexive and it becomes *correspond* or put it in the intensive form and it means *inscribe*. It's such a precise and artistic language. There is so much literature written in Hebrew and each era has its own linguistic characteristics. Biblical and Talmudic is so different from medieval and today's modern Hebrew the way it's spoken in Israel..."

"Whoa, Tyra. Is this the shy little girl I used to know speaking? And maybe the New York school system doesn't need

Hebrew scholars, but the world, well, I'd like to think we need them." He laughed again.

"I acquiesced and told her I would major in English also so that I could teach English and have that to fall back on, so here I am! But I have to say, it's a pretty difficult language and some times I did cheat."

"You, cheat? I don't believe that."

"Well, I used English translations of poetry and Biblical texts."

"Oh, Tyra, that's not cheating. Even rabbinical students do that!"

The two of them burst out laughing. Tyra was happy. It felt like old times.

"And how are your parents? Such good people."

"Okay. Working hard."

"And Jessie? Married?"

"No." The expression on her face changed and she looked down as she described Jessie's job in the hospital.

"Come, Tyra," Vicki called out. "Let me show you your room. Soon it will be Shabbos."

August 22, 1966 5:30 P.M.

Dear Mom, Dad and, Jessie,

As I got out of their car at the bus station, she kissed me and said, "We hope you'll be our adopted daughter this year." Thus ended a most wonderful visit with the Singers!

Now from the beginning. I got a lift to Kiryat Yismach Moshe (where they live) with two guys I met at the university. They were spending the weekend in Ashkelon and kept asking me to change my plans and spend the weekend with them! Knowing your daughter's fine and upright character, I stood firm in my original plans and arrived at the Singers safe and sound. The kids recognized me and hugged and kissed me. It was just wonderful seeing all of them again.

They live in a small but very modern and luxurious area. The apartment buildings are three stories high with large terraces. The outside of the buildings are very colorful, adorned with lawns and trees. They have a large apartment and it really is lovely.

They were very friendly to me and we spoke quite a bit about their decision to move here and mine to study here. They are happy. In fact, the Rabbi looks and acts like a twenty-year-old kid. They felt that there was no future for them and especially their kids in New York and life for them here is ideal. He teaches in a Talmudic academy and feels so gratified in helping develop the intellectual pursuits of his young students. He seems to be even more dynamic here than before, if that's even possible.

It's a little difficult for them because they have such a large brood, but they started well because they brought a lot of their appliances and stuff from the States and anyway, they're determined to make ends meet because they love it here so much.

The pace of life is altogether different and one can feel like a human being all the time. Friday night dinner was a typically Shabbosdik meal with lots of singing. It felt very good and I was very happy to be with such a warm family.

After the kids went to sleep we walked around the town. For a change I had so much to talk about, that I could hardly shut up. The four kids sleep in one room on two double beds. They arranged it that I slept on one bed alone and it's been a long time since I slept on anything so big and comfortable.

We went to shul on Shabbos, (luckily I knew enough to bring a cardigan as all my summer dresses are sleeveless), and loafed in the afternoon. P'nina taught me how to play chess and I even won a game. She is quite a young lady- she has very long hair and is very dark. She's not quite twelve and she reminds me a little of how I looked when I was her age. In fact, I even brushed her hair in a bun the way I used to brush mine!

Batya is still gorgeous and the boys are wild as ever. They have the tiniest pais- Vicki tried to cut them off but the boys wouldn't let her because all their friends have them. It's easy to see in such a large family the responsibility that the kids have for each other. They fight like anybody, but they always look out for the next one.

Late in the afternoon, Vicki and I went to her neighbor's where all the women in the Kiryah (town) meet on Shabbos to discuss the parsha -portion- of the week. They first talked about all the problems of the Kiryah: the kids make too much noise on Shabbos afternoon and don't let the parents rest, the garbage isn't collected often enough, etc. and it was like a real yentas' club. After the meeting we went back home and it was already after Shabbos.

We spent the night talking- of course they asked for you and Jessie, Grandma and Grandpa and Vicki said, "Here we are- the Singers and Tyra Miller talking in the Middle East!"

The community is basically composed of people from America and England and there's really no need for them to speak Hebrew. They're here for years and Vicki's first studying in an Ulpan this September. She can hardly speak any Hebrew. The kids picked up beautiful accents and intonation patterns.

The reason the community is so nice is because these people immigrated and brought all their furnishings from the States or England.

Sunday morning we got up early and picnicked in the Galilee (about two hours from their home). There was a beautiful lake and we swam and ate all day long. The sun was hot and I got a beautiful tan. The ride through the Galil was just amazing. It's full of floating mountains and the light is incredible. In the crevices there are many Arab villages where they still use candlelight at night.

At the picnic spot itself, there was a flat piece land and all of a sudden a steep incline - that's the mountain. The lake is paved at the bottom and sides but the water is fresh and flows from a brook running down the mountain. The kids and I followed the brook until the entrance of the mountain which was a cave. The lake is in the shape of a figure eight and at one side in the middle there's a little island of rocks with trees growing up from them. The place is called Mayan Harod and is in the Gilboa Mountains- the place where King Saul was supposed to have died.

The day was just beautiful and I really wished you could have been there too, resting and enjoying yourselves. This country is so full of beauty and wonders that I really hope you'll come see for yourselves.

We stayed until after supper and left around 6:30. The kids- all four of them fell asleep in the car. They asked if I wanted to sleep over and leave early Monday morning but I thought I'd go back. After all I must have been enough of an imposition.

I got back to Jerusalem at 10:30, but missed the last bus to the university, so I had to go into town and wait 45 minutes for the last bus to the dorms. Finally got back at 11:30 and found two letters from you. That's it for now. Take care.

Love,
Tyra

Dear Tyra.

It was wonderful seeing you. You must come again soon. Communications are terrible- so just show up when you have time. You left your toothbrush here, so I gave it to a very nice Brooklyn boy, Paul. He is studying at HaRav Ben Zvi Institute for a year. He's very nice and since he said he would be going to the University this week, he offered to bring your toothbrush to you. Keep smiling!

Love, Vicki

Tyra had organized all the ingredients and mixing bowls she needed to make a noodle pudding and made two trips from her dorm room down the hall to the kitchen. She had finished her Ulpan assignment and didn't feel like running out with the other American students. She had hoped Irit would be able to come visit, but it seemed they were always missing each other. Perhaps tonight Irit would pop over. Tyra was anxious to use some of the kitchen wares Irit helped her pick out at the *shuk*- the open-air marketplace- the week before, especially the Palestine pot- the tube cake pan that you could bake anything in on top of the stove. Her grandmother used them a lot and everything she made in them came out great. But then, everything Hana baked came out perfect.

"Be quiet," Irit told her, as Tyra watched her cousin bargain and get a lower price for each item. "You must do this. It's expected. Otherwise, they laugh and you waste money."

Tyra shuddered. That wasn't exactly what a shy girl looked forward to doing, but as they say, when in Rome. By the time they found the fourth item she needed for the dorm, Tyra tried her hand at bargaining with the vendor, and she didn't do too badly at it.

"My grandpa would be proud," she said.

"You could be better," Irit admonished.

Tyra decided to try the trick that she learned from Vicki during her visit- if you melt the sugar in hot oil before mixing it in the cooked noodles, the noodles turn brown and syrupy and really sweet as they bake. Scrumptious, Tyra thought as she was measuring out the sugar. *I better start watching myself,* she thought. For the first few weeks she was in Israel, she ate four times as much as she did in the States, and was amazed that she hadn't gained an ounce. She attributed that to all the hiking and touring. But after only five weeks, the pounds piled on and she gained more than three kilos, almost seven pounds.

She was stirring the hot sugar into the pot full of noodles.

"I'm looking for Tyra Miller," a slim American fellow said coming into the kitchen. Do you know her?"

"That's me."

"Wow! That's easy. I'm Neil. I have your toothbrush. Rebetzin ..."

"Paul. You mean, you're Paul. Vicki said..."

"Oh, Paul told me Rebetzin Vicki asked him to bring you your toothbrush, but something came up and since I was coming to the University anyway, I told him I would drop it off to you."

"Oh. Well, thanks." She held out her hand and took the toothbrush he pulled from his back pocket. It wasn't wrapped. She laughed to herself. She tried hard not to laugh out loud. She would never use that toothbrush again- back pocket- unwrapped. What happened to her traveling case? "It was nice of you to come out of your way. Are you studying at the same yeshiva as Paul, too?"

"Yes. For a year. And I have relatives in Jerusalem, too. I graduated Brooklyn College in June and want to get a degree in social work when I get back.

Tyra put the mixture into the Palestine Pot and put in on the stove to bake.

"I was graduated from," Tyra said.

"You mean, you're not a junior?"

"No, I mean you say, I was graduated from, not you graduated. And to answer your question, no I am not a junior. I'm a grad student, studying Hebrew Lit, but I also majored in

English." Tyra began to gather up all her utensils and ingredients to bring back to her room.

"Yea. I mean yes, I can tell."

They both laughed.

"Hey, let's take a tour of Jerusalem."

"Not now. I'm baking."

Neil walked over to the row of burners and shut the flame under the pot. "Not any more."

There was something charming about him. "I really can't let all these ingredients and the hard work go to waste. Some other time, maybe."

Just then, Carol, another American on the program, walked into the kitchen. She was disheveled, her arms full of groceries from the Supersol in downtown Jerusalem.

"Here. Let me help you with that," Neil said, as he grabbed a bundle and put it on the counter.

"Thanks. The bus was so crowded. I don't know what I was thinking," Carol said, surveying the wall of small refrigerated cubicles. How is all this going to fit?

"You can put some in mine. Just leave room for the Palestine Pot. By the way, could you do me a big favor? Could you shut off the kugel in an hour, please, and I'll be back to put it in the refrig when it cools." Tyra said and looked at Neil as he nodded in approval. Tyra went to the burner and turned it on again.

"Sure." Carol said as she starting putting her things away.

Tyra and Neil walked to her room with the utensils, where she put them down, picked up a cardigan, and they went downstairs.

They walked through the campus grounds to the road and he stopped at the parking spot on the street, bent over, stretching his arm inviting her to hop on.

Shocked, her mouth was agape. "Oh, no! No way, I'm getting on that. I thought we were going for a walk."

"Come on, it's great. She's my cousin's. He's in the Reserves for a month and said I could keep it warm for him. There's nothing like it. The wind at your back. The chill on your cheeks. I'll show you a thrill. Come on, there's nothing to it, once you get on."

Tyra stared at the motor scooter. She hated heights, held her breath every time Sid drove over one of the New York bridges, and she held her breath a lot since they were always visiting relatives in Jersey and Brooklyn. Dawn and Ricky would coax her onto the roller coaster at Rye Beach, but she remembered having lots of fun after she got on.

Here, in Jerusalem with all the hills and valleys, dark, narrow roads, Oh my...

"O...kay," she said, as Neil grasped her waist and helped her on the seat.

"Grab my waist, tight," he said, as he revved the engine. "Holding on? Here we go!"

The scooter chugged up the mountain, sputtering back-fires. She jumped from the noise and her fingers jabbed deeper into his sides. They passed the new Knesset and the Israel Museum. Bright stars shone from above and lights flickered all around them, peeking out of the mountains. They zoomed down the hills toward Kiryat HaYoval, Ein Kerem and saw the tall, gleaming Hadassah Hospital. The longer they rode, the more she loosened her grasp around Neil's waist. She breathed in the mint-fresh, crisp air deep into her lungs. His long, curly locks swirled around his crocheted kippah and her long tresses whipped her cheeks, getting stuck inside her mouth. She tried to wipe her hair from her lips, but she wasn't brave enough to let go of Neil's waist, even for a moment. She was invigorated, joyful and giggled as they made their way around the sharp curves, dipping downward to the left and to the right, close to the pavement, on this glorious Holy Cyclone.

Yom Hamishi (Thursday) 25/8/66

Shalom Zelda,

Mah shelomach? -How are you?- That's all the Hebrew for today! Since I wrote last I met some more family in Rehovot. They were wonderful. They even had a wedding in Jerusalem last week and invited me to come along. Tomorrow I'm going to Haifa for the weekend.

I went to the Ministry of Education looking for a part-time English teaching (high school) job- the first time I went (yesterday) the office was closed. Today the woman in charge of this area was out. Oh well.

The Ulpan is a total waste- I've been cutting more than I've been going. The teachers are recent graduates of the university who are trained to teach in elementary education. Consequently, they ask for doctors' notes or a note from a leader explaining why we cut. You can't lean back in your chair but must sit straight. If you look in your bag for a pen you are cautioned to "pay attention." You know me- that's not exactly what I go in for- oh those elementary school teachers! Oh, I forgot- you're one (but I'm sure you'll be a lot better! Let me know how it works out- teach!) My parents got a letter from the Board of Education (my mother contacted them a few times explaining my situation) and my medical exam has been postponed to August 1967- I guess that's a good sign.

Tonight they're having a party to celebrate the first month of the Ulpan which is over. Only one and a half months to go- not soon enough.

There are loads of fellows in this place. The Israelis come to the dorm looking for rich American girls- it gets to be a pain after a while.

I spent this past Shabbos with my Rabbi from the Bronx who moved here a couple of years ago and it was just wonderful seeing some familiar faces. They invited me for Succos.

Best wishes for a healthy and happy year. Write soon.

Love,

Tyra

"Come in," Tyra responded to the knock on her door.

Neil opened the door cautiously, glancing at the girl who was lying in bed cuddled in blankets surrounded by scattered, crumpled tissues. Her eyes were puffy and teary, her nose red, and her hair a mess. "Oh, what happened to you? You look awful."

Tyra thought one of the girls who stayed in the dorm for Shabbos came to visit her. When she saw it was Neil she almost died.

"Thank you very much. I don't feel bad enough," she said.

"I didn't mean it like that. I'm sorry. You don't feel well?" Neil had a sincere tone of concern in his voice.

"I don't know where I picked up this wicked cold from. All I know is I'm falling behind in my work already."

"Don't worry. You'll catch up. Let me bring you some hot tea," and before she could answer, he went down the hall to the kitchen.

They spent the afternoon sipping tea, talking, it seemed about everything. He even asked her when her birthday was. She asked him why but he wouldn't tell her, thereby peeking her curiosity about his interest. He doted over her, asking if she was cold, if he should close the window, if he could bring her something to eat.

"I'm going to *daven maariv* now, alright, Hon?" he said at ten after six.

Hon, she thought, relishing in the affection he afforded her. "No, it's too early to go."

"This is the one thing that comes before you."

Not bad, she thought. *Coming second only after Hashem.* Tyra was happy with the way things were going with Neil. She felt comfortable with him.

"I can't believe it took so long to get a minyan in Jerusalem. We had to wait until 6:40 to start," Neil said when he came back to Tyra's room after Shabbos.

"I told you it was too early." She laughed.

"Are you feeling well enough to go to *S'lichot* tonight on Har Zion? Rev Zemer will be there. I really want to go with you."

"No. I just need to sleep. But you go."

"I'll get us tickets for his concert next week." He kissed her on her cheek and left.

The concert hall was mobbed and during intermission, Tyra and Neil pushed their way up to the stage to greet Rev Zemer.

"Hello, friends," the Rav shouted to them over the melee of pushing and shoving. "Yes, I will sing Esso Einai for you," he said, acknowledging Tyra's request. "Come to my party backstage after the show."

Walking back to their seats, Neil bumped into a college friend. "Let me introduce...."

"No need," Tyra cut him off. "Hi, Peter." Then turning to Neil, she said, "We know each other from Seminar. Small world, isn't it?"

Peter had been living in Israel for two years, working as a social worker with a group of poor, delinquent teenage boys, and was with his fiancée who was a native of Amsterdam.

"We were good friends in school, weren't we? Neil said.

"I was two years ahead of you. I came here after I graduated. You know how it is, drifting apart and all," Peter said.

"Was graduated," Neil said, laughing.

"What?" Peter said.

"Private joke," Tyra said punching Neil in the ribs. "Don't mind him."

The party broke up when the manager kicked everyone out and locked up the building at one in the morning. The singing and dancing spilled onto to the streets. The residents in the apartment buildings stuck their heads out screaming for everyone to shut up. At three o' clock a man in a third floor apartment threw out an empty can from a window shouting 'shut up' in Hebrew. The police came by and dispersed the crowd. Tyra, and Neil were heady with laughter. They headed back to the university dorms with two of Neil's classmates who joined up with them at the party.

They were exhausted after the long trek on foot across town and flopped on the lawn in front of Tyra's building. The pre-dawn air was crisp and fragrant. After a few minutes, they went into the kitchen and made some strong coffee and toast and went back outside to catch the sunrise in its entirety. It was already 5:30 and teeny streaks of orange were just beginning to peek out of the dark sky.

"It's time to get back to daven," Neil said looking at his watch. It was six o' clock. The other boys said goodbye and started to walk ahead. Neil drew Tyra close, wrapped his arms around her and kissed her. It was a kiss she didn't want to end, and she was happy. She felt comfortable leaning against his strong body and her arms held him more tightly with each lingering second of the kiss. Suddenly he pulled away from her.

Tyra felt her insides smart and tried to hide her hurt and confusion.

"Got to go," he said. "It's getting late. Got to daven. I told you, that comes...."

"First. I know," she said, trying be nonchalant, not believing a word of it.

September 14, 1966-Erev Rosh Hashanah

Dear Dawn,

I'm with my family in Haifa now to spend Rosh Hashanah. I'm just about hysterical and can hardly see what I'm writing. I got up at 5:30 today so I could get to town early enough to see the Ashrei dock. I got there after it docked but just as they were pulling up the ramps. Eitan saw me from the deck and we were talking there until he was able to get his shore-leave pass. Before I saw him I was hardly even excited- two months is a long time, but as soon as I saw him, I felt differently. After a while he came down and we calmly ran towards each other. It was quite unemotional. I waited with him in Customs. They're quite strict with the crew. As we were standing in front of the officer, Eitan sneaked through some boxes of cigarettes and I put them in my bag- it's a good thing we didn't get caught. I've been smoking quite a bit- one pack a day- but I'm cutting down. He also gave me a compact.

We were walking around and I found it difficult to talk to him. The first thing he said when he saw me was why am I so sad- I don't look good- I'm not eating enough. I feel so utterly bad now because I was under the impression that we'd be able to spend a lot of time together- he leaves next Thursday. When I asked him when he was coming to Jerusalem, he said he couldn't- he has to work and only has one day off. He said he'd try but he doubts that he can.

We returned to the port and were sitting more or less alone by the gate- I couldn't get through. I said that we're always saying goodbye and he said he never said goodbye- only l'hitra'ot- au revoir. He said he'd see me- he didn't know where or when- but he must. The ship doesn't dock in Haifa until May or June. I asked him if he'd remember me after such a long time and he said he couldn't help but remember me. He thinks *of me whenever he's on deck or in his cabin or other places we were together on the ship. He had to wait until I stopped crying because I wanted him to remember me happy. Anyway, we dropped hands, he walked to the boat and I walked to the bus- completely opposite directions. Coming back here I kept looking back at the sea- I tried not to- it has been a wonderful past so far, and I should look forward to the future- but I don't feel that now. I'd give anything to have those luscious nights outside on deck with him....*

Meanwhile when it rains it pours. I met an American who graduated from Brooklyn College the same day I graduated. He stays down the road at a yeshiva and will study there for a year. He's 21. We met two weeks ago. It's a long story- he returned my toothbrush that I left at my rabbi's house, and we've been spending a lot of time together. He came up the first Shabbos afternoon and went out Saturday night. He came up Sunday and went to Tel Aviv to hear a symposium. Ben Gurion was one of the speakers. His name is Neil. He came up during the week and asked me to eat in town; but, I told him I'd make dinner at the dorm. I made a tuna casserole, salad, chocolate pudding and melon. We went to a concert to see Rev Zemer. We have so much in common. He used to go to seminars also and knows a lot of the same people I do, including Rev Zemer. He's very easy to talk to and lots of fun. I think he likes me too much. He's very sweet.

The problem is that now I'm torn between a fine, religious boy and a gorgeous hunk of man. Neil makes me feel like a decent human being. Eitan- like a woman. I'm so confused and know not what I want out of this life. Don't know how I'm going to get through Yom Tov here.

Wishing you a sweet year.

Love,
Tyra

Tuesday September 13, 1966 9 A.M.

Dear Zelda,

I have a gigantic favor to ask of you- I've been cutting Ulpan more than I've been attending (I heard last night that if you get kicked out you can't attend the university). I haven't gone since last Thursday. But it's legal. I have a bad cold. Anyway, I'm way behind in my work and I was wondering if you can make up a copy of the review of Jeremiah in English and send it to me as soon as possible. The exam is right after Succos and not only do I have to pass, but I have to pass with the highest grade so I don't have to study in m'chinah —preparatory- four hours a week during the regular school year. I'd really appreciate it. Then I only have to catch up on my vocabulary, literature, grammar and Jewish studies. What a pickle I got myself into.

I couldn't get a teaching position here, but I volunteered to teach Hebrew and English to immigrant children between the ages of 10-14. I start next month and I'm looking forward to it.

Well- there was no water in the dorm last night and it's absolutely black this morning as the lights in our room went out too. The place is falling apart.

Today is your second day of teaching —how is it working out? I keep thinking that I could have been teaching now, too, and I'm beginning to wonder whether I made the right choice — too late now. Happy New Year.

Love,
Tyra

SIX

BITTER STEPS

As soon as Tyra stepped out of the elevator she knew something was wrong. The usual Friday afternoon mouth-watering smell of hot, freshly baked chaleh loaves wafting through the hallway gave way to an unpleasant smoky whiff of burn which Tyra followed into her grandparents' kitchen. The oven had been shut off, but the four loaves were nearly burnt, retrieved barely a second before total ruination. Hana always made a tray of extra flecktls, crisp and crunchy, just the way Tyra loved, but today all the thinly braided doughy strips that topped the Sabbath bread were burned sour.

"Oh, Grandma, not another attack?" Tyra said when she got to the bedroom and saw Hana sitting on the bed, moaning quietly, gently keeping her lips separated to avoid any extra pressure on her face. The attacks were becoming more and more frequent and debilitating. The dentist extracted one tooth after another until he realized that Hana's teeth were not to blame for such excruciating pain. He finally recommended she see a neurologist who diagnosed Tic douloureux, a neuralgia of the trigeminal nerve that caused sudden shocks of indescribable facial pain, the worst pain in the world, one which had driven people to commit suicide.

"There are two new treatments in the works, but until they're ready, this injection should bring you some relief," the neurologist, whose office was on Mosholu Parkway, said as he described how he would locate a teeny loop inside Hana's upper gum and insert a long needle filled with a combination of lidocaine and narcotic, injecting the fluid right into the nerve, bringing on temporary relief for hours, or sometimes days, quieting the nerve until the caress of a gentle breeze or slight vibration of a whisper would trigger another unrelenting spasm.

The shot seemed as devastating as the neuralgia itself. Death by gallows or death by guillotine- a gruesome choice Hana thought as she sat stoically, observing the doctor prepare the syringe. She was not bitter nor did she question why she was the one chosen for this plight. It was her nature not to complain, and she would shake her index finger in front of her mouth if anyone started to speak ill of a friend or neighbor, warning in a whisper, *lashon harah-evil speak-* and just as she did not speak badly of others, even more so, she would not of God. "Don't worry, Doctor," she encouraged, to bolster him as he administered the horrific shot, "do what you have to. I'll be alright."

"Mrs. Siegel, you call me anytime, day or night, if you need me. I mean it," the doctor told her as she and Kaye left his office. Sheldy met them there. He tried to take them home whenever he could.

Kaye woke Tyra at seven in the morning. She and Sid were ready to leave for the new hospital. Tyra wanted to go too, but Kaye said it was no place for a young girl. Jessie's second surgery would take hours. The extra months in the cast didn't help, and they were all trying to be stoic but optimistic.

"Don't forget your lunch, Tyra. I put it in the fridge last night."

Yawning, stirring out of her fitful sleep, she said, "I didn't want to forget it, so I put it in my bag last night."

"Oh, Tyra," Kaye let out a sigh. "I try so hard to make it easy for everyone, and now your lunch is spoiled. We have to get to the hospital and I have to make another sandwich."

"I'm sorry, Mom. I didn't want to cause any trouble, and I was afraid I'd forget it. I'll do it. Tell Jessie I'll be praying for her."

Tyra sat up in bed, and as soon as she heard the front door close, she let out sobs. *Mom and Dad have it so hard,* she thought, *so filled with worry and disappointment.* She tried to be perfect and not cause them an iota of extra trouble. She longed to bring them happiness, but she messed up again.

School was a blur that day. She didn't socialize with her friends or concentrate on her schoolwork, and at three o' clock, she walked down White Plains Road as if by rote, unaware of the people or traffic around her.

She was surprised to find the door locked when she reached the synagogue, and after she knocked for what seemed an eternity, she finally gave up and began to walk home, feeling more despondent than ever.

"That was Rabbi Singer," Kaye told Tyra when she hung up the phone. "He wanted to know how Jessie made out today. He told me the door was jammed, but by the time he heard the knocking and got to open it, you left. He ran after you, shouting your name, but you must have been in a fog, and then you turned the corner."

"Why is there so much suffering, Mom?"

"Everybody has his own fate. You must try to be happy, Tyra, and find your own place. Just because Jessie is having a rough time doesn't mean you shouldn't enjoy yourself."

It certainly wasn't the best answer, but it was the best Kaye could come up with. She shook her head, embraced Tyra and stroked her hair. It was easier for Kaye to deal with everyday details and fulfill the obligations expected of her than to try to figure out what she had done to bring God's wrath upon her and her family. "You'll come next time I go to the hospital. Jessie wants to see you, too."

"Hey, Greg. Sign my petition," Tyra said as she handed him the clipboard and pen. It was Tyra's second year as class secretary, and all her friends were used to seeing her walk the halls with a clipboard.

"Sure," he said, starting to write. "What's it for?"

"If I get twenty kids to commit, we can have Hebrew as a foreign language in ninth grade next year."

"Whoa! Italian is my only hope for a "C." You've got to be kidding," and he handed her the blank sheet.

Tyra cornered Ricardo Perez and his friend, Elias at the end of the corridor. "Here you go," she said, sticking her clipboard under their noses.

"We love you, Ty, but we could use a B or C, and you know we speak Spanish at home."

"Ricky, *el burro* can't help you, even in the Bronx. The whole textbook is about that stupid burro. Do something way out, for a change."

The idea was ludicrous. Why should her Puerto Rican and Italian friends be interested in learning a language written backwards in pretty but strange letters when the Jewish kids wouldn't even sign up? "Too hard," they said, or "couldn't wait to get through with the Bar Mitzvah."

Tyra would talk to Rabbi Singer about her options, which looked pale at the moment.

The hospital had moved to a new location. The building was modern, but the trip from the Bronx was more difficult and time-consuming, adding a crosstown bus to the express and local trains.

Instead of huge wards on the floor, there were only four patients to a room, and Jessie's room faced the East River. She could look out and see Circle Line tour boats and motorboats sail back and forth, and people walking and biking in the path that ran along the river's edge.

Best of all, Nurse Slater retired, and the staff seemed kinder than ever.

The teens had more of a social life, too, as the usual adolescent banter filled the cheerful solarium at the end of the hall. They would meet there as if attending a school social, the girls all made up in the latest Max Factor and Revlon products, wearing their ruffled bed jackets, and the guys in their clean, crisp pajamas. The animated kidding and jostling brought life into the stretchers, as if they were moving back and forth, the wheels transformed into the dancing feet of teenagers yearning to be normal. Irwin and Judy were two other scoliosis patients, but they had mild cases, and both expected to have excellent results. And it was obvious that Irwin Zimmerman had a wild crush on Jessie, as he laid mesmerized by her face awash and glowing in the rays of the sun streaming through the huge picture windows.

Jessie's roommate, Enid, usually stayed in the room, too weak to enjoy the solarium. It seemed to Tyra that of the two girls laying side by side, Jessie, despite everything, was far better off than Enid. Jessie was able to keep up with her school work, even when home instruction was interrupted during surgery. Jessie had a beautiful face, and when she let her hair grow while she was in the walking cast, it was dark and wavy, falling into a thick glamorous pageboy. Her nails were pretty, too. Spending all that time in a body cast protected them from breaking, and she would polish her nails over and over, almost as soon as they would dry, she would redo them in a different color. Her friends were always bringing her bottles of polish- every new shade, every brand. There was a never-ending cycle of polishing nails and reading books while the polish dried, and when turning a page caused a smear, the cycle would start anew.

But poor Enid- she was so frail and twisted. The bones of her arms were so skinny, they seemed almost to be put on backwards. So much of the time she needed oxygen to help her breathe. She looked more like a child than her thirteen years as polio conquered her whole being. Her voice was so weak, so sadly befitting the tiny features of her small face and distorted body. Her parents brought her all the way from Pennsylvania because there was no place like Manhattan Orthopaedic Hospital at home.

Tyra felt shy and awkward when she walked over to introduce herself to Enid. She hadn't yet acquired the knack of chit-chat that Jessie had, or of making people feel at ease and being able to talk about anything and making it sound interesting, like her mother. So she just slid Enid's fragile, tormented hand ever so gently onto her palm and stroked it carefully.

"You have such pretty nails, Enid. I like the color."

"Jessie did them for me before. She's great. You're so lucky to have a sister."

"Sure am," she said convincingly. Enid didn't know how domineering and stubborn Jessie could be, how she could monopolize the dinner talk and just as Tyra would nudge her way into the conversation, the meal would be finished and everyone went about their business, cleaning up or reading the newspapers. But people loved Jessie. She always made a good impression- likeable and generous.

"I have an eight year-old brother," Enid continued. "I feel bad for him. I know he misses my Mom a lot. It's hard for him." She paused for a moment to catch her breath. "It must be hard for you, too."

Judy and Irwin were better off than Jessie- Jessie was better off than Enid- and Tyra was better off than all of them. Did her having too much take away from the others and cause them to have less? It all seemed so confusing and unfair. She thought about that during the subway ride home that night, and she would ask Rabbi Singer about her responsibility for other people's fate. In the meantime, she decided to bring Enid a present the next time she would visit.

Tyra couldn't give Enid *Cinderella* or *Beauty and the Beast*. A paint by numbers set wouldn't be good either, because Enid wasn't strong enough to hold a paintbrush.

Kaye was annoyed and impatient with Tyra's need to analyze and shape every detail of what should be, could be and would have been. "Don't agonize so much, Tyra. People are strange- either they will find fault no matter what you do or they will appreciate whatever you do. Enid is sweet. You can't go wrong."

So Tyra finally settled on a copy of her favorite book about Chandra, the girl who lost her way and found herself in the most mystical *Enchanted Garden*. The book was filled with gentle words and wispy, pastel-colored illustrations. It was a good choice; Enid loved it, and thanked Tyra over and over. "Would you read it to me?" she asked Tyra one time when she was particularly tired. Enid's family had returned to Pennsylvania briefly to take care of business. Enid was alone and the blues lay over her face like a dark, flimsy veil.

"Why," Enid asked, "does the story end so unhappily? She loved the garden and it was taken away."

"Maybe, Tyra answered, "it ends in the middle of the story, and like all of us, Chandra will have to find her way back on her own. Maybe the writer figures she won't be there for Chandra all the time. Maybe she wants you to help her get back."

When Tyra looked up, she figured Enid was floating somewhere inside a beautiful dream, for she had nodded off, and the sadness of a few moments before transformed into a winsome smile.

"Where's Enid?" Tyra asked on her last visit before Jessie's discharge, which was scheduled just before the High Holy Days. Tyra looked around to Enid's corner, and she got a sick feeling in her gut. It wasn't just that Enid was not in her bed, but there was a smell of disinfectant, and all the gifts, cards, the gentle *Enid* things were cleaned out.

Jessie's eyes were red. "She died during the night. Toughen up, kid. You should know by now, crying doesn't help."

Tyra walked down the hall. *Dreams, happily ever-afters, enchanted gardens-* all vanished. *No Cinderellas here*, she thought. The solarium was empty.

Enid's death was hard for Tyra to comprehend. She never knew anyone that young who died before. When she learned about what happened to the Jews at the hands of the Nazis, that too was impossible- the sheer numbers—she couldn't fathom. Tyra knew she had been born in the proper time and generation for the person she was. It was an ordained gift from God and she thanked Him many times for not being a Jewish child in Europe in the Forties, for she would have been far too scared to die, and too weak to survive. She was given the blessing of belonging to a safe generation in a strong country, able to merely observe history happen around her without suffering any hardship or danger herself.

She still couldn't comprehend the horror of what she had learned the very first time she was made aware of Nazi atrocities. It was in a seventh grade assembly in junior high. The students were wearing mandatory white shirts, navy ties for boys and dark skirts for girls, sitting properly, respectfully, silently. Especially silently, for if a student was caught merely whispering, a lengthy detention, embellished with a stern lecture from the dean would ensue. The lights were dimmed and the projector's buzz whirred throughout the auditorium. Without any explanation from the teacher about what they were going to see, the scratchy black and white newsreel images flashed on the screen in front. "American soldiers march into the Auschwitz concentration camp passing under the sign, Arbeit Macht Frei," the narrator announced in his deep matter-of-fact voice. Some of the soldiers covered their mouths and noses, and some even cried. The bleak compound in Poland was dotted with mountains of shoes and valises, mounds of Jewish bones removed from crematoria–ashes from the ovens like trays of burnt Friday night *flecktls,* and the skeletal remains of living ghosts salvaged by the allied liberators. "The number of Jews exterminated is estimated…" Tyra heard the narrator's voice but the rest of his words became indistinguishable to her. *Jews? Exterminated?* She must have misunderstood. Her father sprayed the bathroom to exterminate roaches. The image on the screen was of a half-man, half-ghost donned in striped pajamas, bones protruding from his ravaged face, the sockets of his eyes deep and empty. He lifted his sleeve and pointed to the numbers tattooed on his arm: *Yes, this is true. This is what they did.* Tyra gaped, wide-eyed and open-mouthed in terror and in horror.

There was that summer in the bungalows when strange Esthy Wilansky would walk around in an hypnotic, vacuous daze, hardly ever muttering a word to anyone but her three children. She came for only that one summer and never returned. She must have been a very cold woman, for every day without fail and no matter how scorching the summer day, she wore the same brown jacket. Whenever Tyra would comment about how strange she seemed, Jessie and the older girls would whisper amongst themselves and motion to Tyra to be quiet. Jessie, in her authoritative tone would order her to `drop it.' Tyra felt left out and unworthy of knowing. One day, though, when Tyra went to the clotheslines to take down the bathing suits, she bumped into Mrs. Wilansky who was hanging up her laundry. As Mrs. Wilansky raised her arms to pin the sheets to the rope, the sleeves of her jacket fell down to her shoulders. She noticed Tyra looking at the numbers spread across her left forearm and dropped the clothespins and the sheet on the ground simultaneously letting out a gasp, as if the ashes from the cigarette perched in between her lips fell and brushed against her skin. At that moment Tyra knew her suspicions had been right, that something happened as significant as it was secretive. But no matter whom she had asked and how delicately she had asked it, no one would explain to her. Now she knew, and understood the silence of the past.

The pictures continued to spin in front of her, but she couldn't make out any images. She was confused at the giggles of her classmates reverberating through the hall, piercing their way into the middle of her head, as if she were worth nothing, her people crushed like stale pepper and scattered in the air. She could barely contain the nausea that tumbled inside of her like bed sheets that got twisted and tangled in the drum of a washing machine.

The teachers were strict, but Tyra never had reason to feel that they were anything but kind. Yet they dimmed the lights in the auditorium, told the students to pay attention, and without explanation or warning, left them to flounder in bewilderment, giggle in disbelief, and gasp in revulsion.

She ran out, not caring about getting a pass or getting into trouble. Just as she made it to the bathroom, she allowed herself to give it up. This time, though, she didn't feel better afterwards.

At first, she couldn't understand how people could be so brutal, but then she remembered how Donna kicked Jessie in the back for no good reason. Hatred started out as small individual deeds from which bigger, societal ones were able to grow.

She learned about the ships that had left the harbors of Europe and sailed to within reach of the shores of Miami and Havana: rickety boats brimming with wretched wanderers who had nothing but their desire to live. Rejected, they were forced to return, either to be swallowed by the sea or consumed in ovens.

"Daddy," she asked, "how come the United States didn't help the Jews? You always liked Roosevelt."

"Afterwards we learned the truth about the State Department. At the time though, we read about the Jews being in labor camps. We thought that if they were working, they were at least eating. People were starving here during the depression, so we thought it wasn't so bad for them. But they just went, like sheep to the slaughter, it was awful."

"You mean it was their own fault, they deserved to die?"

"No. No, of course not. We should have done more, but things were not so easy here- there were quotas. Your mother couldn't get a job because she refused to change her name.

But we too were like sheep, who let the wool be pulled over our eyes."

"How could a thousand Jews at a train station not overpower ten, twenty, a hundred Nazis?" Jessie said. "If I were there I would have been in the Rey-sis-tahnce," she continued, enunciating every syllable with a European flair. "Tyra would have hidden in a closet somewhere."

"Come on, girls. Stop. Be nice to each other." Sid said.

But Jessie straightened herself up even more, persistent and smug. "You should have named her Tyrun."

Tyra's cheek reddened, once again straining to hold back tears so her sister wouldn't see. She fled the room, screaming, "They should have named you Tyrant!"

"Rabbi, where was God? How could He have let this happen?" Tyra asked Rabbi Singer at the next Hebrew school class and waited for him to answer.

"God gave man free choice, to do good or evil."

"But, Rabbi, doesn't God take into account exceptions?" She recalled a particular hike in the woods. The youngsters from the bungalow colony were meandering, picking clusters of wild huckleberries from scattered bushes, the purplish juice staining their fingers as the popped them into their mouths. Then they came across a round porcupine crawling slowly along the cow path. The boys started to throw rocks at it, and the calm ball blossomed into a furious fan of erect and brittle steel-gray quills, like hundreds of gleaming knitting needles stuck into an oversized pin- cushion. Only the quills were not as tough as they seemed, for they snapped into fragments as the stones bore down on his body. He shrieked in agony and even though Jessie broke through the boys' circle trying to shield it, she could not. The rocks pelted Jessie, too, all the while Tyra stood watching, paralyzed with fear, crying, wanting to help, but afraid of getting hurt. The porcupine yelped until the moment of its death, and when the woods turned silent, the boys ran off.

Rabbi Singer looked forlorn. The man who loved to challenge his students could not assuage Tyra's anguish. There was no word to describe what happened or any explanation, for what was done to the Jewish people could not be justified. "God told Abraham to look to the sky and the Jewish people would be as numerous as the stars. The Nazis destroyed our heaven."

"Why did they just pack their valises? All they cared about was their stupid valises. Why did they need their junk? Why didn't they fight?"

"They packed their suitcases with the things they thought they needed, for their future. Tyra, they brought what was familiar- they packed their bags with hope. Hope. That was what they took. How could they believe what would happen to them?" Rabbi's eyes were moist as he spoke in a soft mellow voice, very unlike his usual fiery dynamism.

"Someday, Tyra, we will learn the truth. Not tomorrow or the day after, but sometime in the future, the awful silence will be broken. Those who did terrible things to survive, and those who did not do enough, they will struggle with their shame until they cannot hold it in any longer, for the burden of silence is more painful than the burden of truth. And those who found, in subtle ways, in little places, their own seeds of courage and integrity, they will tell their stories so we will never forget what they suffered, and never let anything like it happen again."

Tyra understood the shame of silence. She could not confide, even to Rabbi Singer, about the porcupine.

"I saw in the newsreel," Tyra said, "that when they came to the train station, the children were torn apart from their parents. I was always afraid that if an air drill was for real, I would be separated from my family, how we would never see each other again."

"Tyra, you have a good family. I have never seen such devotion in any congregation. Go home, and ask your Grandpa what he knows about the war."

There were no answers. Nothing made sense. How could people be so cruel, so indifferent?

Tyra could not sleep for weeks. *Hatred, violence. Fear, silence.* She was imprisoned by the mellow sounds of the discordant words replaying in her head, and whenever she closed her eyes, she saw the piles and the ghosts, and forced her eyelids open.

Kaye saw her suffering and tried to comfort her. As for the silence, Kaye said she thought some victims must have felt shame, the shame of surviving when their families perished, and the shame of doing awful things in order to survive. "The very things that are hardest to comprehend," Kaye started to say but hesitated. Her voice cracked and Tyra saw a bulge in her mother's throat. They were sitting at the kitchen table, and Kaye toyed with the wedding band on her finger. After a moment she started again. "...have the most impact. I'll never understand why God and all the doctors and operations couldn't make Jessie straight. All I know is that it changed everything for me."

"What did Grandpa do during the war?" Tyra asked.

Kaye told her. "At least Grandpa took action and helped out." Lazer and his landsmen at the synagogue did not believe the implications of the short articles tucked away in the back pages of *The New York Times*. *Not so bad for Jews who worked in labor camps, earning their food. People went hungry in America during the depression.* Lazer and the men remembered the Poland from which they came and why they fled, and they were not fooled. For truth, they relied on *The Forward* and clandestine messages from the old country. Seeking help from the Joint Distribution Committee in Manhattan, they scraped up whatever they could to rescue relatives who were in grave danger. When Lazer's cousin, Baruch, left for Palestine before the Nazis came to power, he begged his sister to go with him, but she was young and in love. "No, Baruch, you are the ardent Zionist," Sofia said. "You go to the Holy Land. My place is here. Soon I will marry Yaakov." But Yaakov married someone else, and by the late thirties, Sofia would surely perish if she did not escape. Able to arrange a perilous, circuitous journey for her, Lazer wanted to sponsor her, but the quotas in the States were filled. So he implored a well-off but reluctant distant cousin in Ottawa, who after some browbeating, agreed to take her in.

When Kaye finished telling her the story, Tyra bolted out of the apartment and ran upstairs. Kaye comforted, Sid rationalized, and Rabbi analyzed. But Lazer was the only one who actually did something to make a difference. Tyra found her grandfather standing at the kitchen table smoothing the crinkled pattern across the taupe gabardine cloth draped over the table. *Whosoever saves one life, it is as if he saved the entire world.* She had studied that in Talmud class. Redeemed by Lazer's steadfastness, Tyra hugged him close, and was buoyed by his chutzpah. At the moment, the instances of brutality and humiliation far outnumbered those of courage and compassion, but in no way could they outweigh the dignity within her grasp.

"What's this?" he asked almost losing his balance by her sudden lurch. "Don't nudge. I didn't finish the hem on your skirt yet." He had promised her a new suit for the High Holy Days. "And I won't make it one bit shorter than I pinned. You be a fine girl in shul. Amerikanehs!" he griped.

She had learned a new way of breathing then–inhaling the tragedy of the past and exhaling both the despair of lessons resisted and the hope of lessons learned.

"No, no, Grandpa. It's not that."

No matter how tightly she wrapped her arms around Lazer's round belly, and how long she stood there holding him, she could not absorb his merit or integrity. That she would have to earn for herself and find her own ways to repair small bits of the world, a bit a time.

She began to understand what it meant to have purpose in life, that God created man in his image to be a partner and together to repair and perfect the world. One thing was certain—there was plenty of cruelty to go around, and Tyra would find causes to fight for, suffering to alleviate, hatred to combat. Oh, yes. There would be plenty to do, plenty.

But it wasn't without a price and in order to understand, she began to read feverishly about Jewish history, the Inquisition, *The Diary of Anne Frank*, and her absolute favorite, *Exodus*, the story of Israel's miraculous rebirth, for which she wrote a book report and managed to tailor it to the demands of at least eight English and social studies classes by the end of high school. And she adopted the routine of reading parts of the six or seven worn and crinkled dailies her father would bring home from the store each night.

Tchotchka knew the precise moment the ambulance arrived. "Here's Jess. Here's Jess," he sang over and over, flapping his wings so wildly, Kaye let him out of the cage, lest he bang himself in his excitement. Jessie was home, just in time for the holidays.

The Day of Atonement was like no other for a Jew, a solemn fast that could leave one spiritually drained from introspection and remorseful for failings in the past year yet balanced with hope and determination to do better in the next. A grueling day of repentance and soul-cleansing, of beseeching forgiveness from God and reconciliation with loved ones. It was a long day, but feelings of exhaustion from the lengthy daytime prayers melted into exhilaration as the hour of sundown approached and congregants, uplifted by the intensity of their supplications, would stand in front of the opened Torah Ark for the entire length of the concluding N'eilah service.

Lazer took his seat near the pulpit early Yom Kippur morning, but not before approaching Rabbi Singer and in a brief plea, confessed he didn't know what to do. Hana, who stayed home because she had another vicious attack, wouldn't let anyone take her to the doctor. She wouldn't even take a pill. "Yom Kippur," she told Lazer in a barely audible voice, "I can't drink. I won't start the year with a sin."

Yom Kippur demanded a lot from a rabbi. Not only did he have to search his own soul, but had to lead and inspire his congregation, all the while courting hunger and thirst. His sermon had to be the best of the year, dynamic and forceful as he elevated his community to loftier goals and spiritual heights. Yet Rabbi Singer focused on Lazer's ache. "I'll think of something, Lazer, as soon as services are over." And that he did. It was magnanimous of him to spend the brief break between morning and afternoon services plodding through the neighborhood in the heat of the day, climbing the five steep flights.

"Mrs. Siegel, you must go to the doctor for a shot. You cannot suffer like this."

"Rabbi, it's Yom Kippur. I can't ride. How can I make Sid drive?"

"Mrs. Siegel, if you don't let Sid take you, I myself will drive you."

Hana could barely speak, but motioned in agreement. She could never let such a righteous man desecrate the holiest day of the year, and she was desperate for the relief.

Sid went to bring the car around and Kaye started to help Hana get ready. "Tyra, honey, go stay with Jessie."

Tyra left the apartment with Rabbi Singer. At the landing of the fourth floor he said goodbye. "I have to get back to shul. I'll say a *m'sheberach*- prayer for the sick- for your Grandma. Be strong, Tyra, and wish Jessie a *gut yontif* for me."

She sat down on a wide step, and could hear the Rabbi's footsteps against the marble stairs becoming more and more faint as he descended the staircases floor by floor.

Tic douloureux, scoliosis- from one apartment to the other, each occupant was a prisoner locked in her own torment. They were all prisoners- a family, and what affected one, affected them all. Equidistant from the fourth floor cell and the fifth floor torture chamber, Tyra looked out of the huge hallway window into the alley and the yellowish-brown brick wall on the other side. There wasn't a sound, but she was deafened by her bitterness. All the questions that she had asked over time went unanswered. That she didn't even cry startled her and from a deep torment within, she heard her silent screams, for Jessie, for Hana, for Enid, and for all the Jews in Europe. *I hate you, God. I hate you.* She hated herself, too, for hating God.

SEVEN

LOST

The Monday night after Yom Kippur, Neil stopped by Tyra's room. Surprised to see him when she opened the door, she asked him to come in.

"No, I can't. I thought you would like to come with me to my Aunt and Uncle's place. My cousin is getting back tomorrow and I want him to have his scooter. We can take the bus back."

Tyra looked at the open books on her desk, and after a few moments of deliberation, she said, "Sure, why not?" Things had been so wishy-washy with them for the brief month since they had met. She actually looked forward to some time with him, almost hoping that the evening would solidify their relationship- one way or the other.

"Uncle Mordechai, Aunt Rifka, I want you to meet my friend, Tyra," Neil said as they were climbing the few stairs to the porch. They had come outside when they heard the scooter approach.

Tyra held out her hand and Rifka grasped it. "It's good to meet you. I like to see my *boychik* with a good girl."

Mordechai nodded his head. "Yes, Yes. Come in. Rifka, make some tea."

They entered the crude, primitive house, each one of them kissing the mezuzah. Tyra was struck by how old the couple was considering they had a son just a little older than Neil. Rifka was wearing a long, plain dress and had a kerchief tied around her head. Mordechai was bent over, the tall yarmulke, more like a soft hat, gave him some extra height.

The kitchen was old. The sink consisted of a plain tub with a faucet and the stove was a mere two burners sitting on a counter. The three sat down while Rifka brought tea and cookies to the table. "You see this table," she said as she slammed her hand gently on the simple wooden rectangle, and sat on a hard, wooden chair. "It's more than a hundred years old. How could a modern kitchen table have the significance of this old, cracked piece of wood? My father, *olev l'shalom*-may he rest in peace- sat and learned Torah here!"

After drinking tea and listening to endless stories of Europe, they walked around the house with Mordechai. He showed Tyra and Neil the bullet holes in the pipes and on the walls, souvenirs of the War of Independence. "During the war, this house was right on the border with Jordan. You must visit in the day, so you will see the surrounding area and how close we were to the Arabs. Such dangerous days."

"Say hello to Yoni tomorrow, and thank him for letting me use the scooter," Neil said as he kissed his relatives goodbye. Tyra thanked them for their hospitality and the young pair left the house, making their way to the nearest bus stop.

Tuesday, September 27, 1967

Dear Mom, Dad and Jessie,
    Last night I went with Neil to visit his aunt and uncle in an old section of Jerusalem called Beit Yisrael, right near Mea

Shearim. The houses were very old and crude, more like the bungalows in the Catskills. The streets were crowded with mule carts and open air stores. Every house had a succah in the making. There were lots of Hasidim with long pais, tall hats and long black coats. Also more "modern" religious people like Neil's relatives. The area was fantastic- I felt like I was walking through a European shtetl.

They are soft-spoken, speak Yiddish and Hebrew, and I could tell they liked me a lot and even suggested that I settle here. It seems like Israelis, whether religious like Rifka and Mordehai or secular like Manya and Barak, want Jews from all over to come and make aliyah. Why should Jews be in exile now that we have returned to our homeland? It's like something is missing- American Jewry is a hand, Soviet Jewry is a foot. European Jewry is the ache that never can go away- all the future generations in perpetuity- gone forever- at least we should be whole today- all of us together to build a great country. I stand here looking at the hills around me and it's like I am stuck in a wonderful way- I breathe in Jewish air and stand between Jewish sky and Jewish earth, Jewish clouds and Jewish wind- Jewish, Jewish, Jewish and it is so unbelievably grand. Amidst all the zeal about Zion- I have never been as homesick and miss you all so very much. Take care.

Love,
Tyra

Sunday, October 9, 1966

Dear Mom, Dad and Jessie,

I guess the theme of this letter will be the famous people your daughter has had the privilege of meeting!

Tonight after supper, we went to hear David Ben-Gurion speak to students from abroad at the University. It was very interesting to listen to him even though I don't agree with much of what he has to say. It was an honor to hear someone who is so well known throughout the world. He feels that just living in Israel is enough for one to be a good Jew. That the land is a land of Jews- Jews who work the fields, pave the roads, build the buildings. (I think I told you Barak spent two years working on the construction of the new Knesset building which was inaugurated on September 30 – so it's really true in the most practical sense- what Ben Gurion says). He said that to live in the Holy Land is a mitzvah. True enough. But there are 612 other mitzvoth and they, too, have to be fulfilled to make this, not an ordinary land, but the Holy Land. He doesn't respect other people's ideas, especially about religion. He was sarcastic and rude, in a sweet kind of way!

During the week, we went into town to celebrate Simchat Torah. Jerusalem was jammed with people and it was so hot, but so much fun. We went to the main synagogue where the Chief Rabbi of the Ashkenazi officiated. They took the Torahs out into the streets and everyone was dancing. One of the boys in the program, David, is the son of the nephew of the cousin of the Chief Rabbi and I was with him when he went up to him to introduce himself. David introduced me too, but, of course, I couldn't shake the Rabbi's hand!

David is studying philosophy and we have gone out a few times. Sometimes I feel we get along well and enjoy each other's company. Then I don't hear from him for a while. I get the feeling I'm not intellectual enough for him.

Academic classes are starting this week and now the fun begins. I will see what I am made of – if I can keep up with Israelis in Hebrew Literature classes- I hope I made the right decision coming here. At least I know we have a wonderful family here, and hopefully Irit will help me with my work like she promised! Will let you know how things go.

Love,
Tyra

Sunday, October 16 4:30 P.M.

Dear Mom, Dad and Jessie,

I'm so glad the hullabaloo with moving is over. There was so much tension with choosing who was going to stay in Shenkar and who was going to move into the older buildings on campus, we had to draw lots. There was almost a riot. I won a room in the basement in Shenkar but I figured that even though it was a better building, it would have been cold and damp in the basement, so I chose to move into Building 2. There are problems with the hot water all over, so we'll see how it turns out.

Just got more or less settled and I'm even too exhausted to write. Went to sleep at 4 A.M. and got up at seven. Just ate a container of cottage cheese and am patiently waiting for the hot water to come on so I can shower. I absolutely refuse to get into a clean fresh bed in the state that I'm in now. I haven't met my permanent roommate yet- and there's a girl that isn't moving out of the room yet- not until the 28th- although she may stay. She's from Morocco and very sweet and very filthy. When I walked in this morning, I almost plotzed. The Israeli girl who moved out was also a pig. When I took off the mattress cover to clean up the bed, I saw apple pits and loads of dirt on the mattress. I had to beat the hell out of it to get it in a sleepable condition. I started sweeping and from under the Moroccan's girl's bed came about three dozen pairs of shoes, dirty bags and onion skin peels. She keeps her food and pots on the floor and has all kinds of crap all over. The Israeli girl left me her closet and shelves in a condition too unbelievable. I had to use a towel to wipe them around as I don't have any rags, and I doubt if I can ever use the towel again. She had rice, crumbs and powder all over. The cleaning lady came in after I swept and washed the floor. I was determined not to bring in a stitch of my stuff until the place was clean. I had to make a million trips back and forth from Shenkar to here. I pulled out my hold luggage from the storeroom- one suitcase was full of toilet paper and the trunk had my winter clothes. Everything's all put away now. I have a stack of summer clothes I'll attack (laundry) tomorrow. There's just about the same amount of storage space-only the winter clothes really filled up the closet. The room is a little wider.

As I was moving, someone came in and said she was told to meet me to see if we wanted to be roommates. She's a 37 year old bio major from Poland who's not religious. We had to fill out questionnaires to specify what kind of roommates we wanted and I said a religious Hebrew major! My madricha-leader-must hate me. Anyway I have no idea who my roommate will be.

It's about seven now and I finally got out of a hot shower. Each shower has its own private anteroom with a bench and it's nice.

The Israeli bitch (excuse the language) who left today didn't hand her keys to the office so I don't have any keys. She also left her food locked in the refrigerator so I can't move my food from Shenkar yet. God knows when she'll get around to doing it. She was so rotten all day and made things difficult for me. She's so dirty and smelly- it's just amazing.

Anyway I'm getting used to this place. I'm getting dressed now as the kids will be over soon.

Monday 3:15 P.M.
Just finished all my laundry and am completely exhausted but we are going into town soon. My party was a smash. We were all in such dismal sad moods and we were so overtired from moving and everything that if we all spent the evening alone we would have gone crazy. I think everyone feels that now we are really going to be on our own- away from the group- in

studies, with our new roommates and we still are clinging to each other.

The dorms in Shenkar are deserted as many Israelis don't come until right before classes start and here everyone is strange. Some kids from Bolivia who live in town and studied in Ulpan came with a record player and great Spanish music. Also listened to Fiddler. We popped popcorn and that was fun. I wore my new robe and it made a big hit with everybody.

I guess the Israelis here think a "rich, noisy American" moved in. Actually I haven't seen or spoken to anyone yet. My roommate studied all night but before she left I introduced her to everyone and asked her to stay but she said she had to study for a test on Wednesday.

She's very friendly and sweet. Her stuff that she keeps outside is neat but the stuff she "hides" under the bed and in the shelves is schlumpy. She's 19 and not religious but from first impressions, if she turns out to be my permanent roommate we might get along well. But I'm not making a definite or firm expectation so soon.

A few other kids are making plans to travel around, but nothing definite yet. We have orientation tomorrow morning and find out about registration. Got your letters today- the first ones addressed to my new building. Glad all's okay. Give my love to all. Take care.

Love,
Tyra

Tuesday, October 18, 1966 5:30 P.M.

Dear Mom, Dad and Jessie,

Nothing much new here. Had orientation meeting today. Classes start Sunday the 30th and I have to plan a program. Saw Peter at the meeting. He's the one from Seminar that we bumped into after Rev Zemer's concert. He invited me to his wedding December 27. She's from Holland and they'll be settling here.

Just took a shower. For the past two days we didn't have any hot water until 8 P.M. We have it until 8:30- 9 A.M. and they shut it off all afternoon. In Shenkar the hot water came on at about four or five and I thought that this building, because it's older, doesn't get it until eight, which is awful. But I guess there was something wrong with the pipes. So everything's working out okay. I heard that the kitchen and the two rooms next to it are full of big black bugs at night. Thank heavens I haven't seen them in there.

October 28, 1966

Dear Tyra,

I think you are being too hard on yourself. Why can't you choose a guy who accepts you for who you are, which is just fine as far as I am concerned. David thinks you're not smart enough; Neil thinks you're not religious enough. My darling daughter, you are wonderful. Of course it's good to improve yourself and be the best you can be, but you should have faith in yourself and make sure the fellow you like appreciates you for who you are. I'm sure these boys are not so perfect themselves, and they certainly have no right to make you feel bad about yourself. Look at your poor friend, Dawn, always pining over that boy who stands her up and gives her a rough time. You know, it's no crime if a fellow treats you nicely. And on that score, don't be so hard on yourself with your studies, either. Do the best you can. I'm sure you are learning and speaking a lot of Hebrew. Get whatever credits you can, but don't worry so much. You'll finish up whatever you need for your master's degree when you get home. Just enjoy the wonderful opportunity you have. I have to stop writing, as if I start washing the pots now, I will be ready to go down to the basement when the laundry is done. So you see, make the most of this exciting time. I love you.

Mom

Friday, October 28, 1966 A.M.

Dear Mom, Dad and Jessie,

I figured out how much money I've spent and got an aver-age of $15 a week. That means I'll have enough until mid-June. Then I started thinking of the black pocketbook I have to buy, the six weeks of vacation and where I will be traveling, gifts, etc., but meanwhile I have quite a bit. I'm off to the beauty parlour for the first time. To be con't.

Sunday, October 30

I had three choices for an updo- the pony, the kookoo, or the chaleh. Since it was erev shabbos, I chose the latter. It came out okay except for the fact they forgot to put the yeast in! The 2 ½ lira hairstyle, after the cost of the bobby pins, hair pins, and Spray Tov-good- as opposed to Spray Ragil —regular- came out to five lira. Considering it's still only $1.66 for a wash and set, that's not bad. Have to get ready for first day of class tomorrow. Will continue soon.

Tyra scanned the students already sitting, waiting for the teacher of the Modern Poetry course to enter. There were an even mix of men and women, mostly in their mid to late twenties.

She took a seat somewhere in the middle of the room. A short, stocky typical Israeli-looking man walked in, perhaps thirty-two or thirty-three, walked behind the podium, set down his briefcase and introduced himself as Professor Doron. During some brief pleasantries and introductions, Tyra thought that class wasn't so bad and started to relax. Then the professor began distributing some mimeographed assignment sheets. She didn't recognize the names of the poets. No, none of the major poets she had studied at Lexington was on his list. Only minor, not so well known poets by American standards would they be studying here, poets she intuitively knew, who would not have had their works translated into English.

Professor Doron called on Tyra during the session, and though she was pleased with the way she discussed an image Bialik used in his famous poem, "The Oracle," Doron managed to make a disparaging comment about her *foreign* accent. He made her feel as if she were from outer space and she was embarrassed in front of the others. Instead of feeling proud of being a wonderful Jew from America devoting a year studying this wonderful language and literature with her colleagues and compatriots, she was belittled for a somewhat deficient rolling "r".

She had a three hour break until her next class and decided to hang around campus instead of going back and forth to the dorms. Luckily she bumped into Irit and her boyfriend Abraham at one of the cafeterias and caught up on gossip during lunch.

At three, she moseyed up to the room for her Master's Seminar in Modern Jewish Philosophy: *Hertzl, Ahad Ha-am and the Role of Zionism in Jewish Thought.* At least she had a similar course in her undergraduate studies so she should do well there. She took a seat around a large rectangular table. There were only five other students who were there first, and three others entered after her. Two other women, six men, all seemed to be in their late twenties or early thirties, all serious, scholars in-waiting. She took out her notebook and waited for the professor to come in. And he did! In walked Professor Doron. When his eyes landed on hers, he honed in on her as if to say, '*What are you doing here, you little squirt?*', if you could even translate that into Hebrew! Then Doron took the only seat left at the table as the professor of the seminar entered the room.

Tyra sunk low into her chair. A disparaging teacher in one class turned out to be a colleague in another. Tyra wished she were back in the dorm. No. She wished she were home in the Bronx.

Monday, October 31, almost midnight

Hi again,

I'm exhausted, but wanted to finish this letter and get it in the mail for you.

Today was the first day of classes. The campus was swarming with Israelis and motorcycles. People were hugging and kissing. It was one great reunion. I had three classes and though it's too early to tell what they'll be like, I understood quite a bit and I hope I will do well.

I met up with Irit after my six o' clock class and we went to her place. It's about a five minute walk across the valley from campus. She's closer to the university than I am. Her apartment is lovely. She shares it with three other girls. She works three full days a week at a small hotel. She's a receptionist, sets the tables for dinner, etc.. As far as I can tell, she deserves a dorm room more than my roommate, whose father is a dentist and has more money than Barak. But here, if you have protectzia- connections- you get ahead.

I had supper there and when I came back I found letter #30 from you and one from Zelda, and I was happy.

The university wants to more than double tuition so there will more than likely be a strike starting tomorrow. Even though I'd rather go to class, I really have to participate or else the Israelis will boycott me! It's not definite so we will see what happens.

Tuesday, November 1, 10:30 a.m.

I have a few minutes before I leave for class. I got up early and went to the Customs Office in town. The officer gave the couple in front of me a hard time with three rolls of film they received. I was plotzing. I didn't want to pay $10 for the five rolls you sent. He looked at the declaration sheet and said I could receive them duty-free. But his sheets said I was allowed still film. After a rigmarole, I was charged L12.50 for instant breakfast. They charged for three boxes, even though they were packed into two boxes, and sixty grush (cents) for being in the post office two extra days. The whole thing came out to one dollar, so even though I could have argued that the instant breakfast was a vitamin, I was so happy he let the film pass, I kept my mouth shut!

To answer your question, Neil is still attentive, when he is here. However, I haven't seen him since ten days ago, but who's counting?

The weather has been beautiful these past few weeks. It's been as high as 90F. Still wearing sleeveless and it's November already

Love,
Tyra

Thursday, November 3

Dear Mom, Dad and Jessie,

We're pretty much settled in the dorm now. My permanent roommate Michal is from Tel Aviv. Sometimes she is sweet, sometimes selfish, so it will be interesting how we get along. Bella's room is down the hall and I am so happy that we will be close. Her roommate, Tirzah, is from Yemen. She is twenty-six, a graduate student in Hebrew Literature. How lucky can I get! She seems really kind and told me she will help me with my work. She is very, very smart. She published two volumes of poetry already and wants to be a professor and writer after she gets her degree. A typical Yemenite, she is short, has an olive-complexion and dark, curly hair.

The dorm is as it was described: old, touch and go hot water- showers are haphazard- sometimes enough hot water, sometimes I have to rinse the shampoo out with ice cold water. The electricity goes out in spurts at night. Romantic, studying by candlelight! Otherwise it's fairly civilized here.

My friend, Olga, from the program comes from Parkchester and we think you and Daddy and her parents should meet soon. We think you would enjoy each other's company and you can compare notes about your daughters who abandoned you this year! Their number is PArkchester 3 6690. Call them soon, It would be good for you to get out and meet someone new. Olga and this fellow in the program, Mike, who is a junior at Boston U, have become an item. He's really sweet, observant.

Have to run.

Love,
Tyra

Saturday, November 5, 10 P.M.

Dear Dawn,

I hope to be hearing from you soon, meanwhile I thought I'd start this. It seems that things are good for a spell of a few days and then they get crummy. Natch, this is the latter. Classes started last week and I think I'm in for a year of sweat and tears. I'm taking difficult courses and I hope I can keep up with the Israelis. My Ulpan literature teacher is in a Master's Seminar I'm taking!

I saw Neil Wednesday. A bunch of couples went on a cook-out. We hiked to a nearby forest and when we got to the hill-top, the guys built a fire- Peter, Mike, Chaim and Neil- and the girls got the food ready for dinner. We all got comfortable,

139

that is as comfortable as you can get arranging your tushies on the cold damp rocks! Anyway, all the others were all cuddled up and there we were, Neil and I, sitting ten feet apart, I finally moved closer to him and asked him why he kept giving notes to other people to give me when he was at the university playing basketball. "Don't you know how embarrassing it is for me to have other people know you are near and don't come to see me yourself?" I asked him. "I didn't have time," he said. I could have killed him. "Don't you get it? Don't you realize how much it hurts that you would rather play basketball than see me? Why did you ask me on this blasted cookout anyway?" And do you know how the creep answered. "You know I'm not seeing anyone else." He turned to the boys and shouted, "Come on. Let's daven Mincha." And all the guys broke away from their make-out sessions and went to the top of the hill and davened.

It really was a beautiful sight as the sun set over the hills of Jerusalem, but I felt so lonely, I thought I would die. I honestly didn't know how I could get through the rest of the night, especially when all the other girls were so much in love and having such a good time.

I don't know why I am so drawn to him. Sometimes I feel like he is a locked strong box and once it is opened, a treasure will be revealed, but obviously I don't have the key. Why do I choose boys with soul who don't have their feet on the ground?

You must think I'm crazy, for each letter fluctuates regarding how we are getting along. I decided that we shouldn't see each other anymore. We don't have an honest relationship. He says many things I know he doesn't mean- rather he means the opposite- as kind of protection from his own feelings. We can't talk to each other as in the beginning and what we have is pretty shallow. Sometimes I feel that I'm no more to him than a piece of merchandise and so I think it'll be best if we break off now. I'm not counting on him asking for an explanation and wanting to start over. He's very independent and even if he doesn't want to, he'll probably walk out very smugly.

It's now 1 A.M. and I just got back from another building where a few of us had a frozen pizza- it was pretty good too. We spent last night and today loafing around, drinking wine and getting high. I'm really exhausted now and tomorrow's a long day. I have a big shopping list to cover and classes. I went to sleep at 1:30 A.M. last night and slept until 1:30 P.M. today. My roommate Michal -an Israeli- went home for Shabbos and I was alone. It's nice having a little privacy.

I got a letter from home saying that you called. Thanks for keeping in touch with my folks. I know they appreciate it. I picked up the package and it was fun looking at all those "American" things.

I left my transistor at the picnic on Wednesday and on Thursday I went back to see if it was still there. It wasn't, but in between, I wound up in the central police station (of course I'm not mentioning this to my parents). I was walking along this mountain road to get to the spot we were at, and a guy started following me. He got pretty morbid as he unzipped his pants and exposed himself. It might as well have been 125th Street on the IRT line. Anyway I screamed like a banchee and some nearby forest workers grabbed him. The police came and I had to ride in a paddy wagon and sign an affidavit at the police station. They put him in jail and he's going on trial. It was just like the time in the elevator when a guy exposed himself. I screamed and he ran away. I was about fourteen, and when I ran into the apartment I was shaking like a leaf. My father called the police, and a few days later, a guy did the same thing to another girl in the neighborhood. Lucky for her, her brothers were nearby and they beat the crap out of him. I had to go to the police station with my father to identify him. I was shaking like a leaf. These days I'm not shaking so much. The stupid thing is that now I have to go to the police station to report the loss of my radio! If not, I'll have to pay duty on it when I return to the States since they will assume I will have given it to an Israeli.

I'll continue this some other time. I'm going to flop into bed right now. Goodnight!

Well it's Tuesday night and you're a real fink. Still haven't written- hey?

Classes are a bomb. It's a wonderful feeling to sit through 20 hours of lectures, understanding only four- which are two classes especially for foreign students. The whole thing is so frustrating that I dread this year now. I can just imagine coming back next year with a blank transcript.

Friday

I haven't seen Neil since the cookout last week. If he doesn't come up tomorrow- Shabbos afternoon- I guess we are finished.

Friday, November 11, 4:30 P.M.

Dear Mom, Dad and Jessie,

I did go on the cookout Wednesday. It was okay. The only thing is that I left my radio there. I went back yesterday to check and it was gone. Now I have to go to the police and report it. Otherwise I will have to pay duty on it when I come home. I'll go crazy without a radio but it's my own stupid fault. It doesn't pay to mail one, but maybe when Zelda's parents come February 7, you can give them another one.

I got another package from Barak. Got the notice at twelve and just made it to the post office which closes at 12:30. I was glad because I figured it was fruit and didn't want it to spoil.

There were six pounds of apples, pears, avocado, raisins and prunes.

Falafel- ground chick peas, grated onions, salt, pepper, garlic. Make balls and deep fry. Put in pita bread with cut up tomatoes and cucumbers. Don't tell me Daddy is that ambitious!

I changed courses again so I have classes from Sunday through Thursday as of now.

There was a strike on Wednesday. It was interesting to hear slogans in Hebrew. The place was mobbed and there were reinforcements from Tel Aviv and Haifa schools. I cut out early though to go on the blasted picnic.

What's something interesting and easy to cook? I'm getting tired of the same old crap. I made fried matzah for breakfast today- it was pretty good.

Love,
Tyra

November 10, 1966

Dear Tyra,

I don't know what you mean about Neil thinking you're not religious enough. If I remember, you keep kosher and observe Shabbos, although you at least put on make-up now. You go to shul and pray too, so what does that mean- you have to wear your sleeves down to your knees! This whole religion bit is crazy as far as I am concerned, but that's beside the point. I think Neil must be nuts if he thinks you're not good enough for him on that score, and so are you for putting up with that. But who am I to talk. Look at all the grief Eric gives me. Did I tell you that he is going with this girl and is standing her up and treating her like garbage, too? I'm waiting for her to ditch him, so I can win him back. I still think I can change him. Anyway, remember what we wrote in our high school yearbooks? How are we going to walk our babies in carriages in the park together if we can't find decent men to have them with. We sure pick lulus, don't we?

Thanks for giving me Ricky's address. I'll get to writing him one of these days. Let me know what happens with Neil.

Love,
Dawn

Tuesday, November 15, 1966

Dear Dawn,

I can't tell you how happy I was to get your letter. I miss you so much.

You won't believe what happened to me today as I still can't believe it myself. After class, I took the bus to the center of the city to do my errands, and after I went to the bank to take out some money, and the laundry to drop off my clothes, I went to the supermarket, the Supersol, which is just like the A&P or Grand Union. When I finished my shopping I left with two mesh bags filled with groceries. Just as I exited the store on my way to the bus stop, shots rang out from on high and every one on the street scurried to take cover. Groceries flew all over the place. Cars screeched to a halt. People were screaming in confusion.

I always thought these mesh bags that come in all different colors were kind of primitive, but Israelis don't have paper bags. They're too busy planting trees to chop them down for paper goods. Now I know another reason for the mesh bags. They're good at holding canned goods in when bags go flying in the streets during Jordanian target practice! The shooting stopped in a few minutes, the all-clear sirens sounded and people started standing up and gathering their belongings. It was wild. We were close to the protective walls along the border and some Jordanian snipers shot across the wall into our streets.

Well, that's all the excitement for today. If you speak to my parents, of course don't tell them about this episode. They'll kill me if they knew.

Still haven't heard from Neil. Anything with Eric?

Love,
Tyra

November 15, 1966

Dear Tyra,

I knew it, and I let your father have it. This is what I was afraid of all along. We've been so worried about what's been going on in Israel and the attacks she carried out on Jordan. By this time you must know the newspapers are full of the Jordan-Israel crisis and we are all hoping it will blow over without a war. This morning I read in the Jewish Press that Syria pledged to make every Israeli household a graveyard. Boy did that set me off. If the American Embassy evacuates Americans, please come home. I don't know why Israel had to start up with Jordan, attacking the village of Es Samu.

This is just a brief note to tell you to be careful and stay safe. Come home if it gets bad.

Mother

November 21, 1966

Dear Mom, Dad and Jessie,

First, please don't worry. I am safe and things here go on as normal. That's how life here is. Israel had to do something to stop the constant border infiltrations from Syria and Jordan. Perhaps they should have gone after Syria rather than Jordan, but it's always a lose-lose situation because of world opinion.

I finally got my schedule straightened out. I have an easy schedule- nine courses or eighteen hours spread over five days. Tirzah, my Yemenite literature major who is Bella's roommate, helped me read a story and write an analysis until three in the morning the other night. She's a doll. I told her I didn't know how to thank her and she said it wasn't necessary. She took me to visit her aunt and uncle in Romema last Shabbos. They have four children and the whole family is very hospitable. Her uncle was loafing around in pajamas and we were sitting eating all kinds of spicy foods which I never tasted before. The Yemenites are a very cultured, educated people, especially in Jewish studies- Talmud, Mishnah and the like. Israelis- the Western Ashkenazis look down on them with the other "Black Jews" (referred to that way because of their dark complexions) from North Africa and the Arab countries who are poor and uneducated. There seems to be quite a bit of discrimination here, too. We had a great visit. The only thing is I feel bad for Tirzah because she is so talented and smart, but her family is almost on the verge of disowning her because she is so OLD- all of twenty-seven and not married. She would like to get married, but would like to love someone first, and she really loves her studies and wants to become a professor. I think I mentioned that once.

I was really prepared for the short story discussion in class this week although the professor didn't collect the written work. All that preparation for nothing! Actually I was really pleased because I had a lot to say. The only thing is I was so self-conscious about my accent. I guess the Israelis will just have to put up with me. I have to read a fifty page story for tomorrow. So busy, busy, busy.

Please save the papers this week as it's the third anniversary of the assassination. Thanks.

Love,
Tyra

November 27, 1966

Dear Tyra,

We had a busy day today. The weather is mild these days but the air has been very polluted. It's lifting now. We paid our respects to Mrs. Sheft. Her son Sam (the doctor), passed away. He had a heart condition for several years and it got him Thanksgiving Day. Everyone was at the chapel and I saw practically everyone from the old neighborhood.

Then we picked up Grandma and Grandpa and visited Aunt Minna and Uncle Izzy. Aunt Minna is hobbling along nicely on her crutches since her fall. She just needs time to heal, and an abundance of patience she doesn't have. They appreciated our visit, although we did get stuck in traffic on the way home and we're all tired now.

I deposited $170 in your account for December. The extra twenty is from Grandpa- He wants to give you ten dollars for Hanukah and 5 each for Hadas and Irit. Please take care of that for him. I want to send you a few gifts but the mailman said that this time of year there are a lot of temporary workers and packages going to foreign countries that aren't insured are easily pilfered, so I will wait until after the holidays.

Meanwhile we are worried sick over what is happening in Israel. The 6th Fleet is standing by in the Mediterranean Sea. I was wondering what the Israelis think of the Americans after the stand they took at the U.N. I'm enclosing a bunch of clippings about the censure. Why don't they ever censure the Arabs? It's the same old story. I'm tired and going to rest and watch some TV before going to bed. Be careful.

Love,
Mom

Monday November 28 midnight

Dear Mom, Dad and Jessie,

There was a strike after all- who knows for how long it'll keep up. It started today. The government decided to raise tuition from 600 to 700 lirot. It was a compromise- they originally wanted to raise it to 1400 lirot. The student government said it wouldn't protest any raise as long as it was less than 200 lirot. Now they say it's a matter of principle and are striking anyway. Yesterday I was against it- today I spent a few hours catching up on my work and the extra time came in handy. They say it'll last at least until Thursday and since I have no classes on Friday, I'd like to travel somewhere. Everyone seems to want to study, though, and I just have a paper which would have been due tomorrow (which I'll write tomorrow) and after that I'll be free. Probably go to the beach in Tel Aviv one day.

Today I got #41. Too bad about Aunt Minna's fall. I hope she'll still go to California. Send regards and get well wishes. I owe loads of letters for a change and should start on some of them.

It looks like the aerogramme Jessie started will get all faded by the time she gets around to mailing it.

Tell me if there's a difference (if it's easier to read my pencil handwriting).

If you can make up a copy of the Hebrew Teaching Certificate, I'd like to hang it on my wall and give the Israelis a big kick out of it.

It's now 2:35 A.M. I've been trying to sleep for two hours. Michal's up too. Thank God for the strike tomorrow. At least I'll be able to sleep late.

I don't know if I told you how shocked Michal was when I told her corn on the cob only takes ten minutes- she didn't trust me. Today I gave her some chicken and tzimmes- she said I cook better than her mother. How's that for international relations!

I'm so hungry I'll get something to eat. I'll get to sleep yet. I hope. Good night- morning or whatever.

Tuesday 10:30 A.M.
Finally fell asleep at about three- just had breakfast and am getting back into bed. Thought of some other things Zelda's parents can take- one or two bottles of liquid makeup and some light colored lipsticks.

Also in the next package put in a bottle of Excedrin and some Pepto-Bismol tablets- not that I need them- just in case. Zelda wants to know if her parents should bring toilet paper. I have enough-I'm on my second roll and I have a whole suitcase full. Boy was that ever a stupid move. Oh well. Take care, you all.

Tyra

Later that night Peter knocked on the door and Tyra was happy for the company. Maybe he could shed some light on Neil's mysterious ways. More importantly, her loneliness and confusion might be assuaged.

"Excited about the wedding?" she asked.

"Am I ever. Yael's whole family is coming from Holland. It's going to be some swanky affair." He sat on her bed.

"I shouldn't have eaten all those falafels this year. I can't get into my nice outfits anymore, Tyra said, berating herself. "Do you want a drink or something?"

"No thanks. Come on, babe, don't be so hard on yourself. You'll look good in a blanket," he said, as he eyed her.

She laughed and sat down beside him. "Maybe I'll lose a few kilos. Still have a few weeks. Listen, do you know what's going on with Neil? You're his close friend."

"No. What do you mean?"

"Well for the past few weeks, he's been really distant. I've hardly seen him. And what's strange is that he sees my friends, the other guys that are around the dorm, and tells them to send me his regards. What's that about? He's on campus, playing basketball, and he tells other people to send his regards….He doesn't come to see me! I'm so embarrassed and hurt."

In a flash, Peter put his arm around her and pulled her down on the bed and kissed her vigorously. As quickly as he did, he pushed her away, propping the two of them up in a sitting position. She was in shock, her complexion white. He stood up, his face red.

The silence seemed to last forever until he sheepishly looked down. "I don't know what happened. I don't know what to say," he stammered. All the while, Tyra sat there looking like a frozen statue, abused, tortured, violated and guilty.

"Tyra, please forgive me. I'm happy. I found the woman of my dreams. I'm so ashamed. Please it was all my fault. I'm sorry. Say something, please."

"I poured my heart out to you about Neil. It's not like I don't feel bad enough about myself."

"Badly…."

"Don't grammar me now."

"Sorry, you're right. Maybe it was my last revolt as a bachelor."

"You guys, you're all rotten."

"Tyra, you know I adore you. You're a good friend. Can we forget this ever happened? You'll still come to the wedding won't you?"

Again, the silence, the long, drawn out silence between two friends who were saddened and perplexed by a misunderstood impulse.

"I guess, if I can find something to wear."

"Listen, about Neil, if he doesn't level with you by the wedding, give him up. You're gorgeous, and a good soul. There are a lot of guys who could fall in love with you in a jif. Other students that met this year are already engaged. Don't waste your time with Neil. Some people are too messed up to fix. Trust me."

Trust, she thought. *How nice that would be.*

Thursday December 1, 1966 1 P.M.
Dear Mom, Dad and Jessie,

Well, it's December 1 and 24 days till Xmas! I got #42 today.

It was sweet of Grandma and Grandpa to give us Hanukah presents. I'll be going to Barak next week- we're off on Thursday and Friday- first two days if classes start again- a four day weekend almost- like Thanksgiving. Oh- remembered another in the skit- something to the effect that America has far reaching influence- here a group of Americans are sitting down celebrating an American holiday in Asia. It's funny- before then we didn't think of ourselves as being in Asia.

The night air is getting very brisk now and today the wind howling down the corridor woke me up. I just finished that paper I was supposed to finish on Monday night. Anyway it's done and off my mind.

Tuesday afternoon Tirzah, Bella and I went up to the Knesset to get into the public gallery as a hearing on the strike was taking place. We stood on line for an hour- got pushed and shoved and naturally didn't get in. We then went to walk around the Billy Rose Gardens in the National Museum. It was dark and the only lights were the spotlights focused on the sculptures. It's arranged in such a way, on slopes all surrounded by stone walls- the ground is just pebbles- no paving, and you can see bare trees lit up against the dark- it was kind of cold, but very striking and overwhelming. Then Bella and I went to a student dramatic production on the other side of the campus. It was good- in Hebrew- and we basically understood.

7 P.M.

Yesterday Bella and I went to Beer Sheva. The campus, with the strike on, is like a morgue and we wanted to get away. On the bus, I thought I `saw a `picture of Ted Kennedy on the front page of a newspaper, but the guy was `sitting about five seats in front of me and I wasn't sure. Then another guy across the aisle pulled out a paper and I guess he saw us trying to read his paper, so he gave us the page and we learned that Ted Kennedy landed in Israel. He was supposed to come to the university at 3:30 today, but didn't. I went and we were all disappointed. Some of the kids in the group caught him at his hotel last night and got into a press conference. Lucky creeps! It would have been great to see a "landsman". We (Americans) would have been in the spotlight for a change. I hope you saved all the newspaper articles about his visit- also if any magazines cover the story- please save too.

Anyway, I saw a camel on the way down to Beer Sheva. It was the first time I traveled south of Jerusalem. We got there at 1:30 and all the stores were closed up so we went to visit a family that Bella knew from home. We asked a policeman how to get there and he rode with us on the bus and then walked us to the door. Nice! He lived around there. The family wasn't home, so we went back to town and went to the Museum of the Negev. It's in a mosque- it was a mosque until the War. We climbed up the minaret 90 steps in a 360 degree angle. They were very narrow and all centered about the pole (not like an open spiral where you can see the top and bottom). We just kept walking and walking until we hit the top which was a very narrow platform surrounded by bars. We saw the whole town and the Negev. Couldn't take pictures though- not allowed.

Schlepped the still camera yesterday and today and didn't take one picture.

The museum houses archeological finds from the Negev. Saw a sundial from the fourth millennium, ancient pottery, and Roman maps. It was all fascinating. The guard's daughter took over for him when he went to eat lunch. She's an eighteen year old girl, very sweet and she must be very lonely as she started talking to us about her problems with her parents (who don't let her go out at all) and the boy she loves (and he doesn't love her). Imagine me giving her advice. I gave her my address and she said she'd write. I'd like her to come and spend a Shabbos with me- I hope her parents will let her.

We left the museum and started roaming around trying to find the "Well of Abraham"- couldn't- none of the natives knew either- instead roamed into a beautiful store and I bought a beautiful, also expensive menorah. It's very striking- eight gold and black lions with candleholders on top and the Shamash is on top of a star which is on top of gold and black arc doors in heavy filigree. It's on a blue stone platform with gold legs. It's a big dust collector and it'll be a mess cleaning the wax off of it, but it was just so pretty I couldn't resist- and I really haven't splurged too much so I'm happy.

From there we went to visit that family again. They had come home from work. We got on the bus at five o'clock and it actually got crowded- like rush hour- it was great! It was pleasant visiting them and we left to catch the last bus back to Jerusalem. I'll continue on another aerogramme....

We were the only two passengers but as the bus was pulling out another girl ran on. The bus driver was very nice and we were kibbitzing around. He wanted to know why we asked for student discount since there's a strike (which will probably be over Sunday) and we told him that when there are classes we don't have time to travel and take advantage of the discount!

On the main road from Beer Sheva we saw army jeeps lined up one behind the other. Soldiers had rifles in hand and steel helmets on. Never saw such "prepared" soldiers before- they usually are more casual. Coming into the hills of Jerusalem I saw a fantastically bright light reflected on the ground. At first I was startled and said- it can't be the moon- then realized it was the projector searching the mountains and border areas for infiltrators. When we got to the station we asked the bus driver what was going on. At first we thought there might have been another incident. He said the entire army is on the alert and in a state of readiness. Things are much more tense than a few months ago. I used to travel to Jerusalem a lot at night and never saw the projector before- but people don't think of it- they go on living and doing what they have to because otherwise- to live in fear all the time- everything would stop. We are all aware of what's going on here and really there's nothing to be afraid of- if anything happens the American Embassy will kick us out and ship us home. Anyway I hope it doesn't come to that.

We got back to the dorm and talked with some kids. One had a whole stack of pictures from the Ashrei and our trips. Saw a couple who spent the day in Tel Aviv- it seemed we all bought menorahs! I stayed up until two listening to Radio Moscow. They had some great musical selections and then heard an English newscast and commentary. I never heard such direct propaganda before. On Vietnam, they said the American housewife is suffering the most with inflation. The government keeps decreasing its funds for social services and increases war funds. They called Johnson a tyrant and our army a regime and some other nasty names. It felt kind of strange hearing a broadcast all the way from Russia.

Finally got to sleep at three. Woke up with the wind howling. It's eight now and I'll go over to Shenkar to eat supper. They took our hotplate away again to fix. I'll come back, wash and set my hair and pack. I'm going to Michal's tomorrow. She's home already, She had a blind date with a medical student from Hadassah Hospital the other night and fell head over heels over him. He lives in Tel Aviv, too, and works in Ichelov Hospital on weekends. I'll mail these now. Hope it leaves the country tomorrow. Don't forget to save the articles on Kennedy. Take care.

Love to all.
Tyra

HI FAMILY,

In Beer Sheva- Picture on back of postcard is of the Marketplace- people are running around with live chickens all over. Shockneh would love it! Having a ball. Will write more when I get back home- to Jerusalem that is.

Love, Tyra

HI DAWN,

Picture on postcard of Beer Sheva- donkeys all over- classes are terrible- I'll never pass-love-life- awful- getting fat, too- I'll never make it through the year. Never been so miserable. Write soon. Am desperate. Need help. Come visit.

Love, Tyra

EIGHT

THE THISTLE AND THE HONEY

They say the groom breaks a glass at the end of the wedding ceremony to bring back to the congregation via a shattering sting of fragility, the reality of sorrow's existence even in times of joy. Surely for the Miller family, pure happiness was elusive. Their joyous moments seemed to be, in part, contaminated with pain or grief. And for Jessie, there seemed to be so little joy, and what there was, was tempered with the cruel blows of life's truths, as if the hand could laugh only if one of its fingers cried. That was the way it was, and all of them tried to savor what they could in spite of the way things had to be.

Jessie was able to enter Paul Revere High School in November of her senior year, and although the two surgeries barely improved, no less correct her curvature, she learned to adjust. She made herself a survival kit consisting of a layer of armor, a lot of spunk, and found a new niche for herself. She was talkative, good-natured to a fault, but stubborn and liked things her way. She would hang around with her friends, some of the same ones who used to visit her when she was in bed. In those days, it wasn't quite as apparent that there were couples in the group.

But now they would be together until the others would pair off to go to the movies or a dance, and Jessie would go home. She would never admit it, but she must have been lonely watching others going places and doing things that normal young people did. Jessie was everybody's pal but no one's sweetheart.

She studied hard in school, for although she excelled during home instruction, she couldn't cover all the required material in the limited sessions allotted. Most of her teachers were compassionate and allowed her a little extra time to make up the work. After all, she needed to graduate and get good enough grades to get into a city college. But Mr. Becker, the Spanish teacher, treated her with disdain from the moment she walked into the classroom. He assigned her a seat in the back, in the last row, as if he didn't even want her there at all. He never gave her partial credit for any of her answers, although he did so for the other students. He refused to give her an extra copy of *El Camino Real* to keep at home so she wouldn't have to carry a heavier load back and forth. And he never let an opportunity pass when he could embarrass her in front of the class. He even threatened to fail her, which of course would prevent her from graduating. So she learned early on how to deal with prejudice and unfairness, a skill she would unfortunately exercise often. She hated Becker, and cursed the stories of the damn burro that did her more harm than good in the Bronx. He was an idiot if he thought he was preparing her for the real world. Tyra thought the real world had taught Jessie plenty of lessons already and that she handled them far better than Tyra ever could.

For a long time, Tyra had pondered over Rabbi Singer's suggestion that she take an entrance exam for the coed Yeshiva High School in Washington Heights, since Hebrew was not going to be offered in ninth grade in her junior high. On the last Sunday in February, she entered the gymnasium at Breuer's High School, nervous and excited about the lengthy three-hour exam. She felt she was answering the secular parts adequately, and although the religious sections on prayer and bible were more difficult, she thought she had a decent handle on them as well. However, when she turned the booklet to the Modern Hebrew language section, the pages became a blur as her eyes filled with tears. She recognized the letters, but she could not even pronounce the words they spelled. They were written without the phonetic crutch of vowels, and the test might as well have been Greek or Latin. She looked around the tables and saw the other students writing away with ease, and she was devastated by her inferiority.

She picked up her belongings, handed the booklet with the unfinished answer sheet to the proctor, and ran into the bathroom down the hall.

Tyra leaned against the cold, white tiled wall and sobbed, tears from her eyes and mucous from her nose blending into a wet mess of humiliation and disappointment. A kindly mother dressed in a royal blue suit, waiting for her child to finish the exam, turned her around by the shoulders, embraced her without a word, and put her hand on Tyra's head. Tyra cried until she choked on her phlegm, and forced herself to stop. The woman spoke, perhaps some words of comfort and encouragement, but Tyra was too overcome to make out the specific words. She could only feel the lady's soft tone. When Tyra pulled away, apologetically pointing to the teary stains she made on the blue jacket, she did hear the woman say, "Don't worry, sweetheart. It'll dry. Everything will be alright."

Tyra stayed when class was over, and when all the students were gone, she asked Rabbi Singer why he told her to take the admissions test, angry, as if he set her up for failure.

"You had your heart set on it, and I didn't want to discourage you. It's a wonderful trait not to be afraid of challenges. Even if you think you might fail, you'll find out where you stand. In all honesty, you would have done very well except for the conversational Hebrew."

"But the other kids, they just knew what to do...."

"Tyra, they went to day school all along. You made the most of the opportunity you had. There are many ways to get what you want. This way wasn't for you, but now that you know how hard it is. If you still want it, you will find a better way to get your dream."

"Rabbi, I studied so hard. I know every word in the prayer book."

"You may not speak fluently, but you are my best student. No one understands like you. Remember the first day of school when I asked the students to tell me who their fathers were? One by one each listed store manager, optometrist, salesman. When it was your turn, I knew I could count on you. 'My father is a good man. He's honest, works hard for his family. He's wise and the closest thing to a saint!' and you started to chuckle."

Tyra was stunned for the moment. Of course she remembered. She was so enthralled with the Rabbi's dynamism and charisma. But she hadn't realized she made such an impression. She was merely stating the simple truth. Yet even now, her modesty prevented her from accepting such praise easily, and she looked down at the floor, and the anger she felt at first dissipated.

"I could see the boys squirm as they realized they missed the point in judging their fathers by the amount of money they earned or the level of education they attained." Rabbi Singer continued, "You led me into the discussion of a person's worth and integrity, and the significance of man being

159

created in God's image. Tyra, you have an understanding soul. Skill is not the only important thing. You have a sensitivity, a compassion, and that counts for a lot, although you may not see it this second."

The shame of her failure and limitations slowly left her as she realized the accomplishments she sought were no longer deserving the importance she had accorded them. Rabbi Singer saw in her a depth, something special, a quality that made her different and stand out from the crowd. "And I might as well tell you," he continued, "I recommended you to the board for the President's Award at graduation."

"Oh, Rabbi." It was not the honor or even the silver candlesticks she would receive at the ceremony that made her gulp. This acknowledgement, she thought, is the true measure of her own worth, her inner beauty.

With a sudden hint of vitality and mischief she told him, "I don't like you anymore, Rabbi." She saw the shock on his face and quickly added, "I love you!" Relieved, he laughed and shook his head in the way only grown-ups do, as she sprinted down the stairs giggling and calling out, "Say hi to Vicki for me."

"You're looking at the proud owner of *SID'S FOOD SHOPPE*," Sid came home one night, beaming. After years of hard work and weeks of negotiating a good deal, Sid was able to purchase a small luncheonette in the food distribution district of the South Bronx.

"It's better to be the boss of a hole-in-the-wall than an employee in a blue-chip," he said, even knowing that he would work long hours six days a week. Of the first generation born in America, he glowed over his efforts to attain a piece of the American dream for his family, and give his children opportunities he never had.

"So you went in with Duvid after all," Kaye said. She had been skeptical all along.

Izzy had come over the house a few times during the past few weeks, each with propositions and pleadings for Sid to take on Izzy's brother, Duvid, as partner and cook. "I'll even help Duvid out with the down payment, Sid. Make sure you get your due," Izzy said. Duvid was the black sheep in the family, a real character. He had a great sense of humor, always had everyone in stitches, except his wife, who got tired of putting up with him and finally got a divorce- the first one in the family.

"Why? He'll only cause you trouble," Kaye said, shaking her head.

"He says he'll change. He's a good cook and besides, Izzy lent him money for his share of the down-payment."

"He's always changing, when he's not off gambling. I hope you know what you're doing."

"Come on, Kaye. Don't be so afraid. We can't stay still forever. It'll be okay. Have some faith." Sid kissed her forehead.

"Faith. Sure." Her words were sparse and heavy with sarcasm.

Sheldy burst into the apartment all enthused, waving an envelope in the air. He lifted Jessie up and spun her around. "Will my fair lady accompany me to see *My Fair Lady* on Broadway?" He said it as a statement more than a question. "Two orchestra seats, for me and my girl."

Jessie couldn't contain her excitement. "For real!"

"Absotively, posilutely! You will have the honor of being my last date before I get hitched. Your crazy uncle did it this time. My bachelor days are just about over." A small wedding was planned for the beginning of May.

"And you will have the honor of being my first date!" She laughed and told him she would plan a shopping trip to get the prettiest dress in the world.

"You've been to a Broadway show, haven't you?" He took Tyra aside. "You don't mind, do you? I want to do something special for your sister."

"No, I've never been to a show before and no, I don't mind." That wasn't exactly true; she never liked being left out. But that was the truth, and she didn't like herself for being as selfish as she was. Kaye had taken her to Rockefeller Center many times for ice skating lessons, and her parents signed her up for a membership at Shorehaven Swim and Tennis Club the past two summers. At first, she didn't want to join. It was too expensive, but Sid insisted. "We can't go to the bungalows while Jessie's in bed, and it will be good for you to keep active and make new friends," he told her. Many mornings she would walk a mile on Bronx Boulevard to Gun Hill Road to catch the bus to Shorehaven instead of taking a city bus north on White Plains Avenue to the connection, all to save the fifteen cent fare. She could save almost two dollars a week if she walked home in the afternoon, too, and she would deduct that sum from the next week's allowance.

That's what parents did, she thought. Everything for the children. One of her friends, Carol, lived in a one bedroom apartment also, on the Boulevard. Her parents slept on the Castro convertible in the living room, and gave the bedroom to Carol and her brother. Not only did they get the bedroom, but her parents had a room divider built-in so they would each have privacy. All for the children. And when her friend Michelle's father died, all the friends were devastated. Fathers aren't supposed to die so young. Tyra looked at Sid differently after that, and she prayed harder for his well-being.

The shopping trip which sounded like it would be fun at first didn't turn out that way at all. Kaye took Jessie and Tyra to a fancy dress shop on Mosholu Parkway. Tyra went along just for the ride, but afterward, she wished she had stayed home. She was going to wear her gold Bas Mitzvah dress to her uncle's wedding. She had only worn it that once, and even though almost two years had passed, the dress fit her perfectly. She still hadn't filled out like the other girls. She didn't even get her period, which made her feel inferior and immature. The dress was just a little shorter as she had grown a few inches, but hemlines were creeping up, and it seemed frivolous to buy another dress she would hardly use. On the other hand, Jessie was going to wear her first fancy dress at least three times- to the show, the wedding and hopefully in June, to her senior prom, if she could get a date.

After much trying on, Jessie chose a sleeveless, black chiffon with a delicate nude lace bodice underneath. She looked radiant, modeling it in front of the mirror, swishing the flare skirt with her graceful fingertips. From the front, you could hardly tell, except for the slight dip of a shoulder. But from the back, there was work to be done. Even the corsetiere from the lingerie shop next door came into the fitting room with several styles of long-lines that Kaye thought would be easier to pad on one side and make Jessie's back look more even. Hours seemed to pass; the store was sweltering, the noise from the elevated trains clanking back and forth grated on all their nerves, but the seamstress and corsetiere conferred, pinned, and worked non-stop. Jessie would be beautiful; they wouldn't give up until the dress was perfect. And no one paid attention to Jessie's protests and impatience as she squirmed around, tugging at the miserable bones in the longline corset. When she couldn't stand it anymore, she ripped the shoulder pads from the dress and threw off the longline, padding and all. "Enough," she screamed at Kaye. "All your talk about inner beauty means nothing. When I look in the mirror, I see me and who I am. Other people see my back, and if they have trouble looking at me, that's their problem and yours. I want the dress, but no corset. I'm only eighteen, damn it, not an old bag."

Kaye was devastated. She just wanted Jessie to have what all the other girls her age had, but Jessie was strong-willed, and with the big box under her arm, she left and waited outside until Kaye paid the owner.

The night of the show finally arrived. Sheldy looked smashing in a dark suit. He came in with a fragrant wrist corsage for Jessie, and a carnation each for Kaye and Tyra.

Jessie pranced out of the bedroom modeling the dress and she was beaming. Kaye approached her, tugging on the right side of the skirt to straighten the hem. "Stand up straight, Jessie. Let's see."

"That's it. I'm not going." Jessie screamed, turning around heading for the bedroom.

"Why did you have to do that, Kaye?" Sid said.

"What do you know?" she answered.

"Always pulling me, straightening me out," Jessie said. "I'll never be straight. When will you get that?"

"Come on, Jess," Sid implored. "You look wonderful. Don't spoil such a nice evening. Mom didn't mean anything. Uncle Sheldy spent a fortune for the tickets. Come on, now. Don't be spiteful. You'll have a great time."

The door slammed with a thunderous boom, an omen that no amount of cajoling or begging or reasoning would change Jessie's mind.

Tyra's head was pounding from all the commotion and tension, but she didn't know what to do, so she just stood where she was fighting back tears.

After fifteen minutes of everyone futilely trying to change Jessie's mind, Sheldy turned to Tyra and asked her to put on a dress. "We're not letting these tickets go to waste, are we?"

Tyra looked at her mother for permission. She wanted to go but it didn't feel right.

Tyra loved the show. The theatre was a wondrous cavern with enchanting chandeliers and velvet chairs. She was engrossed in the music, swaying back and forth to the voluminous sounds of the instruments, and could hardly believe her eyes when the whole orchestra descended into the pit after the overture. The costumes were like nothing she had ever seen before and her hands were beet red from clapping during the standing ovation at the end. Sheldy treated her to cheesecake at Lindy's afterward. They bought an extra slice for Kaye, Sid and Jessie to share.

When they got home, Jessie came into the kitchen to see what was going on.

"How was the show?" She looked straight at Tyra.

Tyra saw Jessie's eyes were red. "It was okay." She changed the subject quickly. "Have some cheesecake. It's from Lindy's. It's de-lish."

"No thanks. Good night."

School was out for winter vacation. Sid and Tyra stole out of the apartment so as not to awaken Kaye. Jessie was already into the third day of seminar. The December pre-dawn air was cold and damp as the father and daughter strode up the hill in the dark and got into the car. Sid drove past the reservoir and made the sharp left turn leading through Crotona Park, whizzing through the Bronx which had never seemed more desolate and calm.

"I don't know why you insisted on coming with me at 4 o'clock," Sid said as he exhaled a puff of smoke from his Tareyton. "You could have come by bus a little later on."

"I wanted to help you open," Tyra answered. It figured that Duvid would wait until her Easter vacation to skip out,

165

probably to Vegas. She tugged her coat around her, hoping the heater would hurry and warm up. Sid called the old Chevy *Old Reliable,* but Tyra just thought of it as old. Something was always breaking down and causing trouble and inconvenience. If she had money, how she would love to buy him a new car…

"Tyra," Sid shouted, "You're daydreaming again. Told you you should'a slept more and come by bus."

"Are you in trouble, Dad? With Mom, I mean, because Duvid ran out this week?"

"Well, she isn't too happy about it." He let out a sound somewhere between a sigh and a chuckle. "But it's my own store. It's better to own a shack than rent a mansion, and someday we'll have a little house of our own. You'd like that, wouldn't you?"

"Sure. I just want everybody to be happy and stop yelling."

They eventually wound up in front of Sid's Food Shoppe. Even though it was so early, earlier than most of the other merchants opened their businesses, Sid had to drive around the block until he found a spot. Alternate side of the street parking days was just another way of adding to the difficulties in the crowded Bronx.

The work was hard and never ending. Sid cooked big slabs of corned beef, peeled potatoes, made endless platters of food as the customers came in throughout the day. Tyra worked the fountain and took cash at the register. The two of them were on their feet, constantly running along the counter and to the few small tables.

"Good egg cream," a customer called out to Tyra. "Lots of foam." Tyra was thrilled.

At one point during a lull, Tyra went across the street to Shockneh's market to pick up two chickens that Sid needed to make chicken salad. Shockneh's work was hard, cruel, and noisy. Chickens clucking about in the back of the store until he picked up one by one, and obeying the strict laws of *schita,* slaughter, he slit the poor bird's neck, then plucked the feathers and kashered it in salt, and packed cartons on ice waiting for the distributor to come get them.

"So he's not using *treif* chickens today, your papa?"

"Daddy's a good man, Uncle Shockneh. You know he has to work hard to make a living. The store's busy today. He ran out. Besides, he knows you'll give him a good price, even if it can't compete with *treif* ones."

"Everybody changes rules to make it good for them. What will be left of us if everyone gives up what *Ribono shel olam* wants?"

"You know what Rabbi Singer says, Uncle Shockneh? A good person is a good Jew and a good Jew is a good person, but one who observes rules without a heart is neither."

"Yeah, yeah," he said, as he waved his hands in front of him in frustration. "Vate a minute." He turned around and walked to the back of the store. Returning a few seconds later, he handed Tyra a paper sack. "Chicken eggs. I saved them for you and Jessie. Don't get them so much anymore, but I know you like them."

"Thanks. I'll give them to Grandma when I get home." She kissed him on the cheek. "Say hi to Aunt Sophie," as she turned around to leave, her arms full of bundles.

"Your papa, he's a good man," Shockneh called out after her. "And you're a good girl to help him."

Time seemed to fly that spring, for everyone but Hana. The facial attacks were becoming more unbearable and frequent. Kaye happened upon an article in one of the daily papers about a doctor in Philadelphia who was experimenting with a hot-water injection that would anesthetize the trigeminal nerve root. The downside was the entire side of the face would be numb forever, like a huge dose of Novocain that never wore off, and made your cheek tingle and feel swollen, distorted and ugly even though it wasn't. But the injection would quiet the nerve and prevent acute pain from recurring. The only other alternative was to have the nerve severed, and after much discussion, the family encouraged Hana to go to Philadelphia with Kaye right after Sheldy's wedding. There would always be time to sever the nerve if the injection didn't work.

Hana suffered throughout her youngest son's wedding, but she held her head up and managed a slight smile every now and then, so as not to spoil everyone's joy. Tyra swore afterward that she saw Lazer brush away a tear or two, although she knew her grandfather would never admit to such a *feminine* gesture. The very next day, Sheldy and his bride dropped Hana and Kaye at Grand Central Station and went off on a honeymoon cruise. Kaye and Hana boarded the 1:15 train at bound for Philadelphia. It was the first time Kaye ever traveled alone and was in charge. She put the two small valises in the overhead compartment, and sat down next to Hana. Kaye smoothed her sleek skirt and patted her hand on Hana's as the train rolled away. Kaye was scared and unsure. Sid was the strong, confident one. Even when he was recuperating from his kidney operation, he would joke with Hana about all the good food she cooked for him, and would reassure Kaye that he would get well, get back to work and make a living. The baby, he said, would be beautiful and all would be fine. Kaye leaned on him for everything, and now as they passed miles of tenement buildings, and dreary industrial zones, she wondered if she would find the hotel without getting lost, if the nurses would be kind and if this decision was the right one. Hours passed and the drone of the wheels on the track lulled the two women into a light sleep. Their heads leaned against each other, and Hana's fine, yellowing tresses fell over her eyes. Her mouth was a little opened as she slept quietly.

When they returned a week later, Hana was numb and full of discomfort, but pain-free and happy to be home.

Sure enough, none of the boys Jessie had a crush on asked her to the prom. Yet she had to endure the endless conversations of her girlfriends who babbled enthusiastically about their dates and dresses. It seemed as though Jessie wouldn't go after all.

"You know what I always say, Jessie," Sid told her while they were watching the evening news. "If you want something done, do it yourself. "It's a whole new world now. Look at that good-looking Kennedy kid from Massachusetts trying to be president. A job for old men. His wife is pregnant and he's a Catholic, to boot."

"What are you talking about, Daddy?"

"Look, some people have money and connections. Others need to get what they want with ingenuity and smarts."

"Are you patenting one of your thig-a-ma-jigs or what?"

"No, silly. I'm not going tell you what to do, but if you want to go to the prom, I'm saying you're clever enough to find a way."

"What makes you think I want to go to the prom?"

"Oh, come on, Jessie." His tone turned gruff. "Stop putting on such a front. All girls want to go."

"Well, I'm not all girls, am I?"

Jessie dialed and let out a sigh of relief after she heard Irwin's voice on the other end of the line. She wasn't in the mood to answer all the questions Mrs. Zimmerman was sure to ask.

"This is some… coincidence. I've been… meaning to call you for a few days now," Irwin said in an unusually halting manner.

"How come?"

"Listen, Jess. I know we're just friends and all that, but I…I would… like…," he kept stammering, "to take you to your prom…if you wouldn't mind. I know the score. I don't mind. I just would like to be with you."

"Sure," she answered without hesitation. "We'll have a blast."

"Groovy. What did you call me for?"

"Just to catch up. See how you did on finals."

The night before graduation, Jessie, proud as could be, strutted around the apartment practicing her *Pomp and Circumstance* walk in her black cap and gown. It was amazing how she could stand so tall and wasn't afraid to march. There were some moments when things seemed to be truly as she had said they were, that she sees herself only from the front and has no problems with that. It is the others who have a problem. Jessie was a force to be reckoned with, and despite the usual rivalries and the extraordinary experiences Jessie's illness contributed to their relationship, Tyra admired her sister's determination and sense of integrity. But sometimes God seemed to test her way too much. During one pass from the living room to the bedroom, she stopped dead in her tracks in front of Tchotchka's cage hanging in the foyer. The shriek she let out got everyone running to the spot. Tchotchka, at the very ripe old parakeet age of eleven years, lay dead on the floor of the cage. Sid poked him gently, gently, just to see if he would stir, but it was obvious that he was gone.

Jessie was stricken with silence for the first time ever. Her face tightened trying to hold in the pain. Tchotchka was never just a pet. Since those hospital days, he knew when Jessie was gone and when she was on her way home. He was her true friend. And now he was gone. Jessie didn't cry, at least, not in front of the family. Tyra tried not to cry. She remembered how Jessie admonished her for doing so when Enid died. But no matter how she tried to hold back, the tears just flowed. Kaye went into the bedroom and brought back a shoebox. Together, she and Jessie wrapped Tchotchka in a clean wash-cloth and put him in a plastic bag, and another, and one more, all so that dogs, cats and other critters wouldn't smell the fresh burial mound and disturb Tchotchka's resting place. Jessie lined the box with tissues, and Kaye placed Tchotchka, wrapped in his shroud, in the little coffin.

"Be quiet when you walk down there," Kaye told the girls. "Try not to get arrested for trespassing on government prop-erty."

Sid took the sealed box in one hand, a small flashlight in the other and with a daughter on each side, left the apart-ment. The three walked down the hill in silence stopping only to get the snow shovel from the trunk of the car, until they reached the Horseshoe in the park.

Tyra held the flashlight as Sid and Jessie dug a small, deep hole, and after several rounds of kissing Tchotchka goodbye, Jessie making sure she gave the last, they placed the box in cavity in front of the Obelisk and covered it carefully.

The sky on graduation day was overcast and held the prom-ise of a fine drizzle. The ceremony took place at the majestic Lowe's Theatre on Fordham Road, the one with blinking stars on the domed blue ceiling and the grand circular staircase leading to the balcony. Jessie marched with her friends and right after the ceremony, she insisted the entire family return home to take pictures. No stopping for a fancy lunch or even ice cream sundaes. They all stood in the Horseshoe and Jessie directed their positions so that no one inadvertently stepped on the fresh grave. She made sure too, that the Obelisk was in the background of each pose, with Tchotchka at her side in the only fashion possible, and her diploma in her hand, she feigned smiles for the camera.

That was the constant Tyra knew all her life. Always a piece of the puzzle missing. Pieces lost and found, never all in the proper place at the same time. Someone missing; others left to yearn. Family never whole and joy never pure. Life hovered on the thistle and on the honey. Nothing was ever perfect, not a dress, nor the weather.

NINE

NEGEV SPIRIT

Sunday, December 4, 1966 8 P.M.

Dear Mom, Daddy and Jessie,

I got #43 and 44 today. Thanks for the clippings- they really got me mad. When Israel said the attack was for retaliation, she meant it. Obviously no one back there knows about all the bombings that have been going on- including one about 1 1/2- 2 months ago on a Friday night in a residential area about 2 miles from the University. I doubt if any newspaper in N.Y. can give an authoritative figure of how many Israeli soldiers have been killed by border infiltrators in the past few months.

The attack was that Israel bombed 10 and not 40 houses as reported by Beirut, Lebanon newspaper sources, which is where if you notice, the news dispatches you've been getting are from. Anyway, things have been quiet on the civilian side of things so don't worry.

I was sorry to hear about Mrs. Sheft's son.

I'm scurrying to find something to wear to Peter's wedding. If I can lose a few pounds, the black, silk skirt will do with the black and gold brocade blouse. So much for self-control. Wish Grandpa were here! Peter invited Olga, too, since they are in two classes together and I had introduced them earlier in the year. Olga and I are chipping in for a present. We saw a lovely set of glasses in town last week- each one a different hue, and we will probably get that.

Love,
Tyra

December 4, 1966

Dear Tyra,

All the neighbors are a flurry! The pope allowed the gentiles to eat meat on Fridays. Last Friday night you could smell steak up and down the hallways-the building smelled like an indoor BBQ, if there is such a thing! It was quite a celebration. We had our usual chicken and soup. It reminded me of when you went to summer camp for a few weeks one year. You refused to eat fish on a Friday night. You thought that Jewish children had to have chicken, and you didn't realize that though the camp was kosher, it had to provide fish for the Gentile children. Oh, Tyra! You were always my sweet, easy daughter, and even though I am happy that you are doing what you want, I miss you more than ever.

I know how interested you are in the Kennedys. A new book came out by William Manchester- The Death of a President. Jackie wanted to sue because she didn't approve, but even she couldn't prevent its publication. I cut out the articles about the JFK anniversary liked you asked.

Do you miss seeing Neil? Will he be at the wedding?

Daddy is a little busy now before the holidays. Every Monday and Friday Freddy comes in late and makes it a rough day. This past Monday he came in at 11:30 because he got drunk the night before and couldn't get up. Otherwise he's a pretty good worker. Daddy can't be too independent because he needs him so badly.

I guess we're all working hard now. That's the trouble with American life today. Everybody works too hard.

I can well imagine the tension going on in Israel because American Jews are tense, too, and I don't mean only us because we have a daughter there, but whoever you speak to prays that everything will be alright. I guess the American Jew is proud of what the Israelis have accomplished in the short time they have existed and part of that is due to the help the American Jew has given Israel and we want the country to be a good place for them to live in peace. But it's not easy for them. They have to spend so much in defense.

Things in Vietnam are getting pretty bad. We lost some planes over Hanoi. Johnson has his hands full.

The only article I saw about Ted Kennedy in Israel was a photo of an Arab talking to him and not letting him get a word in edgewise. If I come across anything else I'll save it. You give me so many little things to do I can't keep up with you.

Now it is late and I must mop the kitchen floor before bed. We all miss you.

Love,
Mom

The ceremony was just over by the time Tyra, Olga and Mike arrived at the hotel. Tyra saw the bride and groom as she scanned the reception hall filled with guests.

"Hi, there." Neil tapped Tyra on her shoulder and she turned around.

"Hi," she said and smiled. "How've you been? Glad to see you."

"Me too."

Their conversation started out awkwardly but they sat down next to each other and throughout the meal they spoke a little more easily, oblivious to all the dancing and celebrating going on around them.

She told him that she started teaching in the poor neighborhood of Romema in a boys' elementary school.

"The boys are ragged but so sweet. The building is so damp and cold. One boy, Yoram, brought me a cup of tea. Another brought a heater up to the room. They want to hear stories of America and astronauts. They have such hopes but hard lives. I feel so bad for them."

"You're a kind person. I've missed you."

"That was your choice. I don't understand you."

"Let's not fight. I envy you. You do things to help people. I sit all day and do nothing but study, bury my nose in books."

"That's important, too. We need people to understand the Law and interpret and analyze." Tyra put her hand on his. He looked so sad, tormented, his head hanging low, his eyes looking down to the floor. "I wish you would let me into your heart. Talk to me. I feel like such a stranger."

"I'm sorry. It's not you. I like you a lot. Be patient with me. Did I tell you you look really pretty tonight?"

December 30, 1966

Dear Mom, Dad and Jessie,

Went to the wedding last night and had a marvelous time. We got there too late for the Huppah —ceremony- but almost everyone else missed it too. Peter looked adorable and it could have been his Bar Mitzvah if Yael hadn't worn a wedding gown! I got into my skirt- it was a little too tight and uncomfortable, but my hair and makeup came out good. We took a picture with Olga's camera but the flash didn't work. The photographer caught Neil, Peter and me once or twice. The food was delicious which was quite a surprise. The seating arrangement as it worked out was quite funny. I had come a few minutes before the guys from the yeshiva. There was an empty seat next to me which I thought Neil would use. Before he came to the table, Joey and his date Ruth came and sat down next to me and by the time Neil had come, there was only one seat at the other side of the table. His friend Zev was sitting next to him. Anyway, your sneaky daughter figured out a way. The guys danced with Peter before the meal began- near the band- and to look I had to twist in my seat. So I decided to move to the other side of the table and sat in Zev's chair- but lest they thought I did it intentionally! I left my bag and gloves at the original place. When the boys came back- I began to get up but Zev had already sat down where I was originally! How's that for feminine wiles?

We left at 11:15 to catch the last bus from the hotel which is quite far out. In fact it's in disputed territory and we could see quite clearly the lights of the U.N. Patrol Force. We had to walk quite a way back to the dorm- we were with Olga and Mike, Joey and Ruth. Neil and I stopped along the way and spoke until 2:30 A.M. We got back to my room at 3. It looks as if things might be working out well- although it's too early to know for sure.

I'm making a huge kugel for Shabbos in the Palestine pot and expect a lot of company. Irit said she will come for lunch and a lot of the kids will be hanging around the dorm this weekend so it should be fun. Take care.

Love,
Tyra

December 29, 1966

Dear Tyra,

Yesterday I received your letter# 52 which was mailed on Monday and I got on Wednesday. This was a record breaker. You said you got my letter #55 with the clippings of Jackie Kennedy, but you didn't mention anything about the Bic pen I stuck in. Did you get it? I assume #52 was written in a hurry because it was late and you didn't have time to write me in detail about Neil. I had a feeling that he would get in touch with you again. However now that you've got me curious I'd like to know a little more about him and the things you spoke about. Don't leave me dangling in mid-air over a little information. So I am also assuming that in your next letter you'll tell me more.

In your previous letter you mentioned something about a two week vacation. Why fore is that? Boy, what a school! When are you going to learn something in that school?

What are you doing New Year's Eve? We don't have anything planned. It really doesn't matter. I can just imagine customs going through the package- it was so compact- we stuck so many things into the Bunny Hugs and if it comes disheveled you know who did it.

Take care and don't forget to please tell me more about your agreement with Neil and why he stopped seeing you.

Love and Happy New Year,
Mom

TEN

THE TORCH HAS BEEN PASSED

Kaye was standing at the stove adding the kasha and browning it in the pan of sautéed mushrooms and onions. Tyra was setting the table for dinner, distracted by the view from the kitchen in the new apartment. They had moved into the two-bedroom corner unit next door a few months before. As Sid used to say, "The luncheonette isn't a gold mine, but it's a decent living." With Sid's earnings and the salary from Kaye's part-time bookkeeping job, they were able to afford the higher rent for the larger apartment. Sid and Kaye finally had a bedroom of their own. The kitchen faced front and Tyra could see the park and Obelisk.

Jessie stormed in and slammed the front door behind her.

Tyra was startled out of her daydreaming and dropped the forks she was holding in her hands.

"I don't know why I ever decided to go to Lexington College in the first place! October 22nd will live in infamy," Jessie said, passing by the kitchen.

"It's 1962, not 1941," Tyra said, fixing up the place settings.

"Shut up, Kiddo."

"Girls, stop the bickering. You're not even home two seconds," Kaye said. "What's the matter?"

Jessie stomped her way into the bedroom. "I don't want to talk about it now," she hollered. "I'll just have to repeat it for Dad."

Kaye winced as the bedroom door slammed shut. Then she turned again to the task at hand, adding bowties into the pan, mixing everything with a long wooden spoon. She stirred mechanically in endless circles, shaking her head in a coordinated rhythm. "Always something," she mumbled.

Tyra could tell that Kaye was agitated, in a state somewhere between anger and worry: angry for what seemed to be the constant conflicts Jessie found herself in and worried because it was her daughter who was suffering.

Kaye glanced at the clock on the wall. Dinner was ready and Sid wasn't home yet. "It'll get cold," she complained, but Tyra knew Kaye was more worried that Sid was late than the food getting cold.

Tyra was not looking forward to supper. Between bracing herself to tell her parents what was on her mind, competing with Jessie's tragedy at college, fireworks were sure to fly. She sucked in a deep breath. The skies were already darkening and she hated when her father came home later than usual. It could be anything- traffic or a straggling diner that delayed her father from closing the store. It wasn't normal for children to worry about parents. It was supposed to be the other way around. But lately crime seemed to be overtaking the borough and the Bronx was losing its charm.

Sid's Food Shoppe had been broken into twice in the past eight months. The first break-in was a shock and Sid learned a bitter lesson. The thugs, unsuccessful in trying to unlock the cash drawer, tore the cash register from the counter and threw it against the mirrored wall. Shards of the mirror and large pieces of the broken plate glass window crunched underneath

Sid's footsteps as he surveyed the damage. Pieces of glass lay across the long counter. Stool cushions were slashed open, the fluffy white batting spilling over the bright red vinyl covers. The crooks made a mess and it cost Sid a fortune to repair everything they destroyed.

From then on, Sid left the drawer ajar with twenty dollars in bills and change in it when he locked up at night. He left the cartons of cigarettes on display in the front window instead of locking them up in the back room. This way there wouldn't be a need for the thugs to destroy anything; they could just take what was there. "Better the bums take whatever stuff quick-and-easy than make a big mess getting nothing," he said.

But it was the brutal attack on Mr. Goodman that disturbed the Millers the most. Mr. Goodman was a sweet man, too old to work as hard as he did. He earned the affectionate nickname of *Pickleman* not only because he had the best pickle business in the neighborhood, but he was generous, too. The half-sours were his best seller—they were crisp and not too salty. Whenever Tyra went to the luncheonette to help Sid, she'd stop by *Pickleman* and he'd treat her to a fat, juicy pickle.

"Things are getting tough around here, *Pickleman*. You should always have some cash on you," Sid cautioned after the luncheonette was robbed the first time. But *Pickleman* was a proud man. "They want from me," he protested, "they'll have to wait until I sell my green babies."

At five o'clock one morning, *Pickleman* was struggling with his full barrels. He was dragging a barrel of sours from his truck to the curb when three hoodlums jumped him and turned his pockets inside-out. But *Pickleman*'s empty pockets filled the beasts with rage. They punched him, slammed his head against the pavement, broke his arms, and beat him to death. The police found him on the street. Dawn began to lighten up the neighborhood and the proprietors and laborers swarmed in the area to begin their usual, arduous day. But this morning was not usual: the blare of sirens and the flashing lights from the top of the police car drew them to the corner where all the commotion was.

"What's going on here?" Duvid whispered as he approached the policemen, almost afraid to find out. But they didn't answer. They just pointed to the spot on the sidewalk that was wet with pickle juice and blood.

"Oh! My God! They slaughtered him like an animal!" Duvid cried out when he caught a glimpse of the bloodied heap that was once sweet, old Mr. Goodman.

Shockneh put his arms around Duvid. "You're wrong," he said shaking his head. "I'm the *shat'chan-* ritual slaughterer- and I have more mercy." Tears ran down his face. "I sing to my chickenlach before I slit their throats."

It was no wonder then, that the Miller women waited nervously for Sid to come home from work. When they heard the key jiggling in the lock, on this night when Sid was later than usual, they breathed a collective sigh of relief.

Kaye greeted Sid at the door with a hug and a real kiss on the lips. Their front-door kisses were always genuine, never perfunctory; comfortable, not passionate. Kaye held her husband, her home complete and steady, now that he was in it. Sid put his arms around Kaye. He was where he belonged, having left the outside world in the hallway.

He set the stack of newspapers he was holding on the stepstool. "I'm starved," he said good-naturedly. "Let's eat so we can listen to Kennedy." He pointed to papers. The Monday afternoon edition of the World-Telegram was on top. The headline read, *"Kennedy Will Talk Tonight on TV, Calls Crisis Parleys."*

Kaye sprinkled a spoon of sugar over the grapefruit, and passed the sugar bowl around the table. "Put some sugar on it," she told Jessie.

"I don't like sugar."

"Contrary. Why do you always have to be so contrary? It's so much better with a little sweetness."

"Umm…. This is a real bitter one," Jess said, seemingly just to annoy her mother, as she chomped on a grapefruit section.

They were eating their grapefruits quietly when Kaye broke the silence. "What happened in school today?" she asked Jessie.

"I got a message during my education class to go to Dr. Lewin's office. It was 2:10- or maybe 2:15. The secretary or maybe it was a receptionist…"

"Get to the point," Kaye interrupted. "You always drag out all the details. Who is Dr. Lewin?"

"Exasperating," Tyra mumbled under her breath.

"The head of the Education Department," Jessie explained. "He told me I'm still allowed to take whatever courses I want."

"So what's the big deal?" Tyra said.

"He told me I wouldn't be able to get a teaching license in New York City. That's the big deal," Jessie said, glaring at Tyra.

"Oh, no. I knew it." Kaye said as she put her forehead in the palm of her hand, as if she had a headache.

"He said that it was the Board of Education's policy not to allow the children to be exposed to anything that might upset them."

"What did you say?" Sid's voice was gruff.

"I told him that that was the point, to teach children how to cope in the real world, that life isn't a fairytale."

"Did that sway him any?" Sid asked.

"Poor Jessie, what are you going to do?" Kaye got up and threw the grapefruit skins in a garbage bag. "Adele, at work, her daughter wanted to teach but they told her she had a hissing "s" and would never pass the speech test. But Adele knew someone who had a contact at the Board, and her daughter got a license."

Jessie hated it when her mother called her `Poor Jessie!' She ignored Kaye and the story about Adele's daughter's good fortune. Looking at Sid, she continued her story. "He advised me to find a field more suited to my capabilities. The nerve of him. I told him I was perfectly capable of teaching children. But he said that with my back being the way it is, I would never pass the physical."

Kaye brought the platter of pot roast to the table and went back to the stove get the bowls of kasha varnishkas and peas.

"I told him that we all had flaws, that he was more handicapped than me. The only difference was that his deformity wasn't as obvious as mine."

"Do you have to be so fresh to people!" Kaye slammed the bowls on the table. "Here, take," she said as she stabbed serving spoons into the bowls. "That attitude won't get you anywhere."

"Oh, Mother!" she said, dragging out with scorn the word mother. "I didn't ask to be born. If you don't like the way I'm living my life, that's your problem."

Kaye pursed her lips tightly. She had heard all this before.

Tyra's head was beginning to ache.

"I'm leaving. I'm not hungry," Jessie said, and started to push the chair away from the table.

"Sit still. We have a serious problem here," Sid said. "We have to figure out what to do. You need to have a profession, to be independent."

"She wouldn't have to worry about being independent if she would find a nice boy." Kaye was frustrated. "You always have to be right, and stubborn. You could get dates if…."

Jessie threw her arms in the air. "I'm not going to pretend I'm dumb just to please fragile boys' egos…"

"Quiet down," Sid said. "What do you want to do, Jessie?"

"I love children. I'll have to figure out some kind of job I can do to work with them. It's a stupid law." She hesitated for a moment. "It's so unfair." Her voice had mellowed by the time she finished her last sentence, and she had a little gleam in her eye, a resurgence of determination.

For a moment or two no one spoke, and the quiet was refreshing. Then Sid put some pot roast on his plate, and told his daughters to take some too.

"Take care of yourself, Jessie. Let someone else fight City Hall. I wonder what Kennedy is going to speak about. It sounds serious," Sid said.

"Salinger said it of the highest national urgency this afternoon," Tyra said, proud of her savvy.

"Hon, please, don't worry about the entire world. You have enough on your plate." Kaye told Sid. She seemed a bit more gentle, as if her strength was sapped out of her.

"As a matter of fact," Sid said, winking at Kaye. "I don't. Pass back that platter. I didn't take enough."

Kaye and Sid laughed heartily. They always shared that sense of timing, the gift of one playing off the other, buoying each other with needed moments of comic relief, the nourishment, the magic that whittled away some of the chronic hardships they endured.

Then Kaye looked at Tyra. "So, tell us what Joel had to say in his letter? You're always so quiet," she said, putting a chunk of brisket in her mouth.

I'm always quiet because Jessie hogs all the conversation, Tyra thought. "He's going to Winter Seminar." When Kaye handed her the letter in the afternoon, Tyra tried to hide the rush from her mother. She ran into the bedroom, nearly ripping the letter itself as she tore open the envelope. She read it at least a hundred times, and memorized every word. But now she spoke in a low monotone, trying to make believe the letter meant nothing, that her feelings for Joel weren't important at all.

"The pot roast's delicious, Kaye," Sid said. "Soft like butter."

"Joel decided not to major in art," Tyra continued paraphrasing the letter. "His father convinced him that his mouth is bigger than his talent, and he'd make more of an impact as a lawyer than some poor struggling artist."

"At least somebody listens to his parents," Kaye said.

Tyra sighed. She couldn't win. "He's applying to Brandeis and Columbia. His father prefers him to stay home."

"Tyra has a boyfriend," Jessie said.

Tyra glared at Jessie but didn't say a word.

Kaye smiled. She wasn't used to Tyra being so talkative. She ordinarily would have had to pry to get that extra little tidbit. "I suppose you're hoping he gets into Columbia?"

Tyra tried to hide her grin. She knew the more she revealed, the more Jessie would torment her later on. Tyra asked for a second helping of pot roast, which pleased Kaye no end.

"Boys, boys. Is that the only thing you ever think about?" Jessie scorned. "Better learn how to be independent," she mimicked.

"Shut up, Jess. You're just jealous," Tyra yelled. Then she looked down. She couldn't look Jessie in the eye, but said with a softened voice, "I'm sorry. I didn't mean that."

Tyra was a little older now, sixteen, and she knew that life was not fair, and that it was an impossible feat for her to be happy and excited while Jessie's dreams were disintegrating at the very moment. That's all she ever talked about for years, teaching kids and how much they were going to love her.

Tyra was older, but age didn't make it any easier for her to cope. She tried to be happy for her own fortune. But when things went badly for her sister, when Jessie was miserable and disappointed, guilt and resentment churned together with all the good things Tyra had. Nothing was clear. Tyra knew all these lessons, but understood none of them, especially why God didn't care.

"Yes, you did mean that," Jessie said. "But it doesn't bother me anyway." Jessie pushed the brisket around with her fork. She didn't like potted meats or anything with gravy. She nibbled on the kasha, dry.

"Can Dawn sleep over this weekend?" Tyra asked as she stood up and without being told, began to gather the plates from the table. Her mother agreed. Turning her back toward the table on her way to the sink, Tyra sucked in a deep breath, trying to garner enough courage to say what she had to. In her typical hit-and-run fashion she mumbled, "Good, it'll be more convenient for us to go to Ricky's birthday party Saturday night."

Fireworks! Here is comes, she thought.

"Oh, no you don't, young lady," Sid yelled, his drawn cheeks puffing up with redness. "You know there's no dating gentiles in this family."

She turned to look at her father. "It's not a date. He's my friend and it's his birthday. His mom is making him a party. I've known him for years. He's eaten by Grandma's a million times."

She had first met Ricky Lopez in seventh grade and they became close. She could confide in him and trusted his judgment. Kaye always said it was good for a girl to have a male friend. A boy would be sincere. Sometimes a girlfriend who is having boy trouble steers you the wrong way, so you can be miserable too. Ricky had Tyra's best interest at heart. He was the only non-Jew she was close to and he would do anything for her. Anything, that is, but sign a petition to study Hebrew in junior high.

"He's a Puerto Rican boy." Sid was adamant.

"When I was your age…" Kaye said.

Tyra turned her back again, walking toward the sink. She mouthed the words her mother spoke, words she had heard so many times before.

"…I could have dated the cutest Italian fellows, but I didn't want to chance falling in love with a gentile. Turn around and look at me when I speak to you. You'd better not be mimicking me. But I didn't want to hurt my parents."

Kaye went to the refrigerator to get the compote for dessert. The kitchen was narrow and Kaye and Tyra bumped into each other.

"I know, Mom," she argued, "but you don't understand, either of you."

"You always start trouble," Jessie said.

"Shut up," Tyra screamed, and walked back to the table. She sat at her place and tried to explain. "You don't think I am going to marry a non-Jew and teach my children the catechism do you? You complained about how religious I was becoming after I came home from seminar last year, and now you think I'd let myself fall in love with a *goy*, a *shagetz*?"

It was true that the more Tyra learned about Judaism, the more she was smitten with the desire to be *machmir*- strict. She tried adhering to the narrowest interpretation of the Law. Tyra began to wait six hours before eating dairy after meat, replacing her family's traditional three-hour separation. She stopped combing her hair on Shabbos, as creating was prohibited, and arranging a hairstyle was creating something, in direct opposition to the essence of rest on the Sabbath. She refused to use make-up too. Writing with an eyeliner was writing just the same. Kaye couldn't stand how Tyra looked when she would leave the house for shul. "How can you go out in public with your hair such a mess? Such a pretty girl like you." Every Shabbos Kaye laced into Tyra.

When Tyra tore up pieces of toilet paper on Friday afternoons so she wouldn't have to tear on Shabbos, that just about blew everyone's gasket and she endured a lot of scorn on that one.

One Shabbos afternoon in Hana's kitchen, Tyra almost started a war. Hana had made a large pot of *chulant* for Shabbos. Tyra loved *chulant.* It was a special dish, usually reserved for a cold winter day. A big pot of stew, it cooked overnight and permeated the whole apartment with an irresistible aroma. Sometimes when Tyra was little, she would sleep "upstairs" on the couch in the living room, just so she could smell the stew as it was cooking, and in the middle of the night, she would get up to "check" it, to grab a little taste of the soft, tender beef, potatoes, onions, beans and barley. Hana prepared it on Friday afternoon, and before sunset, she would light a low fire and cover the burner with the *blech,* an aluminum sheet. She would then set the big pot of *chulant* on top of the *blech* where it simmered all through the night, and by Shabbos afternoon, the flanken fell apart with the touch of a spoon, and the barley doubled its size. Tyra had walked back from shul with Lazer, and when he began to fill a bowl of *chulant* from the the big pot which had been warming overnight on the *blech,* Tyra told him he was doing it wrong. "Grandpa," she said, "you have to remove the pot from the flame first, and then scoop out the *chulant.* Otherwise it's still cooking, and you're not allowed to cook on Shabbos."

"Me you have to tell I can't cook on Shabbos!" Lazer's cheeks turned as red as beet borscht.

Tyra cowered at the loudness of his scream.

"A zai g'zukt to de zayde!" Like that you talk to a grandfather! he yelled. "Since when you make such a *rebbetzin?"* His English was always worse when he was angry.

"Shrai nisht. Don't shout," Hana said, and when Lazer stormed out of the kitchen, she turned to Tyra shaking her head just slightly. "You shouldn't talk like that, Tyraleh. Grandpa goes to shul every day. Is not good enough?"

"Grandma," she explained, I want to be strong, disciplined." Deep within her though she thought the more she observed, the closer she would feel to loving Hashem.

"I didn't mean to cause you and Grandpa problems." She walked over to Hana and put her arms around her waist. "I'm sorry."

Soon after that Shabbos afternoon, Tyra gave up the additional, self-imposed constraints. She couldn't stand Kaye's nagging; she felt bad about causing extra work for Hana and tension between her grandparents. But the truth of the matter was that all that extra devotion, observances, and attention to details just filled up time, not her heart. Worse than anything, it didn't make her feel any closer or kinder toward God.

Kaye put the large container of cooked fruit on the table, and started to spoon it out into small glass sundae dishes.

"When have I ever done anything to make you distrust me?" Tyra searched her father's eyes for an answer.

When Jessie caught Tyra's glance, she brought up two fingers to her lips and blew, reminding her younger sister that she sneaked smoking cigarettes. She didn't have the nerve to remind her father that a long time ago, he had given permission for her to smoke when she turned sixteen. She knew that at the time he was just putting her off. He would never allow her to smoke at sixteen.

Tyra felt a bit of shame coursing through her as she peered at Jessie. Then she turned her sight back to Sid, who hadn't caught Jessie's gesture. "He's a good friend and I won't hurt his feelings by not going," she added.

Tyra got up to leave.

"How's his mother doing?" Kaye asked. "Wasn't it his father that was killed a few months ago?"

"Get back here," Sid said. "You can go with Dawn, but you must be back by midnight."

"I don't want any," said Jessie as she motioned away the glass dish Kaye put in front of her.

"A curfew? You never gave…." She stopped short, right in the middle of her protest, tired of all the fighting and tension. At least she got permission to go to Ricky's party. That was good enough for now. "The fruit's good, Mom."

"You're the good daughter. You like com-POTE," Jessie said to Tyra with attitude, accentuating the last syllable.

"You never do anything," Kaye screamed at Sid. "You let the girls get away with murder." She went to the refrigerator and put back the container of leftover compote.

"Come on, Kaye. That's not fair." His voice started to rise, then as if he wanted to stifle his own anger, he added in a softer, slower way, "I have problems of my own."

Sid got up and walked over to Kaye. He stood behind her and rubbed her shoulders. She sighed and leaned back a little toward him. "Everything will be all right," he told her.

"Sure. You're the one who sleeps at night. Why does God punish us so? We're not perfect Jews but we're good people."

The sisters looked at each other, Jessie shrugging her crooked shoulders and Tyra swishing the features of her face together while raising her eyebrows at the same time. Sometimes it seemed that the only time they shared camaraderie was when they managed to get their father in trouble with their mother.

As Kaye was the one to absorb the brunt of Jessie's every crisis, every let-down, Sid was the one to bear Kaye's anguish. Tyra observed it all but didn't know how to reconcile her own needs and responsibilities. She understood none of it and had no place to go.

"I'm going upstairs," Jessie said as she pushed her chair back, got up and left. She didn't slam the front door this time.

Sid's hands slipped off Kaye's shoulders and fell at his sides. He started to walk out of the kitchen, glancing at Tyra. "Help your mother with the dishes."

"But Jessie…" she started to protest.

"Jessie had a rough day. Be a little more compassionate."
He kissed her on the cheek and scooped up the newspapers
from the stepstool in the corner. He made his way toward
the living room. Usually he would turn on the television set,
sprawl out on the sofa, and doze off to the drone of the newscasts, snoozing easily from sheer exhaustion. But tonight he
turned on the television set and sat up straight waiting for the
president to speak.

Tyra came trailing behind, draping the damp dishtowel over
her shoulder as she flopped down next to him. Kaye sat next to
her knitting bag at the other end of the sofa just as the speech
was about to begin. Kennedy's face looked ghostly pale and
his shoulders seemed less broad as the cameras opened with
a wide angle shot of the Oval Office. But his voice thundered
with determination as he informed the American people that
the Soviet Union was preparing offensive missile sites on the
"imprisoned island" of Cuba. Long-range ballistic missiles would
soon be "capable of striking Washington, D.C., Cape Canaveral,
or any other city in the southeastern part of the United States.

*"We will not prematurely risk the costs of worldwide nuclear
war in which even the fruits of victory would be ashes in our
mouths…but neither will we shrink from that risk…."*

Sid groaned and shook his head.
"Daddy, could we die?"
"Shh. Listen."

*…It shall be the policy of this Nation to regard any missile
launched from Cuba against any nation in the Western
Hemisphere as an attack by the Soviet Union on the United
States, requiring a full retaliatory response…*

Kennedy outlined America's plan during the rest of the speech. A strict quarantine of all ships bound for Cuba would be imposed and "any found to contain cargoes of offensive weapons would be turned back." Emergency meetings of the Organization of American States and the United Nations Security Council would be held.

Kaye picked up her knitting when Kennedy's speech was over. "This is a grave situation. Very grave," she said, her voice mellow. She was too exhausted, after work, after the tense dinner, to be anything but mellow. She shook her head studying the skirt she was knitting, but her thoughts were with the President's speech. The skirt was almost finished, and she wondered if she would ever get the opportunity to wear it. The stitch was a complicated shell pattern and she worked it up in a soft champagne-colored yarn. She spread out the large clump of woven yarn on her lap. Knitting was the only real hobby Kaye enjoyed. She worked quickly and every stitch was pulled perfectly even. She followed intricate patterns from books and magazines. It was rare to see her working on the same project for more than a few weeks. She knitted far more sweaters than she could wear, and loved to give cardigans and baby outfits to this cousin or that nephew or a friend's child. She was an artisan with yarn the way Lazer was with fabric. She became so adept and proficient at it, that she even sized patterns on her own that would fit Jessie, taking inches from one side and added them to the other.

She studied the last rows she had knitted on the round needles the night before so that she could pick up the design on the right row. "It's easier to check it first than to rip later." That was her motto. She and Sid seemed to speak the same way after so many years.

"What does a quarantine have to do with anything? He's not talking about a contagious disease like tuberculosis or typhoid?" Tyra asked her parents.

Sid explained that it was a blockade. "A blockade is an act of war. Kennedy's smart. Maybe he doesn't want to back Khrushchev into a corner. He's leaving him a way out."

Tyra appreciated her father's keen understanding of world events and politics. Although he hadn't had the opportunity to go to college like Kaye's friends' husbands, he was well-read and never afraid to speak his mind. Whenever they got together at informal Saturday evening visits, boisterous debates about taxes, welfare, segregation or some other issue of the day filled the room. Sid kept the facts he read in the newspapers stored in his head as though it were a safe deposit box safeguarding a cache of gems. He argued his points one by one, never intimidated by their college degrees.

Once after such a visit, Tyra went over to her father and kissed him on the cheek. "You're the smartest man I know. You should be a politician."

He laughed. "No, I just tell it like I see it. They'd make chopped liver out of me," he said. Besides, I'd have been an engineer, not a politician. Just think, sweetie, of how great it would be to spend your life thinking how to create new things and find solutions to problems."

Jessie came back, arm and arm with her grandparents, one on each side. "Poor Grandma and Grandpa. They shook their heads the whole time. Tell them it's going to be alright. And I thought I had problems with my future. Now we might not even have any future."

Kaye let out her sigh of hopelessness. She had several in her repertoire, each having a distinct pitch and volume, each revealing her frame of mind. One was a throaty grunt, signaling her determination. A whispery whimper indicated an awareness that she was being called upon to fulfill a task no one else could do. The loudest was the Florence Nightingale groan- the acceptance of taking care of the sick—lately either Hana who had circulation problems or Lazer, who struggled with a heart condition. Tonight though she sighed her sigh of powerlessness. It was a silent gasp of breath. How could she fix the world's problems when she couldn't even solve her own?

"So nu. What's going to be?" Hana asked, walking toward the Chinese red armchair, reaching out for the armrest as she lowered herself into the cushion.

"Ach, the President, *esht zayre gutten man, un schtarka.*" The president is good, very strong, Lazer said. "That *mamzare* Khrushnik- he should swallow his tongue- it should come out his…"

"Papa!" Kaye screamed.

The next morning Tyra was in a fog when she walked to school. Phrases from the president's speech spun around in her head. *The cost of freedom is high* and *Americans have always paid it.* The autumn air was crisp, the last of the birds were chirping- most had already migrated south- closer to Cuba and nuclear danger.

Rays of sunshine sparkled in between the almost bare branches of the trees lining the street. When she passed the church at the top of the hill, the church that her friend Camille had asked her to attend when she was little, she was breathing hard which struck her as odd, since she had plenty of time and didn't intend to walk as fast as she had. The shrubbery on the church's lawn was nearly bare, and lacked the vibrant colors of the spring flowers. Tyra stared at the cardboard placard staked in front of the barren chrysanthemum bush scrawled with a handwritten message that read: *Pray for Peace—24 Hour Confessions.*

She turned the corner where the stores along the avenue were getting ready for a new day of business. Trucks were clogging the avenue and the morning traffic was slow. Cars were weaving between the double-parked vehicles and the pillars of the el and trains were noisily grumbling in both directions overhead. But today, men in hats and overcoats on their way to work, lingered at Grossman's Appliances, watching the television screens, listening for the latest news about the missile crisis. Tyra stopped by the store, too, and walked inside, listening to a man in Kansas showing a reporter his basement fallout shelter. "When I finish, we're gonna have enough supplies to live here for three months," the man bragged, pointing to shelves piled high with canned goods, toilet paper and jugs of water." Lucky for him, she thought, a little envious and scared, as she made her way down the avenue.

Truck drivers were unloading cartons of goods, flinging them through the open metal doors on the sidewalks to the basements of the stores. These cellars would make terrific bomb shelters she thought. Roomy if not dank, and fully stocked with canned and paper goods, anything one could want while waiting for the radiation clouds to dissipate. The honking of horns blared intermittently, but Tyra heard only a muffled din.

She wondered if the supplies would ever be consumed or if the world would blow up before she even got to school. As Tyra approached the old school building, she could almost touch the solemn veil of stillness that hovered over Paul Revere even as the throngs of students converged on its entrances waiting for the bell to ring and the doors to open. The brightness of the morning shone in defiance of the uneasy tension of the situation. The breeze whipped through the branches of the large oaks, planted in measured intervals in the concrete, growing out of the sidewalk around the school. The leaves, from which the autumnal colors had already faded, were strewn on the cement. Tyra felt as though she were clearing her way, her arms pushing through a fine mosquito netting, the kind that covered carriages and protected babies from pesky insects disturbing their naps with annoying hums and bites.

Tyra searched the crowd for her best friend Dawn Kasoff, and for Ricky and his friend Elias Rivera, but she couldn't find any of them. She headed for her first period class. She would catch up with everybody in homeroom, between first and second periods.

"Hey! I've been calling you and calling you." A hand grabbed Tyra's shoulder. "Can't you hear, or what?" Dawn said, shaking her head, her wavy hair bouncing and glistening under the lightbulb in the stairwell as she climbed the stairs..

Tyra turned around and practically fell into Dawn's embrace. "Oh, I'm in such a fog, I guess. I'm sorry."

"What are we going to do?"

The students swarmed around them, continuing their ascent while the two friends fell behind, stopping to find a corner to stand in, out of harm's way.

"I wanted to call you last night, after the speech, but my parents wouldn't let me," Dawn said, and added as a sarcastic afterthought, "for a change."

"What did you do now?" Tyra asked.

"Nothing. Lenny told them I messed up his science experiment, but anyway it doesn't matter now. Can you imagine- the whole world might disappear in a mushroom cloud and all they care about is my brother's stinkng project."

Dawn always told Tyra she wished she had had a sister instead of a brother. "A sister like you," she'd say, since Tyra and Dawn were closer than sisters. And Tyra would laugh. "Not if she's like Jessie, you wouldn't. You don't know how lucky you are, not to have anyone boss you around." It was the perennial grass is greener phenomenon- the girls with curly hair straightened it and the straight haired girls got permanents.

Tyra envied Dawn's curly hair, with all the bounce and body. She never understood why Dawn envied her straight, limp tresses that she herself couldn't stand.

The late bell for first period rang and the girls shrugged at each other. "Might as well cut. We're late anyway," Dawn said. She never needed too much of an excuse to miss class.

"Oh, I don't know about cutting," Tyra said.

"What good is algebra going to do for you now? We're all going to be pulverized any second," Dawn said, "just like in that book—*On the Beach.*"

Tyra was still in a daze.

"Are you listening?" Dawn said, trying to get her friend's attention. "What's going to happen?" She shook Tyra's shoulders. "We're supposed to grow up and get married and push our baby carriages in the park together. We promised."

"Too many things happen in this world. I don't understand any of them. I don't know where God is either," Tyra said.

"God didn't build the missiles. Anyway, you're supposed to be the religious one," Dawn retorted.

"Hey, girls. We've been looking for you," Ricky said as he and Elias walked over to the corner where the girls were sitting on their notebooks on the cold floor. "We went to your first period class and figured you were both together since none of youse was in your class."

"Neither of you were," Tyra corrected.

Ricky laughed. "Even now you care about grammar! How come *youse* aren't in class then?"

The two boys crouched down on the floor next to the girls, forming an unintentional circle.

"You're hopeless, Ricky. Hopeless."

"Nice of Kennedy to tell Khrushchev to get his missiles out of Cuber." He mimicked the president's Boston accent. "He couldn't wait until after my party."

"Do you want the Communists to walk all over us, Ricardo?" Tyra became even more serious now. She always called him by his full name when she wanted to make a point. "What do you want Kennedy to say- `Here Nikki, take New York. No- how about Washington first, so Ricky can have his party?"

"Kennedy can do no wrong for you. Wonder how many maids will be cleaning his fall-out shelter. And he probably has a movie theatre there, too. We'll be crouching in our closets or taking cover under these stupid seats."

Tyra was confused at Ricky's bitterness. He came from a patriotic family. His father had been a colonel in the army. He was killed in a freak helicopter accident on duty just a few months before. And like his two older brothers, Ricky was planning to enlist after graduation.

"If we live," said Elias.

"Yeah. I head for the army. If we live," Ricky mimicked.

"You could go to community college," Tyra told Ricky. "You don't have to go into the army."

"The Lopezs love America. We serve. That's what we do. My father would expect no less." His eyes became watery.

"Ain't it great we practiced those air-raid drills in elementary school?" Dawn said trying to ease the tension. She jumped up from the floor and dropped down clumsily to the floor, curled up, covering her head with her lanky arms. "Safe!" she screamed. The others burst out laughing, and when the brief moment of relief passed, they put their arms around each other and started to sing quietly, swaying back and forth:

When you walk through a storm
Hold your head up high
And don't be afraid of the dark...

Tyra felt her eyes tearing up, though she struggled not to fall apart. She would keep busy, make the best of it, make whatever time she had left count.

When the grumpy, gray-haired dean of discipline turned the landing and saw them moping on the floor, he told them to get back to class before he'd write them up for cutting. "I'll be back in ten minutes. I don't want to see you here."

The cold clicks of his footsteps faded as he continued up the flight of stairs.

"I'm going home," Ricky said. "You guys coming or staying?" Ricky pulled himself up from the floor and the girls followed suit.

"Don't cut out, Ricky. You could get in trouble," Tyra said.

"My mother's alone. If we're going to die, I don't want her to be alone."

Tyra knew full well how Ricky was feeling. She wanted everyone to be together in a crisis like this, but that was impossible. Lazer was working at the tailor shop in the garment center, Sid was at the luncheonette, Kaye was at her bookkeeping job, Jessie was at school and Hana was in the house, probably baking. The Millers could never be together. They were destined to be irradiated separately, which was sure to be more frightening, more terrorizing than if they were together, to know their fate, to comfort each other, and to go to heaven together. Tyra felt like a child, like the third grade student taking cover under the desk in elementary school. Would she ever stop being so scared?

"I'm staying," Dawn said. "The farther away from my family, the better."

Ricky hugged each of the girls. His eyes were still teary. "See you tomorrow," he said, and with a shrug of his broad shoulders, added, "Maybe." Then he darted into the corridor, making sure no one was around. The hall was unusually still, and he hurried toward the exit. His frame was sturdy, broad, and rugged-looking from the back.

"Ricky, your jacket. Don't forget your jacket," Elias called out, waving it in front of him. But Ricky didn't turn around, and Elias flew after him. "Bye," he called out to the girls, and in a few seconds, the boys disappeared through the exit.

"What book were you talking about? The one about nuclear war." Tyra asked Dawn as they were collecting their things to go to class.

"*On the Beach.* I read it for a book report in History last year. Shute, Nevil Shute was the author. It was good too, but scary. Who knew?"

"Let's go. I want to stop at the library for a second."

"Oh, don't tell me! Miss Goody Two Shoes is going to do some extra credit now. We might not even be around."

"No, come on," Tyra coaxed.

"Where are your passes, girls?" Mrs. Whitestone, the librarian asked, as the girls entered the library.

"Please, Mrs. Whitestone. I need to get a book on my way to class."

Dawn shrugged her shoulders and gazed quizzically at the librarian, who was distracted and looking at her wristwatch.

"Mrs. Whitestone, are you okay?" Tyra asked.

"Oh," the librarian gasped. "My daughter called from Stonybrook last night. You know, after the speech. She's a wreck, all alone. I'm so worried." Her voice trailed off and her eyes misted. "I'm sorry, girls. I shouldn't make you nervous. Sure. Get what you need."

Tyra weaved through the tall stacks of the fiction section, leaving Dawn at the counter rifling through the stack of newly returned books. When she got to the back of the section, she studied the volumes on the shelf until she came across the one she wanted. She took it down and leafed through the pages.

Such a popular theme, the end of the world scenario. Now she was in one of her own, for real. She returned to the counter to check out the book.

"Try not to worry, Mrs. Whitestone. I'm sure your daughter will be fine." Tyra felt so uncertain of her words, she didn't know how she found the courage to speak them. She turned away from the counter and walked toward the door.

"Hey, wait for me," Dawn called out, running after her. Dawn took Tyra's hand. "Otherwise, I'll lose you," she said. They made their way down the flight of stairs. Suddenly Tyra stopped short and held Dawn back. "If we live through this awful thing, we'll wind up pushing our baby carriages in the park, in the Bronx, forever," she blurted out. They glanced at each other and burst out in a fit of endless giggles that eventually brought tears to their eyes. All their conversations about running away, their plans of finding that great, exciting world somewhere- and they still would wind up in the Bronx!

Walter Cronkite said on the news Tuesday night that it was like "time standing still". The Organization of American States voted unanimously to support the United States and with that approval in tow, President Kennedy, at 7:06 P.M., signed the naval quarantine to take effect at ten o'clock the next morning.

Mr. Solomon entered second period World History Honors class at nine forty five, just as the bell rang. He sat down, pulled off his horn-rimmed eyeglasses and set them on the desk blotter. Rubbing his palm over his scalp toward his neck, he said, "Class, I don't feel that it is appropriate to teach from the curriculum today. I want to talk about what is going on with our country, and what it means to us."

This was an honors class. The students were bright and aware of Kennedy's speech, and the impending deadline. Twenty two Soviet tankers and freighters were bearing toward

Cuba and in fifteen minutes, American sailors would have orders to turn them back.

"We have to have hope," he said, and he began to tell about his experience in the camps during the Nazi extermination of the Jews. Students had an inkling that Mr. Solomon was there and lost his family, but no one ever spoke of it, least of all Mr. Solomon himself.

"I suffered. I can't begin to tell you the terrible atrocities I saw. I thought I would never live, yet here I am. It's true. I still, to this day, feel isolated and disconnected from the past. I have no parents or brothers or sisters aunts, uncles, cousins, anyone who shared the details of my life. It's as if I were dropped like an alien from the sky, not coming from anything, not being part of a family, a tradition, just like a stranger, an atom all alone without any DNA, no genetic code, a lost link with no one standing behind me to push me ahead."

Tyra raised her hand, and Mr. Solomon acknowledged her.

"Are you glad you were born?" As the words slipped out of her mouth, she gasped, and clutched her stomach. It was a stupid thing to say, and she heard the whispers of her chiding classmates. She hated herself for being so stupid. "I'm sorry, that's not really what I meant..." she said haltingly. "You know, to suffer so much. Wouldn't it be better not to have witnessed any of those things at all?"

"No. No, Tyra. It's a good question. It is perfectly apropos. "Even though I saw such things, I couldn't, I wouldn't describe to you, and my connections have been obliterated like bleach rots fabric, I found a way to go on. I have hope. When you find out where your feet are on the ground, you start to walk from there. There is no other way to go but forward. You can't go back. There's nothing to go back to, and if you stand still, you would start to sink. No. You find a beautiful person to share the remnant of your life with, you get married, have children, and you go on to make a future. Slowly you start to build for your children a past, a history, a tradition. You construct a connection. When you are this close," he said, pinching his thumb and index finger together, "when you are this close to death, you know exactly how much your life means to you and you don't want to die."

The room was motionless, silent, and sober. Mr. Solomon's words were like a hypodermic filled with Novocain. By the time he finished speaking, the injection took hold, numbing his spellbound students.

"But you, class," he said, his voice taking on a new power, "you are our hope, the new generation, like my children, your energy and dreams will fix the world. Look at the Peace Corps President Kennedy established last year. Young people putting their own careers and material gain on hold, traveling the world over to teach and feed, to build, to give hope to those who have none. Yes, dear children, life is as high as it is low. And we must have faith that this will pass. Pray for the President to have the wisdom to get us through this. Mankind cannot sustain another massive burnt offering, another... holocaust."

"Look!" one of the boys called out, his voice racing as he pointed to the clock above the door. "The deadline. It's almost time." He took out a small pocket radio, and Mr. Solomon nodded his head. The boy turned on the radio and they listened to the news. "The American blockade has just taken affect," the reporter announced at the beginning of the broadcast. Forty Russian ships, Cuba-bound, bolting toward the imaginary line drawn by President Kennedy, dotted the waves of the ocean like chocolate sprinkles floating on melted marshmallows on the top of a cup of hot cocoa. Would they stop? Would they break through?

Even before the determination of the Russians would be tested, Americans across the nation emptied store shelves of supplies and groceries, hoarding provisions for their families, the lucky families stocking their fallout shelters. The Bronxites, without the luxury of private homes and land, would have to crowd into the basements of their building, in the laundry rooms and next to the furnaces, if it should come to that.

Two ships, the Gregoryn and the Kimosk, were closest to the destination where man's destiny would be determined. Time was standing still, the world was holding its breath and even the sophomore high school history class was quiet.

"It looks like they're stopping," cried out a reporter on the radio. "Yes, they are stopping!" His voice was animated, excited, and a cheer went up in the background. The kids in the class cheered also. Two ships were turning around. Mr. Solomon lifted his head and arms up to the sky. He was still the man of faith he always was. How else could he have survived and made sense of the world? There were a total of forty ships, and a nuclear submarine was escorting them. It was the closest Soviet missiles ever came to American land. The Navy boarded and searched the Maluka, and finding only paper goods bound for Cuba, let it pass. For the moment there was relief, a release of the tension. But it was only a brief reprieve.

Tyra stayed home on that Thursday, the twenty fifth of October. She curled up in the blankets and began reading *On the Beach.* The hero, Lieutenant Commander Peter Holmes of the Royal Australian Navy had to prepare his wife Mary for the final moments of life as the cloud of radioactive dust approached the island town of Port Phillip Bay, the last place on earth to be smitten by radioactive fallout. She read relentlessly, only stopping to watch Adlai Stevenson give his "Until hell freezes over speech" to the special session of the United Nations' Security Council. She loved Stevenson. In 1956, when she was a little girl, she watched the Democratic convention on television with her father and sister. She listened to his acceptance speech as presidential candidate. He spoke with visions of a prophet in metaphors of a poet. But people made fun of him, calling him an egghead throughout the campaign. He lost to the war hero, General Eisenhower. Tyra didn't care for Eisenhower. He was old and spent more time playing golf than working in the White House. Every now and then he wound up in the hospital with a heart attack. She liked him even less after Sputnik, the first spaceship, was launched by the Soviet Union in 1957. He demanded that American children become more proficient in math and science. He ordered schools to create more sophisticated and difficult programs so that American youth could compete with Russians. That did not thrill Tyra at all, since she was terrible in arithmetic. Throughout elementary school, Sid would spend endless hours trying to teach her how to comprehend the basics- subtraction and multiplication tables. Then percentages and fractions. It was hopeless, and by the time she was in high school, when the demands of geometry—the proofs and the theorems—were beyond Sid's scope, he hired a tutor for her. Without the special help she surely would have failed. One of the boys in Rabbi Singer's collegiate youth group came to the house every week, and explained to Tyra with limitless patience, the shapes, degrees, and concept of pi that eluded Tyra. He offered to tutor her for free. "Rabbi says I could use an extra mitzvah," he said, but Sid wouldn't hear of it. "But the deli man knows how a young hardworking boy like you needs some money in your pocket," Sid said, insisting on giving Mel four dollars a week.

Kaye suspected that Jessie had a crush on Mel, although Jessie never admitted to it. Every week Kaye would bake either angel food cake or ruglach or some other treat that permeated the apartment with such a delicious, inviting smell, it might inspire the blossoming of a romantic inclination. After the lesson, he would stay and talk to Jessie. He would ask her advice on how he could get this other girl who didn't look at

him twice interested in him. Jessie gave him honest suggestions, and all along, she would have given her eye-teeth for
him. He never saw what was right there in front of him. And
still Kaye baked.

The tutoring sessions got more uncomfortable for Tyra as
the year progressed. She felt Mel's eyes on her, as if he wanted
more from her than correct answers. Once he pulled his chair
behind hers and she felt his hot breath on her neck as she
fumbled with the protractor. By the end of the session, when
Kaye came into the kitchen to slice the banana cake, Tyra was
ready to burst. Later on in May, Melvin said he had tickets for
the Yankee game. "My dad bought us tickets, but he's got to
work. Will you come with me?"

"Are you kidding!" she chided. "I hate baseball, but Jessie
loves it." Before he could say a word, Tyra called out toward
the bedroom, "Hey Jess! Mel's got a surprise for you. He's taking you to the Yankee game. Come here."

Jessie strutted into the kitchen. "What's this about
baseball?"

"Mel's got some tickets for the Yankee- Red Sox game, and
he wants you to go with him, being you know the game so
well."

"I'm a Giants fan," she said brushing up against Mel's
shoulder. Her tone was cool and matter of fact. Sauntering
past Tyra, she whispered, "Mind your own business."

Mel snickered at Tyra as he scooped up his books and fold-
ers from the table.

"Thanks for the lesson, Mel. I think I understand the angles
now." As he turned his back to leave, she grit her teeth.. She
could barely contain her despair. Again, she was put in the
awful and frequent position of being in the middle and failed
to turn it to Jessie's advantage.

At the end of the year, Tyra passed the Regents exam with
a grade of ninety-one, and no one was more shocked than she.

Sid was proud. He snuggled his arm around her shoulders, needling her, "You could have passed with a sixty-five and we could have saved a bundle!"

"Yes or no, Mr. Ambassador? Don't wait for the translation!"

Tyra thought he was wonderful. The diplomats were sitting around the Council's horseshoe table when Stevenson addressed Mr. Zorin in front of the entire world. "Do you deny the Soviet Union is placing intermediate and long range missiles in Cuba? I am prepared to wait until hell freezes over! And I'm prepared to show the evidence...." He displayed, for all the world to see, the low-altitude surveillance pictures taken by American U-2 pilots.

Tyra picked up the novel again. The lieutenant had to convince his wife that she had to administer the injection of cyanide to their baby first. But she protested. The baby wasn't sick yet. If you die, he explained to his wife, who will be left to prevent Jennifer from endless vomiting as her skin would burn away from her bones? He showed her the red box with two vials- one pill in each—in case one got messed up. He told her she had to have courage.

Tyra visualized the last scene of *On the Beach* in her mind's eye and the end of the world would look exactly as Nevil Shute described it, the sadness of mothers making sure to kill their babies before they ingested their own dose of poison. In a moment of tragic recklessness, yesterday's fiction would metamorphose into fact, and no one would be alive to change the proper Dewey decimal number on the book's spine or make corrections in the card catalogue.

Tyra and Dawn walked sluggishly the long way west on Gun Hill Road after school on Friday. Dawn wanted to pick up her overnight bag early, before her parents got home from work.

"We still have time to stop in at Izzy's, don't we?" Tyra asked. It would be good to get in from the cold, blustery air, before they continued their way to Dawn's house.

Uncle Izzy's eyes lit up when Tyra and Dawn entered the candy store. "Hey, what's two pretty dolls like you'se lookin' so glum for? The world didn't end yet!" he said as they walked to the end of the counter and propped themselves up on the last two stools. In a flash, Izzy slid two large mugs of hot chocolate, piled high with whipped cream and sprinkles down the counter.

"Tell me which cruds are breaking your heart and I'll give 'em a what-for," he said.

The girls laughed. Tyra twirled the spoon around, waiting for the drink to cool. Dawn studied the mug, like an alcoholic nursing a drink, as if she would find solutions to broken puppy loves written in code lurking in the swirls of cream.

Dawn Kasoff lived near Mosholu Parkway, just a few blocks from Izzy's store. The boys from that neighborhood, including Eric Shuman, Dawn's one and only true love, attended Clinton High School, but the girls had a choice of attending the all-girls Walton High School or the co-ed Paul Revere. Dawn chose Revere.

Dawn was tall, slim, and her dark hair contrasted starkly against her porcelain white complexion and made her angular facial features stand out. Except for the Friday night parties at Mosholu when Tyra chose to spend Shabbos at home, it seemed they spent every waking hour together, in school or gabbing at Izzy's, or at least talking on the phone. They even started to look and dress like one another. They shared outfits but competed with their hairstyles, one trying to outdo the other, seeing who could create the most unique style of the day.

Dawn was generally a flighty, fun-loving teenager, more concerned about boys than books. She was outgoing, forever making arrangements—a real social director. Tyra met her the first day they started Revere High School. Shy and unassuming, Tyra was terrified she would spend her high school days left out and alone, but Dawn was drawn to her from the moment they sat next to each other that first morning in biology class, and Tyra was relieved and comfortable, gently easing her way into the circle of Dawn's neighborhood friends.

"What did Eric do now?" Tyra asked.

"It's what he didn't do. He didn't show. I waited all last night, and he didn't even call." Dawn took a sip and called, "You make good hot chocolate, Izzy."

Izzy winked from across the counter. "Gotta fatten you girls up. Boys like a little meat on your bones." He scooted down the aisle and disappeared in the back room.

"You shouldn't let him be so rotten to you. If you don't demand respect, you won't get it," Tyra said.

"I love him. I don't know what to do."

"Well, you shouldn't always be there for him, no matter what crap he pulls. Keep him wondering. Treat him like dirt for a change. See how he likes it."

Tyra gave a lot of advice considering she didn't have much luck with boys either. She had a secret crush on one of the boys in the youth group at Anshei Shalom, but he was dating someone else. And Saul bugged Tyra to death, and she couldn't get him to leave her alone. "But I know this much, I wouldn't beg a guy for anything. Hard to get, that's me. Not that that works," Tyra laughed. It was hopeless. "Love's for the pretty girls with the good personalities and the big *chachunkers*. Not the flat-chested ones like us.

"*Chachunkers?*" Dawn chided and laughed.

"Well, you know," Tyra said, her cheeks turning red.

"All I know is that I'm tired of being a good girl. It's time to be nice!"

Tyra pulled out Joel's letter from her pocketbook. It was totally crumpled and stained. Though she had poured over the letter hundreds of times, Tyra's heart was once again racing with excitement.

"Columbia," Dawn said, you've got to get him to decide on Columbia. Then you can see him all the time."

"I know. It's too much to hope for. Listen to this. This is the best part…"

"Love, Joel," Dawn interrupted, mocking Tyra. "I heard it a million times. Why don't you get a local boyfriend so you can be happy? You're so afraid of getting involved."

"It's not that. I go out plenty on Saturday nights, but…," Tyra's voice trailed off. Even with her best friend, Tyra felt as though she was violating some deep, private family secret. "Hey," she said, changing the subject, "why don't you come to winter seminar in December. It'll be fun, and you can get away from here, meet some nice boys, boys that have more on their minds than you know what."

"What!" Dawn protested. "Eat kosher food and sit around all day Saturday doing nothing, no thank you. And I bet you study Talmud or Torah or whatever it's called. I'd rather die. And besides," Dawn continued, it's bad enough I have to go to shul with you tomorrow. Oh God, don't tell me I have to tear up the toilet paper when we get home!"

"You're hopeless. You know that? It wouldn't be so bad to pray tomorrow anyway. Maybe God can knock some sense into Khrushchev and Castro both."

"You need anything else, girls?" Izzy asked as he dropped two thick pretzel rods on the counter for them. "Just remember this," he said. "Don't let 'em boys get fresh with you. Give 'em what they want, and you're goners. Keep it mysterious. Have an air about you. They don't want you to play hard to get, but they won't respect you if you don't."

Izzy certainly knew what he was talking about. Tyra remembered the neighborhood talk about Betsy, the chubby girl who lived in a modest private house down the block. When Betsy was in eighth grade, she'd let the boys from the avenue trek down to the park with her and they would all crawl into one of the thick bushes lining the bicycle path. Rumor had it that two boys at a time would slip their hands under her Banlon pullover while the others watched. Braless, she was an easy conquest and they would feel her up, each boy having one breast to himself. Then Betsy would lift her sweater up to her underarms for them so they could cup their hands over the pendulous, elongated mounds that hung down low on her chest toward her stomach. But the soft, flabby heaps could not be contained within the boys' palms, and the bosoms flopped over the groping fingers like globs of toothpaste oozing from the tube and then dripping down the sides. The boys would lick the big brown aureoles until their tongues would tire and their cheeks ache with glee, and they would suck the nipples until they turned red and tender. The boys knew that, not because they cared about hurting her, but because it was then that she stopped giggling and started to whimper. When she finally pushed them away and told them to leave her alone, they abandoned her in the bushes, and sauntered up the grassy slope, mocking her behind her back, mooing like cows and barking like dogs.

Tyra had a taste of how it felt to be humiliated by a boy. All she wanted was a little affection and security, things she thought were innocent and sincere, yet what she did backfired on her. She was completely misunderstood, and brought upon herself shame and loneliness. It happened at the Blueberry

Bluff Bungalow colony outside of Rockridge in that last August of 1962.

The Millers were spending a two week vacation with Hana and Lazer in the two bedroom bungalow. All of them were going to Brown's Hotel one night to see Steve Lawrence and Edie Gorme. Kaye loved the way they sang, but Sid said he'd prefer to have a few laughs with Shecky Greene who was performing at the Nevele. Kaye said she really wanted to see the young couple and offered to see another comedian the next time.

It was nice to see Kaye rested and dressed up for a change. Her full satin skirt crinkled against the metal kitchen chairs and the halfway dilapidated refrigerator as she moved across the crowded bungalow.

"Come on, Jess. Hurry up, will you?" Tyra shouted as she banged on the bathroom door. "You're only doing make-up. Unlock the door. Let me in."

"I'll be out in a second. Hold your horses."

"Ma, do something. We'll be late." Tyra said as she tried to put the finishing touches on her hairdo without the benefit of the looking through the double mirror in the bathroom.

Kaye's demeanor changed in an instant, all of a sudden looking haggard. "Shh. She'll be out in a minute."

Tyra hated the sympathy Kaye extended to Jessie, yet she understood why things were the way they were. "You have to look out for each other," Kaye said over and over again. Tyra remembered the scolding she got in the bungalows a few summers before. It was on movie night, and Tyra searched the grounds for Jessie to tell her the movie was about to start. She called out her name, asked everyone around if they had seen her. Finally, without success, Tyra went into the casino about fifteen minutes after the movie started, found her friends, climbed over the row of people to get to them, and sat down. She hardly enjoyed the movie and felt guilty because she couldn't find Jessie. When she returned to the bungalow after the movie, Kaye laced into her.

"Why didn't you tell Jessie the movie was starting? She has so little pleasure as it is."

Tyra tried to defend herself but to no avail. What else could she do? She went into the bathroom and cried, trying to be as quiet as she could so no one would be able to hear her. Meanwhile Jessie had bopped in at midnight. She had a great time hanging out and joking with a bunch of college kids from town.

Jessie had this strange power to ruin the entire family's evenings at parties or weddings. She could make everyone miserable. "How much make-up can you put on?" Kaye would scold. "If we don't leave now we'll be late," Sid would prod as Jessie holed up in the lone bathroom doing God knows what. She always took forever to get ready, and the second any of them would say even one word to her, she would get her back up. "Go without me," she'd yell, all huffy and puffy, and no amount of pleading or cajoling would get her to change her mind. And off they would go, Sid, Kaye, Tyra, Hana and Lazer, feeling badly and angry at the same time, and throughout the evening, their joy would be diminished while thinking of Jessie languishing alone at home all night, missing out on the food, the dancing, the celebrating of other people's happiness....

"Jessie, you can't pull this crap all the time. If you don't come out now, we're leaving without you," Sid said, his cheeks all red, his chest heaving with the anger it contained within.

"Give her a few more minutes," Kaye said in utter frustration.

"I'm not ready. I'll never be ready. Go without me," Jessie screamed from behind the locked bathroom door.

"That's it. I come up for a vacation and this is the thanks I get. Let's go," Sid said, grabbing his jacket from the kitchen chair and waving his arm for everyone to leave.

Just then the bathroom door opened and Jessie announced, "I'm ready." Her eyeliner and shadow highlighted her hazel eyes. The deep brunette tones of her shoulder-length hair contrasted gracefully her fair complexion.

"Hallelujah! Let's get out of here," Sid said.

The next Saturday night, Sid and Kaye went to a show by themselves. Jessie didn't want to go and Tyra made plans to hang out with her friends. She stopped by Madelyn's bungalow and the two girls walked to the casino to meet up with a group of teenagers on their way to a get together at the lake. Some of the boys already left with a pail of ice filled with cans of soda and beer. Tyra and Madelyn hummed along to the tune *Earth Angel* they heard coming from a portable radio from the dock.

Two boys approached them when they reached the clearing. One introduced himself to Madelyn, and they started some light hearted banter.

"Have a coke," Mike said, as he handed Tyra the cold, slippery glass bottle, wet and drippy with melted ice from the bucket.

"No thanks. I'm not thirsty."

She was thrilled Mike came over to her. She had noticed him earlier in the summer, and they had exchanged casual glances. She found his muscular physique and slick pompadour appealing. He was eighteen but hadn't graduated high school yet. Not Tyra's usual type, but it was summer, a time of frivolity and vacation.

"You don't have to be afraid. I didn't spike it."

She laughed. "I'm not thirsty."

"Let's walk over there," he said, pointing to the rickety dock. They left the crowd of teenagers sitting around the campfire laughing, drinking and making out. He took her hand and they walked to the dock. The three rowboats that were tied up to the pier were smacking rhythmically against the water, making soft, foamy waves splashing onto the rocky bank of the shore. Before he even said "come on," Mike jumped into one of the boats and held his hand out to her. She almost lost her balance as she climbed in and the boat rocked. They laughed and then sat on the wooden benches facing each other. The night was peaceful; patches of white reflections of the moon bounced on the rippling water, making abstract designs on the surface of the lake; soft, cool breezes caused the boat to sway back and forth.

Mike lifted the rope from the tether and grabbed the oars.

"What are you doing? It's too dangerous," she said.

"Don't be scared. I'll protect you," he said beginning to row effortlessly and slowly toward the other side.

The hypnotic beat of the oars skimming the water calmed Tyra as the intermittent momentary sprays of lake water landed on her face, the mist for sure smudging the make-up she had only a short while before struggled to apply after Jessie relinquished the bathroom. Set to a precise pattern, as if he were accompanied by a metronome, Mike's powerful chest heaved back and forth, and in those beats when he leaned forward, closing in on her, glancing intensely at her face, smiling, she felt her insides quiver.

"This is spooky," she said.

He laughed and told her to relax. She heard the din of laughter and music coming from the shore, and soon enough the rowboat came to a rest in a thicket of tall reeds.

He put the oar handles in the locks, and leaned back sucking in a deep breath. She asked him about his family, his likes, the standard list of questions Kaye taught her to ask and which she practiced diligently in front of the mirror to get over her shyness. He was carefree, refreshing, and the more he spoke with candor, the more she felt at ease.

She began to talk about the new movie in town and about hitchhiking plans to Liberty in the coming week. He scooted over from his bench to sit next to her and pulled her toward him. Slowly his arm slid from her shoulder toward her waist. Her stomach dropped as though she was falling from the apex of a roller coaster. She pointed toward the sky crowded with constellations and stars. In what must have been a unique phenomenon, they counted seven falling ones. Her father was never a very religious man, but he would say that there had to be a God when observing the power and complexity of the universe. The brisk mountain air brushed against her face and she understood Sid's awe of nature. Mike guided her face towards his and he kissed her. She started to shiver.

"You cold?" he asked, and draped his jacket over her shoulders. He was tender and she enjoyed his hovering over her.

"Let's go back. This is creepy being out here, away from civilization. What if there are creatures below?"

She heard him laugh and then the clanking of the oars against the metal locks. The boat rocked harder as Mike shifted his weight back to his seat. He shoved the oar against the bank of reeds, pushing the boat around, and that he fulfilled her request without protest provided her with the strange combination of relief and power.

The sounds of the earth were so low and quiet. The ripples of water beat softly against the banks; the croaking of frogs, the clicking of crickets competed against the silence. The lights of the heavens were high and sparkling and space voluminous, a testament to God's majesty. The evening was as placid as the water and Tyra felt a serene, subdued feeling of happiness. They hopped out of the boat and their feet crushed twigs beneath them as they negotiated the narrow dirt path. When her foot got caught on a clump of bramble-bush, he bent down to untangle her leg. He rose and pulled her close to him. They kissed on the lips, and she melted, her body leaning into his so close, she almost came through on his other side. But when he pushed his tongue into her mouth, she froze. Her stiff body jerked awkwardly the moment his cold, damp fingers groped the bare skin of her waist under her sweater. She pulled away from him, nudging his arms off of her, still gripping his wrists.

"Shh…. Take it easy," she whispered as she took his arms and put them around her shoulders.

He lowered his head into the crick of her neck, and put his hand under her top, in the front this time, and his palm crept up her bare midriff toward her bra.

She pushed him away and glared at him. "Don't push me," she said. "Why are you spoiling it?"

The combination of joy and nervousness she felt, and the brief moments of pleasure were shattered as soon as she regained her senses. She was getting in too deep. She would have to give too much. She was losing control. She had enjoyed the tingling inside and out, as he caressed her. She wanted to lose herself in the comfort of his arms and make him happy. But it was wrong. How could she be self-indulgent and self-respecting at the same time? She didn't know how and she hated herself for being stupid and immature. She turned and left him, the moon lighting the way on the narrow, rocky path to the top of the hill, back to the lawn, to safety.

"You don't have to run away. You could just tell me to stop," he yelled out at her.

She continued without turning around, without answering him. The other kids must have heard him and she felt sick with shame.

"Hey come back. I won't make you go all the way." You could trust me."

She didn't answer him, and scratched her leg on the thick brambles as she stepped up her pace.

"Tease," he called out. "You're nothing but a prude," he added, his voice trailing in the breeze.

Her eyes started to burn, just as they had when Jessie once plunged her spoon into a half-grapefruit and drops of tart juice squirted right across the table into Tyra's eyes.

Somewhat calmed that the bungalow was dark when she reached the porch, she opened the screen door. It squeaked in the stillness, the squeals and squawks of nocturnal critters adding to the otherwise dormant environs. She dropped into the soft, lumpy mattress on the cot and sank her head into her hands.

"What happened to you?" Jessie asked.

Tyra jumped. "Oh my God! You scared me half to death. What have you been doing?"

"I was reading. I just turned out the lights. Mom and Dad aren't back yet. I hope they're having a good time."

"Then you should've gone with them, if you're so concerned."

"You don't understand anything. They need to get a life for themselves. They can't protect me forever. None of you respect me. Anyway what happened to you? Boy trouble?"

"Leave me alone. You wouldn't understand anyway." Tyra couldn't confide in Jessie. How could she talk about boys and love? And if she did, Jessie would throw it up to her somewhere down the line, like a bullet out of nowhere, striking her completely off balance, revealing her secrets and confidences to anyone near, embarrassing her to death. She smothered herself underneath the chenille blanket and feigned sleep.

"Good morning, Mr. and Mrs. Bungalowites!" the loud, sing-song voice of the old, white-haired lady proprietor billowed over the loudspeaker at the ungodly hour of seven. "The bakery truck is on the premises. Repeat. The bakery truck is here now. Pick up your orders of fresh onion rolls and bagels. He'll be leaving in ten minutes."

Lazer had just left for his morning walk in the *fresha luhft*, crisp air. He let the screen door slam. No one should waste such a beautiful day. He hated when the girls slept late.

219

The Miller sisters were stirring in their cots, both disturbed and annoyed by the door, and grating voice of the nagging owner, which now accentuated the bustle in the kitchen.

Kaye was standing over a frying pan, sizzles of hot oil splattering as she slid breaded kippered herrings in to fry. Hana was scrubbing and peeling a big pile of little white potatoes to boil.

"Such sad news today, I hope it shouldn't spoil your breakfast," the owner continued over the P.A. system. "The headlines this morning says Marilyn Monroe committed suicide last night. Repeat. Marilyn Monroe found dead in the nude. And Bungalowites. Don't forget Bingo at the casino at eight o'clock sharp tonight!"

Tyra shot up in bed as did Jessie.

"*Oy. A shanda,*" Hana said. "Such a beauty." Her cheek started to twitch and she patted it with the palm of her hand.

"I don't believe it, Kaye said. So, so tragic. Go figure. A woman who had everything, money, looks, men."

"She was just a tramp," Sid said.

"I'd do anything to have her bust," Jessie called across the bungalow, "instead of padded bras and falsies."

"*Oy vey, what kind of talk is this? Yiddishe madelach.*" Hana said in her usual, gentle manner. Tyra started to giggle.

"It's a shame. She didn't have any self-respect." He shook his head, glancing at his daughters. "See what happens," he added as if he was waving a red flag in front of them.

"Oh, hon. Have a little sympathy," Kaye said. That's the way these starlets have to get to the top. It's the moguls that are the bums."

Sid offered to go to the main house to get the onion rolls and no doubt, the Sunday paper. He trotted down the stairs and the screen door flopped three times against the wooden frame- clunk, clunk, clunk- until it stopped vibrating.

"Maybe he'll fix it when he gets back," Kaye said to Hana. "It'll be easier than nudging the owners to do it." She put the platter of fried herring on the table shaking her head. "Such a beauty," she mumbled. "All she wanted was to be loved." Turning her attention to the fresh pot of coffee brewing on the stove, she told the girls to get washed up for breakfast. "Daddy'll be back in a minute."

In an unusual act of unison, they both protested. "Not now," Tyra said, and Jessie added, "Not hungry."

Tyra curled herself in the covers, too agitated to go back to sleep, too sluggish to get up. *Was it so wrong to want to be held, to feel safe,* she thought. *She just wanted to feel worthy of being protected. Was that so terrible? Why did things have to be so complicated? Maybe it was better to be a tramp than a tease. At least the boys got what they expected they would. No leading on. No stopping short. No games. But look what happened to Marilyn. Why did guys have to be such creeps?*

"Do you think we'll ever fall in love and get married?" Dawn mused, stirring the gooey remains of her cocoa in Uncle Izzy's candy store. "Assuming we don't blow up, that is."

"I want to find a guy like my father. He's not real romantic or anything like that. Jessie and I are always bailing him out, rushing to get a last minute birthday or anniversary present for him to give my mom, but for the important stuff, there's nothing in the world he wouldn't do to make her happy. He's always rubbing her neck or back, and he hardly ever yells."

"Oh! My, God! Tyra. Just the thought of marrying somebody like my father gets me nauseous. My parents hate each other. They really do. I've never seen them kiss each other, not even on the cheek. I'm always walking on eggs, and I just want to get through the day without a blow-up or getting punished. And Lenny, he knows just what to do to get them on my case. I wish I could run away. Swear you'll never tell," she pleaded, "I can't hold it in anymore. I sneak into the liquor cabinet when they're not home. Sometimes, I feel like I can't stop drinking."

Tyra was horrified. Dawn's eyes looked downward and Tyra saw tears welling up. She never saw Dawn look so sad.

Dawn was right about her parents. The Kasoffs were big, imposing people, cold enough to make Tyra feel unwelcome when she visited. "Here's a tuna sandwich and applesauce," Mrs. Kasoff said one of the few times she allowed Dawn to invite Tyra for lunch. "That's sufficient," Dawn's mother said. True the amount of food was sufficient, but it was the revelation of annoyance in Mrs. Kasoff's voice as she uttered the word *sufficient* that made Tyra feel that she was a burden, intruding on Mrs. Kasoff's routine. Kaye or Hana couldn't stop offering Tyra's friends food when they came to visit.

Dawn was embarrassed by her mother's coldness to her friends. The Kasoffs constantly belittled Dawn and compared her to her bright and gifted younger brother, Leonard. Their favoritism was obvious and distasteful, and Tyra disliked them for it. She felt stiff and uncomfortable in their presence, and even tried to plan her visits to Dawn's house when she knew her parents wouldn't be home.

As bad as things were for the Millers, as much as Tyra wanted to run away, too, drinking never even occurred to her. "Dawn, you can't do that. Please, you've got to get a grip. My life isn't so great, either. Jessie is always fighting at home. I need you to stick around for me, too."

"I'm sorry. It's just that I'm doomed."

Tyra didn't know how to answer, but one thing bothered her. Dawn's family was healthy. They didn't have to be miserable and loveless. They had a choice. Even so and stranger still, Tyra would never trade places. Never.

"Come on, Dawn. You scare me. Besides, we promised, friends forever, pushing baby carriages in the park."

Their conversation was interrupted when Izzy shouted to a few schoolboys who came into the store and hovered around the comic book racks. "Buy them books or get outta here. Takin' up room and wrinkling the pages! Tell you what- if the world blows up in that big black mushroom cloud…" He spread his hands over his head making the shape of a giant mushroom, "and if it sn-e-aks…" He dragged out the sylla-bles… "into your bedroom through the window and swe-eps over you at night when you're in your beds, and your skin disintegrates into a piles of sand, then you—you don't have to pay me for the damn things." The boys looked at Izzy like he was crazy and ran out of the store.

"Uncle Izzy, Tyra said, you're so mean." Dawn laughed.

Izzy turned to them and threw his arms up in the air. "If the world blows up, at least I don't have to mop this damn floor anymore."

He swished the mop past the girls and told Tyra to tell her father that he expected Duvid to come back in a few days.

"What do you mean. Where is he?"

"Oh my goodness. Didn't your father tell you? He ran off some where to gamble last Sunday."

Tyra remembered her father telling Kaye that he had prob-lems of his own. But he hadn't said what they were. Now she understood why he had been coming home later than usual this week.

Tyra was just about to complain about Duvid's irrespon-sibility and the trouble he caused. After all, he had ruined a week of Tyra's summer vacation when he disappeared on one of his gambling binges and Tyra went to the store to help her father. But when she glimpsed Izzy's eyes lowering to the floor, she discerned, for the first time, an uncharacteristic expres-sion of shame and embarrassment on her uncle's usually jolly face. It was Izzy who had pleaded with Sid to take Duvid as a partner, to give him an opportunity to make something of himself. But Duvid had repeatedly managed to spoil things for everyone. The yelling in Tyra's house these past few days was unbearable. Kaye continually admonished Sid as though he were a child. "I told you not to take Duvid on. Look how hard you have to work. And I guess you'll pay him, too." Sid would say that it wasn't so bad, that when Duvid did work, which was more often than not, he did a good job; he opened at four and started the pot roasts and corned beef and served breakfast to the earliest of the workers coming into the neighborhood. "I wanted to give him a break. Everyone deserves a chance," he said. "People don't change," Kaye countered.

Tyra felt bad for her father. She had helped him out in the store once before when Duvid ran away. She saw how hard he worked, how he ran back and forth on his feet all day. Tyra felt bad for Izzy, too, and held in her resentment. She wouldn't have had the guts to say something anyway.

The chilly afternoon grew raw and dark.

"If we leave now, I can pack before my parents come home from work, and just leave them a note," Dawn said.

"Good idea. We have to get home for candles anyway."

The sun was totally hidden behind the clouds as the girls got up to leave. Tyra kissed Izzy on his cheek. "Thanks for the drinks."

Izzy called out, loud enough for everyone to hear, "Remember—no *chuppy*—no *schtuppy*!"

Tyra was horrified. Her cheeks were burning red. "Uncle Izzy, how could you?" She tried to hide her face in the shoulder of her coat and told Dawn she was ready to die.

Dawn giggled and smacked Tyra playfully on her arm. "Oh God," she stammered, barely getting the words out. "I thi–ink I'm gon-na pe-e-e. You're so lucky. I wish I had an uncle like that."

Ricky's party was as sad and low key as the entire week since the President's speech. His relatives were out in force, mostly to support his mother as they celebrated Ricky's first birthday since his father's death.

Mrs. Rosa Lopez was tall and her wavy tresses fell on her shoulders. Her black blouse had a low, V-neck ruffled collar. Her tight black skirt was too short and too tight for her age. It might have looked better if her calves weren't thick and her stomach was flat.

"So Ricky tells me you eat kosher," she told the two girls. Ricky approached them as they stood in the foyer. Mrs. Lopez added, "I made the rice and beans without meat special. Ricky sweet-talked me." She winked at Ricky and pulled him close to her, pecking him on the cheek. "I don't see why my food isn't good enough for you." She paused for a moment, giving the girls a once-over. "You two are pretty for Jewish."

"Come on inside." Ricky looked at his mother with squinted eyes as he grabbed Tyra's arm on one side and Dawn's on the other, and marched them into the living room. "Meet the rest of the gang. Elias should be here soon."

Tyra knew Ricky for years, but this was the first time she was in his house. A big wooden cross hung on the wall in the foyer. A carved wooden end table in the corner of the living room was covered with a white lace tablecloth. A small statue of Mary was set in the middle with two lighted candles flanking it, the shadows flickering on the wall. "We always have one lit candle, but since my father died, we have two. Extra light to guide his soul to heaven," he explained.

"He must be there already, don't you think?"

"I guess so," Ricky said. His family was religious. They were close. His grandparents were retired and lived in the apartment with them. "We'd never put them away," he told her once. After they all ate, the relatives stayed in the kitchen while the kids joked around and danced to Latin music. Then the relatives came into the living room, flanking Mrs. Lopez who was buried under the weight of a huge cake, a Valencia,

Ricky's favorite, a soft sweet cake moist with fresh pineapple, aglow with nineteen birthday candles.

Ricky's aunt and uncle drove the girls home. When they popped out of the sedan, they cuddled together in the cold, windy night. Tyra looked up as they hobbled into the courtyard.

"Looks like they're waiting for us," Tyra said, pointing to the kitchen window with the lights on.

"You called to tell them we'd be late."

"I just don't know why they won't get it. Ricky's a great kid. We're just friends." Tyra took in a deep breath. "Let's take the stairs- it'll take longer that way."

"Good idea."

"You don't have to worry." Tyra assured Dawn. "The most they'll do to you is tell you that you're a bad influence on me. They'll kill me."

Tyra jiggled the key in the police lock until she heard the latch release and the metal pole slip into the open position so they had enough room to enter. Kaye was sitting by herself in the kitchen.

"Hi, Mom. Couldn't sleep again?"

"Did you have a good time? You too, Dawn?"

Tyra grabbed Dawn's hand at the side of her coat. Tyra expected a grilling, but Kaye was calm.

Kaye got up and walked over to Tyra, helping her off with her coat. "Don't worry. Everything is okay but the police called about half an hour ago. The store was broken into. Daddy went down to check out the damage and file a police report. Jessie went with him. They'll call when they get a handle on things."

"Oh gosh. I'm sorry, Mom. Is there anything I can do?"

Kaye shook her head. "At least Jessie got to go out on a Saturday night, too. By the way, Joan called me before. She's making a surprise birthday party for Howard." She turned to Dawn and explained, "our dentist, next Saturday night. Assuming this Cuba thing turns out okay."

"That's nice. You're going, aren't you?"

"Oh, I don't know." She sighed with that familiar gasp of tiredness, the one where it hardly was worth the effort to try to have a good time.

"Go, Mom. You and Dad will have a good time. Besides, next weekend I'll be home studying for midterms, even on Saturday night."

Kaye looked at Tyra and smiled sadly. "Probably. Thanks. I hope they come home soon. Tell me, how was Ricky's party?"

"It was nice, easy going. A few friends were there and some of his relatives. His mother made this special dish for us, and she didn't use meat so I could eat it.

"The one with the meat looked good," Dawn said. "But I felt funny, like I'd be betraying our heritage if I ate it."

"I see Tyra is a good influence on you," Kaye said.

The girls laughed.

"His mother sounds nice." Kaye said.

"Well, she's really proud of Ricky.

"So a Puerto Rican mother *qvells* over a child, too," Kaye said with a chuckle.

"She beamed at him the whole time. They're a pretty close family. But I got the impression she'd prefer Ricky just to have Puerto Rican friends."

The thieves had made the biggest mess yet, and it took Sid and Jessie almost until dawn to clean everything up. Sid was drained and limp when he entered the apartment, but Jessie was bubbly and animated by the excitement of talking to the police and the hubbub of filling out reports and talking to detectives. "Did you hear," Jessie said, "Khrushchev ordered the dismantling of the missiles? It's over. Heard it in the car on the way home. We are going to live!"

The librarian was standing at the check-out counter as students were filing in and filling up the seats around the tables for a library lesson that Monday morning. Mrs. Whitestone was chipper and talking with some students.

"How's your daughter?" Tyra asked.

"I spoke to her last night. She's coming in for Thanksgiving. I can't wait to see her," she said as she smiled.

"That's great. I came to return the book I borrowed last week."

"Just leave it on the counter. I'll take care of it."

Tyra wondered if the librarian's newfound kindness would last after the tension of the past week was forgotten. "No, No. I want to do it myself. Really."

"Well, then. Let me process it first," she said as she took the book, stamped the card and put it back in the pocket. Then she gave it to Tyra.

Tyra walked to the fiction section and moseyed down the aisles, slowly taking in the view of thousands of volumes she still hadn't read. Judging from the dust on the mahogany shelves, not too many others read them either. When she reached her destination, she lifted the volume in her hand, studied the letters on its spine, and kissed the cover gently, just the way she kissed the siddur and chumash (prayer book and bible) at the end of services. Then she squeezed *On the Beach* onto the crowded shelf, sandwiching it between novels written by Shuler and Siddone. She breathed in a deep breath, felt her lungs fill up with serenity and composure, and she smiled.

It could have been that, with a blink of the eye, either Kennedy's or Khrushchev's, the entire world could have disintegrated in an instantaneous nuclear conflagration. In these last six days, man had the power to destroy the universe God had created in the first six.

Blessed art Thou, O Lord our God, King of the Universe, who has given mankind the wisdom to prevent an unprecedented act of tragic recklessness; who has generously allowed us to retain our fiction as fiction, and our non-fiction story to continue; who has permitted us to preserve in tact and accuracy, our Dewey Decimal system and card catalogue. Thank you, my God, for sustaining us with our lives, as blue as they may be, and the most important of all, for keeping us together- even though we can't stand each other.

ELEVEN

WIND BEFORE THE SAIL

Tyra loved the leadership seminars sponsored by Jewish Youth Institute of Higher Learning. They brought together young people from all over the northeast and Canada, young adults who were thirsting for knowledge, searching for raison d'etre. Mostly from non-orthodox homes, each had a seed of Yiddishkeit planted somewhere in his or her background, and the desire to nurture it with learning burned a path to seminar. That was good for Tyra. It was what she needed. A way to cleanse herself of the bitterness she harbored by surrounding herself with people who knew wisdom was there for the finding, and joy was in the learning.

Study sessions throughout the day interspersed with recreational activities provided opportunities for young adults to nourish friendships that would last for years to come. Rap sessions with learned men who sought nothing more than to share their love of God and Judaism, and bequeath the heritage to the next generation, helping find the balance between the old European ways and American progress, bridging the gaps between individual fulfillment and societal needs with a stabilizing ethical and moral core. Men were racing to the moon on the high road, and firebombing churches and lynching colored people on the low one. God needed to be somewhere in the universe to bring order to it- to fit science and faith alongside one another and harmonize new challenges and dilemmas with steadfast moral, Talmudic principles set down generations before. Seminar was just that place for young people to hash out the complexities of society and find ways to be good Jews.

Tyra couldn't wait for the seminar in December. She would see the friends she'd made in years past, and best of all Joel would be there from Massachusetts. Of course, Jessie would be there, too, as an advisor, so Tyra already felt smothered knowing that she would be "looked after," told what to do, and when to do it, just as it was in the house, just as when they were kids, just as always.

Rabbi Singer was going to go with his family and he told Tyra that since she would already be in college by the coming summer, despite her young age, she would be eligible to serve as an assistant advisor. "I'm going to put in a good word for you," he told her, and he had plenty of clout. It was because of him that Jessie was allowed to be an advisor in December. She faced so much prejudice because of her appearance, as if that determined her ability to think or to lead. It seemed people were more concerned about the reactions of others to Jessie's condition rather than Jessie's feelings or capabilities. Rabbi Singer stood his ground with the director, who had his reservations about hiring Jessie. But because Rabbi Singer knew Jessie so well, he was genuine and unflinching as he vouched for her talents and determination, and the director needed Rabbi Singer, as his seminars and discussion groups were the most popular with the students.

Jessie always seemed to take the high road and try to achieve what others told her she wouldn't be able to or that she didn't belong or worse yet, didn't deserve. That just seemed to get her back up even more, and with each setback and rejection, she became more obstinate and steadfast. A little obnoxious, too. The family, especially Sid, for whom Jessie had enormous respect and affection, gave full support and encouragement to fight the world, so to speak. Jessie started a two-year medical assistant program. She liked working with people who needed help, and if she couldn't teach, it seemed helping the ill was perhaps even a better choice for her. Jessie also had a natural affinity toward young people, especially those afflicted with medical problems, and in the medical field she could flourish. Her compassion and intelligence would be appreciated and the unique empathy she possessed would be put to good use.

Because of all the exposure she had to hospitals and medical procedures, she had a propensity for the field, and medical terminology, a foreign language in essence, came second nature to her. If only she could have adapted to Spanish like she did medical terminology, she might have had an easier time in high school. Jessie wasn't one to shy away from blood either, and where Tyra had to close her eyes at gore, Jessie was right there, borrowing everyone's fingers to practice her finger-stick skills for school. Uncle Sheldy was the most willing guinea pig, and Hana would do anything for Jessie. "So gentle, you are, Jessie," she would say, praising her eldest granddaughter's prowess, barely wincing as the lancet pricked her plump middle finger. Tyra was the most uncooperative of all, nearly being dragged to the chair. Jessie dragged her arm out from under her, to get a good grip. "Ow!" Tyra screamed more than once. "I thought you were gentle." Jessie said she didn't get enough blood, and needed to stick the index finger of Tyra's other hand. "No way," Tyra protested, but the others cajoled her into giving in. After all, Jessie needed to pass her course.

Human nature hadn't evolved since Jessie was a child, and she still suffered at the hands of her fellow students in the Medical Arts School of Fifth Avenue. It seemed that those who kick you in the back when they're young and not so innocent, grow up to find other vicious ways of being mean. Even though young adults who chose to work in a profession with sick people, to bring them comfort and healing, weren't able to see Jessie past her deformity. The other students taunted her, excluded her from parties, and mocked her as she passed them in the hallways. What did they think? That the sick were beautiful, that ill people lay in bed with bright white linens, peaceful and happy, like wounded soldiers in the war movies, whose bandages were always spotless, no blood on amputated limb wounds? Or Hollywood starlets dying of leukemia, laying peacefully in bed, bodies not contorted and writhing in pain? Why would anyone want to be with someone weaker, suffering, indebted, if he had no compassion himself? Even some of the teachers made it rougher on her than the other students, as if she needed to prove that it was more important for her than the others to fulfill the course requirements.

Tyra hoped that Duvid wouldn't fly the coop again and go off on a gambling tirade like he did the previous year. Tyra missed seminar so she could help Sid in the store. She'd handled the fountain pretty well, but adding up the checks and giving change at the register proved a challenge. Still she worked hard. She took the bus in early and stayed late most nights, waiting for Sid to close, coming home with him. "Go home, sweetie. Take the bus," he'd say at three or four o'clock, after the lunch rush. But she saw how hard he worked, especially since he had to open for Duvid at four in the morning to get the corned beefs and briskets started. Every now and then she would catch a glimpse of him as he grasped and rubbed his bursitis-inflamed shoulder. Even if she could just help mop the floor and scrub the counters, it would be better than running out, leaving all of the clean-up and next day's set-up for her father.

She worked in the shop for the entire week Duvid pulled his disappearing act. Jessie said she would give up seminar to work in the store, the self-sacrificing martyr that she was, as if she hadn't given up enough good times in the past.

"Daddy asked me to go in," Tyra protested in her typical whiny voice, emphasizing the word *me*. "You always have to trump me, don't you. Just go to seminar and have a good time."

"You're such a baby, Tyra. I like helping Dad. You did it last time. What's bugging you, anyway?"

"Nothing's bugging me. But Daddy asked me, and I want to stay. That's all." Tyra couldn't bear having a good time at seminar while Jessie stayed home. She knew that Jessie was putting on her martyr act, lying about wanting to stay behind, not seeing her friends at seminar.

They both turned to Sid as if he were King Solomon. Which daughter would he award the sacrificial prize to?

"If you both stay, maybe I'll go to seminar!" he laughed. Then his lips tightened and added in a soft, tired voice, "You missed a lot, Jess." He patted her on her shoulder. "I want you to go. And, winking at Tyra, "you can help me." She walked over to him and kissed him on the cheek, thrilled that he stuck up for her. "Next time, you can help, Jessie," he said.

"What do you mean, next time," Kaye chimed in. "There better not be a next time. The guy's more trouble than he's worth. He'll get you in jail one of these days with his bookie comrades. It's about time you lay down the law and throw him out. I told you from the beginning..."

"Aw, come on, Hon. I couldn't have started the business without his help." His voice was stern and bellowed out of pursed lips. He had had enough. "And there won't be a next time." He left the room, flicking the newspaper in front of him in a rare display of anger.

Hana was starting to talk about the menu for Thanksgiving still two weeks away. And there was plenty to be thankful for. "You think Kennedy's so smart mit Khrushshev?" Hana said. Several times in the past few weeks since the Cuban crisis, Hana made sure the family knew how difficult it was to get along with Lazar. "Kennedy, Shmennedy. I should get the prize, the vay I handle Lazar." She loved to plan ahead, making a mental schedule of all the chores to be done, getting ready for the festive meal with all the relatives. First they'd purchase the groceries, then the produce and of course Uncle Shockneh would pick out the plumpest turkey and soup pullets and send it home with Sid.

Tyra heard that the City University system would be sending out their acceptance and rejection letters for the spring semester before the holiday. She had applied to the Manhattan campus of Lexington College, where she would be able to take Hebrew as her foreign language. She applied to Stern also, just as a lark, to see if she would get in. Nowhere in the world would she get such a complete and intense Jewish education, but even with a partial scholarship, the expenses would be far too difficult for her family, and she certainly didn't have the grades for a full scholarship.

She thought it was pretty cool that she would graduate from high school in January, right before her seventeenth birthday. It had been a blessing to being born right after the war, at the onset of what would later be known as the baby boom generation. The public schools were under enrolled more than ever in 1950, because five years earlier the men were overseas fighting the war, not home making babies. As a result, there weren't enough five-year-olds to fill the kindergarten classrooms, and the Board of Education lowered the age requirement to four instead of five. Tyra's generation of youngsters filled kindergarten classrooms throughout the city. Tyra also skipped a year of junior high by taking on the extra responsibilities of the SP class which combined the eighth and ninth grades. And then, because she couldn't stand wasting time, she doubled up in the final English and history classes in high school and was able to graduate mid-year and start college in January. All the better too, not to waste time in classes where the students, except in the honors classes, fooled around, cheated and couldn't care less about their futures. Tyra had plans. She wanted to make something of her life, to accomplish things. Joel was definitely going to law school in New York and she had to keep up with him, to be interesting. Now that she was almost in college herself, she felt more mature and able to handle a serious relationship. Their correspondence had brought them closer and though she went out on casual dates in New York, she never accepted offers to go steady with any one. Joel wrote her often, and she memorized every word, cherishing every innuendo of his feelings and intentions.

Tyra shook out the umbrella as she entered the lobby of the apartment building and walked up the two steps to the bank of mailboxes.

"Hi, there," she said to Johnny, the mailman who was dropping mail in a steady beat, the sounds of different sized envelopes making soothing "plop, plop" sounds as the parcels made contact with the metal boxes.

"Don't tell me you're going to stand and wait until I get to your side again? Why don't you come back in twenty minutes? I'll be done then."

"It's okay. I'll just wait." She thought about asking him to flip through the bundle that her mail would be in, but she was afraid to take the chance, since he had refused just a few days before.

She stood in the corner, leaning against the wall at the foot of the stairs, brushing off the rain from her gray tweed coat, the hand-me-down from Jessie that Lazer altered for her after the summer.

Plop, clink, plop. Sounds the envelopes made as they fell into their respective places in the boxes. Hard steady raindrops tinkled against the walls of the building and the sounds of the mail and the rain became indistinguishable.

Tyra stood there, antsy, shifting her weight from one foot to the other, biting her nails as she waited.

"Well, sweetheart, if you're gonna stand there watching me, chewin' your fingers like they're lamb chops or somethin', I might as well get rid of you before you drive me to drink. What are you waitin' for anyway, gold?"

"College letters. I told you, didn't I?"

"College! You old enough for college. Gee. I never would have guessed. Why didn't you say so?"

Still considering herself to be scrawny and flat-chested, Tyra felt humiliated by the mailman's assessment of her, and all the joy of succeeding in her studies to date shriveled inside. She lowered her head, staring at the marble tiles on the ground.

"In that case, let me see what I can do for you," as he bent down swiftly, totally unaware of the impact of his words on Tyra, and sorted through the bundles in his brown U.S. Mail pouch in big black letters. Finally, he said, "Okay, this is it." He flipped through the envelopes, stopping at one point. "Here we go." He handed Tyra an easily recognizable Con Ed bill for her father, and then an official-looking envelope addressed to Tyra from Lexington College.

"Thanks a bunch," she said as she took the envelopes.

"So did you get in?" he asked. "Hey, where'd you go?" he said, looking around as Tyra's rapid footsteps up the stairs echoed through the halls and gradually faded away.

"We are pleased to inform you..." Tyra's eyes lit up as she read the letter in the quiet of the bedroom. Jessie was at school and Kaye was still at work. But as she continued reading, her smile shrank and tears welled up in her eyes. That joy could be tempered so swiftly with disappointment seemed to be the curse of the Millers. Accepted to the college of her choice so that she could study Hebrew, but not to be accepted at the campus where Hebrew classes were given. All because her average was a half a point below the required 85% needed for admission.

"Stop sulking," Kaye said later, as Tyra was setting the table for dinner. "You should be happy to get into a free college. You can transfer after a while. I missed out on all of college because..."

"I know, Mom. I heard the story a million times. The lousy math teacher gypped you of an eighty five and you were short a half a point..."

"Be quiet. Since when are you so disrespectful?"

Jessie, who had been within earshot, floated into the kitchen for a drink; although, it seemed to be at that precise moment, just to torment her sister.

"Yelling at your precious daughter," Jessie said to Kaye with a glint in her eye. "What did she do now, Little Miss Perfect?"

"Stop it already," Kaye screamed. "I've heard the same things from you two for fifteen years." She shuffled a bunch of utensils in the drawer looking for the ladle. "Grow up already. I'll probably hear this attitude for the next fifty years, if I should live so long... if you don't kill me first."

Jessie ignored Kaye's plea. She turned toward her sister. "We all know you're disappointed because the Bronx campus is all-girls. Can't you live without boys for a semester?"

"Shut up, Jess. I'm not a tramp." Tyra's face turned red and her eyes filled up. "You're just jealous," she screamed, feeling sick to her stomach as the words came out.

"Hebrew, my eye. It's really Joel. Admit it. He'll be at Columbia. Isn't that right?"

Jessie's belittling tone cut through Tyra like a new razor blade on a sunburned leg. She couldn't tell if her cheeks turned red although they felt hot, and tears, which she tried desperately to hold back, welled up in her eyes.

"Bitch," Tyra muttered under her breath. She was afraid to be heard. If Kaye told Sid, he might punish her for cursing, like he did years before when Tyra called Jessie a f—ing bastard. "You're insulting your mother," he screamed, "saying she wasn't married when she had your sister. We're civilized in this house," he said banishing her to the bedroom, warning her not to curse at her sister ever again, "or else." Tyra was trembling. She had seen her father only once before so furious, with reddened cheeks and fists pounding in the air.

"That's enough," Kaye hollered. She slammed the pot she had been carrying from the stove onto to trivet. "You're so mean to each other. Can't you both try to be like normal caring sisters. Two girls," she mumbled, "I always wanted two girls so they could be friends. I never had a sister, but boy I wish I had two sons right now."

Jessie shoved her way through the crowd, and boarded the bus. *Sure*, Tyra thought. *She'll sit in the back so she can watch me.* Why couldn't she do something on her own? Why did Rabbi Singer have to arrange for Jessie to go to seminar, as an advisor no less? Tyra was only an assistant advisor, and no doubt Jessie would find ways to boss her around. At the last seminar, Tyra was talking to Joel outside her bunk. "It's light's out," Jessie shouted as she passed by. Tyra thought she would die. She met Joel at that seminar, just a few weeks after the disaster with Mike in the bungalow colony. Joel was different. He spoke softly, told her of his dreams, expressing his idealism, and he made her feel important, unwittingly and subtly lifting her spirits, boosting her self-esteem. Despite his puny, narrow frame, she was attracted to him. They even looked liked they belonged together—two bamboo sticks in the middle of a redwood forest. They met in the dining hall, and struck up an easy conversation and became good friends in the course of the week. They corresponded throughout the fall, and he even signed his letters with "love," which Tyra took very seriously. She would see him in a few hours, and her heart starting racing already. She climbed up the three steep stairs of the bus entrance.

Stop yakking and get on the bus, she thought as dozens of young people were milling about the depot, hugging and kissing between suitcases, friends reuniting from all parts of Jersey, Long Island and the boroughs of New York. For many it was the first time they had seen each other since seminar last summer. It was cold and Tyra huddled in the gray plaid woolen coat Lazer had made for her that fall.

She squeezed down the aisle and took a seat in the middle of the bus, passing by her sister who was sitting behind the front wheels. Of course Jessie wouldn't have sat in the back, on top the rear wheels; it would be too rough a ride for her fused spine. Tyra scolded herself, torn between guilt and anger. She would never be free.

She moved into a window seat, and as she was fidgeting, trying to get comfortable in the seat, she heard a bellowing voice call out her name.

"I'm so glad you're here," Marlene called out loud enough so that all the kids on the bus could hear. She wrapped her tweed coat tightly around her chubby body and flopped into the aisle seat next to Tyra. "I was looking for you outside. Guess what? I checked with the director and he assured me I would be in your bunk. Isn't that great? You're going to be my assistant advisor. He promised."

When Tyra could get a word in edgewise, she asked Marlene to fill her in on the troubles she was having with her family. She liked Marlene, who was fourteen and a freshman in Paramus High School. They met at the previous summer seminar and Marlene, who was outwardly energetic and jovial, confided her insecurities and parental tensions to Tyra.

Tyra was happy to be an assistant advisor this time. She liked the idea of helping people, of making a difference in someone's life, just the way Rabbi Singer was so important to her. He brought out the very best in Tyra. In public school she had to struggle in endless hours of study to achieve the grades she did. But with Rabbi Singer, Judaic lessons came naturally, especially the wonders of Jewish history and the analysis of *p'sukim* in the Torah. The language of prayers rolled off her tongue like Lazer's bolts of silk, and what was even greater satisfaction was that not only did she pray in Hebrew, but she understood and felt in Hebrew as well. Rabbi Singer made her feel important and smart. "One day, you are going to be a great teacher," he told her, "because you care." And she believed him.

"I thought a lot about what you said last summer, that I shouldn't demand my parents keep a kosher home for me, and you were right," Marlene said as she leaned her head against the seatback, looking straight ahead as the bus started to pull away from the station.

"Well, that is a lot to ask of parents, to change their whole way of life for something only their daughter finds meaningful. So how have you been managing your food?"

Marlene heaved what Tyra thought to be an embarrassingly huge chuckle, again seeming to alert everyone on the bus. Marlene pointed to her ever bulging torso, and said, "Not too well, as you can see. I've turned almost total vegetarian, and the weight still piles up." Her outward nonchalance defied that tinge of frustration which was revealed in her tone. "Actually," she continued, "I reached a compromise with my folks. I spoke softly to them, just as you suggested, and I asked them why they should be so upset if I decided to keep a few dishes separate in my room, and eat just about everything but the meat and chicken Mom cooks. Like I said to them, 'what do you care if I eat cheese before or after meat?' My father thinks the whole idea of religion and kosher is ridiculous, but I finally got my mother to agree, as long as I eat a balanced diet and all. She thinks the discipline might be helpful with my studies and stuff like that."

"It's funny, how different people have to struggle for different things," Tyra said. "I never had to think twice about Kashrus. It's been handed to me on a silver platter all my life."

They laughed at the silly way Tyra's words came out.

"So, Miss Vegetarian, what's your favorite vegetable? Tyra asked.

"Raisinets!" Marlene started to giggle.

"You're impossible. Maybe you would feel better about yourself if you did exert a little more discipline, and if you lost a few pounds you might have a better attitude about your social life. It might even improve."

"Gee, thanks for your input. Maybe I should go talk to the director and get out of your bunk. Do you always have to be so serious?"

Yes, Tyra thought. She was always so serious and she wished she could be lighthearted. *But life was serious. It was a gift, and too many people suffered too much in order to try to have a good one. In every generation, Jews fought to be free from oppression and now Jews in the Soviet Union were struggling to survive. Too many Israelis struggled to defend the tiny homeland. All the ailing, like Jessie and Hana, who tried so hard to get by one day at a time without pain. What else was there but to be serious, not to waste a moment?*

It took an hour for the bus to pass through the wide, bus-tling, store lined Route Four and then suddenly the scenery changed to mountainous wilderness. The noisy babble swirl-ing throughout the bus quieted down to mere whispers as the tired seminarians dozed off. Marlene fell asleep and her head drooped lazily onto Tyra's shoulders. She was happy that Marlene fell asleep, for that meant she wouldn't have to make endless conversation during the long ride. She was always awk-ward when it came to small talk and found it difficult to talk about minor details. She snuggled up to the side of the bus carefully so as not to jar Marlene's head, and leaned her own head against the window. When she exhaled, she could see the fog clear from the window, and she observed the steady rhythm of the fogging and the clearing of the glass in concert with her breathing. As the bus chugged up the narrow, wind-ing pass toward the peak of Wurtsboro Falls, she became mes-merized by the sight of the massive mountain range encircling the steep gorge and valley below. Snow flurried gracefully onto the tops of the tall pines like the sprinkling of powdered sugar on a tray of fresh jelly donuts warm from the oven, melt-ing as it landed. She imagined Joel's face on the other side of the window. The campgrounds weren't too far, and soon they would be together. She closed her eyes and began to doze.

Buses from Hartford, Springfield, Allentown and New York converged into the potholed parking area simultane-ously. High school kids and collegians poured out of them in mass tumult running around, slipping here and there on leftover icy patches on the concrete trying to find their friends whom they haven't seen since summer. Jessie caught up to a few in her group from Bridgeport, and Tyra was wandering around, stepping in between rows of suitcases being unloaded from the bellies of the buses, searching for Joel. It was freezing cold and the skies turned a bleak gray, a sign of an impending snowfall.

"Hey, kid," Joel said, tapping Tyra's shoulder. She turned around and her eyes popped open and she smiled. "Why, don't you look great!" he said giving her the once-over.

"Hey, you," she countered, taking hold of his hands in a restrained greeting, even as restrained as it was, too physically demonstrative according to Jewish law. They caught up on events at home and school, and after a while, buses roared away, leaving gusts of black exhaust fumes in the parking lot. Kids walked off with their luggage and just a few suitcases remained scattered here and there on the concrete. Joel and Tyra, still holding hands each took a step toward each other, and Joel pressed his lips against Tyra's forehead. They had made up to meet in front of the dining room before dinner, and parted ways. Tyra searched among the left over pieces of luggage for hers and not finding it, she sprinted toward the row of cottages away from the main house. She was assigned to Cottage # 4 which she would share with an advisor and six high school seminarians. The girls were busy unpacking and chatting when she walked in. She looked around but didn't see her luggage.

"Did anybody see a blue suitcase?"

"No. But it's so cold in here," Marlene said, huddling up, looking like an old lady. "Can't you do something?"

"As soon as I find my valise, I'll see if I can get us a heater for the cabin." She was already being a leader, and she was proud of herself. She was just about to go to Jessie's room in the main house to see if Jessie had her stuff, when Jessie barged into the cottage without even knocking. "Did you take my bag from the parking lot?" She was annoyed and Tyra felt humiliated being scolded in front of her girls.

"No. I was just coming to ask you the same thing."

"Oh no! I sense something bad here," Jessie said.

After searching the main house, and a few phone calls from the director to the bus company, it seemed the driver inadvertently left the Miller's two suitcases in the hold of the bus. The supervisor of the bus company assured the director that the driver would drop off the suitcases on his return run in a few days.

"A few days!" Tyra screamed, her eyes popping out of her head. "How can we manage without any of our stuff, my make-up?"

"You know what Daddy would say, don't you? Improvise," Jessie said, bothered more by the time she wasted packing than by the missing bag. "Well. Let's go scavenge up some clothes from the girls. Tomorrow we'll get a ride into town to get some toiletries. And stop looking so glum. It's not the end of the world, and you'll still sweep Joel off his feet." Jessie laughed with that nasty, know-it-all tone that Tyra despised so much.

"Shut up," she said, looking around to see if anyone over-heard Jessie.

After the soup course was served, Rabbi Singer and Rev Zemer got up to dance in the center of the floor. Although they were about the same age and build, they looked totally different. Rabbi Singer wore dungarees and a knit pullover, while Rev Zemer donned baggy black pants and a puffy, long-sleeved white shirt, tails sticking out along with his *tzitsis* (ritual undergarment). The teenagers called them Singer and Singer and while the rev strummed on his guitar, jumping up and down like a matchstick to the lively beat of a *hora* melody he was composing on the spot, the rabbi who was standing opposite him, hopped and squatted low, flailing his legs out in front of him in an animated *g'zatzkah,* which left him breathless. Hundreds of seminarians stood around them singing, clapping and jumping, the rickety planks of the wooden floor shaking and vibrating violently. "He's worse than Dovid," Mrs. Singer said, half-joking to Tyra who was standing alongside of her, watching as her eight-year-old son ran into the center to dance next to his father.

The hall was filled with the fury and joy, vibrations and sweat, the spirit and spirituality transporting the ordinary diners into a higher world of holiness. Finally the director approached the microphone. "Please, everybody," he shouted several times, "take your seats. We need to finish serving dinner. Please...." But his pleas only exacerbated the crowd's disobedience and vitality. In an instant, several boys seized Toby and Ralph and lifted them onto chairs and gave each a corner of a handkerchief. They were a great couple who met at a seminar two years before. They announced their engagement the past fall and were planning to get married at the next summer seminar. Toby's parents did not approve of her marrying someone so orthodox, a rabbinical student, no less. Her parents wouldn't make her a fancy wedding with hundreds of relatives, abundant hot and cold smorgasbords, billowy gowns and abundant floral arrangements. Her parents wouldn't even attend their wedding. They were experiencing what many first-born American Jews were.

Life in America for the first generation American-born Jewish parent was strange, posing some interesting dilemmas, leaving worried parents grappling with what they thought was best for their children. When the Janolskys, a pleasant couple who lived on the sixth floor in the apartment above Lazer and Hana, were told by their daughter, Estelle, that she was going to marry a heretofore secret boyfriend by the name of Gregory Malone, they became both irate and distraught. It was all Estelle could do to finally gear up the courage to tell them about him, and they swiftly began a tirade and crusade to get her to change her mind.

"A *shaygetz*. I won't stand for it," Mrs. Janolsky cried. "God gives me chance for one son-in-law, and look at what I get. A goy. *Mahatunim*, I want," she said, referring to the Yiddish word meaning parents of the groom, "people like me; we want the same things for our children…and look at what I get- *mahagoyim*," she said, enunciating every syllable of the term she unwittingly made up to describe her utter contempt and heartbreak at the prospect of having an in-law family out of the religion. Mrs. Janolsky wailed repeatedly day and night. Her husband's temper was much worse. He threatened to sit *shiva* for his only child. "I told you, you give the girl too much freedom, let her go off like she pleases. Now look at what you've done."

Hana would hear them moan and pace back and forth in the apartment above. "They make me crazy," she complained to Tyra once. "All the time, they carry on. He blames her, she blames him. A *zuchen vey*. I can't even hear my stories on the television. Let the poor girl live her life. Once you're in love, it's too late. Your mother, she never went out with a *shaygetz*. She knew this, to take such a chance. A good girl she was, and that it would break my heart. Just like you, Tyraleh, *myna shana madeleh*."

The Janolskys refused to attend whatever kind of wedding Estelle and Greg would have, even though Estelle said she would have kosher food for them. Greg's parents also refused to participate, so for all practical purposes, the young couple started their married life alone but for the justice of the peace who officiated.

Estelle invited her parents to dinner for the first time. "Please. Get to know Greg. He's wonderful. Give him a chance," she pleaded.

Mr. Janolsky rejected the offer.

"What am I to do?" Mrs. Janolsky cried. "Sit *shiva* like my father would have done for me, God forbid, if you were a *goy*? I won't lose my child."

"You go alone," Mr. Janolsky told his wife. And she did. After a time, she saw how kind Greg was and how happy he made Estelle. She grew to like him, even love him, and during Estelle's first pregnancy, she convinced her husband to visit, for the sake of the future grandchild, whom Estelle promised to raise as a Jew. And he did.

"Mom, would you ever sit *shiva* for me if I married a *goyishe* boy? Tyra asked her mother one night during the episodes when the Janolskys were screaming at Estelle.

"Do you know what that would mean? I never dated a non-Jewish boy just for that very reason. Sometimes you have to prevent things from happening and control your life."

"I know. But would you and Daddy sit *shiva* for me?"

"Oh, God. I would never be able to speak to you again. Or know my grandchildren. Sitting *shiva* for a child who intermarries is far worse than sitting *shiva* when an ordinary person dies."

"What do you mean?"

"When a person dies, you mourn for seven days, you remember all his good deeds and everyone sits around and tells stories about the person and they laugh and cry. Every year on the anniversary of his death, the *yahrzeit,* you light a candle. You say *Yiskor,* the memorial prayer and *Kaddish* in shul at the holidays. You remember the person with love and he is with you all the time in loving memory."

Tyra was spellbound by her mother's explanation.

"But," Kaye continued, "when a parent sits for a child she disowns, she sits only for an hour, gets up and says, 'her name is never to be spoken again.' It's as if the child never lived. It's just an awful, awful thing." Kaye's voice choked up.

Tyra's face paled and she wiped away tears from her cheeks with her nubby, nail-bitten fingers.

"Tyra, sweetheart, I can't be like the Janolskys. You are my life and my joy. But just don't test me. I had enough."

Tyra wrapped her arms around Kaye's waist. "I promise."

It was a confusing time for the first generation, at least in Tyra's circle of relatives and neighbors. Born in America, they were generally less religious than their European parents. They were consumed with the desire to assimilate into the real American society, where they would be free from the embarrassing, old-fashioned ways. Some even changed their *too-Jewish* last names to get jobs or be admitted to medical or law schools. When they themselves became parents, like Kaye and Sid, and the children grew up, they, too, dreaded those words, that their future daughter-in-law would be a *shiksa* or future son-in-law a *shaygetz*. So they tried to intensify the Jewish identity for their children that they distanced themselves from in their own youth. They sent them to Shabbatons in different communities, overnight gatherings from Friday sundown to Saturday night where young people would learn the nuances and intricacies of the Shabbath and observe it to the fullest.

They sent them to weekend conclaves and weeklong seminars where they would study with learned rabbis, young modern orthodox rabbis and cantors who had the ability and love to inspire them and teach them the wisdom of the Torah and how incorporating these precepts could enrich their lives. The rabbis showed them how the philosophy and law of the Talmud could lift them to a higher plane, that by utilizing the proper techniques of prayer: focusing straight ahead, to concentrate on God, standing erect and leaning back and forth, to move closer to Him, restraining coughs and even sneezes, in attempting to overpower the physical world and ascend to a higher spiritual plane where a true communion with *Hashem* could be achieved. That there was an actual correlation between their observance of *mitzvot* and the intensity of their spiritual satisfaction and with every bit of newfound Jewish *awareness*, came a greater respect for those heroes and martyrs whose courage and faith saved the Jewish people from extinction time and again, in *Eretz Yisroel* of the past, throughout the Diaspora and in the modern State of Israel. The ultimate success of these seminars brought fear into parents who thought their children would soon become too religious and alienate themselves from their relatives and friends. They might become judgmental, exhibiting the annoying "holier than thou" attitude, separating themselves into a narrow, rigid path of righteousness, denying opportunities and progress in the modern world. So the parents, the first generation born in America, had difficulty finding that perfect balance: either they were at risk of losing their children to assimilation or worse- intermarriage, or else, losing them to repentance and strict observance of Torah, or worse- to the State of Israel. And if teetering on this tightrope wasn't bad enough, there was always the not so subtle question that gentile skeptics enjoyed throwing out like an arrow, making it even harder to maintain a shaky balance and almost impossible to explain to the younger generation: *Where is your loyalty? If the United States goes to war with Israel, are you an American or a Jew? Therefore, how can you be both?*

The dining room captain was annoyed that the dinner service was running way behind schedule, and after reassuring the captain, the director took the microphone in hand again, urging the crowd to take their seats. But his pleas seemed to embolden the frenzied seminarians even more, at which point they lifted up onto chairs other couples who were going together or seemed to be. Tyra and Joel were lifted up, too. He was laughing, slipping and sliding in the chair, thoroughly enjoying himself. He flicked the napkin over toward Tyra several times, but she had dug her fingers into the sides of the seat so tightly that her fingers turned red from it, and she wouldn't let go to grab to napkin, not for dear life. Tyra was laughing and hanging on, and in the midst of all the tumult and joy, she caught a glimpse of Jessie dancing in the circle, singing and stomping her feet. Tyra's guilt at that moment was like a hot branding iron searing her skin. She gritted her teeth and closed her eyes to block out the pain. Jessie must be wishing, too, that she would be lifted high in a chair with some smart, gorgeous fellow holding the other side of a handkerchief. The shaky movement of the dancing below disoriented her. She felt dizzy and lightheaded. Her face turned pale. The next she knew, the rest of the meal was being served, and she had no idea of how she got to be sitting at her table.

"So you like, no, love to sing. I noticed you last night in the dining room. In another world you looked- so entranced," Rev Zemer said, as Tyra approached a shady spot under a grand oak tree during the afternoon break.

Rev Zemer had one leg up on the sole wooden Adirondack chair, strumming on his guitar, working out a new *niggun*-tune.

"I love to sing. It's like I'm in another world. If only I could carry a tune," she laughed. "You know, when I was in junior high I tried out for chorus, I wanted it so much, and the teacher gave me several chances to audition. She finally whispered to me, `You're flat,' and told me I could be in the class if I became the attendance monitor. I was so embarrassed, I thought I'd die. Sometimes she'd let me join the alto section if one of the girls was absent! Oh gosh!" she exclaimed, realizing at once how inappropriate the double entendre was. "I'm so sorry," she said, blushing and ashamed of her stupidity. Just one more reason why it pays to be quiet. She hardly ever spoke so incessantly and look how foolish it turned out.

"Ach," he sighed. "What a foolish teacher. Didn't she know that you carry your tune in your heart, not your vocal cords? You should always sing. It delights *Hakodesh Baruch Hu.*"

She couldn't believe that so effortlessly he took her awkward mistake and turned it into something so spiritual. But that's the kind of person he was, Zachariah Zalmonoshiavitz, a scholar and folk singer with a special soul. His long Polish name was an inexorable one, hardly ever spelled the same way twice, and impossible to pronounce. Even as a child, he had learned to avoid the awkwardness of his name and introduced himself simply as Zemer. Now that he was older, the teenagers at seminar accorded him the title Rav out of respect, and called him Rev Zemer, the Singing Rabbi.

Rev Zemer's appearance defied his scholarly reputation. He dressed like a sloppy Hasid: a white shirt, sleeves rolled up, half tucked in black baggy pants with his *tzitsis* hanging out. What set him apart was that he didn't just perform his music; he shared it, teaching others to sing, telling the meaning of the words. "You know, children. *Hashem* needs you. Your voice is holy to Him." As he spoke in a whisper as he twizzled the unkempt long strands of his curly black beard. When he finished speaking, he would strum and slowly start to hum, and only after the melody was repeated over and over again, growing in strength and volume, and until he and his audience were swaying and humming to the tune, only then he would sing the words, and teach them, one phrase at a time. Totally engrossed in his songs, the notes floated up on high as if to serenade *Hashem*, and one did not need to know the translation of the Hebrew to understand whether a particular tune was song a of joy or a lament, for everything with Rev Zemer celebrated life.

"So, Jessie is a problem for you? She's a wonderful person," he said. "Is that why you look so sad?" the rabbi asked as he leaned his chin on the guitar.

"I didn't know it was that obvious. It's so private; I shouldn't even talk about it. It's not fair to Jessie." Tyra always kept her feelings to herself, but tonight she felt as though she would explode. She needed an ear, someone to understand, and though she even felt guilty about verbalizing that which was so deeply painful to her for reasons she didn't even understand, she blurted out the unplanned words in syllables alternating with the hesitating gasps of her sobs. "It's as if someone tied a chain around my heart and keeps pulling it down, down, until I'm so low, I can only see beneath the ground. Why should I be happy when she's not?"

"Just because she's lonely now, doesn't mean she won't have a turn in the future. Nor should you waste the opportunities you have now. Each person must live every day and use the opportunity God has given, for in one moment the future is untold, and in the next it's gone. Do you think Jessie would be happier if she saw you deny yourself happiness?"

"No. Of course not...I don't know." She let out a sigh as she shook her head in frustration. "Everything you say is true, and I agree with you. My mother's been telling me this for years, and my grandmother and Rabbi Singer, too. My brain understands. I just can't get it to feel that way."

He looked at her with immense sadness, stroking his beard, squeezing the tip into a point. Then he started to speak, deliberately, slowly, in a melodic sing-song rhythm. "In all of the Torah, there are 613 commandments, and in not one of them," he said emphasizing the word one, "does *Hashem* command us to *feel* anything. One must respect or honor his parents. But not even the Holy One, blessed be He, can force us to feel a certain way. He knows that maybe, *has v'halelah*, God forbid, there are parents who don't deserve to be loved; still they must be respected. *Hashem* doesn't command us to love our neighbor. But we must not covet him. God commands us to do or not to do. But He leaves our feelings to us, to learn how to control them, *b'rtzono*, for the good. And this, my sweet dear Tyra, is your job, to redirect your feelings and take control, to take your potential for happiness and make it real, so that your happiness will make others happy as well."

She heard his every word and though he made perfect sense, and she would try to do as he said, she didn't think it would work; there was nothing he could do, nothing anybody could do. "I'm sorry. I don't mean to be so weak. But please, let's keep this talk to ourselves. I don't want to violate Jessie's privacy any more than I already did."

The educational highlight of the entire week was the presentation by the noted Rabbi Eliezer Kaplan, president of the Association of Orthodox Rabbis of America and the head of the first delegation of rabbis to tour the Soviet Union for the express purpose of establishing religious contact with the oppressed Soviet Jewish community. Personally risking his own safety, he penetrated the Iron Curtain, smuggling *tefillin* and siddurim in his baggage, speaking to Jews whose lives, just by showing up to hear him speak in the cities of Vilna, Riga, Kiev and Leningrad, were in danger.

"It's a very hard, bitter life for the Jewish people in the Soviet Union," Rabbi Kaplan said. "They deny us our places- the shul*s*, the kosher butcher shops. They forbid us our professions- no rabbis, no *mohels* (circumcisers). They even take away our time."

Our time. What does he mean? And he seems so solemn, so pensive, Tyra thought. Apparently others were struck by his words, as a total hush fell over the hall.

"You know of the few things our group was able to smuggle, the things that brought the greatest joy were the little pocket calendars- Jewish calendars. The communists are very clever. They know how to destroy a culture- a way of life. They forbid the printing, even the possession of Jewish calendars, for if you don't know when is Rosh Hashanah, and when is Sukkos and Shevuos, you forget, you don't observe, bingo- you forget to be a Jew."

Seminarians were touched by the denial of religious freedom for their counterparts in the Soviet Union. They were inspired by the risks the delegation and the Russian Jews took by sneaking in and accepting Judaica items, respectively. At Rabbi Kaplan's suggestion to start protest groups, a steering committee for SASO- the Struggles Against Soviet Oppression was formed on the spot, and the seeds of a vibrant and serious organization took hold. Before the evening was up, Joel started a letter campaign to synagogues, and petitions to the Senate and Congress. Other seminarians brainstormed ideas that they would take they would take back to their local communities even after seminar was concluded later that week. As the session was ending, Rev Zemer approached the microphone and on the spot began to sing a rousing refrain of what would become the movement's credo: *Am Yisroel hayom umahor- am l'olam vo'ed.* The people of Israel today and tomorrow- the people forever!

Tyra thought she might get involved and perhaps participate in a protest march at the U.N., but she wasn't sure how involved she'd become. How much change could she bring about? She certainly didn't have the guts to smuggle anything to anybody anywhere.

After the session, Joel went to the art barn to paint, and Rabbi Singer called after Tyra to stay for a moment.

"Listen," he said, motioning for her to sit down. He sat down in the chair next to hers, tilting it so he could face her. "My wife and I made a major decision recently, and I need to tell you about it. I have to tell the Board of Directors when I get back, and I don't want you to hear it from the neighborhood."

Tyra was puzzled. She couldn't imagine what he was talking about. He couldn't be getting a divorce. That would be impossible; they were such a happy family.

"We decided to make *aliyah* at the end of the school year. We're going to move to Jerusalem."

"Oh, Rabbi, you can't. You just can't leave!" Tyra was crushed. "What will we do without you?"

"You'll be fine." His eyes glanced downward toward the floor. He had formed some very close relationships in the small congregation, and although it was his choice to leave, it wasn't without a sense of loss. "It's hard to explain. I love the families at Anshei Shalom. Well, some of them," he qualified, chuckling. "It's just that they don't need me so much anymore. They don't ask enough questions, and the old men, they probably feel they know more than I do, even though I am the one with *S'micha*"- ordination.

It was true that there was some tension in the community. Rabbi Singer praised those members who were good people, although not overly observant. "Who is the better Jew," he would ask during a sermon, "the man who observes every tiny detail of Shabbos or *kashrus*, but ignores his elderly parents, or the man who needs to work on Shabbos, but manages to take his in-laws to visit the relatives in Brooklyn, and helps them with the cleaning and the bundles, and schleps them to their doctors?" Sometimes, when he spoke like that, Tyra thought he spoke with Sid in mind, for her father treated Lazer and Hana more like parents than in-laws, and more like beloved individuals than nudnicks. The elders in the community argued with the Rabbi. They felt he gave permission for the younger generation to be lax about the laws. But the Rabbi felt just the opposite, that by loosening the grip a bit, by embracing them and not being judgmental and critical, they would cling more to the tradition and assimilate less.

"But the real crux, Tyra, is that we don't have to be a people in exile any longer. We have our own place. Why should we submit to the whim and pleasure of another power? Why do *frum* store owners have to be subjected to blue laws? Do you know how hard it is for Mr. Solomon- he barely ekes out a living from his dry goods store- and the other shopkeepers to be closed Shabbos and Sunday, too? One Shabbos, should be enough. Don't you think so? Why should we struggle in the Diaspora when we have our nation, finally, finally, after thousands of years? Why should any Jewish kid have to sing Xmas carols in school, or fight to take an SAT exam for college on a Sunday instead of Shabbos?"

"But, Rabbi, you always helped us fight these battles. What will we do without you?"

He was already deep in his sermon, ignoring her as if he weren't talking to an individual, but his congregation, as if rationalizing his imminent forsaking of it. "And then there is the issue of the Soviet Union. Israel should be a nation for Jews who are free to choose Her, not just a pipedream for those who are enslaved around the world.

These are my questions that I ask myself and the answers are clear. The greater the *aliyah*, the stronger Israel will be, and it is the Jewish people's obligation to make her secure, so that we can live the way God intended for us to live, and can you imagine the joy to observe in a land where Judaism exudes from the streets and the air, the masses, not the minority?" His voice was strong and enthusiastic, as if he had already been transported to the Holy Land.

Tears were streaming down Tyra's face. He didn't even care about her, and she was ashamed of her selfishness and for Rabbi Singer to see her that way. "The shul won't be the same without you." She barely choked out the words as she got up and turned to leave. She tried to be polite and sophisticated, but her voice was cracking. "How could you?"

"Please don't be angry. We'll miss all of you, but this is our mission."

"I'm not angry, Rabbi," she called out. "It's just that I don't know what we'll do without you." Her voice trembled and she whispered so faintly, she didn't think he could hear her. She hoped he couldn't.

Without thinking twice when she left the main house, she headed straight for the arts and crafts barn. She drew her coat tightly around her as she plodded through the slushy path, studying the imprints made by her boots in the yellowish-white snow. She daydreamed along the way, of falling into Joel's arms, as if he were Troy Donahue cuddling Sandra Dee in the lighthouse in *The Summer Place.* He would console her of the great loss Rabbi Singer's move would bear on her, and kiss her gently. Of course they would stop far short of doing anything they would be ashamed of, for Jewish law was very clear what was expected of young people before marriage.

Joel's grandfather had been a respected rabbi in Europe and when he had immigrated to Brookline, he led a small congregation until his death in 1962. He wanted his son to become a rabbi, but Joel's father followed his own heart and became a lawyer. Joel was an outsider in his own future as his father and grandfather fought constantly about Joel's purpose in life- each tormenting Joel- one wanting him to cling to the old world traditions and the other urging him to take his thriving law practice and propel it into a greater conglomerate. Tyra understood his angst and frustration, and it was those things that made him quiet and inward, too. She knew what it was like to be torn, and she felt for him. Sometimes, when she was quiet and had that reflective look in her eyes, he would ask her what was wrong. "Nothing," she would answer, keeping her pain to herself, not wanting him to know how weak and selfish she was, not willing to betray Jessie's privacy. But they could sit comfortably together, his arm around hers, her head drooping on his shoulder. She didn't need to converse, and she felt less shy with him than anyone else. With Joel, she could just be.

All Joel wanted was to paint his heart out and empty his mind of all the bottled up images it contained. If only he could devote himself to his art and transfer to canvas where these revealed images could reside in the open and relieve him of his inner torment, the torment revealed in the depth of his eyes. It was that passionate seriousness reflected in his gaze that drew Tyra to Joel in the first place. He too was pulled and torn from the middle, and Tyra learned from him that conflict and suffering didn't only have to revolve about disease and deformity, but the more coveted, loftier ideals of talent and self-fulfillment.

Tyra opened the door to the barn cautiously as if not to disturb Joel who was lost in his painting. She stood quietly for a moment watching him as he paced back and forth from the table where his still-life props were set, adjusting the scales of justice and twisting the *tefillin* around her as if each one was strangling the other in a bizarre dance of the wicked and tormented. The *tefillin* he had inherited from his grandfather, a final treasured gift of expectation and guilt. The brown leather straps were worn and cracked by years of piety, the parchment within the boxes replaced recently to keep its *kashruth,* religious integrity, intact. An oversized volume of Talmud, used, read, whose pages rimmed in gold was lying opened to the section Joel's father referred to in a big case involving business ethics. Tyra closed the door and started to walk across the barn to the back where Joel was. The studio was crowded with easels and paints. There were two tables with molds for ceramic statues and a kiln was tucked in a far corner. Tubes of paints, brushes and cans of varnish and turpentine were scattered all around the cavern-ous space, and crumpled rags were lying haphazardly on the floor. If she didn't know better, it looked as if Jessie came and left a mess.

She glanced at Joel's canvas and saw the impressionistic image of a distorted lady of justice, out of proportion, mystically tall and curvy, whose face was composed of elongated features- an overpowering nose, unevenly arched dark eyebrows hovering over beady eyes which seemed to oversee everything about her. The straps of the *tefillin* were wrapped three times around her, but her expression was strong and it was impossible to distinguish whether she was the tormentor or the tormented. Joel remained oblivious to Tyra's presence. She found it curious that he was fussing so much with his props and symbols when the image he was painting was so intensely expressionistic and heretical. Nonetheless, there was something so gripping about the canvas which exuded a ghostlike eerie suffering, and the more she studied it, the more she understood and the deeper she was drawn into it. Despite the electric heater that was plugged into the corner, the barn was cold and drafty, and she shrugged off a chill, huddling in her coat. She didn't know whether she called his name too softly for him to hear or if he were lost in his still-life, probably a bit of both, but he continued to arrange his props she approached the easel.

"Joel," she whispered. "Why don't you just paint? You're not even doing a still-life." She tapped his shoulder.

"Ahhhh!" He turned around and screamed, as if he were surprised by a mugger, and Tyra jumped backward as she gasped.

"For heaven's sake," he said. "Want to give me a heart attack?" She could tell he was more annoyed than amused.

"Did you know about Rabbi Singer? He's making *aliyah*."

"Not now. I've got this concept, this image. It's strangling me," he said as he grabbed his throat, as if the straps of the *tefillin* were twisted around his neck, choking him. He walked back and forth, viewing his table, struggling to place the straps of the *tefillin* with the proper angle of light hitting it. "I've got to get it out and I just can't get it right."

"But, I don't know what I'm going to do. They're everything to me."

"And everything's about you. Leave me alone. I need to do this." His arms were flagellating in exasperation. A tress of his shiny pompadour had fallen onto to forehead, and he slicked it away. Despite the raw chill in the barn, beads of perspiration gathered over his brow.

Tyra's cheeks burned; she could barely hold back tears at his recrimination of her. She backed away three steps, turned around. When she reached the door, she heard him call out, offering an apology. "Later. We'll talk later."

Like hell we will. She had her needs, but not at the expense of her pride. *Nobody talks to me like that and gets away with it,* she thought, and then the dangling participle popped up in her head like a piece of toast from a toaster, *except Jessie.*

Speaking in his mellifluous voice and poetic rhythm, with a hint of genuine European accent, he began. He put his foot up on a stool, and leaned his body over his guitar, clutching it so close to his body as if it were stuck to it like glue, stroking it ever so gently, so as not to disturb the serenity of God's domain.

"*Yesterday, my friends,*" Rev Zemer said in a whisper as the pick in his fingers slid down the strings,

> "*I spoke to a person who is suffering…*
> *I don't know the solution,*
> *and I was sad that I couldn't make things better.*
> *I returned to my bunk*
> *to prepare the melodies for the liturgy*

261

I picked up the siddur,
the prayer book, (he explained to those who might
not know, ever careful not to make anyone feel less
worthy)
You know my friends, people pray and think the answer is that
Hashem gives them what they want
But the truth is,
when you pray with your whole heart and soul,
the answer is not that Hashem does what you pray for,
it is that He listens,
and when someone pays attention to you,
you know you are worthy,
and when someone hears your pain,
you know you are not alone.
And you know my friends,
for me a miracle happened
and the holy book fell open to a page
on its own accord,
the Hand of Hashem Himself
put His blessed finger on the exact place,
Psalm 121,
and the lines bolted out in front of me
and the rest of the page receded into a blur,
and I was struck,
that we may not have answers,
but none of us,
has to be alone.
And this is the melody,
that poured out from my heart,
and as I sing it,
follow along,
and to the special person who helped me last night,
thank you, for releasing this composition from my soul."

Tyra was struck by the impact their talk had on Rev Zemer. He understood exactly how she felt, for she was more articulate with her feelings and with her eyes than with her words. He was the one who gave his time, offered compassion. Yet it was she who made him realize his own limitations, his inability to bring understanding into her confused and sorrowful world, and now he was the one who thanked her.

Rev Zemer started to sing the refrain, holding the first syllable for a long double note... and he strummed a chord at the end of every phrase, a lingering, mellow, full-bodied string of notes that vibrated through the semi-circle of seminarians huddled around in blankets, sitting on the ground, the notes flickering all around the flames of the campfire.

"Es-so ainai, I lift up my eyes,
el-l heharim, to the mountains,
may-ayin ezri yavo, from whence my help will come."

During the song, Joel had edged up closer to her. He grasped her hand and she turned around startled. "Are you crying?" he asked, as tears fell down her cheeks "I thought you were just snifling in the cold air."

"You wouldn't understand," she said as she pulled her hand out of his, turning her back and walking away. She even had a faint smirk, pleased with her strength to not only resist his appeal, but to rebuke him as well.

At two in the morning, a fire truck careened its way through the curvy mountain roads into the camp premises and stop short in front of the arts and crafts barn. It was ablaze and throngs of seminarians and advisors ran toward the commotion. In minutes, the entire structure was demolished into a pile of charred rubble. The smell of burnt wood and paints permeated the cold night air. Tyra found Joel in the crowd, and despite her fear at being rejected, she grasped his hand.

Joel was quiet and shaken. His eyes glazed at the debris. He didn't move, and he let Tyra's hand rest motionless in his.

"I wonder which pile my canvas is in," Joel said, shaking his head in disbelief and despair. All his creativity, his devotion, destroyed. "I couldn't even do it once, no less replicate it now." His voice was low and downtrodden, his height squashed, his body bent toward the ground, as if a hunk of steel were plopped on his back, weighing him down. Tyra felt a touch of satisfaction. He must have felt as abused and alone as he made Tyra feel the other night when she was heartbroken after learning of Rabbi Singer's upcoming *aliyah. Serves him right.* But her meanness upset her as well. That's not the way she was raised. Her gentle, tender grandmother, Hana, would be horrified. Without a word, she grasped his hand and squeezed it, a silent gesture forgiving him his prior rejection of her. Oblivious of her kindness, he slithered his hand out of hers, turned away from the crowd of teens who were milling around watching the firemen plough through the wreckage, and stumbled back toward his bunk.

Tyra stood still, once again crushed by this boy and by her keen sense of empathy. Angry at her own stupidity, she grit her teeth until a sharp pain shot up from her jaw all the way up her cheek toward her temple. An image of the fire that had barely been put out in front of her lent itself to the image of Hana suffering the hot, searing, burning pain of tic douloureux.

In what used to be the corner of the barn, a fireman who had been rummaging through the piles of ash and remnants of things that used to be- cans of paint, stirrers, pottery shards, bent down and picked up what looked like a long strap with two boxes attached to it. The fireman held it up in front him, examining it curiously, jiggling the strap, the boxes dangling a little dance of their own as he walked toward the crowd. Tyra started to breathe hard. The fireman was holding a miracle. Could it be that Joel's grandfather's precious *tefillin* survived the carnage. Tyra ran toward the fireman. "Please, sir, what you have in your hand, it's very special."

"You don't say? It looks sort a strange. What is it?"

She explained the significance of how a devout man wrapped his head and his heart in God's commandments, every morning, to remind him of how he was to live his life that day. "Here," she said, as she reached for the box and pointed to where the parchment was kept. "It's very old, and coveted. It belongs to the artist who was painting here before." Except for being worn, it seemed to be intact, oblivious to the fire it had just been part of.

The fireman shook his head as if all of this, the fire, the weird strap that men wound around their heads and arms, was a bizarre as well as awesome scene out of the twilight zone. "It's the only thing that survived."

"That's truly in-cred-ible," she said slowly, trying to grasp the enormity of the find. "It's a miracle. She reached out her hand to touch it gently, as if her soft caress of the worn, cracked leather could damage it whereas the inferno couldn't. "Can I give to the boy who owns it?"

He held it out for her to take. "Be careful," he said. "It's still hot and dangerous around here." He turned and walked to the fire truck where all the other firemen had gathered, putting their gear back on the truck, getting ready to leave the scene.

The seminarians, too, started to dissemble now that the drama was winding down. Tyra saw Marlene walking toward the bunks. "Wait up," she called out, and as Tyra caught up to her, she put her free hand through Marlene's arm, and the two walked back slowly to their bunk. They climbed the three rickety stairs and Tyra went straight to her bed. It was impossible to distinguish the noise from her exhalation of a deep sigh or the swoosh of air that escaped from the thin mattress as she plunked herself down.

She caressed the *tefillin* that were still in her hands, and as she leaned forward, she pressed one of the phylacteries against her forehead. After a few peaceful moments, she stuffed the *tefillin* in her near empty cubby holes. The suitcases still hadn't been returned and the sisters were still "improvising" with their friends' clothes. Tyra would give the *tefillin* to Joel in the morning. She was tired and confused. God took more than He gave. Joel missed a miracle, Rabbi Singer was abandoning the congregation for Israel, and Jessie, at the age of twenty, still had not had a real date.

Tyra got up early to catch Joel right after morning prayers, on his way to the dining room for breakfast. She saw him walking alone and ran up to him, grabbing him by his arm.

"Joel, wait up. I have to tell you something."

His face was pale and he had bags under his eyes. "Not now, Tyra. I'm not inter…"

She cut him off. "But you don't understand. Something fantastic happened last night…"

"I lost everything last night. Everything went up in smoke and all you can think about is you. Did they find your precious lost suitcase and what, did Rabbi Singer decide to stay in America after all?"

"Joel, please, can you just listen?" Tyra was crushed once again. She had been excited to share a modern-day miracle with him and instead he cut her down, missing everything special. She tried to hold back tears, but to no avail.

He looked at her, shaking his head and continued on toward the dining hall, stooped over and broken.

For Tyra, seminar might as well have been over right then and there. She felt like hiding for the next few days, which she knew would be torture for her. She returned to her bunk, where she decided she would make no further effort regarding Joel. He was a lost cause. How much hurt could she endure? She fingered the fragile *tefillin* in the cubby, deciding to mail them to him when she returned home.

"Dad says we should pack half our clothes in each of our bags in case one of our suitcases gets lost again," Tyra said as Jessie was folding and packing a small pile of clothes stacked up on the bed. It was late August of 1963 and the sisters were preparing for summer seminar. In ordinary circumstances Sid's advice would have been appreciated and followed, but Jessie just continued packing without saying a word.

"Why are you taking such a small satchel, anyway?" Tyra prodded, annoyed at being dismissed by Jessie.

"I'm tired of being weighed down by clothes that don't look good anyway. Even with those damn corsets and girdles," she said, pointing to her underwear drawer, "Mom thinks it's such a good idea." With that Jessie picked up a week's worth of them which she had taken out to pack, and stuffed them back into a messy overstuffed drawer, slamming the drawer shut with a sigh of approval. "I'm freeing up!" she said with that stubborn lilt of pride in her voice, color coming into her cheeks, giving her a spark of energy.

"But you need a costume for the masquerade party and a formal for the farewell banquet," Tyra insisted, oblivious to the frustration Jessie was struggling with, "and an outfit for the talent show."

"If you want to be a paper doll fashion-plate, go ahead. Be my guest. Just leave me alone."

Tyra's eyes smarted. She never got used to Jessie belittling her, pushing her away; and, although she did it all the time, it still hurt. "Fine," she screamed, "but when you freeze your tush off in the dead of night, don't come to me for an extra sweater."

By the time the sisters arrived at Penn Station, Tyra was dragging her valise down the crowded passageway toward the ticket counters. Jostled and spun around by a hurried morning commuter, Tyra's eyes smarted when the corner of her hard luggage slammed into her knee and she groaned in pain. "Damn, my stockings ripped," she said looking at Jessie with both admiration and resentment who, for spite it seemed, was swinging her tote-bag freely, weightlessly from her shoulder, whistling the best whistle of any girl Tyra knew. "We're early. Let's rest for a second."

She put her suitcase on the ground and sat on the edge of it without even waiting for Jessie's consent.

"Listen, Ty, I'm not going to seminar with you. Sorry I was so mean to you last night, but I didn't want Mom and Dad to get wind of it. And close you mouth," she said to her shocked sister, "you look like a goon."

"What do you mean? Where are you going?" Her heart started to race, fearing for her mysterious sister, apprehensive about being alone.

"I can't tell you. Rabbi Singer will ask you about me. Just tell him I'm helping Dad at the store."

"You mean you want me to lie, don't you?"

"Whatever."

"What if something happens? How will we know where you are?"

"I'll be home the same night you get back. I'll meet you right at this ticket counter between four and five. Don't worry. And just in case, there's a letter in my corset drawer- then get

268

the police." She chuckled. "Stop being so mortified. I'll be fine. I'll be back."

Tyra watched from her seat on the bus as Jessie walked away. A sickening feeling came over her even before the bus closed its doors and made way to the meeting point at the Red Apple. *What kind of a sister am I? What if something happens to her? How could I leave her go off like that? How could I be so irresponsible? Are Mom and Dad going to have a fit like when I didn't bother finding Jessie before the movie started in the bungalow colony?* "You have to look out for your sister. Don't be so selfish next time," Kaye had admonished then. *Why? Why? Why?* The questions reflecting Tyra's inadequacies were piling up in her head like a beehive hairdo teased from the crown twelve inches into the air. Her head started to throb and she looked to make sure she had her Emperin with her. She would take them as soon as they stopped for a roadside break. But it all wasn't her fault and the anger she felt was eating her up. *Why is Jessie doing this to me? How can she put me in such a bind? How can I let her control me and she does whatever she wants?* More whys? And where? *Where was she?*

Seminar had lost its magic. Joel didn't come. He hadn't even responded to the several casual notes Tyra had written him. Despite her show of independence and her genuine hurt, she cared about him, and wondered what he was doing and if he ever recovered from his loss at the barn. She had his *tefillin* for months, and had just gotten around to sending them to him. Despite the friction with Jessie, her bossiness and pushiness, Tyra missed her being there. They belonged together. Their parents thought they were together, and Tyra was uneasy and felt guilty at the deception, even though she had nothing to do it. She was consumed with where she was, who she was with and most of all, if she were alright.

Tyra went through the days and motions of seminar list-lessly and without the fervor and exhilaration, the sheer joy she had always felt with the others. The prayers were hollow, the songs in the dining hall were pale, and she hardly got up to dance. She just kept wishing the week would be over and she and Jessie both would be home.

The highlight or really the low point of seminar was Toby and Ralph's wedding Wednesday. On Tuesday night, Toby went down to the lake escorted by a few of her best friends who encouraged her to dunk in the frigid water and recite the blessings of immersion. You could hear Toby's squeals as she splashed in the icy waters and could only imagine as she ran into the open towels held lovingly by her friends waiting to warm her up as she ran back onto the shore.

Tyra didn't get it. Kaye would do anything for Jessie to have a wedding, have a man take care of her, love and shelter her. Yet here was a young couple, alone, getting married on an empty tennis court- without any family to share the excitement- just a few friends, some acquaintances and tons of strangers, semi-narians all, standing as witnesses on a tennis court far away in the mountains during a seminar retreat. A wedding without a luscious smorgasbord, fabulous flowers and bouquets, musi-cians and ball gowns. Toby wore a simple white shirtwaist dress and a crowd of boys carried Ralph on a chair down the length of the tennis court to meet his bride and cover her face with a veil in the *b'dekkin* ceremony. And if the whole situation wasn't sad enough, the skies opened up in a cold, blustery rain and everyone got soaked throughout the entire ceremony. Toby's pretty curls fell into straggly strips around her face, dripping raindrops and smudging her delicate make-up, leaving differ-ent colored marks all over her face. But just at the end, when Ralph smashed the glass to hearty bursts of *Mazel Tovs*, the sun started to come up, and people started to point up to the sky. There was a beautiful rainbow that blossomed out of nowhere from the lakes in the valley all the way to the mountains on the other side. It was as if a miracle happened, and you could hear the mutterings of seminarians and rabbis reciting the blessing when they see a rainbow. *Baruch atah Adonai Elohanu melech haolam, zochar habrit v'ne'eman b'vrito v'kyam b'ma'amarro,* (Blessed are you Lord our God, King of the Universe who remembers the covenant and is faithful to the covenant and keeps His word), and the hosts of 'Amens' as people witnessed each other's proclamations of God's promise.

On the last Friday morning of seminar, four ninety-minute classes were scheduled simultaneously, four rabbis giving talks on different aspects of Judaism- one on the history of Hasidism, another on Zionism, and one on the role of storytelling and legend from the Talmud. But it was Rabbi Singer's class that was always packed and only those who showed up too late to get a seat filtered into the other sessions. It had grown into such a problem that at winter seminar there was talk of assigning students to sessions arbitrarily to even out the attendance and most important, spare the other rabbis of hurt feelings. But since this was the last seminar before Rabbi Singer's *aliyah,* the administration decided to leave things the way they were, rationalizing the students wanted as much of Rabbi Singer as they could get before he left. Surely the other rabbis would find this perfectly natural and not take offense. It would be hard to mandate a course of study for seminarians who came lovingly and voluntarily to find their own level of spirituality. Seminar was going well: inspiring the young generation of Jews, arming them with knowledge, stirring them to action, strengthening the link from generation to generation.

Tyra got to the lecture hall early and got a prime seat in the front row. This was Rabbi Singer's last speech, and kids filtered in left and right to hear him. The buzz of chatter and scraping of metal chairs moved here and there to accommodate friends sitting together came to a grinding halt when the rabbi walked in the room. Suddenly a burst of applause rang out, and the rabbi raised his arms in protest, motioning for everyone to quiet down, as a faint blush exposed his humility. He approached the lectern, put down his folder, and without any introductory comments or salutations he began, his thunderous voice vibrating through space.

"*Zedek, zedek, tirdof.* Once a young student of mine asked what good was our Torah in a world that didn't obey- where there was so much cruelty and evil. And I remember feeling so bad for a person so young to be overwhelmed by such anguish and anger. She felt so deeply. And it is a wonderful quality to feel and be aware of what is happening in the world and not to turn your back on the experiences of others. What am I getting at?"

He stopped speaking as he surveyed the audience in front of him, grabbing their attention, catching their gaze, sucking them in. He winked at Tyra who was sitting right in front of him. When he was satisfied that the audience was interested, that their curiosity needed to be quelled, he continued.

"Feeling. Being sensitive, that is only the first step. "*Zedek, zedek, tirdof*'. Who knows what that means? It is the phrase that is written above the Holy Ark in every synagogue in the world. "Justice, Justice, Pursue." Why say justice twice? Because it is so important it must be repeated. And justice- the word in Hebrew comes from the root, righteous. It is good to be compassionate, sensitive and help other people. But it is harder to mete out justice- just as we have free will to choose our way- we must know that our choices have consequences, and sometimes our deeds call for punishment, for lessons to be taught- for justice to be served."

By now, Rabbi Singer was out of breath. His fists were closed and shaking in the air. Beads of perspiration were dripping down his cheeks. The room was silent as the spellbound class followed Rabbi Singer's every word, every gesture. Not a single drop of spittle winding up in his moustache went unnoticed. Tyra didn't quite know just where his thoughts were leading them. She didn't possess that special quality of intellectual prowess she saw in her friends or those who stood out. She felt inferior because of it, skeptical that no matter how diligent she was, it was a skill beyond her reach. Nonetheless she was riveted, engrossed, sitting upright and forward in the chair waiting anxiously for the rabbi to reveal his purpose.

"Do you know what happened yesterday? It was in the newspaper this morning. Things are changing in this country. And I am so proud that our young people, Jews, are taking part and making it happen. Replacing injustice with justice."

Slowly Tyra seemed to pale. She felt a heavy fog draping over her as the rabbi's words sounded more and more muted until she heard only a garbled murmur swirling around her ears but not coming into the canal, where the syllables would be heard, each loud and distinct, with its own special meaning. Now nothing made sense. She filled with worry, like an unattended bathtub just about to overflow. She shrank back against the chair as her worry began to mix with guilt, the all too familiar guilt that was always nearby, ready to pop up and spoil whatever peace there was. She should have known. *Stupid. I'm so stupid.* She was full of recrimination and condemnation. She hadn't even had a clue.

"Jessie," Tyra cried out, as she saw her sister approaching their meeting place. "I was so worried. Where were you?"

"I'm fine. Can't you see?" Jessie answered. "I had a great time. The march was out of sight…"

"March!" Tyra exclaimed. "Oh my God," she said, raising her hand to her mouth in shock. "I knew it. Where? Was it dangerous? Are you okay?"

"Stop being so melodramatic. All I know is that there's a lot of injustice in this world and I'm not going to stand by on the sidelines."

It was just like Jessie to be daring and fearless. Tyra was simultaneously in awe and jealous of her. Maybe that was the blessing in disguise of scoliosis. What the deformity took away from Jessie's height, it gave back to her in stature.

"You have to be committed to something, Little One. Otherwise, nothing gets done. All of life is risk- just one big chance after another."

Little One. Tyra lingered on the words. She didn't call her Kiddo as usual, she thought. She was still her condescending self, but a little more gentle.

Jessie smiled. "Come on. Let's hurry," and together they walked briskly through the station and down the stairs until they got to the shuttle to the IRT line.

"Come on. Tell me." Tyra hated to beg for tidbits of information, but that was one of the ways Jessie used to keep the upper hand over her. She was always excluded from Jessie's confidence; she was never good enough or old enough to share. Why should now be any different?

"Wait until we get settled," Jessie said.

They got off the shuttle and walked through the tunnel to the platform of the IRT line. When the train came, they settled into seats for the noisy, shaky ride home through the underground, Harlem and the Bronx.

"Okay. Now let's talk. You first," Jessie said, smug and overbearing, knowing Tyra would cave in. What's the latest from seminar?"

"A lot." Tyra filled Jessie in about Ralph and Toby's wedding- the mikvah, rainbow, Rabbi Singer and Soviet Jewry. Now, you tell me. What did you do?"

"Listen, Tyra. Mom and Dad will kill me, so please keep quiet," Jessie said as the subway roared through Harlem.

"Just like that. Keep me in the dark and expect such a humongous favor."

"Well, that's just it. I didn't tell you before because if you didn't know, you wouldn't be able to say anything and neither of us would get into trouble. I went to Memphis where we marched and helped Negroes register to vote."

"Tell me everything. I knew you went down South. Start from the beginning."

"Sure you did. After I left you, I went to the Trailways bus station. The bus was filled with college kids and we went down to Memphis, singing songs. It was great. So much spirit, but we didn't know what we were in for. We ended up at a Comfort House, a three story rickety building, you know, like one of those old main houses in the bungalow colonies. Two representatives from SNIC, a tall fellow in his mid-twenties, and a girl about the same age came on the porch. 'Listen up,' the girl shouted. 'Each room inside has four beds, so count yourselves four girls or four boys and take the first available room till y'all accommodated for. Wash up, settle in and report down to the main room in thirty minutes for snacks and instructions.' The boy was much softer. He thanked us for coming and told us, 'It not pretty here, so watch out for yourself and each other.'"

"Who did you room with? Tyra asked. "What were the girls like?"

"That's another story. I wound up alone. I kind of noticed the girls were eyeing me…"

"So what hap…

"Wait. I'm getting to that. The boy from SNIC, he came over to me and invited me to stay at his house. 'It's more comfortable than the Comfort House,' he said, laughing at the irony of it. 'More private, anyways.' His name was Colter and he thanked me for coming all the way from New York to help change the world. We got to his shabby, wooden cabin. His mother was a gas. She looked at me like I was from outer space. She said I was cute except for the monkey on my back."

"That's awful. I'm sorry," Tyra said shaking her head.

"What are you sorry for? Then she said something like us Jewesses coming down invading their land, sticking our noses, long noses at that, where they didn't belong. So you know what I told the bitch?"

"Oh, I could just imagine."

"I said, and just like this too," Jessie said, with her hands on her crooked hips and her head held high, 'We were slaves once too, and they had cotton over there in Egypt as well.'"

"There was cotton in Egypt?" Tyra was shocked.

"I don't know, Kiddo. I just thought it was a good thing to say at the moment. She softened up after that, so I guess it worked.

"The next morning we walked up and down the dirt paths in teams of three with at least one boy in each group. Colter, Debbie, another New York girl, and I knocked on the doors of shacks, explaining to the residents how important it was to register to vote. Despite how dangerous it was to them, most signed up on the spot. Most made their marks by x, and we got almost seventy signatures the first day alone. It wasn't easy though, as the white townspeople stood around taunting us, pelting us with trash and raw eggs, calling out, 'Go home nig-ger-lovers,' 'Jew-bastards' and the like.

"A rock came hurtling through the air towards my cheek and Colter grabbed me and threw me down to the road, shielding my face with his broad hands. The rock grazed his shoulder. He winced but didn't utter a sound.

"'Oh, God. Thanks,' I said, panting. I can't believe how shaken I was. Then the marshals blasted us with water hoses to break us up and sic dogs on us, too. The dogs barked so loud and jumped so ferociously, that for the first time in my life I was terrified of animals. Me, of all people. No wonder why the survivors hate dogs- remember that old Mrs. Wilensky in the bungalows?"

"The lady with the numbers on her arm that used to hang laundry all the time?"

"Yes. Remember how she was so afraid of dogs and the boys used to make fun of her. Well, now I can understand why. And to tell you the truth, I think the cops down there were more vicious than the dogs.

"Anyway I fell down to the ground, and people were falling all over me. I broke my glasses in the melee."

"You should be careful, Jess." Her voice reflected the concern she felt despite the usual tension. "You can't afford to get yourself injured," she said trying to wrest Jessie's knapsack from her lap.

"Leave it. I'm fine. I can manage. I always do, don't I? Besides, the Jews in Russia will never get out if it's up to you and your pussy attitude."

Tyra stopped dead in her tracks as her cheeks reddened with shame. She felt like a crumpled up piece of tin foil that Jessie tossed into a garbage pail. *Gentle,* she thought. *Not quite.* But maybe she was right. Tyra was all feelings and no action. She needed to get involved, to **do** something. She needed to discover what it was. She would. As soon as Tyra felt that determination, she felt uplifted, like her life mattered, that even though she wasn't as smart as she wanted to be, or as socially savvy as some of the popular girls, she would make a difference.

"Colter helped me up." Jessie continued without even noticing the effect she had on Tyra, as if nothing happened between them.

"Colter. That's a pretty romantic name."

"Life down there is no easy picnic for them. Afterward, he took me to his house. Colter and I washed up and the bitch gave us something to eat. He was really gentle. We took a long walk down this dirt path and we sat in a little knoll off the beaten track. He could tell I was bruised, I guess from the way I was squirming and uncomfortable. He rubbed my hump-it didn't bother him at all. He saw my scar and traced it with his fingers. He said my incision looked like broken railroad tracks. Mom would get a kick out of that. She always complained the doctors butchered me and tore my skin apart like hungry dogs. Grandpa is more of an artist, she used to say, his hand-stitched hems almost invisible. Anyway, I thanked him for taking the brunt for me, and helping me in the melee. Do you know what he said?"

"No, tell me, and what did he look like?"

"He said he had taken plenty of brunting before and it looked like I had taken plenty of brunting myself. I love that word brunting. It's not a real word, but it says so much. He showed me his scars too- he was whipped and beaten all the time when he was a kid. He was so sweet. He had broad shoulders, not too tall, and real curly hair." Jessie had that gleam in her eye, that little tease that always drove Tyra crazy.

"Oh my God, Jessie. Colter was Negro, wasn't he? Daddy will kill you."

"He was so gentle. After a while, my back spasms relaxed, and the burning stopped. I felt so good. He pulled me toward him and we…."

"Don't stop now, Jess."

The ice seemed to melt between the sisters. Jessie even gave Tyra a few tidbits about Colter, enough even to let on that theirs was not just a social justice commiseration but a romantic liaison. If they weren't encumbered by their baggage, they would have reached over to hug each other.

"Did you lose… oh my God, you didn't."

"Stop with the 'oh my gods'. You're so annoying. Did I or didn't I? Do hunchbacks have more fun? Only your hairdresser knows…"

"Shut up. You're obnoxious."

"Lose. I spent my best years in a hundred pound plaster cast while all my friends were partying. How much more time do you think I have to lose? And you and Mom sit around and mope on Saturday nights for me. Don't think I didn't know."

Jessie didn't lose her virginity so much as she gained her sexual validation, and though she had a delicious taste of passion and tenderness, she still didn't have a real date, and it broke Tyra's heart. She could barely hold back tears. No matter what she tried to do for Jessie, it never seemed to be good enough or appreciated. All the suffering Jessie's back caused her made her learn how to put up a front, and no one could tell if what she said was sincere or not. The elusive Jessie. Tyra couldn't stand it.

"Oh Jess. Mom and Dad will kill you."

"Only if you tell them. It's strange, Mom and Dad teach us to be kind and fair and generous. Daddy helps out strangers all the time. And when it comes to us, they're so protective and narrow-minded, afraid for our safety, afraid of anything different. They don't want us to jeopardize anything or take any risks. It must be a Jewish thing."

"I know," Tyra said. "They just don't want us to get hurt. Don't be so hard on them."

"Hurt!" Jessie raised her voice. "They should know better. You know how to spell *Life*? H-U-R-T. Life." She enunciated each letter as if reciting a second grade spelling exercise. "Let's get home, Kiddo. And don't rat on me either."

"And stop calling me Kiddo. I can't stand it anymore."

They descended the stairs of the el in silence, walking the rest of the way together, each with unequal amounts of spiritual exhilaration and physical exhaustion. Jessie was determined to change the world, and Tyra would think about how she would try to change the world.

Kaye was preparing veal cutlets for dinner when the girls arrived home. "How was seminar?" she asked, grabbing each one around their shoulders, pulling them so close to her that their satchels flopped against their legs. "I missed you so much. It was so quiet around here."

"Great. Seminar was great." Tyra answered as they dragged their suitcases to the bedroom. Jessie, not wanting to lie, kept her mouth shut and quickly stole into the bedroom.

Kaye turned her attention back to the cutlets that were sizzling in the skillet. She shook her head and smiled in disbelief. "What's going on with you two? It's never so quiet."

"Tyra." Kaye called after her. "There's a letter for you on your desk. I think you might be interested right away."

Tyra dropped her bags and her heart throbbed as she recognized the handwriting and tore the envelope in a flash.

Dear Tyra,

You have no idea how much you mean to me. You gave me new hope and because of you I found myself.

Tyra was beside herself with joy. She couldn't wait to see him next, perhaps on his next trip to New York when he would settle in to the dorms at Columbia.

That morning when I received the package you sent with my grandfather's tefillin, I realized that I had to take a risk and stand up for myself because God knows, my father wasn't going to help me. I guess I am a terrible disappointment to my great rabbinical grandfather and to my father as well. I am not going to be a rabbi nor a lawyer. When you made me see the miracle of those tefillin that survived that awful fire, I thought I lost everything that night of the fire: all the art that was within me went up in smoke. But when I held those worn boxes treasured by my grandfather that survived that devastation, I

knew that I was born to treasure my talent and my true love.
So screw Columbia and law school. Tyra, I know you are...

Tyra's heart sank as she read. She could barely see the letters on the pages. So this is my reward, she thought, of being honest and smart and helping...

proud of me. For the first time I feel free. I am ready to explode.
I can't wait until my paints fly on canvas with abandon and
joy, without the heartache of my father's yoke on me, but that
can wait. I will always have my talent. But what can't wait is
our people's freedom. I am going to the Soviet Union as a repre-
sentative of SASO. I don't know how things will work out, and
hopefully I won't get arrested and sent to Siberia, but I must do
something. Am Yisroel hayom umachor!

Thank you, Tyra. I don't think I would have ever realized
my purpose were it not for you.

One more thing. Forgive me for being a real creep.

With love always,
Joel.

Just like that. That's it. Tyra crushed the papers in her hands, the fountain ink smearing on her fingers from her tears. He was a wonderful boy but she was not his true love.

One night, when Sid came home particularly late, and Kaye was already playing mah jongg, he went upstairs to Hana's house for supper. Hana had cleaned up the kitchen and after serving Sid a plate of pot roast and potatoes, she sat down with him and rested. The years of hard work and pain had taken a toll on her. Her eyes were tired and sunken into her face, but her skin was still pure and smooth. Her salt and pepper hair had changed to an almost pure white. Tyra still put blue into it every few months to hide the yellow streaks. Thyroid problems added even more

281

weight to her already abundant torso and wide hips, and poor circulation caused her to limp when she walked.

"You work so hard, Sid. It's time you should take it easy a little. Maybe sell the store and get a job someplace," she said, her voice gentle and tired.

"I wish. This is so good," he said as he put another piece of meat on his fork.

She started to sing a little ditty she had sung to her grand-children throughout the years:

Moishe had a candy store
Business was so bad
Asked his wife
What to do
This is what she said:
Take a bissel kerosene
Spill it on the floor
Take a match
Give a scratch
No more candy store.

"Mama," Sid laughed wryly, barely able to speak with his mouth full of food, "I can't give up the store. Not now. Not yet. It's a good living."

"*A shrara arbeiter*, you know vus dis means, a hard worker, you are Sid. You should have it a little easy now."

He was tired, but enjoyed eating the late meal. "Isn't it something, Tyra going to college." He said it, not as a question but as a statement.

"You should be proud. And Jessie, the *kindah*, (children) at the hospital, they love her. She works so hard for them. Only she is so stubborn. It be good if she meet someone, to take care of her, keep her company. It no good, a girl always to be alone."

"Yes, I am proud. They're good girls. Don't worry. Jessie's a strong girl. She'll be alright."

In the mid-sixties crime was spreading into the residential neighborhoods of the south Bronx, where Uncle Shockneh bore the brunt of it. He had gotten old and tired. His thick hair turned gray, but he still worked hard in the chicken market, a few blocks from where he lived on the wide, pretty, tree-lined Southern Boulevard opposite the Bronx Zoo. Gangs thrived there, too, taking even more advantage of the elderly European immigrants who populated the massive pre-war buildings. On three separate occasions, each during his late Shabbos afternoon trek to shul for *Mincha* and *Maariv* services, Shockneh was beaten, thrown to the ground and robbed of the only material item on his person. Of course, he would never have money in his pockets on the Sabbath, but he always wore a beautiful watch. He loved watches. He was proud he could tell time in English. As if to prove his resilience, he bought a new watch after each assault.

The two great nieces visited him in Montefiore Hospital as he lay recuperating from the last attack. Jessie bent over and pecked his forehead gingerly. His face was swollen, housing a large cut on his cheek which had been stitched together, the eye above closed shut, red, black, blue and nearly popping out of its socket.

"Why do you keep wearing watches, Uncle Shockneh?" Tyra scolded as she focused her gaze on her beaten, battered uncle. She was weak with fear and anger at the wickedness of animals who could ravage this dear sweet man.

"I have no children to worry for me," he whispered.

"Uncle Shockneh," Jessie said as she reached for his hand and squeezed it, "we love you, Tyra and I. Don't say something like that."

"You'll get better before you know it. Just do what the doctor says," Tyra said.

"Even though I have no chicken eggs for you anymore? They send them to Russia for *gourmet*," he said, pronouncing the "t".

Tyra laughed. "Gour-may," she said accentuating the last syllable. "The t is silent. And yes, we love you anyway." She stroked his forehead. "I learned in Hebrew class what your name means. Remember I used to ask everybody what your name meant and nobody knew. Well, your name is as amazing as you are Uncle Shockneh. Hebrew words are based on consonants…"

"Conso…vus?" Shochneh asked.

"Don't worry; it doesn't matter. Just listen. If you take away the vowels, o and e, which makes it Yiddish, and replace them with two I' s and an e, the word becomes *Shi..chi..neh*, which means the Presence of God, like *Hashem* is always with you. Isn't that beautiful? It fits you to a "t", too."

He looked at each of his great nieces, grasped their hands, placing them on his chest. "Promise me, you will name a child after me."

"That's for Tyra, Uncle Shockneh. I'm not getting married, so I won't be having any kids."

"Oy, don't talk like that," he said. "You got to have hope, always."

"Well, if I would have a kid, I would definitely have you hold him during the *bris*," she said, laughing. "You got to hope, you know!"

He could barely chuckle, but you could tell he cherished his nieces' affection. "If I have a watch for them to take, maybe they be happy with it. No watch and no wallet, maybe they kill me."

"Then maybe you should *daven* at home, and stop putting yourself in danger. Grown-ups aren't supposed to look for trouble. That's our job," Tyra said, half-jokingly. "Why bring trouble on yourself when there's plenty of the real kind to go around?"

"*Oy vey, shaina maidel.* How you understand? What if I be tenth for the *minyan* and they need me? They can have my watch, but they can't take my soul. Never, God forbid." For emphasis, and with great conviction, he repeated, "my *n'shumah*, never!" When he patted Tyra on her head as if she were a little child, she felt shame and anger both swirling in her stomach.

Tyra was at a low point. She was jealous of Jessie's strength and adventuresome spirit, the way she took a stand against prejudice and injustice. Even though she hated Joel for hurting her, she yearned to have his idealism and absolute courage, as he planned to sneak into the Soviet Union- the possibility that he could be arrested by the KGB and sent to Siberia didn't even faze him, or if it did, he kept it as hidden as the Judaism he wanted to expose to his people who were enslaved by Communism. Even old and frail Uncle Shockneh's unswerving devotion to Torah was nothing short of inspiration. The people who were so important in her life had honed great meaning in their own lives, while she was safe, safe in college where not only was she studying the language and literature she loved, but she was also majoring in English. Opportunities teaching Hebrew were scarce and Tyra knew enough to plan for contingencies, to plan a future of security, even if it were devoid of meaning and joy.

They were just about finished with dinner when Tyra tried to be nonchalant as she broke the news. She had been nervous throughout the meal, hardly eating, merely pushing the food around the plate. She hoped her voice wouldn't shake as she began. She wanted to talk to her parents alone, but she knew she could never get Jessie out of the way.

"I want to go to Israel after I graduate," Tyra said. "I want to start my master's in Hebrew Lit and where better to do that than in Israel?" She thought it was nothing short of a miracle

285

that in a mere nineteen years the Jewish people made this tiny barren space a haven for the bedraggled remnants of the world's despised, and transformed indignity and torture into pride and achievement.

Kaye's demeanor changed in a second. A long day at the bookkeeping machines, a crowded ride on the train, a hard walk up the hill carrying bundles for dinner, now this. "No. Absolutely not. It's too dangerous."

"The letters of the country don't even fit into its spot on a map," Tyra said. "It's so tiny and look what they've accomplished. Come on, Mom, please. You know I always wanted to learn how to speak Hebrew fluently and live the history of our people. I worked like a dog to graduate with honors in Hebrew. It's so exciting. Don't I deserve it?"

"No. I mean, yes you deserve it but no, I won't allow it. You should think about your future, get your teaching credentials solidified. Get a good position in a good school." Kaye was adamant.

"That's the point, Mom. I'll become fluent and so knowledgeable in literature. I'll make a fantastic career using my expertise when I return." She looked at Sid. "Daddy, help me out. I've never left the Bronx, except for the bungalows. I want to travel –to see what the world is like." She could tell her father was touched by her pleading, but he didn't say a word. "This is the Sixties. It's time for expanding one's horizons, for change."

"You just want to run away from us. Admit it," Jessie chimed in. "Tyrun, they should have named you."

"Shut up, you jealous bitch."

"Girls, enough," Sid said, shaking his head.

"And I made up my mind," Tyra continued. "I got a scholarship from the American Alumni of the Hebrew University to help out and I'm going." Tyra's face was red and her whole body was shaking with defiance.

"You what?" Kaye screamed. "You applied for a scholarship behind our backs!"

Jessie drew her fingers to her mouth pretending to smoke. "Why should you be so surprised? That's the way Tyra always does things. She doesn't have the guts…"

"Shut up, Jess. What do you expect? How can I be up front when you all jump down my throat? Besides I'm going one way or the other. I will join *Shayrut L'am* if I can't afford to study at the university."

"What's shay what?" Sid asked.

"*Shayrut L'am.* It's the Israeli equivalent of the Peace Corps. Volunteers work in the poor slums or agricultural areas. I can do social work or teach immigrants." Tyra looked at Sid, begging him for intervention.

"Look, Kaye. It's better if she studies at the university so she can get her master's degree and make a life for herself than let herself be taken advantage of as a volunteer. She's grown up now. Think about it."

"You always let them do whatever they want. It's too dangerous with the fighting and wars there all the time. And I'm always the bad one," she said, looking at Sid. Then she turned to Tyra. "Stay here and get a job. And be happy for what you have."

"Yes. Have a perfect little job, a perfect little life, where every child has a straight back. And I won't fall in love so I won't get heartbroken. And I won't have any children because they may not be perfect. And I won't have any excitement because I shouldn't take any risks." Tyra glared at Jessie.

"What do you want from me, Kiddo? My life is just great. I didn't ask to be born."

"You make every one suffer because you're miserable. If you were…"

"Shut up all of you," Kaye's voice was shrill. "I'm the one that hasn't had a day's peace since you were born," she said, looking at Jessie.

It was ten minutes after eleven when Tyra finally came out of the bedroom. She had failed to persuade her parents to let her study in Israel after graduation, and she had been sulking all evening, trying to come up with new arguments, reasons, anything to sway them. The others were in the living room listening to the news. Kaye was knitting a brown and orange sweater, Jessie was half reading, half watching television and Sid was dozing on the sofa. Tyra walked toward Kaye and bent down to kiss her on the cheek. "I'm sorry about some of the things I said before. You're a good mother. I don't want to hurt you."

"I know. I just want what's best for you."

"I know. But I have to go to Israel. I need to prove to myself that I can handle being independent. That I don't have to rely on you and Daddy for everything."

Sid had awakened from his doze. "Your mother and I discussed the situation fully and we decided that it would be better if you would start your master's at the university than stick yourself in the wilderness with volunteers. We will give you the money you need for the year, and then you can come home and finish your degree here. Is that a deal?"

"Oh, Daddy. It sounds like a good plan. Oh, my God! Thanks so much."

"A good plan isn't good enough. You have to promise that after the year, you'll come home. No foreign entanglements, no excuses. A solemn promise." He glanced at Kaye who nodded in approval.

"I said okay. Don't you trust me? Okay, I promise. And thanks so much." She went over to Sid and hugged him, and then she put her arms around Kaye.

"Thanks, Mom. I'm so happy. And when I get a teaching job here, I will pay you back- every penny."

"Good for you, Tyra. You always get what you want. You'll do fine." Jessie got up and left the room. "And don't forget to write," she screamed from the other side of the house.

Twelve

Broken

January 2, 1967

Dear Tyra,

I just got back from Winter Seminar and I am so enthused. Rev Zemer was fabulous as usual. He said he saw you and a bunch of other former seminarians in the fall. Have you seen Rabbi Singer and his family?

I decided that once I get into college next fall and live in the dorms, I will be able to observe more fully concerning Kasruth and Shabbat. I am spiritually ready to make that commitment now, and I will observe whatever I can without causing stress with my parents. I am hoping to get into Stern to major in Jewish Studies and Hebrew. I have been really studying hard to improve my grades and hopefully get a scholarship. I daven three times a day, and I feel such a closeness to Hashem. I also decided to respect the body He gave me and I already lost ten pounds. I feel more energetic, too.

Tyra put the letter down for a moment, drew a deep breath. She was proud of Marlene's newfound maturity, even as it highlighted her own shortcomings, about faith, weight, everything. Then she began reading again.

I am full of love and hope and I know I can accomplish good things with the life Hashem has blessed me with. You have been such a good friend and role model for me, and I am so grateful for your friendship and guidance over the years.

I miss you and can't wait to hear about your latest escapades in Jerusalem. Write soon.

Love,
Marlene

Friday, January 6, 1967

Dear Mom, Dad and Jessie,

I got back yesterday and this is the first chance I have to sit down and write. It's 12 o'clock now and I'll have until Shabbos to write if I need all that time.

We woke up at 4:30 Monday morning to get an early start. The first place we stopped at was an archaeological dig in the Negev called Momshet. We saw the public bathhouses, the remains of a church from the sixth century. It had a mosaic floor from the Roman-Byzantine period- the kind of floor Michener talks about in The Source. Some people, like Daddy, are so wise they don't make mistakes. Me, I just learn from the mistakes I make. I finally thought it would be worth shlepping the movie camera. Took lots of film. When I wanted to film these ancient ruins, the trigger wouldn't work. I forgot to check the batteries. I also brought along my still camera and the two rolls of film I had, so I managed to take some pictures. I'll be sending them back soon.

We then rode to Avdat, another archaeological site. Saw ruins of church, wine press, caves people lived in. It was a community built on top of a mountain and from the top you can only see dry desert land and it's hard to believe that this was once a thriving community- that people actually lived there. On the way back on Wednesday we saw the Ain Avdat-well or water source about three miles away that these people used.

On Monday, after leaving Avdat, we continued traveling south and stopped at Mitzpeh Rimon. This is a huge crater that was a mountain millions of years ago. Water flowing down ate away at the land, hollowed it out and split the mountain. We stood on top of a cliff as the guide explained it to us.

From there we traveled to Eilat without making any stops. We ate in a restaurant (the food was delicious all during the tour). The spirit was high all through the trip, too. We were singing a lot and it was really fun. From there we went to the youth hostel, got settled and went to the beach for a campfire where we sang and danced. From the shore, on a clear day, you can see Jordan, Egypt and Saudi Arabia! The Eilat port is a very strategic point and was fought over during the Independence War.

We woke up at six Tuesday morning and after breakfast and a short ride through the desert we stopped at Mt. Amram-250 meters above sea level. It took five hours to get up and down but it was the most memorable part of the whole trip. I feel terribly inadequate about not being able to describe it, but I'll try.

We started climbing and when we got up to the first big cliff, the guide, Professor Har El of the archaeology department here, explained the different rock substances. There's sedimentary, sandstone and limestone. Each is a different color and it's fascinating to see all these major rock materials at one time- white, red and black. We kept climbing as if there were no top to reach. When we got high enough we saw the Red Sea which was farthest away, then a large piece of desert wasteland, then the range of mountains we were on. It was a hard climb but not very dangerous if you were sure of your footing. I went slowly and carefully and every few seconds would stop and look at the scenery- it changed with every step. It was sad to think that this would be the only time in my life that I would be at that particular place- its utter beauty and magnificence cannot be described or contained in a photograph.

While climbing I felt a sudden closeness to God- not a personal God but the God of the Universe, of Creation- the God of an age very far away in time from our own. The kids were singing and because of the canyons there was a strange echoing quality in their voices and there was an eerie feeling about the whole thing.

We got to the first landing- I was third from the last to get there. Everyone had rested for quite a while by the time I got there, but that happened all day long- I was always in the back. I got angry, rather annoyed, at the kids who would hurry me up- they were in such a rush to get to the top that they probably didn't see half the beauty of the climb up. They didn't care if the person in front had sure footing- just as long as he didn't hold them up.

At the first rest point the kids were told that if they were tired they should go down from a path, if they weren't they should continue climbing to the very top and descend from there. Physically it would have been very easy to stop at that point- it was strenuous and tiring. But I would have never forgiven myself had I stopped- especially after seeing what I would have missed. I was tired but not that tired and so I continued. We climbed for about another 45 minutes and when we reached the top we took a lunch break. It was 11:15 and it took about two hours to get up. The top was just rocks and when we started climbing down all the falling rocks jingled and it sounded like background noise for a movie during Xmas- only it was much too hot for snow!

From here we could see the Harai Edom- the Red Mountain Range- for in the afternoon, the peaks are red in the sun. This range is in Jordan. The way from that point started out easy. We just walked across the mountains until we reached the cliff going down. After a while though it got treacherously difficult and for the first time I got frightened. I never liked heights too much but going up and looking down didn't bother me at all. But then the going down got rough. Before the really hard part came, we had to walk along a path and the width of the land was the path itself- it was quite narrow and there were two drops on both sides. Then came the hard part- the cliff- it was steep-full of stones. The beginning was easy. I sat down and slid- with all the sand and rocks rolling underneath me. But then I had to stand and just hang on to the rocks along the sides and get down slowly, concentrating on every step. There were two girls in back of me and a guy and girl were in front and the five of us got down after everyone else had met in the valley of the canyon and had rested and left. The only ones left were two guides.

In the valley these gigantic rocks and cliffs were red and we had to climb under and over and through them. We caught up with the others and got a warm greeting! We thought we were at the bottom when we realized as we came to another cliff that we still had more to climb and jump down. One of the guides was helping everyone get down a steep rock and when he saw me he was quite surprised- you see I wasn't at the end this time. I had quite a reputation by the end of the day- every guide knew me and asked how I was doing all through the day! Didn't know you had such a brave kid in the family!

After a while we finally got down and had to walk about an hour through the desert to meet the buses on the road. When we got out of the canyons there was a desert plain and the most surreal live painting I have ever seen- an endless carpet of thick, yellow flowers as far as the eye could see with the Red

Mountains behind them. God is DaVinci and Chagall rolled into One! I can't describe the feeling that I had walking in a "never, never land" in a make-believe world.

There was one point, before we reached the first cliff to descend that I had the weirdest feeling- I could see no one in front of me nor in back and even though I knew there were a hundred and fifty people somewhere around, I felt absolutely alone on top of a mountain in the middle of a desert. It's an aloneness that can never be experienced in New York- that's for sure.

We got to the buses about 3-3:30 and from there we went to see the Pillars of Amram and some nearby caves. I had no film left with me but I got a postcard of it and soon I'll be sending home postcards of the places I saw. The pillars were formed or cut out from the sides of the mountains by the rains that ate away at the sides. The desert was absolutely different from the way I expected it to be. I had pictured something like the Arabian desert with nothing but sand and dunes. As we were walking from the bottom of the mountain to the buses I realized how wrong my expectations were. There is dirt- lessoil- rather than sand and there are many little rocks and stones making walking very difficult. The land isn't smooth- rather there are places that look like they were eaten away and it's necessary to climb down into the holes and then climb up out of them. Then there are hills- splits in the land- almost like what dried up rivers look like and you either have to jump over or climb in and out of them. There are all kinds of desert plants and bushes-green and yellowish in color. I spotted one flower- blue- and no one was there to warn people not to step on it this time.

Just as the desert was different from what I expected it to be, so were the mountains. One can not really know what a mountain is until he climbs it and goes through it like we did- and even so I'm sure we missed a lot. A mountain from afar looks just like a protrusion from the ground. One can't see all the intricacies- the cliffs, the canyons, the valleys. It was just so fantastic and so magnificent- the beauty overwhelming.

The first stop on Wednesday was at the Pillars of Solomon and the copper mines at Timneh. I felt a little nauseous and didn't climb up to the mines. After that we went to "Petria"- the Hebrew version of Petrified Forest. I guess three days of eating oranges caught up with me. We were walking the desert and the caves of Timneh known as Solomon's Mines when I found myself in need of a bathroom- however for miles and miles the expanse was sheer tan desert sand and tall pillars of immense stones reaching toward the sky. I was desperate and walked far, far away from the crowd and found a crevice to hide in and do my business, covering it up afterward with a giant rock. I guess you can say, "I sat and shat" in the Holy Land! Can you imagine all the mounds of human waste absorbed into this majestic ground- from Moses, Joshua, David, Aaron, Miriam and on and on for millennia. Everything is so sacred here and to think I added my contribution to the Negev! I guess that's where the expression Holy Shit comes from!

Love,
Tyra

January 8, 1967

Dear Marlene,

I was so happy to learn that Seminar had so much meaning for you. Seminar's job is to plant and you are the blossom! The love of Hashem that you have found is the greatest gift- you have found what most people don't even search for. I pray, study and observe, all in a struggle to achieve that love that has come so natural to you, and I am not there yet.

295

Two things which I learned from experience which helped me. First, try hard and go slow. There is a danger in coming home from seminar completely inspired and making a total commitment, one that falls by the wayside after some discouragement or loneliness. It's more important to observe one mitzvah with dedication and joy than many haphazardly- that is to say on a shaky foundation. Set a pace you can follow- the most important thing when climbing a mountain is sure footing- I know. I climbed a mountain in the Negev and I was the last one to reach the top, but I enjoyed every moment going up, although sometimes I could hardly breathe! It's the same growing in Judaism. It's not always easy, but it yields great pleasure.

Secondly, don't let go. There were times when I used to think I could "forget" about observing this or that- just this once, out of laziness or tiredness. But that is how the foundation starts to weaken. So even if there are times when you have to force yourself, try. It can't be all inspiration and spontaneity all the time- and just because it isn't, it doesn't mean it's not worthwhile. That's why the pace you set up front is so important. Try to make it so that every mitzvah is not a burden, but a joy to fulfill.

In closing, Marlene, I want you to know how privileged I feel because you wanted me to know your most inward thoughts. You'll never know how much your trust in me means to me.

Wishing you much success in your studies. Have fun, too, and write soon.

Love,
Tyra

January 24, 1967

Dear Tyra,
You wouldn't believe how hot it was today-74 degrees! June in January. It's been the hottest January on record.

296

Look Magazine printed the first installment of that Kennedy book I wrote you about. I tried to get a copy for you everywhere, but they just fly off the shelves. I'm enclosing a few reviews about the book for you.

I wanted to call you to hear your voice, but the rate was $12 for three minutes plus seventy five cents for tax. You have to be a Rockefeller for that, so I guess we'll just have to continue writing for now.

Aunt Sylvia is so excited about her trip to Israel with her sister. She can't wait to see you. I'll send a care package for you with her. Enjoy your visit. I'm sure you'll show her a nice time in Jerusalem.

Love,
Mom

January 30, 1967

Dear Mom, Dad and Jessie,

The one thing that's so weird and wonderful in Israel is that everyone seems to know or know of everyone else. I went downtown to the hotel where Aunt Sylvia and her sister are staying, but they weren't back yet from their tour. I sat in the lobby waiting, and there was a young couple sitting, also waiting for someone. We got to talking, and it turns out the woman was Sylvia's sister's niece! The five of us had dinner together at the hotel. Sylvia is loving every minute of the trip and for a seventy year old, she certainly has a lot of pep. Her sister though is a kvetch- the bus is too bumpy, the weather too hot, etc.. But it was a fun evening. I invited them to the dorm for Shabbat lunch. Neil will be coming, too, and I will ask Irit and Abraham also.

Speaking of Irit and Abraham, they are really an item now. They have been dating for two years and she is head over heels in love. He is quite the hatik- a real good-looker. The only thing is, I notice how he hovers over her and interferes with her social life and appointments. Even at dinner with Sylvia, Abraham made Irit order a steak which she didn't want. She wanted eggplant salad. She gave him a dirty look, but finally acquiesced but hardly took a bite. I felt terrible that Sylvia had to pay so much for it, but she didn't seem to mind. Irit is such a headstrong and stubborn girl. From the moment I met her she reminded me of Jessie. Hadas is more like me- quiet and refined! Anyway, I don't know why Irit would put up with him, but who am I to judge? After all, I haven't been so wise in the romance department this year myself.

Love,
Tyra

February 4, 1967

Dear Mom, Dad and Jessie,

Do you remember the man in the desert who stood over the lone blue flower? Well, I've been seeing him around the dorm recently. He always wears denim overalls and a kova temble hat. (That's a pointy hat that looks like a stupid little dunce cap). He takes courses at the university but isn't really a student. He just audits the classes he likes. He doesn't work. He comes from a well-to-do family somewhere in the Midwest, Iowa, I think, and he lives on stipends his family sends him. He comes around at night and manages to get meals from the girls in the kitchen. I would call him a loafer. He seems to have taken a liking to Tirzah and loves her spicy food. I warn her not to let him take advantage of her but she seems to like his company. He changed his English name from Oscar to Azariah because when he studied The Ethics of the Fathers, Rabbi Azaraiah said "if there is no Torah, there is is no derech eretz- decency or good manners- and if there is no decency, there is no Torah." In any event, he is quite a character. I annoy him no end and I still call him Oscar because I don't think he has manners or decency! He's just a schnorrer! He says he is a true mensch and he will prove me wrong some day. Tirzah almost has to pull us apart with our banter!

Love,
Tyra

February 6, 1967

Dear Tyra,

You know how hard it is for me to write so you know this is important. I am very disappointed that you are not keeping us up to date with what's going on in regard to that boy, Neil. Sylvia came back from her trip and said that she met him and the two of you are wild about each other. He told her he is planning to settle in Israel, that there is no place in the world as wonderful for a Jew to get married and raise children. You know I had to do a lot of convincing to get Mom to agree to let you study in Israel for the year and now she is really giving me a hard time and a cold shoulder, blaming me for giving you this opportunity. Things are really tough in the house now and Mom is miserable. You better write soon. Call if you can, never mind the money, and set things straight.

Love,
Dad

February 10, 1967

Dear Mom,

I got Dad's letter, and I am so sorry that there's been a terrible misunderstanding. When I told Aunt Sylvia about Neil, she must have assumed our relationship was much more than it is. So let me say outright, I am not serious about him, and especially have no plans to marry him and settle in

Israel now. I can't imagine why she would say that. The fact is, Neil is pretty messed up. Half the time he says he wants to make aliyah-emigrate- and the other half he says he wants to go back to the States to finish up his studies. The worst part is that he's so hot and cold toward me, I am absolutely miserable. I never wrote you about this because I didn't want to worry you, but since Sylvia stirred up trouble, I might as well try to set your mind at ease. Neil stands me up half the time and I never know whether to believe his excuses or not. The communications here are non-existent- there is one public telephone on the dorm side of campus, and what's the chance of getting a phone call? People give messages on slips of paper, but who knows if they're ever delivered, to the right person, and on time, so if he doesn't show up, I don't know if it's because he tried to let me know something came up or if he just forgot or even worse, didn't care.

I try to find out what's bothering him, but he says everything's fine, that it's not my fault, and frankly I am confused and don't know why I am still trying to make a go of this relationship. I see in him something very gentle and giving, idealistic and spiritual, but it just doesn't translate into him being a mensch toward me. I remember what you wrote a few months ago, about choosing someone who likes me for who I am, and I am slowly coming to the conclusion that although I might be lonely and miss him, I will have to give him up if things don't change.

Even his friend, Peter, told me recently that if I can't get him to level with me, I should stop wasting my time with him, and he knows him better than anyone.

Please don't aggravate yourself over me. I promised I would come home after the year and you can hold me to that. And please tell Daddy not to be angry at me.

Love, love, love,
Tyra

Neil,

This is ridiculous. I spend half my time writing to people thousands of miles away and now I have to write to you- you who lives ten minutes from me because you don't have the guts to talk face to face. I have tried very hard to be patient with you and understand you, but if we can't even talk face to face, I guess there's nothing good between us. I have seen in you a good soul, someone who strives to reach the heights of goodness and devotion to Hashem. I have so admired you for that. But you have made me feel so bad about myself, like I'm not good enough or worthy of your love. Well, I have realized as much as it hurts, that you are not honest with me. I am good enough. I'm not a nun but I'm not a tramp either. I don't know what is truly bothering you, but I do know that I am not your problem. You are your own problem and until you level with me, I see no reason for me to keep getting hurt by you. I'm not interested in finding anyone else- you have meant too much to me- but I think it's time for us to end this nonsense.

Tyra

February 14, 1967

Dear Tyra,

In the beginning, you had such a grand time on the boat and a wonderful summer, I was happy for you and didn't have a chance to miss you because I was with you – your letters did that for me. But now as time goes by, it's six months already, I want to talk to you or see you. That's why I write, no matter how tired I am. You are not as happy as you were, with your studies not going as well as you'd want, and you seem to be lonely now that you are not seeing Neil.

Truthfully I did wonder why Neil stopped seeing you and I didn't understand why you didn't say. I don't know whether you want my opinion or whether your feel the situation is ended but I'll tell you how I feel about it and then it's up to you. You must realize I don't know the boy at all, if he is forward or shy, rich or poor etc.. All you've said is that he's sweet and considerate which in itself says quite a bit.

I believe a girl should be proud and independent to a certain degree. I also believe if a girl thinks a lot of a boy, considering his qualities are good, she doesn't let him slip through her fingers too easily. Neil may have felt he was getting too involved and was not prepared for it. Or maybe you were too needy. But if it had been me, I would want to know why. I'd be curious enough to find out why and I would have asked him very simply if he was peeved about something that you may have said during that blasted picnic. If it were me I would have dropped him a Chanukah card saying Chaim said he wanted to speak to you and not having heard from him- you hoped he was okay- something simple- not too mushy. Then if he made no attempt to get in touch with you at least you would have tried. If you showed a little concern it wouldn't have been so terrible. Sometimes a girl has to push a little (not much). Or maybe he felt he couldn't get anywhere sexually with you and wanted to break away for that reason. Only one other thing entered my mind and this only a mother can tell a child although I don't think this pertains to you as I know how meticulous you are about your appearance, but make sure your hygiene is good in Israel. And eat healthy foods- enough kugels- it's too hard to get the weight off once it gets on. I notice every time you ask for slacks, the size goes up!

I sort of got off the subject but I would be frank with Neil and not be afraid to resume a friendship. If you want to know the truth this is what I did with your darling Daddy. Someday I'll tell you all about it. Anyway this doesn't mean I want you to grab Neil for a husband but knowing now you can get along without him if you have to, I would try to get to the bottom of it. I know you are a wonderful girl and everybody that knows you has made me feel so proud of you. I also trust you and have

faith in your judgment. Sometimes mothers are wrong, too. I
gave you my opinion and whatever you do is alright with me.
Nothing is rosy all the time but for most of the time- be happy.

I'm getting tired now. Will watch Peyton Place and go to
bed. I hope you will enjoy your birthday despite this disappoint-
ment, knowing the next year will be happier than this one.
Remember you can always come home earlier if you want to.

All my love,
Mother

Tyra put on a long sleeve blouse and a knee-length skirt and hurried to catch the #22 to Rehov Agnon. After the twenty minute ride, she got off the bus and walked the five blocks in the cold rain to the yeshiva. She entered the courtyard where one of the rabbis tried to stop her telling her she was forbidden from entering the dorm building. Ignoring him, she ran past, afraid if she hesitated, she would be turned away.

"You owe me an explanation," she said, as she stormed into Neil's room. Neil was pouring over a text of Talmud and jumped out of his chair when he heard Tyra's voice coming out of nowhere.

"What…What…"he stammered.

"I said, you owe me an explanation. You played me for a fool and I want to know the real reason."

He stood in front of her, his head low to the cold, terrazzo floor.

"Well, say something," she said.

"You were right in the note you sent. It was my problem. I made excuses blaming you but it wasn't you at all." He stopped as if he were finished.

"Well, do I have to pull teeth?"

"When I met you, I really liked you. You were sweet, educated, and… and really attractive." He could barely look at her, casting his eyes down to the floor.

"Am I going to have gray hair before you finish? Could you look at me for God's sake. Am I invisible?"

"I'm sorry. I guess I'm embarrassed." He paused once again. "I came to Israel and promised myself I wouldn't get involved with anyone. I would just study and try to find myself."

"Where did you get lost?" Tyra was exasperated. "Spit it out, will you?"

"There was this girl. I was going with her for two years in college. I thought we would get engaged after graduation, but she said she wasn't ready. I was shocked. She came from a revered, *frum*- religious- family. I thought she would want to get married and have a bunch of kids, but she said she wanted to travel and have some freedom before she got saddled with a large family which was what was expected of her. I was crushed and decided to come to Israel and learn. Then I met you, and was totally confused."

Tyra's anger overpowered her hurt feelings. "You were really mean to me, the way you were so dishonest. And you think that's the way to achieve *kavanah*- holiness and closeness to *Hashem*?"

"I'm sorry. I didn't mean to hurt you. Is there something...."

"Yes. You can start by telling me the truth- the whole truth."

"I don't understand. I did."

"I don't buy it for a second, Neil. We all have break-ups and disappointments. You don't think I haven't had my share of heartaches. But we move on. So what's the real story?"

Neil slumped back into his chair in utter silence, and Tyra sat on his bed. "I'm not leaving. You owe me an explanation for all the hurt and embarrassment you caused me and my family."

"Your family?"

"Never mind that now. The truth."

"When I met... you, I...I... really liked you," he stammered. He hung his face low and covered it with his hands. He couldn't speak anymore.

Tyra felt sorry for him. "So? That's a good thing. To like me? Well." Her sympathy was quickly fading to impatience,

"You don't understand. I wanted you." His voice was almost screaming. "I wanted to grab you and kiss you and go into you. And you let me have sex."

"Sex. What! Are you crazy? We didn't have sex. We were affectionate. We kissed and hugged. Is that so terrible to want some warmth and closeness?"

"You know it's not allowed."

"For whom? Only for those who choose it. Thanks for making me feel like a slut."

"Well, I was torn and you didn't help me. You encouraged me and I hated you for it."

"Really? You didn't seem to mind it at the time. You never voiced any concerns."

"You brought out the worst in me. The *yazeh harah*- evil inclination. There. Are you happy now?"

"You should have been born a Catholic. You would have made a wonderful priest, You have no idea how to treat a woman according to Jewish law, starting with honesty and dignity."

The door slammed so hard, the walls shook.

February 16, 1967

Dear Mom,

I have never felt like such a fool. Neil and I broke up for good, once and for all. I really mean it. We finally had a long talk and it turned out that while for all these months I felt like I wasn't good enough for him, not religious enough, not educated enough, not idealistic, not devoted enough- it turns out he has been locked up inside about a former girlfriend and he used me on the rebound- to try to get her out of his system. I was such a fool. I had no inkling, not even a suspicion that another girl was involved. And that wasn't the worst of it. He is so confused about so many things which I can't even begin to explain in a letter. He even said he wasn't sure whether he wanted to settle in Israel or not! At least I have decided that I will never again allow myself to fall so completely for a guy who can string me along and make me feel so bad about myself. I don't think I deserve that- if he's not settled and mature I want no part of him. I'm so sorry that you had so much aggravation about my relationship with him, and that it was all for naught. I feel bad but I'm a big girl. It will take some time to get over but I will try to accomplish what I set out to do this year. Please don't worry about me. I'll be fine. Take care.

Love,
Tyra

Tyra saw something more than just a relationship during her time with Neil. In the moments she observed him davening, swaying back and forth, swathed in his huge *tallis,* or wrapping his *tefillin* around his head and arm on the top of the hill at sunrise, she thought maybe he would be the one to bring her back to the God she longed for. *Heal Jessie. Let me find you,* she thought. Yes. She believed in the existence of God, so it was possible for her to be observant. But He was not the God she wanted, so her belief was bitter and unpleasant, and her observance to a God she despised was not easy. Neil's love for *Hashem* would help soften Tyra's heart. The finality of their break-up was a double loss for her and she sank into a despair she never knew before.

Monday, February 21, 1967
Dear Mom, Dad and Jessie,
    I left a message at the hotel for Zelda's parents that I was sick and couldn't come to the hotel, so they came to the dorm

Saturday night, which was really nice of them. They look great and are having a wonderful time. They brought me all the gifts you sent. I have to get used to the radio again- it's been such a long time. I wore the gorgeous pajamas and robe last night during my surprise birthday party! And Jessie, the dress is just "wow". Thanks for everything.

I figured that the kids were going to do something for my birthday; I just didn't know what. But since I had 102 degree fever, the doctor came to the room early Sunday morning. She told me I had a virus, gave me some medicine and told me to stay in bed. She said it must be hard when you're sick and you mother's not around to take care of you! I had been alone all morning because everyone had classes. After she left Bella came in, then Tirzah and Olga. Then Irit came with a beautiful cake that had my Hebrew name on it. She said I should keep it in the refrigerator until all the kids come at five! I told her I wasn't supposed to know! Irit made me lunch (mashed potatoes and sour cream) and straightened up my things. She came this morning, too, and just left. She brought me all kinds of groceries and she absolutely wouldn't take any money. She said she'll come tomorrow, too.

All day yesterday kids kept coming in and I also got a whole stack of birthday cards and put them on our little table. Bella gave me a beautiful pair of delicate hanging earrings, Miriam a ceramic ashtray, Edna a pottery vase and Irit said she'd paint it. Then Olga and Mike gave me two Hebrew poetry books and Tirzah a beautiful Hebrew poetry book by religious poets. Tirzah yelled at me, "Why did you tell Bella to call the doctor? Why didn't you tell me?" Really all the kids are great and I feel very lucky. Then another couple came in with a big bundle of beautiful tulips and other flowers which we put in the new vase and a book by Agnon. One I had read already but my copy's a mess. Then Yael and Peter came in- they gave me

*three books of poetry in English, thank heaven. I feel so happy
to have such a good group of friends.*

*The mail just came as I am writing this and I got your let-
ter of the 14th. For God's sake, Mom, stop analyzing. I didn't
mother Neil. I didn't lean on him because I was lonely. I just
liked him. I'm a little unhappy but not miserable and I'm not
coming home yet. Just forget the whole damn thing. Okay?*

*By the way, I straightened out some of my closets this week.
I got all the film together. I have 1000 feet of movie film and
64 still shots left. It's about 680 liras worth if I'd bought it
here. I'm going to start filming soon.*

*I don't mean to be harsh but all this writing back and forth
has caused so many misunderstandings and anger this year.
It's so hard communicating long distance.*

I love you. Tyra

March 1, 1967

Dear Tyra,

*I don't know what to do with my crazy daughters. Your sis-
ter finally is settled in a wonderful job. Except for one woman
who has it in for her, she is well-liked and the patients adore
her. Now she has to start up being a witch. Can you believe?
Jessie came home from work last night all excited about meeting
this woman at the hospital. Our dinner was one long diatribe
about how this well-dressed, tall lady talked to her during her
break yesterday in the ladies' room. She introduced herself to
Jessie and asked her what she did. Jessie described her job to this
Gene in great detail, as you can imagine. Gene asked her if the
other lab techs who are men got the same salary. Jessie said, "Of
course not. I think I get 60 cents to their dollar." The woman
asked her if she worked as hard as the men. Jessie said no and
told us the woman looked astonished. Then Jessie told her, "I
work ten times harder, stay later and do a damn better job, too."*

"Ah, that's more like it," Gene said. "Do you think it's fair that you get paid less?"

"Don't get me started on fair, Miss…"

"Meyer. Just call me Gene. Anyway, Jess. I'm part of a new organization to get equal pay for women. I'm here today, talking to the hospital administrator about this very issue. We could use a young woman like you to help us organize and bring about awareness in society for women's rights."

"I know something about rights. I've been fighting all my life to get some."

"I could tell that you've probably had it harder than most, and that's why you would be perfect for our group. How about coming to a meeting tomorrow night? We call ourselves WICHEN- *it stands for* Women in Charge-EqualityNow. We're not really a group of witches although some men think so!" She let out a bellow of a laugh and gave Jessie a business card and wrote the address and phone number on it. So that is where your sister is now. I just hope she doesn't antagonize her boss and get in trouble and risk her job for other people's causes. And you. What are you up to these days? Gone are the days when I can strap you both in the carriage and keep you safe. Tough as nails, I'll get yet.

I'm enclosing a letter from Ricky. As you can see from his envelope, he is stationed in Viet Nam. I hope he is okay. Let me know.

As for Neil, time will make it better. You sound like you have a strong attitude. Try to enjoy yourself as much as you can. You enjoy traveling and seeing the country, so distract yourself. Just be careful. Try not to worry about your studies. Do the best you can. You will finish up when you get home. And everything will turn out well. You'll see.

Love,
Mom

March 1, 1967

Dear Tyra,

I lost your address in Israel, but I know your folks will send this to you. I'm finally getting used to the misery here in Cam Ranh Bay. We live in a tent with nothing but dirt for a floor. We walk a mile to shower and there is no running water. Every night we have to burn human waste. This by the way is the safest place in Viet Nam.

The people here are shy and have way-out customs. They are poor but hardworking and proud of what they have. GIs look down on them and treat the women like trash. Americans have a lot to learn about other people before we get respect from them. Leave it to us to make a mess of thing no matter where we go.

I went to a village not far from base. The homes are run down and the people dress in rags. The girls are pretty and hang around the bars. The biggest shock is that their families encourage them to resort to prostitution. There are no streets, just alleys. The market is open and the insects are there for the taking. There is little if any sanitation. I couldn't eat anything but tried a Vietnamese beer. It was just awful and the bar smelled like a fish factory. The day taught me one thing- we really have it easy back home and I'll never knock the States for as long as I live.

The tension that developed in Israel recently worries me. If it gets too bad, please go home. Promise.

Write soon. How's Dawn? Haven't heard from her at all. It's so lonely here.

Love,
Ricky

Thursday, March 2, 1967

Dear Mom, Dad and Jessie,

I saw the play, "The Land," and enjoyed it. I understood most of the Hebrew. The audience was as polite as ever! About three fights broke out during the performance. If I were an actor

I would have walked off the stage. On the way home Tirzah and I walked through the side streets near the shuk- night is the only time the shuk is clean. Then we stopped off to see her aunt and uncle. They're really nice. Her uncle is highly educated and has a fantastic sense of humor. Some of their friends were there and they drove us home. Afterward, Tirzah told me the friend is treasurer of Hadassah Hospital.

Last night I started a megillah —scroll- for Ricky to go in the package I'm sending him. It's on toilet paper and the kids signed the cutest things. I hope it cheers him up.

This morning Bella and I got up early to go into town. The weather was beautiful and I planned a whole day of filming in Jerusalem. When we got to the museum, the motor conked out. I was so disappointed. We took a bus into town and went to the camera store. The salesman told me the batteries are corroded. I will bring him four new ones, and if it's not that, I don't know what to do. Do you think the sun's too strong and it's too hot here? I have lots of work before the semester is over on the 24th, so maybe I'll wait until vacation to check it out. Dad, please don't be mad at me about the camera. I really do try to take care of it. It's just that I have no luck with it. That's it for now.

Love,
Tyra

March 2, 1967

Dear Dawn,

I got your letter yesterday, which was one of the worst days since we broke up- so depressed and lonely. I have a ton of work the last week of the trimester and then have a six week vacation. I haven't done a stitch of studying- par for the course.

Have you written to Ricky yet? I'm putting together a Purim package full of candy, funny books and yesterday, on a roll of hard, brown Israeli toilet paper, I started a megillah. Loads of kids signed some hysterical stuff. I'll send it next week.

I'm cutting all my classes today except my last one from 6-8 P.M. Then I'll go to Peter's. I have to talk to him. I'm going crazy. All I do is eat and smoke (at least one pack a day) and eat more. I don't have the patience to sit and write. I can't sleep either. Haven't gone to bed before 2:30- 3A.M. all week- get up 7ish. I'm ready to fall off my feet but too overtired to fall asleep. What a crummy, bitchy letter- sorry-really.

The weather's been beautiful. Looks like spring is on her way.

How's school coming along? Please write soon and a lot so it'll take up some time. I'm just going bats. Damn it all.

What a waste of a letter. I ought to sign off now because if I don't I'll just keep rambling like an idiot. Take it easy and please write soon. I need help.

Love,
Tyra

Sunday, March 12, 1967 2 P.M.

Dear Mom, Dad and Jessie,

I got your letter Friday, which is always nice as there's no mail on Shabbos, and one today with the photos. As far as sending a package, I could use a few cotton dresses (nothing wild or loud). Everything else I could get here. It's a pretty civilized place after all. Irit will be graduating so I guess you can send a gift for her. She always compliments my pajamas so a pair for her would be nice.

Friday the weather was beautiful (today it's pouring) so Tirzah and I decided to get up at 6:30 on Shabbos and walk to shul and from there walk all over Jerusalem. We davened at Hachal Shlomo which is the seat of the Chief Rabbinate.

We heard a beautiful choir. I want to go to as many shuls in Jerusalem as possible before the year is up.

After services we walked to Rehavia which is the most lovely suburb- Eshkol and the president live there. Then we visited Tirzah's friend and then her aunt and uncle. The kids, grandchildren and cousins were there. They were all warm and hospitable. Then we walked through the shuk which was all closed up for Shabbos. We crossed to the other side of town. It was three-ish and all the people were leaving their houses to stroll. We walked through Mea Shearim and the old sections including Bucharin which is where I teach. We stopped at another uncle's but no one was home so we climbed to the roof as it was the highest building (five stories) and it's right on the border. From there we could see a little border fence running parallel to the road on our side. Beyond that we saw the Old City of Jerusalem, the part that used to be ours before the war- Har Hazofim- where the original Hebrew University and Hadassah Hospital were. We bumped into Tirzah's friend and went with him to his brother's place. The brother, who is a teacher and was positioned on Har Hazofim when he was in the army, explained the surroundings and the military tactics. From their windows you can see Jordan and it's fantastic to think that people really live right there. I asked how it felt to always be in the Jordanians' sight and he couldn't even describe the constant gravity of the situation. We drank coffee bean skins and cinnamon with hot water- a wild taste!

Then Tirzah and I walked to the Mandelbaum Gate and went into the courtyard of a destroyed house in no man's land- kids play there all the time. We continued through the other side of Mea Shearim (the entire city is a circle) and watched groups of girls and boys playing.

Tirzah took me to visit an old friend of her mother's. I thought the man there (who was in his pajamas and a jacket) was her husband but he was her son and he had three sons. They were nice and the man was sweet and adorable. We ate different Yemenite foods- burnt spicy chick peas, homemade pita, pickled liver, spicy chicken with pickled chopped herb soup, beer, wine, tea and fruit. At one point the man forgot my name and called out, "Hey, Amerikai' it," and handed me a fork with the liver on it! I felt at home there.

Tirzah came to Israel when she was seven. All these people are Yemenite, too. They're gracious and sweet- simple and casual. There seems to be a misunderstanding about them. The Ashkenazim lump them together with the other Sephardim from Arab and other North African countries like Tunisia, Algeria and Morocco. But from what I've seen, Yemenite standards can be compared to Ashkenazim. The customs are different but the values are similar. The people I met are very well educated-especially in Torah and Talmud. They're neat and pleasant, and the kids are integrated with the rest of the varied Israeli society.

By the time we left, Shabbos was over and we borrowed money for busfare. We got home eight-ish, absolutely exhausted-but what a wonderful day. The weather was great. We ate in every house. I saw a tremendous part of Jerusalem. It is a city of contrasts. I saw the most beautiful and the filthiest- magnificent homes next to old ruins- hard to believe people really live in them. I saw many of these places when I first arrived but now I have a much better concept of Jerusalem as a whole. It's a difficult place to understand because in essence it's one big circle surrounded by Jordan on three sides. In the beginning I thought the Mandelbaum Gate was so far away- an isolated place- but it's quite an integral part of the community and highly populated.

Time is really going fast and when I think that there are only four more months left I get terribly upset- it's just awful. Student flight schedules are coming out in a week and I have to decide which countries to tour on the way home. Oh well. Time's flying.

Daddy, better watch out! The mailman saw the photos of Mom and Jessie. He asked me if I have two sisters!

Thanks for sending Ricky's letter. He's as safe as he could be in Vietnam, but very lonely.

That's about it. Have to finish some work I didn't get to last night.

Love,
Tyra

March 16, 1967

Dear Zelda,

It was great seeing your parents last month. I love my new radio. I was accepted to graduate school next year and hope to take nine credits at night if that's allowed.

I'm back in circulation again. I was asked out by seven Israelis- went out with three, stood one up. One was a typical Sabra- with the "Oh, Tyra don't be a child" bit! Another one, after two dates told me he loved me. It's fun if nothing else. I still miss Neil terribly but that's life.

I got a letter from NYC Board of Ed. My licenses were revoked. Why? Because I didn't show up for a medical appointment in August 1967- five months from now! I hope I can start teaching in September.

My tests next week are in Jewish Philosophy and History of Hebrew Language which is terribly difficult, especially since I didn't do anything all year. I'm going to miss not speaking Hebrew next year. But I'm learning Arabic curse words so I can blow my top and no one will even know!

Tell me about your summer plans to Israel. Maybe we can meet here in July.

Love to all. Tyra

March 16, 1967

Dear Tyra.

Please don't be mad at me for not writing. I don't know how to tell you this so I just will. Lenny is dead.

"Oh, my God," Tyra gasped, raising her hand to her mouth as her face turned ashen. She started to read the letter from the beginning again, hoping the words would change, praying she read it wrong the first time.

It happened a couple of weeks ago. He and his friend Arnold were canoeing and they drowned. The police said it was an accident, but tell me how the deaths two college kids, drunk out of their minds, stoned on weed, canoeing in the middle of Lake Kiamisha in the middle of a thunderstorm could be considered an accident. He was so stupid, I could kill him. They dredged the lake for three days before they found the bodies and my parents were devastated. I feel so awful. He caused so much trouble between my parents and me, and used to gloat about it, but he was my brother. Do you know at one point, I heard my mother cry out to my father, "Why wasn't it her?" But you know they always favored him and hated me. I don't know what's wrong with me. I don't have any pity for them. Didn't you tell me once that God doesn't command us to love our parents? I forgot what that discussion was all about, but what does God say about hating your parents? All I know is that I am miserable and I can't wait to get out of here. I am so desperate and alone, and can't stand being near them.

As far as Ricky goes, please don't expect me to write to him. I could barely get this letter off to you. Please write soon.

Love, Dawn

March 20, 1967

Dear Dawn,

I don't know what to say. What a heartbreak and how lonely you must be. If only you could just pack up and come here to spend some time with me. We are so different but you have always been my best friend. I can tell you anything and we really understand each other. We could really give these Israeli guys some grief, too, for a change.

I think the discussion we had about God referred to the fact that all the commandments require us to perform an act or deed- a mitzvah, and that even God cannot command a person to feel a certain way about another human being- to love someone- love comes from the heart- it is a feeling- and feelings cannot be forced. Hence a child must respect a parent, but cannot be commanded to love him. Perhaps you should talk to a rabbi to help you through Lenny's tragic death- accident or not. I have always found, that even though they don't have the answers to life's tragedies and problems, and they are only human themselves and there are no real solutions, rabbis are comforting and have said things that I could hold on to which make things a little easier for a while.

Until this happened, things had been going so well for you. Please stick with school and keep up with your job. And please, please, don't start drinking again.

Don't worry about Ricky. I'll let him know. Write soon.

Love,
Tyra

March 20, 1967

Dear Ricky,

I was so happy to get your letter. I think of you all the time. I love being in Israel. I am studying my tail off. It is very hard but it is exactly what I wanted to do. Israel is an amazing place, and everyone, even girls, under the age of fifty is a soldier at one time or another. It is always dangerous, the border is always a few feet away. I can't tell you all the "incidents" that happen on a day to day basis but when you live here, it's just the way it is, and you get used to it. Otherwise you'd wind up in a psych ward.

My love life is crazy- the Israelis are strong and gorgeous- the Americans are screwed up, and I don't expect anything serious to happen this year, which will please my parents no end!

Enough about me. As far as Dawn is concerned. Some bad news. Her brother Lenny drowned in a terrible accident a few weeks ago and she is forlorn. She sends her love to you although she isn't in the state of mind to write much these days.

I hope this package gets to you by March 26th which is the Festival of Purim. After the destruction of the second temple, the Jews were exiled to Babylonia and Persia. In Persia, Haman- a high-ranking official tried to arrange a total annihilation of the Jewish people. He almost succeeded but we- a strong and stubborn people- were saved and the king ordered Haman to be hanged. The story is told in Megillat (Scroll of) Esther. It is a joyous holiday and there is a custom that everyone sends platters of candies, cookies and fruits to their neighbors. It is called Shalach Manot- the sending of portions- and this is my portion to you! There's also another custom that even in our greatest joy because we were saved, we must think of others and give charity. We must think of others who are worse off than we. I think it is very beautiful to think of someone else when you yourself are happy. That's what it means to be a Jew. I hope you enjoy the goodies and the scroll!

You think your latrine is bad. The megillah-the roll of brown paper- this is what Israelis call toilet paper- I call it cardboard- and that's why it was so easy for all my friends in the dorm to write on it and send you messages of love and wishes for your safety- also riddles, jokes and puzzles. It also proves your friend —me- is as crazy as ever! I hope it fills up lots of your free time with entertaining laughs knowing that there are many of us, me especially, who care about you and pray for you all the time. War is a horrible place to be and I can't wait for you to get home.

Write soon. Be safe.

Love
Tyra

March 20, 1967

Dear Tyra,

It kills me to know that you are so unhappy at this time. This was supposed to be such a wonderful year for you. It seems all you girls are having boy troubles- Irit with her possessive one, and your roommate is a romantic, starry-eyed girl altogether. Tirzah with all that pressure on her. You're young women still. Study and prepare yourselves to be independent in your futures. Have a good time, but don't let your hearts get broken. The important thing is to choose the right person when the time is right. Look at your father and me. We struggle every day to get by, but who better to struggle with than the one you love? Than the one who loves you and who tries to do the best for you? Hopefully, your life will be easier than ours. No struggling for you, this is what I pray for, my darling daughter.

Make the best of what is left of the time in Israel. Think of all you have accomplished so far. When you return you will finish your studies and get a good teaching job. You will find a good man to love, this I know.

You can't judge people on the basis of their passports. Our family knows better than any how wrong it is to judge by appearance rather than quality. You have good sense and when the time is right you will choose a man you will be happy to share a lifetime with. I just hope it will be someone closer to home.

Love,
Mom

April 23, 1967

Dear Mom and Dad,

It sure would be easier to send a card than to think of something original to write, but there aren't any decent cards here. Congratulations for sticking it out for twenty seven years- here's at least to twenty seven more! L'chayim! Now Jessie can join in. I had so many invitations for Passover I didn't know how to choose. I went to a family in Petach Tikvah and they were super nice to me, warm and friendly. Everyone else argued and was hurt that I didn't accept their invites but I could only be in one place. It's not easy being in such demand. Seriously, everyone is so hospitable here, it's just amazing. You should have seen the supermarkets. Everything was turned upside down in honor of Passover. I don't think you could have found a trace of chumetz if you tried. Not many items have labels, but on each shelf there are sheets of papers saying which products by which companies are kosher for Passover. Everything is in Hebrew and it's nerve-wracking. I didn't have patience so I wound up with coffee, matzah and chocolate!

I got a letter from the Director of Seminar. He offered me an advisor position at the summer seminar starting August 24th. I would love to go and have to answer him within the next two weeks but I wanted to clear it with you first. I want to make sure there aren't any objections leaving home so soon after my return. I should be home by the 14th. Let me know.

We're on vacation now and I will be traveling around the country, trying to see places I haven't been to yet. Don't expect too many letters but I will send postcards in the next few weeks. I will return to Jerusalem in May for Independence Day celebrations and then I will really crack the books for finals. Promise. Don't worry about me. I'm doing okay.

Love,
Tyra

PART TWO

JERUSALEM OF GOLD AND STEEL

THIRTEEN

JERUSALEM OF GOLD

May was a glorious time of year in Jerusalem, and because of the exceptionally excessive winter rains, the city was more beautiful than ever. The hillsides had broken out in a bloom of color. Thousands of dainty *rakefot*, the fragile, red-petal wildflowers, carpeted the rocky slopes outside the dorm building creeping toward the valleys below.

It was good for Jerusalem to be joyous, Tyra thought. For her there was a bit of sadness, especially when she would walk along the strip of Rehov Yaffa, closest to the border with Jordan. Jerusalem was a divided city. The Palmach could not hold on to the most holy places during the War of Independence in 1948. Jordanians seized the Hebrew University and Hadassah Hospital on Mt. Scopus; they captured and defiled the Kotel, the Wailing Wall in the eastern part of the city, as well as the ancient cemetery of Har Hazaitim. Tyra couldn't fathom how anyone could crush tombstones and use the rubble to make roads, roads inscribed with bits of engraved Hebrew letters memorializing the dead, trampled on by vehicles and donkeys and their dung. The more she thought about it, the angrier she became.

Walking along the border, especially close to the high walls that were built to protect Israelis from barrages of gunfire and mortar attacks, accentuated the restriction of those parts of the city. Tyra likened the feeling to an incision on one's body that did not heal, always smarting, yearning for what one could not have. Yet she admired the pragmatism she saw all around her. It seemed to her that Israelis didn't have the luxury to pine for what they had lost. They were too busy building new: the new Hadassah nestled in the slopes of Ein Kerem, the new campus in Givat Ram, and synagogues to take the place of the Wall. Perhaps the Temple would be rebuilt in another time, but this was now.

The capital had been gearing up for Independence Day celebrations. More than two thousand soldiers had taken up residence in makeshift tent-camps around town in the last two weeks. One encampment sprung up overnight in the adjacent valley, a mere rocky, dirt path away from the dorm. There were as many soldiers swarming around the city as there were wildflowers sprouting up from the ground, either to march in the parade or protect the people. The best, most modern equipment of Zahal- the Israel Defense Forces, were to be marched about and displayed. The city was bubbling and the celebrations, the fireworks, the parties, the concerts, all of it would be great and exhilarating.

Tyra looked out of her dorm window, the scene a reward for all those months of cold, searing dampness that pervaded the stone buildings and terrazzo floors, causing even young bodies to ache, making them huddle around kerosene stoves that never gave off enough heat for lasting comfort.

Tyra sat on the bed, sipped a cup of tea and began to pour over a complex story by Shenhar, one characteristically heavy in symbolism and laden with biblical references and proper but unfamiliar archaic usages. She put the cup on the desk to turn a page of the text, and with her free hand, stroked her hair off her face and placed a tress that had fallen over her eye behind her ear. She was full of frustration. The story was difficult to comprehend and she did everything she could: underlined key phrases, looked up words in the dictionary, and reread the passages, but to no avail.

Tea. She was determined to lose the fifteen pounds by filling up on tea. She missed the ease of being slim and lanky as she was all her life, although Barak told her recently that she looked radiant. "Israeli men like women with meat on their bones." But she was tired, almost ashamed to ask her mother to keep sending new clothes, each bundle filled with garments a size larger than the last. Enough, she decided. She vowed to give up the warm freshly baked breads she loved. Funny. She hardly ate bread in the States, just Grandma's *chalehs*. She imposed an embargo of *g'lida*, hardly as rich and creamy as the American ice cream she remembered and especially, and the hardest to resist since she loved it the most, falafel, especially from the Yemenite kiosks. "Nobody made falafel as wonderful and fresh as the Yemenites," Tirzah, said, and she was right.

May was a new beginning for Tyra in terms of her studies as well. She had cut classes for almost two months, since March, to get away from Jerusalem and Neil. Tyra had tried to find solace in hitchhiking through the country. She explored Israel with the zeal of a prophet. She knew the wadis, crevices and craters of the Negev, and the streams, hot springs and hidden lakes of the Galilee. She traced the paths of Abraham in the south, near Baer Sheva and Isaiah in the north, along the Carmel, and she cloaked herself in the history of her people as if it were Joseph's coat of many colors, with all the strengths and frailties it represented. So that even though she was broken-hearted, she was happy in her heritage and comfortable with the places she was in.

Final exams were soon approaching, and somewhere between Mitzpeh Rimon and Arad, she decided to salvage the studies she started in October. She returned to Jerusalem to see if she could garner sympathy from her professors and make up all the work she had missed. The year should not be a total loss; no matter what, she wanted to get credit for the seminars and courses she had taken and would go on to complete her master's degree in the fall, after she'd return to New York as scheduled.

Tyra sipped the very last drop of tea, dropping her head all the way back, when she heard a knock on the door, and the quiet spell of determination was broken as Bella barged into Tyra's room.

"Come with me to the army camp, Tyra," Bella said. Her smile was big and her voice, enthusiastic. She was swinging a newly pressed khaki uniform on a hanger in the air. "I have to bring this to a soldier in valley. He needs it for the parade tomorrow."

"Can't," Tyra said pointing to the stack of papers on the desk. "I have to finish this dissertation. Don't tell me you ironed clothes for a stranger. Your boyfriend Bernardo must be delighted."

"He wouldn't mind. It's no big deal. You shouldn't be so bitter just because Neil was a creep. These are our boys. It's the least we can do. They'd die for us."

"You see a war around? I have to study. After all, I can't be a total failure." A sound came out of her mouth, a cross between a sigh and a laugh. "How could I ever face my parents?"

"There are no classes till next week. Come on. When Tirzah gets back she can help. She's the real brain around here." With her free arm, Bella dragged Tyra out of her chair and pulled her toward the door.

Tyra laughed. She was used to Bella barging in, making her presence known, not only because of her bulky, solid size, but her energy and lightheartedness as well. "Wait," Tyra called out as she nearly lost her balance. She scooped up her shoulder bag and the Super 8 movie camera stored on the shelf in the corner of the room. "Might as well be prepared."

The two girls made their way down the winding snake path toward the army camp. Tyra began to feel lighthearted and jovial, slipping and sliding down the steep, rocky hillside. She was stiff and clumsy, one hand grasping the air for balance and her super 8 movie camera in the other. Bella skip-hopped down the crude dirt path, holding the hanger at shoulder height, too high for comfort, making sure the long sleeved khaki shirt she had just washed and ironed didn't drag on the ground.

Sunday, May 7, 1967 3:30 P.M.

Dear Mom, Dad and Jessie,

Jerusalem is bustling with about two thousand soldiers preparing for Independence Day next week. The latest military equipment—there is even a rumor that a Mirage jet will be displayed during the parade. Can you imagine, the streets will serve as a runway for it! We have two days off from classes and our crowd is planning a real wild party.

Bella and I took a walk down to the army camp in the valley, not even five minutes away from the dorms. I took my movie camera and started to film a regiment of paratroopers during a drill. An officer came over and told me to stop. But you know me, I filmed anyway. The guys started to make faces and we just cracked up; the camera was shaking in my hands. A group of foot soldiers was listening to an officer giving them instructions for the parade, and as I filmed them, they started to turn around to the camera and make faces. The officer gave them hell, and he also kicked us out. I was surprised he didn't take away my film, but typically, the army's bark is smaller than its bite. When he turned back, we hid under a truck, and after a few minutes, a couple of sailors came by and started to kibbitz with us.

There's a lot of excitement about the Independence Day celebrations. Everything stops and the people live it up.

Tuesday, May 17, 1967

Hi Again,

Sorry I didn't get to mail this letter sooner but I got so caught up in the celebrations and will fill you in now. Sunday night, Tirzah, Bella and I sneaked into the stadium on campus for the big ceremony. It was jammed and all the dignitaries were there- Ben Gurion, Rabin and Eshkol. The music was wonderful and everyone was standing, dancing at their seats. The fireworks were fantastic and at the end of the ceremony, huge beacons of light shone in the dark, cloudless sky making Magen Davids encircling the heavens. Can you imagine, here in Jerusalem, even the sky is Jewish!

Barak snagged six tickets to the annual Song Festival at Benyanei Hauma Monday night. They are so coveted and hard to get. It seems Barak is a very amiable person and although he is only a simple carpenter, because he worked on the Knesset, he knows a lot of people in the government, and got the tickets for his daughter and her friends. That's what you call protektzia. Life is so much easier here if you know the right people. Otherwise, we would have had to listen to the concert on the radio. Of course, Barak made sure one ticket was set aside for me and Irit told me I could bring Tirzah and Bella, too. The songs in the contest were beautiful, but the special song that was commissioned for the occasion, Jerusalem of Gold, was absolutely magnificent. The words told of the longing the Jewish people have for the Old City- of praying at the Wailing Wall, and of being able to travel to the Dead Sea via the shorter route through Jericho, which of course is off limits now because it's in Jordan's hands. The melody was so haunting that when the concert was over, thousands of people streamed out of the theatre humming it into the parking lot.

We got back to the dorms and celebrated with an all-night party with the South American crowd. Bella and Bernardo are a real item- he puts her on a pedestal. They'll probably get engaged soon. We had a blast dancing to La Bamba. Luis stuck a long-stemmed rose in his mouth, hopped up and down, and had us all cracking up. By dawn, mostly everyone was sprawled out, sleeping in the social hall.

Later that day, Tirzah, Irit and I went into town to see the parade. We were able to sneak up to the front using our feminine wiles to get past the guards, but it was hardly worth the effort- maybe a thousand marching soldiers and a few jeeps- no tanks and of course the Mirage was nowhere to be seen. There were rumors that the government didn't want to antagonize the Arabs by flaunting our might. Irit said that Barak heard there were rumblings of trouble with the Arabs and a call-up of reservists.

Sleep's been at a premium these days, so if I survive these shenanigans, I'll write again soon.

Wednesday

Dear Mom,

I promise I will get to the post office to mail this today, promise!

So sorry I won't be there for Grandma's and Grandpa's 50th. I thought it was so cool of you to have their party in the Israeli nightclub, in my honor. I ordered a hand written scroll which I hope will be ready by next week, so I can mail it in plenty of time. Fifty years of marriage- I can't believe two people could spend their whole lives together. I can't even keep a boyfriend for more than a couple months.

I addressed this to you Mom, because now that my year in Israel is almost up, and because it was you who bore the brunt of it, I want you to know how much it has meant to me. I know you didn't want me to come, that you were afraid for me, but all in all I have been safe. I feel safer walking through town at night here than walking from the subway station at home. In fact, since I've never been on a plane before, I am more afraid of flying home than I have been of Arabs trying to push me into the sea.

I have accomplished what I set out to do regarding my studies in Hebrew Literature for my master's degree and have attained a level of fluency that I am proud of. Studying did not come easy to me, especially in the two master's seminars. All I need to do is complete two papers and pass my final exams. You'll be happy to know that I will be returning home without any "foreign entanglements," just as I promised you and Dad last year. Bella and I decided to spend two weeks in France, Italy and England. Since it's on the way home and will hardly cost anything extra, we might as well take advantage of the opportunity. I can't wait for you to meet her. I don't think you will mind if she stays with us for a few days before she goes home.

Mostly I wanted to thank you for encouraging me about my studies and especially comforting me about the debacle with Neil. I don't know how I would have gotten through it without your help. And also for taking the time to write long and newsy letters. I know you are tired after work, and the last thing you need to do after dinner is to spend hours writing. But you kept me in touch with the family, and believe it or not, even though it may sound so exotic that I am away and having exciting experiences, I have missed all of you terribly and all has not been perfect. If it weren't for your letters, I don't know how I would have gotten through the rough spots.

I can't explain this feeling, but even though this year has been far from perfect- being that my love-life and studies fell below my expectations, there is something so extraordinary about living in Jerusalem that makes me feel so complete and worthwhile. This feeling has grown within me almost from the very beginning, and I can never put my finger on describing what it is exactly, though I try and try. Hopefully, now that the year is coming to a close, I will be able to articulate soon exactly what it is that I feel.

Love,
Tyra

FOURTEEN

CAUTION: BORDER AHEAD!

The year away from Jessie's watchful eye didn't bring Tyra the love and freedom she sought. Rather her troubles from the past tagged along, not so much as a valise that could be separated from her or lost, but as an appendage, gripped around a vital organ, a permanent guest imposing on an unwilling, grumpy host.

The year was a tough one for Israel as well, filled with infiltrations, sabotage, danger, and numerous, blatantly biased Security Council meetings and condemnations. The Soviet Union was arming the Arab countries to the teeth while America was mired in her own problems in Vietnam. Since May tensions were oozing under the surface. Israel was as alone as Tyra, but Israel would have the courage. Tyra feared she wouldn't.

"*K'dai lach.*" Her professor assured her that her effort would be worth her while when he would return from the reserves. The practicality of her earning the maximum twelve credits she could use for graduate school, the idealism of fighting for one's country, and the fear of dying for the homeland tore her apart like a heap of sweet *chaleh* dough divided into three parts for the braid. *Flecktls.* All of a sudden she thought of *flecktls*, the miniature braids Hana, her beloved grandmother, made extra crisp just for her. She was so lonely and homesick. Her mind was wandering aimlessly as her legs carried her automatically to the dorms when the still silence of the heavy *hamsein* air was pierced by the radio's six beeps, like wooden toothpicks jabbing a mound of rising *chaleh* dough.

Six beeps. Steady. Staccato. Piercing. *"Zocharayim tov. Hasha'ah shalosh v'henei ha'chadash'ot."* (Good afternoon. The hour is three and here is the news.) The announcer of the State's radio station, Kol Yisroel, the Voice of Israel, billowed confidently in Hebrew over the airwaves. The afternoon broadcast began like every other, on the hour, and on the half-hour, and whatever the time, day or night, hustle in grocery stores or chit-chat on busses would halt as the people would pay heed to the news of the moment. The longer the silence of the audience, the more trouble there was. In this land of never-peace, perhaps war, what would a new day bring? Sabotage, infiltration, snipers, a border skirmish? Tension had been steadily increasing over the past few months, and this day, May 18, 1967, brought the region closer to war. Much closer.

U Thant, Secretary General of the United Nations, complying with Egypt's request, the strong, steady voice continued, *withdrew U.N. Peacekeeping Force from Sharm el Sheikh and the Straits of Tiran.*

The logic of it was so simple, yet the wisdom of it defied logic. Egypt, so overburdened by her attack of Aden, could not sustain a war with Israel. Yet she had to threaten the tiny country in an attempt to save face with Jordan and Syria, who accused her of reneging on her agreement with them. How much would Gamal Abdel Nasser risk for his people, and what price will Israel pay?

335

As a result of the UN decision to pull its troops, Israeli trade via the Red Sea to Africa and Asia ceased to be protected. Israel's economy was already wretched from an excessive, disproportionate defense budget, and could hardly withstand a cessation in commerce. Nothing to do but wait and see.

Despite the efforts of Israelis to go about normal daily life, they awakened as they had for the past nineteen years almost to the day, on guard, and just three days past Israel's nineteenth Independence Day, to the threat of war.

Tyra found herself torn again. On one side, she had to placate her family and reassure them she was safe. On the other, she had to summon up all the strength within her for she knew the right thing to do was to stay. How could she run out on her people, her relatives after all they had done for her? She was a Jew; Israel was the Jewish homeland. She belonged here. Why should the burden fall strictly on Israelis? True, she couldn't fight in the army, but she could help. There was plenty to do to keep the country functioning during the state of emergency. If only she could be brave, like Jessie, like her father, like her Uncle Sheldy.

A little more than a week had passed since the U.N. troops pulled out of Egypt. Israel was in a state of preparedness. Technically classes were still in session, but hardly anyone was on campus. Tyra didn't even know if she could earn any credits toward her degree back in the States. Fifty percent of the men, students and teachers alike, were drafted in the first wave of a reserve call up. Classrooms were near-empty and the campus was a semi-ghost town, except for the women, foreign and Arab students who were of course exempt from the military. Soldiers from the makeshift encampment in the valley below dropped by to get cigarettes, some real food, or a shirt laundered. Mostly they came by for some chitchat. School was the last thing that mattered now. Somehow poetry takes on a bizarre meaning when the fifty-two year old chairman of the Department of Hebrew Literature of the Hebrew University of Jerusalem dons military fatigues and sports an Uzi on his shoulder as he patrols somewhere along the Syrian-Israeli border.

When she returned from her classes, Tyra picked up a special delivery letter along with some notices that were slipped under the door to her room. She put the unopened letter on the desk. She knew what it would say. It was the third special delivery letter in as many days. "Come home," no doubt. Please, help me have the courage to stay, to do my part for my people. Don't break me; don't make it easy for me to be a coward. I'm terrified as it is. Help me be strong. No. "Come home, Tyra. We're worried." No doubt. She would deal with the letter later.

She grabbed her basket of toiletries, and turned on the dual current electric rollers so they would be hot by the time she finished her shower. A flick of the switch from 110 to 220 volts, and she could use them in Israel, a real convenience- top of the line- no adapter or transformer necessary. Her parents had given it to her as a gift for her trip. She ran her fingers through her knotted tresses. She loved styling her hair. Even in high school, she took pride in wearing her hair differently every day.

Tyra would set her hair before going to dinner. The academic routine had been broken; Israelis were already reporting to their reserve units; classes were half-empty. Despite the crisis, there was an all-out effort to keep the routines of daily life as normal as possible. Mail was delivered, banks were open. That is why she too decided to keep her routine, to pretend things were normal, that in the words of Israelis, *yeyeh tov*, everything will turn out good. She walked down the corridor to take a shower. She had just enough time before the crowd would show up. It seemed her room was the focal point for the *chevrah,* the group. Maybe it was because of all the good nosh she always had on hand, the nosh that cost her twenty pounds. Kaye sent packages with everyone who traveled to Israel during the year, and along with a tin of her grandmother's home baked *mandelbrodt,* there was a new pair of dungarees, always a size larger than the last.

Her shower done, she knew she could not avoid reading the letter much longer, but she did take a few extra seconds to unwrap the red strip of the pack of Tareyton's and crinkled the cellophane in her palm. She had been smoking for nearly six years. When she was fourteen, she asked her father for permission.

"Everybody's doing it," she pleaded.

"You're too young," Sid said. "When you're sixteen, you can smoke."

He said it just to placate her. After all, two years was a long way off. But Tyra didn't forget. She wasn't the kind of daughter to sneak or do things behind her parents' back, but she held in a little corner of her mind that her father did give her conditional permission to smoke, and the day she turned sixteen she started huffing and puffing. Tareytons. The same brand as Sid. She didn't remind Sid either, as she already had his permission, but she didn't smoke in front of him, or Kaye or even Jessie. Jessie would probably tell on her. As usual, Tyra avoided scenes, confrontations and the risk of being refused. She was eighteen before she had the courage to light a cigarette in the presence of her parents. Now, as she drew the match to the end of the cigarette, she saw the yellow of her fingertips. Her teeth had been stained as well. Even her sundresses and polo shirts had become speckled with tiny burn holes here and there where hot ashes would inadvertently settle on the fabric.

It was an expensive habit, too. A pack of American cigarettes cost four lira- more than a dollar thirty. Israeli cigarettes
were cheaper, but they burned sour, and were not as coveted.
Luckily she still had a stash of duty-free cartons she managed
to hoard throughout the year. This carton she just opened was
one her great aunt Sylvia brought duty-free for her from the
airport in March.

Tyra was disgusted with the habit, and tried to stop many
times. Now during this unbearable crisis, the fear and the tension, she would make an attempt, at least to cut back- to be in
some control. She always expected more from herself, always
trying to improve during the bad times, when it was harder. If
she could break the habit, attain the victory then, it would be
twice as sweet.

She picked the letter up in her hand, and fingered the
red and blue stripes along the edge of the airmail envelope.
No matter how far she traveled away from home, she felt
tied to her roots. Had God bestowed upon her a double portion of grace and beauty, and in doing so, halved what He
gave to Jessie? Tyra felt the excess with guilt and sadness, as
one wears a woolen overcoat in a drenching rain, the heavy
weight of the sopping fabric bearing down on one's spirit,
leaving it damp and shapeless. She resented God and Jessie
both for making her miserable. Though others saw her as
thoughtful and generous, she criticized herself as being too
selfish. And when they admired her confidence and capability, she saw herself as wimpy and indecisive. So far away,
she was able to create the allusion of being free. Merely
tethered to a long, loose string, the letter she was about to
read would yank her back to the real world, like the ball
attached to an end of a rubber string bouncing against the
paddle.

May 20, 1967

Dear Tyra,

    Our anxiety is not only for you as our child but also for Israel and our people.

    We're all glued to the television. I've used the phone in the office like crazy and my boss doesn't say a word. I hope your passport is handy. Please get on a plane- now.

Love,
Mom

Luis came by the dorm to pick her up for dinner at the Mensa. He had liked Tyra from the beginning, but she discouraged him. Tyra had that gift of making people feel comfortable. She was never a talker, but she listened attentively and her friends learned they could count on her. It was like that with Luis, too, and they enjoyed a good friendship despite his disappointment. He was great fun to be with and happened to be the best dancing partner she ever had. The South American *chevrah* would party in the social room, play poker and dance Latin dances to the music of El Choclo or La Bamba. Luis had a short, squat body. His curly hair was messy; his mustache was thick and untrimmed. Standing erect, with a long stemmed flower in his mouth and a bent elbow behind his back, like a matador, he would encircle Tyra and grasp her waist, dipping her so low that the ends of her flip would touch the floor. They were just friends, but he made her sparkle, and brought the life out of her, making her giddy and childlike.

They were walking back from dinner when he asked her if she wanted to go to Building #4 at ten the next day to change the dorm into a field hospital. "A medical contingent from Hadassah is coming and they need help. Want to do it?" There was no amusement in his tone now.

Most of the male students were in the army, and their rooms were needed for this new purpose. The volunteers would learn first aid, scrub the rooms and stock them with supplies, roll bandages and practice emergency procedures.

Tyra hesitated for a moment. Hospitals and the like were not her thing, but these were special times. "Sure. Come by in the morning. Let's walk over together. Okay?"

There would be a lot of work to do; she should try to get some rest. She needed to get the letter over with. She sat at her desk and wrote a few words to comfort her folks. Then she would try to get some sleep.

Monday, May 22, 1967

Dear Mom, Dad and Jessie,

I received the invitation to Grandma's and Grandpa's 50th anniversary party on June 10th, and regret to inform you that I will not be able to attend as all students are drafted to guard the borders of Jerusalem- until June 11th- wouldn't you know!

Actually, I'm writing to clarify the present circumstances as certainly you are concerned, and I want to reassure you. Please, please don't worry.

It's all a matter of Arab politics. Egypt screwed herself up but good, the U.N. can drop dead and everything else is just as normal as ever. In the last few incidents between Jordan, Syria and Israel, the first two claimed that Egypt finked out of their agreement to come to their aid. Things have been quiet with Egypt in the past few months- most probably due to Egypt's role in Aden. Egypt's excuse was that she could not start up with Israel because of the U.N. Emergency Forces stationed on the border. So after enough pressure, she gave in and gave the U.N. an ultimatum to withdraw some, not all, of her troops. The only decent thing U Thant did in terms of strategy was to withdraw all the U.N. Special Forces. Egypt didn't think the U.N. would pull out altogether. She just had to ask them to save face with the other Arab countries. So now she has no excuse not to fight Israel but most of her forces are in Aden- so she's in a pickle. Meanwhile Israel doesn't anticipate anything to happen; nonetheless, she is completely prepared. There was a partial reserve draft over the weekend and every tank and air attack unit is fully prepared.

The situation is serious- the people are angry. They've stocked up on provisions, and they are willing to fight. But no one really believes that anything will happen. Israel's nose got caught in the bungling of Arab politics. Because Israel is so prepared, the Egyptians would be at a loss to surprise us, and you know surprise is war's best weapon.

Dovid, the leader of the American Student Opportunity Plan (ASOP), explained to us that the situation is similar to the one before the Sinai Campaign in 1956, but now there are ONLY seven instead of ten Egyptian soldiers to each Israeli soldier, so we're in good shape!

Everything is almost as normal as ever- we're even making a surprise birthday party for Bella tomorrow night. The only thing is I won't be traveling on the Western (Egyptian) border of the Negev. We went to the beach in Ashkelon last Shabbos- it was crowded and the water was great. Don't worry.

Love to all,

Tyra

She looked out the window as she sealed the envelope. Of all the Arab soldiers, the Jordanians were the best. They were trained by the British Legion. They had a reputation for being the bravest and most skilled. She had seen Jordanian soldiers countless times throughout the year as they patrolled the rooftops all along the border in the city downtown. They were armed with stern expressions on their faces wearing dress uniforms. These most capable, fearless Arab soldiers were the closest to Tyra, for when she looked out of the window of her dorm room, she could see the barren hilltops of the Jordanian landscape in the not so far distance.

Everything that Tyra wanted to leave behind, to run from- the pain, the hospital smells, the sadness, was right here. What if she had to help a soldier who was wounded, whose leg was blown off, or whose mind went berserk? Jessie was good at this stuff. She worked with sick children in Manhattan Orthopaedic Hospital now. She was the one who drew blood, hooked up mouthpieces to patients' respirators and taught them how to breathe. Tyra ran from hospitals and sickness. Always timid, always shy. If only she could be sure she would be able to meet the challenge.

Even six thousand miles away, the past was with her. Unwanted and uninvited, configurations of ghosts and spirits popped up and prevented an easy sleep. Tyra was never one for sleeping. Even when she was a child, Kaye would come into the bedroom, sit on her bed, and stroke her head to comfort her. "Sleep, little one," she would say. "Everything's alright. Life is good." But despite the gentle comfort Kaye offered her daughter, Tyra was never assured. She felt the heaviness in Kaye's words, as if she herself wanted to believe the things she spoke but couldn't. Life wasn't good. Kaye was always full of worry. Kaye never slept well either.

Tonight, as Tyra lay in bed, she tossed and turned, angry at herself. She would need strength tomorrow. There was much to be done, and she should get her sleep, but she tossed and turned restlessly as her thoughts conjured the long-ago frightening image of that white-haired, white-capped, white-uniformed, white-stockinged, white-shoed Head Nurse who patrolled the stark white corridors of Manhattan Orthopaedic Hospital in wide, chunky heels, whose every footfall thumped against the slick tiles of the Ninth Floor, warning the approach of the The Warden, Harriet Slater, R.N., who injected potent doses of dread into patients and especially little sisters.

FIFTEEN

OLD WOUNDS-NEW WOUNDS

The crisis intensified during the night and on the morning of May 23rd, the nation awoke to the somber realization that another threat of war had been made. The quiet of the early dawn was spoiled by an overly nervous American student who must have likened himself to Paul Revere riding through the colonies with a lantern in his hand yelling, "The British are coming; the British are coming!" It was six thirty-five when he ran up and down the corridors of the girls' *shikun* banging his fist on every door. "Get up. The Straits are closed. Nasser closed the Straits. Get up," he hollered, as if the students could do something. They couldn't do anything. Tyra didn't bother to turn on her transistor radio. She already missed the six thirty newscast. *Kol Israel* gave no minute to minute updates. It offered no special bulletins. Regularly scheduled programs were never interrupted. This was Israel. Each day percolated its own emergency, and if every infiltration or act of sabotage or sniper shot warranted a break into the normal programming, stability and calm would be worn away. National sanity was one weapon Israelis could not afford to lose. In Israel, one waited for the six beeps every thirty minutes, at the top of each

344

hour and the bottom, and Tyra would wait until seven o'clock to hear the news for herself.

A flurry of activity accumulated in the hallway as girls tied belts around their robes, rubbed sand from their eyes, and peeked out of their rooms to check the commotion in the corridor. The modern-day Paul Revere explained that Egypt declared an official blockade of the Straits of Tiran. Israel's sovereignty was violated, commerce to and from Israel was jeopardized, and the ever crucial oil supplies coming from Iran via the Straits would be forced to return.

Jerusalem was quiet. Hardly any cars were on the roads. The army had already confiscated private vehicles, which for the most part were given over by citizens voluntarily and with their blessings to the military. Public transportation was drastically reduced and young boys who knew how to drive took over their fathers' bus or mail routes. The Dead Sea Scrolls, displayed at the modern museum across the valley from the campus, had been lowered from the Shrine of the Book into the underground vault for safekeeping. Sadly, there was no way to protect Chagall's vibrant stained-glass windows of the twelve sons of Jacob. The massive, colored-glass walls of the synagogue at the new Hadassah Hospital in Ein Kerem were sitting ducks, a lone bulls-eye in the center of a verdant Judean hillside. "Don't worry about the windows," Chagall said. "Worry about Israel's defense, and I will create even more beautiful windows."

Jerusalem, usually bustling, crowded and noisy, attained the demeanor of a ghost-town, bearing muffled sounds of life at ten percent the norm, the air heavy and hot, hard to breathe in because of the dry *hamsein* sand blowing in it.

Tyra remembered how enthralled she was the first time she walked down Yaffa Road to Zion Square in the center of the new city. Eyes wide open, she grabbed in every detail: the pushing and shoving of the crowds, a shop of hand-made

Yemenite jewelry adjacent to an electronics store, the tantalizing, unfamiliar smells of exotic foods which whetted her appetite. She was amazed and happy that all of it was kosher, and it was difficult for her to choose from the array of warm donuts, sizzling falafel balls, and hunks of schwarma roasting on skewers in kiosks set up right in the middle of the sidewalks. She sampled everything, one by one, eating as she walked. Such an uncivilized sight. People actually eating in the streets, and now she was one of them! The policemen on the corners directing traffic were Jewish. Firemen were Jewish. Sanitation men were Jewish. And so many soldiers- young and baby-faced, girls as well as boys, younger than she, wearing their casual green uniforms and lugging machine guns. Only once did Tyra remember seeing soldiers in the States- a convoy of jeeps and trucks passing the Millers on the New York Thruway during a return trip from the Catskills. She and Jessie kept waving, trying to get the attention of the cute ones, soldiers who would be stashed away in distant places, waiting just in case the Cold War turned hot. But here, soldiers weaving through throngs of pedestrians were part of the landscape- as indigenous as olive trees in the Judean Hills or salt in the Dead Sea. Israel, a giant bungalow colony, a comfortable place where everyone seemed to know one another, where in troubled times, they could depend on each other.

Tyra was reluctant about going to the first aid course. Her memories of hospitals were disturbing and she never had her mother's knack of comforting the sick. She lacked the instinct of knowing whether to apply ice or heat in an emergency, and the sight of blood left her weak and jittery. Always shy, she never was good at making small talk, and felt awkward while visiting sick relatives. But now she was glad she had decided to participate. Nasser's imposition of the embargo, an act of war by Geneva Conventions, made war more probable than possible. First aid might come in handy.

Tyra and Bella decided to walk the forty minutes to the main post office on Rehov Yaffo, rather than wait for an Egged bus that might or might not come. They could always hop on if one came by along the way. They wanted to send telegrams home and stock up on aerograms and express stamps. Streets were crowded with housewives and children stocking up on food and supplies.

Once they reached Rehov Melech George, they stopped at Nissim's Falafel Kiosk which they often frequented during the year. Tirzah, Bella's roommate who was a Yemenite Jew, told them that the *Taimani's,* or Yemenites, made the best falafel, and introduced them to Nissim, the owner. Nissim was not there though; he had been sent up to his reserve unit. His wife was trying to run the business. It was one thing to cook for her brood of seven children in the comfort of her home, but especially during the hamsein day, the smoke, the hot oil, along with her worry about Nissim made her grumpy and harried. "*Ayn davar.* Take your time," Tyra said, while she and Bella stood around, waiting for the balls to get good and crisp.

By the time they reached the post office, it was mobbed, mostly with Americans and other foreign residents. When they approached the express counter, the clerk asked them if they were afraid.

"Of course, a little," Tyra said.

"Well, I'm here now. You don't have to be afraid," he said smiling.

Bella added, "Of what, you or the war!" The people standing around laughed.

The telegram window was even more jammed. An old man called out, "What's going on here? You have to wait an hour and a half to send a telegram."

"*Mazav hamor,*" the clerk behind the window shouted. "Don't you know we got emergency?"

An emergency, Tyra thought. Even after all her time spent in Israel, it still grated on her, the sound of English sentences without the use of indefinite articles when Israelis spoke English.

Pushing alongside the girls was a short, Southeast Asian fellow wearing a United Nations uniform.

"Sorry, girls. Didn't mean to step on your feet. Where are you from?"

"You're from the U.N. Why do you care?" Bella said, as she shook her head with a touch of scorn in her tone.

"I know it looks terrible. We're trying very hard. What's your phone number? Maybe I can visit you? " he asked, looking at Bella.

"You've got to be joking," Bella said, and the girls started to laugh, and were still laughing even as they walked down the steps onto the street.

"Men will be men. Even a war can't stop them." Tyra said.

There was a strong sense of comradeship and solidarity, a lot like the way Americans behaved during the Cuban Missile Crisis of 1962, and as they walked through the city, strangers waved and greeted each other saying "*Yeyeh tov, Yeyeh tov.*" It'll be good. The mood was solemn, but not morbid. Smiles were hopeful while eyes were filled with worry.

The post office was close to the border of the Old City, and Tyra could see the high protective walls that were built along the border in 1948 to protect Israelis from Jordanian fire. What if the Jordanians broke through the walls? No, Eskhol assured King Hussein that Israel wouldn't attack Jordan first. Hussein for sure, would stay out of the war.

When they got to the corner, they took up places on line at a makeshift Magen David Adom station. Two ambulances were parked on the street, and nurses were helping the passersby who were donating blood.

"Come on, Tyra. You look so pale, and you didn't even donate yet. Get a grip," Bella encouraged.

Tyra kept taking deep breaths until it was her turn.

The *shikun* lobby was bustling and crowded with all the foreign student volunteers and medical staff when Tyra and Luis entered. The rooms were empty as the Israelis were already in their reserve units, and by the end of the day, the bottom two floors of the dorm would be converted into a makeshift hospital for those wounded on the Jordanian front.

A dark-haired IDF medic walked to the center of the lobby. "My name is Uri Gavron," he said and immediately and without any pleasantries began describing the symptoms and treatment of shock. At once, his deep, imposing voice commanded attention and the buzz from the volunteers ceased while they scurried to sit on the floor. "Where there is external bleeding, give warm drinks," Uri instructed in his terse, stilted English. He demonstrated the use of tourniquets on pressure points, and showed how one should tie a tourniquet with a pencil or stick to add pressure. He taught the necessity to relax the pressure every twenty minutes for five minutes.

They could barely keep up as they rushed to scribble every word he said. Yet he continued without pause, as if he were speaking to the air. So rushed, so much to cover. He described how someone bleeding internally should be treated. "Drinks forbidden, but keep lips moist, best with lemon. If fainting, lower head and slap face. Rub hands with alcohol," he said.

Struggling to keep up, Tyra felt totally frustrated and skeptical. She envisioned bombs bursting in air, soldiers bleeding in the streets and wondered where one gets lemon in the middle of a war.

Uri told them the proper way to move an accident victim on a makeshift stretcher. "Remember, do not move the wounded unless you have at least eight people, four on each side of the stretcher. Stand staggered, not directly opposite each other."

Two of his staff demonstrated CPR as Uri described the steps, and Tyra asked if they should come up and practice. Uri was annoyed by the interruption. "No time. We need to set up another field hospital across town." Tyra's face felt hot and red at his gruff dismissal.

When he finished all the points on his list, he packed up his gear without even saying thank you to the group. He probably just didn't want them to get in the way. He slowed his pace and brushed by her as he left. "Don't be afraid," he told her. "You Americans aren't used to this. Vietnam is not in your backyard, not like here. Don't worry for courage. God gives it to us when we need it. Remember, courage will come." He glanced around the crowded room and added, "It's good you all stay to help."

Tyra was shocked at the change in his manner. He put his hand on her cheek and asked her her name. She told him, and he said, "Come see me at Hadassah, Tyra, when the *ba'alagan*, craziness, is finished."

His hand was soft, and the initial disdain she felt toward him changed to mild attraction. He was good-looking, of medium, solid build. His fingers were stubby but strong. Most of all, he seemed so confident, so self-assured. It was a strange sight she observed as he left the building. A doctor carrying his life-saving black bag on one side and his Uzi on the other. She prayed for his safety. *Baruch atah Adonai, Magen Avraham*- Blessed art Thou O Lord, Shield of Abraham.

The students stayed behind to scrub the floors, disinfect the beds, furniture and bathrooms. They rolled bandages and arranged the supplies neatly in the cabinets. It was hard work and after several hours, the hospital smell overpowered her. By the time she and Luis left for the cafeteria on the other side of campus, she breathed in the smell, and because the air was heavy with the *hamsein* stillness, there was no way for her to clear her lungs, and the burn lingered.

She didn't feel like eating, but the others would congregate there, and as long as the Mensa was still in service, it seemed like a good idea to take advantage of a hot meal. You need your strength in times like these. Neither she nor Luis were energetic enough or inclined to speak. He too was under pressure to return home to Argentina. They were hot, tired and parched. She grasped his hand and in the heavy silence befitting the oppressive heat, and the comfortable silence of their friendship, they climbed up the steep dirt shortcut to the cafeteria. Tyra was troubled and homesick. She knew her parents looked to her to bring joy into their lives, fulfill the dreams they had for her, and she couldn't blame them, considering all they went through. Obligation was crushing her. She knew another telegram or special delivery would be waiting for her, urging her to return. *Come home, Tyra.* She displaced their pleading by memorizing what Uri had taught about shock, shrapnel and wounds. But Uri's words about courage took over and spun around in her head many times over. *Remember what you learned and don't worry for courage. Courage will come.* The two mantras blended into one and kept spinning. *Courage will come. Come home.* Which would she choose? How could she choose? Surrounded by friends, strangers, brethren all, never did she feel so scared and so alone.

Tyra picked up the postcards and blue-stenciled announcement from the American Embassy that were slipped under her door.

May 23, 1967

AMERICAN CONSULATE GENERAL
JERUSALEM

Due to current situation, the American Consulate General advises all American citizens to depart from Israel immediately via the first available transportation. They should make their own travel arrangements with commercial transportation companies or travel agents.

Americans who do not have valid passports should get in touch with the Consulate General to obtain such documentation.

Those citizens who are permanent residents of Israel should obtain exit permits from the nearest office of the Ministry of Interior.

Those subject to Israeli military service should obtain permission from the nearest office of the Ministry of Defense to depart from Israel.

Tyra crumpled up the sheet of paper. Thanks America, for all your support, she thought. Johnson had already announced the United States would remain neutral. He had his hands full with Vietnam, and her thoughts went to her high school friend, Ricky, who wrote to her earlier in the year from Cam Ranh Bay. He called it the safest place in the country. But how can anyone be safe in war?

She skimmed the postcards. Heaven forbid there should be at least one telephone in the lobby so she could keep in touch with people. Communication was primitive, behind the times, and annoying. The frequent letters she wrote throughout the year were usually a thrill for her, a way of remembering tiny details that surely would be forgotten after time if they weren't recorded. But now, writing was a chore, and an inconvenience. If only the country were a little more modern. A cousin near Beer Sheva wanted her to stay there, another in the north wanted her to go there. The last was from Vicki, the rabbi's wife.

Tyra- If you are in Jerusalem, please stay with us until the crisis blows over. Our home...

Tyra visited them when she arrived and because of them, she met Neil. A fluke turned to disaster, but they meant well and she still loved them in spite of it. Vicki wanted her to meet

Paul, but then there was that mix-up with the toothbrush Tyra left at the Singers, and Paul's friend Neil was the one who brought it back to her. Neil-Paul. Their initials separated by one letter of the alphabet. Neil-Paul. Each name, four letters. Neil-Paul. One syllable, and a final *l*. Would her life be different today if Vicki's intuitive choice was the one that materialized? But now was not the time to muse about if's and could have been's.

She glanced at the card once more before she dropped the mail on her desk.

... is yours. Be safe.

Love,
Vicki.

Tuesday, May 23 7:45 P.M.

Dear Mom, Dad and Jessie,

I really don't know how to begin. I know that you're all worried but as of now there is nothing to panic about. I got a telegram this afternoon when I got back from class and I sent one when I went into town a few minutes later. It's true the situation has changed since the last time I wrote. Then the country was in a state of preparedness. This morning we all got up early at the news of the blockade at the Gulf of Tiran and it really surprised everyone. No one expected that Egypt would do any more than chase out the U.N. The situation is serious but we can only wait it out to see what happens. There's no use predicting what will be. Meanwhile, life is going on as normal minus a few things. There's a slight reduction in public bus transportation due to the fact that buses and bus drivers were drafted. Classes are in session and there is absolutely no panic. The people are fantastic and it reminds me a lot of how it was during the Cuban Crisis. We're all hopeful. As of now, there is no reason to flee. Trust me to decide the right thing to do.

Irit came today in the morning and I went over to her place for lunch. Everything's okay with her family. Last night we made a party for Bella. It was lovely. Before then, Neil came up. Friends, friends we will always be!

I can't think of anything else to write. I bought a whole stack of aerograms and will try to write at least once every 2, 3 days. I'm sending this to your office so you don't have to wait all day until you get home.

I was planning to tour the Galilee from Sunday to Tuesday, but because of the situation I decided to stay in Jerusalem. Irit wants me to go to Haifa but I'll be here until the situation blows over. Please don't call here. I will keep you informed of my plans.

Please don't worry too much. Wouldn't you know that after I sent the telegram, we went to eat falafel. Life is just as normal as ever. Seriously, it's tense but not drastic. Keep calm. Love to all. Will write soon (unexpress). Take care. L. Tyra

SIXTEEN

NIGHT VISION

The mostly religious neighborhood of Mussrare was one of the oldest and poorest in Jerusalem. From the edge of a hill, Tyra saw the road that led to the original Hadasssah Hospital and Hebrew University on Mt. Scopus. Only a tiny part of the amphitheatre could be seen in the distance, and the whole area fell within an inaccessible strip of no man's land, enclosed and cut off by twelve-foot tall barbed wire fences. It was on that road in 1947 and 1948 that the convoys bringing water and provisions to Hadassah were constantly attacked and decimated, a stinging defeat for the Palmach of old, and a terrible loss of life. The primitive and squalid apartment buildings of Mussrare were pockmarked where numerous randomly scattered bullet holes landed during the past twenty years.

Tyra took part in a contingent of volunteers from the university who organized an assembly line of sorts to fill sandbags and fortify shelters in the ultra-religious neighborhood.

An old, stooped-over woman in an cotton print housedress was walking down the street. Her head was wrapped in a scarf, with only little snips of gray strands hanging out. She hobbled down the deserted block shouting, "Water, water," as she carried a pitcher and some small cups on a tray. Tyra and her group were putting down their shovels to sit on the sidewalk for a brief rest, and the lady offered them refreshment wholeheartedly, grateful for their help in an old forgotten neighborhood that was never spared enemy fire. At least the religious were helping this time instead of hindering. They opposed the existence of Israel because the Messiah hadn't come yet, but even they knew that if Israel were destroyed now, the Messiah would be farther away than ever. Even the Hasidim were in the army for this one.

They picked up their shovels again just as the elementary school let out early for the day. Curious, the children ran over to see what was going on, and they joined in, piling up the sandbags. Tyra and a dark-haired girl, maybe ten years old, made eye contact, smiled and started to talk. The girl pointed out her apartment down the block.

"Would you like to sing an American song?" Tyra asked, and she taught them the words and hand movements. One by one they started singing. Singing and shoveling, singing and piling.

Where is Sunday? Where is Sunday?
Here I am. Here I am.
How are you this morning?
Very well, I thank you.
Run away. Run away.

In spite of the tension, the children were quite cheerful, but when they got up to the Thursday refrain, they stopped singing as the beeps of the one o'clock newscast signaled the start of the news. A blaring cacophony of beeps and static echoed through the neighborhood as residents in apartments and people on the streets raised the volume of their radios and transistors and news of Nasser's speech earlier that morning gripped their attention. Since May 23rd, when Nasser blocked the Gulf of Aqaba to Israeli shipping, the United Nation's Security Council was in almost continuous session and American and Russian warships converged into the Mediterranean Sea. On May 27th, Nasser threatened to shut the Suez Canal and the flow of oil to Europe if the West intervened on Israel's behalf. Now his words were broadcast from a meeting earlier that morning of the Arab leaders who converged on Cairo to sign military pacts. "We intend to open a general assault against Israel. This will be total war. Our basic aim is the destruction of Israel."

Even before the newscast was over, shots rang out from a rooftop in no man's land, as if the Jordanians were buoyed by the announcement of the bold Arab ambition against the Jewish state. Children and volunteers alike scurried for cover behind an old apartment building. There were reports that four Jordanians were seen in the area, and that was the third time shots were fired in the area that day.

A few of the little girls started to cry and a policeman came by and told them to go home. They scattered except for one who cried out, "I can't. My house faces Jordan." Tyra grimaced at the worn policeman and then walked over to the lone girl.

"Don't be afraid. The bad guy ran away," Tyra said, as she stroked the girl's curly hair. "Hold my hand and we will walk home together. Come. Tell me your name. Mine is Tyra."

"Ye..Ye..hu..dit," the girl whimpered, trying hard to stop her crying.

They walked the few blocks hand in hand until Yehudit was safe at home and Tyra tramped (hitched) her way to the dorms.

She approached the grounds of the *shikun* during sunset, and by the time she entered into the lobby, it was night. Strange how there is hardly any dusk in Jerusalem. As Tyra approached the entrance to the campus, a thousand tones of reddish gold shimmered in a land where dusk comes and goes as quick as the shuffle of a deck of cards, and just as the cards are arranged in a completely different way with each mix, so to the city has an entirely new appearance, a soft, transparent dark drape floating down covering the hilltops one by one. And like millions of fireflies suddenly escaping from a big glass jar, tiny lights springing forth from within the treetops, quicker than stars fill the sky, adorning the beguiling Holy City in a bejeweled crown, made even more precious at that very moment because of her vulnerability.

Dusk in Jerusalem still fascinated Tyra, even after nearly of year of observing the awesome transition from day to night. In the Catskills, the sun would set leisurely; shades of golds and reds, pinks and oranges splattered across the sky, slithering into shapes both familiar and strange, conjuring wistful fantasies from the forms they took. Here, the distinction between light and dark took but a quick moment, a mere shadowy haze descending from on high, a sheer gray veil drifting like a coverlet over the rolling slopes, like angels tucking the Judean mountains into bed for a night of calm and of peace. Never as at this moment, right now, did Tyra feel as heavily, and with intense certainty, the presence of God. They say there are no atheists in foxholes. Tyra was never a non-believer; she always believed in God. But she vacillated between a gentle, loving faith and a bitter anger toward Him. At this moment though, with the entire Jewish people in grave danger and virtually alone amongst of the nations of the world, the Miller story of struggle and heartache paled, and Tyra's heart softened as she implored God to protect her people. "No more millions, not again," she whispered. Never as this moment, right now, did she yearn for the assurance of God's watchful, protective eye.

She was tired. The day's work was rigorous and the accompanying tension added to the exhaustion. Her straight brown hair was disheveled and limp, her sleeveless cotton shirt damp and unkempt. From the way she dragged herself across the hall, the small tote bag slung over her shoulder seemed to be heavier than its size would allow.

She was glad it was dark as it was the darkness that obstructed the panorama of endless and majestic rolling hilltops and valleys, lush and green for a short distance, and then starkly delineated by white, stony Jordanian slopes way off as far as the eye could see. At least it was the night and not the protection of the glass walls that hid the massive, comforting slopes. Out of her line of vision now was the threshold of heaven, the closest place she had come to reach her own spirituality, her sense of purpose. She ached for the serenity of those hills, their presence violated by the need to protect the city from their enemies. She was lonely, homesick, and of course, afraid. The huge glass walls of the sleek modern building were dressed for war, wearing multiple rows of dingy white strips of cloth, pasted crosswise, sideways, vertically and diagonally from corner to corner. That was the student project last night. A civil defense activity a day keeps the nerves away. Not quite.

She climbed the staircase up to the second floor and entered her room, glancing through the open window at the Jordanian hilltops across the valley. Below, on her desk, she saw her papers strewn about, and the texts. She had been struggling to compose a thesis for the Master's Seminar in Modern Hebrew Poetry with Dr. Yarkon. The whole year was a struggle. She remembered the first day she entered his class, ten students sitting around a conference table. She understood his first few words of introduction, and then labored to understand every word thereafter. An American, with just a few years of college Hebrew Literature behind her, competing with Israeli graduate students was absurd. Her confidence was shot. Even graduating from Lexington with Hebrew

Honors didn't mean much in Jerusalem. Prose was hard enough, but poetry was impossible to understand. Plodding through archaic structure and high vocabulary proved to be a hopeless challenge. Now the paper was just sitting around collecting dust. The instructor in the undergraduate course in Zionist Essay chided her for signing up for his course, too. "Welcome, *Geveret*, Miss Miller. So you think you can understand Jabotinsky and Ahad Ha-am?" Tyra almost died when he walked in and took a seat at the conference table as a student in Dr. Yarkon's class. Nor could she tell which one of them was the most embarrassed.

Tyra picked up the special delivery letter that was slipped under the door and sat down on the bed. She was tired and dusty from the day's work in Mussrare. Hamsein had been brutal for a week, the air was heavy, the extreme heat so parching, and the grit from the sandbags lingered in her mouth.

May 26, 1967

Our Dearest Tyra,

    Daddy called the State Department today only to learn that they issued warnings to all Americans in Israel and told them if they didn't evacuate, the Embassy would not be responsible for their safety.

    He is so upset; he forgot to order meat for the restaurant. Things look so grave. Nasser's army is much better prepared than you think. They are armed to the hilt with Russian MIGS and tanks.

    It's time for you to leave. If you wait any longer, it will be too late. Please. I beg you, come home.

All my love,
Mom

Tyra started to cry even before she finished reading the letter. She couldn't take the pressure, the waiting, her fear, her family's fear. She cried hard and afterwards, she felt a little lighter as if a valve released everything that had been building up. She walked down to the shower room, determined and strengthened. She returned to her room refreshed and clean, and struggled to write a convincing combination of words that would allay her family's concern.

May 28, 1967

My Dear Family,

I'm so sorry that you are so worried. I sent two express letters and several postcards during the week. Hope you got them.

We're all encouraged by the worldwide support we've been getting- it really makes a difference. Volunteers from all over the world are coming to help. The news broadcasts have been virtually the same since last Wednesday and I must say that it is a little nerve-wracking, the waiting, that is. We still hope for a diplomatic solution.

Today I helped clean up a poor neighborhood. The little children were a delight, but they know something is wrong- their fathers and brothers are away in the army. It's a pity they have to be afraid.

You said some things were vague. The group does not travel back to the States together. We all go our separate ways. As I said, I made temporary plans with Bella. As far as the money- we have to buy airplane tickets now and will get back $344 from the ASOP in a while. So what you're putting in won't be really used. If you understood that you're great- anyway you should know I'm not a spendthrift....

You said Daddy assessed the situation the same way I did in the first express letter I sent. The next day I wanted to confess how ignorant I am of politics- but that wouldn't look too good for Daddy! How's Jessie? How about a line or two, Stinker!

Please try not to worry. The people are terrific and there's still time. I'm careful and I'm not doing anything stupid.

Love,
Tyra

Tyra felt a little dishonest, the way she put an almost nonchalant take on the situation. She really wasn't lying to her parents. It was anything but stupid to help fortify the border neighborhood with sandbags. A little dangerous, perhaps, but not stupid. And she knew they were worried enough.

Tyra's room was quiet since her roommate Michal went back to Tel Aviv. Her father and brother were called up, and she didn't want her mother to be alone. As usual, Tyra seemed to have a room for herself only when circumstances were dismal, like when Jessie spent all that time so long ago in the hospital. She finally found a volunteer teaching position in Katamon, another poor neighborhood on the outskirts of Jerusalem and spent the last few nights teaching. It was crucial for these teenagers, who had jobs during the day to help their families make do, to continue their education at night. High school education was not government-funded, and once they would turn eighteen they would be drafted into the army.

Tyra unfolded a crisp, mint green aerogram from the stack she bought the week before, and started a letter to her friend, Zelda. They had majored in Hebrew at Lexington together, and Zelda, being the angel she was, sent hard to find translations of literary works that helped Tyra throughout the year. Tyra wanted to finish the letter before Bella came by. Zelda was the friend of Tyra's who Kaye liked most of all. She was a fine, religious girl, but not too religious, just traditional enough to make her parents proud. She was pretty, but not in an overly made-up way. Kaye said she had a good head on her shoulders. She was smart and practical. She got high grades and a good teaching position after graduation. Although she studied Hebrew with Tyra, she had no interest in flying off to speak a language no one in her family would be able to converse with her in. She searched and found a husband-to-be at a singles weekend at Grossinger's. Kaye said she had her feet on the ground, too, and the only time they would leave it would be when her bridegroom, who was an established pharmacist, would take her on a honeymoon to Israel. If only Zelda had been a better influence on Tyra.

May 31, 1967

Dear Zelda,

The room is dark and shadows from the flashlight are flickering on the walls. We cannot use electric lights. We tacked up heavy, opaque fabric over all the windows in the dorm buildings. The blackout is official and I feel like I'm roaming around London in a black and white World War II movie. Headlights of the military vehicles are painted black, and jeeps crawl about the streets like bugs that hum and whiz from unseen spaces in the night- you know they're buzzing about, but you can't smack them because you don't know where they are. I just peeked out, and the forced unnatural darkness made the stars lower and moon brighter and I can see the silhouettes of the hills encircling us. Is this our place in the universe? The multitude in the heavens- our people- the seed of Abraham? Oh, Zel, we are so outnumbered.

The Israelis have such an air of confidence and ability, and yet we are so outnumbered. There is so much trust and faith, and even so, how can we not be afraid?

There is such great solidarity- socialists and capitalists, kibbutzniks and city slickers, Moroccans and Yekkers, Hasidim and epicursim, the poor and middle class, all struggling together. The threat of annihilation from without brings peace within. The crime rate in Haifa declined so drastically that the city sent its policemen to help with the harvesting!

Israelis want peace so badly- live and let live, yet they must be posed for war, always ready. It's a daily existence of schizophrenia that should drive the entire nation insane, yet I see a resolve, an acceptance of the way things are, and the constant hope that things will get better. Hatikvah.

We've been so encouraged by the enormity of the world-wide support we've received. Volunteers are coming from all over-helping with mail routes, driving trucks, kibbutz and hospital work, whatever needs to be done.

Time is going slowly, and everyone's nerves are shot. The news broadcasts today sound as if they were tape recorded last Wednesday. We hope for a diplomatic solution, but there is a jitteriness that suggests fighting will break out before the night is over.

The room, the corridor, the campus, the night, everything was so eerily quiet, she took a break from writing, and flicked on the transistor. The stillness was violated as she heard the venomous messages the Arabs broadcast around the clock, on multiple airwaves, messages in every language, sparing no one from the threats. *"Every Israeli backyard will be a graveyard,"* be it French or English. She kept spinning the dial, but to no avail, and when she heard in Yiddish, *"Egyptian martyrs will finish what Hitler started,"* she clenched her teeth so hard, an acute pain jolted from inside her left cheek up to her forehead. Poor Grandma, she thought. Poor Grandma, as she lifted her left hand to her cheek. Preferring silence, she clicked off the radio.

Isn't there any place in the world for Jews? Our few kilometers are green and their millions of dunams are barren and sandy. They just can't stand us having anything. Maybe Apollo was just a conspiracy to rid the world of Jews. We should pray for a new moon, a full moon, a Jew moon. Maybe that's the only place for us.

One thing for sure, I have no interest in traveling around Europe on my way home as I had planned- Europe lost its allure- with Israel being in such great danger. Who knows what things will be like when this is all over? I refuse to imagine.

The university is unofficially closed, but will try to arrange for tests and transcripts for foreign students if they leave so they won't lose credit.

I'm glad we'll be in the two courses with Dr. Josephs next semester. I've mastered reading the newspaper and my fluency is great. I've been told my speech is getting more colloquial, but my use of idiomatic expressions gets me into trouble because I am still too literal. You should hear my guttural rolling "r"!

Don't read this to my parents- they'll probably get more upset than they already are. Love to Melvin and your folks.

Tyra

"I can't believe Bernardo did this," Bella cried as she stormed into Tyra's room, handing her a note. "How could he go back to Chile now? Two weeks ago we were talking about getting married. Now, not even a good-bye."

"The year is almost up. You just got caught up in the future and the heartache of farewells. What did he say?"

"His parents threatened to cut him off if he didn't go home. They're terrified."

The two friends, drained and tense, embraced. "Let's go eat," Tyra said. "Kugel or cheesecake?"

"Both," Bella said, and they giggled nervously, hoping to find relief from the endless waiting.

"I have to go to my folks in the Galilee tomorrow. They keep insisting, and they won't take no for an answer any longer," Bella said, as they walked to the kitchen.

"I know. My relatives too, want me to go—to Haifa and to Ashkelon. Maybe I could send half of me up north and half down south," Tyra answered, meanwhile thinking of what she would do without Bella.

June 1, 1967

Dear Mom,

I finally got a job teaching English in night school. I'm taking over for someone in the reserves, and will continue until the situation ends. It's in a poor neighborhood, and the students work during the day. The seniors are really restless- probably because they were due to be drafted into the army for their regular three-year stint after graduation, which would have been in a few weeks, and they feel like they're cheating, leaving the real job to the older men in their families. I have a ninth grade class of thirty brats, and everything I did flopped. Kids started fighting, and there was so much noise, no one heard the bell ring. I'm hoping Sunday night will go better- I'm running low on Excedrin!

You'd think that I'd be losing weight these days. We have a new motto- Eating more and enjoying it less. If this keeps up, I'll be able to wear Grandpa's pants!

Speaking of which, the Chief Rabbi (you remember, I met him on Simchas Torah, during a truly joyous moment), declared today as a fast day. He said that all Jews must bear the burden in this crisis.

I find it awesome that I am here now, in the place of our forefathers who sat in days of old, heeding the supplications of the prophets, beseeching God's mercy in abstinence and fasting. I've always read in books that in every generation enemies rose up against us: Syrians, Persians, Hellenists, Romans, Italians, English, Spanish, Polish, Russians, Germans. Now they arise in our generation, and it is we who are on the page.

I've been thinking a lot lately. If Grandma and Grandpa didn't have the courage to leave Poland, they probably would have perished in the camps and I wouldn't have been born. You know I don't want to cause you extra worry, but I've enjoyed Israel all year. I have been treated like family, adopted by everybody, and I can't run out on them now. There is much work to do; it certainly isn't glamorous, and if I don't do it, someone else, for sure, will. But my place is here- Israel fights for all of us, and God will not let us down.

Love,
Tyra

In a history of five thousand years, precise with pilgrimages based on the calendar and fasts born out of danger and mourning, a new fast had been created, and Tyra was part of a living history. Was this the excitement, the thrill the Jews of Persia, three thousand years before, felt when they too created a fast as Haman conspired to destroy them? And what of the irony, that Haman himself was hanged from the very noose he had set aside for Mordechai's death? Hadn't God heard their supplications them and answered their prayers? Was he listening now?

As a unique and spontaneous page was added to the liturgy of the Jewish people, Tyra fasted this newborn fast, conceived in the present, and serving as a link in the chain, history in the making. She fasted with gusto, appetite, determination and spiritual intent. Unlike other fast days of her youth, which left her empty, this one nourished and enveloped her in a veil of *kavanah*- devotion. It brought out the faith which had been trapped deep inside her for so long.

SEVENTEEN

FROM SACKCLOTH TO BANLON

June 1, 1967

Dear Mom, Dad and Jessie,

I've been writing just about every day. Have you been getting my mail? You probably got a telegram from ASOP N.Y. and that's why I'm sending this express to explain or try to at least, what's going on. ASOP N.Y. requested Foreign Students Office to evacuate us- now- when there isn't even an official evacuation by the Embassy. Yesterday we had a meeting with the Foreign Students Advisor and the Vice President of the University. He said the decision to leave now or to stay meanwhile is an individual decision. To all those who are staying, they are being as helpful as possible. Volunteer work is being organized as group efforts. Everyone must report to the office as to where he is at all times, so contact can be maintained. The University is unofficially closed and they will try to arrange tests and transcripts so that we won't lose credit. They also said that if and when a student decides to leave, they will try to facilitate his trip. In other words, the University and Foreign Students Office are being extremely cooperative.

Well, that's about it for now. Please try not to worry. Will write again tomorrow or Sunday.

Love,
Tyra

June 1, 1967

Dear Tyra,

It is late and just a few words to keep you informed. We are all exhausted watching the news all day and night.

You ask questions even rabbis can't answer. Maybe that is why we're despised; because we try to do the best we can, and others think that we think we're better than they because we're chosen. Chosen for what? All I know is that I believe in reincarnation, that all the miserable, cruel souls just roll around from one generation to the next, one place to another. It's always the same. Nothing ever changes but the fabric. Today it is us, only we are dressed in Banlon and polyester instead of robes of sackcloth tied around the waist with braided twine.

Meanwhile, we are all worried sick. Please come home now.

Love,
Mom

Had yesterday's fast already worked? Was it God or the Egyptians who let the American aircraft carrier, the USS Intrepid, pass through the Straits on the morning of June 2nd? Had the crisis played itself out, as Israelis had been debating of late? After all, with everyone prepared and all sides on guard, all borders fortified, surprise was lost. Perhaps Egypt could back off, even temporarily, just to capture a moment of surprise in the future. Surely, the Arab League would concur; they couldn't accuse Egypt of failing in her commitments to destroy Israel. Maybe relief was on the way.

The slight hope of the morning's events came too late for the Miller family. Hana and Lazer were about to celebrate their fiftieth wedding anniversary on June tenth, the Golden Jubilee- a time of rest and renewal. It was anything but that for the Miller family, and the trend of celebrating milestones tainted with pain or illness or now war continued.

Imagine, fifty years of two people, always bickering, yet totally devoted to one another and their family, reaching such a milestone. Kaye had planned the festivities to mark the occasion. It was to have been the grandest celebration since the bar mitzvah of Kaye's nephew. Kaye invited the entire family. She wrote Tyra of the plans for the party, and Tyra could tell Kaye was excited. She booked the Israeli Café Ra'annah in Manhattan and wrote details of the menu, kosher, of course, the centerpieces, the entertainment. Tyra knew she wouldn't go home for the party, but she had already ordered a parchment scroll from Tirzah's cousin who had one of the most beautiful collections of personalized art work she had ever seen. Tyra knew Lazer would really treasure it.

Tirzah's cousin Oded was a scribe and his calligraphy was ornate and perfect. He had soft gentle features, a deep olive complexion, and was perhaps a centimeter or two taller than Tyra. He was of the typical Yemenite *look*. It seemed that almost a third of the soldiers in the army were of North African descent, dark complexioned, short and slight of build. In the States, they would probably be rejected by the army because of their stature, and here they were the rock and standard of Israel's defense. In Israel Oded flourished as both a soldier and an artist.

Oded was generous to Tyra, too. He gave her a good price by virtue of her friendship with Tirzah, and even sent Tirzah a letter from the front and told her to tell Tyra not to worry that he was called up; he would work on the scroll in the tent at night and send it back to Jerusalem so Tyra could send it to the States in time. But by now Kaye had cancelled the party. "We're not in the mood to celebrate," she told the owner of the nightclub, who was an Israeli. He had refunded Kaye's deposit without a blink. "Who could celebrate with Israel's survival on the line?" he told her when he handed her the check. "I go home tomorrow to Eretz, to join my reserve unit."

Friday, June 2, 1967 10:30 A.M.

Dear Mom, Dad and Jessie,

I'm starting a letter because I missed the Friday pick-up and I'll continue this tomorrow and mail it Sunday. I haven't heard from you since Tuesday and I hope that nothing's wrong back home. I hope it's just because the mail might not be getting through. The weather's been very hot the past few days. It's hamsein and today it's 33 degrees Celsius in Jerusalem and 41 in the Negev- almost 106 degrees Fahrenheit- which is just horrible for our boys. It's very hot and air is very heavy.

Things look a little better now. Intrepid passed without incident, so it looks like Egypt's biding her time too. Also Lebanon didn't join the Egyptian-Jordanian Pact. A commentator said that if Syria joins, she'll have to fight in her major cities whereas Egypt will be fighting in a desert and if and when the moment comes, Syria just might not want to take the risk or damage.

1 P.M. Listening to English news on Kol Yisroel. Crime declined in Haifa so drastically in the past two weeks, that the city decided to have policemen help with the harvesting!

Was supposed to get up at 6 today to- don't crack up- dig ditches but didn't make it- slept till 12. Went to movies with girls tonight. Coming back got lift with soldiers (just like Independence Day, Jerusalem is flooded with them (Israelis, not Arabs). A whole bunch came for hot showers in the dorms.

There's a base at the Museum not far from the University and they invited us to coffee in their tent. Considering the situation it's an obligation to oblige. They were giving us all kinds of information- like the "games" taking place along the borders in the South. An Israeli tank moves to one side and the Egyptians have to protect that area on their side, then the Israeli tank moves to the other side and it keeps up all day. Tonight one of the guys was a watchman and he saw a young couple go into the museum grounds and he had to get them out because he didn't want the watch dogs to hurt them, but he didn't know how because he's afraid of dogs! They had us cracking up. They invited us back to visit and to bring cards and play for matches. Their morale is really very high and that's the strongest weapon we have. These guys feel the situation with a passion- it means something to and for them- it's not like Vietnam where the boys regret going and don't know why the hell they're there. One of the saddest things is to see an Israeli who wasn't drafted- he tries to hide from embarrassment.

I know it's very difficult for all of you now. I heard that one New York newspaper headline was "Israel fears extermination." Between stuff like that and all the bulletins (there hasn't been one special announcement yet here-everything waits for the regular newscasts), the tension must be very high. I'd love to suggest that you cut out newspapers and T.V. until this crisis is over but I know it's impossible. Try to keep in control of the situation and take things realistically and calmly. Worrying won't help so be strong.

Love to all,
Tyra

Bella barged into Tyra's room waving a telegram in her hand. "See this? My father wrote that all the American students returned home. "Come home immediately.'"

"I guess all the parents are trying to do everything they can to get us to come home," Tyra said and the two friends burst out laughing, aware of the ruse. Despite all the pressure, the telegrams, and their own fear, not one American student from the program had left Israel.

"I'm going to Kibbutz Negbah later, to help out in the apple orchards," Tyra told Bella.

"I'm going to my family in the Galilee, too. Be careful."

Their nervous giggles turned to worried sobs as they embraced.

"Let's be strong," Tyra said as they backed away from each other.

"See you later, alligator," countered Bella.

"In a while, crocodile."

The Independence Day celebrations of just two and a half weeks ago had been toned down to quell the rage of the Arabs. Israel's leadership thought it best not to flaunt its statehood and military might in the faces of the nations who despised her. The old guard of Israeli politics changed during the early sixties and was losing its grip. Ben's Gurion's fearlessness and chutzpah gave way to Eshkol's passivity and accommodation. The country was undergoing massive changes, changes the Arabs could interpret as weaknesses and use to their advantage.

In the few weeks since preparations for Independence Day so much had changed. There was an inkling of trouble then, and rumors of a reserve call up, but still there was hope that all would pass. Even Tyra seemed to adopt the inexplicable Israeli mentality of mild optimism tempered with a resigned sense of uncertainty. *Yeyeh tov- it'll be good,* and continued planning for the all night parties and wild celebrations. But instead of music and dancing, the *chevrah* turned to talk of what Israel meant to them, of not having to fight against scheduled exams on Saturday, as in their native countries, of being able to eat in any restaurant in Jerusalem because all were kosher, of how wonderful that Jews from all over the world had a place where they were accepted, and especially of how awesome Jerusalem was cloaked in the spirit of the Sabbath every seven days, and how God-awful it would be if Israel would be no more.

EIGHTEEN

I Lift My Eyes to the Mountains

The kibbutzim in the northern Negev along the Gaza Strip were struggling. The normal work force was depleted by the military call up, and things were even worse since the Egyptians opened up a blaze of mortar and machine-gun fire against Nahal Oz on Wednesday, May 30th. Civilian farmers were under attack, and members of the other kibbutzim in the area dropped their own work and ran to help the farmers put out hundreds of acres of fire in the ripe wheat fields. The crops didn't wait for the crisis to be over, and at Kibbutz Negbah, the apple trees had to be pruned or the entire crop would rot on the trees.

Two soldiers in an army truck waited in front of the Administration Building at the University for a group of volunteers they would be driving to Kibbutz Negbah. Before students in the ASOP could leave campus, they had to sign in with the leader so that each one's whereabouts were known, accounted for, and could be contacted. Although the most agricultural thing Tyra ever did was to pick blueberries during summers in the Catskills, and she wasn't thrilled with the thought of sweating in the hot fields, she knew she needed to do something useful. Bella had just left for the Galilee. She knew the other kids from the program, but they were just acquaintances. They, like she, were leftovers, hanging around Jerusalem, looking for something to do while the country waited.

The Intrepid had sailed through the Straits unimpeded earlier that morning. Did God respond to yesterday's fast or did the Arabs respond to the new unified Israeli government, with Moshe Dayan as the new Minister of Defense and Menachem Begin and Yosef Sapir as ministers without portfolio? Had the crisis worn itself out as some officials pondered? The waiting was nerve wracking. Even Chief of Staff Major-General Yitzhak Rabin told the troops, "I know the effort for a soldier to wait under high tension is no lighter than it is in actual combat." Nothing was certain but the uncertainty itself.

The roads were quiet. About fifteen volunteers, mostly girls, sat in the back of the open truck for the three hour journey. The hamsein was still relentless. It was 31 degrees Celsius in Jerusalem, but by the time they reached the Negev, it was 41 degrees. The roads were dry and dusty, and the tires kicked up clouds of sand that circulated around the students. It was hard to imagine how soldiers armed to the hilt with heavy war gear could manage to function in such conditions. Tyra passed around a pack of Tareytons, but it was just too hot, even for chain smokers to smoke. The pack came back to her unopened, and she threw it back into her tote bag. Some passed around oranges, which was a far better choice, for the oranges sections were sweet and wet.

The driver, a lieutenant in the Border Patrol named Boaz, pulled over to the side of the road for a quick stretch break. He turned up the volume for the noon newscast. The announcer told of the evacuation of all the children in Eilat, the southernmost point of Israel, the place from where on a clear day, you could see the Sinai in Egypt on one side and Jordan and Saudi Arabia on the other. At least the children were safe. Then the newscaster announced births of children whose fathers were soldiers somewhere along the fronts. "Dani B. of Rehavia, your wife Ilana gave birth to a healthy boy- 3.2 kilos, and he looks just like you!" On and on the list continued, giving the longed for information to men who could not enjoy the thrill of seeing their newborns, but rather had the solemn task of protecting their very lives. So a nation rejoiced publicly, cherishing the renewal of life, knowing that life goes on. The newscast concluded with a hearty "Mazel tov!"

"Can you take the heat?" Boaz said as they stood around the truck after the newscast was over. He called her *yefai' fi'ah,* pretty one.

She laughed, looking down at her shorts and sleeveless shirt. She felt sloppy and fat—just like a farmer. "You're not the only one who cares about this country. Here, have a cigarette, anyway."

Boaz jumped at the Tareyton Tyra offered him. "American cigarettes, a dream. Too bad they're so expensive here."

"I know. Everyone who comes from the States brings me a carton, duty-free. I want to stop, but it's hard."

"You can't smoke in trees. You'll start a forest fire!" he said, and they both laughed.

"You're a real Smokey Bear," she said.

"What?" he asked.

"Never mind. I'll look ridiculous trying to smoke on a ladder picking apples anyway."

She offered him the pack and he smiled as he took it from her.

They took up their places and continued on the journey. The truck pulled into the dirt road entrance of Negbah, and Boaz dropped off his cargo of volunteers. Tyra wished him luck and he drove off. The kibbutz consisted of a semicircle of bungalows, with a larger school building on one side, some storage huts in the back, and an A frame building that housed the large communal kitchen-dining room. Some of the children were digging up green lawns, turning them into trenches, while others were filling sandbags and piling them up in front of the *miklat*- shelter.

The orchards were visible in the background, a green dot standing up in the barren expanse. The harvesting was already finished for the day. It was just too late to go back into the fields in the heat of the afternoon. They would get up at 4:15 the next morning, Shabbos, eat breakfast and make their way to the orchards, where they would harvest until noon. Rifka, the teenage kibbutz leader, gave the students a tour of the kibbutz and showed them to their quarters- a row of barracks with cots and rudimentary cubbies for personal items.

Tyra settled in and washed up, and took a walk around the premises. She was drawn to the *miklat* where some youngsters were still piling sandbags, fortifying the entrance to the shelter. She walked over and tossed a few bags onto the pile.

When she was in elementary school, the students had to practice air raid drills. Children had to hide in closets. It was just so ludicrous and terrifying. Tyra remembered those drills clearly. The buzzers would unexpectedly blare throughout the halls and the teacher would call out, "Take cover." The students in the sixth row would crouch underneath the fifth row seats, making sure to protect their heads with their arms and cover their eyes with their hands. Each row of students moved over, one row farther away from those huge windows. The luckiest, the first row students hid in the wall-to-wall closet. They would be the safest. The safest against what? An atom bomb? It never mattered to Tyra where she hid. She was always scared, just because she wanted to be with her family. If she were going to die, she wanted for them to be together. Even if she were safe, she would just worry about where her parents or grandparents were. How cruel to be separated from those you loved. They would each die alone, her parents and grandfather at work, Hana in the kitchen, Jessie in junior high, and Tyra in a closet in P.S. 13. She was too young to understand that the world would be pulverized; she just worried that if her family died separately, they would not find each other in heaven.

She wondered what was it like for these Israeli children now, and she descended the stairs into the narrow tunnel. It was dark but for the light bulb hanging from a piece of twine in the middle of the space. Some children were stacking pillows and blankets on one side and jugs of water on the other. They were laughing, their voices animated. They seemed older than their years; they were used to this life near the border, exposed to sporadic shelling and gunfire. They were brave, and curious about her. She told them where she was from, and her family, and of the excitement of city life in Jerusalem.

The more Tyra saw of the kibbutz, the more it reminded her of a camp. The dining room was set up just like the camp in Catskills where she attended Leadership Seminars from Jewish Youth Institute of Higher Learning, with long narrow tables and benches or plain metal chairs. But then there was spirit, singing and joy. Tonight, only reserve, exhaustion and concern.

Rifka's mother was in charge of the dining hall that night. She was very friendly, and the conversation waxed nostalgic and calm. She pushed as much boiled chicken and potatoes as she could; she wanted everyone to feel at home.

The food was the typical Friday night fare, and lit candles in plain glass holders adorned each of the tables, along with a bottle of wine and chaleh loaves. It was not a religious kibbutz, and no one said the Kiddish or the Hamotzi before they ate. The absence of the men was obvious, and Tyra could only imagine how crowded the room would be on a normal Friday night. Way back in the room, at the far end of a table, a young man, perhaps nineteen or twenty sat alone. He ate quickly and was the first to leave the hall. He limped, and used a wooden cane to steady his gait.

At the end of the meal, the *kol'boh*, the steel bowl, was passed from one person to the next to collect chicken bones, fruit peels and other refuse from the meal. Tyra didn't mind the steel bowl anymore, although it had stunned her the first time she ate at a kibbutz earlier in the year. What seemed so uncivilized then was just so practical now. True equality- socialism at its best. Why should one person have to clean up after the others! After dinner, Tyra's group sat with the residents and listened to the English newscast. The Israeli Bond drive was doing extremely well, surpassing all expectations. "So that's why the crisis," old Yossel said, and everyone laughed. The Friday night movie was a Polish one with Hebrew subtitles called *The First Day after the War*. It took too much effort to translate, and the content wasn't exactly uplifting, so Tyra slipped out and took a leisurely walk to her quarters. She gazed in the dark at the shadows of the trees and buildings, and she jumped when she heard gunfire.

"It's nothing," the fellow with the limp said. Again Tyra was startled as she hadn't noticed him sitting in the dark on one of the wooden crates surrounding a tree. "There's an army base nearby. They're just practicing. They do it all the time."

Tyra saw the red flashes off in the distance.

"Can I sit here with you? I'm Ty...."

"Tyra. I know. The children talked of you. I'm Moshe. Moshe Boshe, the children call me." Pointing out to where the flashes were coming from, he added, "They play war games. All week long, our tanks move to one side, and the Egyptians move theirs. Then we move ours to the other side, and the Egyptians move theirs back again. All day long, back and forth. I know from my brother."

Tyra could see how forlorn Moshe was, telling of his brother's contribution, while Moshe himself was rejected from the army because of his deformed leg. She could tell by the way he chided himself, deliberately mispronouncing the word *boshah,* which meant shame, so that it rhymed with his name.

"You shouldn't be so hard on yourself, Moshe. What happened to you, it's not your fault."

"It's not fair, I have to sit here while they protect me."

"Fair is for the world to come, not here, not now," Tyra said, tapping her hand gently over his.

"God punished me twice. My brother has all the girls, too," he added with a sardonic chuckle.

Tyra told Moshe about Jessie's scoliosis, the problems she had with people because of her condition, how they excluded her, how cruel they were. "I thought it was men mostly who couldn't get past a woman's looks. I see girls can be pretty superficial also."

"You are very pretty. You must have plenty of *haverim.*"

"My friend Ricky's in Vietnam," she added, changing the subject. "He said that he would give anything to be home, that most of the soldiers there felt that way, especially since they learned of all the protests in the States. They're risking their lives and for what? Even the Vietnamese don't want them there." Tyra added the story of one of the boys in college who had hay fever, and the night before his medical exam, picked a bunch of ragweed and put it on his pillow. By the morning, his eyes were red and swollen; he was congested and could hardly breathe. He showed up for his medical exam and was rejected, no questions asked!

"Well, we are home. That's the difference. You better get some sleep. I shall take the girls to the orchards at quarter to five in the morning."

Tyra was just about to ask, when he interjected. "I made a tool I could use to put my bad foot on the clutch so I can drive." Then he walked her to the girls' bunk.

Tyra offered to wake up the girls at four fifteen in the morning for the harvesting. She never was much for sleeping, and refused to allow herself to doze for fear of missing the alarm

381

and failing to wake up the crew in the middle of the night for harvest duty.

She took in the sounds of occasional gunfire that woke up the babies in the nursery and chickens in the coop, the crying and cackling. When the gunfire stopped, and the babies and chickens settled down, the buzzing of the crickets, the hoots of owls, and weird howls of unfamiliar desert critters were heard in an orchestra of nocturnal life, keeping time to the repetitive tick-tock of the alarm clock Tyra had buried under some clothes in the closet.

She popped out of bed at 4:15, right on time. It was still dark; the moon and stars still shone but less brightly as they were fading with the onset of first dawn. The roar of one air force jet flying overhead in the desert sky jolted the sluggish dawn calm out of Tyra. Another day. More tension. As promised, Moshe picked them up in the truck at a quarter to five and they were in the orchard by five. The kibbutzniks showed them how to place the ladders and how to determine which apples were ready to be plucked and which needed to stay. The orchard was huge and it was amazing that with a little bit of organization, they were able to methodically prune the trees, even with the water breaks that became more frequent as the morning progressed and the sun got hotter. The singing was a big help, and spirits were high. The work was tedious, but necessary. They sang the rallying songs for Soviet Jewry composed in the early sixties against Soviet oppression of Jews when Russian Jews were forbidden to practice or learn about Judaism. At that time, the meager bits of news smuggled out of the Soviet Union indicated that the more vocal dissidents were forced into labor camps, or even worse, admitted into mental institutions and deemed mentally insane and tortured with mind-control drugs. The songs were the inspiration for the American idealists of which Tyra was part, to demonstrate at the United Nations and petition United States legislators.

The girls composed words of their own to other songs, too, and they sang impromptu words that were clever and apropos. To the tune of "Go Down, Moses," they sang:

Go Dayan, Moshe, way Day'an Egypt land.
Tell ole' Nasser, let our ships sail through.
If in peace you don't let us live-
We'll knock the socks off you.

Go Dayan, Moshe, way Day'an Egypt land.
Tell ole' Kosygin, let our people leave."
Our little corner in the world
He will not take away!

Go Dayan, Moshe, way Day'an Egypt land
Tell ole, Nasser,
The Tiran Straits you blocked to us-
Let our ships sail through.

For a little while the tension dissipated with the singing and even a little horseplay, apples being tossed around from one volunteer to the other, during the intermittent water and rest breaks. By twelve, the work in the orchard was over. Rows of wooden baskets laden with the fresh crop were lined up in the field and when Moshe stopped by, the workers relayed the bushels onto the truck. When they were finished, they piled into the truck for the brief ride back to the kibbutz to freshen up and eat lunch. Tyra was exhausted from the work as well as the sleepless night, and there was a knot in her stomach. She was bored and restless, knowing the rest of the afternoon would be wasted milling about. She didn't belong in Negbah. She had to get back to Jerusalem. She would feel more at ease if she were there. She could continue teaching where she would accomplish more working with students. That was her raison d`etre. She tried the outdoor pioneer stuff, but she just wasn't suited for it.

Rifka's mother tried to discourage Tyra from leaving, but to no avail. She became the center of attention as the kibbutzniks, including some of the children she had told her New York stories to at the shelter and Moshe crowded around her, trying to convince her to stay. She kissed them goodbye and they wished each other safety. None of the other American girls wanted to go back to Jerusalem, and though she was a bit leery, Tyra made her way to the main road by herself. She waited under the shade of a tamarisk tree by the side of the road, getting more and more nervous as the waiting seemed interminable in the utter quiet and desolation, and she became more uncertain that a vehicle would come. The kibbutz leaders warned her not to leave. She was alone, defying civil defense regulations. She couldn't return to the kibbutz. It would be too humiliating. A breeze kicked up, and as if a miracle occurred, she perceived a slight break in the hamsein. Finally she saw a military vehicle in the distance coming from the south. As the truck approached, she ran into the middle of the road and flagged it down. At first, she thought it was passing her by, and she jumped out of the way while screaming for it to stop. Luckily, the jeep screeched to a stop a few hundred yards past her and she ran towards it, her tote bag bopping along on her side.

A soldier hopped down from the back and started to yell at her. "You have to get back to where you belong. You're not allowed on the road."

"Listen, I *am* trying to get back to where I belong. Can you give me a lift?"

"Are you from Negbah?" he asked.

"Yerushalayim," she answered. "I have to get back to Yerushalayim."

"We can't take civilians. If you get hurt, we get in big trouble. It's too dangerous."

"How can you explain to your officers that you left a lost American stranded in the desert to die. Then you'd really get in trouble. Wait a second," she pleaded, and reached into her bag for another pack of Tareytons. "Here. Please, take it."

She saw an officer jump out of the jeep from the driver's seat. "Can't take the heat, yefai'fi'ah?" He laughed.

"Boaz," she screamed. "You *mamzeh*! You knew it was me and you let me squirm! Come on, please. I need to get back to Yerushalayim."

The lightheartedness she saw on his face before quickly turned to a foreboding seriousness. "Why? You can help here. It's dangerous. There's been some activity further south. Go back to Negbah."

"I can't explain. I just need Yerushalayim. If war breaks out, that's where I have to be."

"*Hal-ah, ha-lah.* Come on. Let's go. Sit in front. You can squeeze in the middle." He chuckled at the idea. "And duck if I tell you to."

As the jeep pulled away, the driver pulled down the visor to help block out the sun's glare. There was a photograph of President Kennedy tacked onto the back of the visor. Tyra gasped as if she had seen a ghost. "If he were still alive, we wouldn't be in this situation," the driver said. She understood how he felt. She still found it hard to believe that her beloved President was gunned down in cold blood. She rode the train in disbelief of the rumors she heard that Friday afternoon. When she walked into the lobby, the super's door was open, and she heard Walter Cronkite's voice. "The President is dead," he announced, and Tyra knew it was true, but couldn't believe it. She always had a hard time believing bad news, holding out hope against hope for bad things not to happen, unable to convince herself of reality. How sharply she remembered those somber days of mourning. She cut out every article about Kennedy in all the newspapers Sid brought home from the store, and saved them in a carton. It seemed that Israelis adored Kennedy, too.

The jeep rode hard northeast to the Crossroads, and as Tyra shook up and down, she turned to look behind her and saw the endless desert, the coarse bramble bushes and stony cliffs, fading in the distance.

Blessed art thou, O Lord our God, King of the universe, Who has enabled His people to bring forth apples from sand; Shield of Abraham, spread Thy wings of protection over your people Israel.

When they reached the Crossroads which led south to Tel Aviv, and north to Beit Shemesh, and then east to the foothills of Jerusalem, Boaz told the driver to stop. Boaz hopped out of the jeep and flagged down an army truck going toward Beit Shemesh and struck up a conversation with the driver. After a few moments, he motioned to Tyra to get out. "You're in luck. They're going to the base in the valley near the university. Good service, yes? Stay put, and be careful." He shook his head, laughing.

She kissed Boaz on the cheek, wished the other soldiers in the jeep well, and grabbed the hand of a soldier in the truck who pulled her up. It was almost sacrilegious for her to ride into Jerusalem on Shabbos. She had violated the entire Shabbos, from sundown the night before when she listened to the news and watched a movie. She rode to the orchards and she picked fruit, breaking the tenets of the Sabbath, disturbing life and rest. Yet what was her choice? Israel was too beautiful a country to be destroyed; she had to do something, to help. Sometimes things had to be broken so they could persist. *Esso einai el heharim ma'ayin yavo ezri? Ezri mayim Hashem.....* The sounds of the song kept repeating in her mind, timed to the bumps of the road, finding a rhythm in the hum of the motor. Rev Zemer composed the beautiful melody for the words from the Psalm. He taught it at a seminar long ago, and Tyra loved it since. *I lift my eyes to the mountains, from where will my help come? My help will come from God.* But soon she heard the soldiers singing too, and realized she had been singing out loud. The narrow, windy mountain road was lined with the burnt out remnants of the Palmach tanks which were attacked and destroyed during Israel's War of Independence. It was called Sha'ar HaGai, and served as a monument to those who lost their lives in battle. The skies were darkening as the truck made its ascent to Jerusalem, and the tanks were visible only in the silhouette of dusk. Stars would soon pop out of the cloudless sky. Three stars and Shabbos would soon be over. The hamsein had definitely broken, and a brisk, refreshing chill circulated through the late afternoon air, carrying the crisp scent of the pine forests. *Good, good for our boys. It will be easier for them, carrying all their battle gear.* The weather would be better for the Arabs too, but they wouldn't make as good use of their fortune. Tyra had broken Shabbos, yet as she entered the dorm, she felt good, as though she honored God as never before.

Shabbos ended and darkness enveloped Jerusalem and the city was returning to its *normal* Saturday night activities. Luis bumped into Tyra in the corridor and asked her to go downtown to catch a movie. Happy to see a familiar face, she agreed.

When the lights went down and the film started, she felt his arm around her. She dropped her head on his shoulder, and thoughts of this crazy year raced through her head. She thought of the men, at least a hundred Israelis, who would have been happy to sleep with her. Sid always used to tell her to play hard to get, to keep her self-respect. "A boy will take what he can get. The good ones will stick around and wait until it's right." Tyra never *played* hard to get; she just was. She hated the games, the strategies. She prided herself on being straightforward and direct. But she was miserable. Neil made her miserable while they were seeing each other, and she was miserable since he broke up with her. "Men, men everywhere and not a one to love," she mused, as if she had won some kind of war of independence of her own, and hadn't slept with any of them.

"Wake up, wake up," Luis said, gently shoving her head upright when the movie was over.

She stretched and yawned, trying to regain a modicum of alertness. "I haven't slept so good in months."

"Yes, picking apples is a good sleeping pill," Luis said. "And I can finally say you slept with me."

"You know your prepositions better than that. I slept on you, my dear, on you!" And for a brief moment, they enjoyed a hearty giggle.

Bus service to the campus had been suspended so they boarded the last bus to Beit Hakerem and from the end of that route they had no choice but to walk the remaining mile and a half to the dorms.

Two soldiers on patrol stopped them as they approached the valley below the dorms. After a brief conversation and cursory inspection of Tyra's purse, they were allowed to enter the campus.

Tyra picked up the letters that were slipped under the door. Kaye had written about the rally at the United Nations and her closing words, "*Come home.*"

NINETEEN

From Whence My Help will Come

Today, June 5, Jerusalem was high. The sky above was a deep sparkling blue, and so imperially high, cloudless, a perfect abode for Hashem. The sunrays glistened upon the plethora of tiny wildflowers, making the reds, lavenders, and yellows warm with color, dotting the mounds and slopes of the terrain with life. The elements were perfect and so out of sync with the expectations of trouble it contained. Today, all of Tyra's feelings of inadequacy, failures and loneliness fell away as inconsequential bits of triviality, for life itself was at stake, the very existence of Israel and the Jewish people were at the brink and who knows how any of it would turn out, and what tomorrow would be like, and if Tyra could live up to the task.

Tyra opened the yellow Western Union. She felt a wrench in her stomach as she read:

CALLED STATE DEP'T. SITUATION GRAVE. MOTHER SICK. FAINTED. COME HOME NOW. UNCLE SHELDON.

The others were sitting around Tyra's room, singing along to the song *Jerusalem of Gold*, which was playing on the radio. "If war starts, let it not be during this song," Tirzah said. The song had become a prayer during the last three weeks, since its Independence Day debut.

Tyra passed around the telegram and her friends shook their heads in commiseration of Tyra's dilemma. "We want you to stay, but we won't blame you if you leave," Tirzah said, and the other Israelis concurred. Most parents of the foreign students put the same pressure on their kids to return home. One student even received a telegram from her father who wrote: EVERY FOREIGN STUDENT RETURNED HOME, which obviously was totally false. She knew she wanted to belong, she couldn't desert, yet she was afraid of the unknown.

Irit stopped by with a tote bag on her arm. She wanted Tyra to go Haifa with her. "Hadas is in Tiveriah and *Abba* is in the *melu'im*, reserves. I spoke to *Emah* on the phone this morning. I can't bear to have her be alone. A ride is picking us up downstairs at eleven. We have ten minutes."

"Irit, I almost got arrested for civil disobedience yesterday." Tyra described her adventures being out on the open roads trying to get back from Negbah. "I have to be in Jerusalem."

Irit shook her head in disbelief and annoyance. "I don't understand you, Tyra. You do such foolish things sometimes. I can't leave *Emah* alone to worry about all of us being separated. What's here? We're your family. We're in Haifa and I can't leave you here alone in such danger."

Tyra couldn't explain that spiritual pull that gripped her, her need to find her own spot in Jerusalem, and once again she was in the middle, wanting to stay where she was for her own mysterious needs, for a feeling she could not define in words nor make any one else understand. Yet she was torn to do the right thing for her family, for she understood Manya's anguish as she did her own mother's. She was tugged between countries, even between cities, and like the *x* in the center square of a tic-tac-toe board, she was pulled in all directions in a game no one could win. Would there ever be a time when what she would want would be good for her family, too?

After some useless banter, she relented. "I'll straighten up and put a few things in a bag," Tyra said.

"I'll straighten up; you pack. We need to be downstairs in five minutes. Hurry." She spoke with a nervous urgency in her voice.

Tyra said her goodbyes to Tirzah and the others, and while she was throwing what she hoped would be enough clothes and toiletries to get through her time in Haifa, air raid sirens started to blare, and in a flash, artillery shells zipped relentlessly across the valleys from Jordan, whistling along the way. All of a sudden, in a blaze and a whir, she belonged. The national waiting was over; all that communal tension was released. It was ten o'clock in the morning and Israel was at war.

Tyra's vacillation paid off. Her indecision became decisive as a mere result of procrastination. When the war started, Tyra was there, not because she made a conscious effort to be, but because she let life happen to her. She belittled herself for not taking a stand, and there was little comfort in knowing she did not run, for she saw no courage in her staying.

All her life she witnessed the strength and courage of others. She observed everything, in silence, from the corner, in the back: Sid gave a helping hand to everyone. Once he even risked his life pulling a stranger to safety from the roar of a subway train. Hana fed the hungry and Lazer clothed the naked. Kaye nursed the sick and Jessie not only nursed the stray animals she picked up; she fought against man's cruelty and intolerance toward others. Tyra watched in silence and saw merit and honor in their lives and none in hers. Nor did she credit her own *cheshbone,* her account, her quiet existence, with worth or purpose. Even now, she did not choose to stay with her people; Israel chose her. Israel picked the time and night to strike at Egypt's air force and Tyra happened to still be there, pruning apples and teaching wayward kids, waiting for something to happen.

"Oh my God," Tyra cried out at the same time Irit screamed, "*Oy va voy, e'mah!*" Tyra picked up her survival bag- the one that she had packed two weeks ago and kept ready for the big moment, if it ever came. It contained her Instamatic camera, the Super 8 and film cartridges, aerogrammes. She would be participant and reporter simultaneously. She scooped up a bottle opener from the countertop. Sid always cautioned her to have her keys protruding from in between her fingers as she walked home from the train station at night for protection. "Punch him in the eyes and run!" he told her. "Defend yourself." New York was dangerous, too. She only had two small keys while she was in Israel, one from her dorm room, and the other to the Sagal's house. They had given her a key when she visited them for the first time. "Our home is yours," Manya told her. "Come whenever you want, and if we're not home, just wait, and take something to eat until we get here." Then she handed Tyra the key. But it was a small key, not the big, heavy one that opened the deadbolt lock of the Bronx apartment, or the long cylindrical one that switched the sturdy steel pole of the police lock from one side to the other. No, Tyra thought, her little Israeli keys would not do the job. Better take the bottle opener with the sharp point. She looked at it for a second before tossing it into her bag. Just in case Jordanians broke through the lines, she would try to take one down with her. She would be defender, too. Sid would be proud, although now he was probably fuming. She took Irit's hand and together, they ran down the staircase.

There was pandemonium as the dormitories emptied out and people scurried, crouching low to reach the shelter. The noise was horrific: the sirens still blaring, the booms of the artillery whistling overhead, and the loud crashes they made when they landed onto their targets. Tyra and Irit had to make it across the lush green lawn to the other side of the residential campus. Then they would be safe. "So much for Haifa!" Tyra screamed.

An Arab student was staggering to the shelter, too. He had been hit by shrapnel; he was dazed and looked like he was in shock. His face was bleeding and his clothes were covered in blood.

Tyra had always considered herself to be an ordinary person. History seemed to happen to special people in extraordinary times. But now, even though Tyra knew she was in an extraordinary, exciting moment of time, she didn't fathom just how special and wonderful she was. She could only think, *Safe. Safe.* She promised her family she would be safe.

Tyra and Irit had to make it across the lawn to the safety of the *miklat*. The sirens, the whizzing of missiles, the booms and vibrations of artillery fire, the smoke filling the air and clouding everything. "Irit, where are you?" Tyra screamed in the moment she realized they were no longer holding hands. Tyra turned around but could not see her cousin in the clouds of smoke filling the air. "Irit! Irit! Where are you? Oh my God! Irit!"

TWENTY

JERUSALEM OF STEEL

"Irit, Irit where are you?" Tyra kept screaming. They had been running together halfway across the lawn to the shelter when all of a sudden Irit had disappeared amid the fray. Students were running helter-skelter. Dust from the exploding artillery shells clouded the air; the booms of the explosions dulled the screams around her. Even if Irit was calling… would Tyra be able to hear her? Where was she?

Her heart pounding, Tyra turned around. She was frantic. Where was her cousin? A shell whizzed over her head. She couldn't see amid the dust and smoke. She started running back to the dorm from where they came. It was instinctive. She just did it without thinking, without reason. "Irit, Irit!" she screamed.

On the way back, she saw the same Arab student still stumbling toward the shelter. He was hit by shrapnel. His forehead was bleeding and he held his hand up to it. His hand was full of blood and blood was dripping down his face. As he continued to falter, two Israelis who were running toward the shelter grabbed his arms on either side and helped him along.

Tyra finally got to the glass-walled lobby, the lobby that the students a few nights before had plastered with strips of cloths to protect it from just what was happening at this very moment, and there Irit was, huddled in the corner, paralyzed amidst the booms of the shelling.

"Irit, Thank God. Come," Tyra coaxed her. "Come, we have to go." Tyra slipped her arm through Irit's, vowing not to let it go until they were safe in the shelter. Still lugging their knapsacks, the girls made their way, slowly at first, out of the building. Then they picked up their pace across the lawn, shells bursting above them, to the building that housed the subterranean shelter. They walked down the flight of stairs out of breath, struggling to take that sigh of relief.

The civil defense officer was bandaging the Arab student that Tyra saw a few minutes before. How weird, an Israeli officer helping an Arab who was wounded by his own brethren. Weirder still, a Bronx coward, saving the life of an Israeli soldier girl who froze in a moment, a beloved girl who enjoyed showing in better times, a photo of herself in a crisp khaki uniform, a cute cap atop luscious curls, brandishing a rifle, a proud but inexperienced soldier, to an admiring, envious American brat.

The vast underground space was lit only by a light bulb set in the middle of the ceiling which cast creepy shadows moving about the room. The cousins signed their names of the registry and took a blanket, pillow, a small jug of water and box of provisions. They scoped out a space along the wall, and proceeded to plop their belongings down and make as comfortable a spot as they could for themselves knowing they would be here for a while.

The shells fell steadily through the night and the people in the shelter found various ways to pass the nerve-wracking time- some played cards, some dozed on and off, some prayed.

At three in the morning, the familiar six beeps of *Kol Yisrael* newscast sounded and everyone sat up at attention. The announcer said something about half the Sinai being conquered and a great cheer arose from the crowd.

"Irit, why is everyone so happy? *Hatzi e-* half the island- we still have to win the other half of Sinai," Tyra said. She was never one to be "half" happy. Everything had to be perfect, complete, for Tyra to be confident.

Irit began to laugh so hard she could not stop.

Tyra looked at her, at first in amazement, then in annoyance. "What," she screamed. "What is going on here? Don't you know there is a war?"

"*Hatzi e*" literally means half island," Irit explained when she calmed down enough to speak. "You think we need to conquer other half? No. *Hatzi e Sinai* means the Sinai Peninsula, all, whole. We bombed 400 Egyptian planes. Egypt surrendered. We won! Tyra. We won." She grabbed Tyra by the shoulders and started jumping up and down, causing her cousin to jump up and down with her.

One front conquered; two more to go. Meanwhile, the shelling of Jerusalem kept up, the noise, nerve-wracking and intolerable, as some shells landed almost on top of the shelter itself.

June 5, 1967 10:26 P.M.

Dear Mom, Dad, Jessie & everyone,

We got up around eight and heard the first special bulletin that Egypt opened fire in the Negev. It wasn't too long till we realized that it was war. The Jordanians have been shelling Jerusalem since 10 A.M. this morning and haven't stopped. Right now I'm in the shelter with Irit at the dorms. She came this morning, helped me pack and straighten up and we were going to Tel Paran but didn't quite make it. I guess you know more details because here on the radio our gains can't be announced, but from the soldiers we've spoken to and the civil defense officer that gave us general instructions, we're in Sinai, burned up an Egyptian airport and one plane of ours downed 2 Migs in Natanyiah. Irit and I will be together from now on. I'm really tired now so I'll continue in the morning. Meanwhile we're as safe as can be expected in times like these so please try not to panic. We'll smash 'em good!

June 5-6 midnight
Saw two of our planes go into Jordan. Saw Arab fire trying to down them - planes got the old city on fire and came back. It's been quiet for about five minutes. Maybe we can finally get- oops- those bastards don't give up. I thought this whole year until two and a half weeks ago was too unrealistic- lots of fun, freedom, and no responsibilities. This sure is a pretty extreme year.

Wednesday, June 7 10:45 A.M.
No cease fire in Jerusalem since it began except for a few hours late afternoon- early evening yesterday. Thought it would be okay to sleep in the dorms with clothes on. The South American guys and I broke up a poker game by candlelight in my room and were leaving and the bombs came very, very close and we ran to a shelter- heard long-range missiles passing over-head. We slept in the shelter drowsing between newscasts. Yesterday afternoon walked to university-with all the bombing-one window in the national library was broken. Picked up fragments of bombs, saw prisoners of war in stadium. This morning- battle in the Old City- heavy fighting. Filmed our planes coming in and out-right now the bombing and shooting is very, very heavy- pounding noise. Alert in Jerusalem still on. This morning it was announced we have Ramallah- main

Jordanian city- broadcasting of Hashemite Kingdom of Jordan now Hashemite Kingdom of Israel. Yesterday also captured Latroon and can shorten way between Jerusalem-Tel Aviv.

Last night in Luis and Arturo's room, we saw a Jordan hilltop exactly opposite the dorm on fire. Arturo asked how it felt to be sitting watching a war. Strange. Very strange. At first we thought the lights were a line of tanks but didn't know whose and we thought it could be a decoy or war games. Then we heard it was napalm and the whole hill was set on fire and is in our hands now. Marvelous!

Last night, like Monday night, stars were very large, bright and plentiful. Last night more freedom to walk around a bit. Monday night- just peeked at the sky from the entrance of the shelter. Just announced on radio that except for certain areas Jerusalem can get out of shelters but we still can hear the battle in the old city and it's still going strong; we're giving them hell which they asked for. It's a miracle that the Old City will be ours even though it's burning- old ruins, new ruins.

Monday bombs from 10 A.M. until yesterday- yesterday evening too quiet. Just announced all clear in Jerusalem.

11:45 A.M.

A shell fell at #16 bus stop in Shikun and our soldiers exploded it. When we came out of shelter Tuesday morning the one thing I did was look at the museum and ask myself if it was still there- bombs were so close- one landed in front of Mensa, one near the geography building near the shul. They fired in this direction to knock out military factory down the valley in Bet HaKerem and instead of hitting it, they hit everything else.

Soldiers just came back from the Old City- we captured it and now soldiers have to search houses - most fled- typical.

After America's declaration of neutrality, it's absolutely shameful. Good old America did it again. Thanks loads.

Tuesday, June 6 11:30 A.M.

After 24 hours without a break it's quiet finally. Resting in the shelter now. Very few people here- in a half hour going to Mensa for a "decent" meal. We heard reports all during the night- we downed 400 planes- 300 Egyptian. We were in Sinai, Jordan. Last night we set the Old City of Jerusalem on fire-today the Old City is ours. If things continue for us like they are now, by the time you get this letter, I hope you will get a telegram saying, "We showed 'em good!" All we can do is pray and it's funny how war brings so many so much closer to God.

Considering they made so much damn noise yesterday and last night, just some windows are broken. All night we heard our planes passing overhead and, more importantly, we heard them coming back. We lost 19 planes to their 400. Miracles. We're going to eat-will continue. Oh, I have my movie camera with me so when we're outside, I've been taking some pictures of planes and stuff. Twelve o'clock- listening to news- Egypt bombed the American and English consulates- so stupid!

There's a lot to write but I have to send this letter out now with the last Super 8 cartridge I filmed. (An attaché is leaving with a sack of mail). So until I write again take care and try not to worry. We knew all along since Tiran that this was going to happen- it was just a matter of time.

Love, Tyra

SPECIAL DELIVERY

June 7- 8:30 P.M.

To all my Dear Family,

I just can't describe the great happiness we all feel now. Fighting in Jerusalem is now over and the Old City is ours-it's unbelievable. We're listening to a lecture in the lobby of

Shenkar about the new map of Israel and Jerusalem. We're sitting in the dark because the war is not over yet, but I thank God that I had the privilege to be here now. There were people who said in the recent past that Israel lost the spirit it once had. Well today was Israel's real Independence Day and as the chief of the Armed Forces announced tonight- we did it alone. It's been very expensive- unauthoritatively, one soldier said that the 3 day battle cost 400 lives just in Jerusalem alone but what they gave us- for them we must rejoice at this moment.

I got your letter today telling me about Arab hatred for us (which is obvious) and the wonderful Egyptian weapons. Weapons don't help when the soldiers leave their boots and run. As for being an American (oh, in your letter you told of America standing firm in her commitment) it's kind of shameful, although her failure was to our good. I have loads to write, but I'm so happy and excited. I'll try to write it all down when I get back to the room (no shelter tonight) and send a letter soon.

Now there is really something to celebrate. Don't cancel the party although instead of the party, why not buy two tickets to the Old City of Jerusalem for Grandma and Grandpa!

Last year I didn't believe that I'd be here when I sang l'shana haba b'yerushalayim. But whoever thought l'shana hazot b'yerushalim ha'atikah- this year in ancient Jerusalem!

I've been with Irit since Monday morning when it all began. She's fine. So is Hadas, Barak and Manya.

Will write soon. Take care. Have a good time Saturday night. Love to all. How much they're losing out- all those who fled the country in the past two weeks. I never thought I'd live to be part of a miracle in the history of Am Yisroel.

Love,
Tyra

June 10, 1967

Dear All,

More war stuff.

It's Thursday, June 8 at 7:30 P.M. sitting in an army base with soldiers. They were telling stories of how gruesomely Arabs lie dead and they laugh and joke and tell how easy it was to rummage through houses and destroy and loot. But these guys have seen their friends blown up and lie in pieces, soaked in blood. And you can see it in their eyes- blank, empty, watery, staring- and their laughing is an attempt to adjust- to get back to what they were only 24 or 48 hours before. But what they went through cannot be forgotten so quickly- if at all.

One soldier looked at a picture of John F. Kennedy which was glued on the wall. He said that if JFK were alive, this wouldn't have happened. It was very touching to hear something like that after the USA was so disappointing- even though it was for the best that she didn't interfere. As Herzog said, "and Zahal did it all alone."

On June 7, truckloads of soldiers returned from Jordan passing through the main streets. Some stopped up the block at the hospital, and the others came down the street. The love the people poured out to them is indescribable. It's a feeling- gratitude, admiration of their courage and guts. It was an interchange of love- the soldiers love the nation and the people they fought for, and the nation's love of them. People jammed together on the street corners cheering soldiers hanging Jordanian flags they captured out the car windows, a picture of Hussein; one soldier wore a pair of red boxing gloves, one sign on back of a tank said, "Zhirut- Zahal," (caution- Israeli Army), another sign "express to Old City." Jordan newspaper- saw Jordanian tanks and arms. They fought hard, but they mustered up the strength to receive and return the people's affection.

On Friday, we saw tanks returning- one soldier was completely submerged in a tank but for his head protruding from the turret. He answered my wave with a tired but affectionate smile.

People filled the streets reading hundreds of notices plastered on the sides of buildings trying to find out who was killed.

One corner was fenced in and made into a prison camp, Egyptians mostly. When we passed by, they were being given water in metal cups. So weird. Not like the WW II movies where Japanese tortured our soldiers and made them grovel.

Am fine. Don't worry.

Love,
Tyra

Sunday, June 11, 1967
Post card from Ambassador Hotel- Jerusalem, Jordan Hi!
All's quiet on the western front, Southern front and northern front. The card is from a soldier who made it back. Get film (movie and still) to me if possible- Jerusalem bigger than ever!

Love,
Tyra

Meanwhile, back in the Bronx on June 12, one of the customers who was sitting in the back of the store, reading the newspaper as he ate, shouted out, "Hey, Sid. Come quick. It's for you." He got up to answer the phone in the booth behind his table. "Collect call from Israel, the operator said," he added, waving the black receiver in the air.

Sid wiped his hand on his soiled white apron as he ran to the booth. "Hello," he screamed into the telephone.

"Daddy, Daddy is that you? I'm fine."

"Where are you? Are you okay?"

"I'm calling from the main post office in Jerusalem. I've been waiting for hours to get a line. It's so crowded here.

Everyone's trying to make contact. I'm fine. I don't want you to worry."

Sid chuckled. "It's too late for that, Kiddo, but it sure is good to hear your voice."

"Daddy, talk louder," she said with urgency, as if they might be disconnected.

They spoke for a few minutes and when the crowd of people became too noisy trying to hurry her up so they, too, could use the phone, she told her father she had to go. "I'll write soon. Tell everybody I love them."

Sid hung up the phone and sank into the little seat in the corner of the booth, relieved and exhausted. He knew he'd better call Kaye at her office to let her know of the good news when his ears were pierced by the ringing of the phone.

"Sir, please deposit twenty dollars for the collect call you just accepted," the operator said.

Sid chuckled again. "Sure, hold on a minute," he told her, and went to the register to get a few rolls of quarters from the cash register. He returned to the phone booth and stood there for what seemed a very long time putting in the coins one at a time in a repetitive motion, causing him to hope that the bursitis in his shoulder wouldn't be aggravated. *Eighty quarters,* he thought and laughed, so indescribably happy that Tyra was safe and well. *It takes only forty quarters to be eligible for Social Security!*

Tuesday, June 13

Hi,

Had tried getting in touch but it was impossible until yesterday when I spoke to Daddy. All's fine here. Irit came up yesterday. We're walking to the Old City for Shevuot. We're leaving about 5 A.M. before sunrise. Weather's extremely hot since yesterday. I hope everything's okay back home and your nerves are getting back to normal. I imagine it was pretty hectic there too. Take care.

Love, Tyra

There was a stack of mail waiting for Tyra when she returned to the dorm- all the pieces that were sent from the States since the beginning of June but were held up en route because the war broke out. She opened Marlene's first, then her mother's.

June 1, 1967

Dear Tyra,

Everyone is so nervous about what's going on in Israel. Are they still holding classes or has school been completely suspended? Everyone is going to Israel now to help out. I'd like to go but my parents would be totally devastated. You see, my brother was just drafted and he's starting Basic Training in a few weeks. I suppose after that he'll be shipped to Vietnam. It's enough of an adjustment for them to get used to his leaving. I couldn't possibly go to a war now, too. So here I am in the U.S. feeling rather useless and sorry for myself. But that's life. My family sends their love to you, too.

We had an Advisor's meeting yesterday to discuss plans for Summer Seminar. So glad to see your name on the list. Can't wait to see you. Toby is pregnant again and Ralph is going to be Rabbi-in-Charge at Seminar. Joel and a committee of bigwigs for Soviet Jewry met with President Johnson a few months ago. Joel's been engaged for a few months and they plan to get married next year. I haven't met her but I hear she is pretty and nice. Very religious, too.

Do you know that Rev Zemer did a beautiful thing? The community had all the necessary money to start building their

*new shul. Rev Zemer took all the money and gave it to Israel
(he bought Israeli bonds). This of course with the community's
approval, but imagine! Can't wait to see you.*

Love,
Marlene

June 5, 1967

Dear Tyra,
*I knew it. War. Oh, Please God, keep you and all Israel safe.
No point in mailing this now. I'm sure there's no postal service.*

Sunday, June 11
*All the neighbors always ask for you. They want to know
when you are coming home and how we are coping. When they
announced on Saturday that the war was over, we decided to
have a celebration for Grandma and Grandpa. The neighbors,
all the family, everyone came over last night. Everyone brought
trays of food and casseroles. I mustered enough strength to bake
a strawberry shortcake. We were exhausted but it was really wonderful to be together with everyone. It turned out to be more of a
celebration for Israel than for the anniversary. I can't describe the
feelings we have of gratitude that our people and you survived.*

Wednesday, June 13
*Daddy was so happy to hear your voice yesterday. It was
good that you called the store- I would have loved to hear your
voice too, but considering the phones were so jammed, at least
you were able to get through and you knew he would be there.*
*I thought you were safe in the shelter. We watched your
film- taking pictures of a jet being shot down. If you were here,
I'd have killed you myself.*
*I can understand why you stayed during the war and I
can't blame you. I am only very grateful things worked out*

well for us and that you were unharmed. And so this episode in Jewish history leaves its mark on all of us. I only hope the victory will not be in vain.

We spend every night in front of the TV watching what goes on at the United Nations. Abba Eban is wonderful, but it seems like a lost cause. Even Grandma, who never curses, when she watched the Arab ambassador said, "He should swallow his tongue and it should come out..." and you know the rest! We are all so worn out and now we worry that Israel will lose in the UN what she won in war.

Love,
Mom

Monday, June 12, 1967 12:45 P.M

Hi all-

The war started a week and a few hours ago. There has been a cease-fire for two days. When I first came here, one the most striking things was that almost everyone was a soldier- young- babies of 18 and 19- as if the army were a game for how could these kids do it. This past week they proved it, and they did a lot of growing up in six days.

Saturday night, June 3 went to the movies. Saturday night, June 10 went to the movies. Similar evenings- only there was a war in between. It's so hard to comprehend- it's too new to be vague or hazy and it was real enough- the bombing, the deaths, the looks in soldiers' eyes- it was all too real to be real at all. It was a miracle, but an expensive one. But the real miracle is that almost all thought it was going to be much, much more expensive and without the miracle. More later.

Jerusalem jutted out like a little finger into the endless slopes of the Jordanian-held Judean Mountains. In 1948 the City of Peace was carved up like a roast, the burnt ends for Jews, the holy Temple remnants and the Wailing Wall ironically dished out to the Arabs. Everyone's blood spilled everywhere in the slicing, the red hue intermingled and indistinguishable in the streets. The Jordanians desecrated the sacred *Kotel* by erecting two public bathrooms alongside it; they smashed the headstones of Mt. Olive Cemetery and built a road from the shattered pieces. How dare they? Tyra's exuberance during this extraordinary Shevuot pilgrimage turned to rage and she needed desperately to turn her thoughts back to the spirit and the miracle of the day. The government barely had a few days to clean up the mess of the Old City and prepare it for this modern ancient pilgrimage, one of the three annual dating back from Biblical times: Succot, Pesach and Shevuot, the celebration of the receiving of the Torah.

How could such huge stones, cold chunks of rocks, grip a nation by its throat, imprison her with a yearning that wouldn't loosen its grip until the remnants were free from the barbed wire cutting them off from her people? Today, throngs of modern Israelites, heady with energy from the crisp, early morning summer air, sated from the fragrance of the abundance of olives in the groves lining the hills, giddy from the scent of the pines circulating in the national forests, pushed toward them, toward their past, toward their future. How could such cold stones hold within them, the living vestiges of a people who had been cut off and who had already gained and lost so much? The girls climbed and danced through the hills and valleys of the new, ancient Jerusalem with a now, possible yearning to get to the Dead Sea via the shortcut which traversed the Old City and the streets of Jericho, just like the song *Jerusalem of Gold* described. Tyra squeezed through the crowds and got up to the wall. She caressed the stones and tucked a blank piece of paper in between the cracks. All the feelings bottled up inside poured out as tears flowed down her cheeks:

Blessed art thou, O Lord, our God, who has remembered your people who have never forgotten the Holy City of Jerusalem, and has enabled us, through courage and sacrifice to return to the foundation of our Temple and the heights of our faith. And please, my dear Hashem, bless my family- my parents, grand-parents, and Jessie with good health, especially Jessie.

Thursday, June 15, 1967 4 P.M.
Dear Mom, Dad and Jessie,
Because we wanted both to beat the crowds and the heat, we got up at 3:30 A.M. and left home at 4:30 A.M. to begin our first Aliyat Haregel (pilgrimage) to the Western Wall. The sky was already light and the air was cool. We walked through valleys instead of the road and we saw throngs of people. We got to Har Zion at 5 and the streets were already crowded. A special road was built during the week leading from Har Zion to the Old City. Every few yards we stopped at the police lines which controlled the number of people entering. We saw people gathering at the mount coming from all the paths in the valleys. They came from all directions. It was a magnificent sight- everybody came- Nuturai Karta, Hasidim, the non-religious, and everyone in between. The contrast of fur strimmels and Kova Tembles, babies in carriages and the elderly. The opening of the Old City was a magnet drawing all the people of the nation together. We walked along the path that soldiers guarded every few feet. And then there were the poles bearing the helmets of those who died. We entered the city at 6:04 A.M. There was a gate and beyond that a courtyard covered with Israeli flags. The area was flooded with soldiers still guarding the place. One of the most striking scenes was that of a soldier standing

on his post- the top of a very high ledge of a building facing the Wall. Standing in his uniform- his rifle - a big cowboy hat-wrapped in a tallis and davening. He was so high up and the scene was so outstanding. We neared the wall and Tirzah and I davened- prayed- Shaharit- morning prayers, and we managed to touch the Wall. We left about 7ish, passing through the streets of the Old City. The way it was built, it was a miracle that we were able to capture it- the streets are narrow and there are so many corners and places for the enemy to hide and wait in ambush.

We left by Yaffa Gate and Yaffa Road, Jordan was a continuation of Yaffa Road, Israel. We walked through what was once no man's land and passed all the rubble left over from 1948 still. We got to the part of the city we were more familiar with- the part we lived in all year. We saw that all the walls along the border were torn down this week. As we left the old city we saw Arabs in a hotel staring at all the throngs of people making their first "Biblical Pilgrimage" to the place of the Temple in modern times.

The only thing that spoiled the atmosphere was the old women who complained about those who wore sleeveless dresses and the long, black-robed Hasidim who spit at them. Of course, I was wearing sleeveless and it just proved that with or without the Old City, Jews are Jews and some don't learn how to mind their own damn business. But thank God, the core of Am Yisroel is the young- they're the doers, the fighters, the getters. As in the days of the Tanach-Bible, those that fought for the "nation of Israel" were basically non-religious. But it's funny, there is such a strong historical identity that even those who don't observe anything feel, and here in Israel if there isn't a lot of observance- there most certainly is a great belief and trust in Hashem, and if one didn't realize that before, he certainly did within the past few weeks. During the crisis Tirzah said

409

that now Am Yisroel is drafting God and He can't desert us now. He can't let Israel be destroyed and if He exists, He'll help. Well, He sure turned out to be some hell of a good soldier!

We got back home about 9:30 and it felt like 4 in the afternoon. We were exhausted and there was a certain sadness, probably the strain and the loss of the war. It's kind of indefinable.

How I wish Grandpa, Uncle Shockneh and all the old men from Anshei Shalom could be here with all of us today to see this miracle.

I took a slip of paper with me so when I got to the wall, I could stick it into a crevice, but I left it blank because I didn't know what I wanted to say. As I approached the huge stones, it came to me. Of course, I had to leave the paper blank because I couldn't write on Yom Tov. I shoved the little folded up paper into a crevice with my invisible prayer and recited quietly what was in my heart.

Love,
Tyra

Tuesday, June 20, 1967 A.M.

Dear Mom, Dad and Jessie,
Nothing much new here except that on Sunday Syria opened fire and Monday Hussein called a meeting between all Arab countries to plan future wars with Israel. Tuesday, Russia accused Israel of being like Hitler's Germany and Egypt is continuing to persecute its Jews. Israel gets first prize for waging a war strictly according to the Geneva principles, despite the fact that the Arabs have been caring for our holy places by destroying cemeteries in Jerusalem and having erected two public bathrooms along the Kotel HaMaarav, and despite the fact that Syria hanged on live television two of our pilots. It's almost ludicrous that one nation, despite being abused so

much, still acts righteously even when those who benefit don't deserve it at all, and when retaliation seems to be the easiest and most natural way of acting. I think Israel has a right to be proud.

As far as my plans are concerned- school is closed until further notice. Arrangements have not been decided yet. Two of my midterms will be counted as finals and I decided not to take any other tests. If I get six credits for the two courses, okay. If not, no big deal. I canceled my July 23 flight to Europe and home. I'll be taking a direct flight from here to New York, probably sometime before mid-August. I have about seven more weeks here. In another week the Jordan territory we captured will be open for touring and there sure are a lot of places to see. That's basically why I canceled out on Europe. After going through these past few weeks, I want as much time in this country as possible. Now the real problems are starting with all the politics and diplomacy. We just hope that Israel doesn't lose in the diplomatic battle. It's about time she does what's good for her. There are so many Arabs around; the problem is what to do with them. Time will tell.

Since the beginning of the crisis, I didn't do any laundry. You wouldn't believe the quantity of clothes I washed yesterday and ironed today. But it was a must. Gone, thank God, are the days when you wear a pair of pants and the same blouse for weeks at a time. After all who needs fashion when filling sacks of sand or sleeping in shelters!

Wednesday, June 21

Hi again-

Classes start Sunday, but I'd like to travel around a little bit first.

My Hebrew has really improved lately. It took about two weeks to learn how to read the newspapers and listen to the

411

newscasts. Just one beaut of a slip I made. Bella and I were kibbitzing with the soldiers in the camp down in the valley the other night. I said something about war strategy and all of a sudden the guys burst out in hysterics. They were blushing and Bella and I looked at each other like they were crazy. They couldn't stop giggling, slapping their hands on their legs. It was amazing. I said it was a really hard war, fighting on three fronts. Well, finally one of the guys squeaked out that I said chaziot, which means brassieres, instead of the word for fronts, which is chazitot. I came to Israel with the hopes of becoming a Hebrew scholar. It seems I have a better chance of becoming a comedienne! It was good to hear the guys laugh after all they've been through, even if the joke was on me.

That's all for now- love to all. Hope Grandma and Grandpa feel okay. Take care.

Love,
Tyra

I still didn't get around to mailing this letter, so I thought I'd open the envelope and add to it.

I got back to Jerusalem today and I'm very tired so I'll just write a few words. I got about nine letters- that's more mail than all month put together. Most of them were your special deliveries. #21 was most recent. After telling me what's going on back home and how miserable everyone feels, I think the war and all was easier for me. Anyway, I hope you all rest up, calm down and feel better.

I was planning to come home August 5- Sunday- but when you told me your vacations are from July 31, I decided to leave on the Sunday before. After all this, I don't want to botch up your vacations, too. I hope you think it's a good arrangement.

As far as writing all the crap before and during the war- don't feel bad. I understand how you felt. Only a lucky few received encouraging letters telling them to do the right thing.

I went up to visit Irit last Thursday. She told me they drafted Barak and he was up North. He and Hadas are both okay. Manya was alone all the time.

Irit is heartbroken. Abraham went back to South America. He wanted her to come with him and get married. He was sick of all the tension and fighting all the time. I asked her why she didn't go if she loved him. She told me she wasn't religious like me, but to leave Aretz- she couldn't. A sabra belongs here like chaleh and wine on the Shabbat table. "My father almost died for our freedom, and I can shoot a rifle if I have to," she said. She chided me for even suggesting she leave. "Two years I drained my life with him."

"Wasted, I corrected her. You wasted two years of your life with him," I said trying to explain the intricacies of transla- tion. I was getting back for half of Sinai! She said, in her sweet English, "Yes, yes. Two years I wasted."

Michal just came back from Tel Aviv. Tomorrow morn- ing we're going to travel around the Western front- Ramallah, Hebron, Jericho- it's great. Will write all about it.

I just read letter #20 again. I'm really glad Grandma and Grandpa were able to celebrate a little. I sent a telegram but I don't know if they got it. When you say I seemed unaware of your concern, the thing that bothered me most during the whole thing was that I knew I was safe and you back there were hearing reports that the University was being bombed and that Jerusalem didn't exist anymore. Irit thought I was crazy for running around trying to send a telegram, but I reminded her that she, too, was a wreck until she called Manya on Tuesday, the sixth. Anyway, I learned a few days ago that no telegrams left the country during the week of the fifth so it didn't help anyway. Well, this is finally it. Bye.

413

Thursday, June 22, 11:45 P.M.

Dear Mom, Dad and Jessie,

I had an absolutely marvelous day and although I'm tired I want to write it all down now as I won't have very much time afterwards. Tirzah and I are going to Ashdod tomorrow for the weekend. It's along the sea and we'll be sunning until Sunday.

Michal and I left at 8 A.M. and went to what once was the border and waited for a hitch to any place in the Gadah HaMaaravit (Western Bank). We waited about one-half hour. Buses, cars, jeeps, army trucks passed, but nobody stopped. I tried stopping a bus rather jokingly as I didn't expect it to stop, but guess what? The driver asked us where we wanted to go and I asked him where he was going. He said he was on a whole day tour! We jumped in! It was a tiyul for teudaiyim- students whose draft is deferred because of studies except in emergencies. This group fought in the Jerusalem area. They were a bunch of nice kids and it was a fantastic day. We started out travel-ing around Jerusalem (Jordan) and saw from the distance the wall of the Old City. We saw from the distance BetLehem. Then we took the road to Jericho. Along the way, we saw the "Shaar Hagai" of Jordan- all the jeeps and tanks that were destroyed and lying on the road. We turned off and went to the Caves of the Dead Sea Scrolls along the shore of the Dead Sea. Saw the archaeological digs of an ancient town of Kalyah. My archae-ology teacher, Yigal Yardin, is there already, exploring the caves. It was funny that the scenery (craters, desert) was the same as that traveling from Baer Sheva to Ein Gedi and then it struck me that it is the same landscape- the boundaries were political, not natural. From there we went to Jericho. On the way we passed a new border post and many Jordanian Army bases which were completely destroyed. Only some lounge chairs were strewn around. One camp that remained intact had an Israeli flag on it. We passed along the River Jordan and the scenery was unbelievable. It's all desert but the bank is one long oasis- just indescribable. We got to Jericho- Arabs around, some stores open. Arabs in buses with sacks of belongings were being transported to Jordan (by their own choice). Trees- red, pink and purple flowers-houses beautiful. From there we went to the ancient finds and the springs. From Jericho we went to Schem. The road overlooked a stream and the plants and trees along the banks were beautiful. Area is mountainous. It was very hot. Then we reached a lower point- cool air, wind blowing, trees and waterfall. It is an army stronghold now, another oasis in the desert. All along the way we saw refugee camps of those who fled in the War of 1948. The huts made of mud and the primitiveness was unbelievable for this day and age.

We got to Schem.

June 25

Schem is a beautiful place. It's surrounded by mountains. Stores were open and the streets were filled with Arab men who loaf. No women were to be seen. The people were very nice and pleasant. We entered a store- something like a small 5&10 and someone kept pointing to things and asking how much. Then he saw a Turkish turban - red with a tassel and asked how much. The guy shook his head and pointed to an older man and it turned out that the hat belonged to the owner and we all laughed and it was really cute. Walking along the streets, the empty soda bottle I snuck into my bag fell and thank heavens it didn't break, but all the men that were standing around kind of chuckled and was I embarrassed. There was none of that instinctive kind of hate and I thought how nice it would be if there could be peace. As the bus passed (with Israeli flags on the front window) the little kids waved at us and we waved back. From Schem we went to Ramallah (where the radio station was) and tonight I heard that one soldier who fought there

415

said that the first thing they wanted to know after they got hold of the city was where the records were!

I had wanted to make a tape called sounds of Israel and in it to record Arab programs in English- their hate filled commentaries against Israel. But the "Broadcasting service of the Hashemite Kingdom of Jordan Ramallah" became Kol Yisroel from Ramallah before I got around to it. That's what happens when you procrastinate.

The road was fantastic. We stopped and bought nectarines from an Arab fruit stand along the way. In Ramallah we roamed around, ate falafel (Israeli falafel is better). It's a pretty Western modern kind of town. It reminded us of Rehov Yaffa- the main street in Jerusalem. From Ramallah we rode to Jerusalem (Jordan). Along the way we passed Atarot, the Israeli airport that we lost in the Independence War of 1948. Also passed the city of Shoafot which is very wealthy. We saw the palace of King Hussein. In one villa we saw our soldiers relaxing on a terrace. Evidently they took over the place! We got to Har Hazofim. Saw the original University and Hadassah Hospital. From the top of one of the buildings we saw the new Jordanian Jerusalem, the new Israeli Jerusalem and the whole Old City- the complete circle of the walls. Now all the Jerusalems are one- ours, and it was just beautiful. We went to the nearby amphitheater and just as we got there, the first concert in all these years began with Hatikvah. We left and rode around the new part of the city. Saw the Sha'ar Ariot- The Lions' Gate, where our paratroopers entered the Old City during the battles, Sha'ar Rachamin- the gate that no Jew can enter until the Mosiach comes, Yad Abshalom and then we entered the Old City through Sha'ar Schem. We walked through the narrow streets, the alleys, steps with huge arches overhead. The men were sitting in the streets smoking their water pipes, dressed in pajamas, kids running around dirty in rags, garbage strewn in the streets which stank, the absolute filth and poverty over-takes the beauty of the place itself. It's built in such a charming way and all its beauty can't be seen through all the muck. The people looked at us and you could see the hate pouring out of their eyes. They called out nasty things and we couldn't wait until we got out of there. We got home about 8:30 tired and dusty, but it was a fantastic day. It was very interesting seeing Pepsi Cola signs in Arabic and weird riding through a desert that seemed to be the most peaceful place and yet seeing here and there the burnt tanks and crushed cars, trying but finding it impossible to comprehend or imagine what had happened there only a week or two before. The raging smell and sour stink of burnt bodies and corpses is one that will never leave my nostrils.

Today classes started. I passed two exams so I'm basically finished. I saw one professor for the first time since before Purim. After the vacation he was sick and then the crisis started. He said he didn't see me in such a long time, he thought I left the country! He might give me credit for the course based on some work I gave him. Two men were in class. Most of the guys are still in the army. It was sad, learning which professors and which students were killed.

I went to town today and the trip is definite. I leave Tel Aviv at eight, arrive in Paris. Have a few hours free. Leave on Air France arriving New York at 5:00 P.M. on Sunday, July 30. I'll get to N.Y. after about 22 hours of traveling and I'm sure I won't go to sleep Saturday night, so I'll be absolutely pooped and it'll only be 5 P.M. there, and I guess everybody will expect to hear about my whole year in one breath, but it'll still be good seeing everyone again.

Reuven, one of the few students who returned to school, was in the Sinai and told us all kinds of stories, too gruesome even to write. He said that the Zanhanin (paratroopers) were

417

really mad. Everywhere they went, they didn't have to fight. Either the tanks led or the Arabs fled. They should have been in Jerusalem for action.

Tirzah's cousin, Ashdod, fought in the Old City and he said that as they progressed he had no one to talk to. They fell by the numbers and what once started as a company of who knows how many, four made it to the end. He was shot in the arm.

Reuven told of how we outwitted the Egyptians, and of tragic friendly fire. That Israeli tanks by error fired on other Israeli tanks because they didn't think that our forces could have advanced so far so soon and thought they were Arab tanks. He said they found two camels that drank 1000 liters of water. Could you imagine the thirst? He said there were sand storms where you couldn't even see a half meter in front of you, and troops on foot had to advance. There's another joke name for the war. The Sinai Campaign was called Milhemet Kadash (Kadash is the name of the Sinai desert). This war is called Milhemet Kad because it's even shorter than the week long campaign ten years ago! Before the war, a vendor in Tel Aviv sold "Eshkol Jokes". Now he shouts out "Nasser Jokes".

Well, I guess that's about it for now. Will probably travel around the Galilee at the end of the week. I'll wait until I hear from you about the date of my return trip- if it's okay with you, I'll make it final. P.S. Start me on a diet immediately- what I lost during the war, I gained back in the victory!   Love,
Tyra

Thursday, June 29, 1967 2 P.M.
Dear Mom, Dad and Jessie,
Nothing much new. Have a test and paper in two courses within two weeks and I'll be finished with school. Speaking with

a lot of soldiers who are coming back to the University or who are stationed in Jerusalem and am hearing all kinds of stories. Reuven said that we wanted the Egyptians to think we were going to enter Sinai through Gaza and so we lined that whole area with carton tanks- meanwhile our forces entered through another area. He told of a Jordanian officer (M.D.) who was in an Afula hospital (a wounded P.O.W.) and they found an order in his papers that when Afula was conquered, he was to take over the hospital! Reuven said he was more worried about the cities than the fronts. The first night was awful- we just heard news of our cities and border towns being bombed, and there was no good news until 3 A.M. when we learned the air force destroyed 400 planes. He said when he came back to the dorm, he walked especially through the University to see exactly what damage had been done. We told him he had to walk any-way because the bus service was suspended since the third week of May. It started again this week.

Another soldier said he was more worried about the peo-ple than the soldiers- at least they had weapons to protect themselves, but if the Arabs advanced inward, there would have been mass slaughter- that's one of their principles of war.

The guys are really great- they're over the initial exhaustion and they're really fantastic the way they talk. One says he sits in class, listens for a few minutes and then he sees the pictures in his mind- the burnt bodies. They can kid about the Arab corpses, but when they think of their friends- I don't know. It's all incomprehensible still.

Tomorrow, Bella and I are going up to Tiberias. We'll stay over at Hadas' place. Will travel around the Kinneret and come back Monday or Tuesday. It'll be the last time this year I'll be up North. These last few weeks will go very fast and there's still a lot to do. Irit stopped in yesterday for a few minutes. Everything's okay at home. They'll be moving as soon as Barak's released from the army.

Thursday, July 4 - P.M.

I started this letter by saying nothing much new. Bella and I went away on Friday and wound up spending the weekend in army camps in Ramat Syria- we even got kidnapped Saturday at midnight, but it's a long story and I'll start out at the beginning.

Thursday night we planned to get up at 4:30 A.M. and leave at 5- destination Tiberias. Natch, we didn't get up until 5:30 and so from the very beginning just about nothing went according to our plans. We had fantastic luck with hitches. We left the dorms around 6:30 and we didn't even have to walk to the main road two miles away. Along the way near the dorm, a soldier stopped. When he dropped us off at a turning point, he was going South- we barely got across the other side of the road when another soldier in a truck stopped and so it went. Only dafka in Nazeret we had to wait about twenty minutes with all the Arabs wandering around. After about six tramps-hitches- (all with soldiers) from Jerusalem, we finally got to Tiveriah about 2 P.M. Hadas left the key with a neighbor as she went home in the morning. She lives in the mountains of Tiveriah and not in the city itself, and from that area you can see the whole city below, the Kinneret and Ramat HaGolan, until last month called Ramat Suriah. It's basically a poor area. Hadas works with delinquent kids. The people were very friendly and we were like celebrities to all the little kids. According to our "plan," we were going to spend Shabbos at the lake, then cross over the lake to Ein Gev on Sunday, and from there try to sneak into the Ramah- Syrian Heights. We still had time Friday afternoon so we decided to travel to Kfar Nachum, the oldest synagogue in the country. We went to the city and walked to the main road to get a tramp. We saw some soldiers and asked them if we were going in the right direction. They said they were going that way and if we wanted we could stand with them. In a few minutes a truck came by and picked up the six or seven of us. One was a younger brother of a soldier who wore an army shirt, carried his brother's rifle and that way was traveling around the Ramah. We asked if there was any way we could get in (it's all politics- the question is who gets the passes). They said they didn't have the authority but we could travel with them to the roadblock and we'd see what would happen. Along the way, we saw the fields that were completely burnt out. We got off at Rosh Pinna and walked until we got a tramp from there until Gadot (a kibbutz on the former border) with a big truck full of soldiers. We were stopped at the roadblock and had to get down. The soldiers didn't even have written permission to get back to their base and the military police gave them a tough time. We got down and asked the guard to try to get us a tramp back to Tiveriah. He apologized for having to do the "dirty work." We told him we understood and he needn't apologize. Bella asked him if it would be possible just to walk to see the Jordan River. He told us to go see a Seren (two stripes) and we went to this Seren's private quarters and asked him. He said we could walk down to the bridge B'not Yaacov, but to come right back. We got a hitch to the bridge and took some pictures. Meanwhile, all the jeeps and trucks that passed stopped and the guys asked us to come with them. But like good little girls, we started walking back. All of a sudden, the military policeman called us and we had to go back to the bridge. The bum just wanted us to take his picture!

We started talking and he asked us what we were doing here. We told him the truth- that we had permission to go only to the bridge. He said he would let us go through if we wanted.

421

After thinking about it for two seconds- we really thought that the Seren- lieutenant, back there didn't think we'd come back if we were already in, but since he couldn't give us official permission, he let us in and left it up to us- so the next truck that came along had two unexpected but quite welcome guests. We got to their camp and they told us not to continue farther to Kunnetra because it was far away and it was getting late- it was about 4:30 or 5 by then. We were sitting around talking- eating Syrian candy which was quite good. Then we ate sup- per- meat, French fries, salad, wine, arak. Then we changed into uniforms as all we had was our purses and the dresses we were wearing. At night it was really beautiful there. We could see the Kinneret and beyond, the lights of all our Kibbutzim on the other side. The stars were out full blast- we saw the dippers, the Milky Way. The air was cold, the area was all open and it was just marvelous. After supper we went into the officer's tent and were kibbitzing around. The relationship between him and the guys was very informal and natural and it seemed to be quite unusual. We drank coffee and ate cake and candy. They prepared places for us to sleep in a truck that was the storehouse for all their uniforms and blankets. In the morning we rode in a caravan of jeeps along the shore of the Sea of Galilee- the Kinneret. We saw two old women sitting on the road and the guys gave them some of the food that they brought for lunch. Then the guys went swimming- natch our bathing suits were in Tiveriah- so we just got a little wet and tried to wash all the dust we gathered during the trip. After that, we went to Kibbutz Ein Gev where we ate lunch. All the "civilians" that passed said, "Good Appetite" and the soldiers kept kibbitzing with the girls and old ladies that passed. When Bella and I went to the ladies' room, the women made sure that their stuff wasn't in our way- kids kept pointing to us as if we were heroines. It was a riot. From there we went up on a curvy, windy dust road to Tel Kazir- a Syrian town. We had to pass a roadblock as each vehicle needed a permission slip and because we were in uniforms we weren't questioned. We saw Syrian fortresses and positions and it was unbelievable that we were able to beat them. All their weapons were so well protected and their bunkers and trenches were just unbelievable. From there we went down to El Hama (mineral springs) a city very low- we descended on bombed out, curvy roads- we saw the bridge of the Yarmouk River- the train tracks between Haifa and Damascus. We walked around the city- the southernmost point of the Ramah and its borders with Jordan. From there we turned to go back to the camp and then go up north. On the way we were racing and going 120 k.p.h. Can you imagine the speed in an open jeep!

The two jeeps were playing leap frog on the burnt out road to Kunnetra. As one passed the other, the soldiers cheered and made haughty gestures of victory. Not to be outdone, the other driver would rev up the engine and leave a trail of dust in an attempt to overtake it. The jeep Tyra was in blew a tire and veered off the road. The soldiers in Bella's jeep howled and hooted with joy but just as they passed the disabled vehicle, steam hissed from under the hood grinding their jeep to a halt. It was quite a sight, six soldiers and two Americans girls milling about on a deserted bombed out road. The girls left the soldiers to repair the jeeps and meandered down a path off the side where a cluster of ramshackle huts lay abandoned. Each was painted in a different pastel color: orange, green or blue. They walked toward the lavender one. The one-room abode was desolate, ghost-like and dusty. All the clothing and kitchen utensils were gone, but the heavier, bigger items of furniture were still there. Tyra could tell that there were curtains or drapes once, which were gone now, too, because the rods and brackets were still hanging above the window frames.

Some Arabic newspapers that were strewn about the room caught Tyra's eye. She picked one up and thumbed through the pages. A political cartoon seemed particularly ironic. Lyndon Johnson, sporting a long Hasidic beard, was a puppeteer controlling the strings of the one-eyed General Moshe Dayan. Tyra couldn't read the Arabic caption but the cartoon's intent was obvious.

Bella meanwhile picked up from the floor a stack of photos left in haste as the occupants fled for safety. In the moment it took Bella to look at the face in one of the pictures, her mood of levity and excitement died and her face turned pale.

The Arab girl in the black and white photo was about ten years old. Her head was covered by a black woolen hood from which only her dainty features peeked out. Even her forehead was covered, accentuating her wide, happy smile.

"War really does a job on people, doesn't it?" Bella said.

"Look out there," Tyra said, waving her arms. They were on the top of the Syrian Heights and could see far below, the kibbutz of Ein Gev and the Sea of Galilee beyond it. "Now they don't have to plough the fields with armored cages."

"And look at this," Bella said, sticking the photo of the girl in Tyra's face. "She's so young, and now she's far away from everything familiar, everything safe in her life. She looks like the same age as Mindel when she was taken."

"Who? Who's Mindel?" Tyra asked. "And this girl wasn't taken. She fled, and they brought it on themselves."

Bella seemed to already be in a trance. Softly she began.

"There was this photograph, black and white, yellowed, with jagged edges in a frame on his nightstand," Bella said. "When I was a little girl and would ask him who the people in it were and why he had it on the nightstand, he would just say "from the Old Country," and shoo me away. My mother would put me off, too. 'I'm busy, now. Later I'll tell you.' But later never came. There was a man, who looked like my father, only much younger, and happier, a woman, two boys and an older girl." Then Bella continued in an almost fairytale manner, a somber story while the two friends sat on the bare floor of a Syrian hut.

Though the man who would become Bella's father was never a husky man, he was a strong one. In the days of plenty, the days of rich meats, soups laden with vegetables freshly picked from the garden, and the tasty Shabbos *chulants* which simmered overnight so that the chunks of seasoned brisket were infused with an irresistible aroma that sometimes would flow all the way into the bedroom and keep him awake at night, tantalizing and teasing him, for he knew he could not indulge, as tradition had it, until after the *Musaf* services the next morning. The potatoes and onions were soft and all of it fell away from the fork in even smaller pieces as one tried to scoop them from the stew pot. But on the day he returned to what used to be his hometown, he was particularly slight, and his pale face was drawn. Though there wasn't sufficient fullness in his cheeks to house deep lines of worry, his flesh had become thin, frail, and anyone could see that beneath the taut pulling of skin over his bony cheeks, that he had aged far more than the length of time he had been gone. His eyes had sunken deep and far into his skull. For his whole life had changed in those three wretched years, and on the day he returned, his gait was sluggish, for he had no energy. Though his musculature was slight and lean in his old life, he had always been spry and productive. But by now his muscle tone had dissipated altogether, and he looked as he felt, shrunken, haggard and inept. He walked slowly, partly from starvation and overwork, and partly from the trepidation of the thoughts that consumed him as he neared the property that was once his. Though he had lived there most of his life, he felt estranged, as a man thrown out of his home by an angry wife, who comes stealing back to retrieve some clothes, or business papers, or a favorite photograph. He could barely recognize the street. He longed to find out what happened to the rest of his family, to reconnect, yet he dreaded information he was hoping to learn and not to learn at the same time. He didn't know exactly what to expect, but he knew instinctively, it would not be good. It would take some time for him to get his bearings, to return to what he forced himself not to forget and grasp what was once familiar and wonderful.

He climbed up the stairs gingerly, trying to avoid the pitfalls of clutter, broken boards and shards of glass. He could barely recognize the apartment. It was bare, stripped of its beautiful furnishings. The still lifes and portraits had been pilfered as were the many ritual sterling pieces and filigreed ornaments. Shimon bent down to pick up a piece of broken piano key from the rubble. He lifted it up and as he pressed it against his ear, he closed his eyes. He tried in vain to hear the sounds of Bashka's rendition of the Moonlight Sonata, her favorite. He lowered the piece of discolored ivory to his nostrils, as if he could sniff the essence of his wife Bashka, but all was gone. It only felt cold to the touch, a dusty crumb of the past, and damp with his tears dripping onto it.

Though he felt weak from the destruction surrounding him, he continued his search into the largest bedroom, and then opened the closet door in the corner of the room. He pried up a piece of floorboard, but the box he was looking for wasn't there. He grew frantic. "I could have sworn it was in this closet," he thought, but then doubted himself. "It's been so long." He became disoriented and shook his head. After all it was three years before that Shimon hid the box. When the rumors warning of the Nazis' plan to send off the Jews to the east became more detailed, more frightening and believable, Shimon filled a box with the most valuable small pieces of the family's jewelry, along with wads of cash, the few bankbooks. Shimon had stuffed the container so full, there was hardly room for the few photographs he set aside. He took the most recent, the one taken of the five of them that winter, outside in the snowy street. The boys were bundled in hats with pompoms and mittens Bashka knitted from fine wool, and Mindel, spunky little Mindel, standing there sticking out her tongue. Shimon slipped the photo under the lid. Then he called Bashka and the children into the room and showed them the box. "When we come back, this shall be for a new start," he told his Bashka and his ten year old Mindel. He pointed out the box to his sons who were only eight and five. Perhaps too young to remember, but Shimon showed them as well. "When we come back," he said motioning to the hidden box. "Don't forget." Then he hid the box under a plank of wood and tightened the screws.

Shaking with anxiety, Shimon walked into the second bedroom, and when he went to check the closet there, he saw that a floorboard had been loosened. He heaved a sigh of relief. Someone had returned. Excited and breathing fast, he wondered who survived. Or was it the Nazis and his hope gave way to fear. He sucked in a big gulp of air, preparing himself for whatever the truth behold. Which relative survived? Who could he prefer and how could he choose? He yearned for each one of them. Perhaps all returned. He sank to the floor and leaned against the closet door. He hands were sweaty and he didn't know what to think: who had come back and where he could find them. Realizing that he may not be alone after all, he became cold and weak. He worried about their state, in what condition they would be. It was too much for him, and he curled himself on the floor, weeping.

"Shimon, Shimon," Tessie whispered.

Shimon stretched and lifted his head to see a soft beautiful face in front of him.

"Bashka, is that you?"

"Shimon, it's Tessie. Thank God. Thank God you came back." Tessie dropped down to embrace him.

Shimon rubbed his eyes until he became alert. He saw that it was his wife's sister who was standing before him. You could tell Tessie and Bashka were sisters by their coloring: their dark hair and olive complexion, but Tessie, younger than her sister by thirteen years, was taller and thinner. Her body hadn't had the opportunity to fill out from childbearing. She was only seventeen when they were separated, and her pretty face was more angular than ever. To Shimon, she looked like a welcome fragment of the familiar.

"The rest of the family," he whispered. "Do you know what happened to them?" he asked, his voice quaking.

"When we got to the station, they pulled us off the train and pushed the children to one side and the women to the other. Mindel screamed and Bashka lurched forward to grab her. 'Stay with me, Bashka,' I said. 'Stay.' But Bashka ran to Mindel. I tried to hold her back. I tried with all my strength, but Bashka wouldn't give up on Mindel. I could hardly keep her in sight. Such hoards of people, but then I caught a glimpse of her scooping Mindel in her arms. I saw Mindel smile. That was it. The last time…." Her voice trailed off.

"And you, Tessie, how did you stay alive? What did they make you do?" There was no energy in his tone. He didn't even know why he asked; he didn't want to know, but he had to say something. What do you say in such a world?

Tessie knelt down on the floor, weakened by the few words she already spoke. She cast her eyes downward, staring at the grains in the wooden planks. "I was too afraid to live…. She paused. "…and too tired to die. Too numb to plan or think about any of it." The secrets of shame and survival would stay silent for a long time. "That's all. No more."

Shimon and Tessie sat on the floor for a few moments in silence. Tessie pointed to the hiding place and then reached into her pocket. "I looked for the box when I came back two weeks ago. I come here every day to check, hoping, praying someone else would come, too." She handed Shimon the photograph. He fingered it and cried.

Shimon and Tessie lived in the crude apartment. He stayed in the room he had once shared with Bashka, but slept on a pile of rags instead of the thick mattress that used to be there. Tessie used the room that was her nephews'. There was no trespass of the other's space, no violation of the Law.

Tessie was too old to be Shimon's daughter and too young to be his mother. But she became for him a little of both and gave him the wherewithal to build life anew.

One time, after six months had passed, they brushed against each other as they passed in the hallway. Each felt a twinge, an echo of desire- for thirty-five year old Shimon, a long forgotten sweetness, and for twenty year old Tessie, a never-known fulfillment of longing.

She leaned into him and he wrapped his arms around her. For Tessie, Shimon was safety, security, the only future she could see. And for Shimon, Tessie was the only remnant of the life he had, the life he built with hard work, determination and reverence. The life that was taken with impunity, as if it were garbage.

They stood there, still, and mute, for a long time, leaning, swaying. Leaning, swaying. Then Shimon loosened his grip and took his palms and placed them on Tessie's cheeks, lifting her head toward his face, until their lips touched. Shimon didn't know if he was kissing Tessie or dreaming of kissing Bashka. Nor was Tessie certain if Shimon wanted her or her dead sister. But it had been such a long time since either one kissed or was kissed, they each dismissed the doubt, as it did not seem to matter at this point in their lives. The kiss felt good.

"We should get married," he said.

"Married," she mimicked. "Are you crazy?"

He turned his head to the left, then to the right, pretending to search for something in the air. "Why not? Do you see something better out there?"

They laughed. They laughed a sad laugh and spoke about the irony of life and the Leverite commandment whereby a man marries his brother's widow, to protect her and provide for her children. But here, it was the reverse. There was no widow. In this case, a woman would marry her sister's widower, comfort him and cherish the memory of his children.

"We will marry and go to America." He told her he had a distant relative in Cleveland.

"Good, Good," Tessie said. "We'll use the box to go to Cleveland, America."

When their baby was born, Shimon wanted to name her Bashka, but Tessie wouldn't hear of it. "You will not live with ghosts forever," she yelled. She was adamant. "Bella. We will call her Bella."

When Tessie handed Shimon the newborn, he felt fire rise up from within his loins. He was energized by his restored fertility. But at the very second he felt pure, unabashed joy, he needed to hold it back. How could he dance with Bella in his arms on the gravelessness of Mindel and her brothers? Though he had been able to love once more, he would from then on restrain himself from enjoying even modest amounts of light-heartedness. Yes, he would build a life, a mirror image of the past. Only he would never forget what he had lost, and would not remember to see the difference in the new reflection.

It took years for Shimon to digest the rich, fatty meats of *chulant*; it would take more than a decade before he and his new wife, his ten year old Bella and two younger sons would escape to America from behind the Iron Curtain. It took a long time for Shimon to become, for the second time in his life, a man.

"Oh my God! I don't know what to say," Tyra said, after hearing the amazing story.

Bella's face was ashen. She fingered the photograph of the Arab girl she assumed, lived in this house once until the war.

"You know, Tyra, my father calls me Mindel sometimes," Bella said. "After more than twenty years, he calls me Mindel." Bella began crying. Whether it was for the Arab girl or for herself, Tyra wasn't sure. Probably a combination. "Once from across the house he called, `Mindel, bring me the newspaper,' and I was so angry, I threw it at him."

Bella heaved more deeply as she sobbed.

Tyra felt terrible for her friend. "My Mom says, 'Someday when you have children, I hope they are as sloppy as you.'"

"What?" Bella chided. "What has that got to do with anything?"

"Just that maybe when you have children of your own, you will know something of what your father is going through."

Bella continued as if she hadn't heard what Tyra said. "He apologized to me and said, `For you I survived. To have you and your brothers and to spit on the Nazis,' he told me. And I yelled, 'What about me, Papa? Didn't you want me just for me? Aren't I good enough?' Then he started to cry. I never saw him cry before. Oh, Tyra. How am I supposed to feel? When I see that photograph from Romania that they keep displayed on the dresser, of him in his overcoat with my aunt and Mindel and my two dead brothers, I feel...." Bella hesitated for a moment. She punched her right fist into her other arm, as if to prove she was real, flesh and blood. "I feel like a ghost...." Tears were streaming down her cheeks. She drew in a breath and continued, "...like my aunt is my mother and my sister is me."

Tyra's face was ashen, as if she, too, were a ghost. She never saw Bella so downtrodden, so distraught. Even when Bernardo ran back to Chile before the war, Bella was more dramatic than heartbroken. Now her eyes were red from crying and Tyra did not know how to comfort her. She had no insight, no special wisdom. She, too, had struggled in vain to comprehend the genocide of her people. The two friends stood frozen in the abandoned, war-torn home. All her life, Tyra thought it was her family that was different. The Millers suffered as Tyra watched her friends live normal, happy lives with their families. All the while Jessie holed up in plaster casts and Kaye crying herself to sleep, full of angst. By now, Tyra learned that many people encountered heartaches of their own.

"I think you are very brave, and your parents, they are very courageous and strong. To go through all that suffering and to rebuild a new life and family. I don't know if I could have done that," Tyra said. "To risk having more children that they could lose again? Did you have to fight with them to come here this year?"

"You know, I never thought of it that way, and no, I didn't have to fight. My father told me I was his special gift for the past twenty years, and if I wanted to be part of Israel, it was his gift to me. I never realized how hard it must have been for them to let me go. You're pretty brave, too. After all, you didn't run home despite all the pressure from your aunts and uncles," Bella said with a chuckle, remembering all the nasty guilt-grams Tyra's relatives sent before the war.

Tyra was bursting. She wanted to tell Bella how she ran back to the glass lobby and dragged Irit out to safety, but she couldn't. It wasn't so much out of modesty, because she wanted to share her accomplishment: the first time she ever felt she did something selfless and brave. But she thought it would embarrass Irit, and even though she realized that everyone, even ex-soldiers like Irit, had weaknesses, she didn't want to expose her cousin's, even for Tyra's own advantage.

Suddenly a grin stretched across Tyra's face and though she tried, she couldn't contain the chuckles that popped out of her throat.

"What's so funny?" an annoyed Bella asked.

"It's just that I thought of Jessie for a second." Tyra recalled the conflicts and aggravation her sister caused. "It seems whether they're dead or alive, sisters always manage to be a pain in the ass."

Tyra and Bella reached out to hug each other. Bella's tears turned into laughter, and Tyra started crying.

"Now I understand why you are so gay and laugh all the time," Tyra said, managing to squeeze out the words.

"What do you mean?"

"Don't you remember, Bella, on the ship I asked you how it was that you always laugh and you told me because your father never did? You said it was a long story and we didn't have time for it then."

Just then a soldier came running up to them. "*Haleh, haleh-hurry, hurry,* " he said. "The jeeps are good. Time to go. To Damascus," he laughed.

The girls wiped their faces and shored up their uniforms. Tyra tore out the page with the cartoon, folded it up and tucked it in her pocket, for a memento. Bella placed the photograph gently on top of the bare, stained mattress, in case the Syrian girl would one day in the future, return in peace.

.... It took the soldiers about 45 minutes to fix the jeeps and it was too late to go to any other places, so we went back to base. We continued riding, going over bombed out roads again, passing through Arab villages. Our jeep ran out of gas and we had to wait on the road for help. The other two jeeps were in front of us so they got back before us. A few trucks stopped and gave us gas. They asked us if we wanted to go to

433

their base in Kunnetra and even though we thought we should leave because we didn't want to burden the guys at the camp anymore, our guys wouldn't let us go. We finally got back around six to the camp. To our dismay, unlike the night before when there were about 20 soldiers, most of the soldiers got back from a 2 day leave and there must have been around 100. We really felt that we were intruding and we went to the truck to get some jackets when one guy came over and asked if we had a few minutes. Why? The captain who returned wanted to speak to us. We thought we'd die! We went into the tent. The captain, 2nd officer and the guys we traveled with were there. He was very nice, friendly-even asked us if we wanted to shower- he'd arrange something!

He asked how we got there and the guys told him that they found us on the bridge and offered us a lift. He asked us our plans and we told him we wanted to travel farther but he said it was too late. We'd sleep in the camp that night and travel with them to Kunnetra on Sunday morning as they were packing up the camp and leaving the area. We left, relieved needless to say, and sat outside and talked to a whole bunch of guys. We went into the officers' tent and ate watermelon. About midnight we decided to go to sleep- this time in one of the little tents - so we took a "walk" and the guard said, "I see you want to walk around alone- there behind the truck!" He said he would keep out all intruders! We got back to the camp and thanked him for his understanding. We barely got settled when some officers barged in- one who must have been around 26 and absolutely gorgeous said "Shin Bet" (security police). He yelled at us to get our stuff together; he was taking us to Kunnetra. We asked if the officer here knows what this is all about? He said, "every-thing's taken care of, no time, get out." As we were getting into the jeep we heard that Egyptian forces were advancing in Sinai. They all started singing and we thought it was to make us feel better, which of course made us feel worse and boy was it frightening riding at night in an open jeep in pitch blackness. We heard all kinds of mises (stories) from the soldiers so we finally realized that the bastards just wanted our company. One of the guys that stopped to give us gas in the afternoon told the officer that there were two girls and they felt that since we spent one night in one camp, it was their turn and they wanted to have a Kumsitz! You would have been proud to hear how we yelled and screamed at the gorgeous officer. We told him that it was not very nice on his part- that we thought more of Israeli soldiers, etc., etc. One of the guys was fixing up a big tent for us to sleep in- with cots too. We put two cots together and he said, "I hope you don't mind if I sleep on this end." We made him sleep on the ground and more than that, it was so cold we took away his blanket and we kept him up all night because we were laughing hysterically. We said at least we could sleep because what they said about Egypt couldn't have been true- they wouldn't let us hear the last newscast. We got up at six and we couldn't wait to get out of there because we didn't want to meet the soldiers from the first camp who were so nice to us. They would think that we were ungrateful. We told the officer how we felt and he said he would explain that he took us by force. We left, got a hitch to Masada, another camp and Druze village, from there got a tramp to Kiryat Shmoneh and was it a nice feeling to be in Israel again. From there we got a tramp straight to Safed where we wanted to visit for a while. It was a taxi but because we had our uniforms in our hands (we didn't want to press our luck and wind up in a military trial), he didn't charge us! We roamed around in Safed and tramped to Rosh Pinna and on the way passed the soldiers we were with Friday and Saturday but, thank God, they didn't see us because we were really embarrassed. We finally got to Tiberias around two o'clock. We took some nice cold showers.

I wanted to take a color picture of my bra which started out nice and clean on Friday. Can you imagine wearing the same stuff for three days, getting filthy in the wild jeep rides! We were on our way to swim in the Kinneret at three and we saw Hadas returning from Haifa. Everything's okay. Barak was home. He was drafted to build for the army. We went swimming and the water was just marvelous. We met some soldiers who were young but really sweet and we walked around the city with them. They were going to Jerusalem the next day. We ate in town, walked around. The people were very friendly. We walked around the shore. A group of kids, 17-18, asked us to have watermelon with them and we ate while dipping our feet in the sea. By the time we left, I think all of Tiveriah knew of two Americans "studying" in Jerusalem who spent the weekend in the Ramah. You probably hear of it as the Golan Heights. We got back to Hadas' at 10:30, spoke until 12. Went to sleep exhausted, got up at 7 instead of 6 (according to our schedule), wanted to go to a few places in the Galil and go back to Jerusalem through Janeen. We got to the main road and soldiers in a jeep- a hitch straight to Jerusalem-can you plotz- but they weren't going through Janeen, so we said we'd get off at Afula. So they suddenly decided to go through Janeen, too. Oh- on the way to Afula we passed the three soldiers we met at the beach. They were trying to hitch to Jerusalem. We waved at them and they grunted! It was cute. We got through the road block without any trouble- like B'not Yakov it was the hardest place to pass through but I guess Bella and I smile nicely. We traveled a little bit when the tire blew and the spare was no good either, so we went back to the roadblock and the two guys went to fix the tires and we waited for them for three hours. One of the soldiers who took some pictures of Michal and me when we were tiyuling in Jordan was there and he gave me the pictures I'm enclosing. We played poker, checkers, ate battle rations and finally they came back and we got to Jerusalem at 4:30 exhausted and filthy.

Well that winds up our adventures. I left out a lot of little details, but it was so full of exciting experiences and even the soldiers think we have a lot of guts.

Love,

Tyra

Thursday, July 6, 1967

Today Tirzah and I went to Bethlehem. We saw the place where Jesus was born, walked through the Shuk. It was strange seeing newspaper stands with both Hebrew and Arabic papers. From there we hitched to Hebron, saw the tombs of Abraham, Sarah, Yitzhak, Leah, Rivka and Yakov. It was an awesome feeling being there, hearing old men davening and old women weeping. We went to the shuk. I bought a sheepskin bed rug and I'm thinking of buying a fur jacket for $10. We got back to Jerusalem. Tomorrow is Air Force Day. Next week I'm going down to Eilat and try to tramp to Sharm-e-Shaik by boat but that's not definite. In any case don't worry. I'm taking your advice and making the most of these last few weeks. Of all the things I've been doing lately, the thing that scares me the most is "flying" home! Take care.

Love to all,

Tyra

I lay in bed tossing and turning. I cannot sleep, worrying about tomorrow. Tirzah wants me to go with her to Hadassah Hospital tomorrow. She distributed the tissues and toilet paper to the soldiers today and they insist on meeting the crazy, spoiled girl who lugged suitcases full of Kleenex from America. I'm told you, Giora, were the one who was most flabbergasted. You're only nineteen, and a grenade blew off your leg just below the knee while you were engaged in hand-to-hand combat in the narrow passageways of the Old City. Tirzah says you need someone to lean on. I will come tomorrow and be that someone.

I am not spoiled, Giora. Israelis think Americans have it great, but my folks struggled for everything we have. We're Bronx Jews, you know, not Rockefellers. Even Manya thought I went to the beauty parlor as soon as I got here, as if that would have been so terrible- just because from day one as a child I learned how to style my hair myself, and took pride in making sure I never went to school looking the same way two days in a row.

My friend back home told me the toilet paper here was rough, and since the ship allowed four suitcases, a trunk, and two duffels, I thought, so why not bring some luxury? But didn't you notice, Giora, that the suitcases were full; after a whole year, they were still full. Doesn't that count? Maybe it was a sign from Hashem that I should have something to give you- my young, courageous defenders, something to soften your burden, something to soften my heart and draw me to Hadassah.

Tirzah said you need someone to lean on so you can practice walking in the corridors until you get used to the crutches. The nurses are too busy, taking care of all the soldiers who are lying on stretchers in the bursting hallways You swore that three months after you get your prosthesis, you will walk without a limp.

Hospitals are hard for me, Giora, selfish as that must sound to you now. The smell still lingers in my head. Maybe we all have our wars. My family's war was over years ago, but there were no victors. I stayed for the war, but I ran from a truce; I still don't know how to make peace. I'm still running.

I run, but the ghosts and shadows stalk me. They have overtaken me and tethered me to the ground. I am stuck and cannot be the person I want to be. I should run toward you, help you, comfort you. You who have given so much and lost so much, for your country, for your people. for people like me whom you don't even know. How is it that

I have the chutzpah to cry to you about my pain. Oh- I shall pray to Hashem with all my heart tonight that I shall find the courage to come to you tomorrow.

I am not like my mother. We call her Florence Nightingale. By necessity she learned when she herself was a child to nurse the sick. It is a blessing to be born into a family where everyone is devoted and caring, but illness is a curse and my mother dealt with it in all the generations- her mother, her husband, her child. And illness is a curse not only for the ill, but for the healthy, who love them and are forced to see them suffer.

Sometimes it's easier to fight the battles than clean up the rubble that's left behind. Jerusalem was a rough one, 125 dead in two hours in the Old City alone. Poor Giora, what did you see? You will not limp, but how are your eyes? Are they clear or tormented with the bloody screams of your dead brethren who fell before you? Are you filled with guilt, too?

I saved someone, Giora. I wasn't trained, I didn't ever in my whole life expect to, but I did. I didn't know I had it in me. I always thought I was a coward and selfish. It just happened; I didn't even realize it at the time. I still find it hard to believe, but my father would be proud.

You are the one who lost a leg, Giora, yet I am the one who is crippled. Giora, I will try to chase away my ghosts, to stop them from tugging and kneading at my heart as if it were a helpless lump of my grandmother's moist, sweet chaleh dough.

They are always there, in that sad part of my heart, the bottom left corner. No matter how I tried to push the sadness away, to make it disappear, it remained, so I decided to just let it be. But I must fortify its border, to contain it, so that it won't spread, like a malignancy, to the other chambers, to the places reserved for joy, where I must make my happiness, and even learn fun.

I have had fun, even giggled hard, but I've never felt truly free, always holding back. How can you be happy when someone close is miserable, and why should two be miserable instead of one; why one in

439

the first place, and if one, why not me? You see, Giora, never ending questions, and only excuses, explanations, but no real answers.

What's the point of surviving, then, and we are survivors, Giora. They tried to push us into the sea and obliterate us. We have been through too much. My name is Tyra and I will come to you tomorrow. We will lean on each other, and together we will weep our path clear of debris and broken cinderblocks, of shards and shrapnel. Perhaps we will find a way to laugh, too.

Sunday, July 9, 1967

Dear Mom, Dad, and Jessie,

In Jerusalem now- will be going to the Old City to mail this as today is the first day the post office will open. The other day Tirzah and I went Bet Lechem and Hebron. Friday I went to the Old City, Har HaZofim and Har Hazatim.

The past few weeks have been one long daze. Nothing can beat the excitement of traveling through Syria last week but it seems ludicrous traveling to all those places every moment remembering the thousand freshly dug graves in the military cemeteries. I've been having nightmares of wounded soldiers. It's impossible to escape from the mental pictures and it's still difficult, and I guess will be for a long, long time to fully grasp that this actually happened- a war, not in history books, but in our very own lives and experiences.

Rev Zemer came to Israel to entertain soldiers and he was at Hadassah last night. I went to see him there. He was so happy to see me and he is so wonderful with the soldiers. Since the very beginning, I wanted to go to visit soldiers but you know me and hospitals. I had given Tirzah all those rolls of toilet paper and tissues I schlepped here and never used to bring to Hadassah and the soldiers loved them! She told them about me and they thought I was crazy, so I finally went to meet them. I've been going regularly and they look forward to my visits. They love the movies I take of them, especially Giora. He's lively and friendly. He was in a jeep when they rode over a mine in Bet Lehem and he lost a foot. He's in a cast and he swears he will walk without a limp three months after he gets his prosthesis. He tries to run down the corridor and hams it up for the camera! He wants to learn English. I told him I'd bring him some homework exercises if he wanted. He didn't particularly care for that! The others are quieter. I write letters to their parents and girlfriends if they can't write themselves because of their wounds.

I feel very badly about leaving just now. I feel I can do so much at this time, especially in social work as there are so many new problems as a result of this war. In relationship to what we went through and what the situation is now, getting an M.A. doesn't seem to be particularly urgent that it can't wait another semester. Teaching English in New York isn't one fraction of the contribution that it would be to work here in social work or rehabilitation. I know I said before I left that I'd come back after a year, and I will, but it seems that the year went so fast and that it's an arbitrary limit of a very worthy experience. I just wonder how I will be able to get along. It seems to be more valuable and even more sensible to stay on now for another little while and come back when I feel that I've done something, than to leave in the middle and always feel incomplete. I know how you probably feel. I know that you all want to see me already and I guess it's even a little cruel to send this letter. But this is how I feel and I'm trying to be as honest as possible, both with you and myself. A few months ago I thought it would be nice to extend the year- there was a lot of fun, and very little responsibility, but I thought all "good" things must come to an end. Now it's completely different. Now it would be staying to do something, to contribute what I can for our people.

As they say, a promise is a promise- I still have a reservation for July 30, but I will wait to either cancel or pay it until I hear from you. As you can see this letter is not a decision- it's written to be kind of a discussion and because it can't be face to face- you got my side first- I'm waiting for yours. I hope you have read with understanding and will not get upset or aggravated, but think of it calmly and come to a decision that will be best for all of us.

Please take care and give my love to everyone.

Love,
Tyra

After Tyra left Giora and the other wounded soldiers during one of her visits, she decided to see if Uri, the soldier who taught first aid at the dorms before the war started, had returned to Hadassah. She didn't really know why, probably just to do her accounting of who was still alive. She asked around and found him holed up in a tiny office which in better times had been a hall linen closet. She knocked on the half open door and peeked in.

"Ah, the American who needs practice. How many hundreds did you save? Or was its thousands?"

"You're a *mamzeh*, you know that?" Tyra smiled, brushing her hair back off her face.

He nodded and smiled, his cheeks turning red, like a little boy get caught doing mischief. "Your name…eh…Tyra…yes?"

"Yes. How are you? Really? How did you make out in the war?"

"I'm here. Yes?"

She could tell from his expression that it had been rough for him and as she approached, he held out his arms and they embraced for a moment. She could feel him softening, if just briefly. "You look busy." She looked around his tiny, messy office, papers strewn all about. "What is a doctor doing with all this paperwork?"

"I am busy. There is so much to do here. Each soldier has so many needs, and there are so many soldiers. It's difficult when their families are far away. To find a place for each one. So what brings you here to Hadassah?"

"I've been visiting. Keeping the wounded company. Helping out. Nothing special."

He nodded approvingly. "Sweet."

"Listen, Uri, I've been thinking…"

He cut her off. "Yes, yes. You Americans, you like to think."

She tilted her head and squinted, a slight smirk flirting on her lips. "Now, now, *Motek*"- sweetie, "be nice. I know it's hard, but try." She laughed.

"Ka'fe?" he asked, walking over to the burner, a silent peace-offering for his gruffness.

"Please. I have an idea. I've been visiting the soldiers here and I know that some of them want to enter the university after they finish with their rehabilitation. What if we set up a preparatory class in English for them so they can do something worthwhile during their stay here in rehabilitation? It will give them something to study and then when they start their university studies, they will be ready. After all, the text books in math and science are in English."

"That is excellent. Let me think about the implementation and bring it up to my supervisor. What do you want to do- teach, make materials?"

"Yes. All of it, of course."

July 15, 1967

Dear Tyra,

I feel that the war has changed you. How could it not? I sense both a deep anger and confusion in you and wish you were here so I could comfort you- It must be very difficult for you to see all the pain and suffering from all the different angles.

I certainly give you credit for exposing yourself to all the hurt, especially helping the wounded soldiers in Hadassah. I know how squeamish you were when Jessie had all those treatments and surgeries.

As far as the soldiers go, I remember when your uncles, my brothers came home from the war, WWII that is, they also were distant and upset. War is ugly, and they didn't want to talk about what they did or saw. After a while, they got jobs, found nice girls and had families. So things do go back to normal and I'm sure all those Israeli soldiers will also find a way to get back to whatever normal life is for them in Israel's usually difficult circumstances. As far as the wounded and injured, well that's so awful and so sad. Their lives are ruined and will never be the same again. It's too bad good people have to suffer. We're here on earth for such a short time, and it's always the same- people never learn how to get along, how to share, how to make peace. Maybe now, there will be a better chance for that.

Take care of yourself, and don't take everything to heart. I know these are hard times. Do the best you can and stay strong. When you come home, you will get into a routine, get a job, meet your friends, eat good food. Your life, too, will get back to normal, and you will be fine and happy. How are your plans coming for your trip home?

Love,
Mom

Tuesday, July 18, 1967

Dear Mom, Dad, and Jessie,

I came back from five days in Eilat with Tirzah. We had the opportunity to sail to Sharm-A-Sheik yesterday but considering the Egyptians are playing with Migs, we decided to come back.

I went to Hadassah yesterday. It was worse as all the guys were having operations on their legs and they're in great pain. I promised to go back tonight.

Yesterday I bought two records of all the songs that came out during the war. A paratrooper, Meir Ariel, used the melody of Jerusalem of Gold to describe the battle for the Old City. He called it Jerusalem of Steel and told of lead and fallen paratroopers, and it's a big hit.

I'm sending six reels of movie film airmail with letter. They're from the 2ⁿᵈ day of war and aftermath. Watch out for them.

I had two oral exams last Tuesday- passed them and passed four altogether. Didn't think I'd make it. Take care.

Love to all,
Tyra

July 26, 1967

Dear Mom, Dad and Jessie,

I wasn't planning to write but I've just heard the news and the first items are devoted to the crisis in the States. We heard that the army failed to keep order in Detroit- that there have been deaths and a thousand wounded. New York must be boiling with riots. I know you all work in lousy neighborhoods and hope you haven't had any trouble.

From here the situation sounds very grave and I'm terribly worried about you and hope you're being careful. We hitched to Hadassah yesterday with an American from Detroit and he told us he called home and he sent a plane ticket to his brother. I wish I could send you tickets. It seems ludicrous to live in a place where you're afraid to leave your own house.

I've received your letters and there's a terrible misunderstanding. From what I gather you seem to feel that I'm going to be some kind of sacrifice for the welfare of Israel. You mentioned something about guilt feelings and a guilty conscience. Well that's not it at all and I hope this letter helps clear up the situation. First you have to understand that I'm not an impressionable, mixed up, confused kid. I know myself and understand why I want what I want and why I don't want what I don't want. I've thought about my decision to stay very carefully and seriously and more importantly, alone. I didn't let anyone influence me from either side. I want to stay in Israel for another few months simply because life for me is good here and I'm not ready to give it up. This is the best time of my life. I'm young and healthy and strong, and I don't want to waste it being cooped up in New York. I've been a little spoiled here. In New York I have had to fight strange men's hands off me on crowded buses and trains. I remember the sigh of relief getting out of an elevator unharmed by the stranger who rode in it, too. It's a shame that you've never been here as it must be terribly difficult for you to understand that life is really so free and pure here. You don't have to keep turning around to see who's walking in back of you. You can come back alone at night without being afraid.

You wrote something about not wanting more tension, worry and sleepless nights. Of course I can understand the worry during the crisis and war, but indeed that was an extraordinary situation. We felt the tension with the Arabs all year long until the war. Now there is no fear anymore. They showed us what they are and there won't be any more trouble for another ten years or so and definitely not in the next four or five months! I remember before I left, all the nights you couldn't fall asleep until I came home from school or dates. I honestly don't think that now you won't worry when, let's say I usually come home at eleven from college and if I'm not home by 11:15, you'll still peek out the window to see if I'm on the way.

I want to stay here another few months when I'll feel ready to come home. Of course, I'm not going to give up my studies. I've worked too hard to stop now. But putting it off for one semester isn't so terrible and I'll start the winter semester in February.

Friday went to Haifa- it was Barak's first day in the new apartment. They finally made it and I'm very happy for them. The apartment is just lovely and we took movies on the terraces. The neighborhood's beautiful - quiet, open and green. Hadas and I walked to the Mediterranean Saturday morning and swam. They send their love.

Well that's about it. I hope this letter cleared things up a bit. You wrote something about helping me adjust. Adjusting to New York won't be that much of a problem as long as I feel that I'm ready to come back. Very simply, now I'm not ready and the most difficult thing to overcome will be the feeling that I was forced to do something I wasn't ready for. I guess you're worried that if I stay now I won't want to come back even in five months from now. When I said last year I was coming here for a year I didn't know what to expect. Now I know. Then I didn't even know if I could have stayed for "a whole year." Now I know I can stay a little longer and come back sure of what I want. Don't forget this was the first time I've been away from home and to stay away "forever" would be impossible. Of course I miss everyone and want to see you all and so from that point, there's nothing to be afraid of. But coming back now - knowing that it's not the best thing and knowing that I can't be calm inwardly- always asking how it could have been and always blaming myself for not taking upon myself the responsibility of carrying out my own decisions will cause many problems and heartaches for all of us. I hope you can understand and I'm sure that if you think logically and try to ask yourselves - to what kind of life you are in such a rush for me to come back to- you will be able to see my point of

447

view. Take care. Love to all. Hoping to hear from you soon. Be careful.

Love,

Tyra

July 31, 1967

Dear Mom and Dad,

I know this has been such a terrible time for you wanted me to be serious and make use of my talent to be independent and contribute to society. These were the values you instilled in me, by your own actions and by providing me with the experiences you felt were worthwhile during my growing up years. I do not see this as disrespectful, just a little off track and more difficult. But temporary, only temporary. I have never taken my life anything but seriously- I never wasted myself on wanton behavior or fell in with shady friends or dabbled in drugs or alcohol.

These past few months have been so very hard for me, too. Jessie would be so fabulous here. I always hated the smell of hospitals. I used to sit in the halls of the hospital and gag while I'd wait for you to come out of Jessie's room. But she would be able to go into Hadassah every day and do what she does best- ordering these soldiers around- showing them how to breathe right and get themselves back to health. She wouldn't let them get away with one iota of self-pity. She would be a great role model. Me, on the other hand, I get weak in the knees every time I walk up the path to the main entrance. I have to take a deep breath and pray that I will be strong. I flirt and help the injured boys write letters to their families and their girlfriends, and I put on a great act, but inside I'm dying. I have to gird myself with imaginary steel bands around me-from my shoulders to the ground, to hold me up. I am an unset Jell-O mold waiting to spill off the plate.

But this new program I want to set up- to teach- this is what I can do. I love teaching. I always did. And I can give back just a little to these boys, these men who gave so much of themselves for us. Don't you see, I need to do this? I know I made a promise, but please- I don't feel like I am breaking it- I just need to put it off for a while.

For all the wonder of being here in Israel, I haven't really been too happy and I think you know that. It's one thing to live in the spiritual realm where every cloud holds the essence of our ancestral past, and every monument is cut away from bedrock and mountains by thousands of years of wind and rain. But I need to walk on the ground, and be connected to my family, and be able to see where I am going. I have really been so lost here- despite the magnificence and the wonder.

I can see myself coming home in maybe six months, after I get the program off and running and see the first students succeed in gaining entrance to the university.

Now at this moment I found a way to do the best I can and in helping others, I will find a sense of my own worth I never had the confidence that I would ever have. No- please be patient and don't consider me disrespectful. You have been great parents and I want you to be proud of me. I need my space. Please, don't be angry.

Don't worry about my getting involved with anyone. I haven't had such good luck on that score, and am giving up on men altogether- for a while anyway, especially now that Israeli guys are so messed up in the head.

Love,
Tyra

EXPRESS

August 3, 1967

Tyra,

I'm tired of all these misunderstandings. And it seems Daddy and I are the ones who are doing all the misunderstanding. Enough already. You have gotten everything you wanted- your language, your credits, even a war. Now it's time to come home. This was a bad year for Israel- all the attacks, the UN, and you have no idea how much I suffered. We held up our end of the deal and now you must do the same. You have felt guilty your whole life, with Jessie, now with Israel. But where are you guilty regarding your own mother? I have been sick with worry for you and I swear if you were here in front of me pleading your case to stay in Israel longer, I would strangle you with my own two hands.

Enough already. You can hate me if you want, but you are to keep your promise.

Love,
Mother

August 5, 1967

Mom,

I got your express letter and even Irit was shocked. We were already looking at apartments to rent together. I have tried to explain how I feel and now you can stop worrying. The war is over and the Arabs won't be bothering us for at least ten years. It's my life and my decision. I will wait to hear from you- maybe you will have a change of mind.

Tyra

August 10, 1967

Dear Tyra,

The last letter I sent was harsh and I regretted sending it the minute I dropped it off at the post office. Why don't you come home as planned? You are making a major decision and it would be good to talk about it face to face. It's only a few hundred dollars and 14 hours. Please come home. We have really suffered. We are worn out and we need to see you.

Mom

The dorm was quiet and most of the rooms were vacant. The Israeli students were long gone and the foreign students were packing up, getting ready for their long trips home. Tyra's room was a chaotic mess as she sorted clothes and kitchen wares she accumulated during the year to leave for Hadas and Irit in piles on one side of the room, discarded the worn out items in heaps in the opposite corner, and folded up the clothes she wanted to take back as well as packed the mementos and gifts she garnered throughout her stay. She wanted so badly to leave her electric rollers for her cousins, but they were listed on her passport when she entered the country, so there would have been a whole lot of *meches* (duty) to pay on the way out, so that was out of the question. The decisions she had to make about each of these items were weighing her down so much so, that when there was a loud, determined knock on the door, she nearly jumped out of her skin.

"It's open," she called out. The words could barely get out of her mouth as she turned to see who was there.

"I'm in one piece so why do you look like you've seen a ghost?"

"You look great," she said as she hurried across the room.

Neil held out his arms wide to grab her and they held each other and swayed back and forth in a cheerful reunion. That his sudden appearance was unexpected made the embrace so much sweeter for Tyra. It was the first time physical contact between them felt wholesome, as if she sensed a change in Neil, in the way he looked at life, at her.

"What happened to you? Where were you? What...."

"Hold on," he said. "I'll tell you if you stop asking so many questions." They sat down on the bed and he began his story, his long, long story...

"I went up to the north and volunteered at an army base as a medic. The battle on the Syrian Heights was fierce. The Syrians were chained to their posts. I couldn't believe it. Chained, actually chained, otherwise they would run away. Our boys were running up the hills. They were steep and rocky. It was hard, Tyra, so hard, and they were dropping like flies. *Hashem, Hashem,* it was horrible. A group of us volunteers shadowed them trying to help but it was useless. We were huddled in a bunker and then, this one soldier, I found out later his name was Ephraim, he was machine-gunned right in the belly and his guts hung out from his body."

"Oh," Tyra gasped, clutching her stomach, as if she could push Ephraim's intestines back into place.

"Tyra, I just ran over to him, put my arms under his shoulders and dragged his body down the hill to get him help. I thought I was going to save Ephraim's life, but in that instant when I ran from the bunker to grab him, an artillery shell landed just in the spot where I had been crouching down." Neil's words were running into each other. He was talking so fast, he was out of breath. "The very second I jumped up to cover him. Could you imagine? I thought I was saving him but he saved me. What a hero he was, and *Hashem,* what miracles he makes."

"It sounds like you saved each other. What happened to him?"

"He's still in the hospital. He'll be okay, I guess, in a while. He'll get a medal, too, I suppose."

"My feelings for *Hashem* changed, too...."

Neil cut her off. "*Hashem* is great. Tyra. The whole thing is miraculous. That's why I am here. I know now what is truly important and I know what a good and kind person you are. I have it all planned out. We can go back to the States, get married and finish our degrees. Then we can make *aliyah* and raise a bunch of little kids and build up Israel and make Her strong so never will the Jewish people have to be threatened ever again. Tyra, what a wonderful prophecy we can fulfill."

Tyra was dumbfounded, thunderstruck. All this talk of a future, a perfect world. She half expected Neil to talk about the coming of *Mosiach* next. All of this spiritual greatness and not one word of love. 'I love you, Tyra.' Not even, 'I like you, Tyra. You mean a lot to me, Tyra.' Just, in nicer words, 'Let's screw and populate Hebron, Tyra!' It was all she could do to keep from giggling, from shaking her head in disbelief, from looking at him as though he were completely nuts.

Tyra was so proud of herself. Neil taught her a great lesson in Self: self-respect, self-worth and self-reliance. She would never ever regress. No man ever would be worth giving up one part of herself, no less all three.

Tyra chuckled to herself. The confrontations with men seemed never to cease. On her agenda was to get to Hadassah one last time to tell Uri of her decision.

The next afternoon, she meandered through the grounds winding up at the Hadassah Synagogue Plaza on her way to Uri's office. She sat down on one of the stone benches and gazed at Chagall's windows-all boarded up, some totally destroyed, others broken here and there. When the Jordanians attacked the hospital, she was overcome with sadness. "I will make them more beautiful than before," Chagall had promised in a radio announcement, trying to assuage the nation of her losses, when he found out about the ruined masterpieces. Her skin turned hot and damp from the searing *hamsein* breeze flowing up from the desert, and she lingered as she watched visitors lugging their packages and goodies, medical staff members scurrying to and from their lunch breaks and duties, and patients, shuffling and limping, trying to get around, back on their feet. She looked at the windows and the people and she observed, and felt their message in her bones. Tyra luxuriated in a peaceful, joyful prayer. Suddenly in defiance of the climate in which she was saturated, she shuddered, a swift chill spiraling within her body, involuntarily shaking her shoulders. She thought of courage. Of Lazer leaving Europe and everything behind to find a better way, and then with hard work and great selflessness, ransoming each of the relatives, one by one, until his family was reunited. Of her father pulling a stranger to safety from the subway tracks. Of Sheldy running through the streets getting help for a bleeding girl. Of Jessie, facing excruciating pain and surgeries with grace, and hardly ever complaining. Of Kaye sacrificing her personal dreams to take care of the people she loved. Tyra had witnessed courage and strength all her life, and now for one brief moment, she knew what it felt like, and she belonged. Courage wasn't nearly as special as she had always thought. It was just natural; it happened just because it had to. There was no time to think about what to do, to measure the risk and weigh the consequences, to be logical. Courage did not cover one as a veil or a cloak, something external that you can acquire. Rather it circulates from within and materializes when the time is right, when it is needed, when there is no room for it to remain inside. The unexpected empowerment and quiet satisfaction was strong enough to last Tyra for a lifetime.

Hot but invigorated from her brief respite in the Plaza, Tyra knocked on the door and opened it without waiting for a response.

Uri looked up from his desk. "Shalom."

"Uri, I feel so bad for leaving you and the program. But I decided to go home. I made a deal and I can't break my word."

His desk was piled up in a mess of administration work and papers. "So you are abandoning us after starting something good here. You will be missed. There are others to take your place."

Tyra was a little shocked at his indifference, yet it gave her a sense of relief. She had carried a heavy load of guilt for no reason.

"Just one question, *havivalah-* darling. When are you going to be your own person? How old are you now?"

"My parents have had a rough time. I don't have to defend myself to you."

"Okay, Okay. Come here. He walked over to her and put his arms around her."

"We had a bird once. Tchotchka," she told him.

"You American Jews and Yiddish!"

"He was so loyal. He would always escape from his cage. My father would chase around the neighborhood with a long perch and always, no matter how long it took, find him and bring him back. We'd be devastated if he got lost for good. He was with us until he died. Don't you see, Uri. I am their loyal bird. I flew away, but I promised to return."

"Tyra, Tyra. So sad." He lifted her chin to his face and they kissed a long, lingering kiss.

She felt his muscular arms engulfing her body, his palms resting on her shoulder and the small of her back. All the wars were over and for a few moments there was nothing but the energy of passion and longing. It was a kiss that made her feel good, from the lips of a man who saw too much, knew what he had to do and had no time to luxuriate in spiritual confusion or misplaced loyalties- a *what could be* kiss, if she weren't leaving.

"I will miss you," Uri said.

Tyra laughed. "Come on, now. You are probably married, even though you say no."

"I am not. Israelis, we do not have good reputation, do we?"

"No, absolutely not," she laughed. Then she became her usual self. "I will miss you, too. Take care of yourself. And thank you for all you did for me." She turned and left.

August 19, 1967

Dear Tyra,

Sending this express mail- wanted you to get this before you leave. Sorry I had to write such a tough letter but I felt that it was the best way to avoid any long term problems. I know this has been a difficult year for all of us. I am glad you were able to achieve what you set out to do and I am proud of you. I don't think I was selfish. In fact, I did not burden you with any of our problems this past year but it seems I'm so tired now, tired of working, worrying, that I must unload a little. Grandma got very ill. I guess the nerves got the best of her and she has a lot of pain in her legs and can't get around. This will pass over. It's another attack and I hope rest and time will soon make her feel better. Grandpa cannot be operated on because it would be too dangerous. His heart, weight and asthma could not withstand it. Daddy is extremely tired and still works too hard. Jessie has not been very well this year and has all she can do to take care of her necessities. She works twice as hard to keep up with the job as she loves it. They show her a lot of courtesy, but still she is afraid of losing her job if she's out sick too much. I am so exhausted from anxiety I could not even write last week, and no one else can take over for me. I'm not really complaining because I know how much suffering there is elsewhere. It's just this incident has drained us all, and I miss you more than ever.

Love,
Mother

August 21, 1967

Dear Mom,

 I just got your express letter, and am so sorry for the toll my experiences have taken on everybody. I guess I was pretty selfish. Hopefully everyone will feel better and stronger soon. I miss everyone more than you can imagine and can't wait to see you next week.

 Thanks for sending the pills and nose drops.

 Here are details if all goes well. (I paid for my tickets today.) El Al- Paris- Flight #211- Air France- Paris-New York Flight #077 arriving Kennedy 4P.M. August 30th.

Love,

Tyra

Tyra hugged Barak and Manya and then Irit once more. Ironic that it was Irit who came to say goodbye at the airport. Today it was Hadas who was busy working in Tiberias and couldn't be with her as she had been on that hot summer day at the port a little more than a year ago.

Tyra walked up the tarmac and took her window seat on the plane, peering out at the ramp until she caught a glimpse of the three relatives waving heartily, knowing they could not see her, but knowing she was looking for them. She struggled awkwardly to buckle the seatbelt through the tears streaming down her face.

She was not alone in her sadness. So many of her friends had troubles of their own- Tirzah, Bella, Dawn, and even the people that came into her life for only fleeting moments carried burdens of their own- Moshe and Enid. Yet it was a blessing that Tyra was always surrounded by people who because of their circumstance, were able not only to appreciate life, but to demonstrate the integrity and resilience that comes from within the bounds of personal suffering. More than that, elevating the purpose of life, Tyra learned in increasing increments, not to feel so alone and so different.

She was, as she had written to her parents, afraid of flying, but not nearly as afraid of it as the war. As the plane settled in a cruising altitude and she saw the land of Israel disappear behind her, Tyra settled into a calmer sense of dread and resignation.

Instinctively she reached for the El Al stationary that was in the pocket in the seatback in front of her. The year was so full of writing, of letters home, of literary papers. What would she do without writing? She would write now, only without any one to address her most private thoughts to, and who would care anyway?

I am the bridge between two worlds and now I shuttle back, sad and sadder, for I belong to both worlds and could only be in one at one time. The pain I tried to leave behind followed me the entire year. Yet that spark emanating from within helped me endure in spite of the burdens that I could not shed.

The year had not fulfilled my expectations. I did not find peace, nor happiness, nor love. I had some of the loneliest, most desperate times ever. I caused even more trouble for myself and Mom and Dad. And Jessie, poor Jessie. Things will never change. Will she ever find love and have all the things that mothers want for their daughters? The year in Israel brought me no comfort, yet there was a bolt of energy that pulsated in me all the time. I began the academic year in pursuit of a master's degree in Hebrew Literature, struggling, immersed in studies one moment, and hitching my way through the most exhilarating travels and interacting with the most interesting people in the next. Early on, for reasons I don't fully understand that even if I would live a hundred years, this would be the most exciting, most memorable, most intense year of my life, as I became a participant in the most bizarre, incredulous existential adventure possible. I know for reasons I can't explain, that no matter how fabulous life may turn out for me in the future, the uniqueness of this year will stand out from all the others and be the most treasured ever. I resolved nothing that I needed to and yet everything is clear to me. God does not exist for us, the Millers, alone. He is far greater than that.

Blessed art thou. O Lord our God, King of the Universe, who has granted me the honor of taking part in a great miracle.

PART THREE

THE LAW OF RETURN

TWENTY ONE

MAGIC

Tyra had fulfilled all her promises to her family. She had taught high school English for three years in the Bronx while she completed her master's degree in Hebrew Literature at night. She grew tired of inspiring young ghetto students to draw in pictures what they could not speak, and teach rhyme to those who could not or did not try to read. One of her students had so much talent locked up inside of him, but refused to do the required reading. Instead he wrote terrific stories of what gang life was like on the streets. When he dropped out, he wrote poetry just for her and then sent his poems to her from prison. When his metaphors and similes crossed the bounds of dreams and visions into the realm of hallucinations and incomprehensibility, written with trembling fingers, Tyra knew he must have gotten drugs smuggled in somehow. When his poems stopped coming altogether, she surmised he had overdosed in his cell, and she grieved for his lost youth and that all her time and encouragement couldn't have saved his tormented soul.

She grew weary, too, of fighting with the students who didn't want to do the reading assignments and book reports she required. "We're going to college anyway" under the auspices of the college-bound program, so "we don't have to work, so there, Miss Miller."

Then there were all the dates she had with the teachers at the school. She started getting a crush on the cute English teacher and they would kid around during their planning periods, until rumors started to fly and the chairman of her department subtly informed her that he was unhappily married. Of course, living in the neighborhood didn't make it any easier, either. When students would enter the subway on Saturday nights and find her sitting with another teacher on their way to Manhattan for a show or ballet, they would snicker sweetly, "Hi, Miss Miller." Then on Monday mornings, her classes would be abuzz with truths and fantasies about her relationship with Mr. Biology or Mr. Business Administration.

The coup de grace was that the one and only Hebrew position was filled by Mrs. Goldblum, who was in her thirty-second year of tenure and would be there for another thirteen until her retirement or until her death, whichever would come first. Tyra would be at least forty-six before she would have a crack at the job of her dreams, if there would be any Jews left in the neighborhood who would want to learn Hebrew by then!

She still longed for Israel. It was time for her to go. She was free and she went.

It was June of 1971. Tyra was living in Jerusalem for almost a year. She had been sharing a spacious two bedroom apartment with Karen, another American *olah hadashah*, new immigrant, in Israel. The sixth-floor apartment overlooked the Central Bus Station, the grand concert hall- Binamei HaUmah, and the Judean Hills in the background. Kiryat Moshe was a wonderful, middle class suburb of Jerusalem. Most older five and six story buildings honed into the gold-hued stone hills in the older neighborhoods were designed to have the entrances in the middle of the structure, on the second or third level, carved out of the mountains, so that one only had to walk up and down a maximum of two floors. But Tyra's building had an elevator with an "American" ground floor lobby. Even more important, the building had central heating, so during the cold, damp Jerusalem winter, she didn't have to huddle next to a kerosene heater.

Israel was different the second time around. Irit was married and had a little boy. Her reunion with Tyra was bittersweet when they fell into each other's arms and wept. It wasn't bad enough that Israelis lost so many people in the wars. They had to drive like maniacs, too. One Friday afternoon Hadas, Irit's younger sister, rode the bus home for Shabbat. A car coming in the opposite direction passed another and couldn't get back in his lane before hitting the bus head on. Hadas and three others were killed instantly and scores others were injured. It was awful. Tyra remembered coming home from teaching that day. Kaye was sitting in the kitchen looking so sad. She broke the news to Tyra. They cried together and Kaye lit a *yahrzeit* candle in Hadas's memory.

"I'm glad I had a boy," Irit told Tyra when they first reunited. "If I had a girl, I would have named her Hadas, and I would have made her into my little sister. I couldn't bear it." The cousins sobbed in each other's arms. Irit had lost her oomph- her sparkle, and Tyra couldn't bear that either.

Things were not much better for Tirzah. She had two girls, and Azariah was in the mental ward at Shaare Zedek Hospital. After the war, he had started roaming the streets of Jerusalem clad in torn robes, carrying a staff, calling out. "Flowers, I am the King of Flowers. Don't step on the Blue Flower, the pride of Jerusalem." He was afflicted with the new mental illness, Jerusalem Syndrome. After the war, some people became so overwhelmed with the reunification of the city and the fact that Jews had access to the holy places for the first time in two thousand years, that they internalized their roles as saviors or messiahs. They would walk the streets in ankle length togas made of bed sheets shouting out psalms, singing hymns or spewing forth sermons pleading for the common folk to lead wholesome, spiritual lives that would indeed make them worthy of the newfound gift of the One Jerusalem.

Tirzah taught in elementary school part time and received a small allowance from Azariah's family in the States. Her dreams of professorship and poetry were put on hold, but her daughters were adorable.

Tyra had heard that Neil had returned to Israel after the war and became an extremely religious zealot. He and his group were becoming somewhat of a problem for the government. He married a young ultra-orthodox girl from a family of nine children. Ironically she looked like Tyra- same height and build, dark hair, too. *I wonder if he ever thinks of me when he looks at her,* she thought, knowing that was a stupid, invalid bout of nonsense. *I hope she's happy with him,* her cynical fantasy continued. He and his bride's entire family, along with contingents of religious immigrants from the States, England and South Africa moved to *Hagadar Hamaaravit-* the West Bank. They were developing a town, Kiryat Hamachpelah near the Tomb of the Patriarchs outside of Hevron. Tyra read an article about it in the newspaper- HaAretz. There was a photo of the newlyweds, too. The wife was standing next to Neil as he spoke at a rally trying to drum up excitement and additional participants in this new venture.

"The Arabs don't want peace, good. They won't negotiate a settlement, good. This is our land from where we were exiled. Hashem promised it to us. Now we shall build up the high ground so they can't attack us. We shall protect the Jewish people and teach Israelis how to become the true Israelites we were meant to be, and we shall make our land holy, as Hashem commanded us to do."

The crowd was cheering. Who is this stranger, who was to be known from now on, not as Neil, but Nachum she was reading about? How did such an indecisive and tormented Neil of the past find such a mission and become such a dangerous leader?

When she first arrived in Israel she went to Hadassah Hospital where she looked up Uri. Happy to see her, they hugged. "Now I *am* married," he emphasized with a chuckle. He looked great, if not a few kilos heavier than when she last saw him. She stopped by the Synagogue and saw the colorful jeweled windows in their rightful places. Chagall did repair them, just as he said he would. To Tyra's thoughtful eye, they were even more beautiful than before. But he left the original shrapnel hole on the bottom left side of the Tribe of Issachar in memory of the war. "Some things should not be undone."

That was it for the old crowd. Here and there in the city she would bump into some of the American students who decided to make *aliyah*. The rest was in the past.

Life was hectic enough, and Tyra didn't miss having a television set. At least she purchased a new imported stereo so she could enjoy her 33 1/3 albums. By far the most inconvenient aspect of daily life was the lack of a telephone line, even a party line, in the apartment. The installation of a phone was expensive, even by American standards, approximately four hundred dollars. The waiting list was enormous, and if a family was lucky, it had just one phone. Extensions- non-existent!

Adon Levital, the downstairs neighbor, looked frightful in his robe as he pounded on the door of Tyra's apartment one morning. Poor Adon Levital. This was the second time in three months his amenability allowing Tyra to use his phone number as an emergency contact got him out of bed at the ungodly predawn hour of six. "Phone call, from America. Hurry, hurry," he said tugging on Tyra's robe as she opened the door. Her heart was pounding, too, as she quickly calculated it was already three in the afternoon in New York, and her folks must have been frantic waiting for the earliest possible moment they could disturb a total stranger, and about what she didn't know except it couldn't be good.

"I'm not telling you what to do. I don't even know if Grandma will still be alive when you get back," Tyra's mother said. "But I know how much you love her. The cancer spread to her brain. She's in the hospital, comatose. The only thing she says is `Tyraleh, Tyraleh,' over and over. It's as if she knows that we are all surrounding her- Daddy, Jessie, Grandpa, Sheldy, but it is you she knows who is missing. I know you'd want to know."

All of Tyra's hard work and determination in Israel was finally paying off. She ways always an overachiever and her persistence got her places her ability alone would not. After months of hounding the director of the English Preparatory Program of the Hebrew University, she finally squeaked her way into the sole position that had become available and she began teaching several classes in English as a Foreign Language to young soldiers who finished their army service. Before they would be accepted to the university, they had to pass entrance examinations in English and needed to hone their skills. It was a plum of a job, with a bit of prestige as well, and that combined with her other part time teaching positions around the city earned her a sum of 1200 liras a month, equivalent to 400 dollars, and quite enviable at the time.

She was at the stage where she wanted to find a real man to build a life with and settle in Israel, not like the idealistic, but immature Neil she had loved during her first year in

Jerusalem, or any of the many flirtatious, charming and irresistible Israelis she was meeting now, but whose motives she could not trust. At twenty-five, she was still holding out for love for love's sake, and would not allow herself to be used as access to a green card, material gain or a passport. Tyra was not in the mood to hand out brooms to clever Israelis who schemed of sweeping gold dust off New York streets!

She was successful. She filled her schedule with coveted teaching positions, and finally snagged that precious job at the university. Yet, living in Jerusalem, her unfettered dream come true, without promises or ties holding her down, she was unhappy. All her friends were married. Zelda already had a bunch a kids, Bella was married, her college friends, even crazy Dawn settled down with Eric and was trying to have a baby. All of Jessie's friends were of course married and raising children. Only crooked Jessie and pretty Tyra were single and alone. Poor Kaye. Was anything good ever going to work out for her dear mother?

Looking out on the city she adored and felt so at home in, she made a mental tally of all the things she would need to do, quickly, at that- arrange leaves' of absence from the schools where she was teaching, prepay rent and expenses, and get in touch with her Israeli cousins. Tyra's mother was transferring enough money into her account to cover the airline ticket which would be even more expensive with an open return date. Tyra was so overwhelmed with all the petty details, and since everything had to be done in person, she knew the day would be spent on autobuses traveling from Romema to Kiryat Yoval to downtown. She had to distract herself from contemplating her grandmother's suffering, or else she'd never get everything done. For the first time in years, Tyra knew where her place was, and at least it was pure consolation not to be torn, not to feel the conflict and the tugging between two countries.

Comforted to be reunited with her family at New York Hospital and relieved she had the opportunity to say goodbye to her grandmother, Tyra tiptoed to the bed and kissed her grandmother on the forehead. "Grandma, I'm back."

Hana Siegel's eyes lit up wide and she murmured, "Tyraleh, Tyraleh." As if she hadn't missed a moment of the last two comatose weeks, Hana asked Tyra all kinds of questions about her life in Israel. "It's good you're back finally," she said.

Tyra's parents, Kaye and Sid Miller, Kaye's brothers, Jessie and the other grandchildren arranged an elaborate schedule, juggling time they could each get away from work, thus insuring Hana would not be alone. Each would watch over her, making sure she was comfortable. Jessie worked next door at Manhattan Orthopaedic Hospital, and she became the foreman of the crew, keeping track of everyone's shift, and filling in whenever work emergencies cropped up in the others' schedules.

They were the ones who kept vigil, and she, Tyra, the one who abandoned them after Hana's surgery, was the one who was rewarded with recognition, conversation and affection. Tyra was embarrassed by her undeserved, preferred status, yet she felt no resentment from them. Rather the family understood it was the illness, and not Grandma's will, that exacted such injustice.

When Hana's condition stabilized, Kaye and Sid took her to their duplex in Yonkers. They converted Tyra's old bedroom into a hospital room with all the necessary accoutrements: hospital bed, commode, part-time nurse, and a loving commitment to care for her for however long it would take.

As the summer progressed, Tyra saw how difficult it was for her parents to work and take care of Hana, and once she would return to Israel, it would be even harder for them. Tyra missed Israel, but when she decided to remain in the States, at least for the time being, she didn't feel as if she were sacrificing anything. It simply was the right thing to do; Israel could wait.

Tyra finagled her way into arranging an interview for the sole English position available for the fall semester at the local high school. Nervous and unsure, she sat in the waiting room along with four other applicants. Why was she always in the throes of so much competition, she wondered?

When she was called into the principal's office, she rattled off her experience, and the more she spoke of her ideals, the more confident she became. She found herself vividly enacting a lesson the students loved in which she incorporated the techniques of ballet to demonstrate the meaning of satire. It seemed that Mr. Oliver Roland was a season ticket holder to the Joffrey, and by the time Tyra got back to the house, there was a message waiting for her: "Report to Personnel Department immediately for paperwork. Teachers report to school on Wednesday. Welcome aboard!"

Tyra settled into a routine, and dated alternately, two men, a toy manufacturer and a chemist, both pleasant and intelligent, but not enough for her to put her passport in a safe deposit box.

One day in January, Aunt Minna and Uncle Izzy came to spend some time with Hana. Hana already had been slipping in and out of consciousness as the pain and deterioration of her condition took a toll on her. Of all sisters, Hana was closest to Minna. She was the youngest, the most modern and chic, and had the most lighthearted marriage of all. She wore her charcoal grey hair pulled back taut into a chignon placed just above the nape of her neck. In years past when Minna and Hana got together during family visits, you could hear them giggling and see them hugging and swaying, Hana enjoying Minna's cheerful escapades with crazy Izzy as Hana strove to keep stubborn Lazar in check.

During that January visit, Minna walked up slowly to the hospital bed and clasped Hana's hand. Too weak to speak,

Hana opened her eyes and tried to smile as if to say, "Minna, darling, I know you are here." Her eyelids flickered, struggling to stay open to take in the sight of her favorite sister as long as possible, knowing it would be the last.

On Tyra's birthday, she and Kaye engaged Hana in what would be her last lucid conversation.

"Mama, don't you think Tyra should get married already? After all, she's twenty-six today."

Hana replied in her ever soft-spoken, optimistic way, "Don't worry. She'll find her magic. You'll see."

Three days later, Hana lapsed into a coma. The family gathered and Hana died with her children and grandchildren surrounding her. They each said a quiet goodbye and left Kaye alone for the final, private farewell.

They went to the back of the house and sat around the kitchen table when the men from the funeral home came. The sages, understanding the despair at this particular time, forbade the family to watch a loved one shorn from her roots, in the state of diminished life, between roaming and resting in peace. When they intuitively sensed the men had driven away, it was Jessie who asked Kaye who should be called first, and slowly arrangements were made. Lazer went to the living room, and sat on the couch. For a lifetime of control and yelling at Hana, he looked like a sheep without his shepherd. Who would keep him in line? For the first time ever, he relinquished his command, and let the family take charge.

Death is not easy to accept, even when the person is old and even when death is expected. After all, everyone knows no one can live forever. "Thank God, she was seventy-two," Lazer said to Kaye one afternoon during the *shiva*. Kaye knew he was referring to what the sages said- that if one attains the age of seventy, one has lived a worthy life and will share in the world to come. Kaye patted his hand.

"I'm fifty years old, and I feel so lost." She looked at Sid, whose eyes were glistening with sadness. "How awful it must have been for you, Sid, being orphaned when you were a child."

"Now is worse than ever, Hon. I just lost the only mother I've ever known."

"What about Papa? He'll be so alone." Kaye said, shaking her head, looking at Lazer, who was sitting mute and uncomfortably on the hard, wooden stool.

"Come, Papa. Get off the stool. It's too hard. Lie down for a few minutes. You need to rest."

Unlike him, he acquiesced and accepted Kaye's arm, as he struggled to lift himself up from the low seat, and together they strolled into the bedroom.

Although religiously it was not required of Tyra, she stopped dating the two guys during the *shloshim*- the thirty day period of mourning after Hana's death. She wanted to stay home and keep Kaye company, distract her, cheer her up. At that time, two teacher friends, a married couple, Joyce and Robby, wanted her to meet one of their friends who had just gotten discharged from the navy. They said he was tall, cute and assured her she would have a good time. "I'm going back to Israel soon. I'm not interested. There's no point," she told them. For weeks, she told them, over and over again. Finally she screamed, "It's the *shloshim.* Leave me alone!"

Tyra entered the apartment one day soon after the *shiva* was over, and saw Kaye sitting on the piano bench. Her fingers were gingerly trying to find the keys to the *Mother's Prayer,* her signature piece from so long ago, the notes that failed to fulfill her innermost yearnings for her daughter, notes that she had now nearly forgotten. Today she was the daughter bereft. Tyra tiptoed toward the piano and sat down, nudging Kaye ever so slightly to move over.

"I'm fifty years old, and now I'm the matriarch."

Until this moment, Tyra had measured Hana's death in terms of herself losing her grandmother, but seeing Kaye struggling with the old haunting melody, she realized how much her mother had lost this year, how much they all lost. "I decided to stay until the end of the school year. I'm always picking up in the middle of things and it's just not right."

"Tyra, you don't have to stay on my account. Don't get me wrong, I'd love nothing more."

"When was the last time I did something just because you wanted me to?"

"That's true enough," Kaye laughed. "You do have a mind of your own."

"It seems I'm always running from one place to another. I've started to make a dent with my students. They're from the black ghettoes and some are so hopeless and bitter. I even got a football player to write a composition on how to play the game. It was pretty clear, too, since the girls in the class understood. I don't want to leave them in the middle; they've had enough disappointments, and it took me a while to get them on my side. Now that they're cooperating, I want to see it through."

"Like I said, just do what you want. I can't be disappointed anymore."

After the *shloshim,* Tyra gave in to Joyce and Robby's incessant pleas. "After all, he was in Vietnam," Joyce said. "You'd do it for an Israeli soldier; how could you refuse an American sailor?" That did it. She couldn't take the nagging any longer and agreed to meet Danny. "But only if we double. I don't want to be alone with him."

The trepidation she felt as she walked to the front door was dispelled as soon as she opened it. He stood there, a good looking, clean-shaven guy, casually dressed in an ivory cable knit sweater, and dungarees with flared out legs as wide as his dark, hourglass sideburns. He was of the build Tyra always preferred- tall, a tad heavier than skinny, a sliver shy of lean. "Hi. I'm Danny. You're Tyra, I suppose."

She sensed a bit of relief on his part as well as she led him into the kitchen for that ominous, overwhelming, obligatory introduction of the relatives. Just her luck, extra ones came to visit earlier and all of them were sitting around the table. "My parents, and Great Aunt Minna and Great Uncle Izzy."

"Hey, you no-goodnik," Uncle Izzy said, slapping his hand on his leg. "You and your flat-foot floogies read every comic book on the racks without buying a one! What are you doin' here, cheapskate?"

"At least we paid for the Bazooka," Danny laughed.

"What's going on?" Tyra said. "Don't tell me you know each other!"

Danny explained that he lived across the street from the candy store Uncle Izzy used to own. Danny's mother always sent him there after supper for a nightly chocolate malted. She spent years trying to fatten him up. `Put more ice cream in his drinks,' she would complain to Izzy.

"And don't be fresh, you hear!" Izzy called out. "She's my favorite niece. Pretty, too."

Tyra thought she would die. "Goodnight, everyone. Don't wait up, please." She grabbed Danny's hand and they both chuckled in disbelief as they ran down the flight of stairs, heading out to meet up with Joyce and Robby in Manhattan.

The evening ended where it had began, in the kitchen, over a long, very long cup of coffee. The kiss was not a sizzling, lusty one. Nor was it just a perfunctory good night peck. It was though, a warm, kind kiss, one that made her feel good, like she could trust him and just be herself. Love at first sight wasn't what she was counting on. He probably wouldn't call anyway. That's the way it seemed to work. The ones you want to call, don't. The annoying creeps, the ones you can't get rid of, do. She certainly didn't want any complications, entanglements, as her father used to say. After all, in a few months she would be going back to reclaim her positions and the life she had made for herself in Jerusalem.

But he did call, almost every night that week. They spoke for long periods of time, and he asked her out to dinner that Saturday night. They sat at a small table in a rustic fish house way out on the Island.

"They have the best lobster tails," he told her.

"I never had lobster. I'll think I'll stick to salmon," she said looking over the menu.

"Are you sure," he said. "You'll be sorry."

They ordered.

"So you never ate non-kosher before?"

"Once every summer in the bungalows, while my grandparents were sleeping, early, early in the morning, we would sneak in a package of bacon. Oh, it was so good! And the taste would have to last the whole year. They would get up and ask, 'What's this smell?' 'What smell, we don't smell anything.' We could hardly keep from bursting out laughing. And every now and then we would go for Chinese food on the Concourse, and instead of getting vegetable chow mein as usual, I would cheat and get spare ribs and shrimp. But that was only once in a blue moon. I guess I was a terrible Jew. And you?"

"My grandparents were religious, but we didn't have too much to do with them, and my parents were pretty assimilated. I couldn't care less."

"So tell me about your time in the navy."

"I enlisted so I wouldn't get drafted in the army."

"Why didn't you teach?"

"I'd rather get drafted!"

"You know I'm a teacher."

"I guess I'm on your shitlist now."

She giggled.

"I asked for a tour in Scotland."

"Scotland. Why Scotland? That's so far away!"

"I had heard they had great looking girls there."

"Oh." Her voice was low. She sounded a little disappointed.

"Oh, come on now," he said. "You're pretty cute yourself. You must have had some guys after you."

She smirked in a flirty sort of way. "As a matter of fact, I've had a sailor of my own, and war hero or two, a chemist, a yeshiva student, a toy manufact...."

"Okay, enough. So my first tour was in Alaska. It was so cold there, I hated it. After a year, they did give me a tour in Scotland. Then I spent some time on an aircraft carrier. I got off six months early and now I have a crappy job. I'll finish a business degree at night and then I'll need to settle in a nice, warm climate. I still shiver from my time in Alaska."

The waitress brought their dinners. The food looked scrumptious and appealing.

"Umm. This lobster is delish." Danny dug in heartily. "Here, taste." He offered her a morsel on his fork.

She studied it, the white chunk with drawn butter dripping down its sides.

"No, no thank you," she said, thinking of a whole live lobster scavenging on the ocean floor.

"Go ahead, try it. You won't be sorry. Promise."

She closed her eyes and opened her mouth. He put the fork in her mouth and she slowly savored the morsel, not knowing what to expect.

"Oh my God," she exclaimed. "Oh, that is the most delicious thing I've ever tasted."

"See, I told you," Danny said. "You can trust me. You want another piece?"

"No, I shouldn't!"

"Is lightning going to strike?"

"I don't know, but it's going to be a busy Yom Kippur. I'll stick to the salmon."

They laughed and continued to eat, each their own meals.

"So how come you're not married with a bunch of toddlers hanging on your skirts by now?" Danny asked Tyra.

"When I was a little girl, my grandmother told me to marry for love- to feel the magic." Tyra could feel tears starting to well up in her eyes. "It just hasn't come yet."

"A real romantic, your grandmother. Sorry about her dying and all."

"She was really special. Thanks."

"Maybe I will be your prince charming."

Tyra reached over the table and put her hand over Danny's. "I think, my dear, for now, you will be my lobster monster. Can I have another bite?"

He put a piece on his fork, dipped it in the drawn butter, lifted the fork up, leaned across the table to feed her, but kissed her lips instead.

From then on they dated almost every Friday and Saturday night. Although they never verbalized or agreed to it, they gave up dating other people, just by virtue of spending all their available time with each other.

They drove to Westchester County, bought sandwiches and Cokes in a local deli and picnicked in the chilly woods of Yorktown Heights. They trekked through the hidden paths of the Bronx Zoo, and found a tarnished horseshoe along the way, which Danny took home, polished and gave Tyra as a memento. "For luck," he said, and winked at her.

They spent an entire Sunday going up to the Catskills searching for the long forgotten bungalow colonies they spent their summers at long ago when they were kids. They laughed at their poverty as they had to pool their money on the return trip. They doled out enough for one burger for the two of them to share in Monticello, which left just enough change for tolls on the New York Thruway on the way back.

The movie and dinner dates in the beginning gave way to the trips across the George Washington Bridge looking for cheap roadside motels on Friday nights. The first time they checked into the Travelodge on the Jersey side of I 95, Tyra looked around the room, fixing her gaze on the gold and navy polka dot drapes and burst out laughing.

"We're twenty-six years old. All our friends are married and having kids, and we're both living with our parents. Neither of us has a place of our own. What's wrong with us?"

Danny grabbed her around her waist, pulled off her jacket, threw it on a chair and threw them both on the bed. "It's just the circumstance of our world travels," he said, as he nuzzled his chin inside the nape of her neck. Slowly they undressed, alternately removing articles of clothing from one another, as if playing an imaginary game of strip polka. Naked and cold, they crawled under the covers. Danny caressed her gently, two fingers of his right hand sliding from her left shoulder down around the curve of her breast. Tyra could hardly breathe, wrapping her arms as tight as she could around Danny's back, digging her fingers into his flesh. She could hold him tight like that forever. He leaned his head against her breast, opening his mouth, taking in her nipple, teasing her with his tongue every so lightly. She thought she would explode. Then he kissed her lips, opening them and finding her tongue with his. She held him with all her strength…she couldn't get enough of him.

One Friday night, after they had a Big Mac and checked in, they got into bed and apparently were so tired after the whole work week, they fell asleep. Tyra woke up in the middle of the night and let out a shriek, scaring Danny out of a dead sleep.

"What's wrong?" he said jumping up.

"It's two thirty. You have to take me home. My parents will be frantic. They'll think we were in an accident, lying in the side of the road somewhere."

"Okay, he said, rubbing his eyes. But not before we have a quickie." He laughed. "It'd be a shame to waste the twenty-four bucks for the room."

She rolled on top of him. "Hurry."

Theirs was a whirlwind blend of friendship, romance and love. After a few weeks Tyra mentally started to unpack her bags. They met on St. Patrick's Day, got engaged on Father's Day and planned a Thanksgiving Day wedding.

"Are you sure you want to marry him, Tyra?" Sid asked. "After all you just met him a few months ago. And it'll be a long time until he finishes school and gets a real job."

"Of course, she's sure. What's wrong with you?" Kaye said. "He's a nice boy. He'll make a good living, too, some-day, sooner than later, I hope." Nothing would let Tyra out of Kaye's reach again, if she could help it.

It turned out that when Tyra introduced Danny to Zelda, they remembered being in elementary school together and recalled wild, mischievous stories. Weirder still, after the wedding invitations were sent, Danny said, "You're not going to believe this but your friend Bella in Cleveland, the one you got kidnapped with in the Syrian Heights, she's best friends with my cousin Mike's wife. They're next door neighbors. Seems they thought it was a coincidence they both received invitations to a Thanksgiving Day wedding in New York, and when they compared them- Bingo!"

"How could everyone know us and we didn't know each other! Where were you all my life?" she said.

"Here," he laughed, "only we didn't know it. I like the way you fit," he said as they hugged, rocking back and forth.

Life is so strange. Their meeting was a coup de resistance. Neither was in the mood to meet anyone new, and neither readily accepted the invitation to double date.

"He's a great guy. Tyra, just once, then I'll leave you alone." Joyce cajoled.

"She's a real piece. You're a fool," Robby teased Danny.

So each eventually gave in- one meeting, one blind date and the incessant nagging would stop. Neither one of them was ready or willing, so to everyone's surprise, the chemistry between Tyra and Danny during that blind date was immediate and magical. The more they learned about each other, the more they assumed their paths had crossed, not once, but numerous times, growing up in the Bronx. Exactly which occasions- a high school party, a visit to Izzy's candy store, brushing past each other along a huge book stack at the Mosholu branch library or slurping authentic New York egg creams or "Kitchen Sinks" in adjacent booths at Jahn's Ice Cream Parlour- would always remain a mystery. But for sure, such encounters did exist. Even though fate seemed to pull them away from each other in those young years, they were bound for one another. It was as if a law of nature had been decreed and ordained– *beshert*. Not even the distance of the world could keep them apart any longer.

Dear Irit,

You know I intended to return to my life in Jerusalem after Grandma passed away, but the strangest thing happened. I fell in love and am getting married to a wonderful guy named Danny. We are so opposite, and he hardly has any Jewish background, but there is something I find very special and honest about him. As soon as we save enough money, we will come to Israel, and together we will show him all the most beautiful places!

In the meantime, can you arrange to close up my apartment, but please keep the stereo, the electric hair rollers, whatever clothes and anything else you would like. I can get whatever I need so much cheaper here. It would be a great favor if you could pack up my books and other personal things and ship my trunk- I will send a check to cover the cost. Thanks a mil, and wish me luck! Love to all. I miss you so much.

Tyra

"The year isn't up. They could wait a few months," Sid said, scooping the newspaper as he was leaving the kitchen.

"Wait a minute," Kaye said, wiping her hands on the dish-towel. Her eyes squinted like a squirrel honing in on an acorn. "They want to get married on Thanksgiving. It's only two months shy of the eleven months of Kaddish. Tyra isn't the one in mourning. She's been more than respectful of Mama. Even Papa agrees. She wants to get married and stay here. *You* were the one who let her go." Her voice was gruff. "No more agonizing for me. No more missing and worrying about Tyra." In a brief moment more of contentment than victory, Kaye swooped alongside Sid, smacking the towel playfully against his shoulder, pecking him briefly on his cheek. "This one's mine."

Tyra had a lot to contemplate as she was about to become a married woman with a home of her own. She didn't know where she stood in terms of how observant she wanted to be, and Danny, he could care less. His parents didn't give him or his siblings any background in Yiddishkeit. A kosher home seemed to be an absolute necessity. "It's something to hang on to," she tried to explain to Danny. "If I give up a kosher home now, I'll never get it back, and our kids will really be assimilated."

"As long as I can eat what I want on the outside, you can do what you want in our home. I don't plan on cooking much anyway."

"I don't get it," she said to Danny. "Zelda never questioned once her belief in God. She always observed. She never doubted. She's stable, consistent. How is that possible? I'm always struggling, going from one extreme to the other."

"You're just doing this to get me to agree to have a kosher home," he said in a half-kidding way.

She laughed. "You already agreed. Tell me, why is it that I love you?"

"Tell me, why didn't I find myself a cute little carefree atheist to love?"

"And why is it that..."

"Come here," He pulled her toward him, kissed her hard and wrapped his arms around her tightly, as if squeezing out all her questions, doubts and troubles, as if telling her, lighten up, stop thinking so much. Enjoy life!

"When we have the money, Danny, let's go to Israel. I want to show you all the magnificent places. You'll just love it."

Still holding each other, they pulled away a little.

"What's so special about it?"

"I can't put my finger on it. It's like even before the ship landed, the country was so overwhelming; not just the physical land, but the centuries, no, the millennia- our history, all the wisdom of our philosophy, ethic and literature; it makes each of us so miniscule and yet at the same time, each one of us is so crucial, so necessary in the continuation of our people's future- to keep us strong for the generations to come. You'll see. I know you will."

"I know I need to make you laugh," and he pulled her close once again.

People always said Tyra was sad, but she didn't feel that way. She was just pensive, intense, weighing the significance of moments and deeds in her life, always thinking about the things she did and worse yet, didn't do, thinking about all the thinking she thought about. But that had been changing. Although she never gave herself credit for all she had achieved, she finally had begun to take notice of all that she was accomplishing. She liked the headway she was making with her high school students. Like the pretty but disrespectful troublemaker in her tenth grade composition class who threatened Tyra from the first day of class. During the second week, Tyra said, "If you don't want to do any work, why don't you consider being the attendance monitor. I could use some help. Let me know." After a few days, the girl asked if the 'position' was still available, and became an efficient class secretary. Within a few weeks, she started handing in more assignments and her tone of voice softened. Perhaps the responsibility and trust Tyra put in her turned her around. Then there were other students who would stop by her classroom after the dismissal bell and just hang around to talk or erase the boards. Yes, she liked the changes she saw in her students.

"That's the difference between you and me," she said to Danny. "You were in the service during Vietnam, but you were living it up in the lush isles of Scotland with the pretty redheads...."

"And don't forget the frigid, remote, awful, miserable tundra of Alaska," Danny interrupted her with his adorable smile.

"Yes, my love, while I was in the thick of a nation turned upside down. And my friend, Ricky, who saw plenty of crap in Cam Ranh Bay." Tyra wondered whatever happened to Ricky. She had tried to get in touch with him when she got back to the States in 1967, but she never heard from him.

"Sometimes you just have to live and not analyze everything that happens. Lighten up a bit." He took her around. "There, see what I mean? You look so sad."

"That's a smart thing for a psych major to say. Don't analyze me, please."

"That's why we make such a great couple- a little serious-ness from me- a lot of.... " He started to tickle her and they fooled around laughing until they started to fool around in earnest.

He understood why she was crying. One night when Kaye and Sid were out and Jessie was working late, Danny and Tyra were sitting on the couch watching a basketball game. He saw tears falling down her cheeks.

"You can't spend your life crying about Jessie. It's not your fault, and it's not the converse either, the more you cry, the happier she is," he said. He covered her cheeks with his palms and assured her everything would turn out well.

Tyra knew he was right. As a married woman, it would be her responsibility to make her man, their home and their world a refuse, a place where every bit of joy that was reserved for them would be savored, for who knew what would befall them in the future. Besides, it was true; nothing she could do would change Jessie's fate for the better. It never worked before, and it still wouldn't. But saying it and understanding it could not make her heart feel it. She tried all her life, and it was no different now. She got up and walked to the other side of the room.

"I love you. I love how you care about your family, the kids you teach. I love how sensitive and kind you are, but I don't want you to cry because of me. I can't deal with that. I want to make you happy, not sad, so you have to figure out how to get over this guilt. You lived your whole life with it, but I can't live my life with it. I love you, but you have to learn how to work it out." He stood up and paced.

"What does that mean, Danny? Are you breaking up with me? Are you walking out?" Tyra felt faint and pale, and sank into the chair. "You're the best thing in my life and you're walking out?" She picked up the object nearest to her, a pillow, and threw it at him. Quiet tears streamed down her cheeks.

"No, I love you, but you have to figure out a way of solving what's been eating you up your whole life. Jessie can't come between us all the time. It's you and me now. Jessie can't be in the middle."

Tyra started to laugh. "All my life I was always in the middle, torn between Jessie and this or Mom and Israel. Now Jessie's in the middle!" Tyra giggled so much, she started crying. Danny walked toward her, stooped down in front of the chair and Tyra buried her face into his shoulder. He held her, stroked her hair. "Sh...Sh.... It's going to be all right."

"Just because you majored in Pysch doesn't mean you know what the hell you're talking about. You only..."

"You don't have to get defensive. I'm not threatening. And I don't want to hurt you. But you've understood the situation intellectually or rationally your whole life. It seems to me that you must be suppressing something deep down. I think if you take a hard look at some things and admit some ugly truths, you will find the peace you need, and you'll realize you're not such a terrible ogre after all."

"I don't know what the hell you are talking about."

"I'll call you tomorrow. There's no point hashing this out any more now. It's not my place, anyway. I'm sure you can figure it out. Besides, we have a couple of months till the wedding. I've got faith in you. I'm Jewish, you know," he said, winking his eye.

His voice had softened the longer he spoke, and Tyra no longer felt threatened by him. By the time he left, she felt an earnestness in him, a yearning for her to be successful, for she knew he didn't want to lose her either.

Danny was Tyra's comfortable enigma. From the beginning, he said he would call, and he did. He promised to take her to the Catskills where they would retrace their summer lives in the bungalows, and he did. He described his future with her in it, and she trusted him. He wasn't an observant or educated Jew as she always assumed her mate would be, but he was ethical, helpful and kind, a true mensch. He was a genuine Jew in that regard. He made her realize that she had been praying the wrong prayers all along. God couldn't make Jessie straight. Even the best surgeons couldn't do that. But God gave Jessie an intractable shell to protect her from the cruelty of the real world and allowed her to prevail in spite of it with dignity and purpose. And now God gave Tyra Danny, a man she loved, a friend with whom she was free and natural. Tyra, for the very first time, was happy. The sages say that God causes everyone to meet a soul mate, but it is up to the individual to choose or reject that "*beshert*" in an act of free choice. Tyra was able to love God for the blessing she was able to see in front of her. Jerusalem and the miracle of the Six Day War would always have a special place in her soul, but Danny had her heart. Her search was finally over.

Lazar used the same pattern to make the three gowns: Tyra's wedding gown, long and sleek with a row of satin-covered buttons down the back, reminiscent of Kaye's gown from years ago; Kaye's gold brocade with wineglass sleeves, and Jessie's lavender trimmed with a fluffy boa around the collar flowing down the back. Tyra's skirt had a full tulle overlay with a short train which set it apart from the others.

It was all Tyra could do to get Jessie to agree to be her maid of honor.

"I don't want to walk down the aisle when everyone will be staring at me," Jessie said. "The older sister, too, to boot," she added.

"Since when are you intimidated by others? Don't you always say that you look ahead? If others see you only from the back, it's their problem? You have to be part of my wedding.

You're my sister. And besides, I don't want to have a circus, with a million bridesmaids and flower girls. Just a simple procession. Just the ushers- and they'll be all for you!"

"Okay. But what about the gown? No corsets."

They burst out laughing. "No corsets. Simple."

Tyra rushed down the stairs one morning, piling into the car Sid was warming up. "Daddy, I hope I pass my driver's test this time. It's ridiculous that you have to drive me to work every day."

"Me, too. I don't understand why you just can't get this parking bit down yet. The steering wheel goes one way, the tires go the other. Just can't get it, can you?" He chuckled good-naturedly.

"Coordination was never my thing. But I have other good qualities. Speaking of which, I just want you to know that the year I spent in Israel, it meant a lot to me. I experienced things I never dreamed of, and I found courage I never thought I had."

"What do you mean?"

"Well, the war".... Tyra thought of the incident running to the shelter and retrieving her frozen cousin, but couldn't bring herself to betray Irit's weakness. "But I just wanted to thank you, because if it weren't for you convincing Mom, I wouldn't have been able to go; and I know you had a lot of aggravation."

Sid chuckled. "To say the least." He reached over and put his right arm around his daughter. "That Danny, he'd better take good care of you!"

The wedding plans were moving full speed ahead, and although Danny hadn't mentioned the Jessie issue at all, Tyra was still troubled about the feelings she still had bottled up inside her. She knew deep down she had figured it out, but she was ashamed and it was impossible for her to say it out loud, for that would make it real, and her shame would be real. But like a child who steals a candy bar, you have to admit, make it up, and move on. Like on Yom Kippur, you have to ask for forgiveness in order to be forgiven.

"Tyra, you look beautiful. You're going to be a magnificent bride," Jessie said as the sisters were trying on their gowns for one of the last fittings.

"Jessie, I've been thinking a lot lately about the things that happened to you, and how hard your life turned out."

"I can't say I would have chosen to have scoliosis. And as long as I had it, it wouldn't have been so bad if the operations were successful, but all things considered, I'm managing to make a good life for myself. And I am very happy for you, really. Danny is a sweet guy. You make a cute couple."

"But Jess, I never wanted you to suffer."

"I know, and you should stop feeling guilty. Life is life. Things happen that we can't change. It's nobody's fault."

"But, Jess. I don't know even how to say this, it's so awful."

"Oh come on, do you have to be so melodramatic for God's sake? Can't we just get the damned fitting over with?"

"You always do this. You always make it harder for me. I just want to admit that after everything, I'm glad it wasn't me. There, it's awful." Tyra burst into tears. "I know I couldn't have survived all the operations, and needles and the convalescent homes and the separations from the family...." She struggled to continue, her throat catching and gulping from her tears. "And the mocking and the loneliness. I never wanted it to be you, but I'm glad it wasn't me."

"Poor Tyra, My Poor Little Tyra," Jessie said. She walked over to her sister, whose tears and mucous were dripping from her eyes and nose, and put her arms around her. "Grandpa will be pissed if you stain the gown and squash my boa!"

Tyra managed to squeak out a laugh amidst her crying.

"That's so unrealistic, not wanting it to be you, as if any of us had control of any of it," Jessie continued. "You can't live on an imaginary stage. You never should have thought that way. I'm sorry you were so miserable. Maybe I should have been more up front, too. Look. I know how badly you used to feel about dating, and leaving me alone on Saturday nights, but I had no idea you took it to such an extreme. It's just not realistic, this not wanting it to be you. You had no control. Like I said before, it's nobody's fault, except maybe that damned nurse who may have dropped me in the nursery when I was born. But that was just a rumor. Anyway, like I said, I wanted Mom and Dad to enjoy themselves, but maybe I shouldn't have been so difficult. I'm not the only one in the world who suffers. You don't need to have scoliosis to suffer."

Tyra thoughts drifted to Tirzah, Bella's aunt, Inid and countless others she had known or knew of. Indeed, even a lone porcupine had to face the ravages of man's cruelty at some point. *Enough,* she scolded herself. *I'm getting married. Daddy says, grab happiness whenever you can. You never know what's around the corner.* For now, it was enough that Danny would be by her side to face whatever that might be.

"Jessie, I never mentioned this, but during the war, I did something I never thought I had in me, something real, for a change."

Jessie was looking intently at Tyra, taking her seriously. "Come," she said, reaching out for her sister's hand, "Let's sit down."

"When Irit and I were running to the shelter from the dorm when the war started, she suddenly disappeared. Shells were exploding all over. Plumes of smoke and dust were bursting in front of us. The noise was awful and I could hardly see. This Arab student was hit and bleeding all over."

"Oh, my God! You didn't write it that way in your letters. And how ironic about the Arab. What happened to Irit?"

"That's what I want to tell you. I couldn't find her and I didn't know what to do, but instinctively I just ran back to the lobby from where we came, and thank God she was there, huddled in the corner, and I grabbed her and dragged her back across the lawn to the shelter."

"She was in the army, wasn't she? She should have been prepared."

"I know. That's what I didn't understand. And that's why I never said anything to anybody. Because I didn't want to embarrass her."

"They say you never know how you are going to act in a situation until you're in it. Tyra, you spent your whole life thinking you were a chicken, and you turned out to be a real heroine."

"I know. I was glad I had the strength to do the right thing."

"Well, it sounds pretty courageous to me. Remember when we were kids? Daddy came home late one night. He pulled a man from the subway tracks. Guess it runs in the family. And it's a good thing you survived. Otherwise, Mom would have killed you herself!"

"Let's just keep this between us, okay?"

"Okay. Just one more thing. Be happy. I'm making a life for myself. Even if I were straight, I don't know if I would want to get married, not now anyway. And you, you're the type that needs to get married."

Tyra could kill Jessie, always that little snide attitude, even in the most intimate of conversations, always her back up, her defensive wall.

"And in a few years, you'll be the homebody, with kids and diapers, and I'll be traveling the world, running meetings and having a blast. So just be happy for all of us. It's a good day, Kiddo."

"I didn't get your response card yet," Tyra said.

"I don't know if I am coming," Dawn said.

Tyra felt her cheeks burn with hurt. She had thought Dawn just forgot to mail the card. "What? How can you ...even think not to come to my wedding?"

"You don't have a clue, do you? You were a bridesmaid at my wedding and you didn't make me one at yours. Why should I come? Give me one damn reason why."

"Oh, Dawn. I could barely get Jessie to agree to be my maid of honor. She didn't want to walk down the aisle with everyone staring at her back. Then to make matters worse, she said everyone would be comparing her to my beautiful straight married friends walking down, too. I promised Jessie that she would be the only girl in the wedding party. She's my sister. I wanted her more than anybody and if it would mean only her, than that's the way it would have to be. I didn't realize you would be so hurt. I'm so sorry, Dawn. Nobody understands how hard it is for me and I can't dare complain because what do I have to complain about in comparison? I'm always in the middle, and I can't please everybody. Don't you think I wanted my very best friend in the whole world standing up for me at my own wedding? I didn't mean to hurt you…"

"Okay, okay. But, at least you could have explained it. I thought you were mad at me or something and I was hurt."

"I'm so sorry. I should have explained. So you'll come?"

"What do you think?" Dawn said as the two of them hugged.

Just before they were leaving for the hall, Lazer called Tyra into the leaving room and motioned for her to sit on the couch next to him.

"Grandpa, I don't want to wrinkle my gown."

"Sit, sit." His voice was stern. She had no choice.

He pulled out a small white bundle from his pocket. "Take this. I want you should have it."

"What is it?"

"It vas Bubbe's. Her *k'nipple.* It was in her nightstand drawer. I found it after she…." His voice trailed off.

"Grandpa, you knew about that?" Tyra was astonished.

"What means you? For sure, I knew. Who you think put extra dollars so she should have *gelt* to buy what she wanted. But I never told. You too, you keep for yourself, a few dollars on the side. Danny, he's a good boy, but you keep for you- to be strong, inde... inde..."

"Independent?"

"Yah, independent."

She fingered the little pouch. She fought the tears welling up in her eyes, not wanting her make-up to smudge. She knew she would treasure Hana's tied-up handkerchief forever, but she would never use one of her own. What good is entering a partnership if you have to hide from your partner? And how can you be afraid of a friend?

"Grandpa, thank you so much for everything." She grabbed him around, and he clutched his arms around her without even a trace of pulling away. "Especially for this beautiful gown you made me. It's so simple and elegant, and the buttons are just fabulous. It's a perfect fit!"

Jessie and Tyra were putting the finishing touches on their make-up in the powder room at the hall, when in a sudden fit of emotion, Jessie hugged Tyra. "I'm really very happy for you Kiddo. Danny is a sweet guy."

For the first time, Tyra didn't mind Jessie calling her Kiddo. For the first time, there wasn't a hint of sarcasm in it.

"You know, just because I'm getting married, I'll still be around for you, always."

"Sisters...," Jessie started to say, then they blurted out together Kaye's moniker, "Sisters are forever," both of them giggling incessantly.

"Stop!" Tyra cried out, tears spoiling her eyeliner, "I can't pee in my wedding gown!"

It was time for Tyra and her parents to enter the alcove behind the translucent drape where she would watch the procession unfold before her presence would be known. Her wedding day, a moment somber and joyous at once was perfect, except for missing Hana. She knew Kaye felt that too, and squeezed her hand as the violin was playing.

Hana had told her when she was a child to wait for the magic. She didn't understand then what her grandmother had meant. Just a few months before, in her last moments of life, Hana assured Tyra that she would indeed find her "magic". She was right and it was all because of her, because she yearned to see her beloved granddaughter once more, that all had worked out as it had. It was as if a law of nature had been decreed and ordained–*beshert*. Not even the distance of the world could keep Tyra and Danny apart any longer.

The ushers walked down the aisle. Then it was Jessie's turn. She took small, deliberate steps, looking lovely in her gown and flowing hair.

Tyra's journey was a long one, from the Bronx to Jerusalem, from bitterness to spiritual comfort, from guilt to acceptance and from loneliness to love. *Yes, she and Danny were a perfect fit- it was magic.*

Tyra embraced the symbolism of the day. Of the *chuppah*, that it was open-sided, flimsy, so that it was not any material matter that would give the young couple strength, but their love and devotion that would carry them through whatever the future held for them. Tyra relished the spirituality of the day which gave her the meaning in her life she had always sought; but there was something different on this day. As she stood behind the drape watching the small march of ushers, Jessie, and Danny walk down the aisle, her heart was light and happy, finally so in love, so comfortable with the man she found by fate and by magic. Tyra so free.

The drape slowly lifted and everyone oohed and aahed as they turned around in their seats to look at the bride. Tyra walked down the aisle with her parents at her side, and midway down the aisle, Danny came to escort her the rest of the way. She kissed Kaye and Sid on their cheeks, and just before she was about to turn to Danny, she gave Kaye another unexpected, spontaneous kiss, as if to say a special thank you for all Kaye did for her, to let Kaye know how good a mother she was and how much Tyra really appreciated her, and only then did Tyra turn to Danny, smile, grasp his arm and together they proceeded to the *chuppah*.

The two mothers and the bride encircled Danny seven times as a symbol of the blending of the two families, of inclusion, of devotion to one another. Tyra savored every word of the ceremony, every sip of consecrating wine. Even though she expected it, when Danny shattered the glass with fervor, she flinched and a smile lit up her face. Danny held her tightly and Tyra felt so comfortable, such a perfect fit, magic swirling all around her. In the stillness of their embrace, she heard the graceful tulle layers of her skirt rustling in the air, sounds whispering, "Tyraleh, Tyraleh."

_ه

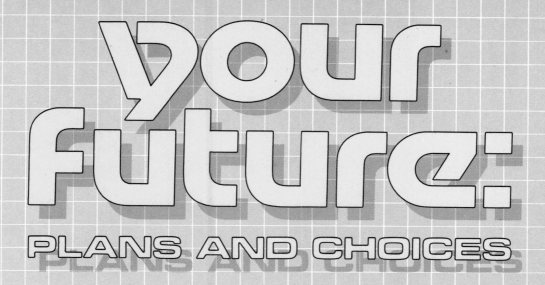

your future:

PLANS AND CHOICES

Willard R. Daggett, Ed.D.

Director
Division of Occupational Education Programs
New York State Education Department
Albany, New York

Published by

P35 **SOUTH-WESTERN PUBLISHING CO.**

CINCINNATI   WEST CHICAGO, IL   DALLAS   PELHAM MANOR, NY   PALO ALTO, CA

ISBN: 0-538-16350-X

Library of Congress Catalog Card Number: 84-50128

1   2   3   4   5   6   7   8   9   K   9   8   7   6   5   4

Printed in the United States of America

Contents

Preface . . . . **vii**

PART I. KNOWING YOUR SELF AND YOUR VALUES

1. Taking Stock of Your Strengths and Weaknesses . .   **4**
    Each Individual Is One of a Kind   5
    Get to Know Yourself   5
    Finding Your Strengths and Weaknesses   7
    Matching Your Skills and Your Interests   14
    Change and You   15

2. Needs, Wants, and Personal Values **18**
    Needs and Wants—An Important Difference   19
    Rating Your Needs   22
    Wants and Life-Style   25
    Personal Values   26
    Your Wants and Your Values   28

3. Establishing Your Identity **32**
    You Are . . . Your Self   33
    Image and the Real You   33
    Presenting Your Image   35
    Physical Appearance: First Impressions Count   35
    Personality—Your Inner Self on Display   41
    Change and Your Image   46

4. Your Changing World **50**
    Change: You Can Count on It   51
    History: The Story of Change   51
    Types of Change: Consider the Source   55
    Reacting to Change   55
    Problems and Decisions: A Question of Source   59
    Preparing Yourself to Deal With Change   60

5. Your Values and Your Personal Code **64**

Your Personal Code   65
Your Personal Code and Change   65
Your Changing Code   68
Elements of Your Code   70
Your Code and Your Personality   75
Challenges and Threats   77

PART II. LIFE-STYLE OPTIONS

6. Your Environment and Your Life-Style **82**

Life-Style: A Design for Living   83
Environment and Opportunity   90
Changing Life-Styles   93

7. Job and Home: Opportunities and Compromises . . **98**

Family Goals: Learning to Compromise   99
Managing the Home   102
Responsibilities of Family Members to One Another   109
Careers and Family Life-Styles   110
Careers and Home Management   111
Managing Conflict in the Home   113
The Family and Society   113

8. Responsibilities, Careers, and Expectations **116**

The World of Work   117
Why Work?   118
Your Future Role as an Employee   123
Responsibilities of Employees   125
Responsibilities of Employers   127
Getting Along at Work   128

9. Friendships, Changes, and Adjustments **132**

Friendships: Relationships You Choose   133
Qualities of Friendship   136
Friendships and Changing Needs   138
Friendships and Your Personal Code   140
Friends Can Be Leaders or Followers   142
Friendships and Careers   142

PART III. MAKING DECISIONS ABOUT YOUR FUTURE

10. Deciding What to Do: An Organized Approach . . . **148**

Problems and Decisions: A Question of Source   149
Using a Process to Deal With Change   150

A Model for Solving Problems and Making Decisions 152
Problems, Decisions, and Your Personal Code 156
Separating Symptoms and Causes of Problems 158
Using a Process to Reach Goals 160
Consequences: Good and Bad 161

11. Identifying and Evaluating Alternatives **164**
Stating the Facts 165
Analyzing the Facts 166
Identifying Alternatives 168
Limit Your Alternatives 169
Considering Consequences 172
Predicting Consequences 173
Contingency Planning 176

12. Selecting and Evaluating an Appropriate Action .. **180**
Selecting an Alternative 181
Making a Commitment 182
Group Problems and Decisions 182
Implementing a Solution or Decision 184
Feedback and Evaluation 188
Contingency Planning 191
Long-Range Decision Making 192
Using Problem-Solving and Decision-Making Skills 195

PART IV. PERSONAL SKILLS FOR YOUR FUTURE

13. Spending Money **200**
Spending to Satisfy Needs and Wants 201
Using the Process Method for Spending Decisions 202
Factors That Influence Spending 206
Life-Style and Spending Decisions 206
Developing Good Spending Habits 207
Planning for Continuing Expenses 214
Using Common Sense 221

14. Developing a Money Management Plan **224**
Planning to Satisfy Needs and Wants 225
Looking at Income 228
Looking at Expenses 230
Preparing a Budget 233
Credit for Customers 238
Types of Credit 239
Credit: The Good Side 244
Credit: The Bad Side 245
Your Credit Rating 246

15. The Smart Shopper **250**

A Consumer's Friends: Caution and Knowledge   251
Be a Smart Shopper: Compare   253
Reading Labels   259
Diet and Health   261
Meal Planning and Shopping   265
Fighting Fraud   268
Consumer Protection   269
Reacting to Fraud   273

PART V. YOUR FUTURE

16. Setting Your Own Course **280**

Your Most Important Decision: A Career   281
Knowing Yourself: A Review   284
Career Information: Where to Look   286
Looking at Career Clusters   291
Matching Yourself to Career Clusters   294
Charting a Course   296
Dealing With Change   297
Your Most Important Ability   299

Glossary **302**

Index **318**

Preface

YOUR FUTURE: Plans and Choices represents the first step of an important journey. The destination of this journey is the selection of a career. This comprehensive learning program is designed to help students begin an organized career selection process.

A vital first step in the career selection process is for students to understand themselves. Students also must become familiar with the concept of a changing world. Identifying life-style goals helps students to determine general career goals. An organized method of solving problems and making decisions is the next step in the process.

Workers are also consumers, and students are given a meaningful introduction into that side of the business world. Finally, students are introduced to broad career clusters. They are shown how to match their skills, interests, and goals with these broad career options.

CONTENT ORGANIZATION

YOUR FUTURE: Plans and Choices has five parts and 16 units.

Knowing Your Self and Your Values

PART I deals with self-knowledge, the changing world, and the individual's personal code.

Unit 1 presents the concept of strengths and weaknesses as characteristics of a unique individual. The importance of identifying individual strengths and weaknesses is reinforced by rejection of "right" or "wrong" judgments about these characteristics. Three types of individual strengths and weaknesses are discussed: physical, mental, and personality traits. Matching strengths, or aptitudes, with interests is pictured as a lifelong process.

Unit 2 discusses needs, wants, and personal values. The concept of life-style is presented as a grouping of general wants. The formation of personal values is discussed, and these values then are related to careers and life-styles.

Unit 3 explains the concept of self. Students are shown how to present their inner selves to the world through development of a positive image. Health, hygiene, grooming, dress, and posture are discussed as key elements of physical appearance. Personality traits also are presented in terms of personal attractiveness and a positive image.

Unit 4 deals with change as a constant factor in life. External change and internal change are discussed as sources of problems and decisions, respectively. Also discussed are the ways in which people can react to external change. Students are encouraged to develop the understanding and the skills to deal effectively with change in their lives.

Unit 5 presents the concept of the individual personal code as a complete collection of a person's beliefs and values. The personal code, or code of conduct, is shown as the guiding force in an individual's response to change. Also discussed are the elements of a personal code and the relationship between an individual's personal code and personality.

Life-Style Options

PART II deals with life-style goals and choices.

Unit 6 discusses the influence of environment on job, career, and life-style options. Life-style goals and expectations are shown as major factors influencing job and career decisions. On the other hand, jobs and careers are shown to have major effects on life-style. Also discussed are the effects of change on life-style.

Unit 7 deals with the interaction of personal and family goal setting. Home management is discussed in terms of the basic roles of family members and their responsibilities to one another. The effects of careers on personal and family life-styles, and methods for managing conflict in the home, are discussed.

Unit 8 presents the world of work as a means for achieving personal satisfaction and life-style goals. Work is viewed as a business transaction between employer and employee. The responsibilities of both employers and employees are discussed in the context of a business transaction. Other major elements include the importance of teamwork on the job and factors that promote good employer-employee relations.

Unit 9 covers the meaning and importance of friendship. Positive and negative effects of friendships on an individual's personal code are discussed. Also examined are ways in which friendships can affect careers.

Making Decisions About Your Future

PART III presents an organized method for dealing with change, a process for solving problems and making decisions.

Unit 10 covers the process method of dealing with change. A model for solving problems and making decisions is presented.

Unit 11 expands upon the first four steps in the problem-solving/decision-making model presented in Unit 10. Emphasis is placed upon the role of an individual's personal code in selecting alternatives. Also stressed is the importance of evaluating the potential consequences of alternatives. Another important element is the need to plan for contingencies.

Unit 12 covers the final three steps in the problem-solving/decision-making model. Differences between individual and group decision making are discussed. Elements covered include the value of an open mind in selecting the best alternative.

The importance of a commitment to a solution or a decision is stressed. Other themes discussed are priorities, feedback, contingency plans, and follow-up.

Personal Skills for Your Future

PART IV covers income management and basic consumer skills.

Unit 13 deals with spending decisions. The process method is suggested as a means of making decisions about spending. Comparison shopping techniques are introduced, and market awareness is stressed along with buying skills.

Unit 14 discusses the critical areas of budgeting and using credit. Again, the decision-making model is recommended as a tool for setting up a personal or family budget. Major types of consumer credit are presented, and the advantages and disadvantages of each are explained.

Unit 15 covers steps that the students can follow to become responsible, well-informed consumers. One of these steps is the ability to understand labels. Elements of smart shopping are explained, including how to recognize quality and value. Guarantees and warranties are discussed, as are ways to avoid consumer fraud. Students are presented with an overview of consumer protection laws and agencies, both public and private.

Your Future

PART V introduces the students to the challenge of career planning.

Unit 16 discusses the choice of a career as one of the most important decisions in a person's life. The decision-making model is employed once again as an organized way of dealing with change. Sources of job and career information are identified. Students then are shown how to relate their aptitudes, interests, and life-style goals to broad career clusters. The importance of identifying educational requirements is emphasized. Two educational goals are stressed as keys to dealing with future change in the world of work. These goals are building a broad base of knowledge and developing the ability to learn.

ACKNOWLEDGMENTS

The manuscript for this text was reviewed during development by two highly experienced, objective educators. The careful readings and thoughtful comments of these reviewers represented, cumulatively, an important contribution to the soundness and quality of this text. Their contributions are acknowledged with sincere thanks.

Elizabeth A. Brown, New York State Department of Education, Albany, NY

Marieanne R. Perault, Sweetwater High School, National City, CA

Knowing
Your Self
and
Your Values

YOU ARE AT AN AGE that will be marked by great changes in your life. It is an exciting time. It is also a demanding time. In just a few years, you will have completed the journey that leads from childhood to adulthood.

Along the way, you will grow physically, mentally, and emotionally. Physical maturity will occur without any special effort on your part. Mental growth will come as a combination of experiences and study.

Emotional growth will require conscious effort on your part. Emotional growth is needed to help you understand opportunities and to plan your future. A major requirement for emotional growth is knowing yourself.

Part I of this book deals with key elements of self-knowledge. In Unit 1, you are shown how to take stock of your strengths and weaknesses. Unit 2 helps you to identify your needs, wants, and personal values. Unit 3 deals with establishing your identity and developing a positive image. Unit 4 covers change as the one continuous force in the world—and in your life. Unit 5 deals with your personal code of conduct and your personality.

Knowing yourself will prepare you to understand the world around you and your place in that world.

1

Taking Stock of Your Strengths and Weaknesses

YOUR LEARNING JOB

When you have completed the reading assign-ments and exercises in this unit, you should be able to:

☐ Identify your strengths.

☐ Identify your weaknesses.

☐ Explain how strengths and weaknesses affect job and career decisions.

☐ Define aptitude.

☐ Rate your strengths or skills according to your interests and your skill levels.

EACH INDIVIDUAL IS ONE OF A KIND

No two persons are completely alike. There are more than 4 billion people in the world, and each one is a *unique* individual. Unique means one of a kind. Anyone or anything that is unique has no equal.

You are a unique person. There may be many people who resemble you. But, no one else on earth is exactly like you.

Even so-called identical twins are not really identical. Identical twins may be almost impossible to tell apart. Still, there are differences. For example, no two people in the world have exactly the same fingerprints.

GET TO KNOW YOURSELF

It is important for you to know yourself. As an individual, you have a unique set of *strengths* and *weaknesses.* Your strengths are your abilities, your good qualities. Your weaknesses are things you don't do as well, or enjoy less.

Physical strength is one type of ability that varies among individuals.
(© Ellis Herwig, 1984/The Image Bank)

5

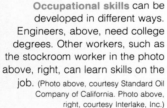

Occupational skills can be developed in different ways. Engineers, above, need college degrees. Other workers, such as the stockroom worker in the photo above, right, can learn skills on the job. (Photo above, courtesy Standard Oil Company of California. Photo above, right, courtesy Interlake, Inc.)

There are no "rights" or "wrongs" involved in identifying your strengths and weaknesses. For instance, it is just as "right" to be skilled in carpentry as to be skilled in medicine. It is just as "right" to have the ability to succeed in sales as to be a skilled teacher.

Individuals who enjoy the greatest success in their *careers* are those who make the best use of their strengths. A career is the course a person follows through his or her working life. A career is usually associated with a particular type of occupation or field of work. Some individuals have more than one career. For instance, a skilled mechanic might attend night school and become an attorney. It is not unusual today for workers to change occupations midway through their working careers. An occupational change may also affect the way a person lives. If so, it is said that the person has begun a new career.

Just as important as making use of your strengths is the ability to recognize your weaknesses. Knowing and accepting your limitations helps you to get along better and to avoid problems or failures.

FOCUS ON YOUR FUTURE

TOM HANDED THE BALL to Marcie and walked, head bowed, from the pitcher's mound. Halfway to the bench, Coach Morrison put his hand on Tom's shoulder.

"Don't feel bad, Tom," his coach said. "You gave your best effort out there. It's just one of those days."

There were tears in Tom's eyes when he looked at his coach. "Thanks, coach. But it's hard to admit that I'm just not good enough to pitch in this league."

"Nobody can be good at everything, Tom. Look at Marcie. She has a strong pitching arm, but she's an average hitter. Your arm isn't that strong, but you're a really good hitter. You also have good fielding skills. Hitting and fielding are your strong points, the skills that make you a valuable player. Why not concentrate on developing those skills?" the coach suggested.

"All right, coach. I'll leave the pitching to Marcie, Bob, and Miguel. As a matter of fact, I do hit better on the days I play third base. I guess I'm more relaxed and can concentrate more on hitting," Tom said.

"That's probably true," Coach Morrison said. "Pitching requires great concentration. It's tough to make the switch from pitching to hitting during a game. Let's just work at making you the best hitter in the Edgewood Little League this season, Tom."

"I'm for that," Tom said. "If I can't do it with my pitching arm, I'll try to do it with the bat." ■

FINDING YOUR STRENGTHS AND WEAKNESSES

Strengths and weaknesses are not limited to any one part of your life. They are involved in each of the basic areas that describe you as an individual. These basic areas are:

- Body
- Mind
- Personality.

Your bodily strengths and weaknesses depend upon your physical makeup. Your mind is your mentality. Your *personality*

7

Professional athletes must have high levels of physical coordination and special skills. (Courtesy Converse Inc.)

is the collection of all your *emotions* and your *behavioral tendencies*. An emotion is a feeling. A behavioral tendency is the manner in which a person usually responds to a change or situation. Your personality also includes your attitudes and habits.

Your personality can be difficult to judge and understand because it involves your feelings. Physical strengths and weaknesses can be measured easily and accurately. Mental abilities also can be tested with accuracy. Personalities are more difficult to measure or judge.

Physical Strengths and Weaknesses

There are a number of conclusions you can draw about your body, regardless of your age or size. Some of these conclusions involve comparisons between yourself and others your age. Comparisons can be made of height, weight, and color of hair and eyes, for example. These are obvious physical *characteristics*. A characteristic is a visible quality, such as being tall.

These kinds of comparisons usually are made among individuals. There are no "right" or "wrong" physical characteristics, only averages based on comparing large numbers of people. For example, a six-foot-tall person may seem like a giant in the company of short people. That same six-footer, however, would appear quite short in the midst of a professional basketball team.

Such comparisons depend on each person's situation. It is "good" for a basketball player to be tall. It is "good" for a jockey to be short and light. Neither condition—being tall or short—has any value in and by itself.

What is important is that you recognize these physical characteristics. Your physical capabilities help determine the kinds of activities for which you are suited. A small, *frail* person, for example, would not succeed at a job requiring the lifting of heavy weights. A frail person is one who is physically weak. However, that frail individual might excel at precise tasks that demand a light, delicate touch.

Think of two people who possess vastly different kinds of work skills: a carpenter and a brain surgeon. The carpenter must master certain skills that involve strength and physical coordination, such as driving nails. The brain surgeon need not be so strong. The surgeon must have great *manual dexterity*, however. Dexterity is grace and skill in physical activity. Manual dexterity is skillful use of the hands.

The brain surgeon does not need the carpenter's strength for lifting or moving heavy objects. On the other hand, a difficult operation may require that a surgeon stand in one place for several hours. Standing in place while concentrating on a delicate task is itself demanding, both physically and mentally.

Your physical skills or limitations will have a major effect on your life. Your physical characteristics may influence your job and career decisions. Your choices of *leisure activities* may also depend on your physical capabilities. Leisure activities are things you enjoy doing in the hours you spend away from job or school. Get to know your physical capabilities. This awareness will be valuable in making decisions that affect your life.

Mental Strengths and Weaknesses

Your mind, like your body, has certain characteristics. You probably have strong mental capabilities in some areas and less in others. This is normal. It is a rare individual who excels in all forms of mental activity.

You may be good in mathematics but less capable in reading and writing. Or, language skills may be your stronger area.

Some individuals are good at *abstract reasoning.* An abstract idea is one that is not associated with any physical object. Freedom and justice are examples of abstract ideas. They cannot be identified through the physical senses of sight, hearing, touch, taste, or smell.

Other people are strong at *concrete reasoning.* Concrete reasoning depends on experience with actual things or events. People who are good at concrete reasoning enjoy working with *specific* or *tangible* things. Something is specific when it is capable of being placed in a particular category. A tangible item has

Carpenters need strength and physical coordination to perform their jobs efficiently.

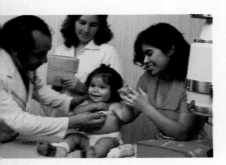

Combinations of skills are needed for some occupations, such as medicine, above. Artists, above, right, express abstract ideas using physical means. (Photo above, courtesy IBM Corporation. Photo above, right, © TRW Inc.)

physical properties. In other words, a tangible item can be seen or touched.

Abstract reasoning skills are important to people in occupational areas such as law, journalism, education, and the physical sciences. Concrete reasoning skills are useful to people engaged in physical tasks. Examples include mechanics, plumbers, dentists, farmers, and assembly line workers.

Some occupations require a combination of these skills. An artist, for example, uses physical means to express abstract ideas. This is true of painters, sculptors, and illustrators.

It is important for you to know your mental strengths and weaknesses as you begin to think about preparing for possible careers. Utilizing your strengths is an important step toward success and satisfaction. Ignoring your weaknesses can lead to disappointment and failure.

Personality Strengths and Weaknesses

People have personality *traits*. A trait is a quality that distinguishes you as a person. Your personality traits are characteristics that describe you.

There are a number of personality traits that relate directly to career considerations. These traits describe a person's general abilities and interests, as illustrated in Figure 1-1. You probably

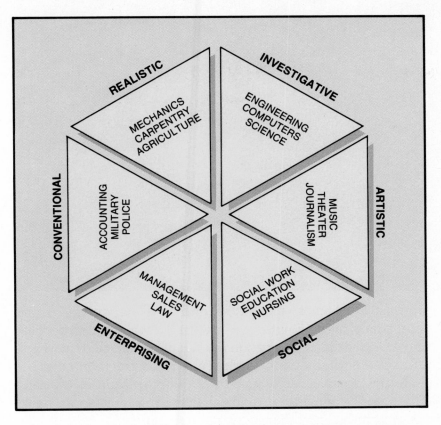

Figure 1-1. Personality traits can be related directly to occupational fields.

will find that you fit into more than one of these categories. Other categories will not match up with your personality.

As with physical and mental characteristics, there are no "rights" or "wrongs." The important thing is for you to identify and understand your personality traits. The better you understand yourself, the better equipped you will be to make decisions about jobs and careers. Personal and job-related characteristics include:

- Realistic
- Conventional
- Enterprising
- Investigative
- Artistic
- Social.

Realistic. A *realistic* person is one who enjoys working with tangible objects. You have realistic tendencies if your hobbies include activities such as building models, sewing, or agricultural

Office occupations are attractive to persons with conventional personalities.

projects. Mechanics, agriculture, and construction *trades* are occupational areas for which realistic individuals tend to be well suited. A trade is an occupation that requires manual or mechanical skill. Another term for trade is *craft.* Construction trades include the occupations of carpenter, plumber, and electrician. Other trades include auto mechanics, machinists, welders, printers, and many other industrial occupations.

Conventional. If you enjoy organized, orderly activites, your personality includes the *conventional* trait. People with conventional personalities tend to enjoy office occupations. Accountants, bookkeepers, and secretarial workers are included in this category. Conventional personalities also are well suited for occupations involving highly structured work situations. The military services, fire fighting, and police work are examples.

Enterprising. An *enterprising* person is usually *ambitious* and *energetic.* An ambitious person is one who has an active desire to succeed or to accomplish tasks. An energetic person has the ability to be active and to use strength in performing work. Do you enjoy taking charge in group situations? Do you find it easy to convince others to share your points of view or opinions? These characteristics are important for career areas such as sales

Investigative individuals often choose careers in fields such as scientific research, above, left. Artistic persons, above, are skilled in activities that require imagination.
(Photo above, left, courtesy of the Walgreen Company. Photo above, courtesy Texas State Department of Highways and Public Transportation)

and business management. Careers in law also tend to appeal to enterprising persons.

Investigative. Are you curious? An *investigative* person likes to learn what makes things work. Do you enjoy taking things apart to see what's inside? Investigative individuals often choose careers in science, mathematics, or engineering. *Research* may also appeal to people with investigative personalities. Research is careful examination or searching for information. In science, research usually is performed with the goal of discovering new facts. Other forms of research, such as in the law, may involve applications of existing facts.

Artistic. An *artistic* person is one skilled in activities, or arts, that require imagination. The arts include music, creative writing, painting, and acting. Artistic individuals often build careers in the fields of journalism, entertainment, music, or art.

Social. A *social* person enjoys working with other people. Do you prefer group activities to being by yourself? If you have a social personality, you enjoy the company of others. Social individuals often choose careers in teaching, nursing, social work, or politics.

MATCHING YOUR SKILLS AND YOUR INTERESTS

Strengths and weaknesses are personal characteristics that help determine your capabilities and limitations. A strength that relates to jobs or careers is called an *aptitude.* Your actual job or career decisions will involve an analysis of your preferences as well as your aptitudes.

Once you have identified the areas in which you have skills, you need to rate those activities. Which skills do you enjoy? What kind of activity would you want to do on a regular basis? Some basic skill areas involve using:

- Your hands
- Your body
- Words
- Numbers
- Analytical thinking or logic.

Analytical thinking is the ability to separate something into its parts and to understand the relationships between those parts. *Logic* means thinking or reasoning in an orderly manner, to produce *valid,* or correct, conclusions.

It is important that you establish relationships between your skills and your interests. The skills you enjoy most may not be those at which you excel. Or, you may have an aptitude for a particular kind of work but not enjoy doing it. These four steps can help you determine how your skills and interests match up:

1. List major skills and rate them from 1 to 5 according to how well you enjoy each one. (Let 1 equal best and 5 equal worst. See Figure 1-2.)

2. Rate the same skills according to your skill levels at the present time. Use the same scale.

3. Compare your areas of interest to your present skills.

4. Determine how skills that are desired but not mastered can be developed.

Matching your skills and interests is an important preliminary step in your search for a successful and satisfying career. It is a step that should be repeated many times during your life.

Skill Areas	Preference	Ability	Plan for Improvement
Work w/hands	4	3	None
Writing	1	2	Concentrate on English courses; increase my reading and writing activities
Numbers/math	3	3	None
Social	1	3	Increase my involvement in school and extracurricular activities; take a course in public speaking.
Analytical thinking	2	4	Go to library and read a book on logic; plan to take a class in problem-solving.

(Rating scale — 1-5, 5 being best.)

CHANGE AND YOU

As you grow older, your interests may change. Your skills also may change. For these reasons, it is beneficial to re-evaluate your strengths and weaknesses from time to time. You may find that your changing interests demand new skills as you mature. Some of your weaknesses may disappear. You may develop new skills to meet the challenges of change.

At this point in your life, your task is not to determine career directions. Rather, you should learn about yourself and develop the ability to match yourself with available opportunities. This ability will serve you well throughout your working career.

Figure 1-2. Matching your skills and your interests is an important preliminary step in your search for a satisfying career.

CONTENT SUMMARY

No two persons are exactly alike. Each human being is a unique individual.

As you begin to think about careers, your first step is to know yourself. You should identify your strengths and weaknesses. There are no "right" or "wrong" judgments to be made about your strengths and weaknesses. Some weaknesses, however, can be eliminated.

Strengths and weaknesses involve three areas: your body, your mind, and your personality. Physical abilities and limitations will have a major effect on all your activities. Mental abilities also play a major role in your career selection. Your personality traits may determine which types of work are suitable for you.

When you have identified your strengths, or aptitudes, your next step is to match them with your interests. You may find that your current skills do not match up with your major interests. In this case, your self-examination can lead to your mastering of skills to match those interests.

Matching your skills and interests should be a lifelong process. Your skills and interests may change as you grow older. The world around you will also change. Your future success and career satisfaction will depend to a great extent on your ability to adjust to change.

CAREER COMMENTARIES

1. **There are no "rights" or "wrongs" involved in identifying your strengths and weaknesses.** If there is nothing wrong with having a weakness, why might you want to improve yourself in that area?

2. **Enterprising individuals are usually ambitious and energetic.** What effect might these character traits have on your career? Why would they be particularly valuable to a person involved in sales or management?

3. **It is important that you establish relationships between your skills and your interests.** How can this activity help you as you begin to think about career choices?

KEY TERMS

unique
strength
weakness
career
personality
emotion
behavioral
   tendency
characteristic
frail
manual dexterity
leisure activity
abstract reasoning
concrete reasoning
specific
tangible
trait
realistic
trade
craft
conventional
enterprising
ambitious
energetic
investigative
research
artistic
social
aptitude
analytical
logic
valid

Needs, Wants, and Personal Values

NEEDS AND WANTS—AN IMPORTANT DIFFERENCE

Every individual has *needs* and *wants.* A need is necessary for your well-being. A want is something that you desire and that you feel will make you happier.

It is important that you understand the difference between needs and wants. Being able to recognize this difference involves making choices. You often have no choice about a need. For example, you must have air to breathe. However, wants almost always involve making a choice. You can choose to get an item you want. You can also choose to delay your action. In some cases, you may change your mind. Suppose, for example, you are thinking about a candy bar as an after-school snack. This is a want, since you don't need to eat the candy bar to survive. You are free to decide either way: You can buy the candy bar. Or, you can decide to use your money for something else. You have a choice. You control the way you satisfy your wants.

Needs and wants help determine a family's interests and preferences for recreation. (Courtesy Texas Department of Highways/Travel and Information Division)

19

Sometimes the difference between a need and a want is less clear. The difference may simply involve a measure of value. For example, a working person may require an automobile to get to and from work. The automobile is a need. If that person decided to purchase a $30,000 sports car or luxury sedan, the vehicle would far exceed the need. That type of purchase would be made to satisfy a want as well as a need.

As a working citizen, you will have many decisions to make about meeting needs and satisfying wants. You will have to exercise good *judgment* in buying the things you need and want. Judgment is the formation of an opinion about something through comparison.

Satisfying needs and wants requires that you use good judgment in making the many decisions you face as a consumer.

FOCUS ON YOUR FUTURE

MIGUEL CALLED TO HIS PARENTS. "Dad! Mom! Come here and look at this model."

His sister Maria was equally excited by the shiny new sports coupe at the front of the showroom. "Oh yes, Mom! Look at the wonderful things inside this car!" she shouted.

Mrs. Garcia put a finger to her lips, a signal for Miguel and Maria to lower their voices. She and her husband were speaking with a sales representative. They were looking at some of the features of a station wagon. Mrs. Garcia excused herself and hurried over to join her children.

"Let me see what has you so excited," she said, looking through a window of the sports coupe. "Oh yes, this is a very nice car. But I'm afraid it wouldn't be right for us," she said.

"Why not, Mom?" asked Miguel. "It's got an automatic shift, radio, and air conditioning—everything Dad said he wanted."

"Yes, Mom. And look," Maria urged. "It even has push-button windows and a sunroof."

"I see all that, and I agree that it is a very lovely car, children. But we need a more practical model. The station wagon will carry the family and all our things when we go on a trip. That sporty car has barely enough room for the four of us. We have to fill our needs before we think about satisfying all our wants," Mrs. Garcia said.

"Well, I just wish they made station wagons with sunroofs and push-button windows," Maria said.

"Look closer," her mother advised. "The wagon your father is sitting in over there does have electric windows. And the salesperson told us that we may be able to have a sunroof installed at a special price."

"All right!" Miguel smiled. "That way, we can get what we need and still have some of the things we want." ■

RATING YOUR NEEDS

All your needs are not equally important. Your needs can be separated into two general categories:

- Physical needs
- Emotional needs.

Physical needs generally involve things. *Emotional needs* have to do with feelings.

Physical Needs

There are two kinds of physical needs:

- Survival needs
- Safety needs.

Survival needs. *Survival needs* are physical needs that you must satisfy to stay alive. You must have adequate food and water. You must maintain your normal body temperature at or close to its normal 98.6 degrees F. Therefore, you need adequate clothing and shelter. Your body also requires minimum amounts of activity and rest. These survival needs must be met before any others are met.

Safety needs. *Safety needs* are physical needs that help determine how well you can function in life. In some parts of the world, people are in constant physical danger from natural forces or wars. They must devote much of their energies to staying alive. You can be a better student or worker if you are reasonably safe from physical dangers. To perform up to your capability, you need to be—and feel—safe at work and at home.

No one lives in a totally safe *environment.* Your environment is your surroundings. Everyday life contains some risks. People who travel daily to and from work on crowded streets and highways face the danger of traffic accidents. Most workers have to deal with some form of risk on the job as well. Some occupations are far more dangerous than others. People who work in dangerous jobs accept the added risks as part of their daily lives.

As a rule, however, more people are injured in accidents at home than anywhere else. This may seem strange, since most people feel safest when they are in their own homes. That very

Serious risks are involved in some occupations. A lion tamer, for example, accepts danger as a part of daily life. (Photo by Steve Castillo; Marine World/Africa USA on San Francisco Bay)

feeling of safety and well-being probably contributes to the frequency of home accidents. Many people tend to be less careful around their homes because they feel safe.

Included in the category of safety needs are *economic security* and an orderly environment. Economic security means having enough income to provide for your needs. You cannot feel safe in the world if you lack the money to buy food. An orderly environment is one in which you can plan your activities and conduct them without great hardship. For example, a working citizen needs reliable transportation between home and job. This may mean an automobile that runs well or some form of public transportation. The important thing is knowing that you can travel to the places you need to reach.

There are no choices involved in meeting survival needs. You must have adequate food, clothing, shelter, rest, and activity. You can exercise considerable control in dealing with your safety needs, however. Choices can be made regarding occupations, recreational activities, and other areas that determine the risks you take. You have some control over selecting your environment. You also have control over your own behavior. Therefore, you can do much toward satisfying your own safety needs.

Emotional Needs

Physical needs involve your survival and your safety. Emotional needs involve your happiness and your satisfaction. Your emotions are your feelings. Emotional needs fall into three categories:

- Social
- Esteem
- Self-fulfillment.

Social needs. Your *social needs* involve being around other people. Everyone has some need to be with other people, to belong to a group. At this point in your life, these needs are probably satisfied by your family and your school. When you go to work, your job may satisfy many of your social needs.

Social needs include being around other people. As a worker, you will become part of a group.

Esteem needs. *Esteem* is your value or worth in the eyes of others. People need recognition for their accomplishments. Successful students usually receive this type of recognition when they bring home a good report card. The extent of this need depends upon the individual's personality. *Self-esteem* is your view of yourself. People need to feel they are making a contribution to the world. They need to respect themselves and to have others respect them.

Self-fulfillment needs. People need to feel that they have reached their *potential*, or that they will reach it some day. Your potential is the sum of your capabilities. *Self-fulfillment* is the knowledge that you have measured up to your abilities. Your report card helps you determine how well you are doing in terms of your academic abilities. Some people set higher goals for themselves than others. Only you can judge if your goals are being met. As you go through life, your opinion of your own progress will determine your level of self-fulfillment.

WANTS AND LIFE-STYLE

When your basic needs are met, you can work on satisfying your wants. Remember that wants involve choices. You can think of two kinds of wants: *specific* and general. A specific want is a certain item, such as a particular video game or a certain style of designer jeans. Your specific wants tend to change as you go through life.

General wants involve *life-style.* Your life-style is the way you live. There are many choices you can make in adopting a life-style. A small sample might include:

Your life-style includes your leisure-time preferences, such as outdoor activities. (Courtesy Aruba Tourist Bureau)

- Living environment. Do you want to live in a large city, a smaller town, or in a rural area? Do you enjoy the changing seasons, or would you prefer living in a warm climate?

- Working environment. Do you prefer to work indoors or outdoors?

- Social interaction. Do you enjoy the company of others, or would you rather live and/or work alone?

- Leisure time. Do you want as much time as possible to yourself? This is a basic life-style consideration when you think about careers.

- Family. Do you want to be married and have children early in life? Would you prefer to remain single? Many people don't know what they want. They just let things happen to them. They have a tendency to drift through life rather than taking charge of their own lives. To reach your potential and achieve your goals, you need to take charge of your life. You should set goals based upon your needs and wants. Then make plans to reach your goals.

- Personal style. Is it important for you to present an image of success? Do you want to drive a sports car and wear high-fashion clothes? Many people prefer an image that draws less attention to themselves. This type of person might drive an equally expensive four-door sedan rather than a sports car. This person's clothes may be expensive but more *conservative* in style. Conservative means relating to traditional style or manners.

As you begin to plan for your future career, you should pay close attention to your general life-style desires. Keep in mind, however, that these general wants also may change as you grow older. Many people change jobs or careers to improve their life-styles.

PERSONAL VALUES

Value means worth or importance. A *personal value* is an idea, a belief, or an opinion that is important to you. A value is the way you feel about something. Your personal values form the basis for your life-style decisions. Your values also guide you in your everyday life.

Actions that support your personal values lead to feelings of satisfaction. Actions that go against your value system tend to be upsetting.

Personal values come from several sources. The major sources of values for most people are:

- Family. Parents usually pass on their values to their children. As a young child, you accept the ideas of your parents without question. As you grow older, you may adopt different values. Changing your values can be difficult.

- Religion. If your family is religious, you probably have acquired many of your personal values from religious teachings. Many people gain much of their sense of *morality,* or right and wrong, from major religions. Religious morality forms the basis for most systems of law. Thus, even nonreligious people acquire values from religions.

- School. Your school activities are a major part of your life right now, both educationally and socially. As you progress through

FOCUS ON YOUR FUTURE

SANDY SAW HER FRIENDS walking up to her front door. She opened the door and stepped outside.

"Hi, Shizu. Hi, Dave. Hi, Kim," she said, as the three approached.

"Hi, Sandy," Shizu responded. "We're going to the movies and thought you'd like to come along."

"Oh, I sure would. But I can't go today," Sandy said. "I have a big homework assignment due Monday, and I've just barely started on it."

"Couldn't you spare a couple of hours, Sandy? There's a really good movie showing," Kim said.

"Sure, Sandy," Dave agreed. "You have the rest of the weekend to do that old term paper. Why don't you come with us?"

"Thanks for asking me. I hate to miss that movie, too. But I'll never be able to finish my assignment if I don't keep at it. Besides, I promised my father that I'd finish

it by noon tomorrow. He's planning for us to visit my aunt and uncle tomorrow afternoon. You go ahead, and have a good time," Sandy said.

"OK, bookworm," Shizu laughed. "We'll think about you while we're enjoying the movie."

"Well, I feel jealous now. But, I'll feel a lot better about myself Monday if I can hand in all my homework," Sandy said. "First things first, I guess." ■

school, the knowledge you gain will add to your value system. As a working citizen, your job or career will have an important influence on your beliefs.

- Friends. Sharing of opinions and beliefs causes you to examine your own values. Some of your values may become stronger if they are shared by friends. However, exposure to different values may cause you to change some beliefs.

- Mass Media. The *mass media* are systems of communication that bring messages to large numbers of people. Included are the broadcast media (radio and television), and the print media (newspapers, magazines, and books). Another *medium* of mass communication is the motion picture industry. A medium is a device or a system by which something is transmitted or delivered. The mass media are important sources of values for many people.

Your personal values form an important part of your personality. Your personality grows and matures largely through the addition of new ideas and values.

YOUR WANTS AND YOUR VALUES

Situations throughout your life require you to make choices based on your values. These include both major and minor decisions. Your values will guide you in making major choices such as a job or career, marriage, and where to live. Your values also play a part in everyday choices such as which program to watch on television.

The most important values involve morality. You face choices every day between "right" and "wrong" actions. The values that guide you in making these choices may be based on religious beliefs. Most people acquire many of their moral values from their families.

Values and Satisfaction

Many of your values are not based on experience. For example, several of your friends may be wearing the same brand of designer jeans. You are about to purchase a new pair of jeans for school. Depending upon your personal values, you may base your selection of jeans on one of several feelings:

- Wanting to be "in style" by wearing the same brand
- Wanting to be a "style setter" by wearing a different brand
- Preferring to make your own choice without considering the preferences of your friends.

Think about values and what they mean. What are you really looking for when you consider purchasing something? The answer is personal satisfaction. Your values help determine what satisfies you. Your values will help shape your decision—and determine your level of satisfaction.

When Values Clash

Values frequently may pull you in different directions in situations that require a choice. In these cases, the value that is most important to you usually determines the choice.

Think of a situation in which two or more of your values might clash. For example, you might have a homework assignment due on a Tuesday morning. Monday night's television schedule includes a movie you want to watch. Your brother or sister invites you to play a new video game. How will you decide among these choices?

If you value success in school, you will decide to do the homework assignment. Either of the other two choices would satisfy a desire for entertainment. Satisfaction from those activities would be brief, however. And, some price would have to be paid the next day for failure to complete your homework.

However, you may not have identified your goals and values, and how your education is a part of them. In that case, you might automatically choose one of the other alternatives. In so doing, you would be placing greater value on immediate pleasure than on responsibility.

Notice that the preceding example made no mention of "right" or "wrong" decisions. This discussion deals with values in terms of personal satisfaction. People's values are not always based on morality. If taking the "right" action seems too painful, a person might choose a more pleasant path. Your personal values determine how great an influence morality has on your behavior.

CONTENT SUMMARY

Needs and wants often are similar, but there is an important difference. A need is something required for your well-being. A want is something that you desire and that you feel will make you happier.

There are physical needs and emotional needs. Physical needs include things you need for survival: adequate food, clothing, shelter, and rest. A safe environment is also a physical need.

Emotional needs involve your relationships with others and your feelings about yourself. The companionship and respect of others is important. Your self-esteem is equally important. You also need to feel that you have reached your potential, or that you will someday.

Your general wants involve your feelings about where to live, kinds of jobs, and leisure time. These wants become specific when you face decisions. The sum of your wants describes the kind of life-style you desire.

Personal values are ideas, beliefs, and opinions that you consider important. Values come from several sources: family, religion, school or work, friends, and the mass media. The most important values involve morality. People do not always make decisions based on feelings of "right" and "wrong," however.

Values often are determined by levels of personal satisfaction. In some cases, doing the "right" thing may bring greater long-range satisfaction at the cost of immediate pleasure. Your individual set of values determines how important morality is to your feelings of satisfaction.

CAREER COMMENTARIES

1. **To perform up to your capability, you need to be—and feel—safe at work and at home.**
   Why is a feeling of safety important to your performance at school or in a job? What happens when this feeling is lacking?

2. **Actions that support your personal values lead to feelings of satisfaction.**
   If an action supporting one of your personal values brought discomfort, what might be the result?

3. **What are you really looking for when you consider purchasing something? The answer is personal satisfaction.**
   How might it be possible to experience satisfaction through the purchase of an item that lacks quality?

KEY TERMS

needs

wants

judgment

physical needs

emotional needs

survival needs

safety needs

environment

economic security

social needs

esteem

self-esteem

potential

self-fulfillment

specific

life-style

conservative

personal value

morality

mass media

medium

Establishing Your Identity

Your self-image is a mirror image of the way others see you.

YOU ARE . . . YOUR SELF

How well do you know yourself? Do you know who you really are? To answer these questions, you need to know your *self.* Your self is your complete person. Your self is your body, your mind, and your personality. Your self is your identity—the real you. As discussed in Unit 1, three basic areas describe you as an individual:

- Body
- Mind
- Personality.

Together, these three elements make up your self. In terms of identity, these elements contribute to your *image.* Your image is your self as other people see you.

You have another image, called your *self-image.* Your self-image is the way you see your self. Image and self-image do not always match up.

IMAGE AND THE REAL YOU

Look in the mirror. Who do you see? Do you see yourself? Is the image you see the same as the one others see when they look at you?

The answer, of course, is no. When you look in the mirror, you see a reversed image of yourself. For example, if your hair

FOCUS ON YOUR FUTURE

CAROL LOOKED UP as John put his lunch tray on the table. "Well, I guess I looked pretty foolish in front of the class," John said, shaking his head.

"Foolish? I didn't think you looked foolish," Carol replied. "Why do you say that, John?"

"Because I got really nervous standing up there. I must have sounded as if I didn't know anything about the topic," he said.

"I'm still not sure what you mean," Carol said.

"Oh, you know. I always feel self-conscious and embarrassed when I have to get up and speak in front of the class," John explained.

"Well, I didn't get that impression," Carol said. "In fact, I thought you were very smooth. If you were nervous and self-conscious, you hid it pretty well."

"Really? That's hard to believe, the way I felt. I wish I could see a movie or a tape of my speech," John said.

"That might help. But then again, it might not. My mother says that we don't

see ourselves the same way others see us. That's because we see ourselves the way we'd like to be, instead of the way we really are," Carol said.

"That's interesting," John said. "I just hope the class saw me looking better than I think I looked." ■

is parted on the left, your mirror image shows it parted on the right.

That is a physical difference. However, there is a more important reason why your self-image may not match the image others see. That reason lies in your attitude.

People are *subjective* about themselves. Being subjective means that, to some extent, you see yourself the way you'd like to appear. Therefore, your self-image is a subjective view of yourself. You have a strong interest in the worth of your self-image.

Other people are *objective* about your image. Objective means that they are not personally involved in judging your image. They see you as you really appear.

Self-image is not always superior to a person's true image. In the story, John was worried about his image. Carol had a better opinion of John's image than he had.

PRESENTING YOUR IMAGE

The image you present to others has two main parts:

- Physical appearance
- Personality.

Your image can be considered a two-step presentation. Your physical appearance usually makes the first impression when you meet someone new. Your personality is revealed more gradually.

There is much you can do in both areas to present a good image. There also are parts of your physical appearance and personality that you cannot change. Your self-esteem depends largely upon the efforts you make to improve those parts of your image you can control.

PHYSICAL APPEARANCE: FIRST IMPRESSIONS COUNT

There is an old saying that first impressions are lasting. When you see a person for the first time, you immediately form an impression.

If the person is well-dressed and neat in appearance, your impression will be *positive.* A positive impression means that you have good feelings about that individual. And, your feelings probably will go beyond physical appearance. You may also feel that person has other qualities, such as:

- Intelligence
- Mental and physical skills
- Ambition
- Reliability.

The point is that good physical appearance does more than make a person attractive. Your appearance says a lot about the kind of person you are.

If your appearance is sloppy or dirty, you usually will present a *negative* impression. A negative impression means that other people will have bad feelings about you. Those feelings also may go beyond physical appearance. Rightly or wrongly, others may see you as a person who lacks ambition, skills, or reliability. Your *reputation* is damaged before you have had a chance to prove yourself. Your reputation is your overall quality or general character as seen by others. When you make a negative first impression, you face an uphill battle to win a good reputation. If you continue to present a negative image, you extend the damage.

Make the Most of Your Appearance

Everyone has limitations in the area of physical appearance. There are some qualities about yourself that cannot be changed. For example, you cannot do much about your height. You may

A positive appearance consists of several elements, including grooming, dress, and posture.

be tall, short, or medium in height. There are advantages and disadvantages to any physical characteristic. A positive approach to dealing with physical characteristics might include these actions:

- Accept the physical characteristic as something that cannot be changed.

- Make the most of its advantages.

- Do what you can to reduce its disadvantages to a minimum.

It is not necessary to be handsome or beautiful to present an attractive physical appearance. Most people do not have the gift of great physical beauty. Some people waste that gift by ignoring their appearance. It is also important to understand that beauty is a subjective judgment. Have you ever watched a beauty contest on television and found yourself disagreeing with the choice of a winner?

Elements of a Positive Appearance

There are many ways in which you can have a positive effect on your appearance. Attractiveness depends upon your efforts as well as upon your natural appearance. Areas in which your efforts can help your appearance are:

- Health
- Hygiene
- Grooming
- Dress
- Posture.

Health. Good health shows. A person who is physically well presents a better appearance than a person who is not in good health. If you are healthy, you probably have bright eyes, an alert expression, and an energetic attitude. Most important of all, you feel well.

Key areas in which good habits promote wellness are *nutrition*, rest, and exercise. Nutrition is the process in which the body takes in and uses food substances. Good eating habits start with maintaining a balanced diet. A balanced diet includes six *nutrients* that you should have each day: proteins, carbohydrates, fats, vitamins, minerals, and water. Nutrients are substances that help the body build and repair itself. Nutrients also provide energy and assist the body in performing its vital functions.

Eating three nutritious meals each day is another good health habit. Meals should be consumed at regular mealtimes whenever possible. Eating snacks and unhealthful treats between meals is a bad habit that contributes to skin and weight problems.

Adequate rest is another important part of maintaining good health. A good night's sleep enables the body to regain strength and energy. Think of your body as a rechargeable battery. Sleep is similar to connecting a battery to an electrical outlet and recharging it. A good night's sleep gives the body a "full charge."

Exercise is the third activity that promotes good health. The type of exercise is not as important as the schedule you maintain. It is important to exercise regularly. Three exercise periods weekly is the minimum recommended by most health experts.

Hygiene.   *Hygiene* is the practice of caring for the body in ways that maintain good health. Hygiene includes care of your teeth, skin, and hair—all of which are important aspects of your appearance.

Oral health depends on two regular practices. One is careful brushing of your teeth, immediately following meals when possible. The other is regular visits to your dentist for professional cleaning and checkups—at least every six months.

Skin care begins with daily bathing. Only a daily bath or shower can remove perspiration and dirt from your skin. Perspiration is a continuous process that can cause an offensive odor. Use of a deodorant is worthwhile to support your bathing routine. However, deodorants are not a substitute for bathing.

Perfumes and colognes should be used sparingly. They are added-on scents and do not have the odor-killing qualities of deodorants.

Your hair is one of the first things people notice. Your hair should look, feel, and smell clean. Clean, healthy hair looks better in any length or style. Equally important is a healthy scalp. Flaking of the scalp, or dandruff, is unsightly and usually causes

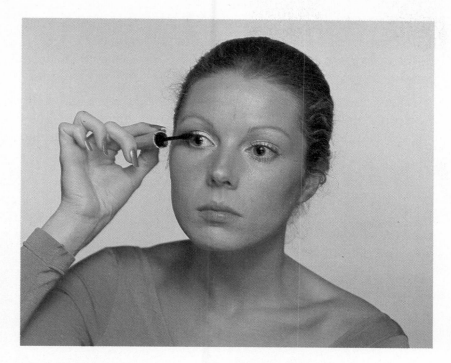

Cosmetics are beauty aids used by most women for facial grooming.

itching. Unsightly "snow" on your clothing and a habit of scratching your head are two revealing signs of an unhealthy scalp. Such conditions are also damaging to your image.

Grooming.   *Grooming* is regular care designed to make yourself neat and attractive. Most grooming practices are *cosmetic* forms of hygiene. Cosmetic means beautifying.

Grooming includes the cutting and styling of hair. Care of the fingernails is another grooming activity. Neatly trimmed, clean fingernails are important for men. Women are also concerned with the cosmetic care of fingernails.

Your face is the other major area of grooming activity. Shaving is the major facial grooming concern for men. Many men wear mustaches or beards. The length and neatness of facial hair makes a statement about a person's attitudes. Most women use *cosmetics*, or beauty aids, in facial grooming. Lipstick, blush, eye shadow, and other makeup products can be used along with moisturizers and other skin care products. Cleanliness, of course, is a basic necessity for clear skin.

Dress. Clothing is a very obvious part of your appearance. The right clothes can enhance (improve) your image. The wrong clothes can be a serious handicap. Your clothes will make a positive statement about you if you follow some simple rules:

Choosing the right clothes has a positive effect on your image.

- Select clothes to match your activities. Faded jeans and well-worn T-shirts are fine for playtime. They are not acceptable for situations in which dress codes are followed. When you

are uncertain about proper dress, find out what others plan to wear.

- Follow fashions and avoid *fads.* A fad is a style that is followed enthusiastically for a short time. Fads often represent extremes of style. It is better to choose well-fitting clothes that stay in fashion for a longer period. This allows you to avoid making the wrong kind of statement about yourself. You also save money by purchasing clothing that will remain fashionable longer.

- Suit yourself. Buy clothes that fit well and look good on you. You are a unique person. Make the most of your own characteristics rather than copying someone else's wardrobe.

- Care for your clothes. Cleanliness and good repair are vital to maintaining a good wardrobe. Dirty and wrinkled clothes are never in style. Match your outfits properly. You will always be considered well dressed if your clothes are neat, clean, and well matched.

Posture. Without speaking a word, you tell the world a great deal about yourself by your posture. Erect posture usually is a signal of self-confidence and a positive attitude. Slouching sends the opposite message. Slouching says that you are negative and unsure of yourself. The way you stand, sit, and walk is a clue to your attitude. Erect posture offers two additional benefits. Good posture makes you feel better and helps you avoid fatigue.

PERSONALITY—YOUR INNER SELF ON DISPLAY

Your physical image is the way you look. Your personality involves the way you act toward others. Physical attractiveness alone does not bring success. More important is your ability to get along with other people.

Your personality is a window through which you display your inner self to the world. The emotional image you project includes positive and negative *traits.* Traits are features of your personality that make you an individual.

If you think about other people, you can identify those traits you find attractive and those you consider unattractive.

Your posture tells the world how you feel about yourself.

A **thoughtful person** cares about others and makes life more pleasant for them.

Remember, those same traits will make you attractive or unattractive to others.

Positive traits that help you project a positive personality include:

- Trustworthiness. A trustworthy person is one on whom you can depend. Having someone trust you is the highest honor you can gain. Loyalty (faithfulness) and reliability (dependability) are important parts of trustworthiness. Together, these are the traits most admired by your relatives, friends, and others close to you. Trustworthiness should be your most valuable characteristic.

- Thoughtfulness. Caring about the feelings of others makes you a good person to know. A thoughtful person cares about other people. Considerate people make life more pleasant for those around them.

- Enthusiasm. Showing eagerness and energy in your activities sends a message that you have a positive attitude. An enthusiastic person is interested and involved. Enthusiasm offers a bonus: It is contagious. You can have a strong effect on those around you if you show enthusiasm.

- Confidence. Let other people know you are willing to take on a job or a challenge. If you display confidence in your abilities, others will share that confidence.

Being pleasant helps you to project a positive image.

- *Ambition.* Ambition is a strong desire for success. An ambitious person works to achieve goals. People respect others who express goals and the willingness to work toward them.

Projecting a Positive Image

Projecting your personality is best done quietly and through natural behavior. Projecting means presenting in a vivid (strong or clear) manner. Avoid being *boastful* or *aggressive.* A boastful person is one who brags about accomplishments. An aggressive person is one who uses force or hostile actions to gain his or her goals. Boastful or aggressive behavior usually accomplishes the opposite of what it is intended to do. Some ways of projecting a positive image are:

- Smiling. Be pleasant (friendly and agreeable) whenever possible. One way of projecting pleasantness is by smiling. However, a smile must be sincere to be appreciated. Your

Paying attention means being a good listener and concentrating on what others say.

behavior should match the situation. Pleasantness is like enthusiasm in this way: It tends to rub off on those around you. The more you give, the more you can expect to receive.

- Paying attention. This means to concentrate on what others are saying. Be a good listener. Showing that you are interested in what other people are saying pays them a compliment. If you seem bored or inattentive, you will be considered insensitive.

- Being agreeable. Respect the opinions and feelings of others—and their right to express them. If you do, your own opinions and feelings should get a more positive response. Avoid being argumentative and challenging. However, exceptions should be made for statements that are damaging or harmful.

- Offering sincere greetings. When you meet someone, especially for the first time, your greeting reveals a great deal about your personality. Shake hands firmly. Don't offer a limp hand, and avoid grasping another person's hand so strongly as to inflict pain. Don't overdo your greetings. People usually see right through false enthusiasm, which can make them uncomfortable and mistrusting.

44

Sincere greetings help you to establish a positive personality when you meet someone for the first time.

Look through the list again, and you will recognize traits that you like or admire in other people. Practice projecting these traits yourself. Make a conscious effort to be friendly and positive in dealing with others. You can practice at home, in school, with friends, and with business persons. If you are successful in projecting a positive image, you should see positive reactions from others. Friendliness is more often appreciated, and returned, than rejected. Having others like and admire you is, after all, the goal of projecting a positive personality.

Poise—Your Emotional Posture

Poise is the way you show your personality traits. Just as posture relates to your physical appearance, poise relates to your emotions. In a physical sense, poise means your *bearing*—the way you carry yourself. A poised person is relaxed and well balanced.

Poise depends on your self-image. If you are sure of yourself, you will tend to be poised. You will have an easy, smooth manner.

Think of any activity—music, athletics, a hobby, or a game—in which practice is necessary for success. When you attempt that activity for the first time, you are unsure of yourself. You may

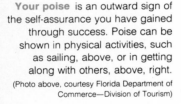

Your poise is an outward sign of the self-assurance you have gained through success. Poise can be shown in physical activities, such as sailing, above, or in getting along with others, above, right.
(Photo above, courtesy Florida Department of Commerce—Division of Tourism)

lose your balance in a sporting event, for example. However, once you have practiced and become familiar with the activity, you gain poise. You become confident of your ability.

Self-confidence in dealing with others is the reward of success in building personality skills. Poise is the outward sign of this success.

CHANGE AND YOUR IMAGE

Your image—and therefore your identity—will change as you grow older. Change is natural and constant. There are some kinds of change that you make happen. Other kinds of change occur in the world around you. Some changes you don't control require adjustments on your part. Some factors that cause a person's image to change are:

- Aging. Your physical appearance will change throughout your life. Your feelings about many things will also change as you grow in knowledge and experience.

- Changing roles. New experiences in your life—high school, work, or marriage and child rearing—cause you to change. Your outlook as a parent would be far different from your attitude as a young student.

Your image will undergo major changes as you go through life. You can work to improve your image through posture, grooming, and wearing attractive, well-fitting clothes. (Butterick Company, Inc.)

• Environment. The world around you never stands still. As you go through life, your image will change to match your surroundings. Imagine what you will be like when you are a senior in high school. Your image and your outlook will undergo major changes in the next few years.

Remember that you can make change happen. You can work to improve your image, both physically and in terms of personality. As you deal with change through the years, you will have many opportunities to strengthen your positive traits. No one is born with an ideal personality. If you work at improving your personality, you will improve your image. In that way, you will be comfortable with your identity.

CONTENT SUMMARY

Your self is the person you are: your body, mind, and personality. These elements of your identity contribute to your image—the picture of yourself that you present to the world. You also have a self-image, which is the way you view yourself.

The difference between image and self-image lies in attitude. You are subjective about yourself. Others see you objectively.

Your image has two main parts: physical appearance and personality. Your physical appearance is the first impression you make on people. That impression can be positive or negative, depending upon your efforts to make yourself attractive. You can be attractive without being beautiful.

Important areas of physical attractiveness are health, hygiene, grooming, dress, and posture.

Your personality is your inner self on display. Positive personality traits include thoughtfulness, trustworthiness, enthusiasm, confidence, and ambition. You can project a positive personality by smiling, being attentive, being agreeable, and offering sincere greetings.

Poise is your bearing. It is your emotional posture. A poised person is relaxed, balanced, and confident.

Change will affect your image throughout your life. Aging, changing roles, and environmental changes are major causes of change in people. You can work to make positive changes in your image and your identity.

CAREER COMMENTARIES

1. **Beauty is a subjective judgment.**
   Write the names of five people whom you consider beautiful or handsome. Ask a classmate to judge your choices. If there are any disagreements, explain the reasons.

2. **Considerate people make life more pleasant for those around them.**
   Think of a considerate person in your life. Describe your feelings toward that person. Is that person held in high regard by others?

3. **Some changes require adjustment on your part.**
   Describe a change that caused you to make an important adjustment during the past year. Was the outcome of the change positive or negative? Why?

KEY TERMS

self
image
self-image
subjective
objective
positive
negative
reputation
nutrition
nutrient
hygiene
grooming
cosmetic
cosmetics
fad
trait
ambition
projecting
boastful
aggressive
poise
bearing

4

Your Changing World

CHANGE: YOU CAN COUNT ON IT

In the midst of a very cold winter, the most constant thing in your daily life may seem to be the cold. The same applies to heat during a summer heat wave. Extremes in weather can cause the feeling that a particular condition will never end.

However, weather does change. No matter how severe the conditions, you know that relief will come sooner or later.

Weather is just one example of a basic fact: Change is constant. Change is the one force in the universe that never stops. You experience change every day of your life.

HISTORY: THE STORY OF CHANGE

History is more than a record of the past. History is the story of change. Major events in history are examples of very large changes. For example, think about the tremendous changes brought about by a war.

Computer chips have helped to shape the dramatic changes that computers have made in the way you live. (Courtesy TRW Inc.)

FOCUS ON YOUR FUTURE

PAUL WAVED A GREETING to the custodian as he passed the principal's office. "Hi, Mr. Johnson. Did you have a good holiday?" Paul asked.

"Pretty fair, Paul. How about you?" Mr. Johnson inquired as he turned back to his work.

"It was great," Paul said. "Say, what are you doing there, putting up a new nameplate for Miss Nelson?"

"Well, I'm putting up a new nameplate, but it isn't for Miss Nelson. You have a new principal, Paul."

"What? You're kidding! Miss Nelson has always been the principal. Did something happen to her?" Paul asked.

"Sure did, Paul. Miss Nelson has been appointed associate superintendent of schools for the entire district. She's taking the position left open when Mr. Davis moved to another district. Mr. Farrell is the new principal," the custodian explained.

"Mr. Farrell? That means we'll have to watch our behavior. He's pretty tough, Mr. Johnson," Paul commented.

"Mr. Farrell is firm, but he also seems fair," Mr. Johnson suggested.

"Yes, I guess you're right," Paul said. "Boy, this sure is a surprise. Go away for one little holiday, and everything changes."

Mr. Johnson looked thoughtful. "I guess change is the one thing you can really count on," he said. "And, you better get to class before the bell rings, Paul." ■

Changes made during recent history have had great influence upon the way you live today. Many of the comforts and conveniences you enjoy have resulted from scientific progress made during the past 100 years. Consider these examples:

- The first automobiles were produced in the late nineteenth century. Cars did not become available in large numbers until the 1920s. Even then, there were only a few good roads in the United States. Your grandparents may remember when a trip

Superhighways have brought great changes in personal transportation habits. (Courtesy W. R. Grace & Co.)

of more than 10 or 20 miles from home was a real adventure. Today, many people drive their cars farther than that to work every day. Personal transportation has been a basic need for most people in the 1980s.

• Jet airliners have made the world seem smaller for the traveler. People have become accustomed to traveling from one coast to the other in less than five hours. International travelers can cross oceans in less time than you can drive across some larger states. As recently as 1945, the main method of cross-country travel was the train. Average travel time was three to four days.

- Personal communication is another area of exciting change in this century. The telephone made possible instant communication over long distances. Most homes did not have telephones until about 50 years ago. Communication satellites now make possible instant communication between people separated by oceans.

- Mass communication 100 years ago consisted of newspapers, magazines, and books. News from distant places was transmitted over telegraph wires. Your grandparents probably remember having a single radio in their home when they were your age. Commercial television was just a dream in the 1930s. Television did not become a basic source of home entertainment until the 1950s. Color television is still newer. Widespread color television transmission did not occur until the late 1960s.

- Computers probably are the greatest single element of change in your lifetime. The first commercial computer was put into use in 1952. Within 30 years, computers had become essential to the operation of business, industry, and government in the United States. Computers also have had a major impact on recreation, as you may recall when you play a video game. Computers have greatly increased the ability of people and organizations to deal with numbers and information. The power of the computer is affecting the life of almost every living person. More important, computers have helped to increase the rate of change.

These changes came about through advancements in science and *technology.* Technology is the application of science to solve a problem or to reach a goal. These kinds of change are considered major because they affect large numbers of people. Changes also occur on a much smaller scale, however. You are probably affected more directly by smaller changes that happen around you every day. You may be more aware of these smaller changes because you often have to respond to them.

Your telephone is your gateway to communication with the world around you.

TYPES OF CHANGE: CONSIDER THE SOURCE

Changes that affect you come from an unlimited number of sources. Some changes occur in nature. As the earth turns, you experience daylight and the darkness of night. This is an example of constant change. Another example is weather.

Natural disasters, such as floods, earthquakes, storms, and forest fires, are dramatic, threatening changes. These kinds of changes require more energetic responses than constant changes.

Other changes are caused by people. People-related changes also range from minor to major. An adjustment in your class schedule is an example of a minor change. Of all people-caused changes, war has the greatest impact.

Regardless of their source, however, these are all changes that you cannot control. As far as you are concerned, change can be separated into two general categories:

Computers have greatly accelerated the rate of change in technology. (Courtesy Hewlett-Packard Company)

- *External change.* Change that occurs from natural causes or by the actions of others is external change. External means outside. External changes are outside your control. This type of change can present you with problems or opportunities.

- *Internal change.* Change that you want to make is internal change. Internal means inside. Internal changes begin from within you—from your own decisions. You are in control of internal changes.

You face change—external and internal—every day of your life. Most of your energies are spent dealing with change. Life is a succession of problems, challenges, opportunities, and decisions. Your personality and your values determine how you react to these changes.

REACTING TO CHANGE

External change can be favorable, unfavorable, or *neutral.* A neutral change is one that has little or no effect upon you. A friend might stay home from school one day with a cold, for example. This type of change has very little effect on you. From your standpoint, it is a neutral change. You notice the change, but you don't have to do anything about it.

Change offers opportunities and challenges. Your ability to adjust to change affects your chances for success.

Many changes do affect you, however. The effect may be minor or major, but you will react to those changes that affect you. In general, you react to change in one of these four ways:

- Opposition
- Acceptance
- Rejection
- Support.

Opposition. If you try actively to prevent or discourage change, you are in *opposition*. First, you recognize that a change has occurred or is about to occur. Then, you try to keep things as they are. You might resist an effort by your parents to change your hairstyle, for example.

Rejection. Refusal to recognize a change is *rejection*. When you reject a change, you take the position that the change should not happen to you. You refuse to accept the fact that the change will happen or has happened. Instead of working to oppose the change, you simply act as if it were not happening. For example, you might refuse to take a raincoat to school, even when a rainstorm is forecast.

Acceptance. Taking a neutral position on a change is *acceptance.* If you accept a change, you do nothing to oppose or support it. You are not against the change, and you do not reject it. You also may not be in favor of the change. You decide to accept the change and its consequences for you.

Support. If you are in *support* of a change, you favor it and try to bring it about. An example might be helping in a family project such as painting or spring cleaning.

These types of reactions indicate different attitudes toward dealing with change. If you oppose or support a change, you are trying to control what happens to you. In rejection, you are refusing to adjust to a change. If you accept a change, you are deciding not to act.

Doing nothing is always an *option* when you are faced with change. An option is a choice. You can choose to let change happen and to accept the results—both good and bad.

Right or Wrong? You Decide

The four basic reactions to change can be chosen at any time, in any type of situation. There is no right or wrong way to react to any particular change. You react to change in ways that are right for you—but not necessarily right for another person.

You may decide, following your reaction to a particular change, that you made a bad decision. This type of conclusion is yours alone to draw. Only you can judge if your personal reactions are right or wrong for yourself.

Reactions Reflect Your Values

You are guided by your values and beliefs in reacting to change. Your personal set of values is yours alone. No one else shares the exact same set of beliefs and feelings. For this reason, no one else is qualified to judge your reactions.

In the same sense, no one else will react to changes in exactly the same way. Your reactions, like your beliefs, are yours alone. In reacting to change, you act alone—by yourself and for yourself.

FOCUS ON YOUR FUTURE

LUIS SAW HIS SISTER approaching their house. He ran to greet her as she came in the door.

"Hi, Juanita. How's everything today?" he asked.

Juanita looked suspiciously at her younger brother. She put her books on the hall table and turned to face him. "When you meet me at the door, you usually want a favor, Luis. What can I do for you?"

"Oh, nothing much, really," Luis answered. "I thought maybe you could help me with a little problem."

"What kind of a little problem?" Juanita asked.

"I was wondering if you could help me with my homework this afternoon" Luis replied. "I have to turn in a book report tomorrow, and I don't have time to finish reading the book. Mom said you got an A when you did a report on this book three years ago."

"How much of the book have you finished," Juanita asked.

"All but the last two chapters," Luis told her.

"It shouldn't take you that long to read those two chapters. I don't understand why you can't do that and write the report this evening," Juanita said.

Luis looked at the floor. "Well, Juanita, there's this movie on television tonight . . ."

Juanita laughed. "Now I get it," she said. "You want me to help you write your book report so you can watch a movie. As I see it,

Luis, you don't have a problem. You simply need to make a decision. Which is more important, the book report or the movie?"

"They're both important, Juanita. That's the problem," Luis said. "Can't you help me for an hour or so?"

"All right, I'll help you. But, you have to finish reading the book first. Then, if you're willing to work hard, we may be able to finish the report before supper. Otherwise, you might as well forget about the movie," Juanita said.

"Thanks, Juanita. With your help, my problem is solved," Luis said.

Juanita turned toward the kitchen. "The decision is yours, Luis." ▪

Choosing clothes in a store is an example of decision making, a change that originates within yourself.

PROBLEMS AND DECISIONS: A QUESTION OF SOURCE

The two basic kinds of change—external and internal—bring different results. Remember that external change happens outside of your control. External change can present you with *problems* or *opportunities*. A problem is a situation that causes you discomfort or that presents a threat. An opportunity is a chance for progress or advancement.

Internal change is just the opposite. You are in control of changes that originate within yourself. These are changes you want to make. This type of change results from a *decision*. A decision is a choice or judgment that you make.

In the story, Luis felt that he had a problem. His sister, Juanita, considered his situation to be one that required a decision on his part. As a neutral observer, explore the possible causes of the situation.

If you consider his homework as an external change, you might conclude that Luis had a problem to solve. His reaction was to ask for help in resolving the problem.

If you feel that Luis could have completed the book report on his own, you probably agree with his sister. Watching the movie on television is something that Luis wants to do. His course of action represents a decision on his part.

Whether the story represents a problem or a decision depends in large part on your point of view. Your values determine how you view the situation. The story points out the similarity between problems and decisions. The only real difference is their source.

Opportunities originate in much the same way as problems. They come from an external source and present you with a situation. It is up to you to decide how to react, how to deal with the situation.

Problem solving and decision making are basically the same. The difference lies in the source of the situation. In dealing with external change, you must first determine the nature of the change. Once you have identified a problem or opportunity, you can decide what to do about it. You can't control external change, but you do control your reaction. Problem solving, then, becomes the same as decision making once you have examined the nature of the problem. Problem solving and decision making are covered in Part III.

PREPARING YOURSELF TO DEAL WITH CHANGE

Change is a constant force in your life. Therefore, your ability to deal with change is a most important skill. Your reactions to change have a major effect on your happiness and success as an individual.

Remember that change cannot be avoided. You can choose to ignore a change. By doing so, however, you give up control over your own life.

The world around you is changing rapidly. The rate at which change occurs is likely to increase throughout your lifetime. Now is the time to prepare yourself to deal with future change. These three preparations will help you to deal with change:

- Understand yourself. Knowing yourself is the first step. Your personal values and beliefs are yours alone. Your values and beliefs undergo constant *modification* as you gain knowledge and experience in living. Modification means change. To understand yourself, you must be able to look honestly at

Moving day is an example of change that can present both opportunities and problems.

your values. This will help you to understand—and to control—your own reactions to change.

- Understand the nature of change. Remember that there are many forces you can't control. Those forces are constantly producing change. Some of those changes will affect you. Some changes present you with problems. Other changes offer opportunities. You also originate, or cause, changes. These are changes you wish to make. Some of your changes affect other people. If you want these changes to be successful, you need to understand how others react to change.

- Develop some practical skills for dealing with change. Part III deals with a *process* for solving problems and making decisions. A process is a series of steps that lead to a known result. Using a process means doing something in an organized way. The process method of solving problems and making decisions can help you deal effectively with change from any source. You can use a process to increase your understanding of change and thus make better decisions.

Your values and beliefs play an important role in the way you deal with change. The next unit covers personal values and their relationship to your personality.

CONTENT SUMMARY

Change is constant. It is a force that never stops. As a result, you need to learn to deal effectively with change.

To understand change, you must identify its source. There are two basic kinds of change: external and internal. External change comes from natural causes or from other people. You can't control external changes. Internal change comes from within yourself. You control this kind of change through decisions you make.

External change can present problems or opportunities. Four general ways in which you can react to external change are: opposition, rejection, acceptance, and support. There are no right or wrong ways to react to change. Your reactions are based on your personal values and beliefs.

Opposition, rejection, or support of a change is an effort on your part to control what happens to you. Acceptance means you allow other forces to affect your life. You always have the option of doing nothing when you are faced with change.

Dealing with change will occupy much of your time and effort throughout your lifetime. Therefore, preparing yourself to deal effectively with change will benefit you greatly. You can prepare in three ways: understand yourself, understand the nature of change, and develop skills for dealing with change.

Using a process, an organized approach, is a good way to solve problems and make decisions. The process method is basically the same for problem solving and decision making. The only difference involves the source of the change. In dealing with external change, you must first identify the nature of the change. At that point, you can decide how to react.

1. **There is no right or wrong way to react to any particular change.**
   If this statement is true, how can you judge the value of your reaction to any single change?

2. **If you accept a change, you do nothing to oppose or support it.**
   Why might you accept a change you do not favor? What is the result of acceptance in such a case?

3. **Problem solving and decision making are basically the same.**
   What is the major difference between solving problems and making decisions?

KEY TERMS

technology

external change

internal change

neutral

opposition

rejection

acceptance

support

option

problem

opportunity

decision

modification

process

5

Your Values and Your Personal Code

When you have completed the reading assignments and exercises in this unit, you should be able to:

☐ Define a personal code and describe its function.

☐ Explain how your personal code guides you in dealing with change.

☐ Explain why your personal code changes as you go through life.

☐ Describe the major elements of your personal code.

☐ Describe the relationship between your personal code and your personality.

YOUR PERSONAL CODE

Your complete set of beliefs is your *personal code*. A code is a set of ideas and beliefs that serves as rules for conduct. The laws of your community, state, and nation are organized into codes.

Your beliefs include ideas about right and wrong. Other ideas included in your personal code include your likes and dislikes, and the values you hold. Your values determine the importance you place on things to meet your wants and needs.

Your personal code guides your conduct. For that reason, your personal code is often called your *code of conduct* or your *code of living.* Your code guides you in every experience you have. Your beliefs and your personality guide your actions.

YOUR PERSONAL CODE AND CHANGE

There is a two-way relationship between your personal code and change in your life. It is accurate to say that each affects the other. Your code and change are related in these ways:

- On one hand, your code serves as a guide in your dealings with change. Your beliefs and values form the basis upon which you react to new experiences. You deal with change

FOCUS ON YOUR FUTURE

Todd took off his hat and stuffed it into his knapsack as he approached the school entrance.

It was raining hard, and his mother had insisted that he wear his new rain hat to school. Todd hated the way he looked in the hat, and he didn't want his friends to see him wearing it. He was sure they would make fun of him if they saw it. He hoped no one had seen him wearing the hat, but his fears were realized.

"Hey, Todd, what are you hiding there?" called David, as Todd approached his locker.

"Nothing. What are you talking about?" Todd asked.

"Come on, Todd. We all saw you wearing the hat," Teresa said. "Let us see it."

"Yes, Todd," agreed Yoko. "We want to know why you hid the hat when you got to school."

Todd knew he was blushing. He wasn't sure which embarrassed him more: the hat or his attempt to hide it. "All right," he said. "Here. Have a good look."

Reaching into his knapsack, Todd removed the hat and held it out for his friends to see.

"Put it on, Todd," said Teresa.

"Yes," urged David. "Let's see how it looks."

Todd put the hat on his head and turned slowly, striking a model's pose. "Are you satisfied?" he asked.

"Hey, that's a neat hat," Yoko said. "No kidding, Todd, I really like it."

"So do I," agreed David. "Where did you buy that? I think I'll ask my folks if I can have one."

Todd looked into his friends' faces. They were serious. They weren't making fun of the hat. They really liked it. Todd was shocked. He took off the hat and looked at it. Maybe it wasn't such a bad-looking hat after all, he thought.

"We bought the hat over at Chick's Sportswear," Todd said. A hint of pride crept into his voice. "The salespeople at Chick's said it was the latest style," he added.

"Well, then, you really shouldn't be hiding it," Teresa said. "What's wrong with being a style setter?"

"Nothing, I guess," Todd said as he hung his coat and hat in his locker. He was relieved that his friends had seen his hat and liked it. The fact that it was a good rain hat took on new importance. Todd had to admit that his parents had a pretty good idea of style after all. ■

in ways you feel are correct or *beneficial*. Something is beneficial if it is good for you or for someone else. Included are your reactions based on considerations of right and wrong.

- On the other hand, your code undergoes change as you gain new experiences. When you learn something new, your personal code is changed as you accept that knowledge. Each new experience has an effect on your code.

In the story, Todd experienced several changes to his code. His friends reacted in a positive manner to his rain hat. Based on their support, Todd changed several of his beliefs.

First, his dislike for the rain hat changed to a feeling of pride. Second, he gained a desire to set a trend rather than following the lead of others. Third, he adopted a new attitude toward the style judgment of his parents. From Todd's reaction, a fourth change can be assumed. That is, he will be glad to wear his rain hat for protection in the future.

Todd's experience was a happy one. The changes to his code would seem to have given him a more positive outlook toward change.

The effect on his personal code might have been far different if his friends had made fun of his hat. Todd's negative feelings about the hat could have been *reinforced*, or made stronger. Also reinforced would have been his *resentment*, or angry feelings, toward his mother for forcing him to wear the hat. Negative reactions by his friends might have strengthened Todd's belief that his parents were poor judges of style.

Opinions are based upon the values in each person's code of conduct. No two people share the exact same set of values. (Courtesy Hit or Miss, a division of Zayre Corporation)

Experiences change the way you look at people and things around you. This is an important part of your growth and development.

YOUR CHANGING CODE

Just as change is constant in the world around you, so is change within your personal code. Each new experience causes some change in your code of conduct. Your personal code grows and develops as each new change comes into your life.

No two persons share the exact same experiences in life. For this reason alone, no two people can share the exact same sets of values or beliefs. Each person sees change from a different point of view and reacts according to his or her code.

Your personal code is very complicated. It is based on your entire range of experiences, and on values that come from your family and other sources. Your code also includes your likes and dislikes. Your dreams for the future are also contained in your code. As you grow in age and experience, your dreams change. Your life is shaped by your ever-changing personal code.

Understanding Your Code

It is vitally important for you to understand your code. You should try to learn why you act the way you do. Understanding your code will give you *insight* into your attitudes and your behavior. Insight is the ability to see the inner nature of something. A person with insight penetrates the surface of a situation and gains understanding.

Understanding your code will increase your effectiveness in dealing with change. Understanding your attitudes helps you to see a wider range of choices in dealing with change.

Shaping Your Code

Understanding your code is one important step. The other is working to shape it yourself.

If you have insight into your feelings and emotions, you can gain control over your behavior and your attitudes. Behaving a certain way in a particular situation may cause problems. For example, you may frequently be punished for coming home late for dinner. Examining your code may reveal that you stay outdoors because your friends urge you to extend your play time. Further examination of your values is necessary to determine which is more important: pleasing your friends or pleasing your parents.

To examine your code, you have to put aside your immediate feelings. Make an effort to judge the facts of a situation. Is it worse to upset your parents by being late, or to disappoint your friends by going home on time? Or, perhaps you are concerned that your friends will make fun of you if you go home on time. By asking yourself these questions, you are seeking the lesser of two evils.

Now ask positive questions. Which course of action does more good for you? Is it more rewarding to make your parents or your friends happy? Which result makes you happier?

In reaching a conclusion, you will change your code of conduct. Either way you decide, you will strengthen your beliefs and your values. Shaping your code, in turn, increases your understanding of yourself. This enables you to deal more effectively with changes in your life.

ELEMENTS OF YOUR CODE

Your code is complicated because it has many parts, or *elements.* An element is the simplest part of something. The elements of your code are all different in their importance to you. Each element plays a different role in guiding your conduct.

One way of separating the elements of your code is by placing them in categories according to their importance to you. Most of the elements of your code fall into one of these categories:

- Laws
- Guidelines
- Preferences
- Interests
- Logical ideas
- Illogical ideas.

Some of these elements have a direct effect on your behavior. Other elements are more general feelings you have about the world around you. Some parts of your code come from outside sources, such as your family, friends, and school. Other parts of your code are developed by your own thoughts and attitudes that come from your past experiences.

Your personal code is too complicated for you to deal with it as a whole. It is more effective to deal with individual elements of your code. This is especially true when you are attempting to shape portions of your code.

Laws

A *law* is a rule of conduct that is very important to you. Laws are rules that you feel you must follow at all times. Some of the laws in your code relate to the *legal laws* of *society.* Legal laws are the rules of conduct spelled out by government codes. Society is the group of people with whom you share common interests and beliefs. Levels of society include your local community, the state or region in which it is located, and the entire nation. You probably feel it is important to obey the laws of your city, state, and country. As you grow older, you will become increasingly aware of these kinds of laws. You will have to pay taxes on your income, for example. You will be required to obtain a driver's license to drive a motor vehicle. As a driver, you will be faced with a large number of traffic regulations, or laws.

The laws of your code of conduct may not always agree with the laws of your community. In such cases, you may choose to follow your own code or the legal law. Of course, if your conduct *violates*, or breaks, legal laws, you may get into trouble. For example, you may feel it is all right to ignore traffic signals under certain conditions. You may decide to walk across the street against a red light if there is no traffic nearby. Your own rules tell you it is all right to risk a citation, or ticket, from the police if you are caught. How well you obey society's laws depends upon your personal values.

Legal laws are rules of conduct for society. Motorists and pedestrians alike are expected to obey traffic laws. (Photo at left, Queen City Metro)

Some of the laws in your personal code may have nothing to do with society's legal codes. For example, you may feel that it is important to treat elderly persons with courtesy and respect. There are no legal laws requiring this behavior. Your own experiences with elderly people, such as grandparents, may have caused you to adopt this rule of conduct. If you break your own personal law, you will probably have bad feelings about your actions.

Your personal code may be tested by a change that breaks one of your personal laws. The change is in *conflict* with your code. Conflict is a condition in which two or more forces oppose one another. Changes that challenge your beliefs can force you to make difficult decisions. If your beliefs are strong enough, you may oppose or reject the change. Otherwise, the change may affect your code. You may change your beliefs to resolve a conflict.

Guidelines

A *guideline* is a rule in your code that covers individual situations. While laws apply all the time, guidelines apply only under specific circumstances. For example, you may have strong feelings against stealing. Your rule might be to notify school authorities if you spot a student taking something from another student's locker. But, what would you do if you caught your best friend stealing? Instead of reporting the incident to school authorities, you might deal directly with your friend. Your *motive*, or goal, might be to have your friend give back the stolen property. An additional goal might be to change your friend's behavior.

Your motive is basically the same in either case—to correct a wrong. But you follow different guidelines in dealing with each situation.

Preferences

A *preference* is something you will select if you have a choice. Your preferences might include a favorite television program, a flavor of ice cream, and a brand of jeans.

As guides to conduct, preferences are less important than laws or guidelines. Your preferences help determine the decisions you make when a choice exists. For example, you might prefer a cola drink. If no cola were available, however, you might be satisfied with another flavor.

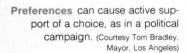

Preferences can cause active support of a choice, as in a political campaign. (Courtesy Tom Bradley, Mayor, Los Angeles)

Interests influence your choice of careers. Your interests may guide you into the world of fashion design, far left, or into scientific research, left. (Photo at far left, © 1984, David Falconer/West Stock. Photo at left, courtesy TRW Inc.)

Interests

An idea or an activity that holds your attention is an *interest.* You might be interested in music, sports, acting, science, or any other activity. Your interests influence your choice of friends, since people who share interests get along better.

Your interests also help determine your choices of games, hobbies, and recreational activities. Interests also can guide you in selecting a career. For example, you might enjoy building models and working with mechanical things. This interest could lead you to explore careers in automotive or aircraft mechanics. You might enjoy cooking and experimenting with new dishes and recipes. In that case, a career as a chef or a baker might be attractive.

Logical Ideas

A *logical idea* is an idea that makes sense to you. Logical means sensible. Your experiences and your own thoughts produce most of the logical ideas in your personal code.

Your sense of logic guides you in making correct decisions. If you hear a forecast of rainy or stormy weather, you know you should wear protective clothing.

Another example of logical ideas might involve going on vacation. If you have to leave early in the morning, you'll probably go to bed early the night before. The logical idea guiding your actions is that you should be well rested before beginning a trip.

Usually, you refer to past experiences when deciding the best way to deal with a situation. The knowledge you have gained through experience helps you to form logical ideas.

Illogical ideas include denials of things that are obvious. This type of behavior usually causes disagreements or arguments.

Illogical Ideas

Beliefs or actions that don't make sense are often based on *illogical ideas.* An illogical idea often develops because you haven't really thought about a situation. For example, you may decide you dislike a certain food without ever having tasted it. Basing such a decision on the appearance or color of the food is illogical. There may be no connection between appearance and taste.

Denying something that is obvious is another example of an illogical idea. If you were to be caught doing something wrong, you would be foolish to deny it. Many people act this way repeatedly, however, in spite of the obvious uselessness of making such denials.

The strongest form of reaction to change is usually opposition. Before adopting such a position, it is worthwhile to find out if opposition is logical. You may oppose something primarily because you haven't studied it thoroughly. A clear understanding of your position may enable you to make an adjustment to your personal code. Making these kinds of adjustments can help you live in greater harmony with the world around you.

YOUR CODE AND YOUR PERSONALITY

Your personality is based largely on your personal code. Your code guides your behavior. The behavior patterns you follow in dealing with other people and events combine to form your personality.

As discussed in Unit 1, a personality trait is a behavioral tendency or pattern. These traits tend to follow the elements of your code of conduct. Some typical personality traits are listed below. You may find that you belong in one category or another, or somewhere in between.

Optimist or pessimist. An *optimist* is a person who usually looks at the positive side of a situation. An optimist usually believes that people are basically good. If you are an optimist, you believe that things will get better. Optimists tend to be happy individuals.

An optimist looks at the positive side of a situation and expects things to get better.

A *pessimist* is the exact opposite of an optimist. Pessimists look at the dark, or negative, side of a situation. If you are a pessimist, you probably tend to oppose or reject change. Even in happy situations, a pessimist will find limited enjoyment while looking out for bad things to happen.

Secure or insecure. A *secure* person is one who is confident of his or her abilities. If you are secure, you have a good idea who you are and where you want to go. You probably are satisfied with your life. A secure person deals with change in a positive, logical manner.

Insecure people usually seem to be trying to decide who they are and what they should do. If you are insecure, you may find it difficult to deal with problems and to make decisions. You may have trouble identifying and selecting *alternatives.* An alternative is a choice or an opportunity to make a choice: In making a decision, it is usually necessary to choose from two or more alternatives.

Extrovert or introvert.   A person who naturally enjoys the company of others is called an *extrovert.* If you are an extrovert, you make friends easily and enjoy the attention of others. Extroverts tend to be successful in sales and in other fields where interpersonal skills are important.

A person who prefers to be alone is called an *introvert.* An introvert is not necessarily unfriendly but may have difficulty meeting and getting to know others. Some individuals would prefer to be outgoing but are too shy or unsure of themselves to try.

Decisive or indecisive.   A *decisive* person makes decisions quickly and with confidence. If you are a decisive person, you are willing to commit yourself to a decision or a goal.

An *indecisive* person has trouble reaching decisions. People who are indecisive spend large amounts of time and energy thinking about alternatives. Even after they make decisions, they tend to keep changing their minds.

Ambitious.   An *ambitious* person is one who pushes to get ahead. For example, an ambitious student might do more than earn good grades. An ambitious student might also stand out in activities outside the classroom. Ambitious people usually seem to have a lot of energy and enthusiasm. People with lower levels of ambition seem content to advance more slowly. These people tend to be satisfied with situations as they are. On the other hand, ambitious people usually seek to make changes.

These are some of the more recognizable personality traits. You can notice them in the people around you. Just as important, you should be able to recognize them in yourself. Remember, personality traits reflect the many parts of your personal code. Your personality and your personal code together determine how you view your world—and how you react to change.

External changes can present problems or opportunities. Your personal code determines which way you view external change.

CHALLENGES AND THREATS

Remember that you can't control external change. Most external changes that affect you do so in one of two ways. External changes present problems or opportunities. How you view these changes depends on your personality and your personal code.

A person with a positive personality will tend to view most changes as opportunities. This type of person will see change as a *challenge*, or a chance to compete. For the person who is optimistic, secure, decisive, or ambitious, change offers a challenge to accomplish something. Change is stimulating. This type of person usually supports change.

A pessimistic, insecure, or indecisive person tends to view change as a problem or a *threat*. A threat is a sign of danger. This type of person doesn't like to deal with change and usually opposes or rejects it.

Each change that comes your way is an opportunity for you to examine your personal code and your personality traits. Changes also provide opportunities to adjust your code. Awareness of your reactions to change can help you improve your personality. By stressing the positive parts of your code, you can overcome those attitudes that may be harmful. These efforts can help you to occupy a more satisfying place in your world.

CONTENT SUMMARY

Your personal code is your complete set of beliefs. This collection of ideas and feelings is also called your code of conduct or your code of living.

Your personal code guides your reactions to change in your life. Your experiences, in turn, change your code. Your personal code grows and develops with change. Your code is unique. One reason for this is that no two people share exactly the same experiences in life.

Understanding your code enables you to deal effectively with change. At the same time, you can shape and adjust your code based on your reactions to changes in your life.

Your code is complicated. Most of the parts of your code fit into general categories, however. These categories include laws, guidelines, preferences, interests, logical ideas, and illogical ideas. Understanding these parts of your code helps you to shape your personality.

Some personality traits are easy to recognize in others. Most people can be considered optimistic or pessimistic, extroverted or introverted, secure or insecure, and decisive or indecisive. Ambition is another easily noticeable personality trait. You should examine your own personality traits. They reflect parts of your personal code.

Think about how you view change. If your personality is basically positive, you probably see changes as opportunities or challenges. If you have negative personality traits, you may view changes as problems or threats. Examining your reactions to change will help you to understand and shape your personal code and your personality.

KEY TERMS

personal code

code of conduct

code of living

beneficial

reinforce

resentment

insight

element

law

legal law

CAREER COMMENTARIES

1. **As you grow in age and experience, your dreams (for the future) change.**
   List three kinds of experiences, or changes, that could cause you to change your dreams or plans for the future. For each one, indicate whether the change is positive or negative.

2. **As guides to conduct, preferences are less important than laws or guidelines.**
   Why are preferences less important than laws or guidelines in determining how you deal with change? How is choice related to preferences?

3. **How you view changes depends on your personality and your personal code.**
   Describe an external change that might be viewed differently by two people. Name the personality traits that cause one person to view the change as an opportunity or a challenge. Also name the traits that cause the other person to view the change as a problem or a threat.

society
violate
conflict
guideline
motive
preference
interest
logical idea
illogical idea
optimist
pessimist
secure
insecure
alternative
extrovert
introvert
decisive
indecisive
ambitious
challenge
threat

Life-Style Options

YOU HAVE ENTERED a period of your life in which you will make many important decisions. Chief among these is the choice of a career path. Before you begin thinking about career options, however, you need to identify some of your basic needs and wants.

Your most important needs and wants combine to form your life-style goals. The satisfaction you achieve in life will depend largely upon how successful you are in reaching these goals.

Part II deals with the major life-style options you need to consider. Unit 6 discusses life-style choices in relation to your personal code. In Unit 7, life-style is viewed in terms of how careers relate to personal and family responsibilities. Unit 8 deals with the relationships between employers and employees. Unit 9 covers friendships and group relationships.

Identifying your major life-style goals will help you to begin narrowing your career options. Understanding change will prepare you for the adjustments you will be facing throughout your life.

Your Environment and Your Life-Style

YOUR LEARNING JOB

When you have completed the reading assignments and exercises in this unit, you should be able to:

☐ Define life-style.

☐ Describe the relationship between life-style and personal code.

☐ Describe the relationship between environment and life-style.

☐ Explain the influence of environment on job and career options.

☐ Describe ways that life-style goals and expectations can influence career decisions.

☐ Explain how jobs and careers affect life-style.

☐ Describe ways in which change can affect life-style.

LIFE-STYLE: A DESIGN FOR LIVING

Think about the way you live. Do you like your life-style, or would you change it if you could? Remember, your life-style is the way you live. At this stage of your life, most of your major life-style decisions are made by your family. However, as an adult you will face some life-style choices.

Basic life-style and career decisions have brought your family to its present situation. If you enjoy the life-style you share with your family, you may seek similar circumstances as an adult. If you are unhappy or dissatisfied, you may choose to strike out in new directions.

Life-style preferences include leisure activities. Many families consider recreation to be a primary life-style need. (Courtesy Indiana Department of Commerce)

Your environment influences your
life-style. Surfing, for example,
is an activity that can be enjoyed
only at certain locations.
(Courtesy Hawaii Visitors Bureau)

There are many factors involved in considering life-style. As an adult, your life-style decisions will include:

- Geographic environment
- Material needs and wants
- Career satisfaction and achievement
- Leisure activities
- Cultural activities.

Geographic Environment

You live in the most highly *mobile* society in the world. Mobile is the ability to move. In the United States, there are no legal barriers to prevent you from living wherever you desire. *Mobility*, or ease of movement, also applies in most local areas.

As an adult, you may wish to move to another area for one or more reasons. You may seek a different climate, a larger or smaller community, or an area where career *prospects* are better. Prospects are chances or expectations of success. Some

people move to warm or dry climates for health reasons. People frequently leave rural communities for the wider job markets of large cities.

Winter sports can be enjoyed by people who live in colder climates. (Courtesy North Dakota Tourism Promotion)

Your environment has much to do with your life-style. For example, problems facing people in colder climates include:

- High costs of heating in the winter

- Snow, ice, and bad weather that can restrict travel and other activities

- The need for expensive winter clothing

- The need to stay indoors much of the time.

People in warm climates don't have these worries. However, natural problems or dangers exist almost anywhere. Some areas are threatened repeatedly by forces of nature such as floods, hurricanes, tornados, or earthquakes. Wherever you choose to live, your environment will have a major impact on your life-style.

TURBO-ZX

Personal transportation decisions are based upon life-style desires. Some vehicles, like this sports car, make a statement about their owners. (Courtesy Nissan Motor Corporation)

Material Needs and Wants

Wherever you live, you will have material, or physical, needs and wants. These material items include housing, clothing, food, transportation, and health care. Think about your present situation in each of these areas. Are you satisfied with your home, your clothes, the food? As an adult, will you want more of these material things? Will you be satisfied to continue the kind of life-style you have with your family? Perhaps you will be satisfied with fewer or more modest physical possessions. Or perhaps you will want more.

Career Satisfaction and Achievement

Much of your life as a student revolves around school activities. Your personal satisfaction depends upon several factors:

- Achievement as measured by grades and report cards
- Relationships, friendships, and harmony with your teachers and fellow students
- Involvement in activities outside the classroom (clubs, sports, music, etc.).

As a working citizen, your job or career will offer similar sources of satisfaction or disappointment:

- Achievement as measured by income level and recognition on the job

- Relationships, friendships, and harmony with employers, supervisors, and fellow workers

- Involvement in work-related and leisure-time activities.

Understanding your personal code and your personality is an important step toward selecting a satisfying career. The ability to get along with others can contribute greatly to your day-to-day satisfaction.

Leisure Activities

Your leisure time is a major life-style consideration. Consider your feelings about factors such as these:

- Working hours and time off the job. Some jobs require long hours. Some other jobs involve working nights, or weekends, or holidays, when most other people are off work. Depending on your hobbies and leisure interests, you may want a job with a limited work day or work week. For example, many individuals and families enjoy weekends at the ocean, a lake, or in the mountains or desert. Some people make large investments in vacation homes, motorhomes and other recreational vehicles, or equipment used in hobbies. If you fit into this category, you may want a job with regular, limited hours.

- Paid vacations. Some employers offer generous vacation agreements. This is particularly important for people who enjoy traveling.

- Investment in leisure activities. Some hobbies or activities are quite expensive. For example, a well-equipped home workshop can represent many thousands of dollars in tools and machinery. Your decision to get involved in a costly hobby or leisure activity may depend on your earning power.

Vacations are an important life-style consideration for people who enjoy travel. (Texas Department of Highways)

Depending upon your personal code, leisure activities may be your number-one concern. Even people who gain most of their personal satisfaction from work need some outside interests.

Cultural Activities

Many people enjoy frequent trips to theaters, concerts, museums, exhibits, and other cultural events. These people are best satisfied by life in or near a major population center.

Cultural interests are best satisfied in large population centers.
(Courtesy The Greyhound Corporation)

Some people like to be involved in cultural activities as participants as well as spectators. Here again, participation may require a large investment of time as well as effort.

Life-style is a very personal area. Knowing your self and understanding your personal code are important elements in any decision involving your life-style. Remember, change will play a major role in your developing life-style. Your ability to deal effectively with change can help you maintain or improve the life-style of your choice.

FOCUS ON YOUR FUTURE

LINDA TOOK ONE LAST LOOK at her bedroom, turned, and walked down the hall. With all her furniture and personal items gone, the room seemed strange. Still, it had been her room for as long as she could remember.

She walked outside and saw her best friend, Jill, across the street. Linda ran over to say good-bye.

The two friends had already made plans to visit each other during the following summer vacation. Linda had mixed emotions. She was sad about having to leave Jill and her other friends. She would also miss the frequent trips into the city that were part of living in the suburbs.

On the other hand, life in a smaller city would have advantages. The family was moving upstate because her father had received a big promotion from his company. Their new house was really beautiful, and Linda would even have her own bathroom.

"Gosh, Jill, my dad just can't wait to get on the road. He's really excited about moving up north," Linda said.

Jill nodded in agreement. "He really loves fishing and hunting, so that area should be just right for him. I guess your brothers will be happy, too."

"The whole family is pumped up about moving. I'm pretty happy about it too," Linda said. She looked at Jill, who seemed a little sad. "I just hope I can find a friend like you up there," Linda added.

"Oh, I'm sure you will, Linda. Just be yourself. And don't forget that you promised to write at least once a week," Jill said. "Even if it's just a couple of sentences, it will help us keep in touch."

Linda hugged her friend. "They're waving at us, so I guess it's time to go. I'll write you a note as soon as we're settled in. If Dad will let me, I'll send a couple of photos too. See you next summer, Jill."

"Good luck, Linda. I'll answer your letters right away. That's a promise," Jill said. ■

Environment affects opportunities as well as life-styles. Agriculture is the main industry in many rural areas. In some parts of the country, agriculture shares space with other industries, such as petroleum production. Fishing is a sport in most areas and an industry in a few places. (Credits: Photo at top courtesy Sun Company; photo above, left, courtesy Greater Milwaukee Convention & Visitors Bureau; photo above, right, courtesy New Idea, Coldwater, Ohio)

ENVIRONMENT AND OPPORTUNITY

Your environment has a major influence on your life-style. Geographic location also determines the kinds of job and career opportunities that may be available.

Obviously, a large city offers a wider range of job opportunities than a small town. However, career opportunities often depend on regional situations. Some areas of the United States have economies that are highly dependent upon one or two industries. For example, agriculture is the main occupation in parts of the Midwest and in the Great Plains states. Logging and lumber industries are vital to the Pacific Northwest. Western Pennsylvania relies heavily on the coal mining and steel industries.

Other areas have become centers for industries that depend more upon human resources than natural resources. A large percentage of the computer design and manufacturing industry is located in Northern California. Finance, higher education, and publishing occupations are highly concentrated in the great old cities of the Northeast.

Shifting Population

The United States is experiencing a major population shift. The Sun Belt, which consists of warm-weather states in the South and Southwest, is making rapid population gains. States such as Texas, Florida, California, and Arizona are growing rapidly.

As populations expand, so do job and career opportunities. People require services. *Service industries* are the businesses that provide those services. Examples of service industries are: food preparation and service, insurance, health care, and retail sales. Service industries are the fastest-growing part of the national economy.

These factors will be important as you make job and career decisions. Continuing change in these areas will affect you throughout your working career.

Some Hard Decisions

People frequently face difficult choices involving opportunities and environment. For example, if a local or regional industry *declines,* or becomes smaller, many jobs are lost. If the job loss is viewed as permanent, the unemployed workers and their families face a hard decision. Some may be so strongly attached to their homes and their life-style that they refuse to seek jobs elsewhere. Others may leave a locality to find work in places they don't like.

Many people knowingly limit their career opportunities because they wish to remain in a small community. Life-style, for them, outweighs career success. Others may do the opposite. They place career opportunity at the top of their list of needs and wants. These people adjust their life-styles to a geographic area or to the demands of their jobs.

FOCUS ON YOUR FUTURE

RICK SWUNG HIS BAG over his shoulder as he and Danny started to walk home from the baseball diamond. "Boy, I sure wish Carlos hadn't moved away from the neighborhood," Rick said.

"So do I," agreed Danny. "He was our best pitcher, and we're going to have a rough time without him."

"Why did the Lopez family have to move into that big house, anyway?" Rick asked. "They had a real nice house right here on our street."

"I guess Mr. Lopez got a really big raise when he got promoted last year," Danny said. "They just decided they wanted to move to a more expensive neighborhood. You can't really blame them, can you?"

"I don't know," Rick replied. "I don't think I'd be comfortable in a big old house like theirs. It seems too formal. I'd be afraid of getting anything dirty in that place."

"You're right. We have all the room we need, and we can relax and be ourselves in our homes," Danny said. "I think I'll probably always live in a house like the one we have now."

"Maybe, but what would you do if you got a good job and made a lot of money?" Rick asked. "Don't you think you'd buy a big house, a couple of expensive cars, and other stuff?"

"Oh, I don't think so," Danny said. "Those things don't impress me. If I had money, I'd use it to travel. I'd like to see the rest of the country and then travel to other places. Someday, I'd like to visit Africa and Australia."

"That would be fun, but I'd much rather drive a sports car and take flying lessons," Rick said.

"It sounds like we both better try to get good jobs," Danny said. "And we probably ought to do some of those things before we get married and have kids of our own. From what I've seen, once you have a family, your life-style changes a lot."

"I guess so," Rick said. "Right now, I could use a change in life-style. I'd settle for a nice reduction in homework." ■

CHANGING LIFE-STYLES

Change is a factor in life-style as it is in every other aspect of living. Your ability to deal with change will affect the quality of your life-style. Some basic changes that alter many people's life-styles are:

- Moving away from home
- Getting married
- Having children
- Changing jobs
- Growing older.

Living on Your Own

You will probably move away from your family at some point in your life. If you decide to live by yourself, your life-style will be far different. You will be responsible for paying the bills, cooking, cleaning, laundry, shopping, and all the regular tasks of everyday life. These things take time and thought. The quality of your life depends largely upon how well you perform the tasks and meet your responsibilities.

Many single persons choose to set up housekeeping with one or more friends. The advantages of this life-style include companionship and the sharing of expenses. Disadvantages include giving up some privacy and having to adjust to other people's habits and preferences.

Whichever course you select, leaving your family is the biggest change of all. Some people make the *transition*, or

Living on your own means taking care of your necessities.

Marriage is a demanding life-style change that requires major adjustments by both parties.
(Courtesy Brian T. Connair)

change, quite easily. Others find it difficult to adjust to life outside the protective environment of their immediate families. Reactions to these changes depend heavily on an individual's personal code and personality and on family relationships.

Married Life

Entering into marriage is one of the most demanding of all life-style changes. A *spouse*, or marriage partner, is more than a friend or a roommate. In terms of life-style, a married couple agrees to share every part of their lives. Furthermore, their commitment is a legal *contract*. A contract is an agreement between two or more people.

Marriage requires that you give up certain freedoms in exchange for a special kind of companionship and support. It is a change—usually a happy one—that requires major adjustments by both parties.

Being a Parent

If you become a parent, you face another major life-style adjustment. Having children requires a great commitment. Parents are responsible for their children's health, safety, and development.

Being a parent can bring great joy. It can also result in deep sorrow. One thing is certain: Parenthood is one of life's greatest experiences.

Couples with children must make basic life-style adjustments. Children require large commitments of time, attention, emotions, and income. Just as single persons give up some freedom to get married, couples give up many freedoms to have children. Your personal code will determine how you deal with the experience of being a parent.

Changing Jobs

Changing jobs can cause significant life-style adjustments, depending upon the circumstances. A change in income—upward or downward—certainly affects life-style. Different working conditions may also require adjustments. Merely changing shifts can alter a worker's daily life, and the schedules followed by other family members.

Parenthood can be a source of great joy or deep sorrow. Being a parent requires a strong commitment.

Changing careers can bring even greater need for adjustment. For example, a factory worker might decide to become a fire fighter. Instead of a regular eight-hour shift, five days a week, the new fire fighter must adjust to an odd schedule. Fire fighters usually spend round-the-clock shifts on duty, away from home. On the other hand, they enjoy longer free periods with their families. This life-style requires a family to deal with some uncertainty and to be flexible in accepting frequent change.

Time Marches On

One form of change is aging. You are growing physically, mentally, and emotionally. Changes in your body and your personality don't stop when you become an adult. Growing older always means life-style adjustments.

Activities people enjoy in their twenties may not be possible physically when they reach their fifties or sixties. This doesn't mean that older people cannot be active. However, they must adjust according to their physical limitations.

Your interests probably will change, too, as you grow older. Remember, your personal code is always being altered by your experiences. Your life-style is an outward reflection of your code of conduct. As your code changes through life, you will find yourself making life-style changes to match your code.

CONTENT SUMMARY

Your life-style is the way you live. Major life-style decisions involve your choice of environment, material needs and wants, career satisfaction, and leisure and cultural activities.

Environment affects life-style and career opportunities. Sometimes these areas are in conflict, and individuals must choose between life-style and career. These decisions are based upon an individual's personal code.

Change has a significant effect on life-style. Major life-style changes include leaving home to live independently, marriage, having children, changing jobs or careers, and growing older.

Your life-style reflects your personal code. Your personal code is changed constantly as you gain new experiences throughout your life. As your personal code changes, you will make life-style adjustments in areas you control.

CAREER COMMENTARIES

1. **Change will play a major role in your developing life-style.**
   Describe two ways in which your life-style has changed in the past year. Identify the change that caused each alteration in your life-style.

2. **People frequently face difficult choices involving opportunities and environment.**
   How would you react if a career opportunity caused your family to decide to move far away from your community? Base your answer on your present life-style, assuming that the move would be to a different type of community.

3. **Your life-style is an outward reflection of your code of conduct.**
   Name three elements of your code of conduct that have a major effect on your life-style. Identify the elements as laws, guidelines, preferences, interests, logical ideas, or illogical ideas.

KEY TERMS

mobile

mobility

prospect

service industry

decline

transition

spouse

contract

7

Jobs and Home: Opportunities and Compromises

YOUR LEARNING JOB

When you have completed the reading assignments and exercises in this unit, you should be able to:

☐ Explain the relationship between personal and family goal setting.

☐ Describe basic roles of family members in home management.

☐ Explain the responsibilities family members have to one another.

☐ Explain how careers affect personal and family life-styles.

☐ Describe methods for managing conflict in the home.

FAMILY GOALS: LEARNING TO COMPROMISE

The family is the closest of all human social groups. Attitudes and values are often passed from one *generation* to another. A generation is a group of individuals who make up a single step in the continuing life of a family. Parents and their children represent different generations. In terms of time, a new generation is said to occur every 20 years.

Each family unit, or *household*, differs from every other household within the same family generation. Two important reasons are:

• A husband and wife bring the influences of two different families to their marriage.

• Each individual within a family structure has a personal code that influences personal and family values and goals.

Family units also differ in their composition. The traditional family unit in the United States has been a husband, a wife, and

Family goals frequently involve home ownership. (Courtesy Century 21 Real Estate Corporation)

Vacations are opportunities for families to enjoy activities different from their normal routine.
(Courtesy Florida Department of Commerce—Division of Tourism)

their children. However, there are many other ways in which a household can be structured. Single-parent families have become quite common in recent years. Three-generation households, including one or more grandparents, also are commonplace. In many families, the husband or wife, or both, may have been married previously. Either or both may bring children of those marriages to the new household. The potential combinations are almost without limit. Therefore, the discussions in these units can be applied to any type of family unit.

Some families seem closer than others. Closeness probably is caused by the ability and willingness of family members to *compromise.* Compromise means that two or more individuals give up some of their wants to reach agreement, or *harmony.* Harmony is an inner calm or peace. For example, you might want to watch a particular program on television. The rest of your family might prefer to watch another show. If there is only one television set in your house, a *conflict* exists. Conflict means opposing needs or wishes. You will probably give in to the majority. If the others recognize your disappointment, they may offer to make it up to you in another area.

Traveling together can be both enjoyable and educational for a family. (Courtesy Virginia State Travel Service)

Compromise may be more difficult to reach when long-range goals are in question. For example, the career goals of individuals may differ dramatically from goals their parents have set for them. If feelings are strong on both sides, such disagreements can last for many years. However, if each side tries to understand the other's feelings, these types of problems usually can be resolved.

Family goals are different. A family may have general or long-range goals. An example might be a desire to move to a different part of the country some day. Another general goal might be a larger home.

Families also have *specific*, or clearly defined, goals. Specific goals usually are more immediate in nature. Examples might be planning a summer vacation or a special family event such as a wedding or graduation celebration.

Family goals are usually shared by all family members. Personal goals may or may not receive the support of other members of a family. The *unity*, or togetherness, of a family is tested when personal goals clash with family goals.

MANAGING THE HOME

No two families are exactly the same. Households differ in size and in the relationships within the family unit. Some families are small and simple in structure—a father, a mother, and one or two children. Other families are larger and more complicated. A single household may contain one or more grandparents. An aunt or uncle may live in the home. One or more of the children may be adopted. If either parent has been married before, there may be *stepchildren*. A stepchild is the son or daughter by a previous marriage of one of the two marriage partners.

Whether small or large, simple or complicated, a family needs one element if it is to function smoothly. That element is a spirit of cooperation. Like any other group, a family needs *organization*. Organization means that each member has a role to play so the group can meet its goals. Each member has responsibilities. When all family members cooperate by filling their roles, a household is well managed. Responsibilities of home management include:

- Income and budgeting
- Home maintenance and upkeep
- Regular cleaning
- Food purchases
- Meal preparation
- Clothing purchases
- Clothing upkeep and laundry
- Care of other family members.

Income and Budgeting

Traditionally, the father was responsible for the income of a family household. However, under today's changing life-styles, traditional roles frequently do not apply. For example, in a two-parent family today, it is common for both parents to work. Another growing trend is for the female adult to be the *bread-winner*, or main income producer, for a family. Many households are headed by a single parent. Older children also may contribute

A growing trend is for a female to be the breadwinner, or main income producer, for a family unit. (Courtesy Sperry Corporation)

to household income if they continue to live at home after completing school.

The family *budget* is primarily the responsibility of those family members who earn the income and pay the bills. A budget is a plan for the organized distribution of family income. Budgeting means planning ahead to take care of the costs of a family's needs. Needs include shelter, food, clothing, transportation, health care, and saving a portion of income for financial security.

Home Maintenance

Maintenance is a greater responsibility if a family owns its home. Maintenance means keeping the home in good repair. Owning a house involves lawn care and yard work as well as maintenance of the structure itself. All of the members of a family can share in these tasks.

When both parents work outside the home, children may assume greater responsibility. Families usually design some kind of reward system. It is important that roles and tasks be clearly assigned and understood.

Home maintenance is one of the responsibilities of home ownership.
(Courtesy The Stanley Works)

Apartment living is different. Renters are expected to avoid damage to property in excess of normal wear. Apartment owners have the responsibility for maintenance and upkeep. Renters, of course, are responsible for maintaining their own furniture, appliances, and other possessions.

Regular Cleaning

Vacuuming, dusting, mopping, and polishing are tasks that must be performed regularly. These responsibilities can be divided in a number of ways. Individual tasks can be assigned more or less permanently, or they can be shared on a rotating basis.

Food Purchases

Grocery shopping often is a family activity. Depending upon the working schedule of parents, one or the other may assume this responsibility. In many families, children are given the major responsibility for shopping. The bulk of food purchases are typically made at regular times, perhaps once a week. Again, working schedules of a parent or parents may determine how shopping is planned.

Meal Preparation

Cooking is another family activity that can be shared. The traditional role of the nonworking mother included doing most or all of the cooking for her family. This is another area that is changing as family life-styles become more flexible. A woman with a full-time job cannot perform the traditional role of family cook. When both parents work, careful meal planning and family cooperation are needed for a smoothly run kitchen. This area of responsibility includes scheduling of meals as well as cooking, serving, and cleaning up after meals. The entire family may be involved in maintaining a healthy, balanced diet.

Clothing Purchases

Value is a major concern in shopping for clothing. Poorly made clothes and garments made of inferior materials do not last. Low prices do not necessarily mean better value.

Style is another consideration. *Fads* are styles that are highly popular for a short time. Fads usually should be avoided. It is better to shop for clothes that will remain in style for a good length of time, as well as wear well.

Wardrobe upkeep is a personal as well as family responsibility.

Clothing Upkeep and Laundry

Each family member should take primary responsibility for the *upkeep*, or maintenance, of his or her own wardrobe. For younger children, this may involve simply bringing problems to the attention of parents. Shoe care, for example, includes polishing leather footwear and replacing worn or broken shoelaces as necessary.

Laundry is another area in which children can play an increasing role as they grow older. Permanent-press and wash-and-wear materials have eliminated most of the need to iron or press garments. Each family member can participate in wardrobe maintenance by hanging or folding clothes properly.

Grandparents can keep active by sharing in the care of their grandchildren. (Courtesy Sears, Roebuck and Co.)

Care of Other Family Members

Another area in which responsibilities can be shared is the care of other family members. Typically, older brothers or sisters share some responsibility for the care of younger children in the household. This responsibility can involve supervision, meal preparation, or any other activity made necessary by a particular family's circumstances.

This family responsibility also may involve care of sick, disabled, or aged family members. Again, individual circumstances determine the type and extent of responsibility placed upon each member of a household.

These are some of the major areas of responsibility that are shared by members of a family. Home management roles are usually determined by factors such as outside employment, age, and need. (For example, a new home may require less maintenance, and certainly less repairs, than an older home.)

An important element in a smoothly running household is cooperation. If family members are willing to work together and to share responsibilities, everyone's work is made easier. An added benefit is that each family member can enjoy the comfort and security of a well-managed household.

FOCUS ON YOUR FUTURE

BILLY OPENED THE DOOR to go outside with his friends. As the door closed, he heard his mother call. He turned and went back into the house.

"Yes, Mom. What is it?" he asked from the front hall.

"This is trash pickup day, Billy. Please take the cans out to the curb before the truck gets here," his mother said.

"Oh, Mom. That's Michael's job. Why do I have to do his work?" Billy complained.

"We discussed this at dinner two nights ago," his mother said. "Have you forgotten? Michael is working full-time this summer, and we have to make some adjustments."

"I guess I forgot. Still, it doesn't seem fair. Michael makes all that money, and I have to do his work," Billy said.

"That's simply not true," his mother replied. "Our agreement was that your allowance would be increased if you accepted the responsibility for taking out the trash. And, your brother is contributing part of his income toward household expenses. You have very little to do this summer except play. It won't hurt you to chip in and help around home."

"Okay, Mom. I guess my turn will come," Billy said.

"Don't be in too much of a hurry," his mother advised. "Enjoy your freedom while you can." ■

RESPONSIBILITIES OF
FAMILY MEMBERS TO ONE ANOTHER

Members of a family have responsibilities to one another as well as to home management. Some responsibilities are determined by the roles of individual family members. Examples of role-based responsibilities include:

- Parents' responsibility for the physical and emotional welfare and safety of their children.

- Children's responsibility to obey their parents.

Other responsibilities belong to every member of a family. Responsibilities shared by all family members include:

- Listening. Each family member owes the others the courtesy of hearing what they have to say. This does not mean you always have to agree with what is said. It merely means that you should be willing to listen to the thoughts and feelings of others.

- Communicating. Each family member also has the responsibility of sharing information with other members. Communication is a two-way process. To communicate, you must give and receive messages. Sharing feelings is also important. Problems are best solved through open discussion.

Communication among family members is an important ingredient of harmony in the home.

- Offering encouragement. Family members should support one another in establishing and working toward goals. You should be confident that your family is behind you in all your activities. In return, you should offer the same kind of support to other family members.

- Attending family *functions*. A function is a social gathering with a special purpose. The family comes first in social planning. Major family events include weddings, birthdays, anniversaries, graduations, and funerals. Other family functions include religious events, vacations, and work projects.

Family members have much in common. They share joy and sadness. A healthy family has *mutual* caring. Mutual means shared by all members. For example, affection is mutual if it is given the same way it is received. When family members have mutual affection and caring, individual responsibilities are fulfilled with warmth and generosity.

CAREERS AND FAMILY LIFE-STYLES

For most individuals, personal life-styles depend largely upon careers. Life-style elements determined by careers include:

- Income

- Work schedule

- Leisure time—amount and frequency.

These same elements also affect the life-style of a family. Income has a very obvious effect on life-style. Income level may determine where a family lives and the amount and kind of possessions its members enjoy. Income level also may influence the type of social activities a family pursues. For example, memberships in many private clubs are expensive and require high income levels.

Work schedules can have major effects on a family's life-style. An example would be a family in which one adult works nights. The person working nights may need to sleep during the day. Other family members have to adjust their behavior to avoid disturbing that individual. Meal scheduling is also affected.

Sharing interests strengthens family bonds. When work schedules permit, many families enjoy shopping together. (Courtesy General Motors Corporation)

Some careers require many hours of work or involve uncertain, flexible work schedules. Many jobs have weekend shifts. Still others require frequent travel. Any of these situations has an effect on a family's life-style. A father who travels frequently may be away from home on some family occasions such as birthdays. Families must learn to adjust to certain career demands.

Leisure time is a basic life-style factor. Some careers or jobs provide a great deal of time off. Free time encourages a family to share leisure activities.

CAREERS AND HOME MANAGEMENT

Careers and jobs play an important role in home management. For example, many families today have two wage earners. When father and mother both work, children usually are expected to share a greater portion of home management responsibilities.

The same is true for single-parent families. A single working parent needs the cooperation of other family members to operate a smooth household.

Work schedule and travel requirements of a job also affect home management. One parent may be absent from the home much of the time. In that case, the remaining family members are expected to fill the gap. Some careers require a high level of flexibility and cooperation by other family members. However, careers that are demanding in one area frequently offer special rewards in another area. For example, many night shifts include *bonus* pay. A bonus is money paid in addition to normal wages.

FOCUS ON YOUR FUTURE

MARIO WAS WAITING at the bicycle rack as his friends came out of the school building. "Hurry up, you guys! I have to get home right away!" he urged.

"What's your big hurry?" asked Steve.

"I've never seen you in a hurry to get home," Benny observed.

"Today is my mom's first day back at work. I have to get home and start cooking dinner," Mario explained.

Benny tilted his head and looked curiously at Mario. "I didn't know you could cook," he said.

"Neither did I," Steve agreed. "Is this something new?"

"Oh, it's not really cooking. I just have to put the food in the oven. That way, it'll be ready when my folks get home from work," Mario said.

"Great! Then you can come with us to the park when you get the oven going," Steve said.

"Not today, I'm afraid. I can't leave the house while the food is in the oven," Mario said. "Why don't you guys come over to the house later, when my folks get home? I got a couple of new video games for my birthday."

"Can we watch you cook?" Benny asked, laughing.

"Absolutely not!" Mario said. "I don't want to make any mistakes. But when I get some more practice, I'll show you guys how to make ravioli."

"That's swell," Steve said, "but are you going to have to do this every day, Mario?"

"Not really. Mom said she'd plan our meals so that I don't have much to do most days. Besides, I don't really mind helping out. The extra money will be nice, especially when Christmas comes around," Mario said.

"I see what you mean," Steve said. "Okay, Benny and I will come over tonight. Don't burn down the house before we get there." ■

Many families experience changes in home management needs when a family member enters or leaves the work force. A mother may desire to resume a career when her children are old enough to take care of themselves. Home management responsibilities then shift toward the children. They may be expected to help with meal preparations and increase their share of housecleaning and laundry chores. One reward for their added effort comes in the form of greater family income.

MANAGING CONFLICT IN THE HOME

Conflict occurs in all groups. This is especially true of families because their members have such close relationships. Typical family conflicts involve jealousy, frustration, and feelings of unfair treatment.

The key to dealing with family conflict is communication. Problems can be resolved more easily if feelings are openly expressed.

Good communication also includes a clear definition of responsibilities and reasonable rules for behavior. Conflicts are less likely when family members understand their roles.

Also helpful in managing conflict is a method for resolving disputes. The method may be determined by the parents or other person in a position of authority. To be effective, any method for settling disputes must be fair and accepted by those it affects. Equally important, the rules must be applied fairly and *consistently.* Consistently means that the rules do not change from one situation to another.

THE FAMILY AND SOCIETY

As an adult, you will have a role to play outside your family, in society. You will have goals, responsibilities, and conflicts. As a family member, you are developing *interpersonal skills,* or skills in getting along with others. You also develop interpersonal skills at school and in dealing with friends.

As a working citizen, your workplace will represent a different type of "family." Your role and responsibilities as a worker are discussed in the next unit.

CONTENT SUMMARY

Families are the closest units in society. How well a family functions depends on the willingness and ability of its members to compromise. Each individual has a personal code and, therefore, individual goals may differ. Family unity can be tested when members disagree on major goals, such as careers.

Organization and cooperation are the keys to effective home management. Individual roles differ according to factors such as family size and the ages of children.

Home management responsibilities include budgeting, maintenance, cleaning, food purchasing, preparation of meals, clothing purchasing and maintenance, and laundry. Assignment of these tasks can depend on which family members work outside the home. Children's ages and abilities also are factors.

Family members also have responsibilities to one another, and to the family as a whole. These responsibilities include listening, communicating, offering encouragement, and attending family functions.

Family life-styles are determined to a great extent by the careers of working family members. Careers determine family income, work schedules, and leisure activities. Career responsibilities can also affect home management arrangements.

Conflict within a family can be managed most effectively if good communication exists among family members. Methods of resolving conflicts should be fair and accepted by all concerned. Rules should be applied consistently. Clearly defined responsibilities and rules of behavior help to reduce conflict.

CAREER COMMENTARIES

1. **Maintenance and upkeep are greater responsibilities if a family owns its own home.**
   Describe ways in which you participate in the maintenance and upkeep of your home. How are such responsibilities shared in your family?

2. **Family members should support one another in establishing and working toward goals.**
   Explain how you might support another family member in seeking goals. Which of your other responsibilities to family members must you meet before you can offer encouragement?

3. **Conflicts are less likely when family members understand their roles.**
   Describe two kinds of conflict that can be avoided when family members' roles are clearly defined. Explain how communication is involved in preventing conflict.

KEY TERMS

generation

household

compromise

harmony

conflict

specific

unity

stepchild

organization

breadwinner

budget

maintenance

fad

upkeep

function

mutual

bonus

consistently

interpersonal skill

Responsibilities, Careers, and Expectations

When you have completed the reading assignments and exercises in this unit, you should be able to:

☐ Describe major rewards of work.

☐ Discuss a worker's responsibilities to an employer.

☐ Discuss an employer's responsibilities to an employee.

☐ Explain the importance of teamwork among employees.

☐ Describe factors that contribute to good employer-employee relations.

THE WORLD OF WORK

More than 100 million Americans have paid jobs. The world of work includes many thousands of different jobs. You are likely to have several different jobs yourself during your working career.

As a worker, you will find yourself with two separate sets of responsibilities. One set of responsibilities involves your role within your family. This includes establishing and maintaining your own household, should you choose to live alone. Your other set of responsibilities involves your role as an employee.

Your level of personal satisfaction will depend largely upon how well you blend these two roles. Blending a career with family responsibilities is not always easy. The roles may frequently come into conflict. Your personal code may be tested—and sometimes changed—when job and family responsibilities force you to make choices.

Your paycheck is one of the major rewards you will receive as a worker.

117

Great demands are made on workers in some occupations, including personal risk and time away from home. (Courtesy Queen City Metro)

For most people, these conflicts present no special problems. However, some jobs or careers demand a great deal of time and effort. If you consider entering such a career, make sure you understand your personal code. Examine your value system to determine if career rewards are more important to you than other, personal concerns.

How you divide your time among work, family responsibilities, and leisure activities represents a major life-style decision. Your personal satisfaction depends upon how well your decision matches your personal code.

WHY WORK?

People work for many reasons. Earning an income is usually the primary reason for getting a job, but it is almost never the only reason. And, of course, there are other kinds of work, such as being a homemaker or working on your house or car. Work offers a number of rewards in addition to money. The value of these rewards depends upon the *expectations* you have about work. Your expectations are the goals you expect to reach. Your goals, in turn, are determined by your personal code. You bring the same value system to any kind of work you do.

118

Rewards of work depend upon your expectations. You bring your value system to any job. (Courtesy Simplex Time Recorder Company)

Rewards of Work

Depending upon your expectations, the rewards of work fall into these general categories:

- Income
- Security
- Pride
- Recognition
- Satisfaction in getting a job done
- Interacting with others
- Belonging to an organization.

Income. The amount of money you earn will depend upon your skills, the value of your work, and your individual effort. Your income will help determine your personal life-style and the life-style of your family.

Security. The feeling that your job will last, and that your income will continue, can be extremely important. Job security is a safe feeling. Security enables you to make plans for the future.

Pride. Pride is a good feeling you have about yourself. Self-respect is a form of pride based on your position or your relationships with others. If you are successful in your work, you will take pride in your accomplishments.

Recognition. Praise for a job well done is an important source of satisfaction for most people. If you brought home a report card with straight A grades, you would expect to be congratulated. Recognition on the job can come from two sources: from an employer and from fellow workers. Each kind of recognition brings a special satisfaction.

Satisfaction in getting a job done. Finishing a piece of work brings satisfaction. You probably have experienced this with your

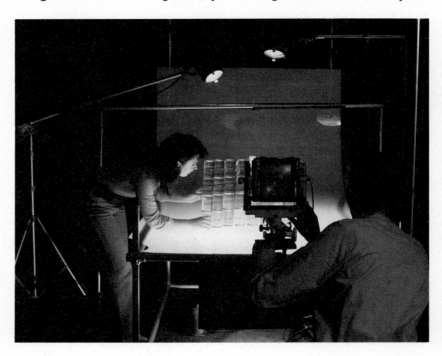

Job satisfaction is particularly important for people engaged in creative work.

homework and with tasks you perform at home. This satisfaction is particularly important to people who do *creative* work. Creative work is performed by people using their imaginations and skills. Examples of creative work include acting, music, writing, photography, painting, and sculpture.

Interacting with others. *Interaction* is the give and take of getting along with other people. Extroverts enjoy the company of others. Some jobs offer the opportunity for interaction with fellow employees. Other jobs, such as sales or nursing, involve dealing with the public. Success in dealing with others—especially in helping others—is a source of deep satisfaction for many people.

Belonging to an organization. People like to feel that they have a role to play and that their contributions count. Belonging to an organization lets people feel that others are relying on them. Belonging also provides the comfort of feeling that you can rely on others.

Interacting with others is a source of job satisfaction for many workers. (Courtesy IC Industries, Inc.)

Your Expectations

Your personal code will determine your major goals in life. These may include success in a career, a rewarding family life, or a particular life-style. Your goals and expectations are the basis upon which you will judge your success or failure.

Your expectations also determine how much satisfaction you obtain from each of the rewards of work. If you set your goals too high, you may be disappointed. Try to adopt realistic expectations. Let your expectations change as you gain experience.

FOCUS ON YOUR FUTURE

JOSE TOOK ONE LAST LOOK in the full-length mirror and decided that his new band uniform fit him properly. He picked up his trumpet and started toward the living room, where the rest of his family was waiting.

"Oh, how neat!" shouted his little sister, Lupe, as Jose marched proudly into the living room. "Are you going to play for us?" Lupe asked.

Jose's mother stood up. "He's not going to play right now, Lupe. We just wanted to see how the uniform fit. It looks just about right, Jose. How does it feel?" she asked.

"Fine, Mom. At first, I thought the jacket was a little tight across the back, but the material stretches. It's pretty comfortable," Jose said.

Jose's father stood and put his hand on Jose's shoulder. "You look terrific, son. If

you play as well as you look, maybe you can make a career out of music."

"Well, Dad, I have a long way to go. But the teacher says I have natural ability. I'm going to work hard at it because I would really like to be a musician," Jose said.

"That's a worthwhile goal," his father said. "But try to be flexible. You may decide later on that you would rather teach music. Teaching is creative, too, you know."

"I hadn't thought about teaching, but I guess that would also be a nice way to earn a living," Jose said. "But right now, I'm just proud to have been accepted into the band. At least I know what jacket I'll be wearing to school most days," he laughed.

Lupe put her arms around her brother. "I don't care about careers or anything like that," she said. "I just want to see Jose march at the football game Friday night." ∎

YOUR FUTURE ROLE AS AN EMPLOYEE

When you enter the world of work, you will be taking on the third major role of your life. Your first role was as a member of your family. Your second role is that of a student.

Your roles as family member and student carry responsibilities and rewards. The same will be true of your role as an employee. Going to work means joining an *organization.* An organization is a group of people who share a common goal.

Work Is a Business Transaction

Work is a process of buying and selling. The relationship between an employer and an employee is a *business transaction.* Business is the activity of meeting needs and wants. A business transaction is the basic act of doing business. Most business transactions consist of exchanging things of equal value. For example, you might receive a new bicycle as a gift. Your old bike may be too small, so you no longer need or want it. You may decide to sell it or trade it for something else you want or need.

Someone else in your neighborhood or in your school may want the old bike. If you and the buyer can agree on a price, you may sell it for money. Or, you may agree to exchange the bike for something else of equal value. A transaction in which items of equal value are traded is called *barter.* In a barter situation, both owners must agree about the value of items to be traded.

Piecework wages are paid on the basis of items produced or units of work performed. (© R. Forbes, 1984/The Image Bank)

When you go to work, you will sell something of value to an employer: your time, energy, and skills. The value you receive in this continuing business transaction is called a *wage.* A wage is payment, usually in money, for labor or services performed according to a contract. Wages are usually based on an hourly or daily rate. Wages may also be paid on a *piecework* basis. Piecework wages are paid on the value of an item produced or a unit of work accomplished. A person who works for wages on a regular basis is a *wage earner.*

Many workers are paid on a *salary* basis. A salary is a fixed rate of pay for services. Salaries are usually paid on a weekly or monthly basis.

FOCUS ON YOUR FUTURE

MICHI HUNG UP THE PHONE. She turned to the club adviser, Ms. Prescott, and shrugged her shoulders. "There's still no answer. I don't understand it. Lois said she would definitely be here," Michi said.

"I hope nothing has happened to her," Ms. Prescott said. "It's not like Lois to miss a project work session, at least not without telling us beforehand."

"What are we going to do now, Ms. Prescott?" Michi asked. "Lois was supposed to bring the materials to decorate the auditorium."

"Let's wait for a few more minutes. If she hasn't arrived by 7:30, we'll have to go to the crafts store and buy some other materials. The decorating has to be finished tonight. Our exhibition opens at 10 a.m. tomorrow, and everyone will be busy with their own projects in the morning. This is really a shame," Ms. Prescott said.

Michi opened the auditorium door and peered into the darkness outside. "I just don't understand it," she said to no one in particular. "Lois is usually so reliable."

Ms. Prescott asked the club members to gather around one of the exhibit tables. "It looks as though Lois is not going to show up tonight," she said. "Michi has been trying to contact her by telephone, with no success. If Lois doesn't get here in the next 10 minutes, we'll have to buy new decoration materials. I'll take two of you with me to the store. The rest can stay busy setting up exhibits."

Just then, a car drove up outside the auditorium. Michi ran to the door. "It's Lois!" she shouted.

Lois carried one of the boxes into the auditorium. Two other club members brought in the remaining boxes. As Lois put her box on one of the tables, she saw that everyone was looking at her. "I'm sorry to be late," she said. "I had to go with my parents to visit my grandmother in the hospital. I didn't realize it would take so long."

Ms. Prescott guided Lois away from the group. The club adviser spoke quietly. "You were right to go to the hospital with your parents, Lois. That is a family responsibility. But, when you realized you would be late for our meeting, why didn't you call?"

"Gosh, I don't know. I guess I thought the other girls would have enough work to keep them busy until I got here," Lois said. "I didn't mean to mess things up."

"Well, no real harm was done, Lois. However, I hope this will be a lesson. When you belong to a club, you also have obligations to that organization. If you cannot make an appointment on time, you should let people know that you're going to be late. That way, the organization can continue to function," Ms. Prescott said.

"Thank you for being so understanding, Ms. Prescott. I can see that my assumption was wrong. If something like this happens again, I'll certainly call," Lois said.

"I'm sure you will, Lois," Ms. Prescott said. "You've always been reliable in the past. Now, we had better get busy with those decorations!" ∎

RESPONSIBILITIES OF EMPLOYEES

Workers have certain obligations to their employers. As a party in a working agreement, an employee's primary responsibilities to an employer are:

- Reliability
- Following instructions
- Loyalty
- Honesty
- Responsibility
- Interest in the product
- Attitude
- Productivity.

Reliability. If you are *reliable*, you are dependable. You show up for work as scheduled, and you are on time. Frequent absence or tardiness reduces your value to an employer.

Following instructions. A good employee follows orders. A business must be organized. If you can't follow instructions, you fail to contribute to the organization. You have little or no value to an employer.

Loyalty. If you are *loyal*, you protect the interests of your employer. As a loyal employee, you would support your employer the same way you support a group to which you belong. You would not speak badly of your employer or do anything that might harm the employer's business.

Honesty. An honest employee is worthy of trust. If you are honest, you do not steal from your employer or cheat in any way. Honesty is an important part of being trustworthy.

Responsibility. Being *responsible* means that you answer for work you do. Responsibilities are duties that you are expected to perform. Major responsibilities to an employer include learning your job and performing it to the best of your ability.

Interest in the product. A *product* is something of value that a business sells. It may be a *good* or a *service.* A good is a physical product such as a toaster or a bicycle. A service is an action that benefits someone. A haircut is a service. As an employee, you should try to make the product as good as possible.

Loyal employees contribute as much as they can to the success of the business in which they work.

Attitude. A good attitude adds greatly to your value as an employee. A *positive attitude* usually improves the quality of your work performance. A negative attitude can affect other employees and reduce the value of your own work.

Productivity. A good employee does more than just show up for work and put in time. It is your responsibility to contribute as much as you can to the product of your employer.

RESPONSIBILITIES OF EMPLOYERS

As the other party to a working agreement, an employer also has obligations. Responsibilities of an employer to an employee include:

- Instruction
- Supervision
- A clean, safe place to work
- Compensation
- Fair treatment
- Opportunity.

Instruction. An employer should explain your duties and your role in an organization.

Supervision. You should have someone available to direct you in your work. A *supervisor* watches the work of others and directs them on the job.

A clean, safe place to work. An employer is responsible for cleanliness and safety in the workplace. Some jobs involve dirty work or danger. The employer should provide ways to control dirt, including special work clothes if necessary. Safety equipment and special training may be needed in dangerous occupations. An example of safety equipment that may be provided by an employer is protective goggles to prevent eye injuries. Employers must provide washrooms for employees.

Compensation. An employer is obliged to pay employees for their work, as agreed. Wages should be paid on a regular basis, on those days set aside as paydays. *Compensation* is an employee's wage or salary, plus other benefits. Typical *fringe* *benefits*, provided by employers, include paid vacations and contributions toward employee health insurance and retirement programs. Some jobs include benefits such as free uniforms, meals while working, and use of a company car.

Fair treatment. An employer has the responsibility to avoid *favoritism* and *prejudice* in dealing with employees. Favoritism means treating some employees better than others. Prejudice means negative feelings or actions against someone or something without just cause. A good working atmosphere is free of prejudice and favoritism.

Opportunity. Any employee should be given a fair chance to succeed in a job. Employees also should have a chance to gain advancement in an organization.

GETTING ALONG AT WORK

The responsibilities of an employee extend beyond duties to the employer. If you go to work for a company, you have an obligation to fit in. There are several ways in which an employee can fit in to an organization.

Maintaining harmony with fellow workers and supervisors is a responsibility of every employee.
(Photo below right, courtesy Union Pacific Corporation)

One employee responsibility is to support the purposes and *policies* of the organization. A policy is a management decision that guides the way an organization functions. A good employee shares the goals of an employer. A good employee also works within the policies of the organization in seeking to reach those goals. Following an employer's policies means being part of a team. Teamwork is necessary for any successful organization.

Another employee responsibility is to accept the job responsibilities that are assigned. This also means staying within the limits of a job. A good employee may ask for increased responsibilities. It is not proper to take them upon yourself without permission.

Finally, a good employee must be able to work in harmony with supervisors and fellow workers. Getting along with others on the job is a responsibility to yourself as well as to other employees. Disagreements are bound to occur now and then. Most disagreements can be resolved peacefully, with satisfaction for all persons. The biggest barrier to this is disagreeable people.

CONTENT SUMMARY

When you enter the world of work, you will have two sets of responsibilities: family and job. Your roles as family member and employee may come into conflict at times. When this happens, you may have to choose between them. Your personal code is tested, and it may be changed by such experiences.

People work for a number of reasons. Major rewards of work include income, security, pride, recognition, and satisfaction in completing a job. Interacting with others and belonging to an organization are other rewards of work. The level of satisfaction you gain from work will depend upon your expectations. Your expectations will change as you grow in age and experience.

Work is a business transaction. You sell an employer certain items of value: your time, energy, and skills. In return for the values you bring to work, the employer pays you a wage or a salary. Your value as a worker depends upon your work skills, productivity, attitude, education or special training, and willingness to work.

As an employee, you have responsibilities to an employer. These responsibilities include: reliability, following instructions, loyalty, honesty, responsibility, interest in the product, attitude, and productivity.

An employer also has responsibilities to employees. Employer responsibilities include: instruction, supervision, compensation, fair treatment, opportunity, and a clean, safe place for employees to work.

Getting along at work involves obligations in addition to your responsibilities to an employer. One obligation is to follow the policies of the employer. Another is to accept the job responsibilities that are assigned. An important part of fitting in is the ability to work in harmony with supervisors and other employees.

CAREER COMMENTARIES

1. **The relationship between an employer and an employee is a business transaction.**
   Describe the elements of the employer-employee relationship that make it a business transaction.

2. **A good working atmosphere is free of prejudice and favoritism.**
   Imagine that, as a worker, you are treated unfairly because of a supervisor's favoritism toward another employee. Describe how such treatment might affect your work. How might it affect your value as an employee?

3. **Following an employer's policies means being part of a team.**
   You have discovered that a particular company policy prevents you from performing your job to the best of your ability. Which obligation do you feel is more important: following company policy or being as productive as possible? How might you best deal with such a situation?

KEY TERMS

expectation

creative

interaction

organization

business transaction

barter

wage

piecework

wage earner

salary

reliable

loyal

responsible

product

good

service

positive attitude

productivity

supervisor

compensation

fringe benefit

favoritism

prejudice

policy

9

Friendships, Changes, and Adjustments

FRIENDSHIPS: RELATIONSHIPS YOU CHOOSE

If you were asked to name all your *friends*, you probably would have to think for a while. You probably know a large number of people your own age. Most of them are *acquaintances*. An acquaintance is someone you know. But an acquaintance is not close enough to share your complete trust and confidence.

A friend is a person with whom you have a relationship based on affection and respect. A friend is someone about whom you care. *Friendship* is a close relationship that usually develops over time. Sharing of experiences and mutual interests helps in building friendships.

One special element of friendship is that you choose your friends. Acquaintances are people you get to know because of circumstances. Your closest relationships probably involve members of your immediate family. However, you don't choose your parents and other relatives.

Friends are people whose company you enjoy. Friends enjoy doing things together.

Building a friendship requires making an emotional investment and sharing feelings. (Courtesy Cosmos Soccer Club, Inc.)

In naming your friends, you probably would mention your closest friends first. As you reach the end of your list, you would be naming individuals with whom your relationship is less close.

Friendship Requires Effort

You have to work at building a friendship. Part of your effort must go toward getting to know a person.

Getting to know someone includes learning some of that person's likes and dislikes. It means getting to understand that person's feelings.

Effort is also required to permit another person to share your own feelings. Doing this means giving up some of your privacy.

Building a friendship involves give and take by both parties. The best friendships usually are those in which the efforts of both individuals are about equal.

Friendship Involves Risk

When you build a friendship, you make an *emotional investment.* An emotional investment means that your feelings are involved in the relationship. There is risk involved in this investment. The risk lies in the hurt that can be felt when a friendship breaks up. Friendships can end for different reasons, including:

- Disagreements. A serious misunderstanding or argument tests the strength of a friendship. If a friendship is weak or one-sided, it can be ended by a strong disagreement. A one-sided friendship occurs when one of the parties makes most of the effort at building the friendship.

- Changing interests. As you grow older, your interests—and those of your friends—can change. A friendship based on a shared interest may simply fade away as each friend moves in a different direction.

- Moving away. Only the strongest friendships survive physical separation. If you move, you will put your efforts into making new friends. If your friend moves, you will seek new friendships to replace the lost relationship.

FOCUS ON YOUR FUTURE

DANNY FELT HURT. His friend Joe had gone fishing without even telling him. Danny had gone over to Joe's house to see if he wanted to play some handball.

When he returned home, Danny slumped into a chair in the family room. He picked up a magazine and began thumbing through it.

His mother came into the family room, a curious expression on her face. "I heard you come in, Danny. Is something wrong?" Mrs. Cheng asked.

"No, not really. I decided not to play handball, that's all," Danny replied.

"Oh, really? What about Joe? Didn't he feel like playing today?" Danny's mother asked.

"Joe wasn't home," Danny said.

"I can tell something's wrong. Do you want to talk about it?" his mother asked.

"Well, when I got to Joe's house, his mother told me that he had gone fishing with Mickey. He never told me he was going fishing today," Danny said.

"Oh, I see," his mother said. "Maybe he knew you wouldn't want to go, Danny. You've always turned him down in the past. Joe knows that you don't enjoy fishing."

"Yes, that's probably what happened. Still, I wish he'd told me. Just going off like that makes me think he doesn't care," Danny said.

"In that case, you and Joe should sit down and discuss the situation. You're pretty close friends. It would be a shame to risk your friendship over a minor misunderstanding. Even best friends don't share every one of their interests, you know. On the other hand, if Joe's company is really important to you, you might make an effort to enjoy fishing," Danny's mother suggested.

"That's a good idea, Mom. I'll tell Joe that I want to go with him next time. Do you think Dad would let me borrow some of his fishing gear?" Danny asked.

"I'm sure he would," his mother replied. "Now, why don't you call Joe's mother and ask if he can come over for dinner tonight? That would be a good opportunity for you to discuss your feelings." ■

QUALITIES OF FRIENDSHIP

There are certain qualities that make friendship different from acquaintanceship. Friendship involves:

- Communication
- Affection
- Sensitivity
- Comfort
- Trust.

Communication.   A friend is someone with whom you share your thoughts and feelings. You may tell a close friend about personal thoughts or experiences that you wouldn't reveal to anyone else. Friends share secrets.

Affection.   Friends like one another. A friend is a person with whom you enjoy spending time and doing things. You care about your friends.

Sensitivity.   Friends get to know each other's attitudes and feelings. Each understands and responds to the other's needs.

Comfort.   You feel relaxed and comfortable with friends. You can act naturally when you are with a friend. A friend is a good person to be with.

Trust.   The final and most meaningful measure of friendship is trust. You can count on a good friend. Good friends should be reliable and honest with you. They can be trusted to keep a secret. They will help you when you are in trouble. Good friends care about you and work to earn your trust. Equally important, you probably feel pride in knowing that your friends trust you.

Each person has his or her own personal code. No two individuals can share the exact same feelings and attitudes. One of the important skills in forming friendships is the ability to recognize and deal with personal differences.

In the story, Danny and Joe differed in their attitudes toward fishing. Having been turned down on several occasions, Joe didn't

bother to invite his friend. Joe's decision to go fishing without telling his friend hurt Danny.

Danny probably would have been disappointed in any event. He wouldn't have gone fishing if Joe had invited him. However, Joe's failure to invite him indicated that Joe didn't care. For that reason, Danny agreed with his mother's suggestion to try joining his friend the next time. Danny was willing to adjust his personal code to maintain his friendship with Joe.

Communication is one quality of friendship. A friend is a person with whom you can share your thoughts and feelings.

FRIENDSHIPS AND CHANGING NEEDS

Individuals grow and develop at different rates. They also tend to develop different interests in response to experiences. These differing patterns can affect friendships.

Friendships that develop at an early age may begin to fade as individuals acquire differing interests. For example, two friends may spend less time together as they begin to develop their individual talents. One person may be interested in music, while the other concentrates on athletics. Differing interests do not necessarily mean an end to a friendship. However, friendships tend to become less meaningful when individuals share fewer interests.

If your interests change, you probably will develop new friendships with individuals who share your interests. This is a normal part of maturing. You may still have the same affection for old friends. However, you now find that their interests no longer meet your needs. Perhaps they feel the same way. Affection remains, but sensitivities fade.

Changes in daily living can also cause friendships to fade. For example, you and your best friend may be a year apart in age. If either of you were to begin high school a year earlier, many of your interests might differ. The differences might be even greater if one of you were to graduate and enter the world of work a year before the other. Still another example would be the differences caused by one or the other getting married.

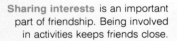

Sharing interests is an important part of friendship. Being involved in activities keeps friends close.

FOCUS ON YOUR FUTURE

MICHAEL CALLED OUT, "Hey, wait up, Alicia!"

The girl continued walking as Michael ran to catch up. "What's the matter?" he asked. "Are you getting stuck-up or something?"

"No, of course not," Alicia replied. "I'm in a hurry to get home so I can help my sister work on her prom dress."

"That sounds really boring," Michael said, shaking his head. "We were going to have a softball game this afternoon. Aren't you coming?"

"I told you, Michael, I have to help my sister with her dress. It has to be finished by next Friday. We can play softball anytime," Alicia said.

"I didn't even know you could sew, Alicia. It's neat that you can do things like that," Michael said.

"Actually, I'm not very good on my mom's machine yet. But, I like to do hand sewing and decorating," Alicia said. "By this time next year, I hope to be making some of my own clothes."

"I guess that means I have to find a new right fielder," Michael sighed. "I was afraid this might happen, the way you've been acting lately."

"People change, Michael. We're growing up, and we have to learn new things. I'm probably not going to get much better at softball. So, there are more important things for me to work on, things I can do as an adult. You understand, don't you?" Alicia asked.

"Sure, Alicia. Actually, I'm going to have to limit my softball, too. I'm starting a newspaper delivery route next week," Michael said. "I decided it was time that I earned some money. I hate being the only one in my family who has to ask for money to buy the others gifts. We're all growing up, I guess."

"We sure are," Alicia agreed. "And I think it's exciting." ■

FRIENDSHIPS AND YOUR PERSONAL CODE

Friendships tend to influence your values and your behavior. When you are very young, your values are influenced largely by your parents and other members of your household. As you begin to develop friendships outside the home, you come in contact with the values of other families. Your friends, in turn, are exposed to your values.

Typical disagreements between friends involve differing preferences of their families. These preferences can involve competing manufacturers of cars, television sets, and other consumer goods. Two families might support opposing sports teams. These are not serious disagreements. However, friends sometimes find their families opposed in matters of religion, politics, and *ethnic background*. Ethnic background includes race and membership in other large groups with common traits or customs.

Minor preferences normally do not cause problems between friends. Major differences, however, can create conflict within each individual. Friends may be forced to question parts of their codes that reflect the beliefs of their families. When your code is tested in this way, confusion can result.

However, you should be prepared to deal with challenges to your personal code. These challenges will occur throughout your life. In some cases, you will reject change and reinforce your code. In other cases, you will react to challenges by altering your beliefs or preferences.

Friendships Build Understanding

Strong friendships often survive major differences. When this happens, parts of your code may remain undecided for long periods of time. You may reject some of the values you learned from your family. Or, you may make slight changes in those values to permit a friendship to grow.

Testing your personal code in this way helps you to develop an *open mind*. A person with an open mind tries to see things as they are, without *prejudice*. Prejudice is an opinion or a judgment formed without thorough knowledge. You can be prejudiced in favor of something or against it.

When friends discuss their opinions and beliefs, they tend to gain understanding of one another's points of view. If their opposing beliefs are very strong, friends may be forced to alter or limit their relationship.

Your capacity for understanding is strengthened, however, each time your personal code is tested. Such testing is a lifelong process.

Friendships Alter Behavior

Friends can have an important influence on your behavior. For example, you might have a friend who is more daring or adventurous than you are. When you are with this friend, you may take risks you would otherwise reject. On the other hand, a cautious friend might convince you to avoid risks.

Merely being in the company of friends can alter your behavior. You may be quiet and shy by yourself, but loud and aggressive as one of a group.

In a related sense, you may be more, or less, obedient when influenced by a friend. For example, you may normally be quiet and pay attention in the classroom. A friend who likes to talk or fool around in class may influence you to do the same. This type of behavior change can get you in trouble.

On the other hand, a friend who is serious about school may help you improve your behavior and study habits.

Taking risks may seem less threatening when you are in the company of a adventurous friend.
(Courtesy Boy Scouts of America)

Group friendships may present important skill-building opportunities. Your relationships within groups help you to develop the ability to adjust to group goals.
(Nawrocki Stock Photo)

FRIENDS CAN BE LEADERS OR FOLLOWERS

You probably know individuals who are leaders and others who are followers.

If you have a friend with strong leadership skills, you may let that individual make group decisions. Your reactions to your friend's decisions are based upon your personal code.

You may have friends who prefer to follow the lead of others. If so, you may find yourself playing a leadership role and developing abilities as a leader.

Being a leader is not necessarily better than being a follower. For one thing, leaders do not always have the opportunity to do what they enjoy. An example might be an airline pilot who is appointed to an executive position. That individual might prefer sitting at the controls of a jet aircraft to sitting behind a desk in an office.

Many individuals with creative skills—both mental and physical—would rather exercise those skills than exercise leadership. For example, it is not unusual for teachers to pass up promotions that would remove them from the classroom.

Relationships you develop with friends will help you to develop attitudes toward the roles of leader and follower. These attitudes, and other parts of your code, will determine which role you prefer.

FRIENDSHIPS AND CAREERS

Friendships can have a major influence on the way you view a career. Your relationships with friends affect your self-image and your ability to fit in with groups.

Good friendships tend to build a positive self-image. If you enjoy the affection, respect, and trust of others, you feel good about yourself. You probably have a positive attitude toward life. People with this type of attitude believe in themselves. They believe they will succeed in any activity.

Equally important, a positive attitude helps you to develop personal goals and the plans to reach those goals. Your goals may change as you go through life. Whatever your goals, you will find them easier to achieve with a positive attitude.

Friendships and Groups

Your relationships with groups provide another important skill-building area. Much of your life involves dealing with, or being part of, groups. In the classroom, you are a member of a group. Other group activities include memberships in clubs, marching bands, sports teams, and other organizations with common goals.

An important element of a group is its common goals. Group members are expected to give up their individual goals in favor of working for common goals. In sports, for example, a team player concentrates on helping the team win. Individual goals, such as batting averages or touchdowns, should be less important than the team's victory. Most sports championships are won by teams with unselfish players.

Your relationships with friends and within groups help you develop the ability to fit in with group purposes. How well you develop this ability will have an important effect on your career decisions.

Team membership involves giving up individual goals to work for team victory. A good team member is unselfish. (Courtesy Verbatim Corporation)

Group Responsibilities

Sharing its goals is only part of your involvement with a group. To contribute, you must be willing and able to accept *responsibilities* within an organization. A responsibility is a duty for which you are expected to answer. Members of a group accept responsibilities. This means that they *commit* themselves, or promise, to do certain things.

There is a saying that a chain is only as strong as its weakest link. The same is true of a group. Each member must contribute for the group to reach its goals.

Group members who fail to accept responsibilities usually become inactive or leave the group.

When you enter the world of work, your job will involve responsibilities. Your value to an employer will depend largely upon how well you accept and fulfill your responsibilities.

CONTENT SUMMARY

Friendships are relationships you choose. A friend is a person with whom you have a special relationship. Qualities of friendship include communication, affection, sensitivity, comfort, and trust.

Building friendships requires effort. Friendships also involve risks, especially the pain that can result when a friendship breaks up.

Friendships are affected by changing needs that result from new roles and interests as you grow older. Friendships also bring challenges to your personal code. You may accept some new beliefs or preferences and alter your code. Other challenges are rejected, and your code is thus reinforced.

An open mind often results when friendships involve individuals from different cultural and ethnic backgrounds. Prejudice usually weakens or disappears in the face of friendship.

Friendships also affect behavior. Individuals gain strength from friends and from group membership. Behavioral changes can be either positive or negative. Friendships also lead to development of leadership or follower roles. There is no right or wrong involved. The value lies in building skills for either role.

Rewarding friendships help you to build a positive attitude and a better self-image. These traits, in turn, help you to develop personal goals and the plans to reach them.

Group relationships are another important skill-building area. Much of your life probably will involve group membership. It is important for you to learn to work toward common group goals and to accept responsibilities within a group. These skills will be valuable to you as a working citizen.

CAREER COMMENTARIES

1. **The most meaningful measure of friendship is trust.**
   Describe two kinds of trust that you have in a close friend. Give examples of past behavior that proved that friend trustworthy.

2. **Testing your personal code helps you to develop an open mind.**
   Describe how a friendship caused you to change an attitude or a preference. Was your previous attitude or preference formed through prejudice or through factual examination?

3. **Group members are expected to give up their individual goals in favor of working for common goals.**
   Identify a situation in which you have placed the goals of a group above your personal goals. Describe your feelings about your relationships within that group.

KEY TERMS

friend

acquaintance

friendship

emotional investment

ethnic background

open mind

prejudice

responsibility

commit

Making Decisions About Your Future

MUCH OF YOUR LIFE IS SPENT dealing with problems to be solved or decisions to be made. The best way to deal with problems and decisions is through an organized approach. The main subject throughout Part III is a problem-solving and decision-making process.

Problem-solving and decision-making skills are especially valuable as you begin to think about a career. The process method is a useful tool for achieving personal goals. Unit 10 presents the process method and a model for solving problems and making decisions. Unit 11 expands upon the first four steps of the model. These are: identifying a problem or decision; analyzing the situation; finding alternatives; and evaluating consequences of alternatives. Unit 12 covers the last three steps of the model. These are: selecting the best alternative; implementing the alternative; and evaluating the results.

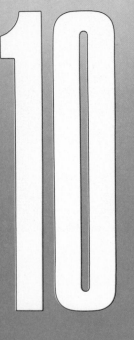

Deciding What to Do: An Organized Approach

Making decisions is a constant process that you must use to reach your goals. (© Craig Aurness/West Light)

PROBLEMS AND DECISIONS: A QUESTION OF SOURCE

Change, as discussed in Unit 4, can be external or internal. External change occurs from natural causes or by the actions of others. External changes are outside your control. Because you have no control, external changes can cause *problems.* Problems are troubles or difficult situations. If a problem bothers you enough, you have to give it your attention and seek a *solution.* A solution is an action you take to eliminate or deal with a problem.

Internal change is change that you want to make. Internal changes begin within you—from your own *decisions.* Decisions

149

are choices or judgments you make to deal with existing situations or to reach a goal. A decision results in a *commitment* you undertake. A commitment is a promise you make to yourself or to others that you will make something happen. You control internal change.

In dealing with change, then, the first step is to identify the source of the change. Is the change external—that is, has it already taken place? Or, is it internal—a change you would like to make?

External change can present problems. The more serious the problem, the more you can benefit from dealing with it in an organized manner. (Courtesy Prudential Insurance Company of America)

USING A PROCESS TO DEAL WITH CHANGE

Dealing with change—whether a problem or a decision—should be done in an organized manner. The best way to do this is to use a *process.* A process is a series of steps that are followed, in a certain order, to reach a planned result.

The process approach lets you deal with change in an organized, clear-thinking manner. There are other ways to reach your goals. However, a process approach is almost always the best way. A process approach helps you to:

- Organize your efforts.
- Consider all the facts of a situation.
- Avoid overlooking any important considerations.

Whether you are dealing with a problem or a decision, mistakes can be costly. The process method helps you avoid mistakes. Equally important, the process method helps you to base your problem-solving and decision-making efforts on facts. Remember, there are no right or wrong choices in either problem solving or decision making. Rather, the choices you make are either *appropriate* or *inappropriate*. Appropriate means suitable or fitting. Inappropriate choices are those that fail to deal satisfactorily with a situation. The process method, then, helps you to select an appropriate action.

Decisions deal with changes you want to make, such as finding a job.

A MODEL FOR SOLVING PROBLEMS AND MAKING DECISIONS

The process approach to solving problems and making decisions involves a series of steps. These steps can be illustrated in the form of a diagram. A diagram that shows a process is usually called a *model.* A model that you can use to solve problems and make decisions is shown in Figure 10-1.

There are seven steps in this model. The steps are the same for solving problems and for making decisions. The only difference lies in the source of the change: external for problems and internal for decisions. The steps in this model are:

1. Identify the problem to be solved or the decision to be made.

2. Make a statement that analyzes the problem or decision.

3. Find alternatives.

4. Think about the consequences of each alternative.

5. Select the best alternative.

6. Implement your choice.

7. Evaluate the final results.

Notice the bar on the left side of the diagram. The bar is connected to each of the steps that represent an action. The bar represents continuing *feedback*, evaluation, and revision of your actions based upon your personal code. Feedback is information that you receive about the results of an action. Feedback helps you to evaluate your actions. Feedback also may identify new problems or decisions. Remember, change is occurring all the time. Changes do not stop happening while you work on problems or decisions.

Your beliefs and attitudes affect each step of the problem-solving and decision-making process. Remember, your complete set of beliefs and values make up your personal code of conduct. Your personal code serves as a basis upon which you evaluate feedback and make revisions to your choices.

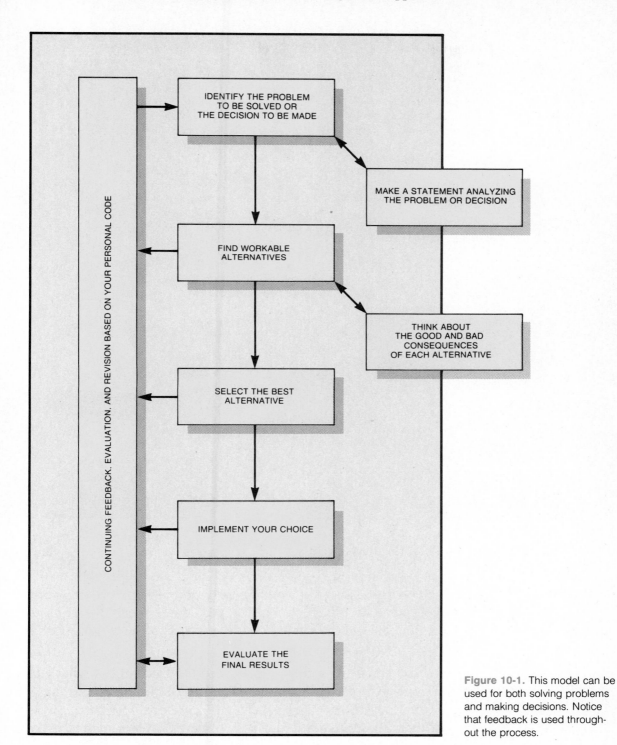

Figure 10-1. This model can be used for both solving problems and making decisions. Notice that feedback is used throughout the process.

Identify the Problem or Decision

The first step in the process is to identify the problem to be solved or the decision to be made. In problem solving, you must determine what has happened. A problem results from a change. Understanding the change helps you to rate the seriousness of the problem.

In identifying a decision, you need to think about what you want to happen. In decision making, no change has occurred. Instead, causing a change is your goal. Therefore, you must analyze the situation and determine how important it is for you to make a change. You may be considering a decision to change something you don't like. Or, you may be reaching toward a positive goal. Either way, you are in control, and the change will not occur unless you act.

Make a Statement That Analyzes the Problem or Decision

In the model, this step is set off to the side. This is because the statement involves an analysis of a situation rather than a step toward change. In preparing the statement, you think about the problem or decision and figure out where you are. Then, you decide on a goal. The statement is used to describe the result you want to achieve.

Find Alternatives

Once you have set a goal, your next step is to think about *alternatives.* An alternative is a solution to a problem or a choice you can make to achieve a goal.

One or more of the alternatives you identify will become the solution or choice that you apply to the situation. Therefore, this step requires concentration. You need to use your imagination to identify the best possible alternatives. You need choices if you are to choose a course of action that achieves your goals.

Think About the Consequences of Each Alternative

As with the problem or decision statement, this step is set off to the side. It too involves an analysis rather than an active step. However, this step is just as important as finding alternatives.

Consequences are the results of your actions. Consequences can be good or bad. For each alternative, you should identify the good and bad consequences that might result. Then, think about where you would be if that alternative happened.

When you have evaluated each alternative, compare the possible results. This comparison probably will do one of two things. It may help you to choose the best alternative for you. Or, it may lead you to reject the alternatives you have identified. In that case, you may want to find additional alternatives.

Making a commitment is a key step in solving a problem or making a decision.

Select the Best Alternative

When you have completed your evaluations, your next step is to select the best alternative. At this point you are making a choice. You are choosing the alternative that offers the best combination of consequences. It should be the alternative that offers the best chance to meet your goal.

The alternative you select then becomes the basis for your commitment. Your commitment means that you accept your chosen alternative and that you will support it through your actions.

Implement Your Choice

After choosing an alternative, you *implement* that choice. Implement means to carry out a plan. You commit yourself to do everything you can to make the plan work.

Evaluate the Final Results

Problem solving and decision making are continuous processes. Change is constant, and therefore you must deal with it all the time. Problems and decisions are not *isolated* situations. Isolated means set apart or removed from others. The consequences of one action usually lead to other problems or decision-making situations.

To evaluate the results of your decision, you need feedback. You need feedback on the results of your decision for three reasons. First, you are affected by your actions. Second, you are responsible for the consequences of your actions. Third, feedback helps you to identify any new problems or decisions you may want to consider.

PROBLEMS, DECISIONS, AND YOUR PERSONAL CODE

Problems and decisions are highly individual. That is, each person looks at a problem or decision based on his or her own personal code. Your personal code guides the values you assign to alternatives. Your code also determines how you react to the consequences of your actions. It is important that you be aware of the values that are guiding your decisions.

FOCUS ON YOUR FUTURE

TRACY WAS HORRIFIED when she saw what her kitten had done. While Tracy was in school, her little pet had decided to play with Tracy's new sweater. As a result, the collar was ripped apart.

She picked up the kitten. "Why did you have to do that?" she asked her pet. "Now we're both in trouble."

Tracy put down the kitten and looked more closely at the sweater. The collar would have to be knit again. Her mother probably would be pretty angry because she had worked hard to finish the sweater for Tracy's birthday.

Even worse, Tracy thought, her mother might force her to give up the kitten. Tracy recalled her mother's warning: "You are responsible for the cat, Tracy. I don't want any problems. If she causes problems, she'll have to go."

Tracy sat on her bed and thought about possible alternatives. She could hide the sweater underneath some other clothes in her dresser. She could tell her mother that the sweater had been damaged at school. Or, she could simply tell the truth and hope that her mother wouldn't take the kitten away from her.

Tracy rejected the idea of hiding the sweater. She would be expected to wear it, of course.

She also decided against telling a lie, for two reasons. First, she would be uncomfortable and feel bad about lying. Second, her mother was not likely to believe such a story. Looking at the ripped collar, Tracy realized that the cause was quite obvious.

Her only workable alternative was to be honest and tell her mother what had happened. Tracy looked at the kitten, playfully chasing one of its toys. It really wasn't the kitten's fault. She didn't know she was doing anything wrong. That's the answer, Tracy thought. She had neglected to put her sweater away when she left for school that morning. It was her fault for leaving the sweater on her bed. Tracy was sure that her mother would accept her explanation. After all, the kitten had been hers for three weeks now, and this was the first problem.

Tracy decided to tell her mother as soon as she got home from work.

Carefully folding the sweater, Tracy placed it in her drawer. She picked up the kitten and went to the kitchen. "I'm going to give you a bowl of milk. But, you'll have to be good from now on," she told her pet. "And I had better be more careful," she concluded. ■

Stress occurs when you face serious problems or important decisions. Stress can be caused by anger, frustration, or worry over problems or decisions.

Problems and important decisions frequently cause changes in your personal code. You should be aware of these changes. For example, you might wear light clothing to school even though the weather forecast predicts a storm and dropping temperatures. If you are caught wearing light clothing in a storm, you may develop a new attitude. The next time a storm is forecast, you probably will dress appropriately. Your new attitude represents a change in your personal code.

Your code is tested, and often changed, for a good reason. Serious problems and important decisions cause *stress.* Stress is personal pressure. *Tension* is another term for stress. Stress, or tension, usually is caused by anger, fear, frustration, or worry. Stress makes you uncomfortable. You may be angry, frustrated, or worried over the results of your decisions.

When stress occurs, you tend to look for ways to avoid that kind of pressure in the future. For example, you may have trouble remembering homework assignments. If the consequences are serious enough, you will write a list of your assignments. In this case, you have learned a lesson from stress. Stress has helped you do a better job of planning your activities. This amounts to a change in your personal code.

SEPARATING SYMPTOMS AND CAUSES OF PROBLEMS

When you make a problem statement, it is important to separate *symptoms* and causes. A symptom is a sign of something else. For example, a sore throat may be a symptom of a cold. You can take cough medicine to relieve the symptom. However, you will still have a cold, which is the cause of the problem.

Another example might be a flat tire on a bicycle. The tire is flat because it lacks air. That is the symptom. You can pump air into the tire, which would be dealing with the symptom. However, if the air leaks out, the tire will be flat again. You have not dealt with the cause of the problem. The cause may be a nail that has pierced the tire. The solution, then, is to remove the nail, patch the tire, and then add air.

Dealing with symptoms may provide relief. But, relief from symptoms doesn't solve a problem. It is necessary to identify the cause of a problem before you can resolve it effectively.

FOCUS ON YOUR FUTURE

CURTIS FINISHED LACING his baseball shoes. He stood up, grabbed his fielder's glove, and walked toward the group surrounding the team manager.

"Hey, Curtis! It's about time you got here!" shouted his friend, Ron.

"Sorry I'm late," Curtis said. "I had to stay after school for a few minutes."

The team meeting broke up. Ron and Curtis jogged into the outfield to practice catching fly balls.

When practice ended, the two friends sat side-by-side while they changed into street shoes. Ron looked at Curtis and saw a concerned look on his face. "What's wrong, Curtis? You've been acting strange lately," Ron inquired.

"I've been doing a lot of thinking, Ron," Curtis replied. "I have a big decision to make. My grandparents want me to spend the summer up at their place on the lake."

"That sounds great!" Ron said.

"It is. But I'd have to go up there right after school is over. That means I'd miss the last third of the baseball season. So, I'm trying to decide if I should forget about playing baseball, or pass up my grandparents' invitation. It's a tough decision," Curtis said, "and I have to let them know by this weekend."

"That is tough," Ron agreed. "But listen. Why don't you just play until it's time to go up north? Coach Williams would understand if you explained the situation up front."

"Not playing would be a tough decision. But, what if we're heading for the play-offs? Can you imagine how hard it would be to leave then?" Curtis asked.

"I see what you mean," Ron said.

"I guess I'll talk to Coach Williams," Curtis said. "Your idea seems best. I can start the season and see what happens. Maybe my leaving early won't be such a big problem. That way, I'll be leaving some alternatives open. Thanks for the good idea, Ron." ■

Graduation is a major long-term goal for students. (Indiana University—Purdue University at Indianapolis)

USING A PROCESS TO REACH GOALS

Effective decision making plays a major role in determining the quality of your life. As you grow and mature, you will assume a variety of roles and responsibilities. Whether in the home, at school, or at work, these roles and responsibilities will involve decision making.

Good decision-making skills help you in two ways. They help you in solving many problems you encounter in your roles in the home and at work. They also help you to reduce the number of problems you face. Appropriate decisions usually bring satisfactory consequences, which tend to eliminate problems.

Decision-making skills also help you to achieve your personal goals and objectives. Think of a goal as a decision you wish to make. Then, apply the decision-making model. Identify your goal and analyze it by making a statement. Next, think of alternative paths by which you might reach the goal. Evaluate each alternative according to its likely consequences and its chances for success. This is a good time to seek advice from others. A person who is not affected by your decision may be more objective about the alternatives.

When you have selected your best alternative, make a commitment to follow through with positive action. Finally, evaluate feedback from your efforts.

Goal-seeking efforts require continuing evaluation of feedback. Evaluation may indicate that you need to revise your plan of action. This is the real value of feedback.

CONSEQUENCES: GOOD AND BAD

The most difficult step in problem solving or decision making is the evaluation of possible consequences. The difficulty lies in the need to look into the future. You cannot be certain about the outcome of a decision because change is continuous. The world does not stop while a decision is being made.

Remember, consequences can be good or bad. It is not enough merely to think about the good consequences of an action. It is just as important to consider the bad results that are possible. It is necessary to compare alternatives according to both good and bad consequences. One alternative may promise the most desirable consequences on the one hand while threatening the worst disaster on the other. Another alternative, while less appealing on the plus side, may be more sensible from the standpoint of risk.

Your personal code will guide you in all these considerations. Remember, your code will change as you grow in age and experience. Decisions you make 10 or 20 years from now may be different from those you make now. The differences will be due to changed values in your personal code.

CONTENT SUMMARY

There are two basic kinds of change. External change occurs from the forces of nature or from actions by others. External change can cause problems. If a problem bothers you enough, you will seek a solution.

Internal change comes from within yourself. It is change that you want to make. Internal change results from decisions you make.

Problems and decisions can be serious. Therefore, it is best to deal with them in an organized, clear-thinking manner. A good way to do this is to use the process method. A process is a series of steps that you take, in a certain order, to reach a planned result.

A diagram that illustrates a process is usually called a model. One suggested model for solving problems and making decisions contains seven steps. First, identify the problem to be solved or the decision to be made. Second, make a statement analyzing the problem or decision. Third, find alternative solutions or decisions. Fourth, evaluate the possible consequences of each alternative. Fifth, choose the best alternative. Sixth, implement your choice. Seventh, evaluate the results of your decision.

Each of the steps involves receiving feedback, making evaluations, and making possible revisions, based upon your personal code. Your personal code affects all your problem-solving and decision-making efforts. Problems and decisions, in turn, may cause you to change your personal code.

In solving problems, it is important to separate symptoms and causes. Dealing with symptoms may not affect the cause of a problem.

Good problem-solving and decision-making skills improve the quality of your life. These skills help you to reduce the number of problems you face, as well as helping you to solve problems. Decision-making skills are useful in reaching your personal goals and objectives.

Evaluating consequences is the most difficult part of problem solving and decision making. The difficulty lies in looking into the future to predict the results of an action. Remember, your actions can produce good and bad consequences.

CAREER COMMENTARIES

1. **Changes do not stop happening while you work on problems or decisions.**
   Describe a situation in which continuing change affected your efforts to solve a problem or make a decision. If you cannot recall such a situation from your own life, describe a friend's situation or an imaginary situation.

2. **You need feedback to evaluate the results of your decisions.**
   Describe a situation in which feedback caused you to change a decision.

3. **The most difficult step in the problem-solving or decision-making process is the evaluation of possible consequences.**
   Why is evaluating consequences a difficult step? Describe a situation in which the consequences of a decision were different from those you expected.

KEY TERMS

problem

solution

decision

commitment

process

appropriate

inappropriate

model

feedback

alternative

consequence

implement

isolated

stress

tension

symptom

Identifying and Evaluating Alternatives

YOUR LEARNING JOB

When you have completed the reading assignments and exercises in this unit, you should be able to:

☐ Explain how a written decision statement helps you choose alternatives.

☐ Describe how your personal code affects your decision making.

☐ Explain why the number of decision alternatives must be limited.

☐ Ask questions that can help you compare the consequences of different alternatives.

☐ Explain why the consequences of problem-solving alternatives are different from the consequences of decision-making alternatives.

☐ Discuss the need to plan for contingencies.

STATING THE FACTS

The first step in the problem-solving/decision-making model is to create a clear picture of the situation. Problems result from external change. If you are dealing with a problem, you must identify and understand the change that has caused the problem. Understanding the change can be more difficult than it seems. You may need to ask yourself some questions: Why is this situation a problem for me? Am I making this situation more of a problem than it should be? Is there another way to look at this situation?

When you consider making a decision, you become the agent of change. The change is your goal. First, you identify the situation. If the situation is complicated, it may be helpful to prepare a written *decision statement.* A decision statement describes

Getting a clear picture of the situation is the first step in solving problems and making decisions. Before you can solve a problem, you must identify and understand the change that caused the problem.

Your goal and the decision necessary to reach that goal. Some examples of decision statements are:

- I want to improve my grades so that I can try out for a school sports team next semester. I have to decide on a program that I can follow to reach this goal.

- I'd like to be able to give my parents nice gifts on their birthdays this year. I want to find a way to earn enough money to purchase the gifts.

- I'll need some new clothes for school next fall, but I'm too heavy for the fashions I want. I need a program to help me lose weight during the summer.

Your goal or purpose should be identified in a clear statement as the first step in the decision-making process. (Nawrocki Stock Photo)

ANALYZING THE FACTS

The second step in the problem-solving/decision-making process is to make a statement that analyzes the problem or decision. This is the step in which your personal code helps determine your *motivation.* Motivation is a combination of desire and determination. Motivation is very personal. You may have high or low levels of motivation, depending upon your personal code.

Motivation can be related to *criteria.* Criteria are measures of importance. Criteria for problem solving or decision making are based upon your personal code. Criteria help you to analyze how important it is for you to seek a change or to make a commitment.

Criteria include considerations such as *urgency.* Urgency involves time. An urgent task must be accomplished right away. If you are trying to solve a problem, you need to determine the seriousness of the problem. How urgent is the situation? In decision making, you need to analyze the importance of the change you are considering. Is this something you feel you must do? Is it a decision that can be postponed?

Another question you should always ask when making decisions is: What will happen if I do nothing? Remember, you are in control in decision making. You are thinking about causing a change. Nothing has happened, and there is no absolute need for you to do anything. Considering the alternative of doing nothing helps you to determine the importance of the situation.

FOCUS ON YOUR FUTURE

HEIDI CAUGHT HER BREATH while she waited for the traffic light to change. She had run all the way from school. Heidi was anxious to see if the puppy was still in his cage at the pet store.

The light changed, and Heidi bolted across the street. She walked into the pet store, said hello to Mr. Benson, and headed straight for the puppy cage.

"He's still here, Heidi," the store proprietor said. Mr. Benson had promised Heidi he would keep the black and tan puppy for her as long as possible.

Heidi wanted the puppy, but she had been afraid to tell her parents. They had reacted negatively when she brought up the subject a few days earlier. Still, they hadn't really said no.

Heidi knew that she would have to make a decision today. Mr. Benson couldn't be expected to hold the puppy any longer.

The puppy had its front paws on the glass, standing on its hind legs and wagging its tail. Heidi looked away. She couldn't concentrate when she looked into the puppy's sad, pleading eyes. She decided that no one could give this puppy as much love as she could.

Heidi also decided on a goal. She wanted the puppy more than anything else in the world. She just had to figure out the best way to convince her parents that she ought to have it.

"Mr. Benson, I've decided that I want this puppy," Heidi said.

"That doesn't surprise me, Heidi. I would have been shocked if you'd said anything else," the store owner said. "But, do you think your folks will let you have him?" he asked.

"I hope so. I just have to figure out the best way to ask them. I'll find out tonight and tell you tomorrow for sure, okay?" Heidi asked.

"Tomorrow will be fine, Heidi. For your sake, and the sake of the puppy, I hope you're successful," Mr. Benson said. ■

Finding alternatives is a highly individual process. This photo, for example, shows an alternative chosen by a person seeking fitness through exercise and diet.

IDENTIFYING ALTERNATIVES

When you have identified a problem or decision and have analyzed your situation, you are ready to select alternatives. Identifying alternatives is a critical step in the problem-solving/decision-making process. The reason is that a problem solution or decision will come from among your alternatives.

Finding alternatives is the point at which you begin to solve a problem or make a decision. The two previous steps involved identifying and analyzing a situation. You attempted to find and understand the cause of a problem or the importance of a goal.

Identifying alternatives is the heart of the problem-solving/decision-making process. The quality of your alternatives will determine the quality of your solution or decision. Finding alternatives should be the part of the process upon which you spend the most time.

Keep an Open Mind

At this stage, it is important to be *open-minded.* Being open-minded means that your mind is open to all possibilities. You also want to *stimulate* your thinking. Stimulating your thinking means you are looking actively for ideas. Depending upon the nature of the problem or decision, you may ask others for suggestions.

One good way to collect ideas is to make a written list. Take all the time you can, within the limits imposed by the urgency of a situation. In general, the more serious a problem or important a decision, the more time you should allow for choosing alternatives.

Your written list should include all the ideas that occur to you. If you make your list open-ended, you can add new ideas and cross out old ones at any time.

Alternatives Should Be Workable

As you list your ideas, put each one to an important test. Ask the question: Will this idea help me to solve my problem or reach my goal?

Alternatives should be workable. Ideas that do nothing to solve a problem or to reach a goal should be discarded. Thinking about unworkable alternatives is a waste of time. For example, skipping a class to avoid a test would not solve the problem of being unprepared. Missing the test would create a new problem.

Each alternative you select should have the potential for eliminating or dealing with the cause of a problem. In decision making, each alternative should move you closer to your goal.

LIMIT YOUR ALTERNATIVES

Being open-minded does not mean that you should consider an unlimited number of alternatives. Too long a list of alternatives will make it difficult, if not impossible, to consider each one adequately. It is good to be open-minded and receptive to new ideas. However, you must take care to limit your list of ideas to a workable number of alternatives.

Limiting alternatives to a workable number is important. Planning a vacation usually involves dealing with limitations on time and money.

A good rule is to match the number of alternatives you consider to the seriousness of your situation. For example, decisions about your career are more important than decisions about clothing styles. Serious problems and important goals deserve thorough consideration of workable alternatives.

Knowing when you have enough alternatives is an important skill in problem solving and decision making. It is always necessary, at some point, to limit the number of alternatives you want to consider. In general, if you list from three to six alternatives, you probably have enough to think about.

Remember that time may be an important factor. The urgency of a situation can modify these general rules. Some problems and decisions require quick action. You may not have time to consider all possible alternatives fully.

There are no specific rules for limiting alternatives, because each situation is unique. Equally important, each individual considers a situation on the basis of his or her own personal code.

FOCUS ON YOUR FUTURE

HEIDI KEPT THINKING about the puppy all the way home. She had to decide on a plan of action, and soon. Before the day was over, she would know whether she would reach her goal.

When Heidi got home, she went to her room and sat at her desk. She felt that she could think more clearly if she wrote a list of ideas.

Thirty minutes later, she had crossed off all the ideas except three.

The first alternative was to ask her parents to buy her the puppy instead of the new bike. They might agree to that. The trouble was that she needed the newspaper route in the fall to pay for the puppy's upkeep. And, her old bike was in no condition to be used on a daily paper route.

The second alternative was to ask her parents to lend her the money for the puppy. If she got the new bike, she could pay them back from her earnings on the paper route. Heidi felt that would be asking too much, however. Also, such a commitment would use up just about all her earnings.

Heidi thought about the third alternative. She could ask for the puppy and for just enough money to fix her old bike. She could fix it well enough herself, if her parents would pay for the parts. That way, she could still take the paper route and save up her money for a new bike. If her parents would pay for the puppy's upkeep during the summer, she could pay them back in the fall. At the same time, she could begin saving up for a new bike.

Heidi thought about the consequences. The most important thing right now was the puppy. Still, she had to have a plan that would allow her to take the newspaper route.

The third alternative seemed to be the best one. Heidi looked at the clock. Her mother would be home from work in about an hour. She would get all her thoughts together and speak to her mother as soon as she got home. Her mother probably would agree, if she could be sure that Heidi would take care of the puppy. Since summer vacation started in a week, that shouldn't be a problem. She would be home to housebreak the puppy and take care of it. If her mother were on her side, she thought, her father would be easier to convince.

Heidi went to the kitchen and opened the telephone directory. The first step, she thought, was to check prices on the parts needed to repair her old bike. ∎

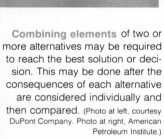

Combining elements of two or more alternatives may be required to reach the best solution or decision. This may be done after the consequences of each alternative are considered individually and then compared. (Photo at left, courtesy DuPont Company. Photo at right, American Petroleum Institute.)

CONSIDERING CONSEQUENCES

Evaluating the consequences of alternatives is the fourth step in the problem-solving/decision-making model. Remember, each alternative can have good and bad consequences. You may not be able to find a perfect solution or decision in most cases. It is important to consider consequences in terms of their appropriateness to your personal code. You should judge consequences based upon your beliefs, values, and preferences. Your goal should be to come up with the best possible course of action in a given set of circumstances.

Evaluating alternatives is really a two-step procedure. First, the consequences of each alternative should be considered. Then, the alternatives can be compared in terms of their consequences. Serious consideration of consequences usually helps you to determine the best alternative.

Sometimes, the best solution or decision may involve combining elements of two or more alternatives. The best rule is to keep an open mind as you evaluate consequences.

Ask Questions

One method for considering the consequences of an alternative is to assume that you have chosen that alternative. Then, ask yourself some questions:

- Will I be better off than I am now?
- Will my problem be solved? Or, will my decision bring me closer to my goal?
- Will I end up with a new problem that is worse? Or, will I be further from my goal?

The answers to these questions will help you to determine both positive and negative consequences of any action you consider.

Be Prepared to Compromise

Alternatives seldom offer only good consequences. Many alternatives represent a trade-off. You may have to *compromise*, or settle for a solution or a decision that is less than perfect. Compromising means giving up part of a goal to reach a decision.

For example, in the story, Heidi wanted a new bike. However, she felt that she could not have both the bike and the puppy. Her choice was to ask for the puppy and postpone obtaining a new bike. Heidi based her decision on values in her personal code. She was willing to work to pay for the puppy's upkeep as well as to save for the new bike. Her decision was not ideal. Instead, it represented a workable compromise.

PREDICTING CONSEQUENCES

The differences between problems and decisions lead to differences in considering consequences of alternatives. In problem solving, you are dealing with a change that has already occurred. In decision making, you are the source of a potential change—or of a decision not to cause a change.

Consequences are the results of actions or change. It is easier to evaluate consequences when you are dealing with change that has happened. You know the situation and the results.

In decision making, you are the agent for change. You are dealing with a change that has not yet occurred. It is more difficult to evaluate the consequences of actions or situations that do not exist. Also, there may be more consequences for each alternative in decision making. Thus, you may choose to spend more time considering consequences of decisions than consequences of problem-solving alternatives.

The time and effort you spend should relate to the importance and urgency of a situation. Be as thorough as you can, because you cannot pick the best alternative without considering consequences. You will have to live with the consequences of the alternative you choose. Be aware, too, that you also have to live with the consequences of rejecting other alternatives.

Urgency is a factor in some problem-solving situations. Your effort should match the level of urgency involved in a change. (© 1978, Rick Dieringer, Cincinnati, Ohio)

FOCUS ON YOUR FUTURE

EIDI TOOK A FINAL LOOK at her figures. They appeared accurate. The cost of buying the puppy would be just about the same as that new bike. She had included the cost of a dog license and shots for the puppy.

Parts to repair her old bike would be about $30. Dog food, dishes, and other necessities for the puppy probably would cost about $40 for the summer. Heidi decided she would offer to pay back those amounts once she began earning money on the paper route. She also planned to take full responsibility for the puppy's care and training. Altogether, she felt she had a good case to present to her parents. Heidi heard her mother arrive, and she knew the time had come to present that case.

"Hi, Mom. How was your day?" Heidi asked.

"Pretty good, Heidi. How about your day? Did you visit your little friend at the pet store?" her mother asked.

"Yes, but only for a couple of minutes. I had to come home and do some figuring," Heidi replied.

"Oh? And how did your figures come out?" her mother inquired.

"That's for you and Dad to decide, Mom. They look pretty good to me. Do you feel like talking about it now?"

"Sure, Heidi. But let me change clothes first, okay?"

Fifteen minutes later, Heidi had explained her plan. Her mother had listened attentively and had examined her sheet of figures.

"I suppose you want an answer right away," she said, smiling.

"I guess I do, especially if it's the answer I'm hoping for," Heidi said.

"All right. Your father and I discussed this situation last night. We felt that your attitude was very positive. We decided that, if you came up with a workable plan, you could have your puppy," her mother explained.

"Well, how do you feel about my plan, Mom?" Heidi asked.

"It seems like a very good plan. I'm sure that your father will agree," she said.

"All right! Would it be okay if I called Mr. Benson at the pet store?" Heidi asked.

"Go ahead and call," her mother said. "I'm sure that Mr. Benson will be just as relieved as I am to have this decision made." ■

Contingency plans anticipate and provide alternatives for the dangers involved in space flights. Backup systems are vital components of space vehicles. (Courtesy Florida Department of Commerce—Division of Tourism)

CONTINGENCY PLANNING

Change is not only constant; it comes from different sources. For this reason, there is always some uncertainty involved in alternatives. A course of action you will take to meet unforeseen consequences of a choice or action is a *contingency plan.* Contingencies occur by chance or as results of unexpected change. When you consider consequences, you should include contingency plans.

Examples of contingency planning can be related to the story about Heidi. One contingency plan would be to set aside some extra money in case the puppy becomes ill. The cost of veterinary care could affect seriously the budget Heidi had projected.

Another contingency might involve a change in her expected earnings. What if the paper route fell through? What if Heidi became ill and was unable to work?

In her position, Heidi could not be expected to deal with such major problems. She would have to rely upon her parents to deal with such contingencies.

Contingencies: Good or Bad?

Contingencies can be either good or bad. They can present you with problems, challenges, or opportunities.

Contingencies usually result from unexpected changes. A contingency can be a problem caused by change that occurs after you have solved a problem or made a decision. For example, you might plan to do a homework project the day before it is due in class. On that day, however, you become ill with a bad cold. The cold is the contingency. Your problem is that you cannot complete your homework on time. A contingency plan might have called for completion of your homework two days ahead of schedule. This would have provided a cushion in the event of unexpected change.

Flexibility Is the Key

The best way to handle contingencies is to plan ahead. Flexibility is the key to dealing with unforeseen circumstances.

Being flexible means that you leave the door open to the adoption of new alternatives when necessary. No one can see into the future. You cannot predict all possible results of an action. But you can prepare to deal with changes that affect your decisions. Think of the most likely changes that can occur in a situation. Your problem-solving or decision-making alternative should permit you to cope with those potential changes. Contingencies are discussed in greater detail in Unit 12.

CONTENT SUMMARY

The problem-solving/decision-making process begins with identifying and understanding your situation. It is important to understand the change that has caused a problem, or the goal behind a decision.

The next step is to analyze the problem to be solved or the decision to be made. Try to understand your motivation, which comes from your personal code. Criteria, which you use to measure the importance or urgency of a situation, also come from your personal code.

In decision making, you should always ask the question: What will happen if I do nothing? Since you are the agent of change, you are not obliged to take any action.

The third step in the process is to find alternatives. Identifying and evaluating alternatives is the heart of the process. This is where you should spend most of your time. The quality of your decision or problem solution depends upon the quality of the alternatives from which you choose.

Alternatives should be workable. They should have the potential for solving a problem or moving you closer to a goal. Ideas that are unworkable should be discarded.

It is also necessary to limit the number of alternatives. Usually, three to six is enough to think about. The number of alternatives should match the seriousness or urgency of the situation. Knowing when you have enough alternatives is an important skill.

In evaluating alternatives, you should consider the consequences—good and bad—for each one. Then you can compare the alternatives according to their potential consequences. Problem-solving consequences are based upon change that has occurred. Decision-making consequences are more difficult to evaluate because you are dealing with a situation that does not exist.

You should be willing to compromise. Problem solutions and decisions are almost never ideal.

Contingency planning is also important. Unexpected or potential changes can have good or bad results. Flexibility is the best way to deal with the uncertainty of change.

CAREER COMMENTARIES

1. **Considering the alternative of doing nothing helps you to determine the importance of a situation.**
   What kinds of questions can you answer by considering the alternative of doing nothing? Why is doing nothing always an alternative in decision making?

2. **You may have to compromise, or settle for a solution or decision that is less than perfect.**
   Why is the ability to compromise an important part of problem solving and decision making?

3. **When you consider consequences, you should include contingency plans.**
   Describe a situation in which a decision you made was affected by an unforeseen change. Did the change have positive or negative consequences? Did you have a contingency plan ready to deal with the change?

KEY TERMS

decision statement

motivation

criteria

urgency

open-minded

stimulate

compromise

contingency plan

12 Selecting and Evaluating an Appropriate Action

SELECTING AN ALTERNATIVE

Step five in the problem-solving/decision-making model is select-ing an alternative. Usually, the best alternative will become apparent after careful consideration of consequences.

In problem solving, there are many potential solutions to each problem. The one you select depends upon your personal code as well as upon circumstances. The best approach is to consider all potential alternatives with an open mind.

In decision making, you use criteria to establish *priorities.* A priority is a rating based on urgency or the overall long-term im-portance of a decision. For example, deciding whether to have a physical checkup is not typically an urgent matter for someone your age. However, having a yearly checkup may be a high priority for many adults. So, priorities can be based upon long-term impact as well as upon urgency. If a decision rates low on your list of priorities, the best alternative may be to do nothing.

Priorities are based upon criteria. The safety of a loved one is a strong priority.

181

A major commitment is required in a decision to join the Armed Forces. The commitment involves a dramatic change in life-style. (National Guard Photo)

Remember, doing nothing is always an alternative in decision making.

MAKING A COMMITMENT

When you have made your selection, you should make a commitment to implement a solution or a decision. Remember, a commitment is a promise to do something. Making a commitment means that you give both acceptance and support to your decision. Your commitment is a vital part of solving a problem or making a decision. If you make anything less than a full commitment, you will weaken your position in the future.

Changing Your Mind

A commitment does not take away your ability to change your mind about a solution or a decision. Remember that change is constant. You may receive new information about a situation that requires you to re-evaluate your choice. Or, a new alternative may come to your attention. If the new alternative offers more favorable consequences, you are free to change your mind.

Contingency Plans as Alternatives

Contingency plans can be applied to new problems, challenges, or opportunities. You should be prepared to deal with unforeseen circumstances. Contingency plans are a form of alternative kept in reserve to deal with unforeseen changes.

The time to plan for contingencies is when you select your course of action. Think about what will happen if new changes occur. For example, you might have relatives visit you from out of town. You decide to take them to the beach on Saturday, which will be their last day in town. But, what will you do if it rains on Saturday? Selecting an alternate activity in case of bad weather is an example of planning for contingencies.

GROUP PROBLEMS AND DECISIONS

Problem solving and decision making can be group activities as well as individual efforts. There are some meaningful differences between group and individual processes, but the steps are basically the same.

FOCUS ON YOUR FUTURE

VINCENT RAISED HIS HAND. He had an idea that he felt sure the class would like. So far, his classmates had been unable to agree on a plan for a class field trip.

Mrs. Davis saw Vincent's hand raised and called upon him. "Yes, Vincent? Do you have another idea?" his teacher asked.

"How about a trip to the State Capitol? We're studying government this semester. A trip to the Capitol would give us a chance to see government in action," he said.

"That's a great idea!" agreed Mary Beth.

"Sure," said Paul, "but what would we do up there? That's a long trip just to walk through a building."

Catherine turned and looked at Paul. "Are you serious? There's a lot to do in the Capitol. Isn't that right, Vincent?"

"It sure is. My older brother, Larry, went up there two years ago with his class. They had a real good time. Our state senator escorted them through the building. They got to sit in on some committee hearings and even met the lieutenant governor. Larry sure was excited when he got home," Vincent said.

Mrs. Davis agreed with Vincent's comments. "I had planned to go on that trip myself, in fact, but I became ill the day before," she recalled. "I remember how disappointed I was."

"If the rest of the class agrees, you may have another chance, Mrs. Davis," Catherine said. "Shall we take a vote now?"

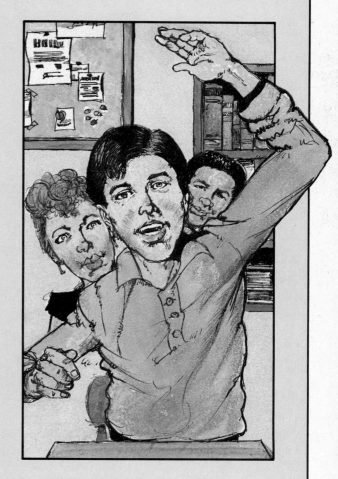

"That would be appropriate," the teacher said. "All in favor of a trip to the State Capitol, raise your hands."

The vote was unanimous.

"All right, then, that's decided. We'll plan a trip to the Capitol in May," Mrs. Davis said. "Everybody think about this over the weekend, and we'll start making plans Monday." ■

An important advantage of group problem solving and decision making is a wider source of ideas. A group usually can identify more alternatives than an individual. This is because a group offers a wider range of experience and a variety of personal codes.

A disadvantage of group activity is that it is more complicated. Since each group member has a unique personal code, it may be difficult to reach agreement. Thus, selecting an alternative can require more time and effort. It may also be more difficult for a group to make a commitment to a solution or decision.

The story that runs through this unit illustrates a number of problem-solving and decision-making situations. Some of the situations require group action, while others are individual efforts.

IMPLEMENTING A SOLUTION OR DECISION

Step six in the problem-solving/decision-making model is to *implement* your solution or decision. Implement means to carry out or accomplish by means of a practical plan.

You should do all you can to implement a decision or a solution. This effort can be quick and easy or time-consuming and difficult, depending upon the situation. For example, deciding what to wear to school should not take up much time or energy. You can implement that type of decision in a few minutes. However, improving your mathematics grade from a C to a B may require considerable time and effort.

Your own priorities determine how much energy and urgency to apply to implementing a solution or a decision. No two individuals have exactly the same priorities. Priorities are determined by the values in your personal code.

If you are working to solve a problem, you should determine what steps are necessary to implement the solution. Then, you should commit the time and energy necessary to carry out that plan. Choosing an alternative is different from implementing it. The solution will not happen just because you have identified it. Action is necessary to put a solution to work.

Decisions also require action. Again, you should determine what steps are needed to carry out a decision. Your priorities will help you to determine the urgency of the change you want to make. Then, follow through on your plan of action.

Group activity is more complicated than individual problem solving or decision making. However, a group has the advantage of a wider source of ideas.

Group Implementation

Group problem solving and decision making also require action. An organization usually has its own goals. The value or success of an organization may depend upon how well its members respond to the need for action.

For example, a group might decide upon a certain work project to raise funds for a specific goal. The decision will not produce results unless group members participate in the work project. Again, action is needed to make a change occur, or to reach a goal.

FOCUS ON YOUR FUTURE

MRS. DAVIS COULD TELL that her students were eager to start when class met on Monday. "Did all of you think about our field trip over the weekend?" she asked. "If so, let's begin to organize this effort.

"Our first step should be to assign some responsibilities. This is a class project, so you should make the plans. I'll help in any way necessary, but the decisions will be up to you. I would suggest that you choose a small committee to organize your efforts. You'll need someone to serve as chairperson. Others should be responsible for finances, planning, and communications.

"Before our election, please be aware that the committee members will have to devote some time to this project. If you feel you cannot make yourself available, don't accept the responsibility. That would only hurt the group's effort."

The remainder of the class period was given over to electing the committee. Vincent, who had suggested the State Capitol trip, was elected chairperson. Also chosen were Mary Beth, finances; Catherine, planning; and Paul, communications. It was agreed that the committee would meet after school and outline a plan of action. Proposals would be submitted to the class for approval the next day.

THE COMMITTEE TOOK SEATS around the teacher's desk when class began on Tuesday. Mrs. Davis took a seat in the audience. Vincent called the meeting to order and asked Catherine to present the committee's suggestions to the class.

Catherine related several basic proposals. First, she said, the committee felt it would be best to charter a bus for the trip. "We know this will be expensive. However, the weather may be quite warm in late May. The trip will take at least three hours each way. School buses are not air-conditioned, and they don't have restrooms. So, we propose to charter a bus. If a majority agrees, Paul will contact Holiday Charters this week. Can we have a show of hands on the question of chartering a bus?"

The entire class expressed support for a chartered bus.

"Fine. That's settled. We also talked about meals. Everyone should have breakfast before meeting here at school. If we all bring our lunches, we can either stop on the way or have a picnic at the Capitol. Vincent says his brother told him that there is a big park across the street from the building. We'll have to discuss what to do for our evening meal after some of our other plans are set," Catherine said. "Mary Beth, do you want to talk to the class about money?"

"Sure," Mary Beth said. "We estimate that the chartered bus will cost about $600. That's a lot of money, but it's our only real expense other than supper. If 30 of us go on the trip, it amounts to about $20 each. We're considering several money-raising ideas. I'll give you details when I've had a chance to do some checking."

Mrs. Davis stood up. "Class, I think this project is worthwhile and well within our abilities to arrange. Let me suggest, though, that you start your fund-raising efforts as soon as possible. Thanksgiving falls next week. You'll have a long weekend to get started with preliminary activities. From that point, we will have six months before the trip. You should plan to complete your fund-raising efforts at least two or three weeks beforehand. Otherwise, you will not be in a position to deal with any contingencies.

"I think the committee did a good job of getting the project off the ground. The rest of you can show your appreciation by cooperating and working with them. Vincent, when will you have your next meeting?" the teacher asked.

"We plan to get together Thursday afternoon to talk about fund-raising projects, Mrs. Davis. Can we report to the class on Friday?" Vincent asked.

"That will be fine," Mrs. Davis replied. "Now, let's get back to our regular work, shall we?" ■

Instant feedback is common at rock concerts and other entertainment and sports events.
(Nawrocki Stock Photo)

FEEDBACK AND EVALUATION

Feedback, as you know, is information you receive about the results of your actions. Feedback tells you whether your solutions or decisions are successful.

Remember that you are involved in the continuing results of your actions. You are affected by the consequences of your actions. You are also responsible for those consequences. Your involvement in a situation does not end with your decision. You cannot take an action and just walk away and forget about it.

Feedback helps you to evaluate how good or bad an action is. Feedback helps you to evaluate the consequences of your decision or action.

Follow-Up

Based upon your evaluation, you may find it necessary to adjust or modify the decision you have implemented. This continuing involvement is called *follow-up*. Follow-up also may involve entirely new decisions, based upon the feedback you receive from earlier decisions.

188

Cheerleaders work to produce higher levels of feedback than normally might be generated during a sports event. (Courtesy Photri)

Feedback frequently gives you new information about existing situations. For example, you might decide to spend a weekend camping at a state park. Upon contacting park authorities, however, you learn that a permit must be obtained well in advance. You then face the necessity of modifying your plans to follow through with your decision. First, you will have to allow for the cost of a permit. Second, you will have to make an earlier decision about a date for your camping trip.

The Continuing Chain of Decisions

Feedback from a decision frequently leads you to make additional decisions. Remember, whether you are solving a problem or making a decision, you are causing a change to occur. One change often leads to another. Thus, decision making can become a continuing chain.

To illustrate, imagine that you decide to buy a used car. Soon after the purchase, you decide to replace the front tires, which have very little tread left. While the wheels are off, you decide to have the mechanic check the front brakes. The mechanic determines that you need brake service. You decide to have the rear brakes checked as well, and they also need service. While the car is on the hoist, the mechanic notices that the muffler is almost rusted through. Your decision to replace two tires has led to a complete brake job, front and rear, and a muffler replacement. One decision has led to another, due to feedback.

FOCUS ON YOUR FUTURE

MARY BETH SHRUGGED. "I don't see any way to get around it. We just have to have that down payment by May 1 to reserve our bus," she said.

"I don't think that's much of a problem," Paul said.

"Neither do I," Vincent agreed. "If we don't have most of our funds by then, we probably won't make it anyway."

"Let's tell the class that fund raising has to be completed before the end of April," Catherine suggested. "And, to get everyone started, let's set some target dates along the way. Otherwise, some people may wait until the last minute."

"Good idea," Paul said. "Maybe we should have monthly targets and reports. I also think Vincent's idea of breaking the class into teams of five or six people is excellent. We can keep a running score and set up competition among the teams."

Mary Beth looked at her notebook. "As I started to report before, the recycling center gave me some prices. They pay $40 a ton for newsprint. Aluminum cans are worth 32 cents a pound, if they are crushed. The man at the center said that it takes about 37 cans to make a pound. So, to raise $300 with aluminum cans, we need about 35,000 cans. That's almost 1,200 cans per student. To raise $300 from newspapers, we need 16,000 pounds, or 533 pounds per student. It sounds like an awful lot, but it's not so bad on a monthly basis. We have five months, so that's 240 aluminum cans and about 100 pounds of newsprint per student per month."

"You must be a mathematical genius!" Paul exclaimed.

"This little calculator I got for my birthday helped some," Mary Beth admitted.

Paul laughed. "Okay, we have our work cut out. Let's break the news to our classmates tomorrow. We'll get feedback from them and from Mrs. Davis and figure out where to go from there."

"That's fine," Mary Beth said. "And we can ask for more fund-raising ideas. If the class can do some other things, we can reduce some of those numbers." ■

CONTINGENCY PLANNING

Part of your continuing involvement with a decision should include contingency plans. Unforeseen changes may occur and require new decisions on your part.

To illustrate, consider the role of an *understudy* in a stage production. An understudy is a performer who learns a part and prepares to substitute in an emergency. For example, an actor or actress might become ill and be unable to perform. The understudy would take the place of the regular performer. In show business, understudies represent a standard form of contingency planning.

In decision making, contingency plans are alternatives to be considered if unexpected changes occur. It is impossible to plan for all possible changes, but it is valuable to identify those most likely to happen. Contingency planning helps you prepare for the unexpected.

Contingency plans are alternatives to be considered when unexpected changes occur. Understudies in show business are familiar examples of contingency planning. (Courtesy Royal Crown Cola Co.)

Long-range decision making includes career selection. Long-range goals are subject to frequent and major revisions.

LONG-RANGE DECISION MAKING

Long-range decision making usually is general in nature. More and more changes occur as time passes. Thus, long-range goals are subject to frequent and major revisions.

When you begin to think about a career, you are engaged in long-range decision making. You are thinking about your future. Remember that decisions you make now are based upon your existing personal code. Your code will undergo change as you grow in age and experience. You may change your mind as new experiences alter your personal code.

External changes also may affect your decisions. An unexpected opportunity may arise in a career area different from one you selected. If this happens, you will have to decide between your long-range plan and the new opportunity.

For example, a person might be building a career as a construction boss for a large contracting company. Suddenly, an opportunity comes along for that person to take over a smaller company as the owner. This situation requires a major career decision. The individual's personal code would help determine that decision.

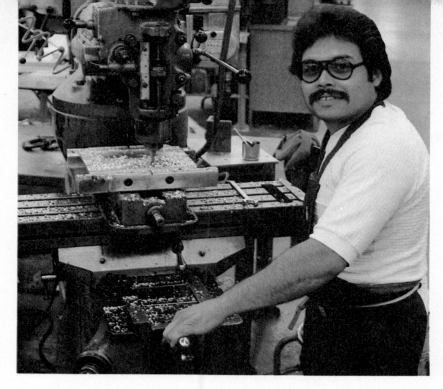

Entrepreneurs usually forego job security for increased opportunity and independence.

The construction boss has a high-paying job with good benefits and a secure future. If he owned his own company, however, he would become an *entrepreneur.* An entrepreneur is a person who invests money, time, and energy as the owner of a business enterprise. As an entrepreneur, he would have the opportunity to earn as much as his knowledge, skills, and ambition permit. However, being an entrepreneur involves risk. He would be trading security for opportunity—and also for independence.

This type of decision requires thorough study of the possible consequences. Changing career direction may also require a major change in an individual's personal code. Part of the commitment to such a change is the willingness to deal with new and unforeseen situations. Realistic contingency plans can be the difference between success and failure.

The process method is the best way to deal with long-range decisions. An organized approach helps you to identify and to understand your goals. The decision-making model also helps you to make a commitment and to implement your decision. Finally, the process method helps you to adjust or modify your decision based on feedback and future change.

FOCUS ON YOUR FUTURE

AFTER HER REPORT to the class, Mary Beth asked if anyone had questions or comments. "We need firm commitments from everyone on what they can contribute," she said. "Otherwise, this project won't work."

Catherine, who was in charge of planning, offered a suggestion. "Each of you should contact your friends and neighbors right away. Ask them to save their newspapers and empty aluminum cans for you. Offer to collect their contributions once a week or more often if necessary."

Mrs. Davis interrupted. "My husband said he would collect your papers and cans in his pickup truck. Now all we need is a place for storage and volunteers to bundle papers and crush cans," she said.

"Vincent and I came up with a signup sheet," Paul said. "We need to have everyone's telephone number. Four volunteers per week should be enough to get the cans and papers ready for the recyclers. We can turn the stuff in once a month."

Mary Beth then told the class that the proceeds would be placed in a special savings account. "My dad works at the bank, and he said he would take care of the account. The money won't earn much interest, but it will be safe. And, we'll always know just how much we have."

Vincent explained that the committee wanted to be sure enough money would be available for the trip. "Our contingency plan is to hold a couple of car wash fund raisers in the spring," he said. "That way, we'll be prepared in case the bus charter fees go up or something unexpected happens. We think it's a good idea to set our fund-raising goal slightly higher. It would be easy to come up short if a bunch of kids got sick or something."

Catherine said that she had visited the local office of the area's state assemblyman. "The assemblyman will meet us at the Capitol. He'll make sure that we get to see everything. We also may be able to sit in on a committee hearing," she said. "The local office will help us finalize plans when we choose our date."

Paul concluded the report. "Mrs. Davis said we could set aside the first five minutes of class each day for the project. The committee will make regular progress reports, and we'll expect the class to be involved. Please let us know ahead of time if you can't make an activity. That way, we can ask someone else to fill in for you. If we all pull together, we should have a really nice tour next May." ■

USING PROBLEM-SOLVING AND DECISION-MAKING SKILLS

You can find opportunities each day to use the problem-solving/decision-making model. Minor problems and decisions do not require much time or effort. However, it is always better to deal with problems and decisions in an organized manner.

The units in Part IV deal with problems and decisions you will face almost every day of your life as a working citizen.

CONTENT SUMMARY

Selecting an alternative is a vital step in the problem-solving/decision-making model. When you select an alternative, you should make a commitment to accept and support your choice.

Continuing change may cause you to alter a decision. You can change your mind as you receive new information.

Contingency plans should be a part of the alternative you select. A contingency plan serves as an alternative to deal with unforeseen change.

Group problem solving and decision making involves the same basic steps as the individual

process. There are two significant differences, however. First, groups provide more sources for ideas. Second, group action is more complicated. It is more difficult to reach agreement and produce a commitment to action.

Implementing an alternative means to carry out or accomplish a decision with a practical plan. Your priorities help you to determine how much energy and urgency you assign to a problem or a decision.

Implementation is an important step in the model. Selecting an alternative is not enough. Change does not occur until your decision is put into action.

Feedback helps you to evaluate the consequences of your actions. Based on feedback, you may adjust or modify a decision. Such activity is called follow-up. Through feedback, evaluation, and follow-up, you are involved in the continuing results of your actions.

One decision or change often leads to another. More often than not, you find yourself involved in a continuing chain of change. Each decision leads to new situations that may require more decisions.

Contingency planning is a means of dealing with unforeseen change beforehand. The use of understudies in show business is an example of contingency planning.

Career planning is a form of long-range decision making. The process method is the best way to deal with long-range decisions. Remember that your personal code will change as you grow in age and experience. Because of continuing change, long-range decisions are particularly subject to alteration.

CAREER COMMENTARIES

1. If you make anything less than a full commit-
    ment, you will weaken your position in the
    future.
    Describe an experience in which you made less
    than a full commitment to a decision. What
    was the result?

2. Feedback from a decision frequently leads
    you to make additional decisions.
    Identify a situation in the past week in which
    you made a decision based on feedback. Also
    describe the earlier decision.

3. In decision making, contingency plans are
    alternatives to be considered if unexpected
    changes occur.
    Think of examples of contingency planning.
    Describe one example that might occur in
    sports, government, television broadcasting, or
    family life.

KEY TERMS

priority

implement

follow-up

understudy

entrepreneur

IV

Personal Skills for Your Future

WHEN YOU BECOME a working citizen, you will have an income. Your income will be the means through which you will satisfy many of your needs and wants. In turn, how well you satisfy your needs and wants will depend largely upon how well you manage your income.

Unit 13 discusses the application of the process method in making spending decisions. The effect of life-style on purchasing priorities also is explored. The major topics covered in Unit 14 are personal and family budgeting and the use of credit. Unit 15 discusses consumer practices that can help you to become a smart shopper. Also covered are consumer protection laws and agencies, and ways in which you can protect yourself against fraud.

13

Spending Money

YOUR LEARNING JOB

When you have completed the reading assignments and exercises in this unit, you should be able to:

☐ Apply the process method in making spending decisions.

☐ Identify major factors that influence spending decisions.

☐ Explain the effect of life-style on buying priorities.

☐ Use comparison shopping techniques.

☐ Identify sources for information to increase your market awareness.

☐ Describe buying skills that help you to develop good purchasing practices.

SPENDING TO SATISFY NEEDS AND WANTS

You probably don't spend large sums of money at this point in your life. Your only source of personal income may be allowances, gifts, and some small jobs such as babysitting or mowing lawns. However, now is the time to begin developing the buying skills that can help you to become a wise *consumer*. A consumer is a person who buys and uses the products of business and industry.

A *product* is something of value that is offered for sale by a business. There are two basic kinds of products: *goods* and *services.* A good is a physical item, such as a video game or a pair of jeans. A service is an action that benefits others. Hair styling and automobile repair are examples of services.

Spending **decisions** are made to satisfy needs and wants. Whether an item is a need or a want may depend upon your circumstances.

People spend money to satisfy their needs and wants. As discussed in Unit 2, everyone has basic needs such as shelter, food, and clothing. The ways in which these and other needs are met is called life-style.

If you had an unlimited supply of money, you could select any life-style you desired. Most people do not possess unlimited wealth, however, so they must establish priorities for the use of their money.

Your income will probably remain small while you are in school. You may decide to obtain a part-time job in high school. However, your parents or guardians will continue to furnish most of your needs and wants. When you become a working citizen you will have to assume major financial responsibilities.

When you get a full-time job, you probably will contribute part of your income for household expenses. If you decide to move away and live alone, you will be responsible for all your needs and wants. If you get married, someone else's needs and wants will become part of your responsibility.

Regardless of your situation, your primary goal should be to make sensible, informed spending decisions. Such decisions help you to obtain the best values for your money. The best way to achieve this goal is to plan ahead. Approach spending decisions in an organized manner. As discussed throughout Part III, the process method is the best way to make decisions.

USING THE PROCESS METHOD FOR SPENDING DECISIONS

Spending decisions are just like any others. The decision-making model in Unit 10 works quite well for financial decisions. To illustrate, think ahead a few years to the time when you may need an automobile. Perhaps you are about to start your first full-time job. Circumstances require that you have a car to travel between home and job. You already have decided that you need personal transportation. Your next decision is what car to buy.

There are no ideal cars available from family or close friends, so you must shop in the open market. Assume that you have determined how much you can afford to spend. Also assume that

you have narrowed your choice to three cars. Using the decision-making model, you have already completed the first three steps:

1. **Identify the decision to be made.** You have determined that you must purchase a car.

2. **Make a statement analyzing the decision.** You have decided how much money you can spend to buy a car.

3. **Find alternatives.** You have located three cars that meet your basic needs.

Having shopped around, you are ready to move on to the remaining steps in the decision-making process. Remember that you should be receiving feedback throughout the process. Feedback may come in the form of advice from persons you trust or from individuals who have greater experience. You should use this

Major spending decisions require careful consideration. The process method is especially valuable when a long-range spending decision is being considered. (© Harry Gruvaert/Magnum Photos, Inc.)

feedback to evaluate your progress as you go. You should also be prepared to revise your attitudes if new information changes your situation. Your remaining steps are:

4. **Evaluate the possible consequences of each alternative.** Compare the cars. You should consider qualities such as economy, reliability, and *utility.* Utility is the usefulness of an item. If you intend to carry large amounts of cargo, you may need a station wagon or even a pickup truck. In this step, you evaluate quality according to your own needs and wants.

Price plays a part in many spending decisions. Pumping your own gas can save you as much as 47 cents a gallon at this gasoline station. (© Pierre Kopp/West Light)

5. **Choose the best alternative.** Select the particular car you identify as best.

6. **Implement the alternative.** Purchase the car you chose.

7. **Evaluate the final results.** This step will continue indefinitely. Your experiences with the car's performance will determine if you made a good choice. Your experience also will help guide you in making future decisions.

FOCUS ON YOUR FUTURE

CHARLOTTE HEARD the newspaper land outside the front door. She put on a robe and went outside to get the morning paper. Removing the string, she laid the paper flat on the kitchen table. She found the advertising insert she wanted.

Sure enough, the designer jeans she wanted were on sale, at 25 percent off. That was what she had hoped. At that price, her mother would have to admit the jeans were a good buy.

"May I borrow the sports section when you're through?" asked her father, as he sat down at the table.

"Oh, Dad. I haven't even touched your precious sports section," Charlotte protested.

"Well, how about letting me have the comics?" asked her brother Phil.

"Here, Phil. Have the rest of the paper. I just want the Henshaw's advertising insert," Charlotte said.

Her mother entered the kitchen. "What's all the excitement?" she asked. Noticing the insert on the table, she nodded her head. "Oh, I see. Those jeans must be on sale. Is that right, Charlotte?"

"Yes, Mom. And they're 25 percent off. Isn't that great?" Charlotte asked.

Her mother was not so enthusiastic. "Well, that brings them down close to the price of the jeans I saw at the discount store. I suppose we can afford that price."

"Don't you think that's a pretty good value, Mom? We'd be getting designer jeans for about the same price as the cheaper ones," Charlotte said.

Her father looked up from the sports pages. "There's more to value than price, Charlotte. Putting someone's signature on a pair of jeans does not make them better as an article of clothing. The appeal of designer jeans is mainly a style consideration. And, I understand why that's important to you. You want to wear a certain brand to be in style," her father said.

Her mother continued. "Just for the experience, why don't you try on both pairs? We can visit both stores this afternoon after school. Let's see which pair fits better and which is better from a quality standpoint."

"Okay, Mom, that sounds fair," agreed Charlotte. "But, if it's close, I'd rather have the designer jeans, okay?"

"If it's close, I'd go ahead and buy the designer jeans," her father said. "One aspect of value is how satisfied you'll be with the purchase. If that particular style is so important, then you may prefer to compromise in some other areas." ■

FACTORS THAT INFLUENCE SPENDING

There are many factors that can influence your spending decisions. Some factors that have a general effect on your values are:

- Family. Most of your strongest feelings and opinions come from the influence of your parents and other family members.

- Friends. As you grow older, your friends tend to have a stronger influence on your preferences. You work harder to earn the approval of friends. Generally, less effort is required to keep your family's acceptance.

- Advertising. Promotion of goods and services reaches you from many sources. Major sources include: radio and television, newspapers, magazines, direct mail, and telephone sales.

- Word of mouth. People who are especially happy with a product frequently tell others. People often boast about the bargains they obtain on particular goods or services. The more attractive it sounds, the more you may be motivated to seek the same or similar bargains.

A common thread runs through these motivating factors: Each has an effect upon your code of conduct. Some may *reinforce*, or strengthen, your existing values. Others may change your opinions or preferences. You should be aware of these changes. Understanding why your code is being reinforced or changed helps you to evaluate your motives.

LIFE-STYLE AND SPENDING DECISIONS

Your life-style affects the way you make spending decisions. Depending upon your family background, you may be *conservative* or *liberal* in your attitude toward spending money. Conservative means cautious, moderate, and tending to maintain existing or traditional views. A conservative person tends to reject risk. Liberal means open-minded, receptive to new ideas, and generous. A liberal person tends to follow new trends.

There is no right or wrong way to view life-style. Each individual holds life-style values according to his or her personal code. However, life-style decisions should be based upon an understanding of realistic limitations.

Needs or wants? Large, expensive homes and luxury cars exceed their owners' basic needs for shelter and transportation. These possessions satisfy wants as well as needs. (© 1977, Craig Aurness/West Light)

To illustrate, you may have a strong desire to own an expensive sports car. There is nothing wrong with such a goal. However, if your income is limited, you may have to sacrifice too many other things to pay for the car. Your personal code will help you to decide how much you are willing to give up for that single want. The decision-making process will help you to determine the consequences of such a purchase.

Individual purchasing decisions frequently are considered from a narrow viewpoint. There is a tendency to overlook or ignore the long-range results of a decision. The process method helps you to take a realistic look at potential consequences.

DEVELOPING GOOD SPENDING HABITS

Spending decisions should be approached in an organized way. There are a number of spending habits you can develop to strengthen your decision-making efforts. This approach also will help you to avoid bad spending habits.

Separating Needs and Wants

You should make sure that your needs are met first. Remember, adequate food, shelter, and clothing are basic needs. They are necessary for your survival. You also have other needs, such as transportation, health care, and recreation.

Attractiveness of a product, emphasized in advertising, often is a starting point in consumer evaluation. (Courtesy Pontiac Motor Division/General Motors Corporation)

You can go beyond necessity in satisfying these needs. At that point, you are dealing with wants. The question is, how far do you want to go in exceeding your needs?

For example, consider your needs for shelter. Can you be satisfied with a modest but comfortable home in an average neighborhood? Or, do you desire a large, luxurious home in an exclusive area? Either choice will meet your need for adequate shelter. Your wants involve the level of satisfaction you desire.

Transportation is another area in which needs quickly change into wants. Say that you need a reliable automobile to get to and from work each day. That is your need. You may decide that your car must have air conditioning, a stereo system, and other optional equipment. These extras are wants. There is nothing wrong with deciding to purchase the extras. However, it is important to be able to identify needs and wants, and to be able to tell them apart.

Recognizing Value

One measure of the *value* of a good or service is its price. Value also means quality, usefulness, and reliability. As a consumer, you should measure the value of goods and services by combining these factors. The real value of a product lies in the combination of quality, usefulness, and reliability—rated against its price.

Appearance and style may be other important factors in determining value, depending upon your personal code. In many cases, attractiveness of a product is a starting point in evaluation. People often begin there and then examine a product for quality, reliability, and other practical factors.

Comparison Shopping

Wise consumers compare before they buy. *Comparison shopping* means to examine two or more alternative choices before deciding what to purchase. In many cases, price is the main factor in comparison shopping. Price is your main concern when you have decided upon the item you want to buy. That type of comparison shopping involves obtaining the best deal from among the available sellers.

Special sales events often lead to hurried purchasing decisions based upon reduced prices. The process method helps you remember to consider other important factors.

Other forms of comparison shopping deal with considerations such as quality, appearance, price value, and trade-in or resale value. The extent of your efforts in comparison shopping depends upon the size and importance of the purchase. For example, you will probably spend more time shopping for a car than for a pair of shoes. Your main goal is to obtain the best possible price on a product that promises the greatest satisfaction.

To illustrate, consider shopping for a video game. You are shown two video games that are roughly equal in operation. One of the games costs $50 less than the other. However, the less expensive product has a history of breaking down after a few months of use. The more expensive competitor is considered to be more reliable. You have to make a value judgment. Would you rather save $50 and take the chance of an earlier breakdown? Or, is reliability worth spending an extra $50? The answer can be found in your personal code.

When you are trying to determine the value of a product, there may be several sources of worthwhile information. Owners or users of products can offer opinions based upon their experience. Consumer advice on many kinds of products is available from government agencies and from private organizations. There are also a number of consumer magazines that offer information on product quality.

Timing of Purchases

When possible, plan to make major purchases at times when prices are favorable. The small appliance on display for $39.95 today may go on sale for $29.95 next week. Watch for sales. Many large companies have sales on certain products at regular times. Some sales are scheduled around holidays and seasonal changes. Off-season prices are often lower. For example, winter goods may be less expensive during the summer, when *demand* is low. Demand is the amount of a product that consumers are willing to buy at a given price.

Some sales are held because the *supply* of an item is too high. Supply is the amount of a product that businesses are willing to sell at a given price.

Many consumer goods, such as cars, television sets, and major appliances, undergo model changes each year. When new models are introduced, the previous year's models often are sold at greatly reduced prices. These sales usually are called *clearance sales.* If price is your main consideration, clearance sales may be attractive. You have to decide which is more important: a reduced price or the features of the newer model.

Timing is important in planning periodic purchases, such as clothing. Prices usually are more favorable during sales, whether regular or special events.

(© Gabor Demjen/Stock, Boston)

Fashion retains value in clothing and other goods. Fashionable clothes stay in style. Avoid fads because they usually last only a short time. Fads also promote impulse buying.

Avoiding Impulse Buying

A good rule for a consumer is to buy with your head, not your heart. *Impulse buying* means making a purchase based on a sudden decision, or impulse. Buying on impulse frequently brings disappointing consequences. The weakness of impulse buying lies in the failure to evaluate alternatives or potential consequences. In other words, impulse buying is the opposite of making a decision using the process method.

Another weakness of impulse buying is that it usually involves a lack of product evaluation. An impulse purchase may be made on the basis of appearance or some other appeal that may be short-lived. Fads tend to promote impulse buying.

Reading Between the Lines

Reading between the lines means to look beneath the surface. Promotional material, whether a printed advertisement or a broadcast commercial, usually gives only positive information about a product. As a consumer, you have to use good judgment in evaluating advertising and sales promotions.

Use judgment in evaluating product descriptions in advertisements and promotions. "New" or "improved" does not necessarily mean a product is better from your standpoint.

Probably the most overused words in advertising are "new" and "improved." New does not necessarily mean better. Improved does not always mean better, either. Sometimes a product is changed in a way that may cause you to turn away from it. You may have preferred the product the way it was.

General claims of product value don't mean much. However, specific claims usually can be proved or disproved. Remember that the claim is only as good as the proof offered to back it.

FOCUS ON YOUR FUTURE

RICARDO LOOKED AROUND. His older sister had wandered over to the garden tool display. Ricardo turned to the salesperson. "Excuse me a minute," he said. "I want to speak with my sister."

Carmen glanced up as Ricardo approached. "Did you find the right electric drill?" she asked.

"Yes, and it's really neat. It's a reversible, variable-speed model, just like Dad said he needed. It's the perfect birthday gift, Carmen."

"I agree, Ricardo, but did you check the price?" Carmen asked.

"Yes. The salesperson said the drills were on sale for 10 percent off. It's only $59.95, but we have to decide right away. The sale ends today."

"Did you say it is *only* $59.95?" Carmen asked.

"Yes," Ricardo replied. "What's wrong? Isn't a 10 percent discount a good deal?"

"Normally, yes," his sister said. "But you should learn to shop around and compare prices, Ricardo. The same drill is on sale at the discount center for $49.95. I know that you like to shop in this store, but do you want to spend $10 for the privilege?"

Ricardo shook his head. "I sure don't. I guess I'll have to be more aware from now on. Say, we could use that $10 to get Dad a set of drill bits for his new drill," he said.

Carmen leaned close and whispered to her brother: "Don't look now, but here comes your favorite salesperson."

"Have you decided yet?" asked the smiling salesperson.

"No, not quite," Ricardo answered. "My sister and I are going to look around some more. Thanks for your help." ∎

Rented apartments are a common form of housing in many parts of the country. Rentals are especially attractive for younger persons just starting their working careers.

PLANNING FOR CONTINUING EXPENSES

As a working citizen, a major part of your income will be used to provide for your basic needs. Shelter, food, and clothing are survival needs. There are many choices available to you in each category. However, these are the first needs you must satisfy from your paycheck. Thus, your decisions in these areas are important to your life-style and to the efficient use of your earnings.

Housing Alternatives

One primary decision is whether to buy or to rent a dwelling. This option probably will not be open to you during your first few years of work. Purchasing a home requires a sizable investment and an established *credit rating. Credit* is borrowing someone else's money for a special purpose. Your credit rating is an evaluation of your ability and willingness to repay a debt. Credit is discussed in Unit 14.

Housing is the largest single living expense for most people. Housing choices depend upon several factors:

- Your income level

- Location and availability of housing

- Your life-style.

Whether you relocate because of work, or simply decide to leave home, there are several housing alternatives to consider. The size and type of community in which you live will determine the availability of these alternatives:

- Rooming or boarding house. These facilities usually include a furnished room, linen and cleaning services, and meals. Rooming houses are becoming scarce. In some areas, however, they are convenient for a single working person.

- Furnished room. This form of rental usually offers greater freedom than a rooming house. You can come and go as you please because no meals are served. However, you may have to eat most of your meals in restaurants.

- Furnished apartment. This is the simplest form of housekeeping. A furnished apartment is equipped with at least basic

Houses are preferred by many people because they offer greater privacy. Houses may be rented furnished or unfurnished.
(© Chris Cross/Uniphoto Picture Agency)

items of furniture. Thus, you have no major expenses for furniture or equipment. However, you may have to buy your own linens (towels, sheets, etc.), dishes, and cooking utensils. Kitchen facilities are available so that you can prepare your own meals if you desire. You are responsible for house cleaning and for maintaining the furnishings in good condition.

- Unfurnished apartment. An unfurnished apartment has no furniture. This life-style represents a major commitment because you provide your own furnishings. If you rent an unfurnished apartment, you may have to acquire one or more major appliances, especially a refrigerator. At this level, you become involved in ownership. You select your own furnishings. However, you must pay for them, maintain them, and move them if you relocate.

- House rental. Many people prefer the greater privacy of a house. Houses may be rented either furnished or unfurnished. In some cases, the renter agrees to perform routine maintenance, such as lawn and yard care.

- Home ownership. For many people, buying a home is a major goal. Home ownership has advantages and responsibilities. Purchasing a home is the most important life-style decision most people ever make.

Consequences of Home Ownership

Buying a home is a major life-style decision for a number of reasons. First, it is the largest financial investment most people consider during their lives. Buying a home is also a major financial responsibility.

For many people, the advantages of home ownership far outweigh their concerns about the responsibilities they must assume. Advantages of home ownership include:

- Equity. As you pay for a home, your share of ownership, or *equity*, increases. Property values also tend to rise, thus making a home a worthwhile financial investment.

- Tax advantages. A large portion of a house payment, especially during the first years of ownership, represents *interest*. Interest is money you pay for the use of someone else's money. In this case, a financial institution has made you a *mortgage loan*. A mortgage loan is a special loan for the purchase of land, especially a home. Interest is a *deduction* on your income tax return. A deduction is an amount that you subtract from the taxable portion of your earnings. The more interest you pay, the greater the deduction.

- Pride of ownership. Your personal code determines how important ownership is to you.

- Flexibility. As a homeowner, you decide how you want your dwelling to look. You are limited only by your imagination, the availability of money, and local land use regulations.

Responsibilities of home ownership include:

- Financial. The down payment on a home is a major investment. House payments tend to be higher than rent. In addition, property taxes must be paid.

- Upkeep. The homeowner is responsible for the maintenance and upkeep of property. Depending upon the size and type of property, upkeep can require a major investment in time and energy. Repairs also are the responsibility of the homeowner. If you have the skills and time to do your own repairs, you can save a great deal of money.

Home ownership involves responsibilities, such as maintenance and repairs. However, ownership also offers rewards in financial and lifestyle terms. (© Craig Aurness/West Light)

- Decisions if you move. You may move to a different area or decide to purchase a larger home. As a homeowner, you have an obligation to pay off your mortgage. You can satisfy this obligation by selling your home. If conditions are unfavorable, you may decide to retain ownership and rent the home.

Decisions about home ownership usually are far-reaching. The process method is useful in making such decisions. The consequences of alternatives can have a major effect upon your life. The decision-making model can be followed in giving full consideration to those consequences.

Food Costs

Consumers in large communities tend to be price-conscious when shopping for food and household supplies. Supermarket chains advertise weekly specials and promotions to attract customers. The careful shopper can save money by comparing advertisements.

However, shoppers are concerned about more than the prices of food. Quality is a major consideration. Other factors that can attract or repel shoppers include variety, cleanliness, and convenience.

Planning is necessary if you want to save money on groceries. This is an area in which small, individual savings add up in the

Eating can be fun when the meal is special. However, grocery shopping is a serious, day-to-day business.

long run. Prices of some food products, especially vegetables and fruits, vary considerably from one season to the next. Many grocery items are less expensive when purchased in large quantities. Rather than merely looking at the price of a package, look for *unit price.* Unit price is the cost of a measured portion of a product. For example, a 10-ounce package of a product may sell for $1.00, while a 20-ounce package costs $1.80. The smaller package has a unit price of 10 cents an ounce. The larger package has a unit price of 9 cents per ounce. The larger package is more economical—as long as you can use the greater quantity.

Home freezers can be a good investment for budget-conscious families. A freezer makes it possible to stock up on certain items when prices are low.

Careful shopping helps you to get the most for your money. There are many variables in food pricing.

Planning meals is another method of holding down food costs. Well-planned menus help you to avoid unnecessary purchases and to prevent waste.

Clothing Costs

Price is a key factor in shopping for clothes. Again, careful shoppers watch for advertised specials. Most stores tend to conduct periodic sales. You should also watch for seasonal bargains. When demand is low, prices often are lower.

Careful shoppers pay close attention to clothing prices, watching for sales and advertised specials.

There are other considerations in building and maintaining a satisfactory wardrobe. Some rules are:

- Dress for your needs. Avoid impulse buying. Look for the kinds of clothes you need for work and for leisure. Your wardrobe should match your life-style. Buy clothing that fits you well and looks good on you.

- Follow fashion. Avoid fads. Styles that have only a temporary appeal may go out of fashion too soon. You don't want a closet full of outdated clothes. Loud or extreme fashions can make the wrong kind of statement about you. The best fashion strategy is to have consistently neat and well-fitting clothes.

- Take care of your clothes. Keep them clean and in good repair. Neat, well-matched outfits are the key to a well-dressed appearance.

USING COMMON SENSE

Common sense and an organized approach to decision making are your best tools as a consumer. When you spend money for your needs and wants, look for the best value for your dollar. The process approach can be most helpful in making spending decisions.

A wise consumer need not be stingy or watch every penny. Your goal should be to develop sensible spending habits. The more successful you are at getting value for your money, the more alternatives you will have for your income. Managing your money is discussed in Unit 14.

The best fashion strategy is to wear consistently neat and well-fitting clothes.

CONTENT SUMMARY

You spend money to satisfy your needs and wants. Your primary needs include shelter, food, and clothing. Spending wisely means getting the most for your money.

Spending decisions, especially for major items such as a home or an automobile, are best made with an organized approach. The process method of decision making works well for consideration of spending alternatives.

Your spending decisions can be influenced by a number of sources. Your family, friends, advertising, and word of mouth are major influences in product purchasing decisions. Your life-style also affects the way you make spending decisions.

Good spending habits include: separating needs and wants, recognizing value, comparison shopping, and proper timing of purchases. Other good habits are to avoid impulse buying and to look beneath the surface appeal of advertising and sales promotions.

Your basic needs—housing, food, and clothing—will take up a sizable portion of your income as a working citizen. Income level and life-style are major factors in determining the type of housing you select. There are advantages and disadvantages to each type of housing, from boarding houses through home ownership.

Owning your own home has more advantages, and more responsibilities, than other forms of housing. Your circumstances and your personal code will determine how you feel about housing.

Food costs can be controlled through careful shopping and planning of menus. Individual decisions may amount to only pennies. However, thousands of grocery shopping decisions can produce large savings over a year's time.

Clothing is another spending area in which informed, thoughtful spending habits can bring savings. Follow fashions but stay away from fads. Neat, clean, well-fitting clothing is your best plan for being in fashion.

Your primary goal in spending money should be to obtain the best value for your dollar. Sensible spending habits will give you more flexibility with your income.

CAREER COMMENTARIES

1. **Your wants involve the level of satisfaction you desire.**
   Explain the difference between a need and a want. Describe a situation in which a need can become a want.

2. **The real value of a product is its quality, usefulness, and reliability—rated against its price.**
   Identify a product for which price is your chief consideration. Identify another product for which quality is more important than price. Explain your reasons for selecting each example.

3. **Rather than merely looking at the price of a package, look for unit price.**
   Describe an example of unit pricing in which a product becomes less expensive as the size of the package increases.

KEY TERMS

consumer

product

good

service

utility

reinforce

conservative

liberal

value

comparison shopping

demand

supply

clearance sale

impulse buying

credit rating

credit

equity

interest

mortgage loan

deduction

unit price

Developing a Money Management Plan

YOUR LEARNING JOB

When you have completed the reading assignments and exercises in this unit, you should be able to:

☐ Discuss budgeting as a plan for spending money so as to satisfy your needs and wants.

☐ Use the decision-making process to set up a personal or family budget.

☐ Explain alternatives for financing major purchases.

☐ Describe some major consumer credit plans.

☐ Explain advantages and disadvantages of the use of credit.

PLANNING TO SATISFY NEEDS AND WANTS

At your present age, you are considered a dependent of parents or guardians. Shelter, food, and clothing are provided for you by others. Until you become a working citizen, your concerns will involve wants.

As an adult, you will be responsible for your own needs. If you start a family and have children, you will also be responsible for meeting the needs of others. In modern society, many needs and wants are satisfied through purchases made with money.

Pioneer families relied upon themselves for most of their needs and wants. It was not uncommon for early settlers to build their own dwellings. Many pioneer families also grew their own food and made most of their own clothing.

However, even pioneers had needs and wants for which they had to pay others. For example, a farmer needed a plow and

Purchases made with money satisfy most of the needs and wants of people in modern society.

225

other tools. Horses needed shoes. Weapons were essential for survival in many cases. These and other items had to be purchased.

Life is far more complicated today. People rely upon others to produce and make available the goods and services to satisfy almost all of their needs and wants. Your ability to satisfy your needs and wants as a working citizen will depend partly upon your income level. However, your spending habits will be just as important.

Living on an Allowance

At this point in your life, your only regular source of money may be an allowance. Spending that allowance involves making decisions. If you use an organized approach, you probably make your allowance last from one week to the next. If you frequently spend on impulse, you may have no money a day or two after you receive your allowance.

The best way to handle an allowance—or any form of income—is to plan your spending. A plan for spending money is a *budget*.

Budgeting: An Organized Approach to Spending

Preparing a budget is an organized approach to satisfying your needs and wants. When you plan a budget, you make spending decisions ahead of time. The process method helps you to think about the potential consequences of your spending alternatives. Evaluating consequences helps you to make sensible decisions that move you closer to your goals.

Planning a budget, or making a decision, is only part of the process. You also have to stay within your budget, or implement your decision. Your success in following a budget may depend upon the importance you attach to your goals. For example, you may want a new video game cartridge. You decide to save half of your allowance each week toward the purchase. After three weeks, however, you abandon that goal. At the rate at which you are saving money, it will be at least two more months before you can buy the cartridge. You decide to do something else with the money you've saved.

FOCUS ON YOUR FUTURE

SCOTT WAVED to his friends, Ron and Greg. "Hey, guys, let's go over to the ice cream parlor," he said.

"Good idea," Ron agreed. "How about you, Greg?"

"I think I'll pass," Greg said. "I want to get home and do my chores before the game comes on TV."

Scott and Ron each bought a double-dip cone. They decided to take a shortcut through the park on the way home.

"I don't understand Greg," Scott said. "He never seems to spend any money. Yet I know that he gets as much allowance as I do. The poor guy doesn't seem to have much fun, does he?"

"Oh, I don't know. Greg usually has some goal he's working toward. I think he said that he's saving up for a camera. He really likes taking photos, you know," Ron replied.

"You mean one of those new auto-focus models? Boy, I'd sure like to have one of those," Scott said.

"Greg has lots of nice things, Scott. He has a deal with his father. If Greg wants something, he saves half of the cost from his allowance. Then, his dad matches that amount," Ron explained.

"That's a good deal," Scott said. "But I could never save money like Greg does."

"Neither could I," Ron said. "But that's because we don't have anything we want that much. Greg makes a plan and sticks to it. That's how he gets so many nice things."

Scott shook his head. "I guess the question is how many ice cream cones you're willing to give up to get a camera." ■

Your income as an adult probably will include the wages you receive for the work you do.

LOOKING AT INCOME

Before thinking about preparing a budget, consider what *income* really means. Income is a benefit, usually in the form of money, that you receive as a result of your labor or your investments. Income can be wages, salary, interest on your savings or investments, or benefits from government or private assistance programs. As an adult, your income will be the money you use to pay for your needs and wants.

You cannot look at income as a simple figure. When you think about a spending plan, you must consider these three levels of income:

1. Gross income
2. Net income
3. Discretionary income.

Gross Income

As an employee, your *gross income* will be the total amount of money you earn on a job. To illustrate, consider a person working a 40-hour week at a wage of $5 an hour. That person's gross income would be $200 that week. However, the employee would not receive the full $200. Portions of that money would be deducted to pay taxes.

Net Income

The amount of money an employee receives after *deductions* is called *net income.* Deductions are amounts subtracted from gross income for taxes and other purposes. Other deductions may be made to pay for worker benefits, such as health insurance and pension plans. Thus, net income is the amount of money that must be considered when planning a budget.

Discretionary Income

Money left over after you have paid your bills and daily living expenses from your net income is *discretionary income.* The final decision-making level in budgeting involves discretionary income. This is not money to be spent on impulse. *Discretion* means the ability to make responsible decisions. The discretion you use in dealing with this portion of your income will determine the quality of your budgeting efforts.

Discretionary income can be used for purchases that satisfy wants. Avoiding impulse buying is an important part of good money management.

229

Mortgage payments on a home are an example of fixed expenses. Regular obligations such as these must occupy top priority in budgeting. (Courtesy Smith, Stevens & Young, Cincinnati, OH)

LOOKING AT EXPENSES

Expenses are amounts of money paid out to satisfy needs and wants. In preparing a budget, there are different kinds of expenses to consider. Three general categories of expenses are:

1. Fixed expenses

2. Day-to-day living expenses

3. Flexible expenses.

Fixed Expenses

Bills that must be paid at certain times are *fixed expenses.* Amounts of fixed expenses are known in advance. Because they are regular obligations, fixed expenses are the first items to consider in budgeting. Examples of fixed expenses include:

- Rent or mortgage payments

- Car payments

- Insurance premiums (life, health, fire, auto)

- Payments for major purchases (furniture, appliances, clothing).

Day-to-Day Living Expenses

More flexible regular expenses come under the category of *day-to-day living expenses.* These needs must be met on a regular basis. However, day-to-day expenses differ from fixed expenses in two ways. First, although some of these costs are regular, others can vary widely. Second, you have some measure of control over these expenses. For example, you can make decisions to increase or decrease the amount you spend for food. Day-to-day living expenses include:

- Food
- Transportation
- Household operation (heating, electricity, telephone, etc.)
- Laundry and dry cleaning
- Personal care (soap, shampoo, hair styling, etc.)
- Pocket money.

Flexible Expenses

Expenses that are most subject to change are *flexible expenses.* You have total decision-making control over planning for some future expenses such as vacations. Other future expenses, such

Food purchases are an example of day-to-day living expenses. These expenses are more flexible than fixed expenses but must be met on a regular basis.

231

as emergencies, are outside of your control. Flexible expenses involve planning ahead. For example, you may decide to put aside money for clothing purchases. It also is wise to have money in reserve for emergencies and other unexpected needs. Examples of flexible expenses include:

- Vacations, recreation, and entertainment
- Clothing
- Medical and dental care
- Newspapers and magazines
- Gifts and contributions (relatives, friends, and religious and charitable organizations, etc.)
- Emergencies.

Entertainment and recreation are flexible expenses. You plan ahead to set aside money for these activities. (Photo below, courtesy American Petroleum Institute; photo below, right, courtesy Salt Lake Convention and Visitors Bureau)

PREPARING A BUDGET

Budget preparation is an activity that is particularly well-suited for the decision-making process discussed in Part III. Fixed expenses usually represent the major decisions affecting a budget. You will have to make life-style decisions about needs such as housing. How much will you be able and willing to spend to meet your need for shelter?

Other major decisions will involve the kind of car to buy and how much insurance protection you need or want. When you make these kinds of decisions, you commit yourself to fixed expenses.

Your day-to-day expenses require continuing decisions. Areas such as food and personal care offer great flexibility in planning.

Some flexible expenses can be postponed or eliminated altogether if you face a need to reduce your budget. For example, careful wardrobe maintenance can help you to postpone some clothing purchases.

The Time Factor

Budgets are designed to cover spending over certain periods of time. Personal and household budgets usually are prepared on both a monthly and an annual, or yearly, basis. The reason is that most fixed expenses must be paid monthly.

At this point in your life, you may find it convenient to plan a weekly budget. You may receive a weekly allowance and be paid for any part-time work on a weekly basis. If so, a weekly budget will help you to match your expenses to your income.

Some workers are paid on a monthly or twice-monthly schedule. Under these circumstances, monthly budgeting matches up well with the receipt of income. To calculate annual income, simply multiply monthly income by 12.

However, many workers are paid weekly or every second week. To calculate annual income, multiply weekly income by 52 or biweekly income by 26. To calculate average monthly income on this pay basis, first determine annual income. Then, divide annual income by 12.

Budget Calculations

In preparing a personal budget, there are some simple steps that can help you to organize your calculations. A simple personal budget sheet is illustrated in Figure 14-1.

Before you attempt to write budget totals in a final format, however, there are some calculations you must perform. These steps, performed in order, will help you to determine your spending requirements:

1. Total your monthly fixed expenses (housing, car payment, insurance premiums, and payments on credit purchases). *Credit,* in its simplest form, is the borrowing of money. The use of credit is discussed later in this unit. Credit accounts include all purchases for which you borrow money, such as major appliances, furniture, and credit card accounts.

2. Total your day-to-day living expenses (transportation, food, household expenses, laundry, personal needs, and pocket money).

3. Add these two figures. The sum represents your required spending total.

4. Calculate your total net income from all sources.

5. Subtract your required spending total from your income.

6. The remainder is your discretionary income. From this figure, calculate how much you can afford for each of your regular flexible expenses.

When you have completed your calculations, the amount remaining is money that you can save. Your savings may include money set aside for special purposes, such as vacations or major purchases. You also should have money set aside to help you to deal with emergencies.

You may have no money left over after subtracting your expenses from your income. In this case, you are living beyond your means. In other words, your income will not support your spending pattern. You need to examine your financial situation and seek ways to reduce your budgeted expenses.

Figure 14-1. Personal budget entries should be organized into types of expenses, starting with fixed expenses.

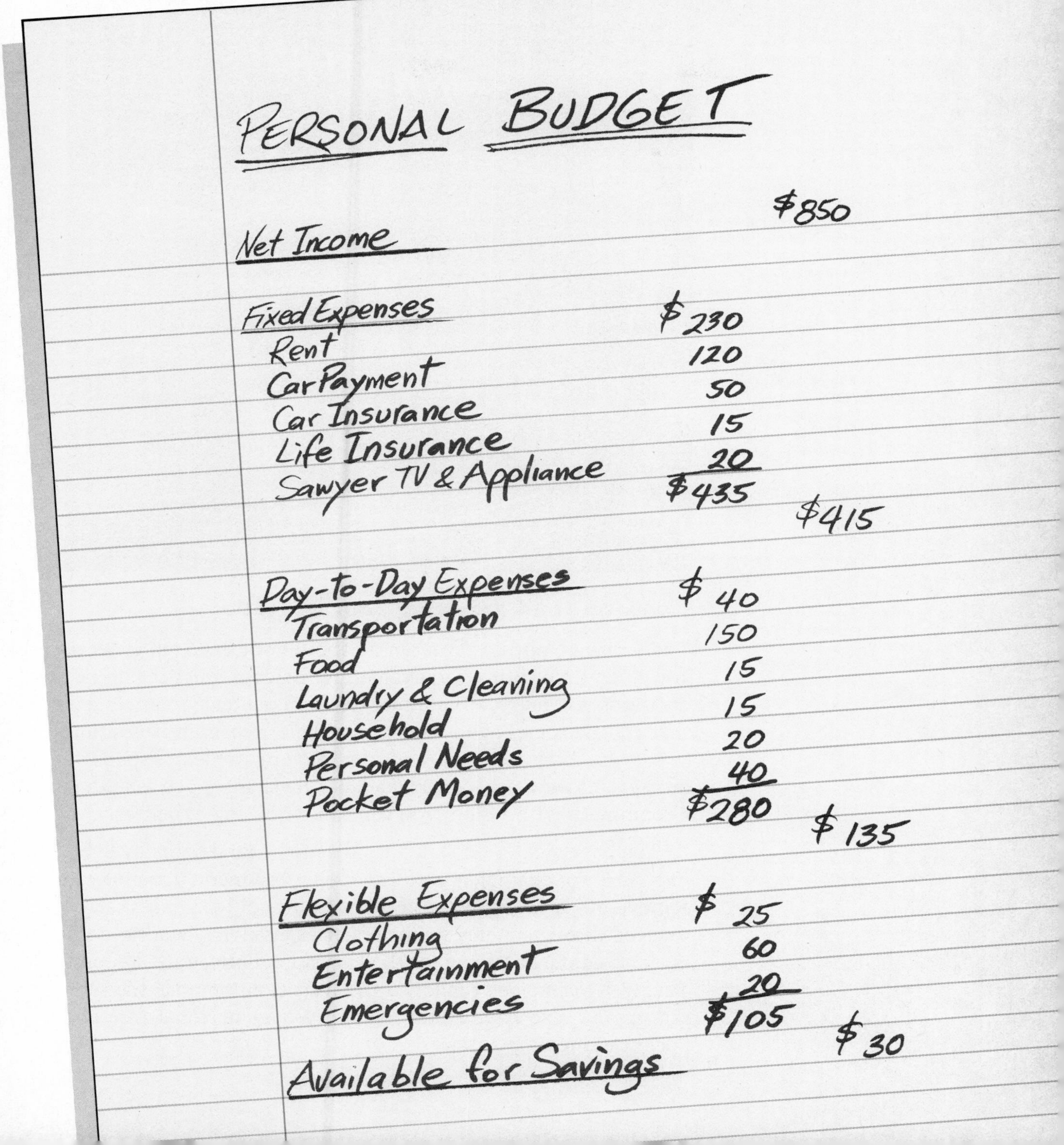

PERSONAL BUDGET

Net Income $850

Fixed Expenses $230
  Rent   120
  Car Payment   50
  Car Insurance   15
  Life Insurance   20
  Sawyer TV & Appliance $435
                                              $415

Day-to-Day Expenses $40
  Transportation   150
  Food   15
  Laundry & Cleaning   15
  Household   20
  Personal Needs   40
  Pocket Money $280
                                              $135

Flexible Expenses $25
  Clothing   60
  Entertainment   20
  Emergencies $105
                                              $30

Available for Savings

Pumping your own gas at self-serve pumps can amount to considerable savings over the period of a year. (Photo courtesy A.E. Staley Mfg. Co., Decatur, IL)

Evaluating and Adjusting Your Budget

There may be nothing you can do about your fixed expenses at any given time. However, evaluating the consequences of past decisions will help you in future decision making. You may feel that you are spending too much in a single area, such as housing. If so, you may want to consider moving to less expensive quarters. Or, you may consider a life-style change such as finding a roommate with whom you can share housing expenses.

You have greater flexibility in adjusting your day-to-day living expenses. For example, careful shopping and menu planning can achieve major savings in food costs. Household expenses can be reduced through energy-saving practices involving heating, cooling, and lights. Shopping for the lowest fuel prices and keeping a car well maintained can lower the costs of automobile transportation. You also have some flexibility over personal care and pocket money expenses.

FOCUS ON YOUR FUTURE

JILL AWOKE WITH A START. The shrill sound of a saw cutting through lumber had ended her slumber. She got up and went to her window. Of course! This was the day work was to start on her friend's house. She had not realized they would start so early in the morning.

When Jill walked into the kitchen, her mother asked her why she was up so early. "School's out. I thought you'd be sleeping late," her mother said.

"Are you kidding, Mom? Who can sleep with all that noise next door?" Jill protested. "I hope they finish the job soon."

"The noisy work should be completed in a week or less," her mother said. "Once the exterior work is finished, you'll hardly know the workers are there."

"It's going to be nice for Dorothy and her family to have a family room. I wonder where they got the money?" Jill said.

"Dorothy's parents got a home improvement loan from the bank, Jill. They've had their home for more than 10 years, so they were able to borrow against their equity," Jill's mother explained.

"What's equity, Mom?"

"Equity is the value of their home minus the amount they owe on their mortgage. In other words, equity is their share of the market value of their home."

Jill finished her breakfast. "That's interesting, Mom. It's almost as if someone paid you for owning your home."

"Owning a home is an investment, Jill. You may put a lot of money and effort into a home, but it's worth it in the long run."

"Well, I think I'll run next door and ask Dorothy if she wants to come over here today. I'm sure she'll want to get away from that noise." ■

In considering any adjustments to your expenses, be realistic as well as savings-minded. Don't make budget changes that you won't be able to accept. Always be sure you have provided for your needs. It is your wants that you can adjust when necessary.

When you have completed all your calculations, write the figures in a final budget format. You may wish to retain your monthly or quarterly budget sheets. This will help you to keep track of changes or adjustments in your income and expenses. Remember, the decision-making process is a valuable aid in planning a budget.

CREDIT FOR CONSUMERS

To understand how credit works, consider borrowing money from a friend at school. You left your lunch money at home, so you borrow a dollar until the next day. True to your word, you pay back the dollar the next day at school. Your friend has given you credit, based on trust.

Consumer credit also involves borrowing money; but there is a difference. Organizations that lend money expect to be paid for the privilege of using their money. The money you pay for the use of someone else's money is called *interest.* The amount you borrow is called the *principal.* In some kinds of loans, there are fees or other costs involved in addition to interest. When these costs or fees are added to interest charges, the total is an overall *finance charge.*

Credit Purchases

Most forms of credit do not involve the exchange of money. Most credit transactions cover purchases of goods or services. When you buy something on credit, you receive the product now and pay for it later.

When you borrow money, or buy on credit, you become a *borrower,* or *debtor.* A borrower or debtor is a person or organization that owes money. The person or organization making a loan is called the *creditor.* A creditor "sells" the use of money to a borrower. As a borrower, you have an obligation to a creditor. You must pay back the money you borrowed, plus interest. If you fail

to pay as agreed, a creditor may take back, or *repossess*, an item you purchased. Repossession usually applies when the item purchased remains under the ownership of the lender until a loan is paid off.

Some forms of credit require that you offer *collateral* for a loan. Collateral is something of value that you own, such as a car or furniture. Collateral is used to guarantee that you will repay a loan. If you fail to make payments as agreed, the creditor may seize your collateral to satisfy your repayment obligation. Your earnings also can be considered as collateral. In some cases, a creditor can *attach* your wages if you fail to make payments. Attaching something means to seize it by legal process, such as a court order.

TYPES OF CREDIT

As a consumer, you probably will use several kinds of credit. Most people do not have enough cash to pay for large purchases, such as a home or a new car. These major purchases usually are credit transactions.

People also use credit for convenience. As a borrower, you would receive statements showing the status of your account.

Obtaining a loan is one way to finance a major purchase through credit.

These statements are useful for record-keeping purposes. Receipts and credit statements are particularly valuable in business transactions.

As a consumer, you will have several alternatives for borrowing money and for buying on credit. Major forms of consumer credit include:

- Real estate loans
- Personal loans
- Installment sales contracts
- Credit cards
- Charge accounts.

Real Estate Loans

A *real estate loan* is a loan for the purchase of land. In legal language, land is referred to as *real property.* Real estate loans usually are made for land that contains a building or buildings.

The majority of real estate loans are *mortgage loans.* A mortgage loan is a long-term loan for the puchase of a home or other real property. A typical mortgage loan may have a repayment period of 30 years.

Personal Loans

A loan in which you borrow money for a special purpose is a *personal loan.* Personal loans are also called small loans because there usually is a limit on the amount you may borrow. Most personal loans are made by banks, savings and loan institutions, credit unions, consumer finance companies, and life insurance companies.

Installment Sales Contracts

An *installment sales contract* is a special kind of personal loan. Installment sales contracts are usually arranged for the purchase of major items, such as cars, furniture, or major appliances. These loans are made by, or arranged by, the seller. A *down payment,* or partial payment of the selling price, usually is required at the

Real estate loans are made for the purchase of land, referred to as real property. Most real estate loans are mortgage loans for the purchase of land containing a home or other structure. (© Chas R. Pearson/West Stock)

Installment sales contracts are a common method of financing furniture and other major purchases.
(© Erich Hartmann/Magnum Photos, Inc.)

time of the transaction. The remainder of the selling price, plus finance charges, is the *balance* of the contract. Under many installment sales contracts, the seller retains *title*, or legal ownership, of the item until you pay the balance.

Credit Cards

The most widely used form of credit today is the *credit card*. A credit card is a small sheet of plastic with raised letters and numbers. Purchases made with a credit card are *pre-authorized* credit transactions. *Authorize* means to grant the power to perform an action. Authorization is permission or approval. Pre-authorized means that credit transactions are approved ahead of time. When a business issues a credit card, it is giving the holder a *line of credit*. A line of credit is the maximum amount a cardholder can purchase on credit.

Credit cards are issued by many types of businesses. The three basic kinds of credit cards are:

- Bank
- Travel and entertainment
- Single-purpose.

Bank credit cards. A *bank credit card* is a credit account with a bank or other financial institution. Bank credit cards are the most widely accepted of all credit cards. Their convenience carries a price tag, however. There is an annual fee for these cards,

242

ranging from $12 to $45, charged by the issuing institutions. In addition, most bank credit cards carry the highest interest rates permitted under law. No interest is charged if you pay your balance in full each month. It is when you carry a large balance that the cards become expensive.

Travel and entertainment cards. A *travel and entertainment card* is intended primarily for business use. Issuing companies charge annual fees that are higher than those for bank credit cards. Not all travel and entertainment cards permit holders to carry a balance. However, most issuing companies have expanded their credit terms in recent years. These cards are particularly useful for businesspersons who travel or entertain clients frequently. Cardholders typically enjoy special rates on car rentals and other conveniences when they use these cards. Many businesses have master accounts, under which they issue cards to their employees. Bills for employee activities are sent to the companies.

Credit cards are the most widely used form of credit today. There are several types of cards designed for different credit needs.

Single-purpose cards. Many businesses that sell to the public issue their own *single-purpose cards.* Examples are department stores, oil companies, hotel chains, and discount and other chain stores. No fees are charged for most single-purpose cards. No interest is charged if the balance is paid in full each month. However, interest rates are high on continuing balances, just as with bank credit cards.

Charge Accounts

Charge accounts are offered by many department stores. Most stores issue two kinds of accounts. With a *regular charge account*, you pay for your purchases once a month. There is no interest charged because you pay in full each month. These accounts are often called *30-day charge accounts.*

The other major type of charge account is the *revolving charge account.* A revolving charge account is a line of credit. If you have a revolving charge account, you can charge purchases up to a maximum amount. You agree to pay back a minimum percentage of the amount you borrow, plus interest, each month. If you pay the entire balance each month, no interest is charged.

Most department stores offer revolving charge accounts. Most bank and oil company credit cards are also revolving charge accounts.

CREDIT: THE GOOD SIDE

If you use credit wisely, you will find that it offers several benefits to you as a consumer. However, your ability to take advantage of these benefits will depend largely upon your decision-making skills. It is important to evaluate all the consequences whenever you consider using credit. Advantages of credit include:

- Use of goods or services while you are paying for them. The majority of mortgage loans, in fact, are never paid off over the period of the loans. Most homeowners could not afford to buy their homes without mortgage loans.

- Opportunities to save on purchases. You may not have enough cash available when a special sale occurs. Using credit, you can purchase items you need or want while they are on sale. By paying your bills regularly, you can save money.

- Free use of someone else's money. When you make full payments on short-term (30-day), or open-end accounts, no interest charges are added. Thus, short-term borrowing costs you nothing.

- Ability to handle financial emergencies. Used wisely, credit can be an effective money management tool. You can use credit to deal with temporary financial setbacks without giving up too many needs or wants.

- Accurate record keeping. Credit bills and receipts help you to maintain accurate records of your expenses.

- Convenience. Some forms of credit make it possible for you to shop by telephone or by mail. This can save you time and transportation costs.

- Better follow-up on purchases. Shoppers frequently find it necessary to return or exchange items that turn out to be unsatisfactory. Returns and exchanges usually are handled more readily for items purchased on credit than for cash purchases.

Bank credit cards are the most widely accepted. They are convenient and offer flexible credit, but they carry high interest rates on continuing balances. (Courtesy First Interstate Bancorp)

CREDIT: THE BAD SIDE

There are risks as well as benefits involved in the use of credit. As in other areas, bad consequences usually result from poor decision making. Potential disadvantages in the use of credit include:

- Greater costs. If you pay interest on purchases, the goods and services you buy are costing you more money.

- Higher prices. You may have to pay more for some items purchased on credit. Some companies raise prices to cover the cost of extending credit.

- Overspending. There is a temptation to buy too many items, or higher priced items, on credit. If you do this often, over-buying results. It is easy to build up your debts to the point where you can't handle the payments.

- Bad decisions. The availability of credit can lead to bad shopping habits. You may be tempted to buy an item right away instead of waiting for a sale. If you become a lazy shopper, you will waste money.

- Impulse buying. Credit availability also carries the temptation to buy on impulse. This is unwise use of credit. If you don't really need an item, and you don't have enough cash to pay for it, don't buy it.

Any and all of these situations can lead to credit problems. Remember, using credit results in a debt. If you use credit un-wisely or too heavily, you may find it difficult or impossible to

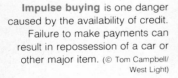

Impulse buying is one danger caused by the availability of credit. Failure to make payments can result in repossession of a car or other major item. (© Tom Campbell/ West Light)

make the required payments. Failure to pay your bills on time can result in repossessions and other problems. Responsible decision making in budgeting and using credit will help you avoid problems.

YOUR CREDIT RATING

Your use of credit also affects your *credit rating.* Your credit rating is an evaluation of your ability and willingness to repay a debt. When you use credit, you are asking a lender to trust you. Think about lending money to another student. You would not lend money to someone you didn't trust.

Lenders look at you the same way. A lender takes a risk in extending credit. If you have a good credit rating, that risk is reduced. Areas that are evaluated in establishing your credit rating are:

- Credit history
- Income
- Assets.

Credit History

Your past record of paying your debts is your *credit history.* Most lenders consider your credit history to be the most accurate indicator of your willingness and ability to pay your bills.

Income

Your earning power indicates your ability to handle debts. A small or uncertain income usually represents a bad credit risk. However, a high income is no guarantee that you will pay your debts. If you have a bad credit history or are heavily in debt, a lender may consider you a bad risk. Lenders look at your obligations as well as your income in determining your ability to pay. You are usually considered a good risk if you earn enough and you have a steady employment record.

Assets

Money and property that you own are your *assets.* If your assets are high in value, a lender can be assured of your ability to handle a debt. Assets also can be used as collateral for some types of credit.

Good decision-making skills will help you make the most of the credit available to you. Used wisely, credit can benefit you in many ways. Misused, credit can be a destructive force in your life.

CONTENT SUMMARY

Budgeting is an organized approach to spending. A budget is a plan that you can follow to satisfy your needs and wants. The two major elements in a budget are income and expenses.

You can look at income in three ways. Gross income is the amount of money you earn by working. Net income is the money you receive after deductions for taxes and for benefits such as insurance and retirement plans. A third level of income is discretionary income. Discretionary income is the money you have left after paying your bills and taking care of your other needs.

Expenses also can be divided into three categories: fixed, day-to-day, and flexible. Fixed expenses are bills that usually remain the same from month to month or change according to a predetermined schedule. Rent and car payments are examples of fixed expenses. Day-to-day living expenses include food, transportation, and personal care items. Flexible expenses include recreation, clothing purchases, and emergencies. Flexible expenses are usually paid out of discretionary income.

Preparing a personal or family budget is a decision-making process. Decision-making skills are valuable in considering the consequences of a spending decision. There are six basic steps in preparing a budget. First, calculate the total of your fixed expenses. Second, calculate the total of your day-to-day expenses. Third, combine the two to determine your required expenses. Fourth, calculate your total net income from all sources. Fifth, subtract your required expenses from your net income. The remainder is your discretionary income. Sixth, decide how to distribute discretionary income to meet your flexible expenses.

Continuing evaluation and adjustment of a personal budget is recommended. Always be sure to plan for needs first. Expenses for wants can be adjusted as necessary.

Consumer credit is a form of borrowing money. When you use credit, or borrow, you take on an obligation to pay back the loan. In business, most forms of credit involve interest, which is a form of rent paid for the use of money. If other fees or costs are added to interest, the total is the finance charge for a loan.

Most consumer credit falls into one of five general categories. These are real estate loans, personal loans, installment sales contracts, credit cards, and charge accounts.

Credit is a useful money management tool when used wisely. If misused, credit can cause serious financial problems.

KEY TERMS

budget

income

gross income

deduction

net income

discretionary income

discretion

expense

fixed expense

day-to-day living expense

flexible expense

credit

interest

principal

finance charge

borrower

debtor

CAREER COMMENTARIES

1. **Discretionary income is not money to be spent on impulse.**
   Why is discretionary income an important area for budgetary decision making? How is discretionary income related to flexible expenses?

2. **As a consumer, you probably will use several kinds of credit.**
   Which kinds of credit do you think you might try to obtain and use during your first year as a wage earner? Explain why each type would be important to you as you begin your career.

3. **An advantage of credit is the use of goods or services while you are paying for them.**
   Identify three consumer goods or services that are frequently purchased on credit. For each one, identify the type of credit most commonly used. Also, explain why credit purchases are most suitable for each item.

creditor

repossess

collateral

attach

real estate loan

real property

mortgage loan

personal loan

installment sales
   contract

down payment

balance

title

credit card

pre-authorized

authorize

line of credit

bank credit card

travel and
   entertain-
   ment card

single-purpose card

regular charge
   account

30-day charge
   account

revolving charge
   account

credit ratings

credit history

assets

15

The Smart Shopper

When you have completed the reading assignments and exercises in this unit, you should be able to:

☐ Describe steps you can follow to become a responsible, well-informed consumer.

☐ Explain how you can use labels and tags in selecting appropriate products.

☐ Describe basic menu-planning and grocery-shopping practices.

☐ Discuss ways to avoid becoming a victim of consumer frauds.

☐ Describe legal remedies available to consumers.

☐ Explain how community and consumer protection and service organizations can help consumers.

A CONSUMER'S FRIENDS: CAUTION AND KNOWLEDGE

There's an old expression that describes the risks you take when you buy something: "Let the buyer beware." This means simply that, when a purchase has been completed, you own the article you have bought. You may have bought satisfaction. But you also may have bought problems.

In dealing with potential problems connected with purchases you make, you find yourself in one of a variety of situations:

- You may be entirely on your own. If you don't like a product, or if it doesn't work as you expected, there may be nothing you can do. For example, suppose you buy a portable radio-cassette player from someone who is moving away from your area. You get a good price. However, a few days later you discover a problem. The radio works fine. But cassettes are being torn up when you try to play them. In this type of situation, you are simply out of luck. You don't have a walk-around sound system. You don't have your money. And you don't have anyone to complain to because the seller is gone. This type of experience can help you build the "healthy skepticism" you need as a smart shopper. *Skepticism* is suspicion. A skeptical person acts as though something can always go wrong. The skeptic expects the worst and does everything possible to avoid negative consequences. One good, skeptical approach to shopping is to know the seller of anything you buy. You should also know whether, and how, the seller will stand behind the item you purchase.

- You may be able to seek satisfaction from the seller. For instance, if you buy the same walk-around sound system in a department store, the situation will be different. The store probably will be there long after you have used up the product you bought. You can come back to the store if something goes wrong with the product. There will be someone available to listen to your complaint. Usually, the store will be interested in your satisfaction with the products you buy. You may pay more for a product in a store than if you buy it used. But you also run a risk in buying used goods. You have to learn what values you want in a purchase. And you have to be ready to pay for those values.

- You may have protection from laws or government agencies. If a product you buy can affect your health or safety, the government may have a say about the item. A number of laws and government agencies exist entirely to protect the consumer. Laws govern the content and construction of some products. Government agencies approve and inspect many items—particularly foods and health-care products. If the government is involved, its presence is usually obvious. There will be labels or markings on products that tell about contents and materials used. Learning why information is included on labels and understanding what labels mean can deliver a lot of protection.

In summary, when you spend your money, you may or may not have protection available if you are not satisfied. One thing you should do before you make any major purchase is to know what protection you can expect. Just as important, however, you

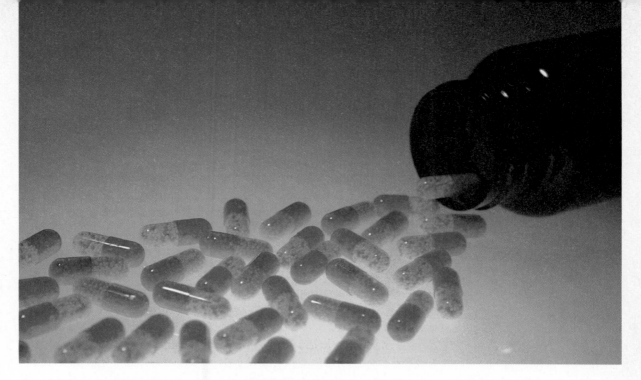

should learn to beware, or be wary, before you buy anything. Know what you are buying. Compare values before you buy. Be sure. Remember that a purchase is a commitment. All these cautions are part of a single picture—a picture of a smart shopper.

BE A SMART SHOPPER: COMPARE

Smart shoppers plan their purchases. Using the decision-making process helps you to develop a clear picture of your needs. This knowledge, in turn, promotes effective evaluation of alternatives. In this case, evaluating alternatives can be called comparison shopping. Remember, comparison shopping means checking and comparing products. Factors for comparison include:

- Prices
- Quality of materials
- Quality of construction or manufacture
- Guarantees and warranties.

Price and Value

Comparing prices is an obvious task for a consumer. You don't want to pay extra for a product simply because you were too lazy to shop around. Most people are concerned with prices when

253

they consider major purchases. This is because large sums of money are at stake. However, carelessness in smaller, everyday purchases can be equally damaging financially. Small price differences can add up to large sums over a period of time.

To illustrate, consider buying gasoline from a dealer who charges four cents more per gallon than a nearby competitor. If you buy 20 gallons at a time, the difference is only 80 cents. However, if you fill up once a week, you will purchase approximately 1,000 gallons in a year. Now the difference is $40.

In some cases, however, it pays to look beyond obvious price considerations. Perhaps the gasoline dealer with the higher prices offers other things of value to regular customers. That dealer may offer maintenance and other services at a better price. Also, the dealer may be a knowledgeable mechanic whom you can trust. In this case, it pays to be a regular customer. The extra cost of the gasoline is an investment in your satisfaction.

Price comparisons also are important from a volume standpoint. Purchasing larger quantities of a product usually saves you money. Remember, unit price is the important figure. For example, if you can buy one pound of dog food for $2.50, or 10 pounds for $15, which is the better buy? The larger package costs $1.50

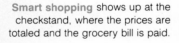

Smart shopping shows up at the checkstand, where the prices are totaled and the grocery bill is paid.

per pound, which is a major saving over the $2.50 price for the smaller package. In some cases, you may have to perform some arithmetic to determine unit price comparisons. However, most grocery markets today post unit prices on their shelves.

Larger packages are not always a better buy, however. A smart shopper also makes purchasing decisions based upon need. Some food items are perishable and must be used soon after they are purchased. Some packaged foods cannot be kept for long periods once their container or sealed package has been opened. Milk is an example. If you use only small amounts of milk in your household, buy small containers. Milk spoils if not used quickly.

Timing also can be important in price comparisons. For example, supermarkets usually run large newspaper advertisements on a certain day of the week. You can check prices by comparing ads for different markets. This helps you to save on the items you need for the coming week. Grocery shopping is an area in which small price differences can add up to major savings over time.

Quality of Materials

Types of materials, and their quality, are of primary importance in judging the quality of a product. Materials determine how a product can be used and how long it can be expected to last. The care and maintenance required by a product also depend upon the materials from which it is manufactured.

Modern manufacturing techniques and advances in chemistry have changed the way some products are judged. For example, plastic components in automobiles were considered unacceptable by most people 20 years ago. Today, however, molded plastics are used extensively in automobiles. Plastic components offer great weight savings over steel and most other metals. Plastic parts also do not rust.

You should learn as much as possible about the qualities of different materials. You can learn through reading or through asking questions of knowledgeable people. Answers to most questions about consumer products can be found in books or magazines available in your public library. For example, you may have a choice between a garment made from a *natural fiber* or a *synthetic fiber.* Natural fibers are cotton, wool, linen, and silk. Synthetic fibers are produced artificially, usually by chemical means. Synthetic materials may have the appearance of cloth made from natural fibers. However, certain characteristics of the two materials will be different.

To illustrate, consider a choice between two sweaters. One sweater is 100 percent wool. The other sweater is made from a synthetic fabric, such as acrylic. Each garment has advantages and disadvantages. The wool sweater may be softer to the touch and provide greater warmth. However, wool requires special care—including dry cleaning or cold-water washing. Wool also is subject to attack by moths. Acrylic garments usually can be machine-washed. Synthetic fabrics do not attract moths.

Quality of Manufacture

You also should learn to judge whether a product is manufactured well. How an item is constructed or assembled has an effect on its *durability*, or how well it will last.

An example is the automobile. In judging quality of manufacture, you can check fit and finish. How well do the body panels fit? Are gaps between panels even? Do doors, seats, and other non-driving components work well? Do windows operate smoothly and easily? There are dozens of points that you can check to judge quality of manufacture.

In clothing, you can check seams for small and even stitching. Examine edges of garments to make sure they are not rough. Are numerous loose threads visible? Are fasteners strong and properly attached?

Take the time to examine products before spending your money. If you are not sure about something, ask a salesperson. If the salesperson can't answer your question, you may do well to put off your buying decision.

Guarantees and Warranties

A *guarantee* is an assurance of the quality or the length of service to be expected from a product. A guarantee usually includes a promise of *reimbursement* if the product fails to match the claims

made for it. Reimbursement usually means replacement of the product or repayment of money spent by a purchaser. A guarantee may be made by a manufacturer or by the seller of a product.

A *warranty* is a manufacturer's guarantee that a product is what it is claimed to be. Usually issued in writing, a warranty sets forth the manufacturer's responsibility for repair or replacement of defective parts. Most warranties are limited, either according to time, or amount of use of a product, or both. For example, most new-car warranties cover major components for 12 months or 12,000 miles, whichever comes first.

You should always take time to read guarantees and warranties carefully. Again, if you have questions, ask the salesperson. If your questions are not answered clearly and to your satisfaction, delay your decision.

FOCUS ON YOUR FUTURE

LYDIA ALMOST SCREAMED. There it was! The album she had been trying to find for months!

She called to her friend Gloria, who was looking at a cassette display. "Gloria! I found that old album!" Lydia cried. "I can't believe it!"

"That's wonderful," Gloria said. "I can't wait to hear it. It's my all-time favorite album, too."

Lydia handed the album to Gloria so she could take a closer look. After a few seconds, Gloria shook her head.

"I hate to say this, Lydia, but this is not the album you've been looking for," Gloria said. "Take a look at the small print at the bottom of the album cover."

Lydia took the album from her friend and looked closely at the cover. She read the statement silently: "The performances in this release were recorded in studios in New York and London. They are not recordings of live performances."

"What does this mean?" Lydia asked her friend.

"It means that the songs are re-recordings, Lydia. This album is not the original live concert. It has the same songs, but no audience in the background," Gloria explained.

Lydia turned the album over and looked at the back of the cover. "Sure enough," she declared. "This album was recorded about five years after the concert. What a shame. I thought I'd finally found it."

"Cheer up. At least you didn't buy it. You would have felt even worse if you had gotten it home and put it on your stereo."

"That's for sure," Lydia agreed. "I've just got to get in the habit of looking more closely at labels," she said. ■

READING LABELS

Federal "truth in packaging" laws require complete, accurate information on the labels of many products. This is especially true for foods and drugs. As a consumer, you can do some meaningful comparison shopping merely by reading the labels of many products.

Labels can tell you many important things about a product. While labels are regulated most closely for foods and drugs, other products also have useful information contained in their labels. You can protect yourself by paying close attention to labels on clothing, appliances, and other consumer goods. Information contained on product labels includes:

- Weight or volume. This information helps you to calculate unit cost.

- Types of materials used in the product. In some cases, such as clothing, this includes the percentages of each material.

- Grade or quality, according to government or industry standards.

- Directions for care or maintenance.

- Directions for safe use. These usually include warnings of potential hazards.

- The intended use of the product and its use limitations, if any.

In addition, food and drug product labels contain special information, required under federal laws. This information includes:

- Directions for use. Medication labels usually include instructions on dosage and on how and when to take the product.

- Directions for care. Some foods or drugs must be refrigerated. Other items must be kept in a cool, dry place.

- A list of active ingredients in the product.

- A list of ingredients in the order of quantity. The ingredient contained in greatest quantity is listed first. Other ingredients are listed in decreasing order of quantity.

Inspecting labels is an important element of smart shopping. (© Erich Hartmann/Magnum Photos, Inc.)

- Freshness of a food or drug item. (Some nonfood products, such as batteries and film, also are freshness dated.)

- Health cautions. Examples are warnings about repeated or heavy use and keeping a product out of the reach of children. (Nonfood product labels may contain warnings such as fire or explosion hazard or need for proper ventilation in use.)

DIET AND HEALTH

Your *diet* is everything you eat and drink. The foods you eat and drink have a major effect upon your health and your appearance. A good diet provides both *nourishment* and fuel. Nourishment involves the chemical building of the body. Different parts of your body need different kinds of food. Bones need one kind of food, for example, and muscles need another.

Fuel is needed for energy. Your body burns fuel to keep you going. The value of foods as energy suppliers is measured in *calories.* A calorie is the amount of heat that can be produced by burning a given amount of a fuel. The amount of calories your body burns in a day depends upon how active you are.

It is important to plan and maintain a *balanced diet.* A balanced diet is one that includes the nourishment and fuel your body needs.

Food Values

The value of foods depends upon the calories they contain and upon their *nutritional qualities.* Nutritional qualities are the ingredients of foods that nourish the body. These ingredients can be divided into three categories, according to their chemical makeup:

- Proteins
- Carbohydrates
- Fats.

All three of these food categories are needed for a balanced diet. In addition, your body needs other ingredients, such as water, vitamins, minerals, and fiber.

Proteins. *Protein* is rich in nutrients that build body tissue. Protein also contains calories. Protein is easily converted into muscle tissue. Meat substances and a number of plant foods, including beans and peas, are high in protein.

Carbohydrates. High levels of fuel, but very little nutrition, are found in *carbohydrates.* Carbohydrates consist primarily of sugars

Carbohydrates are found in starchy foods, such as bread, potatoes, pasta, rice, and popcorn. Most people should limit their intake of carbohydrates.

and starches. High sugar content is found in candies and many soft drinks. Examples of foods high in starches are potatoes, rice, and bread.

While your body needs some carbohydrates, you can easily exceed that need. It is easy to take in more calories than your body can burn. When this happens, your body turns carbohydrates into fats. Excess fats cause weight gain and impair your health.

Fats. *Fats* are chemically similar to carbohydrates. However, fats contain twice as many calories, by weight, as carbohydrates. Fats include the slippery white substance at the edges of some meats, such as steaks and pork products. Butter is almost pure fat, as are many cooking oils. Some fried foods, such as french fried potatoes, are a combination of carbohydrates and absorbed fats.

Every balanced diet should include some amount of fat. Care is necessary in controlling the amount of fat in your diet. Too much fat leads to rapid weight increases. Most people should limit the fat in their diets.

Other elements. A balanced diet also should provide adequate water, vitamins, minerals, and fiber. Water is necessary to life. Your body can survive longer without food than without water.

Good nutrition might include munching on fresh vegetables rather than junk food or sugary snacks.

Chemicals that cause other chemicals to be used by the body are *vitamins*. There are vitamins in most of the foods you eat. Vitamins help the body to absorb food. A balanced diet usually contains all of the vitamins you need.

Vitamin *supplements*, usually in the form of capsules, are sold by most food and drug stores. Some of these substances may benefit your body. However, you should discuss your diet with a doctor or nutrition expert before taking large amounts of vitamins. Overdoses of some vitamins can be harmful.

Minerals are chemical elements found in nature. Iron, calcium, and copper are examples of minerals. Iron in your blood helps to absorb oxygen. Calcium is a major substance in bone structures. Milk is a good source of calcium.

Mineral supplements, also available in food and drug stores, should not be taken without a reason. Before taking any substance into your body, you should know what it is—and why you are taking it.

Fiber, also known as *roughage*, is food that helps move other substances through the body's digestive system. Roughage aids the body in eliminating waste. Cereals, bread, and lettuce are examples of foods containing fibers.

Food Groups

The substances your body needs are contained in the four basic food groups. A balanced diet must include foods from these basic food groups:

- Meat
- Fruits and vegetables
- Cereals and breads
- Milk.

Meat group.   The *meat group* includes meats, poultry, fish, eggs, nuts, dried beans and peas, and peanut butter. These foods are rich in protein. Two or more servings daily are recommended.

Fruits and vegetables group.   All fruits and vegetables are included in the *fruits and vegetables group.* Recommendations include a citrus food or other source of vitamin C daily. A dark green or deep yellow vegetable or fruit should be included in the diet at least every other day. Four or more servings daily are recommended from this group.

Fresh fruits provide nutrition and good taste, whether included in meals or eaten for snacks.

Cereals and breads group. The *cereals and breads group* includes cereals, bread, cornmeal, rice, and spaghetti, macaroni, or noodles. A balanced diet calls for four or more servings daily. These products should be whole-grain, fortified, enriched, or restored.

A balanced diet includes daily servings from the cereals and breads group and the milk group.

Milk group. Milk and milk products are included in the *milk group.* Cheese, milk beverages and desserts, and yogurt can satisfy part of this requirement as sources of calcium. Children, especially teen-agers, have the greatest calcium requirements for building healthy bones and teeth. Adults also need calcium, but in lesser amounts.

MEAL PLANNING AND SHOPPING

Planning is the key to maintaining a balanced diet. The basic rules are the same for a single person and for a large family. Only the numbers change.

Menu Planning

A *menu* is a list of dishes to be served at a meal. A menu also may refer to the meal itself. In a restaurant, a menu is the list of meals or dishes available to be ordered.

Menu planning, or meal planning, can be an enjoyable activity, especially if you have help. One readily available source of help is the large selection of cookbooks available in stores. Cookbooks come in many varieties. Some cookbooks specialize in easy or quick meals for working individuals. Others offer ideas for preparing certain kinds of foods, such as baked goods or casseroles. No matter what kinds of meals you wish to prepare, a cookbook exists to show you the details.

Menu planning is important at home, just as it is in a good restaurant. Cookbooks and family recipes help make meal planning enjoyable. (Photo courtesy of Norton Simon, Inc.)

Cookbooks contain *recipes.* A recipe is a set of instructions for the preparation of a meal. A recipe includes a list of ingredients. Even inexperienced cooks can produce attractive, healthful meals by planning ahead and following recipe instructions.

Meals can be planned for a week at a time. This permits a week's grocery shopping to be done in a single trip to the market.

Planning Your Shopping

Effective, economical shopping also requires planning. The best method of planning a grocery shopping trip is to make up a *shopping list.* A shopping list includes all the food and nonfood items needed by a household for a given period.

A smart shopper will plan a week's meals before shopping. All ingredients listed in recipes should be noted. Check supplies on hand to determine which items must be purchased. These items then are included in your shopping list. The shopping list should include household needs, such as paper products, soaps, cleansers, and products for personal hygiene and grooming.

Planning ahead saves money and helps to eliminate mistakes. Shopping in an organized manner is one of the keys to being a smart shopper.

Selecting meat is easier if you have planned ahead to determine your needs. Organized shopping is smart shopping.

FIGHTING FRAUD

Consumer fraud occurs in many forms. Again, the better informed you are, the less likely you are to become a victim of fraud. An important part of being informed is knowing some of the most likely forms of consumer fraud. Areas in which you should be particularly cautious include:

- Door-to-door sales. Always request identification and a city or county permit from a door-to-door salesperson. If you have any doubts about the person, the company, or the product, don't do business with that person.

- Mail-order sales. In many cases, you are buying a product without actually seeing it. Read mail-order advertisements carefully. Be sure you know exactly what you are ordering. Never send cash through the mail. Keep a record of your order, and the payment you send. Before you buy, be sure you have a good reason. Check to make sure the item is not available in a store. Remember that you have to pay postage or shipping charges. Is the price still attractive when these extra costs are added? Finally, mail-order deliveries require time. Can you wait several weeks to receive your order?

- Telephone sales. Be especially careful of telephone offers. Many telephone sales operations are thoroughly honest. However, one danger is that you may be tempted to make a quick decision in a telephone conversation. Doing business this way is one of the most hazardous forms of impulse buying. Remember that before the telephone rang, you probably had no knowledge of, or intention to buy, the item being promoted.

- Auto repairs. Most people have very little knowledge about the mechanical operation of the vehicles they drive. There are some informational actions you can take. Read your owner's manual and familiarize yourself with the vehicle's maintenance schedule. Consult friends, neighbors, and family members for recommendations of reliable shops for maintenance and repairs. Ask questions about work suggested by the person who writes the service ticket. Check costs before agreeing to have extra work performed on a vehicle.

Shopping by telephone requires extra caution by the consumer. Be sure you know what you are ordering, and keep accurate records of all transactions.

It helps to be a regular customer at service stations and repair shops. The operators get to know you and your vehicle.

- Sales. Stores sometimes sell a quantity of an item at a low price. Be prepared to find that the item has been sold out. If advertising for the sale indicates that it is "limited to the quantity on hand," you are out of luck. Otherwise, you should be able to obtain a *rain check* on the item. A rain check is the store's promise to sell you that item at the sale price at a later date. You should be alert for a dishonest practice called "bait and switch." An item is advertised at a bargain price as bait to attract customers. When customers try to buy the item, they are told there are no more left. Instead, the salesperson tries to sell them a more expensive product.

CONSUMER PROTECTION

Consumer protection services are provided by both government and private organizations. Government involvement, in terms of both laws and agencies, exists at three levels: federal, state, and

Federal agencies and those of states and local governments are responsible for enforcing consumer protection laws.

local. Federal agencies responsible for protection of consumers' rights include:

- Food and Drug Administration (FDA)
- Federal Trade Commission (FTC)
- Consumer Product Safety Commission.

Food and Drug Administration (FDA)

The *Food and Drug Administration (FDA)* has several functions. One is to test and evaluate new drugs to determine if they should be placed on the market. The FDA is concerned with effectiveness of drugs as well as safety. Another major function is the enforcement of truth in packaging laws. The FDA can force a company to change an inaccurate label or to remove that product from the market. Food producers also come under FDA regulations. Packaged foods must be labeled correctly as to ingredients, nutritional content, and artificial coloring. The FDA also enforces standards for cleanliness in the processing of foods.

Federal Trade Commission (FTC)

The *Federal Trade Commission (FTC)* regulates many aspects of *interstate commerce.* Interstate commerce is business involving transactions in more than one state. Responsibilities of the FTC that are most directly related to consumers involve advertising and truth in packaging. The FTC regulates advertising to make sure that product descriptions are stated clearly and accurately. The agency also requires that product labels be truthful and complete. Clothing manufacturers, for example, must include care labels on their products. Care labels contain directions for washing or dry cleaning.

Consumer Product Safety Commission

The *Consumer Product Safety Commission* has a triple role. First, it sets safety standards for products. Second, the agency tests products to determine if they meet those standards. Third, it enforces the standards by removing any dangerous products from the market.

Most states have regulatory agencies that perform similar functions in commerce conducted within the borders of a single state. States also establish standards for the professions, such as law and medicine, and for some other occupations. Licensing and certification programs are used to administer these standards.

Interstate commerce is regulated by federal agencies such as the Federal Trade Commission and the Interstate Commerce Commission.
(The Association of American Railroads)

States also have agencies that regulate businesses within their borders. Business that is conducted entirely within a single state is called *intrastate commerce.*

Local governments also play a role in consumer protection. Health standards for public eating establishments, for example, are enforced by county health departments. Many counties have departments or bureaus of weights and measures, which inspect scales and other measuring devices for accuracy.

Private Consumer Groups

Private consumer groups also play a large role in consumer protection. Some consumer organizations perform a "watchdog" service. They check on consumer complaints and call public attention to offending businesses. Some groups sponsor and promote laws to increase consumer protection.

An organization that promotes legislation is called a *lobby.* Lobbyists study issues and report findings to their *constituents.* Constituents are people who authorize others to act for them. The people who live in a district represented by an elected legislator are constituents. Lobbyists may urge constituents to contact their lawmakers on behalf of proposed legislation. Lobbyists also deal directly with legislators.

State legislatures make laws regulating businesses conducted within state boundaries.

REACTING TO FRAUD

You have more than a right to seek a remedy if you feel you have been victimized by fraud. You have a responsibility to report the incident. However, such action should be taken only after you have made a serious effort to settle with the company.

Dealing With Businesses

You can contact a local company in person or by telephone. Present the facts and give the company a chance to respond.

If your problem involves a company located elsewhere, present your claim in writing. Provide all the facts: date and place of purchase, name and other identification of the product, and price you paid.

If possible, photocopy any mail orders for expensive items. If you pay by check or money order, photocopy that as well. The same applies to catalog or other special orders from a store. If you pay in advance, note the number of the check or money order. Keep any receipts for future reference.

There are two good rules to follow for all kinds of purchases: First, keep accurate records. This includes advertisements, store receipts, checks or money orders, and credit card receipts. Second, do not give up possession of your records. If proof of purchase is required, photocopy your original documents and submit the photocopy.

Seeking Help

There are numerous alternatives open to you if a company fails to help you with a complaint. A good place to start in most communities is the local *Better Business Bureau (BBB)*. A private agency, the Better Business Bureau is organized to improve local business. Two goals of the BBB are to eliminate false or misleading advertising and to find solutions to consumer complaints. Most BBB offices do not make recommendations regarding individual businesses. However, the BBB can and will caution consumers about businesses that are the subject of frequent complaints.

You can also get help from state or local government consumer protection agencies in many locations. Such agencies

Consumer complaints should be made in writing if a business is not located in your own area.

usually can be located under the government listings in the white pages of your telephone directory. If you are still unsure, your public library should have the information you need. Some local police departments also deal with fraud cases. At the very least, the police can advise you on where to file your complaint. Local prosecuting attorneys and state attorneys general usually investigate reports of fraud.

As you improve your knowledge and skills as a consumer, your chances of falling victim to fraud will decrease. Still, fraud can happen to anyone, even the most cautious consumer. Thus, you need not feel embarrassed if you become a victim. The responsible action is to report any case of fraud to the proper agency. Your actions may help authorities to deal with fraudulent business practices. Equally important, you may help other consumers to avoid the same experience.

CONTENT SUMMARY

Caution and knowledge are a consumer's best friends. It is good to be skeptical when you consider a purchase. A cautious consumer is less likely to buy problems.

Knowledge also is important. You should know what you are buying. You also should know the seller. You should be aware of what protections, if any, you have against disappointment.

Know what you want in terms of value before you make a purchase. Higher value usually carries a higher price. Decide how much you are willing to spend before you begin shopping.

Comparison shopping is one good way to get the most for your money. Areas for comparison include price, quality of materials and manufacture, and the value of guarantees and warranties. Price comparisons can be made between brands, between sellers, and between volumes of the same product. In checking prices, look for unit price as the true gauge of value. Always pay close attention to the wording of guarantees and warranties.

Labels can tell you many things about a product. Labels should include information such as weight or volume, materials used in the product, and grade or quality rating. Other information may be required, such as intended use and instructions for use and care of the product.

Labels on food and drug products also may contain instructions for use and care, lists of ingredients, and health warnings.

Planning ahead is the key to efficient, economical menu planning and grocery shopping. Your body needs adequate amounts of proteins, carbohydrates, and fats. A balanced diet consists of substances from the basic food groups: meat, fruits and vegetables, cereals and breads, and milk.

Cookbooks are available to guide you step by step through any kind of meal preparation. Recipes include lists of ingredients. Menu planning can be done on a weekly basis. Then, grocery shopping can be accomplished in a single trip to market. A complete shopping list helps you to purchase all the items you need, in the proper quantities.

There are several areas of business in which you should exercise special care as a consumer. These include door-to-door sales, mail-order buying, and telephone sales.

A number of federal agencies have consumer protection as their main area of concern. These agencies include the Food and Drug Administration (FDA), the Federal Trade Commission (FTC), and the Consumer Product Safety Commission. State and local governments also have agencies that work to safeguard consumer rights. Finally, private consumer groups seek legislation to prevent fraud and unfair business practices.

If you think you are a victim of fraud, you should attempt to gain satisfaction from the company. If this fails, you should report the incident and seek the help of government or private agencies. As a responsible consumer, you help other consumers when you report fraud.

CAREER COMMENTARIES

1. **Knowledge and caution are your best weapons as a consumer.**
   Describe a purchasing decision you made in the past month. Did you use the process method in reaching your decision? Were you satisfied with the quality of the item purchased? Describe any comparison shopping techniques you used.

2. **Be especially careful of telephone offers.**
   How would your response to a telephone offer differ from your response to a newspaper ad or a store display? Rate these forms of product information in terms of your ability to make a sound decision.

3. **You have a responsibility to report an incident of fraud.**
   In your community, where would you first seek help as the victim of a fraud? What kinds of information would you need to provide to an agency offering assistance?

supplement

mineral

fiber

roughage

meat group

fruits and
vegetables group

cereals and
breads group

milk group

menu

recipe

shopping list

rain check

Food and Drug Ad-
ministration (FDA)

Federal Trade Com-
mission (FTC)

interstate commerce

Consumer Product
Safety Commission

intrastate commerce

lobby

constituent

Better Business
Bureau (BBB)

V

Your Future

CAREER PLANNING is one of the most important challenges you face. How you meet this challenge will have a major effect upon your future life-style. Knowledge and an organized approach are vital elements of your career planning strategy.

Unit 16 discusses the process approach to career planning. Using the process method, you first review your self-knowledge. Next, you explore sources of career information. When you have identified broad career clusters, you can relate them to your aptitudes, interests, and life-style goals. After selecting one or more broad career goals, you can identify an educational path to follow. An important concept discussed in Unit 16 is that you must be prepared to deal with change throughout your career.

Setting Your Own Course

YOUR LEARNING JOB

When you have completed the reading assignments and exercises in this unit, you should be able to:

☐ Describe methods for effective career planning.

☐ Identify and use sources of career information.

☐ Identify and describe broad clusters of career opportunities.

☐ Relate your aptitudes, interests, and life-style goals to broad career areas.

☐ Select broad career goals and identify educational requirements for each career area.

☐ Explain why you must be prepared to deal with change during your career.

YOUR MOST IMPORTANT DECISION: A CAREER

"What kind of work do you do?" That is one of the first questions people usually ask new acquaintances. If a stranger asked you that question today, you would say that you are a student. How will you answer that question in 10 years? In 20 years? In 30 years?

Your answer to that question at any particular time will describe the state of your career. Remember, a career is a course you follow through your working life. Your career is your identity as a worker.

With rare exceptions, satisfying careers don't just happen. You have to plan ahead to set your course in the world of work. At

Your career is your identity as a worker. Satisfying careers require individuals to set their courses in the world of work.

Career paths can lead in many directions. Your abilities, preferences, and life-style goals are major elements in the career planning process. (Center photo, © Eugene Richards/Magnum Photos, Inc.; photo at right, courtesy IBM Corporation)

this stage of your educational path, career planning is a process that consists of these basic steps:

1. Know yourself. Identify and understand your personal strengths and weaknesses, your interests, and your values. Using this knowledge, you can determine your primary life-style goals.

2. Understand basic career options. Identify all career information sources available to you. Select alternatives based on information about broad occupational clusters.

3. Match yourself with career options. Use the decision-making process to consider the consequences of potential career decisions.

4. Reduce your options. Eliminate career areas that you feel would not satisfy your interests, abilities, and wants.

5. Choose one or more broad career areas, or occupational clusters. Identify current employment opportunities that apply to these broad occupational clusters.

6. Identify the educational requirements for these broad career areas, or broad occupational clusters.

7. Working with your guidance counselor, set a tentative course of study that will help you to meet these requirements.

Choosing a career path is one of the most important decisions you will make in life. Your career choice will have a great effect on your life-style. As an adult, more of your waking hours will be spent working than in any other activity. Much of your personal satisfaction will depend upon your occupation. Job-related satisfiers include:

- Income and security. The amount of money you earn will have a major effect on your life-style. Job security is equally important to many workers.

- Opportunity. Feeling that you have a chance to succeed and gain advancement contributes to a positive attitude toward your work.

- Achievement. One of the greatest satisfactions you can have is the knowledge that you have done a good job.

- Recognition. Having others notice and think well of your achievements gives you an important feeling of self-worth.

- Social contacts. Much of your time will be spent working. Friendships you develop through your job can be a source of great satisfaction.

- Leisure opportunities. Different careers make different demands on a person's time and energies. Life is not all work. Many people prefer to devote a large share of their time to interests outside of their jobs. The type of career you choose will determine the amount of time you have for leisure activities.

Leisure time is a major consideration for many people. Opportunities for leisure activities vary greatly among careers. (Aruba Tourist Bureau Photo)

Personal characteristics are vital considerations in career planning. An outgoing personality is a requirement for jobs that involve high levels of interaction with others.

KNOWING YOURSELF: A REVIEW

Before beginning your examination of career information sources, review the knowledge you gained in Part I. Think about your strengths and weaknesses, your interests, and your values. Review your list of interests and skills related to occupations.

As you think about career fields, pay particular attention to your personal characteristics that relate to work. Are you realistic, social, enterprising, artistic, conventional, or investigative?

Consider your personality traits. Are you outgoing or shy? Do you prefer working alone or with others? Are you punctual? Do you prefer a set routine and regular hours, or do you work best on your own schedule? These traits, along with your mental and physical skills and limitations, will be matched to job descriptions.

Be honest with yourself in identifying and evaluating your personal traits. There are no right or wrong characteristics. The important thing is to make the most of your strengths while working to minimize your weaknesses.

FOCUS ON YOUR FUTURE

MARK SAW ERIC'S BIKE in the rack in front of the newspaper office. "Good," he thought. "We can talk as we ride home."

Mark went to the counter, where Eric was turning in the receipts from his delivery route. "Hi, Eric," Mark said as he placed his own receipt book on the counter. "It looks like you beat me again."

"Hi, Mark. A lot of my customers weren't home, so I got through early. How did you do?" Eric asked.

"Oh, fairly well, I guess. Listen, I want to talk to you about collections while we ride home, OK?"

"Sure," Eric replied. "I'll wait for you out at the bike rack."

As the two friends rode home, Mark seemed disturbed. "What's wrong?" Eric asked.

"Oh, it's just that I hate doing collections at the end of the month. I don't like asking people for money, and I always feel like I'm intruding and disturbing them," Mark explained.

"Really? You shouldn't feel that way. You're providing your customers with a service. They ordered that service because they want to read the newspaper. They know it's not free," Eric said.

"I know that, but I'm still uncomfortable," Mark said. "And I'm really weak at trying to get new customers."

"Why don't you come along with me one day next week, after we finish our

deliveries?" Eric suggested. "You can see how I do it, and maybe you can pick up some pointers."

"Hey, that would be great!" Mark said. "I'm just not the selling type, I guess. But watching you might help. At the least, I might get a more positive attitude."

"That's exactly what you need," Eric said. "You have to believe in yourself and in the product you are selling. If you're positive about what you're doing, other people will tend to react to you more positively. My mom and dad are both in sales, you know. And they always remind me that a good salesperson has to like people. I like people, and I enjoy dealing with them."

Mark laughed. "That all makes good sense. Now, if I can just make myself believe it." Mark looked at Eric and smiled. "I guess it's no secret what kind of career you're thinking about," he said. ■

CAREER INFORMATION: WHERE TO LOOK

There are two general sources of information about occupations: printed materials and nonprint sources. Make use of both kinds of sources to collect information. Remember, at this stage you are not making a decision. You are merely gathering information. The more knowledge you gain, the better will be your ability to evaluate alternatives.

Print Sources

Print sources of occupational information include:

- U.S. Department of Labor publications and bulletins
- State, county, and local government civil service bulletins
- Publications of trade associations, labor unions, educational institutions, large companies, and professional societies
- Magazines, books, and brochures available in school guidance offices and public libraries.

You may be aware of only a limited number of occupations. For a better picture of the variety of occupations in the United States, consult the *Dictionary of Occupational Titles (DOT)*. The *DOT*

Look in the library reference section for printed information on occupations. Books, magazines, and brochures should be available in school and public libraries.

is the most complete reference guide to jobs and careers. This publication of the U.S. Department of Labor lists more than 20,000 occupations. That massive list may be of limited use to you right now. However, you should be aware of the nine primary occupational classifications listed in the *DOT*:

1. Professional, technical, and managerial
2. Clerical and sales
3. Service
4. Agricultural, fishery, forestry, and related occupations
5. Processing
6. Machine trades
7. Bench work
8. Structural work
9. Miscellaneous.

Highly useful in your career information search will be a companion publication to the *DOT*, the *Occupational Outlook Handbook (OOH)*. The *OOH* is published every other year by the Bureau of Labor Statistics of the Department of Labor. The *OOH* contains current information on many occupational titles and on employment trends. The kinds of information published for each occupational title are:

- Nature of the Work
- Working Conditions
- Employment
- Training, Other Qualifications, and Advancement
- Job Outlook
- Earnings
- Related Occupations
- Sources of Additional Information.

Even more timely information is available from another Bureau of Labor Statistics publication: the *Occupational Outlook*

Up-to-date information about many occupational titles and employment trends can be found in the *Occupational Outlook Handbook (OOH)*, published every other year by the Bureau of Labor Statistics of the Department of Labor.

Quarterly (OOQ). The *OOQ* is published four times a year to present the latest information available on the fast-changing labor market. The *OOQ* contains up-to-date information on employment trends, employment outlook, and new occupations.

Helpful job descriptions can be found in *civil service* bulletins. Civil service is the system of employment used by most government agencies. Civil service uses competitive examinations for hiring and promoting workers on the basis of *merit.* Merit is a person's value or ability on the job.

These and other print sources of career information should be available in your school guidance office and in your local public library.

Nonprint Sources

There also are a number of nonprint sources available to you. Two of the best sources are close at hand:

- School counselors
- Family, friends, and neighbors.

As you progress through school, you will have one or more counselors. A counselor's value lies in the ability to find meaningful information and to relate that information to your academic needs. This is more important in career guidance than personal knowledge of specific jobs or occupations.

Your most readily available source of occupational information is right at home. Your family and friends may be able to give you valuable information about a number of occupations. Personal contacts frequently serve as sources of firsthand personal experiences in various jobs.

Other nonprint sources include government and private organizations. The number and availability of these sources vary among different types of communities. They are more numerous in large cities. Other nonprint sources include:

- Civil service offices of government agencies
- Employment or personnel offices of private businesses
- Commercial employment agencies

- Chambers of commerce, trade associations, and other business organizations
- Private and community-sponsored counseling services.

A good place to start looking for career information is your school counseling or career guidance office.

These sources are particularly useful for information about jobs and careers available in your area. If you live in a rural area, you may find it necessary to visit a larger community to use these sources.

Government Assistance

Each state has an agency that specializes in employment services. The names of these agencies differ from one state to another. Names and addresses of these agencies can be found in the *Occupational Outlook Handbook.* Look under the heading, "Where to Go for More Information."

Accounting is one of the jobs listed under the occupational cluster of *Administrative and Managerial Occupations* in the *Occupational Outlook Handbook (OOH)*. There are 20 broad career clusters in the *OOH*, each containing related jobs.

LOOKING AT CAREER CLUSTERS

The *Occupational Outlook Handbook* lists 20 major occupational clusters of related jobs. A brief introduction to each cluster is followed by detailed descriptions of individual jobs within that category. The *OOH* is a reference work and is not designed to be read from cover to cover. The organization of the *OOH* makes it easy for you to locate useful information about occupational areas and specific jobs. The 20 occupational clusters listed in the *OOH* are:

- Administrative and managerial occupations
- Engineers, surveyors, and architects
- Natural scientists and mathematicians
- Social scientists, social workers, religious workers, and lawyers
- Teachers, librarians, and counselors
- Health diagnosing and treating practitioners
- Registered nurses, pharmacists, dieticians, therapists, and physician assistants
- Health technologists and technicians
- Writers, artists, and entertainers
- Technologists and technicians, except health
- Marketing and sales occupations
- Administrative support occupations, including clerical
- Service occupations
- Agricultural and forestry occupations
- Mechanics and repairers
- Construction and extractive occupations
- Production occupations
- Transportation and material moving occupations
- Helpers, handlers, equipment cleaners, and laborers
- Military occupations.

There are a number of factors to consider when you examine career clusters. Each of the following factors can be related to your aptitudes, interests, or life-style goals:

- Initial income
- Income potential
- Prestige or status
- Job pressures
- Repetition of tasks

Figure 16-1. Occupational clusters can be rated according to factors that are important to you as an individual. You can assign added value to factors that fit in with your strengths, weaknesses, interests, and life-style goals.

RATINGS OF OCCUPATIONAL CLUSTERS

OCCUPATIONAL CLUSTER	BEGINNING PAY	INCOME POTENTIAL	PRESTIGE OR STATUS	FREE OF PRESSURE
INDUSTRIAL PRODUCTION	1	2	3	1
OFFICE WORK	3	2	2	1
SERVICE INDUSTRIES	3	3	2	1
EDUCATION	1	2	1	1
SALES	2	1	2	3
CONSTRUCTION	1	2	3	2
TRANSPORTATION	1	2	3	2
SCIENCE AND ENGINEERING	1	1	1	1
MECHANICS AND REPAIRS	2	2	3	1
HEALTH SERVICES	1	1	1	2
ART AND DESIGN	1	1	1	2

- Interaction with others
- Educational requirements
- Physical requirements
- Promotion opportunities
- Projected employment opportunities.

Answers to these questions can be found in the *OOH* descriptions. Each occupational area can be rated according to these factors, as shown in Figure 16-1.

FEW REPETITIVE TASKS	SOCIAL INTERACTION	FEW EDUCATIONAL REQUIREMENTS	FEW PHYSICAL REQUIREMENTS	OPPORTUNITY FOR ADVANCEMENT	PROJECTED EMPLOYMENT OPPORTUNITIES
3	3	1	3	3	2
2	2	1	1	1	1
1	1	3	2	2	2
1	1	3	1	2	2
1	1	2	2	1	2
1	3	1	3	3	2
3	2	1	3	3	2
1	3	3	2	2	2
2	3	1	3	3	2
1	2	3	1	2	1
1	2	2	1	3	3

MATCHING YOURSELF TO CAREER CLUSTERS

Your next task is to match your aptitudes, interests, and life-style goals to the descriptions of career areas. This comparison requires a thorough examination of your personal code. Remember, you are not trying to pick a specific career at this point. You are trying to identify broad potential career paths. One way to narrow your choices is to make a chart, such as that illustrated in Figure 16-2. Take the following steps:

1. List all the occupational clusters to which you feel attracted for any reason. Using the *OOH* or another reference source, identify the specific career areas that appeal to you within each cluster.

2. Using the list of factors illustrated in Figure 16-1, rate each career area according to your needs and wants. Use a scale of 1 to 5, with 5 being the highest rating and 1 the lowest.

3. Using the same list of factors, rate each career area according to your strengths and weaknesses. Use the same rating scale.

4. Using the same list of factors, rate each career area according to your interests. Use the same rating scale.

5. Begin to narrow your list of options. Eliminate those career areas that you feel would not match your needs and wants.

6. Eliminate those career areas that you feel would not match your strengths or aptitudes.

7. Eliminate those career areas that you feel would not match your interests.

8. Rate the remaining career areas by adding your ratings for each one. The highest possible score on this chart would be 15. That score would indicate your highest rating for aptitudes (strengths and weaknesses), interests, and life-style goals (needs and wants).

Think about the decision-making model introduced in Part III. Steps 1 through 7 above represent the third and fourth steps in that model. Those steps are to find alternatives and to evaluate potential consequences of each alternative. Step 8 above

RATING OF OCCUPATIONAL CLUSTERS

NAME: Marci Bracken

CAREER CLUSTER	NEEDS	WANTS	STRENGTHS	WEAKNESSES	INTERESTS	SCORE
Administrative	3	3	4	-2	2	10
Teaching	3	2	5	-1	3	12
Sales	2	3	3	-1	3	10
Agriculture	4	4	3	-2	3	12
Construction	2	2	3	-3	2	6
Production	3	2	2	-4	3	6
Military	4	3	4	-3	2	10

(Scale = 1-5, 5 being best)

represents the fifth step in the model: choose the best alternative. In this case, you may choose more than one alternative.

Your next step is to determine how you would prepare yourself for the career areas you have rated highest. Again, refer to the *OOH* or other reference works available at your school and seek assistance from your guidance counselor.

Figure 16-2. Match yourself to career clusters by noting how they match your needs and wants, strengths weaknesses, and interests. Rating occupational areas in this way provides a meaningful comparison.

CHARTING A COURSE

At this point, you are ready to move to the sixth step in the decision-making process: implementing your alternative. You do this by charting a course through school.

To prepare for this planning step, identify the educational requirements for the career areas you have chosen. The *OOH* is a valuable guide for these choices. When you have identified the basic educational requirements, discuss them with your counselor. Your counselor can advise you in several ways:

- Set a direction. Determining your next educational moves may be critical in helping you reach necessary objectives. This is especially important in those areas, such as mathematics, in which prerequisites are necessary for advancement.

- Estimate your abilities. Your past performance in school and results of intelligence and aptitude tests are helpful in selecting an educational path. You may not be aware of some strengths or weaknesses that could affect these decisions.

- Keep your options open. In many cases, it may be better to avoid heavy concentration in one educational area. You may

A plan of action is needed for career preparation, just as for a computer program. Charting a course involves identifying the steps required to reach a goal. Continuing education can be an important element in many careers.

change your career goals several times before you complete high school. Remember, the world of work is changing rapidly. You may want to follow a path that will let you delay final decisions as long as possible.

Keep in mind that you are not trying to choose a career at this stage. However, your self-assessment and your study of career areas should prepare you to make appropriate decisions as you prepare to begin your working life.

DEALING WITH CHANGE

Regardless of which career path you follow, you will have another lifelong occupation: dealing with change. In most career areas today, individuals are expected to change occupations between three and seven times during their working lives. These changes are caused by several factors:

- Some traditional industries are shrinking or going out of existence.

- Job skills may be altered by *technological advances*, such as machines that perform tasks formerly done by humans. *Technology* is the application of science to achieve practical goals that meet needs.

- New occupations—and new opportunities—are being created in a changing job market.

- Your own interests and needs may change as you grow in age and experience.

The increasing rate of change presents new opportunities and new challenges in the world of work. The time has pretty much passed when an individual could train or study for one lifetime job. Even those who remain in a particular career today must constantly update their skills and knowledge. Otherwise, change will overtake them.

Effective career planning is a life long activity. Your career plans must account for the role that change will play in your life. In some career fields, this means preparing for supervisory or

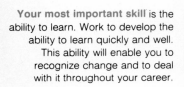
Your most important skill is the ability to learn. Work to develop the ability to learn quickly and well. This ability will enable you to recognize change and to deal with it throughout your career.

management roles when basic work skills have been mastered. In other career clusters, you must be prepared to learn new skills or techniques as industries change.

Many career fields require some form of *continuing education* or skill development. Continuing education is schooling designed to update or upgrade a person's knowledge or skills related to his or her occupation. In some cases, continuing education will involve going to college or technical or vocational schools. In many cases, employers will provide on-the-job training or job advancement courses. The important thing is that you be aware of these opportunities and be ready to utilize them.

Sources of Information

Most of the information sources discussed in this unit will be useful during your working career. Wherever you live, your public library will be a useful source of printed career information. Community colleges and vocational schools have career guidance and job placement offices. When you become a worker, your own employer may have career advancement programs. Employee training and educational programs, in fact, are a major attraction today in recruitment of new employees.

Motivation for Success

Your own attitudes will determine how effectively you deal with change in your career. One valuable strength is a positive attitude. Your attitude is positive if you view most changes as opportunities or challenges. If changes usually seem like problems or threats, check your attitude.

The best way to cope with change is to use the problem-solving/decision-making process. This organized approach is particularly valuable in career decision-making situations.

YOUR MOST IMPORTANT ABILITY

Everyone should have one educational goal in addition to meeting specific requirements for a chosen career field. That goal should be to build a broad base of knowledge. The broader your educational experience, the better will be your ability to deal with change.

Even more important, you should develop the ability to learn. Without this skill, you may be left behind by the forces of change. Learning skills help you to see change approaching as well as to deal with it. A person who learns quickly and well is usually at the front of progress.

As you progress through school, then, remember that the most important skill you can develop is the ability to learn.

CONTENT SUMMARY

One of your most important decisions will be the choice of a career. To make an effective choice, you must first know yourself. Next, identify your basic career alternatives. Then, match yourself with opportunities. When you have selected one or more broad career areas, determine your educational needs. Finally, set a tentative educational course.

Job-related satisfiers include income, opportunity, achievement, recognition, social contacts, and leisure opportunities.

These are factors that should be matched with your aptitudes, interests, and life-style goals.

There are two general types of career information sources: print and nonprint. An especially helpful print source is the *Occupational Outlook Handbook (OOH)*, published by the Bureau of Labor Statistics of the U.S. Department of Labor. The *OOH* groups careers into 20 occupational clusters. Each job or career is described according to the nature of the work, working conditions, employment, job outlook, and earnings. Other factors discussed are training, other qualifications, and advancement; related occupations; and sources of additional information.

Jobs can be rated according to factors that relate to your needs and wants. Initial income, income potential, prestige, pressure, repetitiveness of tasks, and interaction with others are some. Others are educational requirements, physical requirements, promotion opportunities, and projected job opportunities.

By matching your aptitudes, interests, and life-style goals to these job-rating factors, you can narrow your career alternatives. When you have selected one or more career areas, you can chart an educational course to meet educational requirements. This should be done with the advice and participation of your counselor.

You live in a time of rapid change. It is likely that you will make three to seven career changes during your working life. Thus, you should seek a broad base of knowledge. The most important skill you can learn in school is the ability to learn.

CAREER COMMENTARIES

1. **Much of your personal satisfaction will depend upon your occupation.**
   How does this statement relate to your present status as a student? What kinds of satisfiers available to you as a student will carry over into your working career?

2. **Regardless of which career path you follow, you will have another lifelong occupation: dealing with change.**
   Identify an adult, either a relative or a friend, who recently has undergone a career change. How was that person affected by the change? Was the change positive or negative? Do you think you might have dealt with the situation differently?

3. **The most important skill you can develop is the ability to learn.**
   Think of one career area that interests you right now. Explain how an ability to learn would help you advance in that career field. What steps can you take in school to gain the ability to learn?

KEY TERMS

Dictionary of Occupational Titles (DOT)

Occupational Outlook Handbook (OOH)

Occupational Outlook Quarterly (OOQ)

civil service

merit

technological advance

technology

continuing education

Glossary

A

abstract reasoning Thinking about a topic that is not associated with any physical object or specific event. Emphasis is on ideas and their importance.

acceptance Taking a neutral position, offering no resistance to a change.

acquaintance A person you may meet and deal with regularly, but do not know well enough to consider him or her as a friend.

aggressive Forceful, pressing hard to achieve a purpose.

alternative A choice or an opportunity to make a choice. Also, a possible solution to a problem.

ambition A strong desire to succeed or to accomplish tasks.

analytical Able to separate a problem or situation into its parts and to understand the relationships among those parts.

aptitude A personal strength that relates to jobs or careers.

artistic Creative; imaginative.

assets Money and property owned by a person or business.

attach To seize money or a possession from a debtor who has failed to pay for a purchased item.

authorize   Granting the power to perform an action; to permit or approve.

B

balance   The remainder of the total amount of a selling price after payments already made have been deducted.

bank credit card   A credit card that can be used for transactions against an account with a bank or other financial institution.

barter   A transaction in which items of equal value are traded.

bearing   *See* poise.

behavioral tendency   The manner in which a person is inclined to respond to a change or situation.

beneficial   Provides a positive result.

Better Business Bureau (BBB)   A private agency that works to eliminate false or misleading advertising and to find solutions to consumer complaints.

boastful   Bragging or talking about accomplishments with a level of pride that may not be justified.

bonus   Money paid to an employee in addition to normal wages.

borrower   *See* debtor.

breadwinner   A main income-producer within a family.

budget   A plan for spending money.

business transaction   *See* transaction.

C

career   The course a person follows through his or her working life. Usually associated with a particular type of occupation or field of work.

challenge   A situation in which a person must use his or her abilities to deal with a difficult situation.

characteristic An identifiable quality of a person.

civil service System used by government agencies to hire and promote employees. Term indicates a distinction between civilian government employees, and members of the armed services or employees of businesses.

clearance sale Special reduction of prices on in-stock items in a store to make room for new merchandise.

code of conduct *See* personal code.

code of living *See* personal code.

collateral A valuable possession that a debtor uses to guarantee repayment of a loan.

commitment A promise to do something; a responsibility.

comparison shopping Examining the value of two or more similar products before deciding what to purchase.

compensation An employee's wage or salary, plus other benefits.

compromise (noun) A settlement of a disagreement in which all parties give up some wants as a basis for reaching agreement.

compromise (verb) Giving up part of a goal to reach a decision or to solve a problem.

concrete reasoning Way of thinking that is based on experience with tangible things or actual events.

conflict A condition in which two or more forces oppose one another.

consequence The result of an action or decision.

conservative Preferring a traditional life-style or traditional manners.

consistent Remains the same in different situations.

constituents People who authorize others to act for them in the creation, enforcement, and interpretation of laws.

consumer A person who buys and uses the products of business and industry.

Consumer Product Safety Commission A federal agency that establishes and enforces safety standards for products.

contingency plan Course of action to be taken if anticipated problems or situations arise.

continuing education Career-related courses of study or training.

contract A binding agreement between two or more people or groups.

conventional As expected, traditional.

cosmetic Relating to outward attractiveness of appearance.

cosmetics Beauty aids that are applied to enhance a person's appearance.

craft *See* trade.

creative Original and imaginative.

credit Borrowing on the basis of a commitment for later repayment.

credit card A small sheet of plastic with raised letters and numbers that is used to purchase products and services on credit.

credit history A record of a person's payments on credit purchases.

credit rating An evaluation of a person's ability and willingness to repay debts.

creditor A person or institution that lends money.

criteria Measures or standards that must be met in problem solving or decision making.

D

day-to-day living expenses Money that an individual or family must pay out to satisfy daily needs.

debtor A person or organization that owes money.

decision A choice or judgment that leads to a commitment.

decision statement Description of objectives to be achieved or problem to be solved by committing to an action.

decisive Able to make decisions quickly and confidently.

decline To become smaller in size or quantity.

deduction An amount subtracted from the taxable portion of a person's earnings.

demand The amount of a product that consumers are willing to buy at a given price.

Dictionary of Occupational Titles (DOT) A reference guide that lists more than 20,000 occupations available in the United States.

discretion The ability to make responsible decisions.

discretionary income Money left over and available for spending after an individual or family pays bills and daily living expenses.

down payment A partial first payment made on the total price of an item or of real property.

durability The ability of a product to maintain its quality over time.

E

economic security Having enough income to satisfy physical needs.

element A small part of something larger.

emotion A feeling that is usually a reaction to an experience rather than to something physical.

emotional investment The involvement of feelings and expectations in a relationship.

emotional needs Feelings that are necessary for a person to be happy and satisfied. Examples include being with other people, having value or worth in the eyes of others, and being able to realize personal potential.

energetic The ability to be active and to use strength in performing work.

enterprising Ambitious and energetic.

entrepreneur A person who invests money, time, and energy as the owner of a business enterprise.

environment Physical surroundings.

equity Percentage or share of ownership.

esteem A person's value or worth in the eyes of others.

ethnic background An individual's race or membership in a large group with common traits or customs.

expectation A result a person believes or hopes will occur.

expenses Money paid to satisfy needs and wants.

external change A problem or situation resulting from causes that cannot be controlled.

extrovert A person who enjoys the company of others more than being alone; talkative and friendly.

F

fad A style that enjoys temporary, exaggerated popularity.

favoritism Treating some people better than others.

Federal Trade Commission (FTC) A federal agency established to guard against unfair business practices.

feedback Information about the results of an action or event.

finance charge Costs or fees added to interest charges on money borrowed.

fixed expenses Bills and other charges that must be paid at certain times.

flexible expenses Living costs that can be varied, adjusted, or planned for.

follow-up Observing or changing a decision after it has been made to make sure it is implemented correctly.

Food and Drug Administration (FDA) A federal agency that regulates the purity, quality, and labeling of foods and drugs.

frail Physically weak, delicate.

friend A person to whom an individual relates with affection and respect.

friendship A close relationship between two people based on shared experiences and mutual interests.

fringe benefit Payments or values received by employees in addition to wages or salary.

function A social gathering that has a special purpose.

G

generation A group of individuals who make up a single step in the continuing life of a family; represents about 20 years.

good A physical item for sale; merchandise.

grooming Regular care designed to make the body neat and attractive.

gross income The total amount of money a person earns over a certain period of time on a job.

guarantee An assurance of the quality or the length of service to be expected from a product.

guideline A rule in a person's code that influences his or her choices.

H

harmony An inner calm or peace.

household Members of a family living within one home.

hygiene The practice of caring for the body in ways that maintain good health.

I

illogical idea An idea that is not sensible. Often results when a person does not think through a situation carefully.

image A person's self as seen by others.

implement To carry out a plan.

impulse buying Purchasing items based on sudden, often illogical, decisions.

income A benefit that a person receives as a result of his or her labor or investments. Usually provided in the form of money.

indecisive Slow and unsure in making decisions.

insecure Describes a person who lacks confidence in his or her abilities.

insight The ability to see the inner nature of some person or situation.

installment sales contract A special type of personal loan in which the seller of an item retains ownership of the item as collateral.

interaction An exchange between two or more people.

interest An idea or activity that holds a person's attention. Also, a fee paid for the use of money.

internal change A modifying or transforming activity that takes place within an individual.

interpersonal skill An ability to get along with others.

interstate commerce Business involving transactions in more than one state.

intrastate commerce Business conducted entirely within a single state.

introvert A person who prefers being alone.

investigative Searching for causes or reasons.

isolated Set apart or removed from others.

J

judgment A conclusion based on weighing of information.

L

law A rule of conduct that a person must follow.

legal law A rule of conduct written down in government codes and enforced by government agencies. Provides a safe and orderly environment for a society.

leisure activity Something a person enjoys doing when not on the job or in school.

liberal Open-minded; receptive to new ideas; generous.

life-style The manner in which a person lives. Shaped by such choices as type of living environment, working environment, social desires, family desires, and personal style or image.

line of credit An amount of money available to a prospective borrower, such as a credit card holder.

lobby An organization that promotes the need for a specific form of legislation.

logic Thinking or reasoning in an orderly manner to arrive at correct conclusions.

logical idea An idea that is sensible.

loyal Protective and trustworthy toward an individual or group.

M

maintenance Activities that keep equipment in good condition.

manual dexterity Graceful and skillful use of the hands.

mass media Systems of communication that bring messages to large numbers of people.

medium   A device or a system on which signals and/or information are recorded, transmitted, or delivered.

merit   Value or ability.

mobile   Able to move or to be moved.

mobility   Freedom, or ease, of movement.

model   A diagram showing a process that can be followed to achieve a specific result, such as solving problems and making decisions.

modification   A change in structure or design, usually intended to bring about improvement.

morality   Standards of right and wrong.

mortgage loan   Money a person borrows for the purchase of real property, especially a home.

motivation   A combination of desire and determination that helps a person reach his or her goal.

motive   A reason for doing something.

mutual   Shared by all members of a group.

N

natural fiber   Cotton, wool, linen, and silk; a clothing or soft goods material that is not manufactured.

needs   Things that are necessary for a person's well-being.

negative   Bad feeling or reaction, particularly about a change.

net income   The amount of money an employee receives after taxes and other fees are deducted.

neutral   Having no effect or reaction.

nutrient   A substance that helps the body to build and repair itself. Provides energy and assists the body in performing its vital functions.

nutrition   The process in which the body takes in and uses food substances.

O

objective Viewed without distortion from personal feelings or prejudices.

Occupational Outlook Handbook (OOH) Reference guide containing current information on occupational titles and on employment trends.

Occupational Outlook Quarterly (OOQ) Reference guide published four times a year to present the latest information available on labor market changes.

open minded Able to view many kinds of situations and people as they really are; without prejudice.

opportunity A situation that provides a chance for progress or advancement.

opposition Resistance, particularly to change.

optimist A person with a positive outlook.

option One of two or more choices.

organization A structure establishing relationships.

P

personal code A set of ideas and beliefs that serve as rules for a person's conduct.

personal loan Money borrowed by an individual to be used for a special purpose.

personal value An idea, a belief, or an opinion that is important to a person.

personality The collection of a person's emotional and behavioral tendencies.

pessimist A person with a negative outlook.

physical needs Things a person must have to stay alive or to live safely.

piecework Wages based on number of units of work completed.

poise The manner in which a person presents himself or herself to others.

policy A management belief or position that guides the way an organization functions.

positive Good feelings or reactions, particularly about change.

potential The sum of possibilities for personal development.

pre-authorized Approved in advance.

preference Selection based on personal values.

prejudice Negative feelings or actions against persons or groups that have no basis in fact.

principal Amount of money borrowed.

priorities A system of ratings based on importance.

problem Result of change, often requiring corrective action.

process A series of steps followed, in a certain order, to reach a known result.

product Something of value offered for sale.

projecting Presenting an idea, feeling, opinion, or the entire self in a strong, clear manner.

prospect A chance or opportunity for success.

R

real estate loan Money borrowed to purchase land or buildings.

real property Land or land with buildings.

realistic Believable, actual.

regular charge account An account in which a person pays for purchases once a month. Also called a 30-day charge account.

reimbursement Replacement of a product or repayment of money spent by a purchaser.

reinforce To make stronger or provide added support.

rejection Refusal to accept, particularly a change.

reliable Dependable, consistent.

repossess The taking of an item purchased by a debtor when payments are not received by the creditor.

reputation The overall quality or general character of a person or organization as seen by others.

research Study and related efforts directed toward discovery and/or development.

resentment Ill feelings about the possessions, actions, accomplishments of another person.

responsibility A duty for which a person is expected to answer.

responsible In charge of certain activities, or duties, and their consequences.

revolving charge account An account that has a credit limit and requires regular, minimum payments.

S

safety needs Requirements for staying out of physical danger.

salary A fixed rate of pay for services.

secure A feeling of confidence in a person's own knowledge or abilities.

self The complete person—body, mind, and personality; identity.

self-esteem The value or worth a person places on himself or herself.

self-fulfillment Feeling of accomplishment that comes from using abilities fully.

self-image The way a person sees himself or herself.

service An activity that meets demands of people in terms of personal requirements rather than through impersonal delivery of products.

service industry A group of organizations providing the same or similar services.

single-purpose card A credit card issued by and usable only at a particular business or business chain.

skepticism Disbelief; suspicion.

social Involving relationships among people.

social needs Urge for interaction with other people or groups.

society A group of people who share common interests, beliefs, or a common environment. Includes local communities, states, and nations.

solution An action taken to eliminate or deal with a problem.

specific Belonging to a particular category.

spouse A marriage partner.

stepchild A son or daughter of only one of two marriage partners.

stimulate To provide reasons or desires that lead to activity.

strength An ability; a good, or positive, quality.

stress Feelings of pressure that make a person uncomfortable, frustrated, angry, or worried.

subjective A tendency to view issues from a personal perspective rather than considering a broader outlook.

supervisor A person who watches the work of others and directs them on the job.

supply The amount of a product that businesses are willing to sell at a given price.

support In favor of, particularly a change.

survival needs Things a person must have to stay alive.

symptom A sign that identifies a condition.

synthetic fiber Artificially produced thread used to make cloth.

T

tangible Having physical properties.

technological advances Improved methods resulting from development of technology.

technology Applied science used for the benefit of people.

tension *See* stress.

threat A sign that danger might result if a certain course of action is followed.

title A document establishing legal ownership of an item or of real property.

trade An occupation that requires manual or mechanical skill.

trait A quality or personality characteristic that distinguishes one person from another.

transaction An act of doing business.

transition A change that occurs gradually.

travel and entertainment card A credit card intended primarily for business use.

U

understudy A performer who learns a part or role and prepares to substitute for a regular performer in an emergency.

unique One of a kind.

unit price The cost of the smallest measured portion of a product.

unity Shared commitment or purpose.

upkeep *See* maintenance.

urgent Immediate, needed as soon as possible.

utility Broadly useful.

V

valid Authentic, acceptable.

value Rating of a good or service based on its price, quality, usefulness, and reliability.

violate To ignore a law or a code of conduct.

W

wage Payment for labor or services.

wage earner A person who is paid on a regular basis for work performed.

wants Things a person desires and feels will make him or her happier.

warranty A manufacturer's assurance, usually in writing, that a product is as good as it is claimed to be.

weakness Something a person does not do well.

Index

A

Abstract reasoning, 9; occupations using, 10

Acceptance of change, 57

Achievement, 283; and satisfaction, 86-87

Acquaintances, defined, 133

Advertising, 206

Affection, friendship based upon, 136

Aggression, defined, 43

Aging, 46, 95

Agreeableness, 44

Agriculture, 90

Aircraft, 52-53

Allowances, 226

Alternatives: contingency plans as, 182; defined, 76, 155, 156; evaluating consequences of, 155, 160-161, 172-174, 204; identifying, 155, 168-169, 203; listing, 168-169; new, 182; number of, 169-170; quality of, 168; selecting, 156, 181-182, 203, 204; workable, 169. *See also* Choice(s); Option(s)

Ambition, 43, 76

Analysis of problem/decision, 155, 166

Analytical thinking, defined, 14

Appropriate choices, 151

Aptitudes: and career choice, 294; defined, 14; tests of, 296. *See also* Skills; Strengths

Artistic characteristics, 13

Assets, 247

Attachment of wages, 239

Attentiveness, 44

Attitude(s): toward change, 57, 299; conservative, 206; of employees, 127; toward leadership role, 142; liberal, 206; positive, 142; posture and, 41; and self-image, 34-35; of skepticism, 252; understanding of, 69

Authorization: of credit card transactions, 242; defined, 242

Automobiles, 52-53

B

Balanced diet, 261-265

Balances, 242; interest on, 243

Bank credit cards, 242

Barter, defined, 123

BBB. *See* Better Business Bureau

Bearing, defined, 45

Behavior, and friendships, 141

Behavioral tendencies, defined, 8

Beliefs, 57, 65; challenges to, 71; decision-making/problem-solving and, 152; modification of, 60-61; and reactions to change, 61, 71. *See also* Personal code

Belonging, 121

Beneficial, defined, 67

Better Business Bureau (BBB), 273

Boastfulness, 43

Body. *See* Physical characteristics; Physical limitations

Bonuses, 111

Borrowers. *See* Debtors

Breads, 262, 263, 265

Broadcast media, 27

Budgeting, 226, 228-238; of discretionary income, 229; of family income, 103; for food purchases, 218-220

Budgets: calculation of, 234; defined, 103, 226; success in following, 226; time period of, 233

Bureau of Labor Statistics, 287

Business, defined, 123

Business transactions. *See* Transaction(s)

Buying. *See* Spending; Spending decisions

C

Calories, 261

Carbohydrates, 261-262

Career(s): changes in, 94-95, 192-193, 297-299; defined, 6; demands of, 118; and home management, 111, 113; information sources on, 286-289; and life-styles, 91, 110-111, 292-294; planning, 281-301; resumption of, 113. *See also* Occupations

Career choice, decision-making model applied to, 294-297

Career clusters, 291-295; considerations in examining, 292-293; matching self to, 294-295; *Occupational Outlook Handbook* organized by, 291

Career planning, 281-301; basic steps in, 282

Cereals and breads food group, 265

Certification programs, 271

Challenges: to beliefs, 71; defined, 77

Change(s), 51-62; in careers, 6, 94-95, 192-193, 297-299; coping with, 299; and education, 299; external, 55-57, 59, 77, 149, 192; as goals, 165; and history, 51-54; and image, 46-47; internal, 55, 59, 149-150; in jobs, 94; in life-style, 93-95; nature of, 61; neutral, 55; as opportunity, 77; and personal code, 65, 67, 69, 95, 158, 161, 192, 193; preparation for, 60-61, 297; reactions to, 46-47, 55-57, 299; sources of, 55, 150; understanding, 154, 165-166; unexpected, 177, 182, 191

Characteristics, defined, 8

Charge accounts, 243; revolving, 243-244; thirty day, 243

Choice(s): appropriate, 151; inappropriate, 151; influences on, 72-73; of life-style, 25-26, 83, 88; and values, 28-29; and wants, 19, 25. *See also* Alternatives; Option(s)

Cities, activities and opportunities in, 85, 88, 90

Cleaning: clothing, 106, 221; home, 104

Cleanliness of workplace, 127

Climate, 85, 91

Clothing, 40-41; care of, 106, 221; expenses, 230; fads, 41, 105, 221; purchasing, 105, 220-221; quality of, 256

Code, defined, 65

Code of conduct. *See* Personal code

Code of living. *See* Personal code

Collateral, 239; assets as, 247

Commitment(s), 156, 182; and changing mind, 182; defined, 150, 182; purchases as, 253

Communication: advances in, 54; defined, 109; in families, 109, 113; between friends, 136

Comparison shopping, 208-209, 253-257; for foods, 218-219

Compensation, 123, 127-128; defined, 127

Compromise: defined, 100, 173; within families, 100-101

Computer design and manufacturing, 91

Concrete reasoning, 9; occupations using, 10

Confidence, 41, 42, 46

Conflicts: defined, 71, 100; in family, 113; management in home, 113; with personal code, 71; of roles, 117

Consequences: of alternatives, 172-174; predicting, 173-174

Conservative attitude, defined, 206

Consistently, defined, 113

Constituents, defined, 272

Consumer(s): advice for, 208-212; information sources, 209, 255; risks taken by, 251-253; shopping methods, 208-209

Consumer fraud: common areas for, 268-269; seeking help for, 273-274

Consumer Product Safety Commission, 271

Consumer protection, 255; government agencies for, 252, 269-272; laws, 252, 269, 272

Contingencies, 176-177

Contingency plans, 176-177, 191; as alternatives, 182; defined, 176; flexibility of, 177

Continuing education, 298

Contracts, 94

Control: and attitudes, 57; in decision making, 166; of internal change, 59; of reactions to external change, 57, 59-61

Conventional traits, 12

Cookbooks, 266-267

Cooperation in family, 107, 111

Cosmetic(s), 39

Counselors, as information sources, 288

Craft, defined, 12

Creative work, 120

Credit: advantages, 244; for consumers, 238-247; defined, 214, 234; disadvantages, 245-246; types of, 239-240, 242-244

Credit accounts, 234

Credit cards, 242-244; receipts, 273

Credit history, 246

Credit rating, defined, 214, 246-247

Creditors, 238-239

Criteria, defined, 166

Cultural activities, 88

D

Day-to-day living expenses, 231, 234, 236

Debtors, defined, 238

Decision(s), 29, 57; analyzing, 203; chains of, 189; and changes in personal code, 192-193; and conflicts, 71; defined, 59, 150; identifying, 154-155, 165-166, 203; implementing, 184-185; on life-style factors, 91; long-term importance of, 181; modifying, 188-189; versus problems, 59-60. *See also* Choice(s); Decision making

Decision making: as group activity, 184; judgment in, 20; long-range, 192-193; and personal code, 156; priorities in, 181; process approach to, 61, 151-156 (*See also* Decision-making model); urgency of, 166

Decision-making model, 202-204; applied to career choice, 294-297, 298

Decision statements, defined, 165-166

Decisiveness, 76

Decline, defined, 91

Deductions, income tax, 216, 229

Demand, in relation to prices, 220

Department of Labor, 286, 287

Dexterity, defined, 9

Dictionary of Occupational Titles (DOT), 286-287

Diet: balanced, 261, 262, 264-265; defined, 261

Discretionary income, 229, 234

Doing nothing, as an option, 57, 166, 181

Down payments, 216, 240, 242

Dress. *See* Clothing

Drugs: labels, 259-260; regulation of, 270

Durability, 256

E

Economic security, defined, 23

Education, and dealing with change, 299

Emotion(s), defined, 8

Emotional needs, 22, 24-25; for self-esteem, 24; for self-fulfillment, 24-25

Employees: responsibilities of, 128-129, 143; role of, 123

Employers: loyalty to, 125; policies of, 129; responsibilities of, 127-128

Employment information, 287-288

Enterprising characteristics, 12-13

Enthusiasm, 42

Entrepreneur, defined, 193

Environment: defined, 22; geographic, 84-85; image and, 47; and life-style, 25, 83-96; and opportunity, 90-91; orderliness of, 23; safety of, 22

Equity, defined, 216

Esteem, defined, 24

Ethnic background, 140

Evaluation, 152; of alternatives, 155, 156, 161, 172-174, 204; and feedback, 188-189; of purchases, 212

Exercise, 37, 38

Expectations, satisfaction in relation to, 121

Expenses: adjustments to, 236, 238; day-to-day living, 231, 234, 236; defined, 230; fixed, 230, 233, 234, 236; flexible, 231-232, 234

External change(s), 59, 150; defined, 55; long-range plans and, 192; problems and, 149; reacting to, 55-57, 77

Extroverts, 76, 120

F

Fads, 221; defined, 41, 105

Fair treatment, 128

Families, 99-114; attending functions of, 110; communication in, 109, 113; conflicts in, 113; cooperation in, 107, 111; differences between, 99-101; encouragement by, 110; and friendships, 140; goals of, 101; as information sources, 288; life-style and, 25, 94, 110-111; mutual caring in, 110; personal values and, 26; responsibilities of members of, 102-107, 109-111; role in, 102, 117, 123; single-parent, 100, 111; structure of, 99-100, 102; supervision of members of, 107; unity of, 101; values influenced by, 206. *See also* Home management; Household(s)

Fats, 262

Favoritism, 128

FDA. *See* Food and Drug Administration

Federal consumer protection agencies, 270-272

Federal Trade Commission (FTC), 271

Feedback, 188-189; defined, 152, 188; and evaluation, 156, 188-189, 203-204

Fiber in food, 263

Finance charges, 238

Financial planning. *See* Spending decisions

First impressions, 35-36

Fixed expenses, 230, 233, 236; budgeting, 234; time factor in payment of, 233

Flexibility: in day-to-day living expenses, 233, 236; of home ownership, 216

Flexible expenses, 231-234

Followers, friends as, 142

Follow-up, defined, 188

Food(s): labels, 259-260; shopping for, 104, 218-220, 267

Food and Drug Administration (FDA), 270

Food groups, 264-265

Food values, 261-263

Frail, defined, 8

Fraud. *See* Consumer fraud

Friends, 283; comfort with, 136; defined, 133; as information sources, 288; values influenced by, 206

Friendships, 133-144; breaking up of, 134, 138; careers and, 142; and changing interests, 138; defined, 133; development of, 138; effort required in, 134; and families, 140; influence on behavior, 141; qualities of, 136-137; and self-image, 142; understanding developed by, 140-141

Fringe benefits, 127-128

Fruits and vegetables food group, 264

FTC. *See* Federal Trade Commission

Fuel, food as, 261

Functions, defined, 110

G

Generations, defined, 99

Geographic environment, adjustment to, 91; and life-style, 84-85

Goal(s), 43; in budgeting, 226; changes as, 165; decisions necessary to reach, 165-166; of employers, 129; family, 101; family support in achieving, 110; long-range, 192; personal, 101, 142-143; setting, in problem solving and decision making, 25, 155; specific, 101

Good(s): defined, 126, 201; used, 252

Government agencies: for consumer protection, 252, 269-272; as sources of career information, 289

Government regulation, for consumer protection, 269-272

Greetings, 44

Grooming, 39

Gross income, 228

Groups: decision making/problem solving in, 182, 184, 185; relationships in, 143; shared responsibilities of, 143

Guarantees, 256-257

Guidelines: defined, 72; versus laws, 72

H

Hair, 38-39; facial, 39

Harmony: defined, 100; in workplace, 129

Health, and physical appearance, 37-38

Health insurance, 128

Home maintenance, 103-104, 216

Home management: and careers, 111, 113; changes in needs, 113; responsibilities of, 102-107

Home ownership, 216-217; advantages of, 216; responsibilities, 216-217

Honesty of employees, 126

Household(s): defined, 99; expenses, 202. *See also* Families; Home management

Housing alternatives, 214-217

Human resources, 91

Hygiene, and physical appearance, 38-39

I

Ideas: illogical, 74-75; logical, 73-74

Identity, 46

Illogical ideas, 74-75

Image: change and, 46-47; defined, 33; physical appearance and, 35-41; versus self-image, 33-35

Implementing choices/decisions, 156, 184-185, 204

Impulse buying, 211-212, 220, 245

Inappropriate choices, 151

Income, 118, 119, 283; credit rating and, 246; defined, 228; discretionary, 229; gross, 228; and life-style, 110; living beyond, 234; management of, 102-103; net, 229

Income level, 226

Income tax, 70; deductions, 216, 229

Indecisiveness, 76

Independence, 193

Industries: decline of, 91; range of, 90-91

Insecurity, 75

Insight, defined, 69

Instructions, 125, 127

Insurance: health, 128; premiums, 230

Interaction. *See* Social interaction

Interest, 228; on continuing balances, 243; defined, 238; rates, 243

Interests: changing, 15, 138; defined, 73; matching to career areas, 294; matching to skills, 14; in product, 126

Internal change(s), 59, 150; defined, 55, 149-150

Interpersonal skills, development of, 113

Interstate commerce, defined, 271

Intrastate commerce, defined, 272

Introverts, 76

Investigative characteristics, 13

Isolated, defined, 156

J

Judgment, defined, 20

L

Labels, 270; food and drug, 259-260

Laundry, 106, 221

Laws: consumer protection, 252, 259-260, 272; defined, 70; versus guidelines, 72; legal, 70-71; truth in packaging, 259-260; violation of, 71

Leaders, friends as, 142

Leadership role, 142

Leisure activities, 87-88, 283; defined, 9; earning power and, 87; and life-style, 25, 91, 110-111, 292-294; satisfaction and, 86-87

Lenders, risks taken by, 246

Liberal attitude, defined, 206

Licensing programs, 271

Life-style, 25-26; aging and, 95; budget adjustments and, 236; and career, 91, 110-111; changes in, 93-95; choices, 25-26, 84-88; clothing and, 220; decisions, 233; defined, 25, 83; and environment, 83-96; of family, 110-111; matching to career areas, 292-293, 294; of single persons, 93-94; spending decisions and, 202, 206-207; transitions, 93-94; and work-schedule, 110-111

Line of credit, defined, 242

Listening, 109

Lists, shopping, 267

Living expenses, day-to-day, 231, 234, 236

Loans: personal, 240, 242; real estate, 24. *See also* Credit

Lobby/lobbyists, 272

Logic, defined, 14, 73

Logical ideas, 73-74

Loyalty, 42, 125

M

Maintenance: of clothing, 106; defined, 103; of home, 103-104, 216; and quality of materials, 255

Manual dexterity, defined, 9

Marriage, 9, 99, 202

Meat food group, 264

Menu, defined, 265

Milk food group, 265

Mind, 33; defined, 7

Minerals in diet, 263

Mobile, defined, 84

Mobility, and career choice, 84-85

Models, for decision making/problem solving, 152, 154-156; defined, 152

Modification, defined, 60

Morality, 28; defined, 26; personal values and, 26, 29

Mortgage loans: defined, 216; payments, 217, 230

Motion picture industry, 27

Motivation: defined, 166; for success, 299

Motives, 72

Mutual, defined, 110

N

Natural fibers, 255-256

Natural resources, 90-91

Needs, 19-25; and career choice, 294; defined, 19; emotional, 22, 24-25; material, 86; physical, 22-23; planning for satisfaction of, 225-226; spending for satisfaction of, 201-202, 207-208; versus wants, 19-20

Negative impressions, 36

Net income, 229

Neutral, defined, 55

Nourishment, 261

Nutrients, defined, 37-38

Nutrition, 37-38

Nutritional qualities: of carbohydrates, 261-262; of fats, 261; of protein, 261

O

Objective view, defined, 35

Occupational Outlook Handbook (OOH), 287, 289, 294, 295, 296; occupational clusters in, 291

Occupational Outlook Quarterly (OOQ), 287-288

Occupations: classifications of, 287; clusters of, 291; dangerous, 127; sources of information on, 286-289; and technological advances, 297-298

Open minded attitude, 169, 181, 206

Opportunities: and change, 61, 77; versus life-style, 91; and long-range plans, 192; matching skills to, 15; versus problems, 59-60; to succeed, 128, 283

Opposition to change, 56, 75, 77

Optimists, 75

Option(s): defined, 57; to do nothing, 57, 166, 181

Oral hygiene, 38

Organization: defined, 102; in family management, 102

Organizations, 121, 128-129

Ownership, pride of, 216

P

Parenthood, 94

Personal code, 240-242; adjusting, 137; challenges to, 140-141; changes in, 67-69, 95, 158, 161, 192, 193; conflicts with, 71; defined, 65; elements of, 70-75; experiences and, 68; and family, 99; and friendship, 140; function of, 65, 67; and leisure activities, 88; motivation and, 166; personality and, 75-76; satisfaction and, 87; shaping of, 69; spending decisions and, 208-209; understanding, 69; and values, 64-79, 156

Personal loans, 240, 242. *See also* Credit

Personal style, 26

Personal traits, and career choices, 284

Personal values, 26-28; sources of, 26-28. *See also* Values

Personality, 33; defined, 7-8; image and, 41-46; and personal code, 75-76; projecting, 43-45; traits, 10-13, 41-46, 75-76, 77

Pessimists, 75

Physical appearance, 35-41; and first impressions, 35-36; and image, 35-41; subjective judgments of, 37

Physical characteristics, 8-9, 33; and choice of activity, 8-9; positive approach to, 36-37

Physical limitations, and aging, 95

Physical needs, 22-23

Piecework, defined, 123

Plastics, 255

Poise, 45-46

Policies, defined, 129

Population shifts, 91

Positive impressions, 35

Posture, 41

Potential, defined, 24-25

Practice, and confidence, 45-46

Pre-authorized transactions, 242

Preferences, 72

Prejudice, defined, 128

Prices, comparing. *See* Comparison shopping

Pride, 119

Principal, defined, 238

Print media, 27

Priorities: defined, 181; establishing, 181; in implementing decisions or solutions, 184-185; in spending, 202

Problem(s), 61; versus decisions, 59-60; defined, 149; identification of, 154-155, 165-166; identifying causes of, 158; versus opportunities, 59-60; symptoms of, 158

Problem solving, 60; criteria for, 166; evaluating consequences of actions in, 173-174; as group activity, 182, 184; and personal code, 156, 158; process approach to, 151-156; process method of, 61

Process, defined, 61, 150

Process method, 61, 151-156; for budgeting, 226, 228-236; of decision making, 61; long-range decisions and, 193; of problem solving, 61; for spending decisions, 202-204, 207

Product(s): comparison of, 253-257; defined, 201; dissatisfaction with, 252; evaluation of, 208-209, 212; interest of employee in, 126; kinds of, 201; labels on, 259-260

Productivity of employees, 127

Projecting positive image, 43-45

Prospects, defined, 84-85

Proteins, 261

Publishing industry, 91

Purchases. *See* Spending decisions

Q

Quality of manufacture, 256

R

Radio, influence of, 27

Railroads, 53-54

Rain checks, 269

Reactions to change, 55-57, 59-60, 61, 75, 77

Reading between the lines, 212

Real estate loans, 240. *See also* Mortgage loans

Real property, defined, 240

Realistic tendencies, 11-12

Receipts, keeping, 273

Recipes, defined, 267

Recognition, 120, 283

Records of purchases, 273

Regulation. *See* Government regulation; Laws

Reimbursement, 256-257

Reinforcement: defined, 67; of values, 206

Rejection of change, 56, 57, 77

Reliability, 42, 125, 209

Religion, 26

Rental of apartments/houses, 214-215

Repossession, 239, 246

Reputation, and first impressions, 36

Research, defined, 13

Resentment, defined, 67

Responsibilities, 117-130; of employee, 117, 125-127; of employers, 127-128; family, 102-107, 109-110, 117; sharing, 143

Rest, 38

Risk/risk-taking, 22, 193, 246; in buying, 251-253; in friendship, 134

Roles, changing, 46

Roughage, 263

Rural communities, 85, 91

S

Safety: needs, 22-23; occupational, 22, 127; standards, 270-271; of workplace, 127

Salaries, 123, 228

Satisfaction: factors determining, 86-87; level of, 121, 208; and personal code, 118; and values, 28, 29

School, and personal values, 26-27

Science, and change, 52-54

Security, 75, 119, 193, 283

Self, defined, 33

Self-confidence, 41, 42, 46

Self-esteem, 24

Self-fulfillment, 24-25

Self-image: defined, 33; friendships and, 142; versus image, 33-35. *See also* Image

Sensitivity to others, 136

Service(s), defined, 126, 201

Service industries, 91

Shelter, 208, 214-217

Shopping lists, 267

Sincerity, 44

Single persons, life-style of, 93-94

Single-purpose (credit) cards, 243

Skepticism, 252

Skills: creative, 142; decision making and problem solving, 160-161; identifying, 8-14; interpersonal, 113; leadership, 142; matching to interests, 14; matching to opportunities, 15; updating, 297-298

Skin care, 38

Smiling, 43-44

Social characteristics, 13

Social interaction, 25, 120-121, 283

Social needs, 24

Society: defined, 70; and family, 113; laws of, 70-71; levels of, 70-71

Solutions: defined, 149; implementing, 184-185

Specific, defined, 9, 101

Spending: attitudes, 206-207; habits, 207-212; impulsive, 211-212, 245; risks taken in, 251-253; timing of, 210. *See also* Comparison shopping; Spending decisions

Spending decisions: home ownership, 216-217; and life-style, 202, 206-207; process method for, 202-204, 207

Spouse, defined, 94

Standards: health, 272; safety, 270-271

Stepchildren, defined, 102

Strengths, 284; defined, 5; identifying, 5-13; mental, 7; personality, 7-8; physical, 7; re-evaluating, 15. *See also* Aptitudes

Stress, 158

Student, role as, 123

Style(s): in clothing, 41, 105, 221; personal, 26; values and, 28

Subjective view: defined, 34-35; of appearance, 37

Supervision/supervisors, 127; in home, 107

Supplements, mineral and vitamin, 263

Support of change, 57

Survival needs, 22; expenses for, 207-208, 214-221

Symptoms, defined, 158

Synthetic fibers, 256

T

Tangible, defined, 9-10

Taxes: on income, 70; on property, 216

Technological advances, 52-54, 297

Technology, defined, 54, 297

Television, and personal values, 27, 29

Tension. *See* Stress

Thoughtfulness, 42

Threat, defined, 77

Time, in decision making, 170

Timing, of purchases, 210

Title, defined, 242

Trade(s): defined, 12; examples of, 12

Trade-offs, 173

Traits, 10-13, 41-46, 75-76, 77

Transaction(s): defined, 123; pre-authorized, 242; work as, 123

Transition, defined, 93-94

Transportation: needs versus wants, 208; reliability of, 23

Travel and entertainment (credit) cards, 243

Trust/trustworthiness, 42, 136

Truth in packaging laws, 270

U

Understanding, capacity for, 140-141

Understudy, defined, 191

Uniforms, 128

Unique, defined, 5

Unit price, defined, 219

Unity: defined, 101; of family, 101

Upkeep, defined, 106

Urgency, 170, 174; defined, 166; and priorities, 181

Utility, defined, 204

V

Vacations, 87, 128

Valid, defined, 14

Values (monetary), of goods and services, 105, 208-209; and prices, 253-255

Values (personal), 60, 61, 65, 68; choices based on, 28-29; in decision making and problem solving, 152, 156; defined, 26, 208; factors influencing, 206; modification of, 60-61; and obedience to law, 71; opposing, 29; personal, 26-28; and personal code, 64-79, 156; and reactions to change, 57, 61; reinforcement of, 206; satisfaction and, 28; and wants, 28-29

Vegetables, 264

Violations, defined, 71

Vitamins, 263

W

Wage earners, 123

Wages, 127, 228; defined, 123

Wants, 19-21, 25-26, 28-29; career choice and, 294; and choices, 19, 25; defined, 19; material, 86; versus needs, 19-20; planning to satisfy, 225-226; specific, 25; spending to satisfy, 201-202, 207-208; and values, 28-29

War, changes due to, 51

Warranties, 257

Water, 262

Weaknesses, 284; defined, 5; identifying, 5-13; re-evaluating, 15

Work, rewards of, 118-121, 283

Work schedules, and life-style, 110-111

Working conditions, sources of information on, 287

Workplace, cleanliness and safety of, 127